THE LAST
ANGRY
MAN

by *GERALD GREEN*

THE LAST ANGRY MAN

THE SWORD AND THE SUN

HIS MAJESTY O'KEEFE (*with Larry Klingman*)

THE LAST
ANGRY
MAN

a novel
by
Gerald
Green

CHARLES SCRIBNER'S SONS

NEW YORK

PRINTED IN THE UNITED STATES OF AMERICA

Library of Congress Catalog Card Number 56-12444

W

For SAMUEL GREENBERG, *M.D.*
(1886–1952)

I called on the king, but he made me wait in his hall, and conducted like a man incapacitated for hospitality. There was a man in my neighborhood who lived in a hollow tree. His manners were truly regal. I should have done better had I called on him.

—*Walden*

The author has taken the liberty of using the actual names of the members of the Bellevue faculty during the years 1908-1912; these men are now part of the medical history of America, and to fictionalize them would be to minimize their stature. All other persons depicted in this book, however, are fictional, and resemblances to persons, living or dead, are coincidental.

—G. G.

*THE LAST
ANGRY
MAN*

I

Hours before the nightbell had commenced its furious buzzing he had been awake, neither mildly awake nor half asleep, but wide-eyed and alert, his mind crammed with the photographic clarity of insomnia. It was an unbearably hot night, hot as only a square of attached slum houses can get, the heat stewing and intensifying in the crib of ramshackle backyards on which his bedroom window looked out. The oversized window fan (he had installed it himself) was no help either. In the early morning stillness it clattered like a jackhammer.

The buzzing had caused him to start, jerking him to a sitting position in the old double bed and triggering an arthritic spark in his lower spine. The luminous face of the dresser clock read three-thirty and he cursed softly and considerately, although he was the only one in the house.

"Aaah, the bastard. The bastards won't let you live."

Sighing, he plopped back on the moist pillow, hoping that the bell-ringer would grow discouraged and return to his tenement warren. Normally it was his wife's function to trudge to the front window and advise the caller *The doctor is not in, he has gone for the evening.* It was a small lie, and few of them ever believed it, but it worked most of the time. But his wife was at the beach for the summer; if the visitor persisted he would have no choice but to undertake the distasteful journey himself. He was too old and too tired for night work. Why couldn't they get that into their thick skulls?

"My dear lousy patients," he said half aloud. "Why don't they bother some young *shtunk* of a specialist? Why always me at three-thirty?"

By now he realized that the waiting game would not deter the nocturnal intruder. The buzzing continued, in long agonized peals, in brief *bzzt-bzzt-bzzts*, and occasionally, to his horror, in the unmistakable beats of "shave and a haircut, two bits."

The impudence brought him up sharply again, and he probed for his slippers at the bedside, swearing steadily and quietly, and, somewhat irrelevantly, framing a theory of nightbell ringers. The shorter and politer the buzz ,the greater chance it was a "regular," someone he had known for years, on a genuinely urgent mission.

1

When they buzzed wildly they were usually transients, people whose own physicians (probably fancy internists and pediatricians) refused night calls, and in a last desperate attempt tried his bell simply because he had been around for forty years. The worst of all were the uncontrollables, the addicts, alcoholics, and loonies, like the one now camped on his stoop.

Padding across the cramped hallway, through the narrow living-dining room, he decided, again without too much pertinence, that it was the fault of the specialists. "The lousy professors should drop dead," he muttered, "let *them* go out at night."

Again, he heard the *dum-di-de-dum dum, dum-dum*. Why, the rat was enjoying a Halloween prank! A neighbor's dog unloosed a resonant protest, and across the street, somewhere in the cage of Negro tenements, a window slammed open. He held the undone pajama string in one hand (finding time to denounce the thieving manufacturers who put out such defective merchandise) and peered through the copper screen. It was an old-fashioned screen, heavily framed in wood and bolted securely on all four sides. Even with his head pressed against it, he could not see the top step; the caller's identity was hidden from him. Below, Haven Place lay peaceful under its normal patina of filth. The skeleton of a ruined sofa, set afire that afternoon by little children, lay bathed in Consolidated Edison lamplight in front of his car. The awareness that it would remain there until he supplied a liberal tip to the street cleaners distressed him briefly.

"Who's there?" he called down. "What the hell is all that ringing about? Haven't you people any consideration?"

Abruptly, the buzzing stopped. From below, the unseen ringer called back.

"You de doctor?"

"That's none of your business. Get out of here."

"You de doctor?"

"You'll find out who I am, you little *shtunk*! I'll come down with a baseball bat and you'll *know* who I am! Get away from here before I call the police."

Then he saw the visitor for the first time. At the mention of *police*, he had leaped from the top step and now stood framed in the brick portal at the base of the stoop. Under the streetlight the doctor saw him clearly: a lithe, brown youth in T-shirt and billowing yellow pants tapering at the ankle. A ridiculous checked cap covered his finely molded head; beneath its tiny brim the prognathous jaw jutted upward, the dazzling teeth arrayed in a magnificent grin.

"You ain't no doctor. You know what you is? You is *sheee-eeee-eeet!*"

The boy cackled happily at the obscene challenge, and from a sleek fat automobile, bright with chrome and gadgetry—it was parked just in back of the doctor's weary black Buick—there emanated an accompaniment of rich laughter. The visitor had come with a party.

"Tell him again, Josh!"

"Yeah, Josh, you tell him!"

"C'mon, man, don't waste no time with dat old man! Das all he is . . . *sheeee-eee-eeeet!*"

The youth they called Josh did a joyous little dance to the car, and opened the front door. "You better look on yo' stoop, old doctor! You been left somethin'!"

"Why, you scum! You bunch of galoots! Is that all you bums are good for?" the doctor cried out angrily. "Is that all you're good for, even with the relief checks? Waking up an old man like me! Your parents should be ashamed of themselves!"

In trying to elicit their sympathy, he sensed a fleeting annoyance with himself. Ten years ago he would have grabbed Myron's baseball bat and plunged into the street, taking his chances. But he was sixty-eight years old now, and it seemed that every year the galoots got bigger and stronger and fiercer. He could think only of his friend Sol Pomerantz the druggist. Solly had fought back, and Solly had died in the emergency room of St. Mary's with three bullets in his chest.

The motor of the fat car hummed, and the driver swung it out arrogantly past his own automobile, racing the engine. Josh poked his head from the window.

"Lissen, you doctor, I ain't foolin' you! You better look on yo' steps! It's a 'mergency!"

A gleeful chorus followed: "Yeah, a 'mergency! 'Mergency! 'Mergency!"

The car sped away, charging through the stoplight at the corner. Once more the street was silent, save for the wailing of a few dogs. The doctor's anger was complete; worst of all, there was no outlet for his outrage. His wife was a good listener, but she was away. His nephew Myron, who lived with him, was not yet home from work. To phone the police and report the incident would only heighten frustration: the cops would smile at him indolently and dismiss the whole business as boyish fun. It occurred to him then that he had better inspect the front stoop. Who knew what those hoodlums would do? In the darkened hallway, he found a faded flannel bathrobe in the closet, pulled it over his shoulders, and started down the canted stairs to the vestibule, flicking on the street lights. There were double locks on both the hall door and the street door, and by the time he had undone them he heard voices outside. It was the apprehensive hum of the slum crowd, assembling for an evening's entertainment.

The outer door met resistance, and he pushed it open slowly. They had been telling the truth. In the half light he saw the lumpish body of a Negro girl. She was resting, quite comfortably it seemed, on her side, legs drawn up under her, arms crossed in the fetal position. Gently, the doctor turned her on her back. She was quite ugly and very black and she had absorbed a fearful beating. Her left eye was swollen to the size of an egg. The mahogany skin was stained a deep purple. Trickles of blood dripped from both nostrils and her lower lip had been neatly split. Instinctively the doctor reached for her wrist. The pulse was firm and strong, and he shook his head approvingly.

By now a dozen people were ringing the brick pillars at the entrance to his house. Others were crossing the street from the tenements. The sidewalk would soon be jammed.

"Any of you people know this girl?" the doctor asked.

An immense woman in a crimson kimono hefted her weight up the first two steps. "She doan look like no one from 'round here," she said. "Someone sure worked dat ole gal over. She daid?"

"Nah," the doctor said, "she's in great shape."

The woman retreated to the safety of the mob, and the doctor knelt beside the unconscious girl. Deftly, his hands probed the leaden body. Aside from the slight nosebleed there was no external bleeding. Her limbs seemed uninjured, and to all intents and purposes the girl might have been enjoying a nap. The doctor stood up again, the fused vertebrae in his back making him grunt, and surveyed the growing audience. Beneath the yellow light of the lamppost there were now assembled at least fifty of his neighbors. It was close to four in the morning, yet so quickly and so silently had they gathered, it almost seemed they had been expecting the incident, that they had been advised beforehand that excitement was imminent, and that each had carefully set slippers and bathrobes near their beds before retiring. There was a score of children, including a few two year olds. Four small boys, half naked, were perched on the wrought-iron railing above the brick barrier. Two of them were twined, dark cherubim, about the doctor's street sign.

"Get off the railing. That sign isn't a public parking place," the doctor snapped. "What do you all want here? This is no goddam party. Don't you people sleep? I'm calling the cops and an ambulance. Beat it."

There was a shifting and a dull murmur in the crowd, but not a soul moved. The big woman who had sought to identify the girl spoke up.

"You doan own de sidewalk. You better take care dat ole gal."

"Who asked you, lady?" he queried sharply.

"You ain't so big," she called back. "How come you doan take dat gal in yo' office? She hurt, ain't she? You a doctor, ain't you? You too good to take care of a sick gal?"

A few voices joined in approval, and soon the mob found a more articulate spokesman. "I beg your pardon, Dr. Abelman, but I think these people have a point." The speaker was an owlish young man, bespectacled and stooped.

"May I say, doctor, my family has known you many years, and I've often heard them talk well of you. I'm rather distressed you aren't taking proper care of that girl. She is entitled to just as much consideration as any one of us. Right, folks?"

"You bet!"

"Das right, das right."

"Yeah, tell dat doctor."

The doctor bounced down the steps and confronted the champion of the poor.

"Listen, you little punk," the doctor said, "your family still owes me for your delivery. I don't intend to have a *schnorer* telling me how to run my affairs."

The young man shook his head in mock assent, and took in his audience with a helpless gesture. "See what I mean, folks? Everyone knows it about Abelman. That nasty tongue of his. Yeah, it's no secret you lose patients every day! No wonder people go to Baumgart! Ain't I right? You know it's true!"

There was a restrained hum of agreement. An elderly lady in a *babushka* smacked her gums in accord; an aggrieved consumptive Italian who long ago had torn up the last of the doctor's reminders for payment giggled in approval; a coffee-colored man in gold-rimmed glasses took up the general assault.

"The least you can do is show some interest in that girl, doctor," he said. He had a pedantic manner of speaking and his tone was respectful. "After all, you are duty-bound in an emergency."

"Oh, emergency, is it?" the doctor asked. "Well, if that guy

Baumgart is so great, why don't you pick her up and take her there? Hah? Why don't you people ring his bell in the middle of the night?"

"Don't be wroth with us, doctor," the coffee-colored man said quietly. "Everyone knows Dr. Baumgart is an *internist*." He accented the second syllable. "He don't make no night calls. You just a doctor for everyday kind of work."

The doctor tightened the worn braided rope of his bathrobe and turned his back. "You can all kiss my foot," he muttered—but this time, softly, so that no one heard him.

The old lady in the *babushka* ogled him with clear amber eyes. "Such a doctor! He wouldn't even cover her up yet, she should be warm! All he is good for is he should holler all day! That's not nice a doctor should do that."

Thus chastised, the doctor returned to the girl. She was now wheezing softly. A prowl car had pulled to the curb behind his own automobile, and two policemen were shoving their way through the crowd.

"I'm sure glad to see you guys," Dr. Abelman said cheerfully. "Take this mess off my hands, will ya?"

The first cop, a pink Irishman with bland, blue eyes, studied him curiously. "Take it easy, Mac," he said.

"Mac? Who's Mac?" the doctor asked. He was honestly confused.

"You. If I call you Mac, you're Mac." He smiled, but the fradulent friendliness did not win the doctor over.

"That isn't my name. I'm a doctor, and I like to be called that. Why don't we try again?"

"What's your name, pop?" The cop kept smiling.

"Read it off my sign."

The policeman, unsmiling, said nothing, and laboriously copied down the weathered gold lettering: SAMUEL ABELMAN, M.D.

The second cop, a young man, Levantine in appearance, was questioning the spectators. Above him, in the doctor's giant Lombardy poplar, two small Negro boys had established nests and were shrieking gleefully. Their voices were alarmingly loud.

"Callin' all cars! Callin' all cars! Lady wid a baby fell on Fulton Street!"

The young policemen looked up at them. "You kids get down! Go home and go to bed!"

"We ain't 'fraid a you!"

"Yeah, you ain't comin' up here! Lady wid a baby!"

The crowd smiled indulgently, a few laughed, and the dark policeman, acknowledging defeat, pushed his way back to the stoop and joined his partner, now painfully writing down an account of the night's events.

The doctor had already described the foul-mouthed young men in the shiny new car, the manner in which he discovered the girl. The older cop was thoughtful.

"Can't figure why they dumped her here," he said. "Maybe they were so hopped up they didn't care. Usually they toss these broads into the middle of the street. Or an empty lot. You say they called this boogie Josh?"

"That's what it sounded like," the doctor said.

"Why didn't you call us right away?"

"Why weren't you here when it happened?"

"You're a fresh old guy."

"No I'm not. I'm a doctor. I expect a little courtesy."

The younger cop intervened. "Frank doesn't mean any harm, Dr. Abelman. He likes to kid around. Dr. Abelman used to treat my family, Frank. You remember us, doc? Kaplan on Blake Avenue?"

"Sure," the doctor said. "Your father had a dry-goods store. You wanted to be a dentist."

"I'll see to it he never looks at my family," Frank said in a flat voice. "I think I heard about you already. Guy who likes to sound off. Well, I'll make sure you do lots of sounding off in court if this case ever comes up. I don't like the way you handled this. Didn't answer the bell right away. That's a doctor's *doody*. Leaving the victim on the stoop. I think we got a good case for negligence here."

The word negligence stiffened the doctor's muscular body.

"Why damn it, cop or no cop, watch your language! Who the hell are you to preach to me? I'm not the criminal! They are! Them! Out there! Sure, sure, I know you guys. Very good at chasing kids out of the schoolyard!"

"And how come you didn't call for an ambulance?" the older cop pursued.

"Ambulance!" the doctor repeated, somewhat meaninglessly. "I just came out!"

Now the crowd had pressed closer, perhaps a hundred people in all, a score of youngsters perched on the railing, four more in the tree, a few squatting on the roof of the doctor's car. The story was being embellished and altered; at the fringe of the crowd it had now been established that the doctor had thrown the girl out of his office. There were dark hints as to why she was in his empty house at three in the morning. The girl herself was stirring, attempting to sit up. One eye opened, the black pupil agleam in the artificial light. The doctor was beside her, his voice soft and comforting.

"All right, girlie, just lay still. I should be as healthy as you are!"

An ambulance siren wailed, brakes screeched. Two attendants in rumpled white suits were unlimbering a stretcher and forcing their way through the throng. One of the children in the branches of the doctor's tree—a daredevil—leaped to the hard white roof of the ambulance and began a merry tap dance.

"Am-bu-lance! *Wheeee!*"

On the narrow steps the attendants lifted the girl onto the stretcher, covering her with a blanket. Her undamaged eye was wide-open and alert. She was talking softly to herself.

"She ain't even hurt," one attendant complained. "All you guys are the same. Won't take 'em in yer office, so you call us!"

He had not directed his remarks to the doctor, but the doctor accepted the challenge. "Do your work, buddy, and mind your own business!" he barked. "Earn your money for a change!"

"Wise guy, huh?" asked the attendant. "Won't touch an emergency case if you can't get a buck out of it, huh?"

"I'll turn you bums in!" the doctor mumbled.

"Okay, okay, cut it out," Patrolman Kaplan shouted. "I made the call for the ambulance from the prowl car. Dr. Abelman didn't *have* to take her into his office. In cases like this, it's better you shouldn't move them. She might have internal injuries. Right, doc?"

The doctor looked at him thoughtfully. "You're all right, young fellah." Then, to the attendants, he added, "A little sedation and iodine and you can discharge her tomorrow."

The audience crowded greedily around the stretcher. In an instant the girl was inside the ambulance, the siren wailed, and the mob watched it vanish.

It was now past four in the morning; from the direction of Rower Avenue the doctor saw the long-legged, clumsy form of his nephew Myron, hurrying home. Myron worked as a night-side copy boy. He normally was home by three, but during the summer months he had been earning overtime by filling in for vacationing desk men. At the sight of the dispersing crowd, the youth broke into a wild sprint and ran breathlessly up the steps.

"What happened, Uncle Doc? What happened?"

"Oh, nothing much. Some *tunkeles* dumped a girl, one of their own kind, on the doorstep. They rang my bell till I thought my head would crack. There were cops, and an ambulance. You know, the usual crap."

"Was she hurt? Raped?" He was a homely, asymmetrical young

man, his pinched face overwhelmed by an anteater's nose and terrorized eyes.

"I don't think so. They took her to St. Mary's. Thank God I got her off my hands. She wasn't badly hurt at all."

"Gee, what a shame, Uncle Doc. Why do they hafta bother you all the time?"

The doctor turned wearily and held the street door open for Myron. "I don't know. Everyone's a specialist today. Professors. Some slob, a guy on relief, told me that tonight. In emergencies they come to me. Even the galoots. To hell with them all."

"Well, it's a damn shame. I bet you didn't get any sleep."

The doctor bolted the street door, opened the hall door and bolted it also. "I can take it, Myron, don't worry about me. After forty years, you think I let these things bother me? They don't bother me *at all*."

Myron looked at his uncle's haggard face. At sixty-eight he looked perhaps seven years older. The eyes were tired, the rumpled gray hairs rose from the scalp like tendrils; the lines around the nose and mouth were like healed wounds. And yet there was something oddly peaceful and triumphant in his face, a look he had seen many times, always when the old man had been frustrated, or beaten down, or cheated. Myron knew just what had happened: in his mind's eye he envisioned the acrimony, the curses, the snarling exchanges, and he wanted to suffer for his uncle. But some unvanquished attitude in the muscular body, the ravaged face, would not allow pity.

He pulled the braided rope tight, and vigorously punched Myron in the forearm. "Come on, we'll have a cup of tea and some rye bread. You think these lice bother me? Not as much as everyone thinks!"

"Yeah," said Myron, "you always say that. But it's a shame anyway, waking you up and pestering you."

The youth followed the doctor into the kitchen. Dr. Abelman pulled the string and the kitchen chandelier flooded the yellow walls with saffron light.

The doctor seemed to be enjoying some private joke. A faint smile creased his face; he turned up the gas under the teakettle.

"You gotta learn it sooner or later, Myron. I learned it early. I admit it hasn't done me too much good, but at least I know it."

"What's that, Uncle Doc?" And he knew the axiom before the old man spoke.

"The bastards won't let you live."

II

THRASHER had rolled the single sheet of mimeographed paper into a child's telescope and was sighting through it. Far below his office, clearly limned within the paper circle, he watched the summer visitors moving lazily about Rockefeller Plaza. The men wore white, yellow, and blue sport shirts without ties. Many of them carried cameras around their necks. The women were in pale, bulky frocks, patently different from the dark sleekness of the dresses worn by the handful of native New Yorkers. He scanned the bustling square, which somehow, in the heat-heavy morning, seemed cool and pleasant. Vaguely, he was jealous of the grinning, satisfied tourists.

"Happy, happy rubes," Thrasher said quietly. "A taste of the big time, and then back to Ames, Iowa. Or for that matter, DeSmet, South Dakota."

A woman and three small boys were posing in front of Poseidon's statue in the rink; a man in a wide-brimmed yellow straw hat was focusing a motion-picture camera on them.

"Roll film," Thrasher said. "Punch up two and dissolve to Brick."

"I beg your pardon, Mr. Thrasher?"

He spun his reedy, slouching figure around in the swivel chair, still sighting through the paper telescope, and framed his secretary in its counterfeit eye.

"Just mumbling to myself, Louise."

"I thought I heard you say, 'Punch up two and dissolve to Brick.'"

She busied herself with a sheaf of papers, eager for him to be drawn into discussion.

"Did I say that? Why in the world would I be muttering about Brick Higgins?"

"I'm sure I don't know." She was a rather pretty dark woman, now approaching a virginal thirty. She had graduated Phi Beta Kappa and *cum laude* from Hunter College, and had hoped for a successful career in magazine work, public relations, or advertising. But so remarkably efficient had she been as a secretary that none of her employers had ever had the courage to promote her. Secretly most of them sensed she was not quite right for responsibilities beyond secretarial work. There was a little too much weight in her hips and legs, and a little too much Bronx in her voice. To their credit, none of them ever told her this.

10

"Louise," Thrasher said thoughtfully, "have you ever studied Rockefeller Plaza? I mean from an—ah—ethnic point of view?"

"Not lately."

"C'mere." He spun around again, leaning his elbows on the windowsill, tapping against his forehead with the rolled paper. "I've been studying it all morning, Louise. And I've decided it lacks one vital essential. As soon as I get out of morning chapel, I am running over to Mr. Rockefeller and giving him, for free, the best advice he ever had since Ivy Lee went to work for him."

"Ivy Lee didn't work for *this* Rockefeller."

"You're not paying attention. What I have to say will change the whole trend of mass communications in America."

She looked at him narrowly, squinting over spectacular horn-rimmed glasses.

"Rockefeller Plaza," he pursued, "needs a scaffold. A good, old-fashioned wooden scaffold, equipped with a family-size gallows for hangings, and a do-it-yourself chopping block for beheadings. 'Take this from this, if this be otherwise.'"

"*Hamlet.*"

"Hunter College English majors! Who needs you! Now let me finish. See, we'd have this scaffold, just like the Spaniards used to put up in the towns they'd conquer in Latin America. Whenever a fellah was in trouble . . . oh, let's say he lost an account, or he backed a bum show . . . or he gambled on a campaign . . . we'd just drum him out of his charcoal-gray suit, strip him of his striped tie and cordovans, and right down to the scaffold. He'd have his choice, of course, the gallows or the block."

"What brought all this on? The Brick Higgins rating?"

Thrasher turned around again, this time unrolling the mimeographed sheet, and holding it high in the manner of a royal messenger reading an edict.

"Isn't it funny what damage a few little numbers can do? It says here, 'Brick Higgins' Bandwagon, 5.8' and underneath it, 'Ted Townley Show, 10.3.' In those ciphers, Louise, lurks disaster."

"Aren't you being terribly, terribly pessimistic? *You* didn't insist on Brick Higgins for the *G & T* show. Wasn't it our friends across the street who went for him? Mr. Whitechapel can't possibly blame you if the show flopped. *Everyone* voted for Brick Higgins."

Thrasher exhaled slowly, leaning back with his arms behind his head. He was joking about it now, bright with quotations, putting on a brave show for his secretary. But below the navel, a little germ of fear was growing much too fast to suit him. He was only thirty-nine; there had been few occasions in his life when he had experienced failure. Seated at the functional blond mahogany desk, awaiting what he referred to as "chapel," he tried to recall the last time he had brushed with failure. He had to go all the way back to high school; his senior year, it was, and he was in competition for valedictorian honors. Everyone knew Woody Thrasher was the brightest boy in New Arabia High. Everyone took it for granted he would be valedictorian. But somehow, unexplicably, he had fallen apart on the trigonometry final. He had passed, of course, but his grade of 74 had dragged his average down so precipitously that some little girl with a lame leg (he couldn't recall her name) had won the honor. Now, studying the deadly figures 5.8, he could remember the freezing in his stomach when he looked at the posted examination grades outside the classroom and had read the harrowing news, *Thrasher, Woodrow, 74.*

"They've moved the meeting up a half hour," he heard Louise say. "Do you want coffee anyway? I heard Whitechapel telling Barbara to send out for lunch."

Little beadlets of sweat gathered under his armpits. "No, I'll skip coffee. I'll be drinkin' bitter beer alone all day."

"It won't be too bad," she assured him. "You're smarter than the whole bunch. And it wasn't your fault."

She shuffled up another sheaf of papers, deftly and smartly, and walked across the heavy-pile carpeting. Thrasher leaped from behind his desk. "Good old Louise! You'll always love me, won't you, baby?"

She paused at the opened door, and in fair imitation of Eve Arden replied. "Madly. Forever."

He grinned appreciatively. "Listen. I wrote a poem just now! Remember what I said about the Rockefeller Plaza scaffold? Well, when they string me up, you can recite it."

He bowed, a small boy at a party.

"Oh they're hangin' Woody Thrasher
"You can hear the ratings drop,
"The agency will wring his neck,
"For turning out a flop.
"Oh they've taken off his cordovans
"And shaved his balding top
"Oh they're hangin' Woody Thrasher in the mornin'."

"Very funny," she said acidly. "Put it to music, at least."

Old man Whitechapel (T.C. in the industry and "chief" to his associates) had, for as long as anyone could remember, enjoyed the reputation of "a man of integrity." He had earned this reputation not through any positive act or series of acts that might be interpreted as signposts of high character, but rather through a well-nurtured neutralism, stemming from deep, unshakable ignorance. He was a thoroughly nice man, decent to his associates, devoid of rancor or meanness, and always ready to head up useful committees or movements. "I believe in being fair to everyone," was a phrase he used in his moments of articulation. Among his clients, whose total assets exceeded several hundreds of millions of dollars, these words never failed to achieve their purpose. Men whose industrial empires stretched through jungle and desert, and at whose word stocks rose and fell with coronary suddenness, would hear the phrase and would be won over. Won over more completely, it should be noted, than if old T.C. had used the fancy charts, graphs, and glazed booklets that the newer agencies were employing.

As is often the case when the man in charge of a complex organization inclines toward silence and neutralism, the people beneath him found themselves in fierce internecine warfare. A cynical former newspaper reporter who held a brief job as a copywriter at T.C. Whitechapel & Associates was heard to say, "There's more high-pressure conniving up there than in the jockey room before a steeplechase." He might have added that the old man himself refused to believe that any such murderous competition sullied his paneled precincts. He himself never fired anyone; high-level losers at Whitechapel adhered to the rules of the game and left of their own accord. If they insisted on hanging on after defeat, their colleagues themselves—indeed their former enemies—would charitably find other employment for them. All in all, it was a good place to work.

Up to the morning when he had seen the 5.8 rating for Brick Higgins, Woodrow Thrasher's progress at Whitechapel had bordered on the phenomenal. At thirty-nine, he was vice-president in charge of radio and television, a position in which he exercised infinitely more power than a half-dozen account executives who earned much more than he did. He had built a solid reputation as the company idea man; a little eccentric perhaps, but offbeat enough to come up with the unusual concept, the eye-catching slant, the different approach.

Thrasher had always felt very much at home in the board room. For almost four years now, he had been the star of the weekly meetings. Respectfully, they would sit at semi-attention listening to the old man's almost inaudible whisper. Only Woody Thrasher, had the right to slouch in his seat, hum snatches of nonexistent tunes, and, on one occasion at least, remove his jacket. It was accepted as part of his role: the company rebel. "A real, bright creative guy, that Thrasher," one of his adversaries said grudgingly, "but I wish he'd stop working so hard at that Greenwich Village bit."

He was late for the meeting, and the room was depressingly silent. The chief, wrinkled, immaculate, self-contained in his withdrawn perimeter, smiled at him automatically. At his right, Ben Loomer, the executive vice-president, cleared his throat noisily, and drawled, "You're late, Woodrow. Two demerits."

The drawl was a particular source of distress to Thrasher. For over a year he was convinced that Loomer, a big-boned slab of a man, prematurely bald and with a round, red face, came from the Far West. Pressing him on it one day, he discovered that Loomer had been born and raised in Brooklyn, East Flatbush to be exact. The drawl was fraudulent; a back door into the agency world, where small-town roots were invariably an asset.

"Sorry, Benjamin. I've got them deep-down five-point-eight blues, and I ain't myself." He slumped into a chair, noticing that no one laughed, and that Tom Finucane, the account executive on *G & T*, winced.

"Okay, Woody, why don't you start off?" Loomer said. "It's as much your baby as anybody's."

Thrasher pressed his fingertips together and buried himself deeper in the chair. He found Loomer's drawl excessively unnerving this morning. He was tempted for a moment to be fresh. But Loomer and he were fairly good friends, and from the stricken faces around the table he knew he would be needing allies.

"Yes, Woodrow, why don't you give us your views?"

Slumped deeply in the chair, he shuddered internally. It was old Whitechapel speaking, in that ghostly whisper, and it was a bad omen. Normally the chief never said a word until just prior to adjournment; at many meetings he was known to remain silent, indeed, half asleep, throughout. The Brick Higgins debacle must have cut him deeply.

Thrasher struggled to a more upright position and leaned over the table, resting his forehead in one palm. "Okay, first things first," he began. "We begin with the assumption it's summer, middle of August. Ratings are always bad in the summer. What were we shooting for? Let's say a fifteen would have kept us happy, fair enough?"

He expected some argument, perhaps *one* assent. But they remained uniformly silent.

"So we came up with 5.8. Not enough to keep *G & T* happy, for sure. Not enough, even in August, to keep any client happy who's ready to spend fifty thousand dollars a week for a network package. And I gather they *are* unhappy."

He saw Loomer look at the old man for a signal, then speak. "Damn unhappy, Woody. *G & T* is ready to take its business somewhere else. They've never been sold on our television department, and you know it. Now that Higgins laid an egg—"

Thrasher interrupted. "Did I or did I not point out that Brick Higgins is a crude buffoon? As I recall it, Parker Theis rammed him down our throat. Why wasn't I allowed to talk to him?" He was feeling stronger and surer; he'd be throwing Shakespeare at them in a few minutes.

Finucane cleared an alcoholic's throat and spoke up. "That ain't exactly right, Woody," the account executive said, "we were *all* in on it. And if anyone had the final say, it was you 'n' me and, between us, it was mostly *you*."

It was another red flag. He usually had fools like Finucane under his thumb, fearful of sniping at him publicly. But somehow Tom had found his courage. His massive fleshy face, framed in the tumbling black curls of a Dublin patriot, was ripe with confidence. The saloon friendliness that used to amuse Thrasher had vanished.

"Well, if that's the case, me bhoyo," Thrasher said airily, "we can be holdin' Finucane's wake tonight. Ever read James Joyce, Tom?"

Finucane smiled; immense predatory teeth and wide ruby gums were exposed. "I ain't an educated fellah like you, Woody," he said jovially, "I'm just a smart high school kid from Dorchester."

Like Ben Loomer's drawl, it was another fraud. Finucane had actually graduated from Boston College; but he had found it more advantageous to play the role of a Scollay Square hoodlum. His clients appreciated it.

"Biographical sketches are getting us nowhere, gents," Thrasher said. He bent over the table, rubbing his hand from his eyebrows back over his skull-cropped thinning hair, and lingering on the spreading bald spot's silken fuzz.

"I take it we're in real trouble. A million dollars' worth of trouble. Now what exactly do the brains at *G & T* want? They suggested Brick Higgins. They practically forced him on us. He laid an egg, and now they want out. Why doesn't someone tell 'em where to head in?"

Finucane looked for help to Loomer. "That ain't their version, is it, Ben?"

"Not quite," said Loomer. He seemed to be speaking with painful slowness, pulling his words like warm taffy, his honest round face trying to be decent to everyone. "The sponsor feels we weren't capable of—ah—creating a new, bright idea. So, they concluded that an established comic like Brick would be the safest bet to sell the line. He did all right sellin' toothpaste three years ago. They claim they asked us our advice and we agreed. They say they had an open mind all along, but that our TV department didn't supply them with anything fresh."

"That's the way I got it, too," Finucane said quickly.

"Is this for real?" Thrasher asked. "Nothing about the way they sneaked off to the network and asked for Higgins, against my advice?"

Old Whitechapel, his hooded eyes half closed, whispered, "Not quite fair to an old client, Woodrow. We have had an honorable relationship with Mr. Gatling for many years. I am sure he would not countenance anything unseemly."

"I hate to say it, T.C., but it looks like their fellahs are trying to blame our fellahs for their own goof," Thrasher said earnestly. He had found that he could contradict the old man, if he used the right compound of boyishness and impertinence.

But the shriveled man in the dark suit and high collar failed to react. He flicked an imaginary fly from his nose, and sank back to his sleepy world.

The mahogany table was pleasantly still. The exceedingly difficult problem of fixing blame had silenced them momentarily. Failure, like success, was eclectic, and to point the finger at one solitary malingerer was a process fraught with anguish.

Individual responsibility existed, of course, but it was rarely emphasized. The concept of *group* success and *group* guilt was more firmly rooted in the board room than in any social worker's doctorate thesis. It was particularly true in the high echelons, where no man could be too harshly dealt with; for if it were proven that one man was fallible, mistaken, wrongheaded, or simply stupid, it followed that *any* of their ranks might be similarly exposed.

Thrasher knew this for the truth, knew it more soundly than any of the other finely groomed men about him. He knew that the Brick Higgins' debacle could not possibly be laid solely at his door. Somehow, in the stumbling, slovenly way in which Whitechapel had always operated, the *G & T* millions would be saved. Then, abruptly, he heard a new voice. A youth named Chilson (he didn't even know his first name) was speaking in the fine nasal tones of the Eastern campus. "I think Mr. Finucane and Mr. Loomer have a point," he heard the boy say. "I've kept a record of our correspondence with *G & T*."

Thrasher jerked upward in his seat. This lean, scrubbed kid with the white-blond hair had been running for coffee two weeks ago. Perhaps he was speaking from ignorance, Thrasher thought. But as the youth edged closer to the table, Thrasher paled slightly. There was a confidence in his movements and voice that indicated he had all the right instincts: his clothes were casual without being conformist, his face was bland and cunning at the same time, and he wore an immense ring, the insignia of some college society, on his left pinky. Actors like Finucane and Loomer could be handled, but the ones who were born to the work, the boys who never had to simulate were the dangerous ones.

"That's right, Ted, you handled the first contacts," Finucane said brightly.

"As I was saying, sir," the youth persisted, "*G & T* asked us twice to furnish them with a list of new ideas. I'm sure I sent the request on to Mr. Thrasher." He turned to Woody, his pink athlete's face nailing the older man with deadly innocence.

They were all looking at him now, studying him with a kind of curious disbelief, a Trotzkyite unfrocked at the weekly cell meeting. And he realized, too, that he was experiencing one of those rare moments of revelation. He was posittive there had been no plot; no whispered exchange of ideas in corridors on how they would "get" Thrasher at the next meeting. It had just happened, spontaneously and naturally, without preplanning, without malice. He was sure, for example, that Loomer still respected him and that old T.C. liked him. But the fixation of guilt was complete; there could be no retreat. Maybe it had been his own fault for backing and filling. Or perhaps he had made the fatal mistake of insulting an old client's motives in front of T. C. It was like one of those one-act plays they used to do at boy scout camp: six men trapped in a submarine, and one must die to save the others. The coward among them refuses to pick straws; so the others, acting in concert, arrange it so that he cannot help but be the victim.

"I hate to say it, Woody, but you kicked this one," Loomer said slowly. "I don't think Ted has to produce any memos or letters. We're all working together on this."

"What do we do now?" Finucane asked, plaintively.

Thrasher turned earnestly to the old man. "Mr. Whitechapel, may I make a farewell speech?"

"Woodrow, no one has suggested for a moment . . ."

He took no heart from the old man's assurance. Whitechapel had never fired anyone in his life, and if they really intended to hang him, they had neater ways. His office would be changed; he would lose some privileges at meetings; he would be taken off certain assignments, invited less to various homes; stripped of minor prerogatives; day by day he would find that his subordinates were being consulted on decisions that were normally his to make.

". . . that you step down. But if you wish to explain your action in the *G & T* affair, please do."

He had lost so much ground, been maneuvered so artfully to a desperate position, that he knew his counterattack would have to be so fantastic that they would have to support him.

"Let me admit right off that I'm partly guilty for the *G & T* problem. Sure, I okayed Brick Higgins. So did all of us here. But he's past tense. You can't sell underarm perfume with a 5.8 rating, and both Brick and his friends know it. Now a problem presents itself: how do we get *G & T* on our side again? What kind of show can we dream up that will get audience? What can we do on that electric machine that will be genuinely different?"

He was a superb speaker, fast and persuasive, and he could change pace in a fraction of a second.

"But before I get into that, I want to discuss a more fundamental problem. It has to do with *values*. I know research will show us that public service can't sell toothpaste, that highbrow shows don't get ratings, that people prefer wrestling to symphony. But did it ever occur to us that we're not just in business to sell?"

Finucane and Loomer exchanged puzzled glances. Thrasher, they knew, was the office culture-seeker. But to defy the entire principle of the shop!

"Let me put it this way. Maybe the idea of using television as purely a vehicle for advertising is wrong."

Finucane interrupted. "Hell, Woody, go work for the bloody BBC. They got plenty of sustaining birdcallers."

Nobody laughed. He was talking beautifully, saving his punch lines, and he welcomed Finucane's jab.

"You're right, Tom, absolutely right. BBC and for that matter most sustaining public service programs are deadly dull. And why? Because the know-how and showmanship in the agencies—the *talents gathered right around this table*—aren't applying themselves to it. We're too concerned with tired comics and loud bands. We let the networks and their hundred-and-fifty-dollar-a-week writers program the educational stuff, the better stuff. *We should be in there pitching ourselves.*"

Loomer scratched his head and grimaced. "Let me get you right, Woody. Are you saying we should offer *G & T* somethin' like Ed

Murrow? Boy, that's good only in small doses. The public's got all they want."

"Yeah," said Finucane, "a man can get a cawlege degree on CBS Sunday afternoons."

"You're right again, Tom," Woody snapped. "But maybe that's because the programs are unimaginative, uninspired. I feel that the *real* world, *real* things happening to *real* people, is what we should shoot for. I've given this a lot of thought, and the way I see this show, it's a natural for a firm like *G & T*."

Thrasher stood up, stretching his arms and then began circling his chair. He was improvising now, stringing words and sentences together with desperate grace. They were all suspiciously attentive. Collectively they had established his guilt; but the unwritten rules permitted him an appeal.

"I've thought about this kind of show for a long time, and maybe we're ready to spring it on a client now. Maybe *G & T*. We start with the assumption that there are millions of people around the country who lead worthwhile, constructive lives. That by itself isn't enough. Of these millions there are thousands whose lives are dramatic, of interest to their fellow Americans, of *such* interest that these other Americans want to know more about them."

Finucane broke in. "That's an old tired idea, Woody. *We the People*, they called it, and it flopped on television."

"No, Tom," he said sharply. "My idea is not the painful studio interview. I say we select our subject carefully. Then we take the biggest mobile unit in the world, eight cameras if necessary, to their house, or store, or laboratory, or farm. And we do the show *live* from there. No actors, nothing phony. Real people, doing real things, exciting things, the kind of things that make our country powerful and unique. And we'll call it . . ."

He paused, looking fixedly out the window at the hard, beautiful New York skyline, halting not so much to find the right words, but to catch his breath and give mind and tongue a respite.

". . . *Americans, U.S.A.*"

"*Americans, U.S.A.*" It was Loomer repeating it, saying it quickly, without his make-believe drawl. "It's got a nice sound, Woody. But I'm not sold on it as a show. Too many imponderables. And to get real people who can sustain a dramatic feeling for one-half hour! How would you do it? Would they re-enact things? Read script? As Tom says, they've tried this kind of thing before."

"It's a matter of technique," Thrasher persisted. "I am convinced the idea is sound. I know it is. But it needs the best writers—an

Irwin Shaw or a Budd Schulberg. The best directors—Gadget Kazan, Josh Logan."

"But *G & T* needs a show right away," Loomer said. "We're lucky we tried Higgins out early this summer and found out he was no good. But a project like this—you'd never get it on the air in time. What makes you think *G & T* will buy?"

Thrasher felt supremely confident, cocky, exhilarated. He had jolted them out of their comfortable bunks. But he had to keep moving to maintain his advantage. He walked to Whitechapel's chair and leaned over the table, facing the old man.

"Chief, I ask you to bet on me. I want personally to produce and supervise this project. I'd like you to call Mr. Gatling and ask him to approve an audition. I *know* he'll buy and I *know* we'll do him a world of good. I'll guarantee a 25 Nielsen, and I'm convinced that the favorable atmosphere we can create with a useful program like this will sell more deodorant squeezers than that Frank Lloyd Wright factory in East Branch can turn out."

The parched little face turned to Loomer.

"What shall we do, Ben?"

Loomer leaned back, squinting at Thrasher. "I'm not totally sold, Woody. I suppose we could get Gatling to play ball for an audition. But . . . heck, you really haven't given us anything concrete. I'd like a rough idea of what the pilot would be like."

Thrasher turned to Whitechapel's secretary, a bloodless, gray woman who tolerated no familiarity from executives of any echelon.

"Miss Vessels," he said, using the bland smile that had disarmed dozens of industrial leaders, "please call up Miss Farber and have her bring a set of bulldog editions to the room."

Just as the air had been poisoned against him fifteen minutes ago, so now he could do no wrong. She rose, glaring, and left the room.

"What's a bulldog edition?" asked Chilson.

Thrasher spun around gracefully. "Teddy, you should do your apprenticeship in a city room and you'd know. Old newspapermen like Tom and myself know, don't we, Tommy?"

Miss Vessels returned with a set of papers and set them in front of Thrasher.

"Okay, Ben, I'm going to prove to you that I can find our pilot program right here in today's afternoon newspapers. I'm so confident that I've got a winner that I'll pick a real person out of some news item and base a half hour of exciting television on him."

He opened the tabloid New York *Record*, scanning the headlines. There was a banner head on page two about a Chinese Nationalist raid on an offshore island. It was *AP* copy, straightforward and unemotional. Below it, there was a United Nations roundup written in the *Record's* snappy, conversational style. No help there. Page two featured a murder case: a young couple in Mineola being held for axing the girl's father. He read the first paragraph quickly, found it too sordid. There were two other stories: a Hollywood divorce and an exposé of tenement conditions in East Harlem. He turned to page three.

On the right-hand side of the page, under a three-column head, he saw something promising. The headline said simply:

VIGNETTE IN BROWNSVILLE:
DOCTOR SAVES GIRL
by *MYRON MALKIN*

He scanned the first paragraph, then the second, and he knew at once he had found the first program.

"Gentlemen, if you'll bear with me, I'd like to read you an account of our first installment of *Americans, U.S.A.* And as I read I want you to think of the *real* people behind this story, and the way we can bring them to life far beyond the power of a rewrite man's slovenly prose."

He began to read. "There is a heart beating within the steel and concrete confines of our great city. Sometimes it beats faintly, and sometimes it beats with vigor, but it is there all the time.

"Early this morning, a reporter saw the heart of the city in the person of an old man, a doctor, one of a vanishing race, the old-fashioned general practitioner.

"It happened Monday morning, in the early hours when the hard-hearted city sleeps, when tragedy stalks the poor of our town.

"At 3:30 A.M., a doorbell was rung in the Brownsville section of Brooklyn; a doctor's doorbell. Dr. Samuel Abelman is sixty-eight years old and has been practicing medicine on the same block for forty years. There are many younger doctors in the neighborhood. But somehow the poor people of Brownsville have come to know that he is the man they want when tragedy strikes.

"In forty years, Dr. Abelman has never refused to answer the call of mercy. This time, he answered the nightbell and found on his doorstep a young teen-age girl, badly beaten, unconscious, one of the city's nameless and faceless, who suffer in the night.

"When this reporter arrived, a crowd had gathered. No one knew the girl, no one had any idea what had happened to her. A few, including the doctor, mentioned a mysterious 'Josh' who had left her there and had vanished.

"The doctor knelt at her side. With the gentleness of experience, he raised her head, took her pulse, listened to her heart. He made a soft bed for her with his bathrobe. Refusing to leave her side, he had a neighbor call for the police and an ambulance. All this time he held her battered head in his lap, and consoled her.

"The crowd was silent; they understood Dr. Abelman. He was their doctor, their friend. The specialists were alien to them, for in the dead of night, alone and afraid, they knew that only the strong hands of the old GP could aid them.

"It was over quickly. The police came, the ambulance arrived. The doctor himself supervised the carrying of the girl into the ambulance. A screeching of sirens, a murmur from the assembled throng—black and white, old and young—and then the incident in Brownsville had ended.

"The cynics say this is a city with a hard mind and a cold eye; but on one street at least there is a heart beating. Ask the tired and rejected poor who bring their sorows to Samuel Abelman, M.D."

Thrasher stopped and dropped the *Record* to the table in front of him. "Now then," he said quietly, "I dare somebody to tell me there isn't a story there."

Finucane fidgeted uncomfortably. "Maybe there is, Woody," he said, "but it sounds to me like a Jewish Dr. Christian."

"You miss the point, Tom," Thrasher said patiently. "Dr. Christian is play-acting. This is *real, real, real!* A real man living a valuable, constructive life. What greater story can we tell? After we tell this doctor's story, we do a hundred others—farmers, forest rangers, research men, nurses—there's no limit!"

The old man was blinking his eyes rapidly; a decision was forthcoming. "Woodrow," he said, "you have made a persuasive case. Ben and I will talk to Mr. Gatling today. I am reasonably certain that, on the basis of my personal appeal, he will remain with us, at least long enough to audition your first program."

Thrasher stood up. "That's all I need, chief. I'll—"

"But let me warn you, Woodrow," he said, ever so softly, "that you and you alone will bear responsibility for satisfying them. We cannot let the client down a second time."

He rose, immaculate, imperturbable. The others did likewise, and Loomer crossed the table to Thrasher.

"You'd better git on your horse, kid," he said jovially. "Shouldn't we lunch with the network genuises today and get some help? Costs? Director? Writer?"

"I'd rather not, Ben. You heard the chief. It's *my* responsibility.

I want to produce it myself. I might even take a crack at writing it. You know I made my living that way before I got rich."

Loomer shrugged, then smiled. "Go to it, kid. I sure admire your nerve. But I wouldn't want your neck right now."

Sweating furiously, his feet strangely airy and detached, Thrasher returned to his office. It was uncanny the way everyone looked at him; the mailroom boys and the file clerks knew already.

His phone rang seconds after he slumped into his chair. It was Ted Chilson.

"Mr. Thrasher," he heard the nasal voice intone, "I think you've got one magnificent idea there. Could you use a bright creative guy like myself to help you? You know—research and legwork? I fooled around with a little writing at Amherst."

"Well, why don't you fool around a little more, Teddy? Try the *Partisan Review*."

He hung up, seeing Louise's disapproving headshake. "That wasn't necessary," she said.

"I know. But I couldn't resist it. Louise, dear, I'll have lunch in today. Get me the address and phone number of Dr. Samuel Abelman in the Brooklyn book."

"What's the matter? You feeling sick?"

"I am dying, Egypt, dying. Louise, I am excessively healthy and sublimely happy. I just want to be assured that I'm a nervous wreck. This agency could stand a few ulcers to give it some class."

Wearily, the artist enervated, he turned again to the window, studying the swarm of people drifting through the steamy plaza; the gawkers, the lunch-goers, the shoppers.

"Louise," he asked, "how does this title for a television show strike you? *Americans, U.S.A.!*"

"It's fatuous and redundant."

He shut his eyes reflectively. "You're right, doll. But so are they."

With private ecstasy, Thrasher was surveying himself in the full-length mirror bolted with immense spurious diamonds to the bathroom door. He had just showered and shaved and he liked his looks. Physical appearance was enormously important in his world; yet pride of the flesh was never to be manifested publicly. But there was nothing forbidding a man's appreciation of his own charms when alone, or almost alone. He was clad only in his white broadcloth undershorts, whiter and richer than the rumpled sheets of the double studio couch from which he had arisen. His body was long, small-boned, and relaxed; he would never be fat, and the notion delighted him because of the numerous former athletes in the business (like Finucane) who were now running to blubber. In the dark, narrow clothing of the profession, he showed too much better advantage. The face was excellent, too: the forehead broad and furrowed with intense honesty, the features small but neatly defined, the pale-green eyes boyish and alert.

Affectionately, he touched the dignified hollows below his cheekbones. They invested his face with a knowledgeable, dedicated mien: the look of an avant-garde artist, a writer of esoteric novels.

He shivered slightly, realizing with some bewilderment that it was the middle of August, a hot spell was gripping the city, he was in a steel-and-concrete apartment in the middle of New York, and yet he was cold. Air-conditioning reminded him of something his father had said on learning that the rich ladies in Chicago took their dogs to barbers. "It's against nature," the old man had stated. "If the Lord had intended that dogs should get their hair cut, he'd have made other dogs who were barbers."

The aimless recollection of his father, that spare and doomed science teacher, reminded him of the mission he faced that morning, and he sat on the edge of the bed, pulling on socks and shoes. "To seek, to strive, to find, and not to yield," he found himself saying aloud.

Fussing with the orange juice and the instant coffee in the minuscule kitchen, she heard him, and moved into view, holding the plastic juice container like a cocktail shaker.

"What are you mumbling about?" She was an angular, lean girl with a colorless and flawless body. Her face had the same neat lines as did Thrasher's, but it was a much younger face, unlined and untroubled. Her wheat-colored hair was clipped close to the scalp. She was wearing only a finger-length white nylon night-gown, and for a fleeting second Thrasher felt a resparking of lust.

"That was Tennyson, lovey, a poet I'm rarely caught quoting. Wasn't he part of that English survey you took at Los Angeles City College?"

"Chaffee Junior College," she corrected. "And I was a social science major."

"With the best thighs in southern California."

She came to his side, embracing his cropped head, sighing as he ran his hands up and down her hairless flanks.

"Enough," Thrasher said. "This is a big work day for Woodrow Wilson Thrasher. I'd enjoy a reprise very much, but I must be off to Brooklyn."

He tried to shove her away, but she persisted. Her arms were quite strong. "Say you love me."

"To quote that drawling charlatan, Ben Loomer, heeeell no."
She hugged his almost-shaven head tighter against the small upright breasts. "Well, say something nice."
"I love to go to bed with you."
"That's all? Good old once-a-week-Alice?"
"Used a dynamite stick for a phallus."
She disengaged him, smiling tolerantly.

He finished dressing rapidly and they sat in the cheerless kitchenette sipping frozen orange juice and synthetic coffee. Now with the night's tumescence evaporated, he had difficulty concentrating on her, making sense out of her conversation, finding an adequate reason for having breakfast in her apartment.

"Why do you always show up here after some big crisis at Whitechapel? It seems we're always shacking up after you've gotten a raise, or won an argument." She pouted.

"Alice, baby, I hate that rude expression *shacking up*. You don't use it well. The fact that you are an assistant television director doesn't give you license to be uncouth. As for your thesis, you're probably right. A form of male expression. When I'm being creative, or being attacked, I have to express myself in the most elemental way. Reaffirmation."

She crinkled her small, perfect nose and lowered the steaming coffee cup. "I just wish, Woody, it were more than plain—well—carnal."

"Please, baby, no more. You know I respect you and I honestly like you. You're never bored with me, I'm sure. Let's keep it that way. No foreign entanglements. End lynching. Free Earl Browder."

"I'm no better than a whore, as far as you're concerned."

"Oh, come off it," he said wearily. "Why don't you look at it this way? Do you get pleasure from our relationship? You do? Fine. Keep doing it. Be like Hemingway. If he feels good when he does something it's moral. Or something like that. And you're the loveliest piece of morality tale I've ever seen."

He said the last sentence with a Groucho Marx inflection, and she giggled. "I'm sorry I'm being a drag, sweetheart. You've got an awful lot of work today, and I shouldn't be pestering you." She spoke with genuine concern, and for a moment Thrasher was attentive. Then he gulped the blistering coffee, rose abruptly, and walked into the disheveled bedroom to use the telephone.

It was almost ten o'clock and he had no intention of going to the office. He was determined to travel to Brooklyn that morning and get the project rolling. Louise, the only person he could trust, would hold the fort for him. Already, with an instinct which Thrasher was convinced was racial, she understood the gravity of his position. She was manning battle stations and drawing up disaster procedures. Her soft, knowing voice was always of deep comfort to him.

"Mr. Thrasher's office."

"Louise, baby, this is Woody."

"Hi. Where have you been?"

"I stayed at the Warwick last night. Got into a poker game with some of the clowns at the network and it ran too long."

She knew he was lying; she always knew. "Win or lose?"

"I broke even. And a good thing, I need the money. Louise, I won't be in today. I'm off to Brooklyn and the first subject of *Americans, U.S.A.* Did you get me that poop on Dr. Ableman?"

"I have it right here. The Kings County Medical Society lists an Abelman, Samuel, M.D., at 1553 Haven Place, in Brooklyn. Phone number is Haddingway 4-0362. He graduated from Bellevue in 1912, so that must be your man."

"Anything else?"

"Just lists two hospitals he's affiliated with."

"Okay. Keep your fingers crossed that he speaks English, likes television, and doesn't make millions through the practice of abortions on his X-ray table."

"What's new at the *schlacht-haus?*" he asked conspiratorially.

"Pretty dull. You know of course that Gatling agreed to hold everything until he sees the audition. Finucane and Loomer called on him yesterday again."

"*Again?*" Why were they returning to the drug empire even after the old man had agreed to Whitechapel's proposal? He sounded faintly hysterical; Louise sensed it. As she answered, he could see her bending close to the phone, turning to the wall to make sure no one overheard her.

"This is not for attribution," Louise whispered, "but Finucane had lunch yesterday with a couple of network producers. Public affairs types . . . Harvard Club. Mean anything to you?"

"Only that Finucane is much too fond of Harvard men for a Boston College graduate. Tom and his friends have divined that *G & T* like the idea of a service show. So . . . if Woodrow falls on his can, they can run to the network and program their own half hour the easy way."

"I'll ask some questions," she said quietly.

"Call you this afternoon, kitten. I can be reached in half an hour at the good doctor's, where I will probably accept a free high colonic just for kicks."

She waited at the other end, expectantly, and he knew, of course, what she wanted to hear.

"One other thing, Louise. Call Mrs. Thrasher and explain that I'll be in Brooklyn all day. She knew about the poker game, but I haven't had a chance to buzz her this morning."

Her puritanical voice, disbelieving, responded, "I'll call her right now. Don't get lost. 'Bye."

Deliberately, he hung up, annoyed not so much at the small deceit he had just perpetrated, but by the fact that it was a shoddy deception and fooled nobody.

Alice was nude now, moving lightly about the nubby carpet and retrieving her scattered clothes. "I must be a pretty hot poker player, huh?" she asked.

He sprung up from the bed, placed a possessive hand on her lean behind, and kissed her abstractedly. "Winners tell jokes, losers say 'deal the cards,'" he said. In one graceful motion he grabbed his caramel-colored attaché case, and was out the door, bounding down the narrow steps of the brownstone.

First Avenue was hot and malodorous under the midmorning sun. He had never quite understood the magnetism of the Upper East Side of New York City. It was part of the mythology of the business; so much so that he could not think of a single person he knew who lived on the West Side. Who lived there? And why was West Seventy-second Street inferior to East Seventy-second Street? Who made the rules? Thrasher never told any of his associates, but, as far as he was concerned, the East Side was ugly: fly-specked, cramped stores, too much traffic and gasoline, decrepit houses. And dog turds—more per square foot than anywhere else in the world. Garbage collected in the gutter, and if you owned a trim, converted brownstone, you probably lived next door to a ruined tenement, inhabited by aboriginal Irish, a ravaged relic flanked by sentinel ashcans. That was the real symbol of the East Side: the brimming ashcan. Yet he had known men who had failed to make the grade because they didn't have the foresight to live east of Fifth Avenue; there were others who went broke seeking an East Side address. It was kind of a *Drang nach Osten* from Madison Avenue. Waiting for a cab, he envisioned platoons of lean, young men in narrow, dark suits moving in phalanx out of the air-conditioned offices, ever eastward, to the lean, spare warrens of the East Fifties, Sixties, and Seventies, to be met at the doors by lean women with short haircuts and flat voices.

A taxi jolted to a stop in front of him and he climbed in. "I want to go to Brooklyn, is that all right?" Ever since the war years, when cabs were scarce and drivers rudely refused long hauls, he had been in the habit of addressing hackies with painful deference.

The driver (the card read: Sal Intrabartolo) turned a troglodyte's head around. "Datsa big place, Brooklyn. Where? Canarsie? Boro Park? Ebbets Field?"

"Wait a second. I have it written here. 1553 Haven Place. Know where it is?"

"Haven Place!" he said incredulously. "Must be near Haven Park. Dat's not so bad. I could find it."

"It's a section called Brownsville."

"Brownsville!" Intrabartolo croaked. "Only dat's the other *end* of Haven Place. Okay, you're in. We'll go Brooklyn Bridge, Flatbush Avenue, Atlantic Avenue. Dat okay?"

"Anything you say. I don't know Brooklyn at all."

The cab lurched off and Thrasher slumped deep in the rear seat, stretching his long legs out, resting his feet on the folded jump seats. He would enjoy the ride. The solitude of the unshared cab, the air whipping through the open windows, would permit him to think, would clear his head of trivia and turn his mind to the vital matter at hand. He understood from his talk with Louise that morning that failure on the project would mean the end of his tenure at Whitechapel. And if Loomer and Finucane were nosing around for a new public affairs program, it meant that *G & T* had liked the *Americans, U.S.A.* concept so well that his colleagues were betting on his downfall and planning an alternate offering. They'd make it painless, to be sure. They'd protect him, and close ranks so he wouldn't look too bad. But his touch would never be the same; never again could he dominate the meetings; his airy quotes from the classics would go unheeded; his daring notions of programming would be deemed crackpot.

Why had it happened? How had it happened? Maybe it was all illusory; maybe they didn't *really* want to dump him. That was the trouble with the whole business. Everything was illusion, fiction, make-believe. He often got the feeling that all of them—not just the agency gang, a really decent and friendly bunch, but the radio and television people, the comic-book writers, the fiction writers, the movie people, indeed all of the laborers in what the seminar boys called "mass communications," were not really at work, but were playing a kind of screwy "house." It was like going to a modern journalism school, where the faculty gave you a "press card" and you were supposed to cover fires and disasters and crash police line with it. No one ever took the card seriously; it didn't even look like a regular working press card. But everyone in the school had to make believe it was real. So it was in his world, the world that paid him thirty-five thousand dollars a year and permitted him to live in North Stamford. Everyone else had a working press card to the world; but the dealers in talk had only journalism school credentials.

The unreality, the illusion, the myths dominated everything. You built yourself a little role and lived it. When you started missing cues and lines, you were in trouble. Old Whitechapel had his role, and a darn good one he had made it. Loomer with his deliberate drawl; Finucane's harsh slum accents; and he himself with his air of the artistic rebel. He knew one man in the business who for years had earned a phenomenal salary simply by belonging to the American Anthropological Association and dropping potsherds and siblings into his conversation.

They were speeding across the ancient, graceful bridge now, and Thrasher sensed keenly his infatuation with the city. He loved it, loved it as only the small-town boy can love it, finding in its jagged skyline and endless variety a stimulation and a *mystique* that no native New Yorker could ever experience. *It's true,* he mused, *the town is run by hicks, like me. Check the rosters of all the outfits that control the thought processes in New York City, and you'll find nothing but country boys.* They came in droves and they outslicked the slickest of city slickers, simply because they were better at make-believe. They started acting from the minute they got off the Greyhound bus and pretty soon their act was accepted. There were some agencies where a North Carolina accent was a requisite for advancement; others where apprenticeship on the Minneapolis *Star-Journal and Tribune* was the key to success; one public relations house where only Tennesseans, and particularly residents of Nashville, were assured of making the grade. His mind dawdled over a curious paradox: the red-necked, wool-hatted politician who accuses sinful New York of corrupting the nation's morals probably has a son heading up the copy desk at the biggest publicity mill in town. Well, in any case, being from New Arabia, South Dakota, had never hurt him.

They were bearing down on the easterly marches of Brooklyn, a section where, as one travels, respectability unravels in arithmetical progression. Thrasher realized that they were, unfailingly, moving into a true slum.

With each passing street, there was evidence of greater decay. Now they were in a neighborhood which, on one side, exhibited a row of gray tenements, not quite slum tenements, and, on the other, a series of semidetached red brick homes—squat, ugly dwellings erected hastily in the twenties. The streets were heavily strewn with paper and refuse and the number of children darting about, in and out of parked cars, had increased markedly. As they rode, Thrasher also made note of the ethnic variations. When they had first entered Haven Place, the people appeared to be well-dressed, middle-class Jews. As the houses became more modest, he noticed a preponderance of blonds and redheads: German and Irish, he imagined. Then, as the streets grew dirtier in appearance, the residents displayed unmistakable Levantine characteristics, and he took them to be Italians and Jews. It was strange, he thought, how the Jews fitted at both ends. He had observed just a sprinkling of Negroes during the ride, but now, as the cab crossed Rower Avenue, he became sharply aware that he was entering a predominantly colored locality.

"This must be the block," the driver said. "You said 1555?"

"1553. It must be on the left, not far from the corner." As he spoke, he felt a dread, exhausting sensation, a kind of visceral defeat. He knew, too, what had caused it. It was the street: the filthy, swarming, noisy street, the kind of street that moaned of poverty, failure, degradation, all the things he had escaped forever, all the stale, and loathsome aspects of life which Thrasher's own clean world denied. You sold your products to the poor, and you competed for their dollar, you entertained them with programs, and you molded their minds with ideas. But it was best to let sleeping dogs and the poor lie.

The cab halted. They were parked alongside a yellow brick two-story house, one of perhaps twenty completely attached homes which ran the length of the block. It was distinguished from its neighbors by an ugly wall of red brick and cast-iron railing which surrounded it. There was no trace of shrubbery, just a cement square within the iron-and-brick bastion. But at the edge of the curb, rising in splendor from dog turds and rusted sardine cans, was a Lombardy poplar of regal proportions. Thrasher looked skyward, marveling at its fantastic height, at the manner in which it had thrived amidst so much filth and concrete. A deflated bicycle tire dangled from a lower branch, and at the top of the trunk, a yellow and black sign proclaimed:

NO PARKING
DOCTOR'S HOUSE

Bolted to the brick fortress wall he saw the doctor's sign, and he was certain of his destination. The flaking gold lettering read:

DOCTOR

S. ABELMAN

Thrasher had one foot out of the cab, and was gazing over the taxicab's hood to the opposite side of the street. A row of tenement houses, swarming with Negroes of every size, shape, and shade, confronted him. He had never seen so many small colored children in his life. Four black youths were playing stickball in the gutter, their naked ebony chests and limbs glistening exquisitely in morning sunlight. They shrieked and danced in a glut of joy; from the crumbling windows and doorways sodden men and shrill women cheered them as they swung broomstick against rubber ball.

"Hit dat! Hit dat! Hit dat damn ball!"

"Wah-wah-wah-wah!"

"You cain't hit dat ball! You chicken!"

"Yaaaaaah . . . you chicken yo'sef!"

"You got a chicken *wing*, das what. Chicken *wing!"*

Thrasher winced. Did they make that much noise all day long? Every day of the week? Why didn't they do it somewhere else? There were also a handful of shabby stores across the street. One was a tailoring shop, and he could see gusts of steam rising from an old-fashioned pressing machine. Next to it was a barbershop, the window fly-specked and filled with ancient circus posters. Next to the barbershop was a nondescript store, with no sign of any kind, which apparently sold everything from ladies oversized bloomers to dolls and cheap chinaware. Across the street, a gray-haired derelict, a stooped white man in dirty overalls, was methodically shoveling freshly deposited horse manure into a battered pail.

"Hey, Mac, that's four twenty-five. You gettin' out or you wanna go back?"

Jerked rudely back to reality by the driver's insolence, he realized Intrabartolo had been watching him, reading the vague terror in his face. He had no idea of the passenger's errand, but he understood this much: *a rich guy who can't stand the stink.*

"I don't blame ya, Mac," he said. "I don't see how the hell these people live myself. I got four nice rooms in the Bronx. Nuttin' fancy, but clean. No boogies, know what I mean?"

He offered no thanks for the seventy-five-cent tip and roared off, narrowly missing one of the stickball players. Thrasher felt his hand tighten over the hard handle of the attaché case. "Alone and afraid in a world I never made," he said softly. Then he walked through the brick pillars, up four concrete steps, and through the unlocked outside door into the hot vestibule. He pressed his finger against the black button that read *Doctor's Bell.*

A buzzer sounded in answer, and he opened the inner door, finding himself in a narrow hallway. A flight of maroon-carpeted steps ran up to the left, and he imagined that a tenant or the doctor's living quarters were above. To his right he saw a small waiting room, complete with bookcase, magazine table, and eight assorted chairs. It was rather cheerful as waiting rooms go, and Thrasher was about to walk in and seat himself, when he heard a voice. At the end of the hall he saw a gigantic colored woman in a white uniform.

"Yo' all wanna see the doctor?"

"Yes, I would."

"He doan have no office hours in de mornin'."

"Is he in?"

She said nothing, but came lurching down the darkened hallway, the spurious dignity of the starched uniform destroyed by her immense feet, shuffling in tattered slippers. Suspiciously, a malign Babe Ruth in blackface, she looked at his attaché case, then asked, "Watchooall wan'?"

"It's a personal matter."

"You ain' a patient?"

"No, I'm not. I would appreciate it if you told the doctor I'd like to see him." What was he doing being so deferential to this colored woman? He was Woodrow Wilson Thrasher and he earned thirty-five thousand dollars a year and had an expense account.

She half turned, one baleful eye fixing him with contempt, and muttered, "Yo'all sit down in deah. I tell him, but I ain' sure he gon' see you."

Annoyed, he walked into the waiting room. The windows and venetian blinds were raised high and through the copper screens he heard again the wild street noises. He sat on the arm of a massive, worn leather chair, and looked out on Haven Place. From this vantage point he had a better view of the opposite side of the street, where the tenements stood. In the ground floor of one of them, a church of some kind had been installed. Vulgar drawings of the Savior and the Virgin were pasted to a dirty glass. A sign lettered by some amateur hand read:

AFRICAN TRUE CHURCH OF JESUS

THE WHOLY UNITED ARMY OF GOD

Thrasher started for a second, hearing a door slam, but no one
appeared, and he imagined someone had entered through a cellar
door below the front stairs. He sat nervously for a moment, then
bounded up and toured the heat-laden, quiet room. The chairs
had a tired, resigned look about them, and he thought of the
thousands of sick, weary people who had sat in the waiting room
over the years. In a metal tray he found a dozen calling cards.

1553 *Haven Place*   HADDINGWAY 4-0362

SAMUEL ABELMAN, M.D.

OFFICE HOURS   *Sunday by*
1-2, 6-8   *Appointment*

Thrasher absent-mindedly put the card in his pocket, then turned
to an old-fashioned mahogany bookcase in the corner of the room.
It stood adjacent to the high double doors, green-shaded from
within, which led to the doctor's office. He was reading some of the
titles—*Half Hours with the Best Authors, The Swedish Gymnast*—
when he heard the Negro woman calling him. She loomed into
view, addressing with with dull animosity.

"The doctor in the yard. He say if yo' ain' a patient, yo' can see
him back deah. You come along wit me."

Obediently, he followed her, through the hallway, to the rear
of the house. The rear room was a kitchen, the walls and woodwork
clean and bright yellow, but possessed of the lumpy irregularity
characteristic of years of painting. Through a screen door he could
see the doctor's backyard, and the first glimpse of it dazzled him.
He opened the door, walking onto a creaky wooden porch, his eyes
delighted by the lovely colors and forms of a magnificent garden.
The area was too cramped and narrow to allow for a formal garden
of the variety his friends cultivated in Rye and Westport. But it
had a wildness, a haphazard beauty, that showed the hand of a
talented botanist. A brick path, the work of an amateur, lay beneath splotches of moist earth, and bisected the narrow yard. On

either side of the path, for about a third the length of the area, were two fenced-in beds. Thrasher had never seen flowers of such intense colors, thrown together so artlessly and yet with such startling effect. Dahlias predominated: huge, cabbage-sized blooms of pale yellows and deep maroons, subtle pinks and flame orange, some compact and fat like pompoms, others with long spiked leaves. Interspersed were lilies, snapdragons, and hollyhocks, all hurling their primary freshness against the sordid slum walls.

He could see no one in the yard. Gingerly, he descended the rotting steps and walked onto the crumbling brick path. A mustard-colored mongrel dog, broad-snouted and splayfooted, padded toward him, sniffing his shoes and honoring him with a few diffident wags. Where the flower beds ended, there was a cleared area of larger shrubs and bushes: lilacs, roses, and forsythia. On either side of the path, now all but vanished beneath the dirt, two gigantic trees formed a natural bower. One was a cherry tree, no longer bearing fruit, but still thick with hard laquered leaves. The other was a magnolia, a gray, gnarled veteran, with four divergent trunks rising from the immense root. Beneath the cherry tree an ancient slatted bench rested, its rusted legs entrenched in the hard earth. It was unbelievably cool and peaceful under the arch of boughs and leaves. The ugly backsides and gawking windows of the encircling tenements seemed effectively blocked off by the rich foliage. A high picket fence fixed the borders of the doctor's domain, and furthered the sense of seclusion.

The rear of the yard presented the most unusual scene. Behind a makeshift chicken-wire screen (designed, Thrasher imagined, to keep the dog out) was an unmistakable cornfield. He could see the tassels and the tall stalks, the fat husks and the floppy leaves, and he smiled in delight. Thrasher had been raised in a land where cornfields were measured in miles; the sight of this ridiculous patch of stalks was pleasing both as a reminder of his boyhood and as a clue to the nature of the man he was seeking.

He saw a short, stocky figure emerging from the green stalks. The chicken-wire gate opened and an old man walked out. It was the same man in dirty coveralls (or so it seemed) whom he had seen shoveling manure in the street just a few minutes ago. There was no mistaking him—he was holding the pail in one hand and an old-fashioned stove shovel in the other.

"I—er—I am looking for Dr. Abelman," he said, realizing at once that it was his own disbelief that made him word his opening remarks so awkwardly.

"Who do you think I am, sonny?" The inflection was gruff and the doctor's voice was sharp, but he was smiling.

"Doctor, I'd like about a half hour of your time, maybe a little more. Could you spare me that now?"

Dr. Abelman squinted at the attaché case. "You guys are getting worse and worse. A half hour! Where you from—Merck? Lilly? If it's vitamins, I don't want 'em. No antibiotics either."

Thrasher looked blank for a moment, then laughed. Having worked on a drug company's account, he realized that the doctor had mistaken him for a detail man—the itinerant good-will ambassadors of the pharmaceutical companies who visit doctors to acquaint them with new items. It was an understandable error, and Thrasher saw the humor of it. The dark, neat suit, the pleasant face, and the efficient little valise suggested a drug company detail man quite accurately.

"I'm afraid I'm not a detail man, doctor," Thrasher said easily. "And I guarantee you I won't mention multivitamins or terramycin."

"Insurance?" the doctor asked warily.

"No, it's about—"

"Air-conditioning? Storm windows? I can't use any of that crap."

"Dr. Abelman, take my word for it, I don't want to sell you a thing. I'm here on a purely personal mission and all I want is a chance to talk to you. It's quite hot, and I'd appreciate it if I could sit down."

The doctor set down the redolent pail and the manure-flecked shovel and gestured to the bench. "Okay, but just don't try to sell me anything. The last nice young *shagitz* I let talk to me sold me twenty dollars' worth of expensive fertilizer. It burned the hell out of my peonies."

Thrasher sat down, setting the case at his side. The mustard-colored dog plodded toward him, licking the case, and then collapsed in a heap beside it. Wiping his hands on his trousers, the doctor sat beside Thrasher, admonishing the dog.

"Get out of there, Diane! Go away!"

"That's quite all right, doctor, I like dogs."

"She's a big dope. I can't teach her a thing."

The dog ignored him, burying its snout under a rear leg. Thrasher had his first close look at the physician now. In the street, where he had seen him at a distance, clad in the dirty work clothes, his impression had been one of poverty and defeat. Now at close range he saw a strong, hard face. The doctor's forehead was high, the nose less Semitic than Amerindian, the lips firm and thin. Steel-gray hair, badly in need of cutting, grew thickly at the sides of the large head; at the crown only a few strands remained, standing upright. The doctor's eyes were a dark gray. They were deeply sunken and surrounded by a network of harsh lines which endowed him with a look of perpetual outrage and suspicion. Yet when he smiled or laughed, the transformation was unbelievable: the same lines that denoted anger were transmuted into something raffish and humorous.

He was a small man, the legs heavy and short, the torso disproportionately elongated. A comfortable paunch was ensconced below his heavy chest. Beneath the threadbare workman's shirt Thrasher saw the shoulders and arms of a physically powerful man. The deltoid and biceps muscles were enormous, the forearms were thick with tough sinews, the hands were square and confident. He could see him as a medical student: black-haired and dark-eyed, the young strength camouflaged beneath a white lab smock.

Thrasher reached inside his breast pocket for the newspaper clipping. He handed it to the doctor, saying, "Here's how I found out about you. A very interesting story."

The doctor, bemused, looked at the column of newsprint and laughed. "That Myron. A good little crap artist, that kid. Why are you so interested in this?"

"Who's Myron?" Thrasher asked.

"My nephew, Myron Malkin, he wrote this."

"I don't understand. Did he just contribute it?"

"No, no. He works for the *Record*. A regular William Randolph Hearst."

Thrasher nodded in vague understanding. He wasn't sure whether he liked this or not. The doctor's indifference to the laudatory article, he thought, might be the product of honest modesty. But the reporter's kinship might easily have discolored the entire incident and set Thrasher off in quest of a misrepresentation at best, and, at worst, an utter fiction.

The doctor was still chuckling, shaking his head as he read the article. Then abruptly he looked up. "So what's all this about? I don't even know your name. Maybe you're a cop?"

Sulfur butterflies and bees darted about in the midmorning light. Overhead a flight of pigeons wheeled and dipped, and distantly Thrasher saw the end of a pole, rag attached, beckoning to them from a rooftop.

"You're right, doctor, I'm not being very explicit. Let me introduce myself. My name is Woodrow Thrasher and I'm in—" he paused, ready to say "advertising," thought better of it, and continued, ". . . television. Do you have a set of your own?"

"Oh yes. My daughter bought me one two years ago."

"Fine. Now, actually, I work for a large advertising agency. I am the head of the television department and it's my job to put new programs on the air. At the moment I'm working on a new television show, something that's never been done before. And that's why I'm here this morning."

The doctor seemed to have edged away slightly. "What's the catch? What are you selling?"

Thrasher patted his forehead with his handkerchief. "Dr. Abelman, I assure you, I'm not selling a darn thing. I'm not a detail man, or a cop, or a salesman of any kind. I am a television executive, a producer."

"What do you want from my life?"

Thrasher leaned forward earnestly and placed a hand on the doctor's knee. His pale eyes fixed the tired face with the palpably honest expression he reserved for eldest sons of company presidents.

"I want to tell your story to the country."

The doctor folded his arms, the gesture connoting a further withdrawal. "*What* story? What the *hell* are you talking about?" His voice was not irate, or even annoyed; merely bewildered.

"Let me explain a little," Thrasher pursued. "I've felt for many years that our country is filled with average, everyday people who lead rich, rewarding, constructive lives. They need not be wealthy or famous. In fact, we stress wealth and fame far too much. My idea is to dramatize these true stories of *real* people doing *real* things. But not with actors. With the people themselves showing how they lead their lives, in the actual environment in which it takes place."

Thrasher rose. "This delightful garden of yours, for example," he said earnestly, "your house, the street you live on, the people who come to you for help, your neighbors who have faith in you—"

Abruptly, Thrasher realized he was talking to no one. The doctor had sprung from the bench with remarkable speed, and had sprinted through the wire gate. At the rear of the cornfield, he heard voices in great argument.

"Caught you! Caught you, you old poop!" Dr. Abelman was shouting.

Thrasher walked into the miniature cornfield. At the confluence of the back and side fences, the doctor was standing, shaking a huge rusted frying pan at a white-haired man in the adjoining yard.

"You're an old sneak, Baumgart! I know you sneak around here throwing trash in my yard! But this time I caught you!"

The neighbor said nothing. He was a straight-backed oldster of medium height with snowy hair and red cheeks. He wore steel-rimmed spectacles and his face had the immobility and hardness of the insular householder. The doctor's violent assault seemed to move him not at all; his eyes were flat and unyielding behind the lenses, and his voice was low and level when he spoke.

"You didn't see it, Abelman. You couldn't prove it."

"Why, you old *futz*, I saw you do it! I know you threw your garbage in here yesterday also! I got a mind to crack your skull with this pan!"

There was not the remotest sign of fear on the neighbor's part. Stiffly, he turned his back, muttering, "You got a fresh mout', Abelman."

"Cook yourself some ptomaine in this!" the doctor shouted. Deftly, he sailed the skillet back over the fence. It landed in a thick cluster of giant weeds, and the doctor turned to Thrasher.

"How do you like that old *futz*? He makes a career out of throwing junk in my yard! He'll get that frying pan back in here later. Nice neighbors I have. Salt of the earth."

He walked away from the fence, dusting his hands as if to rid himself of the unpleasant encounter.

"Why in the world should a grown man want to throw garbage in someone else's yard? They collect that stuff in the street, don't they?" Thrasher asked plaintively.

"It's a long story, Mr—what did you say your name was?"

"Thrasher."

"Mr. Thrasher. It's a long, long story. Take my word for it, they've been pulling that kind of stunt for forty years on me. Oh, I catch 'em now and then, but there's too many of them."

The vagueness of the doctor's comments troubled Thrasher. There was a ring of psychotic imbalance in his remarks, and he was just as happy not to pursue the line of questioning. Too many of who? Was *everybody* throwing junk in his yard?

The Negro woman materialized on the wooden porch. "Yo' lunch is ready now, doctor," she called. The indolent dog, who had failed to abet her master during the argument in the cornfield, now ambled to her feet and plodded toward the house.

"Look, sonny, I still haven't the vaguest idea what you're talking about. I don't go on any television shows, and I'm not an actor. Maybe I didn't understand you properly. Why don't you join me for lunch, and maybe you can explain it better?"

Thrasher was delighted by the invitation. "Oh, I wouldn't want to put you out, doctor. I can eat in a restaurant and come back."

"Restaurant! Here? In this slum? Don't be silly."

He followed the short, heavy figure through the sunlit yard to the house, weathering a venomous look from the colored woman. The dining room was on the second floor, and they ascended the slanting steps, Thrasher thoughtful and silent as he trailed his host.

At the head of the stairs, they made a hairpin turn around a hallway wall. The front of the upper story was a combined living and dining room—long, narrow, and cluttered with dark, solid furniture. The walls, lumpy with age, were covered with mud-hued grasscloth. A series of immense original oil paintings, all in a neorealistic style that revolted Thrasher, dominated the wallspace. In the dining area, nearest the street side of the old house, a large round table had been set for two. It was apparently part of a set of aged oaken furniture: the buffet, china closet, and chairs were all of the same dark, brooding mien. The windows were thrust wide open, and through the copper screens the bright-green sun-daubed leaves of the doctor's poplar lent a cheerful note. In the backyard it had been delightfully still; now, in the house, the savage voices of the stickball game ricocheted about the room. It almost seemed they were playing inside the house.

They took turns washing their hands in a large bathroom off the hall. While the doctor was gone, the Negro maid set the table. A half-dozen plates of attractive foods were placed on the spotless tablecloth: small hamburgers aromatic of garlic, four or five varieties of cheese, some large, foreign-looking rolls, a bowl of mashed potatoes, a bowl of stewed mixed fruit, and a large percolator of coffee.

In the doctor's absence, Thrasher studied the appalling paintings. Before departing for the bathroom, the old man had bragged about them.

"Pretty great stuff, heh? One of my patients gave them to me after he ran up a big bill. The poor guy is dead now. Never made a nickel on his paintings."

Silently, Thrasher wondered how large the bill was. No matter how minute, he thought, the atrocious landscapes and florals on the doctor's walls could hardly have been adequate recompense for even the bandaging of an ankle.

He had his back turned to the hallway and was studying, with internal shudders, an impossible summer woodland, splotched with fulvous yellows and toxic greens, when he heard a new voice.

"Hiya."

Thrasher turned around. The newcomer was a distressingly thin youth, perhaps twenty-three or -four, with the knobby knees and round shoulders of a basketball substitute. Thrasher could see him warming up: all fancy form and reverse English, but no real drive. A growth of dull blond hair, excessively wavy and uncombed, rose from the cramped face, the most arresting feature of which was a caricature nose. He wore three things: a white T-shirt laced with holes, a pair of wash-worn basketball shorts, maroon with black piping, and a set of yellow-rimmed spectacles held together over the youth's immense nose by dirty adhesive tape. He was barefoot, and had apparently just awakened.

"Good morning," said Thrasher pleasantly.

The youth exhaled violently through puffed cheeks, and collapsed in an ungainly mauve armchair. "Wow, what a night," he said wearily, "I worked till four in the morning." His voice had a ring of both defiance and self-pity.

He had to be Myron, Thrasher thought, Myron the eternal bench-warmer, the second-stringer. His hunch was confirmed when the doctor returned, smelling strongly of medical alcohol.

"Mr. Thrasher—that's right, isn't it?—this is my nephew, Myron Malkin. He wrote that masterpiece about me. The one you read." Then, hurrying them, like an impatient camp counselor, he said, "C'mon, c'mon, let's eat."

They sat at the round table, Thrasher removing his dark jacket and draping it on the back of his chair.

"*Ess, kindelich, is dein America,*" the doctor said quietly.

Myron scowled and, with a flick of his index finger, pushed the taped bridge of his spectacles back. "I don't think Mr. Thrasher understood, Uncle Doc. Uncle Doc makes a joke like that whenever we eat. He said, 'Eat, children, it's your America.'"

Thrasher looked grave. "I think it's quite charming and appropriate," he said. "After all, it is *our* America. All of us."

From the street, the barbarous noises intensified.

"*Wah-wah-waaaah!*"

"You chicken wing! Chicken wing!"

"An' de batteh is deh great Willy Mays!"

Myron jerked his thumb toward the window. "And *theirs,* too?"

There was something in the way the starved young man was studying him, some intonation in his voice that told Thrasher he had an enemy on his hands. Myron was scrutinizing him: the button-down shirt with the perfectly blooped collar, the dark-green tie with the almost invisible dark-blue parameciums, the brown suit with its sedate lapels. Thrasher knew he was being appraised, and that in Myron's slum-nurtured intelligence the appraisal was accurate and uncomplimentary.

"You ain't a patient here," Myron said flatly.

The doctor had made no attempt at explaining Thrasher's presence, leaving him dangling in the alien environment. Spearing a hamburger and inserting it deftly in a fat onion roll, the doctor spoke.

"Myron, Mr. Thrasher is a television fellah. He's a writer or producer, you know, your racket. He wants to do a program about me, but I'll be damned if I understand him."

Myron leaned back from the table, crossed his flamingo legs, and inserted a thin wedge of Swiss cheese between his teeth.

"What kinda program?" Suspicion clouded the ugly face.

"It's not on the air yet, as a matter of fact," said Thrasher. "It's just in the blueprint stage. A simple idea—a half-hour visit to typical Americans. We'd bring the mobile cameras right to location. To this street and this house, for example. And tell the story right on the spot."

"You got the idea from the article I wrote?"

"Yes, that's a fair statement."

The blond young man leaned over the table, again shoving the slipping glasses back. "Why don't I write the script? Who knows Uncle Doc better than me?"

Dr. Abelman looked from one to the other with some annoyance. "Wait a minute, wise guys. Who said I wanted to do this? Don't be in such a hurry, Myron. I don't know anything about this young man, nice as he is. How do I know it's not a racket? Look, I'm no chump."

The old man had been at the table not more than five minutes, but already he had gulped two hamburgers and a slice of cheese, and was already tossing a cup of steaming coffee down. He dabbed at his lips with a paper napkin—still folded at his place setting—and rose. Thrasher noticed he had been sitting at the edge of his chair, as if anxious to get a head start on leaving the table.

"I got office hours now. Myron, you ask Mr. Thrasher what this is all about. I'll see you later."

He walked in quick steps to the threshold, turned and waved at Thrasher. "If I don't see you again, young man, nice to have metcha. I always enjoy meeting other people. These slobs I have to work with—"

His voice trailed off, and he was gone. Thrasher heard the creaking steps and a fleeting panic gripped him. He was convinced he had a "winner" in the doctor—the cornfield alone would make the show. But the crabbed old man was acting as if the whole incident was a pointless prank. Of course he had no way of knowing what it meant to Thrasher. But couldn't he at least have been more interested?

He found himself pouring coffee for the nephew, trying to avert the distorted eyes across the table.

"No kiddin', Mr. Thrasher. What's the real story on this program? Where you really from?"

Thrasher settled on the direct approach. "Myron, I am the vice-president in charge of television and radio for T. C. Whitechapel. Ring a bell?"

"Yeah. A twenty-million-dollar bell. Right?"

"Twenty-one million, seven hundred thousand, Myron, as listed in *Printer's Ink* last month. Isn't it a little strange for an editorial-side guy to know things like that?"

The flattery was not wasted. "I got lots of time for reading on the night desk. I ain't gonna be no night-desk man the rest of my life, Mr. Thrasher. I want something like what you got."

"Myron, apparently you know about Whitechapel. Now what do you know about *G & T*?"

"Proprietary drugs. Take a look in Uncle Doc's medicine cabinet. Any outfit that can *give away* so much stuff must make jillions on what they sell." Then his face brightened. "I get it. Whitechapel has the *G & T* account. You wanna put on a new show for them. And you want Uncle Doc to be the subject of the first show. What a tie-in! Drug company—family doctor!"

"Frankly, I hadn't thought of the association. But everything else is accurate. It has to go on the air by the end of the month."

Myron was shoveling stewed prunes into his mouth.

"*G & T* got any television shows now?"

Thrasher waited a second before replying. "Yes. The Brick Higgins Show. Do you know it?"

"I'm workin' that time of night. So they'll have *two* shows?"

Thrasher was beginning to weary. He was on strange ground, dealing with strange people, in a setting as foreign to him as a Kaffir kraal. "No, Myron. Brick Higgins was a failure. This is a brand-new show. We start from scratch."

The weedy figure assembled arms and legs and stood up. Myron ambled to the mammoth buffet and pulled open the top drawer. First, he found a toothpick and placed it between his teeth; an instant later, after rummaging about, he produced a worn black office ledger, turning again to face Thrasher.

"What'll that show cost *G & T*?" he asked slyly.

"It's hard to say. I can't see it's any of your business."

Thrasher knew what was coming; but he was surprised that this ramshackle youth, with his doomed-to-fail ambition, was so quick to react to the smell of money. He was sure the intruder could be handled, but he resented the young man's diversionary threat to his plan—a plan which was having more than its share of pitfalls without this offensive boy.

"Okay, an approximation. An ava-ridge."

Thrasher hooked a finger over his upper lip and looked out the heat-misted screen, into the sparkling yellow-green mosaic of the Lombardy poplar.

"Production costs might run a company thirty thousand dollars for a program like that. Of course, the network time would vary, depending on what hour it went on."

"I catch. Thirty thousand just to produce it. That's for writers, directors, engineers, huh? And then more on top of that for the time. Like maybe fifty thousand dollars for a half hour?"

"Maybe. Could be more."

"And what does the agency get? What do you get, Mr. Thrasher?" The distorted eyes were leering at him, the makeshift spectacles were descendent upon the droopy nose, but Myron did not flick them back into position.

"I repeat, Myron, none of this is your business. An agency, as you well know, gets fifteen per cent of what a client spends. That should be fairly simple, even for you, if you can multiply and divide. As for my salary, I'll just let you guess."

Myron cradled the ledger in his skinny arms. He opened it and slammed it shut a few times. "Never mind," he said charitably. "I got a good idea. Know what Uncle Doc earns? A year?"

Again he opened the account book, studied a page with aggrieved myopic eyes as if he had discovered some new intelligence there, and closed it, tossing it back into the drawer. He leaned over the carved high back of his uncle's chair and looked arrogantly at the agency man.

"I bet you went to Yale."

"Oh, God, spare me this," Thrasher said, rising. "Myron, you're rude and boorish, and you're also stupid. Yes, I earn a lot of money, but I work for it. No, I didn't go to Yale. I worked my way through a small college in the Middle West, like most successful people in mass communications. Ambitious idiots like yourself like to think that it's Yale or Princeton that makes for success in our line. But that's why *you* remain failures—you're too busy being jealous and living off your own cheap misconceptions. Ah, the hell with it. Why try to explain it to you?"

Thrasher slipped on his jacket. He reached for the attaché case and started for the stairs.

"Wait a minute, Thrasher," Myron said. "Let's stop kidding each other. You still wanna do this show with Uncle Doc?"

"I'd sure like to try. I happen to have a lot of confidence in it."

"Want me to help? Consultant . . . research."

Thrasher smiled. "We can work something out."

"Okay. I'll work on the old man. If anyone can convince him, I can."

They started toward the stairs, Thrasher handing Myron his card.

"I'd like to hear from you before the week is over. It's pretty important to me. If you can't talk him into it, I have to make other arrangements. And if you *can* get him to agree, I have a tremendous amount of work to do. Can I depend on you?"

"You'll hear. Think you can get me seventy-five a week?"

"I'll take care of you."

At the bottom step, Thrasher was able to peer into the waiting room. The doctor was talking to a New York City policeman. The latter, alert with automatic pencil and pad, was taking notes. Thrasher and Myron paused in the doorway, the doctor acknowledging their presence fleetingly, then resuming his colloquy with the law.

"How should I remember so much? I got other things on my mind," he was protesting.

"Not even the make of car?" the policeman asked. He was a dark, sorrowful young man, suggesting more a social worker or a graduate student.

"All cars look alike today," the doctor said flatly.

The policeman—he was, in fact, Patrolman Kaplan, who had been present the night the girl had been dumped on the doctor's doorstep—looked appealingly at Thrasher and Myron.

"I'm trying to explain to Dr. Abelman that this is a serious matter. The girl who was left here that evening—medical examination revealed she had been raped, several times, as a matter of fact—"

"It'll never hurt her—" interrupted the doctor. Patrolman Kaplan ignored him, continuing, "and what happened to her is only one in a series of depredations by this gang. They beat up an old man, for no reason whatsoever, in Lincoln Terrace Park a week ago. The business with Leueen Harrison, that's the girl the doctor took care of, is the most serious so far. But who knows when they'll murder someone? And just kids. *Kids!*"

The doctor leaned over and placed a solicitous hand on the policeman's shiny blue knee. "Look, sonny, you're a nice boy, so I can talk to you. What do you want from me? You want me to go out and catch them for you? I should be a decoy and get klopped on the head so you can come rescue me? It's your job to find 'em. String 'em up! But don't bother me."

"That's just the trouble," Kaplan said patiently. "There are so many of them—they operate the same—"

"Aha!" cried the doctor. "Coming around to me!"

"That's not what I meant. They're just kids. Sixteen and seventeen. The gang we're after is called the Twentieth Century Gents, but they could be any one of fifteen gangs. There was a day when a police force could keep track of criminals because you had records on them—descriptions—clues. But the trouble is—"

"The trouble is, young fellah, that *everybody* is a criminal. Am I right or wrong? Being a hoodlum is now the *rule*, not the exception. We should change our laws so they apply to crooks, and make believe that the lawful people are the exceptions!"

The cop jerked his cap over his head. "You're very hard to talk to. You shouldn't be so intolerant of your neighbors, doc."

"Oh, I am, am I? What do you suggest we do about these Century Plants—what did you call them?"

"The Twentieth Century Gents."

"Yeah, a lovely bunch. What'll you do if you catch 'em?"

The policeman stood up. "I believe they can be rehabilitated," he said. "It's not an easy job, but it's something all of us should work on."

"Rape? Robbery?" the doctor asked. "Where do you begin? And what good do you do rehabilitating five or six in one gang? You said yourself there are fifteen gangs—just in this neighborhood."

The young officer made a gesture of despair. He was sweating torrents in his dark, tight-fitting shirt, and his black-stubbled face face was heavy with fatigue.

"All right, Dr. Abelman, have it your way. But do me a favor. The leader of this gang calls himself Josh the Dill. We're positive he's the one who raped the girl. It's not his real name, of course. But we suspect he lives within four or five blocks of here. You have a lot of colored patients, don't you?"

"Of course I do, and they are damn fine people! You won't find any scum like this Josh of yours in my office."

The doctor's spirited defense of his Negro patients surprised Thrasher; he had sensed a touch of bigotry in the old man's earlier outbursts. Apparently the policeman had been thinking along similar lines.

"You know something, Dr. Abelman?" Kaplan asked. "Maybe I shouldn't say this, but I think you're inclined to be intolerant of colored people. That's not a very progressive attitude."

"Intolerant?" the doctor cried. "Me? Listen, sonny, I call a galoot a galoot, no matter what color he is. I fought Irish galoots when I was a kid and I've thrown Jewish galoots out of my office. And I'll let you in on a little secret, Mr. Patrolman. If you commit a crime or behave like a son-of-a-bitch, you should be punished for it. You, a cop, should know that."

Patrolman Kaplan sighed. "Sure, sure. But that's only part of the problem," he said. "I wish I could debate this with you a little, doctor. But I have to go. Don't forget—they call him Josh the Dill."

"Who sent for him?" the doctor asked.

The policeman nodded at Thrasher and the nephew and, leaving, remarked to no one in particular, "Some job, a cop. If I had better marks, I mighta gotten into dental college."

The doctor addressed Thrasher and Myron. "What does he want from me? Suppose that little rat shows up here? That's all I need is to turn him in. They'd crack my skull for me some night."

He turned, walking through the massive green doors, through the darkened office. There was apparently a third room at the rear, and silhouetted in the light from the backyard, Thrasher could see the doctor sit at his desk, rest his feet on a lower drawer, and pick up a book.

"What does he do now?" asked Thrasher.

"He waits for patients," Myron answered. "Most of the time they don't come."

"His practice isn't too good?"

"The dispensaries and the free clinics took all the poor people. If they got any dough at all, they want specialists, professors. And Baumgart took a lot of Uncle Doc's old-timers."

Thrasher started to ask a question, then stopped. He detested failure, feared it. Failure had a smell, a taste, a size and shape. And he felt he was surrounded by it now. Not just in the street with its profane rabble, not just in the asymmetrical young man in basketball shorts, but in the very person he was risking his future on. His mind was suddenly darting about aimlessly—excuses were forming themselves into sentences—and he was talking quickly to Loomer, to Whitechapel, to Finucane.

The old bastard is crazy—nothing more nor less—leave it to me to latch onto a loony

When I saw the curettes under the kitchen table, well—

If only the old crackpot spoke English!

Okay, T.C., I booted this one. But there are a million good stories.

The alibis, as they grew hair and teeth in his mind, helped him not at all. That was the trouble with the Big Gamble: you had to pursue it all the way. He could come back, humbled and apologetic, and admit defeat. He could make some wonderful jokes about it, plead for time, go out and find another *American, U.S.A.* But it would never be the same. Victory, if it came, would be partial.

"Uncle Doc used to do pretty well," Myron was saying, almost as if reading Thrasher's mind. "It's only since the war."

The agency man had sat down, the tan case on his knees. "Myron, do you mind if I rest here a minute or so?"

"Good idea. Listen, if some people come in, you might get some ideas for the show." He had entered the project wholeheartedly, Thrasher noticed with some revulsion. "I gotta go get dressed."

The weedy figure vanished up the stairs and Thrasher leaned back in the abraded leather seat. Why had he panicked so when Myron had indicated that his uncle's practice was negligible? After all, financial success was not going to be the yardstick for choosing subjects for *Americans, U.S.A.* He ran his hand lightly over his forehead, surprised by the accumulation of sweat and the coolness of his skin. He began to calm down: the doctor's dwindling practice would not have to be stressed in the program. Surely he had some patients, some colorful, interesting people; people who were grateful to him, depended on him, loved him. He assured himself it could be worked out, that his distress was unwarranted, that with Myron's co-operation he could get the old man to agree to the television program.

The door buzzer sounded, a second buzzed in return, and a dumpy woman of middle age, in a faded blue cotton dress, entered. At her side was a small, terrified boy, clutching his injured right hand against his breast with the protective grasp of his left hand. Through the green-shaded doors he saw the doctor rise, flick on an overhead light in the office, and beckon to the pair.

"He broke his hand," the woman said shakily. "I told him he shouldn't play baseball with the big boys!"

By leaning over, Thrasher could peer through the half-opened doors which the doctor, in deference to the heat, had left ajar. The physician was squinting through steel-rimmed spectacles at the boy's hand. Suddenly he looked up.

"Aren't you Kalotkin?"

"Yes, doctor. You treated my husband two weeks ago."

"That's what I mean. He never paid me. Two dollars for an office visit and three for a house call. He said he'd send it over. I never saw it."

She seemed to shrink back slightly. "I'm sorry, doctor, I don't have it with me."

He dropped the boy's hand. "So how do you get the nerve to come in now? What am I, a chump?"

"But, doctor, it's an emergency. He was playing baseball."

The doctor studied her glumly and looked again at the tearful boy. "Sit down here, sonny," he said. He lifted him onto an aged examining table and peered at the injured hand.

"It's a beaut," Dr. Abelman said. "The whole thumb is out of joint. I'm going to hurt you a little."

Thrasher could see him tugging at the malformed thumb. A shriek of intractable pain slammed and crashed around the small room.

"Hey, not in my ear, Charlie," the doctor said.

Gently, he shoved the boy to a supine position. With his left hand he held the thin arm extended, and with his powerful right hand he began a deliberate manipulation of the thumb. The boy's voice was alarmingly loud: Thrasher had never heard such a variety of shrieks. They rose and fell like banshee wails, sometimes sustaining the same shrill note like a factory whistle, then coming in abbreviated, terrified gasps. Through it all the doctor continued his resolute battle with the thumb, paying no attention—or so it seemed—to the unbearable noise.

Above the din, he heard the doctor say, "Okay. Brace yourself, sonny."

He saw the doctor's right hand jerk back quickly, and heard a distinct *crrrrrack!*

The boy was sitting upright, his face sodden with tears. "It don't hurt!" he cried happily. "I got my throwin' hand back!"

With a deft move, the mother yanked the boy from the examining table. One hand on the scruff of his neck, she slapped him fiercely on the cheek.

"What's the matter you annoying Dr. Abelman over *nothing*? Nothing wrong with you and I gotta bother the doctor? I'll teach *you!*"

With remarkable speed, she flew from the office, dragging the screaming boy, through waiting room and foyer, and then into the street.

The doctor walked into the anteroom. He spoke to Thrasher, but the agency man got the feeling that the words were for the world at large, and that the speech would not have been altered had the room been empty.

"How do you like that trollop? *Nothing!* A complete dislocation, and I almost go deaf listening to that little *momsa* yell in my ear! And she yanks him out of here before I can even ask for my two bucks! I'll tell you something—she did it *deliberately*. She knew goddam well I worked for the money, but she had it all figured out, as soon as the thumb looked right again! Oh, those lice!"

He turned away, then looked over his shoulder at the visitor.

"What are you still here for? You like it here?"

"I'm just resting, doctor. You don't mind?"

"No, make yourself at home."

He returned again to his reading in the rear room, and Thrasher looked at his watch. It was half-past one. Office hours would run another half hour. Thus far he had seen little to lend itself to his project; indeed, each additional clue to the doctor's life depressed him more and more. Yet he felt constrained to sit through the remaining thirty minutes. Time dragged in the breathless, chair-crowded room where so many sick people had come with their troubles. A pretty little colored girl delivered a specimen of urine in an empty wine bottle; a detail man, haggard and polite, left samples of a new antibiotic; a starved Italian with sideburns and gold teeth pleaded for morphine, telling the doctor, "I love you— really I do," and was bodily thrown out by the old man with a warning never to return.

It was close to two when the buzzer sounded again. The companion bell sounded several times, but no one entered. Thrasher could hear shuffling in the enclosed vestibule. He rose, opened the door and observed a tableau out of the middle ages. Thrasher had read *The Wall* and *Thieves in the Night* and had seen the arty photographs and oil paintings of Orthodox Jews in the museums. But at close range, in the flesh, they were a completely new experience, a bit unnerving.

There were two callers. One was a tall, austere man with large vague eyes and heavy, drooping features. A disorderly growth of hair and beard, steel gray and frizzy, surrounded the patriarchal face. The whiskers descended halfway down his chest. He wore a true stovepipe—a high beaver hat, shiny black, tinged with green— and a black cloak of a material resembling grosgrain. It almost reached his feet. His companion was considerably shorter and was hunched over a black cane. A black Homburg, undented, rested atop a Biblical face, crossed by a thousand jagged lines. Twin curls of white hair dangled beside each parchment ear; the snowy beard, stained yellow around the mouth, was large and full.

The tall man surveyed Thrasher contemptuously, brushed him aside with an imperious gesture, saying in a thick accent:

"Go 'vay. It's my next."

The shorter man followed him and they entered the waiting room, not taking seats but standing squarely in the center of the carpet. The big man peered through the open doors, saw his quarry, and called out in a voice strengthened by decades in the pulpit, "*Reb Abelman, cumm a-herr!*"

The patriarchs then greeted the doctor with a flourish. Each made a lengthy speech in Yiddish, Thrasher imagined (or was it Hebrew?) and the doctor seemed rather pleased with their visit. He smiled at them with obvious respect, returned their exuberant greetings, and shook hands warmly with the white-haired gentleman in the Homburg, who appeared to be a guest of the tall man.

The conversation was beyond Thrasher's comprehension, but at length he divined that the tall man was requesting a favor on behalf of the other. He pleaded, rolled large soft eyes to the heavens, invoked the deity, and gestured energetically. Dr. Abelman's reaction appeared to change after a few moments. Cheerful at first, he now manifested annoyance. At length he reached inside his pants pocket and extracted from a shapeless wad two single dollar bills and handed them to the tall man. The latter in turn gave them to the white-haired visitor, and both, nodding Old Testament heads and muttering Oriental syllables, began intoning what appeared to Thrasher to be a prayer. They turned from the doctor, stopped in front of Thrasher, mumbled an encore, and left.

Thrasher smiled at the doctor. "What was that all about?" he asked. "I was in the woods, I'm afraid."

"The *bushes* would be more like it," the doctor laughed. "That's one of my pals, Rabbi Piltz. He's an old fraud."

"He's a patient?"

"A pretty good one, too. But every time some buddy of his shows up with a charity he drags him in here first. I figured it out once. He and I broke even for the year. That included a GI series on my part, so you can figure he did pretty well."

"What were they saying after you gave them the two dollars?"

"It was for some Yeshiva—a Hebrew school—in Newark, and they were asking the Lord to bless me, and for all the students to pray for me."

Thrasher was solemn and thoughtful. "I think that's rather touching."

The doctor gestured helplessly. "Who knows? They included you at the end. Probably figured you were a good Jewish boy and needed it."

Dr. Abelman pulled a watch from the pocket of his sport shirt. "Two o'clock. That's all for me this afternoon. I have some more manure to put down, so I'll say goodbye, Mr. Thrasher. I hope you learned something here."

Thrasher noticed he was carrying a book with a dark-green cover.

"What were you reading inside?" he asked.

"*Concord and Merrimack Rivers*," the doctor answered.

"Oh. Travel book?"

"Stop kidding me. Thoreau."

Thrasher was too impressed to feel his own embarrassment. "Really? Do you like Thoreau?"

The doctor held up the bok for Thrasher to see. It was the Riverside edition, the covers functional and severe. "He keeps me going. I'd go nuts without him. I can reread this five times a year and never get tired. Thoreau and the backyard. The bastards would drive me nuts otherwise."

He walked to the window. "Some day, I swear, I'll get out of this lousy neighborhood! I know I'm getting on, but that won't stop me. I don't give a damn if I live for *one more* year after I move. But *I have to get out.*"

Abruptly, as if suddenly discomfited by this baring of his desires, he left, passing through office and consultation room and, Thrasher imagined, into the sanctuary of the cool yard with its protective trees and fences.

He had stayed much longer than he had intended; nothing had been resolved, and much had been confused in his own mind. His hand on the bronze doorknob, he saw Myron bounding down the stairs, now dressed in a bulky beige suit of cheap rayon.

"Well? Learn anything?" the nephew asked.

"He had eight visitors. A cop, a detail man, a girl with a specimen, an addict he had to throw out, a lady with a little boy who cheated him out of his fee, and two old men who shook him down for two bucks. So he came out loser four dollars on the afternoon's work."

Myron pushed the drooping spectacles back up his nose.

"Some days are worse than others. He does better weekends. He say any more about the show?"

"Nothing. I'm depending on you, Myron."

The blond youth looked about him furtively. "Look, you want to lock this up?" His voice connoted conspiracy.

"Now look, Myron, I've already agreed to take you on—"

"To hell with that. Do something for *him*. Get him outa the neighborhood. Help him get a house in a nice section."

"You mean pay him? Money for a house?"

"Why not? With all the dough in your operation? What's a lousy few bucks to help him out? Let me tell you somethin'. Uncle Doc and Aunt Sarah are the only people in the world I owe anything. And I'm gonna get it for them. A big house on Republic Street. Why should he be forced to stay behind—hold the fort, on the goddam frontier? You know that Baumgart who used to live next door? He's only thirty-three. He grabbed Uncle Doc's patients and he moved to Republic Street. A mansion! Uncle Doc won't talk about it, but it kills him."

"He talked about it, Myron. He mentioned to me he'd like to get out."

Myron seized Thrasher's wrist and the latter felt his skin prickle under the youth's clammy grasp. "Eight thousand bucks. That's what he needs. There's a beaut of a house ready to be sold. Not too big, just right. Ya got time? I'll show it—"

Thrasher pulled his hand away. "Not now, Myron. Don't push me. You miss the whole point. If we have to—well, bribe your uncle, it defeats the while purpose of what we have in mind. You wouldn't understand, so don't make me explain. Where can I get a taxi?"

The nephew stepped back.

"Walk toward Rower Avenue and then toward Eastern Parkway. They never come by here. An' remember what I said. You come across for the house, and I'll deliver Uncle Doc."

"Let me hear from you, Myron. I won't promise you a thing."

He stepped into the steaming vestibule, locked between the two doors, feeling suffocated, immersed. The burning sun, cooking the asphalt and concrete of the street, assaulted his eyes; the stench of garbage and dog's leavings assailed his nose. He needed his home, his cool, clean, functional house in North Stamford, and he wanted to escape to it without stopping at the office, where the crisis would again confront him, where he would have to answer questions, attend meetings, be wary of his enemies.

Wearily, he descended the steps, pausing at the ugly brick bastions, where an aged, squat woman stood to one side, inspecting him with hostile eyes.

"I beg your pardon," said Thrasher, "where is Rower Avenue?"

She was perhaps sixty, fat and round, her black hair severely bound in an immense bun. Her face was healthy and small-featured. Across an inflated bosom, her stout arms were folded resolutely, and Thrasher got the impression she had been waiting for him.

"What's the matter you went by Abelman?" she asked.

"I don't understand you," he said pleasantly.

"You went by Abelman," she repeated. "Why you didn't go by my son?" She extended a pudgy hand. It held a doctor's calling card, and he could see the name: SEYMOUR BAUMGART, M.D.

"You shouldn't go by Abelman," she insisted. "He is a *gonoph*, an *anti-Semit*. Everyone knows it."

Thrasher realized at once what she was up to. Apparently this was a regular practice: while her husband threw garbage into the old man's backyard, she intercepted the doctor's patients and drummed up business for her successful son. He felt a deep disgust, a desire to make known his allegiance to the angry old man he had just left.

"I don't see it's any of your business," he said firmly.

She shook a finger at him. "You'll find out. Abelman's patients die. He is a crook. My son has got all the new machines. All the young doctors are smarter, everyone knows it. Abelman knows nothing. He'll cheat you."

"Excuse me," said Thrasher, "you're wasting your time." He tried to brush by her, but her immobile body effectively blocked him off.

"You better go by my son, by Dr. Baumgart, mister," she said darkly. "You go by Abelman, you'll drop dead. His patients all go by my son, he should cure them."

Furious, he moved her aside, and tried to escape. A hand reached out and grabbed his vented coattail.

"Don't be such a wise guy," she continued. "I'll tell you what's else about Abelman. He sleeps with that *schwartzer*. The whole neighborhood knows it."

Thrasher spun about. He was a man who rarely got angry, but he was burning with an uncontrollable fury now.

"Dr. Abelman is a fine man, madam," he said firmly. "And you are a disgrace to your religion. You should go wash out your filthy mouth and pray for yourself."

The assault did not move her.

"I intend to *keep* using Dr. Abelman as my family doctor," he lied, "and I will recommend him to all my friends."

His heart pounded relentlessly; the weakness and lassitude had left him, and he felt buoyed up by his spirited defense of the old man. He exchanged a final glance of hatred with her and set out in search of a cab.

III

THRASHER could not recall when he had so enjoyed his home. He lay on a redwood chaise on the flagstone patio of his ranch house, his body luxuriating in the delightful ebb of fatigue from his limbs. He wore only a pair of plaid Bermuda shorts, and at his right, on a redwood table, was his evening meal: a pitcher of iced tea and a plate of chicken salad. It was the time of day when the suburban houseowner experiences redemption: the mortgage, the leaking basement, the crab grass are all forgotten in the warm dusk of late summer. Across the lawn, his son, Woody Junior, was tossing pop flies to himself, settling under the lazy softball with the false grace of a ten-year-old, and catching it at his waistline with a ragged fielder's mitt. Thrasher rather enjoyed the notion of the boy—a white Anglo-Saxon Protestant whose father was in the top five per cent income bracket—consciously imitating the style of an illiterate Alabama Negro's son. Baseball bored him, but he had always felt a deep rooting instinct for colored athletes. Musing, he realized that these sentiments were not completely unselfish. It was easier to cheer for a Negro half-miler or fullback, an accepted member of the celebrity world, than to be sympathetic to a million savages living in a crime-ridden slum. In the long run you felt just as generous cheering for the few famous ones.

His wife had been visiting the people to the rear, an elderly childless couple named Schultheis, and he could see her now, twisting through the wild thickets separating their property, her tanned arms cradling a paper sack filled with peaches from the neighbor's tree. She was a lean, leggy woman, flat-hipped and flat-chested with large, sharp features and short, sun-bleached blond hair. It suddenly struck Thrasher, seeing her in faded denim shorts and one of his old white oxford shirts, that she looked unnervingly like all the women with whom he had had affairs. It was disconcerting: they all had that spare, narrow look. Where were all the fat women? Didn't anyone like girls with big busts and wide hips any more? Earlier that day he had tried to think of anyone he knew living on the West Side of New York and had failed. Now he could not call to mind a single wife (or mistress) of any of his acquaintances who leaned to fat. He sighed, sipped his iced tea, and smiled, hearing his son warn his mother, "Watch it, Dusty, it's all mine!"

The lopsided ball dropped into the mitt, and the boy pantomimed the dainty steps preceding the throw to the infield.

"Move over, bones," she said, sitting at his side on the chaise. She rested the paper bag on the flagstones and looked with mock puzzlement at the newly plucked peaches.

"I couldn't offend poor Millie," she said earnestly. "I just *had* to take the damn peaches. Maybe Tessa can take them home and cook them tomorrow."

"Toss one here," Thrasher said, "I'll eat it alive."

Gingerly, she picked one up, a small, greenish fruit, hard as carborundum. "Really, Woody, you don't have to carry that sincerity bit into your own backyard. Old lady Schultheis will never know if Tessa takes them home."

"Ann, baby, maybe I really want to eat a peach."

"Martyr. Isn't it awful how the home-grown stuff isn't really as good as the store-boughten?" She threw the peach at him, and defiantly he bit into it, wincing at the hard sourness.

"I like this peach and I'm going to finish it," he said. He stroked his wife's thigh, and she looked at him curiously.

"Is this the new Woodrow Thrasher? What did that doctor do to you? Testosterone in elixir of Vitamin B?"

He bit again into the unripe fruit. "Don't remind me of my burden. I'll think about it tomorrow."

He had given his wife a complete report on the adventure in Brownsville, a rarity in his relationship with her. They had been married eleven years, and when they were young and poor, they were alive to each other's interests, aware of each other's opinions. Now, he told her almost nothing of his work; she rarely asked. Ann had been a fair actress: a girl from New Bern, North Carolina, who had always played the lead in the class play. New York had meant cold-water apartments with other, thin ambitious girls from small towns, a few years of dedicated work with off-Broadway groups (above garages and stables mostly), and one minor part in a legitimate play which folded after three performances. After the war, when acting jobs were becoming available in television, she was married, then pregnant, and then the lady of a ten-room house. She enjoyed domesticity and was a capable and conscientious wife; but both she and Thrasher understood that love (whatever it was, over and above lust, which had also fled) had long vanished. They had expected far too much from marriage—two young, creative, and ambitious people, refusing to recognize that married life is compromise, and that the wild absolute love of the romantics is illusory and deceptive. They had settled down to a dutiful relationship, respectful of each other's wishes, sympathetic, quick to support and defend one another, like an older and younger brother.

"Tell me more about Dr. Aaronson," she said. She bounced off the chaise, sitting on a cushioned redwood chair, her muscular legs jackknifed in front of her. In the fading summer light she seemed a teen-ager, and his own fatigue reminded him he was a year shy of forty.

"Abelman, dear," he said, "Samuel Abelman."

"Why did I say Aaronson? That must be the name of the new family I met at the PTA last night. There's a new Aaronson and a new Feinstein."

She had changed a lot in eleven years. Back in the prewar and war years she had been a battling liberal, taking him to parties where people sat on the floor and sang "*Freiheit*" and some other song which went to the tune of "There is pow'r, pow'r, wonder-working pow'r," Ann wasn't really anti-Semitic, he assured himself. She hated bigots and Nazis and narrow-minded people as much as she always did; but more and more he found her making acerb little comments about the increasing incursions of Jewish families in her own, her very own, Connecticut. "I don't mind the bright, creative people," she had once said, "they're like us . . . like Gray Mandelbaum, who edits *Women's Life*, or Tex Fine from *L & J*. But those cloak and suiters! Woody, I'd dislike them even if they were Episcopalians and behaved the way they did."

It was dark now, the evening soft and sweet-smelling, the rustic furniture and hedge-bordered patio assuring them of their security and achievements. Ann flicked on a yellow insecticidal lamp. Thrasher lifted the arms of the redwood couch, stretching himself out full length, resting his head on interlocked hands.

"Now consider me your father, Mr. Thrasher," Ann said in a vaudeville Viennese accent. "We will start with free association. When I say a word, you say the first word that comes into your head. *Ja? Festeht?*"

They had a running joke about analysts. To their friends who ran to the couch, they had one answer: *be creative, be interested, be domestic.* He chuckled mechanically at her. She was still a pretty funny dame with the comic accents and intonations, a lot better than half the incompetent girls you saw on TV.

"Let's get back to the Brooklyn story," she insisted. "You still haven't told me what's next."

"I honestly don't know. It's his move."

She frowned. "That's not like you, Woody. How did you get in a spot like this? I mean, one where you're at the mercy of some nutty old doctor? Why didn't you leave yourself an out before you made the hegira to Brownsville?"

He turned to his side, facing her, head resting on his left hand.

"I haven't booted this one yet," he assured her. "I have a feeling that goofy nephew will deliver."

"Suppose he does. Then where are you?"

"I got me a show."

She scratched her head vigorously, a small-boy gesture of confusion. "If you ask me, dad," she said, "your troubles just start once Dr. Abelman says okay."

"Why do you say that?"

"Well, frankly, Woody, you didn't sound too convincing telling me about friend Abelman. Why in the world should anyone want to watch a half hour of television about some old failure? Let's be brutal about it. People don't like failures."

"Is that the platitude for the night?" he asked. "You bring to mind a late-lamented television producer I once worked for. After a three-hour discussion of whether we should do a pitch for the Toy Fair, he decided in favor of it, because, as he put it, '*Kids like toys.*' We could draw up a whole list and call it Thrasher's Hypotheses. *Kids like toys. People don't like failures.*"

"But they don't," she insisted.

"What makes you sure he is a failure?" He found himself a little on the defensive.

"You said so yourself."

"It was a snap judgment. Besides, these things are relative. Maybe the doctor is a financial failure. But, for Pete's sake, is that the *only* standard of success? Besides I can't back down. If the doctor consents to play his own life for the greater glory of *G & T*, I'm obliged to follow it through. I got no choice. None."

"You could admit you were wrong. You could find another character. Someone who didn't curse so much and wasn't so *obviously* a flop."

In the still country night he heard the flat *plop* as the ball landed in young Woody's mitt.

"Isn't it kind of dark for baseball, coach?" he called out across the lawn.

"Night game, pops. Two out in the eighth. I'm Maglie."

"Why don't you do a program about Willie Mays or Sal Maglie?" she asked. "They're famous and they're minorities. You'd have big names, social conscience, and sports all at once. You'd get the dolts, the eggheads, and the children in one swell foop."

She was shrewd and knowledgeable, he thought, looking at her well-preserved figure. It had been a long haul from New Bern and the frame cottage of a letter-carrier, but she had made the transition without noticeable strain.

"This isn't going to sound like your dear husband, Annie," he said wearily, "but I've almost got a damn compulsion to follow through with my aging physician. The old man of the sea—I'm Sinbad."

He hoisted himself into a sitting position, his face lined and pensive in the jaundiced light of the insecticidal lamp.

"Dammit to hell, I liked the old guy. He did everything to make me dislike him, and yet—I don't know what it was. Pity? He didn't need mine. Did he make more sense than most people? I don't *think* he did. He sounded paranoiac half the time. Imaginary people against him; always fighting some nonexistent enemy. Did you ever read *Tartarin de Tarascon?*"

"De Maupassant?"

"I don't know who wrote it. I had to read it in Freshman French at State. It's about this middle-aged bourgeois who fancies himself a big-game hunter and adventurer. He plays this imaginary game in which he leads an attack and then defends a castle against his sworn enemies. But you never know who they are. He calls them *'Ils.'* "

"Eel?"

"*I-l-s.* Means 'they.' It's nobody really, and yet it's everybody. That's the feeling I got spending a day with old Abelman. Everyone was fighting him, and yet nobody was. They were *Ils.*"

"Plain persecution complex, sounds like," she said. "The books are full of that stuff. He's old and frustrated. It figures."

Thrasher frowned. "That's only part of it. That's why I almost feel impelled to work this thing out with him. If I can get across to people what's troubling the guy, what's *right* with him as well as what's *wrong* with him, I've got a program."

She stood up, stretching her tan arms, the electric light winking on the golden hairs. From a patio in the vicinity they heard loud laughter, the predrunken gaiety of greetings, the generalized early evening exchanges of an outdoor party. Thrasher looked sourly in the direction of the laughing.

"Who's noising it up tonight?" he asked.

Ann paused a second before answering him. "The Doersams, I guess," she said offhandedly. Chuck and Doris Doersam were the community "characters." Chuck was charitably referred to as a "free-lance writer," a description based on an article on fox-hunting he had sold to an outdoor magazine seven years ago. He was Harvard-educated, widely traveled, well read, and perpetually drunk. All his neighbors and friends participated in the little fiction about his "writing," all of them also being aware that he was able to enjoy this enviable status, his forty-six-thousand-dollar home, and the endless parties, because of a brace of generous inlaws who had never quite recovered from the honor accruing to their ugly daughter. An invitation to a Doersam party was the supreme merit badge of the community.

Thrasher and his wife were silent, each rotating the same disturbing thoughts, each a little ashamed for showing their concern so baldly.

"How do you know they're entertaining?" he asked quietly.

"Hattie Loomer told me." The snap and confidence had suddenly left her voice, and she sounded whiny. "She made a big deal of it when I met her in town. You'd think she and Ben were real buddy-buddy with Chuck and Doris."

"The moving finger writes," he said archly. He and Ann had been early initiates into the Doersams' circle. They were "regulars," members of the close in-group of "artistic, creative people" who lingered on, long after the agency and network dolts had left to relieve their baby-sitters.

He stood up, annoyed by the creakiness of his joints, and hugged her. "Don't worry, cookie, we'll start our own parties. I always rated the Doersam group as kind of halfway between the Aqua Velva after-shave club and the Sanka Inner Circle. As Dr. Abelman would say, what do they want from our life?"

"But why should they leave us out?" she asked plaintively.

"The word is out, Annie. Woody Thrasher is about to have the blocks put to him. I haven't surrendered yet. And don't you worry. We'll go ring Doersam's doorbell and run."

"I guess I am being horribly upper middle class," she said. "We could be overestimating the whole thing. I'll show 'em. I'm going to spend the night reading Kit Marlowe."

"That's tellin' 'em, tiger," Thrasher said, hugging her closely.

She pushed him away, not ungently. "You're too smart, Woody, thats your trouble. Smarter than all of them."

"Louise told me that yesterday. Everyone says I'm smart."

He looked at his son, a bony, blond copy of himself, now sitting on the edge of the chaise and determinedly pounding a small fist into the pocket of the ragged, oiled glove.

"Woods, do you think your old man is smart?" he asked.

He didn't look up, but answered, "Yeah, you're smart."

"That wasn't very convincing. Go ahead, ask me something, anything."

The boy closed one eye tightly and pointed a finger at his temple. "You don't know too much about baseball, anyway," he said, "so I'll ask you a sports question."

"Shoot."

"Aaaah—who holds the National League record for home runs?"

"Hack Wilson, Chicago Cubs, 56."

The boy stood up, happily puzzled. "How come you knew, pops?" There was genuine admiration in his voice.

"Out where I grew up, in South Dakota, you were either a Cub fan or you were nothing. So I was a Cub fan."

"*Nobody* was a Giant fan?" he asked incredulously.

"Nobody."

"What drips. The *Cubs!*"

Across the richly fertilized lawns, the tenderly trimmed hedges, and vitamin-infused arbors, they heard the voices at the Doersams' party, now raised in a ramshackle rendition of "My Gal Sal."

"Why don't they shut up?" his son asked. Thrasher hitched up his drooping trunks and pushed the boy ahead of him toward the house. "They're happy, Woods, just plain happy. You wouldn't refuse them a little joyous singing?"

"Nuts. I wish they'd shut up," he repeated.

The doctor suffered from migraine. The seizures had begun shortly after he had opened practice (more than forty years ago) and could be counted on to strike with a kind of deadly regularity, about every ten days. He had been to headache clinics, to specialists, to the physicians he respected most, and no help had been forthcoming. It was largely hereditary, he told himself. His mother had suffered from the same seizures, and so did his daughter, but to a lesser degree. He had tried a catalogue of drugs, old and new, nose drops, sprays, oils, pills, and had even subjected himself to a painful cauterization of the nasal passages, when it was suspected that the swelling of the turbinates set off the migraine. But the headaches continued, bringing with them intractable, numbing pain; a kind of heavy sensation throughout the body, a loss of orientation and balance. He would awake with the aura: the imaginary blinking of lights around the bed. The first twinge would be along the left temple, accompanied by a swelling of the left nasal passage. Within ten or fifteen minutes after rising, the pain would diffuse about his skull: an iron vise clamped around his crown, sending agonized bolts down the back and sides of his head and neck.

Years ago he had ceased taking medication for the attacks. The relief they gave was a fraud, a trivial and temporary blunting of the pain, which wore off in an hour's time and left him in torment when the pure agony returned. He had one basic rule about his headaches: *don't go to bed, keep working.* He often told himself it was a bad rule, that a sedative and a nap would be better. But the doctor accepted each attack as a personal affront, and effort by some mysterious enemy to get the best of him. Sometimes the pressure and the pounding were so severe he would gasp in agony; but he refused to lie down, refused to alter his schedule. If he meant to work in the cornfield, migraine would not deter him. If he had to make a call, he made it. If a patient wanted a GI series, he took the pictures. Stubbornly, he told his wife, "No sonofabitching migraine will get the best of me!" And so it had continued through forty years: unrelenting warfare in which neither side gave ground.

The morning following Woodrow Thrasher's appearance at his office, Dr. Abelman awakened with a classic headache. He saw the flashing lights, and blinked his eyes, hopeful that he could make them vanish. The blinking was a useless gesture, he knew, but he always tried to dispel the evil harbingers of pain. Sitting on the sweat-dampened mattress cover, he felt the arthritic tightness in his lower spine, mumbled something about "goddam fused vertebrae," and swung his feet to the summer rug on the bedroom floor.

"You louse," he said. It was his standard greeting for the headache, a preliminary exchange with the villain. His left nostril was almost closed; already the twinges were darting up his left temple. It would be a beaut, a real all-day beaut. Dressing, he decided to keep busy even if his work proved light. It had been a bad summer, and he could not expect many patients or calls. He would work in the garden in the morning, remain in the house for office hours, and after two o'clock he would visit the medical library and round out the day in its cool confines with some new literature.

He was downstairs by eight-fifteen, and since Jannine had not yet arrived, he walked into the vestibule, unbolting the street door and stepping outside for his daily morning survey. For over four decades he had lived on the same street, and each day he had found it necessary to check on the condition of his property on rising. He lived in constant expectation of disaster, a fear which had intensified in the last ten years, the period in which the disintegration of the neighborhood had been most precipitous.

This morning his fears were realized. The street bore the pug marks of the teen-age vandal. All along the block, garbage pails and bags had been upset, the malodorous contents strewn about sidewalk and gutter. The cars parked along Haven Place had not been spared either; tires had been slashed indiscriminately. His own aged Buick rested lumpily on four collapsed shoes, looking abused and forsaken. There was a final infuriating touch, an act so aimless in its viciousness that it had made him wince. The cast-iron pole of his street sign had been twisted backward over the brick bastion, so that the black placard with his name on it practically touched the interior pavement. On its peeling lettering, the night raiders had exploded a paper bag of garbage, and his name and title lay beneath a layer of eggshells, sardine tins, and coffee grounds.

The sordid tableau unloosed a new flight of painful darts in the agonized cage of his brain. Outraged, he left the stoop, walking through anteroom and office to his consultation chamber, finding time to be irate with his neighbors, none of whom had bothered to clean up their sidewalks, and none of whom (he was certain) would complain about the depredations.

Seated in his black leather swivel chair, he dialed the number of the nearest precinct house, shutting his eyes in protest against the crashing in his skull.

The voice striking his ear was too loud, and he knew the headache was reaching its peak.

"Semmy-seventh precinct, Sergeant Felice."

"Sergeant, this is Dr. Abelman at 1553 Haven Place. I want to report vandalism."

"Yeh."

"A gang of galoots ran wild on my block last night. The tires on the car were slashed. How can I make calls today? There's garbage all over the place—"

"What do you want us to do? Come clean it up for you?"

The doctor held the receiver away from his tortured head, squinting at it in mingled disbelief and contempt. Whose side were they on anyway? Why always the smart remarks?

"Officer, I'm trying to be helpful. My sign was bent and covered with garbage. I should think you fellows would want to know these things." He was uncomfortably aware of his temperate, almost pleading attitude.

"Yeh. Okay. Haven Place? Did anybody see the kids who did it?"

"I don't know. I didn't."

"So what do you want us to do? I can't change your tires or paint your sign. If we catch 'em we'll let you know."

"All right, all right," said the doctor, his voice unnaturally low and soft.

"What you say your name was, Petey?"

"Petey? Who's Petey? My name is Abelman."

There was a pause as Sergeant Felice's mental processes meshed. "Yeh, I heard about you. The guy who made all the trouble a couple nights ago. I know guys like you."

Dr. Abelman laid the receiver down. He sighed: an audible, defeated noise. There it was: he had made the trouble, he was at fault. The galoots, the corner bums, the loafers, went on forever, and the police made believe they weren't there. Why bother trying to find ten kids who dump garbage pails, when twenty more will turn up tomorrow? It was easier to get snotty with the injured parties. How dare they ask for protection? The random thoughts ricocheted about his head, each aggravating idea generating a new stab.

There was only one solution. *He had to get out.* Everyone else had gotten out. He was being left alone in the rotting slum. Electricians, shoemakers, barbers, and appliance salesmen were all moving away from Haven Place to respectability. Only he, of the early settlers, remained. He was left in isolation amidst the bursting garbage bags, the slashed automobile tires, and the wild shrieks of the stickball players.

In the recesses of his middle desk drawer he found a smudged calling card, squinted at the telephone number (his vision was blurring as the migraine intensified), and dialed.

"This is Dr. Abelman. Is Mr. Dannenfelser there?"

"This is Danny, doc. What can I do you for?" The specious heartiness, the vulgar familiarity, acted as an abrasive.

"I want to talk about the house."

"You know the story, doc. I can't change it."

"Tell me again how much cash I need."

"They want twenty grand, doc. And at least sixteen in cash money."

"I can get ten thousand cash."

"No good, doc. We been through this a dozen times."

"I know, I know. I can raise twelve thousand cash, no more."

"Not a chance."

"Do me a personal favor, Danny, tell 'em that. I *want* that house. I have to have it."

"Doc, please. You know I wanna help you. How many houses I've taken you through? Twenny? Thirty? I've given you more time than any client I got and I ain't made a nickel on it."

"Go back and tell 'em twelve thousand, Danny. Then call me. Be a good boy and do it for me."

"Awright, doc, only for you." The agent's voice was warm and reassuring, in the way one comforts a hurt child.

He had to tell someone, he needed backing and encouragement. Upstairs, Myron was asleep, and normally the doctor was careful not to disturb his nephew's drugged slumber. But the occasion demanded an audience. Quickly, he walked up the steps, entered Myron's cramped bedroom where the youth lay sprawled naked on the rumpled sheets, and shook him.

"Whassamatta? Whaddyawan'? Oh—Uncle Doc!"

"Myron, I've made my mind up. I'm through with Brownsville. I won't stay here any more. I'm moving. Those bastards cut up my tires and ruined my sign last night. That's the end. The lice won't torture me any more. I'm buying that house on Republic Street. I just told Dannenfelser to get it for me."

Myron sat up in bed, his face puffed and confused, but his mind alert and fully comprehensive of what his uncle was saying.

"Uncle Doc, we talked about this a million times. You can't spend sixteen thousand dollars on a house. It'll clean you out."

The doctor smiled raggedly. "Who said anything about sixteen thousand? I got Danny down to twelve!"

"What's the difference, twelve or fifteen, Uncle Doc? It would still clean you out. You asked Aunt Sarah?"

He pounded a hard fist into his palm. "No, dammit, and I'm not. Let her stay in Long Beach. For once, I'll settle the deal. I'm moving, that's all. I have had enough of this vile mess. No one stops me this time, you, or Sarah, or anything."

Myron rose awkwardly, reached for his faded basketball trunks, and drew them up his spindly legs. The myopic eyes searched the maple dresser top and located the spliced eyeglasses. Delicately, he hooked the spectacles over his protuberant ears.

"Uncle Doc, lissen to me," Myron said deliberately.

"You won't change my mind, I can tell you that."

"Now, just lissen a minute, willya?" He guided the doctor to a chair alongside his bedroom window. Below they could see the flowering beauty of the backyard, the bright dahlias and the thick foliage.

"Uncle Doc, you can't give up all your savings for that house. You ain't a kid any more. You need that dough. Now, let me finish! I'm gonna get you the dough. Don't ask me how, I just know I can get you whatever you need to move."

"Who are you kidding, Myron? On your forty-two fifty a week from the *Record?* What will you do, win the Irish sweepstakes?"

The nephew's index finger pushed the adhesive bridge back up the slope of his nose.

"Naaah. I got a plan. Remember that guy Thrasher who was here?"

"Who?"

"Thrasher, they guy from the advertising agency. You know, he wanted to do a program about you."

"Oh, him. The *shagitz.* What has he got to do with it? He wanted to make an actor out of me. What am I, a Boris Thomashefsky in my old age?"

"Never mind. He wants to do a show with you, let him. But we make him foot the bill. I'll see to that."

The doctor folded his arms, looking up in astonishment at Myron's drooping face. "You're crazy, Myron. Why should he pay me? Who am I to him?"

"You're plenty to him, plenty. Just let me take care of that guy."

The doctor got up, waving Myron away with a deprecating gesture.

"You're dreaming, sonny boy. I'll get my house, and I don't need that *shagitz* from the television. An actor!"

"Uncle Doc, I'm callin' him up right now. You're gonna see him, too."

The doctor paused at the threshold, then, without turning, said, "Let him wait till tonight. My head is killing me. By tonight I'll be better. What am I supposed to say to him?"

Louise briefed him as soon as he arrived. He had barely begun shuffling the papers on his desk when she was at his side, bringing him his morning coffee, a set of newspapers, and a concise report on imminent problems.

"Dylan Thomas is still brown-nosing Gatling," she said. "He took him to dinner last night."

Dylan Thomas was their private pseudonym for Finucane. It was a nickname which had its origin in Finucane's cascading curls, which lent him a fleeting resemblance to the poet. But both Thrasher and Louise understood that the charm of the comparison for them lay in a deeper, nonsensical kind of association. They had always called Hymie, the boy who delivered the newspapers (and who owned a 1955 Buick), "the bicycle thief." Neither could explain why, and yet both concurred that Hymie was unquestionably "the bicycle thief."

Thrasher sipped his coffee. "Why doesn't someone invent a tasteless container?" he asked. "To hell with the turbojets. Just take the cardboard out of my morning coffee."

"Loomer is getting up a bee-yoo-tiful brochure on *Americans, U.S.A.* It should hit the columns next week. *Variety* will probably call today."

Thrasher winked at her. "Let Loomer talk to them. Might as well get him in on it. We don't even have a show yet, so it's a good idea to involve everyone."

"Don't count on involving people too deeply," she said gravely. "Says who?"

"We had a secretaries' lunch at Shor's yesterday. After the second martini, there were no secrets. Loomer may like you and Finucane may fear you, but you're *it* this time. They'll play along because the chief has approved the project and because we're in trouble with Mr. Gatling. But, honest, Woody, they aren't wishing you well."

He leaned back, clasping hands behind his neck.

"*Ach . . . zo . . .* like the German submarine commander says. Well, you can't blame 'em. But how do I explain all this to that crazy doctor in Brownsville? He still doesn't know what I was talking about."

She rearranged the papers, then started to leave. "Oh, there was one call before you came in. A Mr. Malkin."

Thrasher lurched forward. "Not Mr. *Myron* Malkin, the poet laureate of Haven Place?"

"He didn't give his first name. Just left a number and asked that you call him. He sounded terribly urgent."

"Not nearly as urgent as I am, sweetie. Get him for me."

The whole picture had changed; things were breaking for him once more. He was sure Myron had called to inform him he had won the doctor over. Already his alert mind was figuring out how long it would take him to write the script; what kind of staff he would need; who to call at the network for assistance—he would need a topnotch director at the very start.

He heard the outer office buzzer and grabbed the phone, hearing Myron's pure New Yorkese.

"Mr. Thrasher?"

"Yes, Myron."

"It's all set. I got Uncle Doc to agree. Now it's your baby."

"Myron, you're doing wonderfully."

"Just two things."

"You mean about a retainer for you? I've already agreed. We can even give you a credit as assoc—"

"Cut that crap. Forget me. I mean Uncle Doc. The *house*. That's how I got him to say okay, he'll act in your show. He owmost went outa his mind this morning. The boogies slashed his tires and ruint his sign. He was goin' crazy, I swear. Was gonna buy a new house, and clean out all his savings, just cause he hadda get out. So I told him you'd help him move. You'd help pay."

Thrasher pursed his lips and frowned. He had no choice but to agree to Myron's terms; at the same time he sensed a deep resentment at the manner in which this overage copy boy was drawing up terms.

"Myron, can't I make you understand that if I pay your uncle, if I give him a big chunk of money for doing this, I'm destroying the whole purpose of showing him to the country as an honest, useful man? He becomes—well, an actor—a phony—like everyone else."

"No. You do it my way. I want"—he paused, as if doing some rapid mental arithmetic, then resumed—"seven, no eight thousand bucks. Enough to help him buy that house."

"I'm not agreeing to anything, Myron."

"Then stay where the hell you are."

Thrasher clenched his fist around the phone and shook it slightly.

"All I will agree to is this. We will make some arrangement to help Dr. Abelman move. But I won't agree on a figure, and I won't put anything in writing."

Myron answered much too quickly, as if he had been prepared to accept minimal terms. "Okay. When do you wanna start work?"

"Today? This afternoon?"

"Make it tonight, after office hours. They're supposed to be till eight, but ya can come earlier, cause it ain't so busy now. I won't be here, but I'll tell Uncle Doc."

"Fine. Myron, one favor. Don't go writing any literary gems for the *Record* about our project. Save your talents for *Americans, U.S.A.*"

"Sure, sure. And save your money for Uncle Doc's house."

Thrasher hung up. He was feeling marvelous. But he needed immediate assistance, somebody technically proficient, and he turned to the network. Normally he would have called one of his executive friends; but he was feeling secretive, almost conspiratorial. He had kept his associates in the dark thus far, and now he preferred equally little interference from the network. *Americans, U.S.A.*, if success it were to be, would be his success. If it flopped, he would fall with it. He had Louise telephone Alice Taggart.

"Alice, sweetie, this is in the nature of a business call."

"Wonderful. Do you need a good A.D.?"

"I will eventually, doll, and I promise you you'll get the job. But first I need a director. Who is young, talented, and in trouble at the moment?"

"Dexter Daw. He's always in trouble."

Thrasher knew Daw by reputation: a wicked caricature of the young man in mass communications—intelligent, a competent technician, fast-moving, utterly unstable, and so incredibly dishonest that his repuation for knavery overwhelmed all his unquestioned skills.

"Is he working now?" Thrasher asked.

"Odd jobs around the house," Alice said. "He's in the bullpen, just like me. What do you want him for?"

"The new G & T show. It's very big, Alice, and terribly exciting. Tell Daw I need him urgently and would like him to work tonight. He can call me before noon."

"What about my job?"

He could see Alice crooking the phone against her bony shoulder, the futuristic lamp on her desk throwing harsh light on the narrow face and the tufts of blond hair.

"In time, dear, in time. I'll request you when we get organized." He paused, feeling the lickerish spark ignite in his groin, and stage-whispered, "In fact I'm requesting you right now. But not for work. I'll meet you at your place at one."

"I hate matinees," she said sadly.

"One o'clock," he said firmly. "Don't undress until I get there."

His day was forming itself into a delicious, integrated whole: the reaffirmation of masculinity and the fulfilment of the artist, all within twelve hours. He started to scribble notes on a ruled pad, aimless yet coherent words relating to the task. He hardly noticed Loomer and young Chilson when they entered.

Loomer placed a dummy brochure on his desk, a handsome, modern sheaf of heavy glossy pages with a plastic binder and a thick cover made of some nubby woven material. An inlay in the shape of a television screen filled part of the cover. The screen showed a montage of typical American faces, and, superimposed on them, the words AMERICANS, U.S.A. Thrasher flicked the cover open and read the introductory paragraph. It consisted of a tiny cluster of words in graceful italics, isolated in the lower right-hand corner.

A new concept in mass communications . . .
. . . a bold, original approach to television journalism . . .
a closer, more meaningful look at our country and
our people, what makes them strong and what makes them
the world's best hope.

Thrasher read it swiftly and looked up at them. "That's splendid, splendid, Ben. Just the kind of pitch we need."

Loomer pointed at Chilson. "Ted wrote it, Woody. The kid turns a nice phrase, don't you think?"

"I think it's very neatly done, Ted," Thrasher said.

"Thanks, Woody." In his Eastern campus whine, the word "thanks" had three syllables. "How's your doctor doing?"

Thrasher got up from his chair and sat on the edge of the desk.

"You guys won't believe it, but it was the old Thrasher magic at work again. I made a wild guess when I picked Samuel Abelman out of the New York *Record*. And, frankly, I was a little scared when I first saw the street—a slum! But only Woodrow Wilson Thrasher would come up with a first subject for *Americans, U.S.A.* who has been a GP for forty years on one block, and—get this, Ben—"

Loomer and Chilson were pointing like golden retrievers, and Thrasher even sensed a physical resemblance in the younger man: he could see a silken brown tail projecting from the vent in Chilson's seersucker jacket.

"—the old character has his own cornfield in the backyard and reads Thoreau!"

Loomer's round face smiled in its best man-to-man fashion. "Well, I'll be darned," he said, "an old guy living in a slum, practicing medicine. And he has a cornfield and reads Thoreau."

"Regularly," Thrasher said. "Dr. Abelman is a scholar on the subject."

"It's fabulous," Chilson said. "It's the greatest."

"How about a meeting this afternoon on the project?" Loomer asked brightly. In Ben Loomer's world, all problems, all crises, all decisions could be resolved by calling four or five people together for three hours of discussion. Meetings germinated in his vast office like algae on a petri dish.

"I'd love to sit in," Chilson said. "Thoreau, gosh! I did a lot of work in Thoreau and Emerson, and I might have a few ideas."

Thrasher shook his head. "I'm not quite ready, Ben," he said. "I'm running out there tonight to start pouring the foundation. But any idea you have—memorandize me." He could afford to be magnanimous, even a little condescending. The Thoreau gambit had put him in total command. They left extending their congratulations, promising their backing and aid. Thrasher yanked open his collar and started scribbling again. He had forty minutes until meeting Alice: the anticipation was often more pleasurable, he thought, than the culmination.

He rode out to Brooklyn again that evening, through the crawling traffic and oppressive moist air, with Dexter Daw. Daw slouched in one corner of the cab, his eyes half shut. He was a slight young man with an oversized, prematurely bald head. His pale-blue eyes drooped downward to a rudimentary nose and mouth, and beneath the protuberant forehead he had the look of a cynical embryo. Daw had started work in television as a very young man, fresh from high school and church dramatic societies. A combination of bravado, fast talking, and some undeniable talent had placed him in the front rank of television directors; but his capacity for offending people constantly prevented him from achieving permanent status. The network retained him at his basic director's salary of a hundred and eighty-five dollars a week—a sum which barely paid for Daw's weekly lunch tab at the better East Side restaurants, where he was on a first-name basis with headwaiters. Every now and then he was thrown into emergencies and new projects where his facile mind worked to excellent advantage. He was twenty-seven years old, drank excessively, and was suspected of being homosexual. Daw was perfectly normal in his sexual habits, but people were delighted to suspect (and communicate) the worst about him. His detractors always coupled the reports of his abhorrent behavior with the footnote that he was close to being a genius. The truth was that he was not nearly so wicked as painted, and far less talented. Daw, who had few illusions about himself, knew this, and would have preferred the true circumstances to have been reversed.

Thrasher had outlined his idea for *Americans, U.S.A.*, and he was pleased by Daw's apparent interest and excellent suggestions. The director talked about the use of old phonograph records as background music; the use of photographs from the doctor's files to tell the story of his early life; newsreel clips of events that could be tied into his career; perhaps the patient who was involved in Dr. Abelman's most dramatic case.

"It's got to be sincere as hell," Daw said. "I mean, we've got to *feel* the whole half hour. Just one false note and we're dead. That's why the writing is so important."

"There's an implied needle there, isn't there, Dexter?"

"Not at all," said Daw defensively.

"You don't think I can write it, isn't that correct? You'd be happier with a regular by-line dramatist, I gather. Some genius who writes hour-long tragedies about young couples in the Bronx who throw out the old father, right?"

Daw closed his sloping eyes. "Oh, Woody, don't give me the frustrated genius bit. I know all about you, or else I wouldn't have agreed to this whore's dream. I know you're the guy who did the American Drama Festival on TV, and that you put that egghead sociologist on as a paid consultant on mass communications. I certainly think you can write it as well as any of these former wire service deskmen. All I said was, the script better be sincere."

Thrasher studied his large, fetal head with curious disgust and settled back in the red leather seat, watching darkness descend over Brooklyn. It was starting to rain, swollen drops which splashed against the taxicab's windows in splotchy patterns. Street odors smothered beneath the fat summer rain, and it was restful inside the protective shell of the cab.

Thrasher heard Daw's lazy voice after a few moments of quiet. "How come you called me through Alice Taggart?" he asked.

"I know her from other jobs," Thrasher said quickly "Sometimes I prefer her judgment to the decisions made by the big wheels."

"You're laying her, aren't you?"

It was one of those unique, pointless assaults so typical of Dexter Daw. It was no wonder he had been black-listed by a half-dozen agencies.

"It's none of your business," Thrasher said.

"Well," Daw drawled, "that keeps it in the family because I used to."

Thrasher looked at him dully. "Dexter, you'll never grow up. The big city was just too much for that little boy from Marinette, Wisconsin. Too much money, too much good booze, too much nooky."

"Saginaw, Michigan," Daw corrected. He dozed off in happy prenatal slumber.

They found the doctor in the rear room, the consultation chamber which Thrasher had never been in. Office hours had just ended, and he was upholstering a footstool. He shook hands with Thrasher and Daw, motioning the producer to his own swivel chair, the younger man to a green leather armchair which bore the signs of the doctor's own haphazard repair work. The physician was sitting on the edge of a brown Morris chair, working an immense needle in and out of the underside of a heavy ottoman, an approximate companion piece to the armchair. His hands worked quickly and with great strength, pulling and tugging the stubborn twine through the leather and the coarse under-fabric. The finished product would be far from a professional job, but sufficiently neat and serviceable.

"I give my metabolisms and EKG's on this chair," he said, "and my *fekokteh* patients don't need anything better. I can do just as good as those crooks on St. John's Place with my own needle."

The consultation room had a warm, used look about it. In the corner, to the rear of the Morris chair, was the metabolism apparatus, shrouded beneath a pointed gray hood like the grand kleagle. An ancient electrocardiograph machine in a glass cabinet stood to one side of the chair. Alongside it was an ornate mahogany bookcase, crammed with medical texts and the doctor's Riverside edition of Thoreau. It occupied a place of honor, Thrasher noticed, on a middle shelf, below Osler's *Modern Medicine* and above Hyman's *The Practice of Medicine*. Opposite the bookcase was the doctor's desk, the surface cluttered with papers, books, a tall, dire-looking sphygmomanometer, and a fancy glass contraption designed to hold two inkwells, pens, and pencils. Only one of the wells was filled, the rest of the desk piece serving as a repository for paper clips, washers, postage stamps, rubber bands, and several small wooden rectangles which Thrasher recognized as the identification tags for dahlia tubers. The walls were done in green sculptured plastering denoting some kind of waves or floral motif, a style long vanished from the decorators' sample books. There were several appalling oil paintings, apparently by the same artistic deadbeat who had created the mammoth landscapes upstairs. Over the desk was a large framed photograph of a handsome man of middle age. He wore a high stiff collar and his hair was carefully parted in the middle. This, together with the yellowing mat and age-darkened oak frame, indicated that the photograph was probably taken anywhere from thirty to forty years ago. The face was wide, the features large and strong, with a distinct Indian cast. Thrasher felt convinced he knew the man.

"You recognize him, Mr. Thrasher?" the doctor asked.

"I—I don't believe I do."

"Harlow Brooks. He was one of my teachers at Bellevue. A great man. *He* had the right idea." The doctor jabbed viciously at the hard leather, pulling the deadly needle upward into the fabric.

"Make a note of that, Dexter," Thrasher said. "We can do a little section on Dr. Brooks. He won't mind, will he?"

"He's dead," said Dr. Abelman. "What are you guys here for, anyway? Myron ran off to work and didn't tell me anything."

Thrasher leaned forward. Outside the August rain whipped at

the narrow windows. It was warm and stuffy within, but there was a tight, self-contained comfort about the room that was not unpleasant. Under the harsh light of the chandelier he watched the doctor's hands manipulating the ball of twine, the needle, the footstool.

"Now that you've agreed to let us do our show about you, doctor, Dexter and myself have to learn as much as we can about you. To do the program honestly and with conviction, we have to start at the very beginning," Thrasher explained.

"Yes," Daw added, "a kind of friendly catharsis, only you can leave out all the dirt and just give us the plain facts of your life. Childhood, growing up, etcetera."

Thrasher looked balefully at Daw, but the doctor did not seem annoyed. He looked up through his steamed glasses at Daw and chuckled.

"Everybody knows the Freud words today, hey, sonny?"

"It's part of our business," said Daw.

"That's just the trouble," said the doctor quickly. "Freud had the right dope. He knew what was going on, and he was the first to figure it all out. But the whoremasters got ahold of him, and then, the way his stuff came out, it made no sense at all."

Thrasher, distressed at being excluded, joined in quickly. "A lot of reputable workers in psychiatry and the whole field of mental health differ with Freud's findings," he said eagerly.

The doctor shook his head, the yellow light bouncing off the high forehead and lighting the vertical gray hairs on his crown.

"Only in details, details. Remember Freud was *first*, first of the whole bunch. He showed the bastards a thing or two. He was no chump."

Thrasher took out a ruled pad, clicked his ballpoint pen so that the nib jumped out, and sat himself at the doctor's desk.

"Mind if I use your desk, doctor?"

"Of course not. It's a little messy, just find room. Say, would you fellows like some ice cream? Or a little cream soda?"

Daw and Thrasher exchanged grieved looks. In their world, you offered ice cream and soda to children; grownups were entertained with alcohol. Yet, even as Thrasher winced, it occurred to him that it was a rather good suggestion; that some ice cream would taste fine at the moment. Thinking about it, he wondered why people always offered him liquor even when they knew he disliked drinking. It gave him a headache and made him sleepy.

"No thank you, doctor," Thrasher said, "Mr. Daw and I ate before coming out here. Perhaps later."

"All right. I always make myself an ice-cream soda before going to bed. You can join me then."

"Fine," Thrasher said. He hunched over the pad, turning sideways to the old man. "Dr. Abelman, why don't we start at the very beginning. Where were you born?"

The doctor made a vigorous knot over his last stitch, snipped the twine with a pocketknife, and upended the footstool. Then he stretched out on the Morris chair, extending his short legs on the repaired ottoman.

"Not a bad job for an amateur, hey? How many doctors you think can upholster?" He was triumphant.

"Not too many," Thrasher said agreeably. "You're quite skilled. As I was asking, doctor, where were you born?"

"Bessarabia," said the doctor. "A village called Brovo, near Kishinev. It's either Rumania or Russia depending on how you look at it."

Daw sat up. "A Rumanian! That's interesting. Rumanians are the most cultured and interesting of the Eastern Europeans, I've always felt. Can you speak Rumanian?"

The doctor smiled indulgently. "My boy," he said, "Rumanians are a bunch of bastards. What did any Rumanian ever do for me? There's two things I can tell you about Rumanians—they use cologne instead of bathing, and they're very good at kicking Jews in the ass."

Thrasher was a trifle upset by the doctor's sudden and thoroughly unexpected reference to anti-Semitism, even on the part of Rumanians. It called for some kind of reasonable rejoinder.

"I think you're being a little extreme, doctor," Thrasher said. "I don't think it's right to condemn a whole nation for the sins of some. I'm sure you don't approve of bigots saying that all Jews are Communists or thieves. By the same token, it's not right to brand all Rumanians as intolerant." He laughed politely. "Offhand, I can't think of any Rumanians I know *personally*—but I'm sure there are many liberal, intelligent, humane Rumanians."

"Step up and see the humane Rumanian," Daw interposed.

Thrasher glared at the director.

"Don't crap me up about Rumanians or any of those other lice," Dr. Abelman said, "they all stink." He sat up in the Morris chair, gesticulating with thick muscular arms.

"You know something about Europeans? They're all full of bull. They're good for one thing: kicking Jews in the ass. I don't mean just Germans, I mean all of 'em—French, Polacks, Hungarians, Russians, the whole gang of thugs. Whenever things get a little tough, whenever one lousy European, say a squarehead, starts shooting Polacks, what do the Polacks do? Do they hate Germans? Of course not! They murder a few Jews and they feel great. *Wonderful!* C'mon, Wladek, the Krauts just burned our farm, so we'll go shoot bullets through Reb Mendelson, that mockey!"

Thrasher, flushed with embarrassment, tried to interrupt, but the doctor had leaped from the chair and was now declaiming loudly, accompanying his speech with comical, hyperbolic gestures. He began by clapping both palms against his pate and staring at the flaking ceiling.

"Oh, those marvelous, cultured, religious Europeans! Well, let me tell you about those fine, gentlemanly Europeans! They're all going to be screaming neurotics in ten years. You know why? *Because they got no Jews left!*"

"You're absolutely right, doctor," said Daw. "Look what happened to Spain. Their whole commerce and finance collapsed after the Inquisition."

"Nah, that's not what I mean," said the doctor with some annoyance. "It's not the commerce or the finance. That's more bull. The *goyim* got the *real* dough, and don't forget it!"

Baffled at first, Thrasher was now intrigued. There was something so frank and outspoken about the old man's peroration—even though he disagreed with a good deal of what he said—that he no longer felt embarrassed.

"It's simple, simple," the doctor said. "What's been keeping Europe going all these years? Culture? Religion? Business? Nah! I'll tell you what—kicking Jews in the ass! *But they got no Jews left.* The Nazis burned six million and the rest beat it. Oh, there's a couple thousand maybe, but they won't last. Then what? You know, when you're used to spitting in a guy's eye every day, it does something for your morale, your character. It kept those Europeans happy for centuries! But what happens when the guy ain't there? Those poor Rumanians! Those poor Polacks! Nobody left to spit on! I give them maybe ten years, and they'll all go crazy. *Meshugeh,* we call it."

"That's a wonderful word," said Daw. "It denotes so much."

Tapping the point of his pen against the pad, Thrasher said nothing. He was having some second thoughts on the doctor's declamation, and he found himself in partial agreement with the old man. It *was* a fascinating thesis: Europeans who had spent centuries relieving their neuroses by abusing Jews. Who would take the scapegoat's place now? It would make an interesting article for the Foreign Policy Association, of which he was a member.

The doctor sat down again, no longer irate or explosive. Indeed, Thrasher had noticed, he had delivered his lecture on European mores without any true rancor or bitterness despite the foul language and the calisthenics. He had merely wanted to set the record straight.

"What do you guys want to know? Let's get it over with," the physician said.

"We were talking about the village where you were born, doctor," Thrasher said. He had written on the pad: *brn Brovo, vllge Bessarabia.*

"It might be helpful," Daw said, "if you tried to recall some incidents from your boyhood. Perhaps one thing that sticks in your memory."

The doctor hooked a finger over his upper lip and gazed reflectively into his rain-swept backyard. He could see the top-heavy dahlias swaying and bending in the night wind.

"I was only five when we came over here."

"Can you recall one person who impressed you? Any event?" Daw persisted.

Thrasher was somewhat distressed at the way Daw had seized the initiative. Dr. Abelman was *his* discovery. At the same time he was rather pleased that the director had entered the project so enthusiastically.

The old man shaded his eyes.

"Who remembers? Who wants to remember? Those goddam Rumanians." He said the last words with a tinge of exhaustion and despair, and for a moment there was a dull silence. It was as if a horde of intruding Rumanians, with their cologne-scented unwashed bodies, all the Codreanus and Gheorgescus, had suddenly crowded into the small office and were inhibiting him.

"Come now, doctor," Thrasher said, "I really can't believe a man of your intelligence would carry a grudge this long. After all, it's more than half a century since you were in Europe."

"What do you know?" the doctor asked. "What do either of you guys know?"

He swung his short legs off the footstool and walked to the window, engaging the lower section in mortal combat a few seconds, before raising it to let in a rush of moist air. Turning, he appeared grave and pensive.

"You keep asking me about that lousy old country," he said. "Okay, wise guys, I'll tell you one thing I remember. I used to have a dream when I was a kid. There was this village street, all mud and wooden houses. And I'm pressing my nose up against the window. It's covered with frost and I can only see through a little circle. There are pigs in the street. That's nothing new, there are always a few loose animals from the *goyishe* farms wandering in the mud. But these pigs are eating the blacksmith or what's left of him. He was a fat drunken Jew who had his shop across from our house. And he's got no shop left. It's all burned down."

Thrasher twisted uneasily in his seat.

"You say you had this dream when you were young?" the agency man asked huskily. "How long did you have it?"

"I still dream about it," the doctor said flatly. "And I'll tell you something else, sonny boy. It was no dream. It really happened. It was a goddam trauma, if you'll excuse one of Freud's words. I saw it when I was an infant in that village."

"That's all you remember about Europe?" Daw asked.

"That's all I need to remember."

"But there must have been *some* happy recollections," Thrasher pursued. "I've read those charming novels about Jewish family life, doctor, Friday night and the candles and—"

"Hoo-hah!" the doctor cried. "A regular Sholem Aleichem! Listen, young fellah, when you can get eaten by a farmer's pig some fine morning, there isn't much room left for happy celebrations!"

Despairingly, Daw leaned forward, pleading with fine white hands, daintily freckled.

"Let's drop Europe for the time being, doctor," the director said, "can you tell us anything about your boyhood in America?"

"Good idea, Dec," Thrasher said. They were both urgently anxious to leave the murky world of Rumanian farmers and their man-eating pigs. "Did your family come to Brooklyn immediately, Dr. Abelman?"

"Oh no," he said, "Brooklyn was for sports in those days, for cake-eaters. The slobs like us went to the East Side."

"Suppose you tell us something about what the East Side was like," the agency man said. "It surely couldn't have been as bad as Europe. Any interesting personality you remember? Anyone at all?"

A wry smile germinated on the doctor's face; the solemnity brought on by his remembrances of Europe had vanished. It was not that he was mercurial or flighty in his emotions, Thrasher realized; rather there was a cushion of nonsensical humor in his make-up that dulled the impact of his frequent rages and ingrained bitterness.

"I'll tell you fellahs something. Know what a *melamed* is?"

"Mlamid?" Thrasher asked. "I'm afraid not."

"It's the word for a teacher, a Hebrew teacher. I had this teacher on the East Side—well, I didn't have him for so long, but that's getting ahead of myself. Boy, was he a beaut! Skinny, red beard, you know, a Cossack in the woodpile somewhere. Did he have an arm for a skinny guy! When he let you have it with those birches, your behind hurt for a week! And never twice in the same place!"

Thrasher and Daw were both eagerly attentive. This is what they were seeking: color, ethnic charm, the real thing.

"Suppose you just start talking about him," Thrasher said brightly. "Anything you remember. He sounds like quite an interesting man."

"He was a son-of-a-bitch," the doctor said.

For Reb Yankele Abelman, the tailor, this was a day of fulfilment. Through the dusty window of the tailoring shop on Ludlow Street (Y. ABELMAN WAITERS' JACKETS) he waved a peremptory goodbye to his wife Malka and his two older children. Then, grasping his son Shmulka by one fat hand, he marched off in stooped, jerky steps toward the *kheydr*, the school for young children. The tailor was a bowed and starved man in his early forties. He clipped his beard short and he wore a workman's cap. Clearly, he was not one of the *sheyneh yidn*, the long-bearded aristocrats of the synagogue's Eastern Wall, the men with soft hands and dreamy eyes who studied the Torah. Back in the old country the shame of his lowly estate had been deeper and more marked; in the village of Brovo, one's knowledge of the law and one's eschewal of manual work were the truest marks of prestige. Here, on New York's cramped Lower East Side, the stigma of being *prosteh*—a common Jew of the shops and factories—was less pronounced. Nonetheless it existed, and Yankele Abelman, the tailor of Brovo, now of Ludlow Street, had resolved that his youngest son would bring eternal joy to his breast by becoming all the things he was not.

Three months earlier, Reb Yankele (the Reb was a grudging term of respect, denoting that the tailor spent one night a week in the house of study, wrestling with the ancient word) had met his wife and two younger children at Castle Garden. He himself had emigrated to the new home a year earlier, bringing with him his oldest son Moishe. Father and son had labored in a shirtwaist sweatshop, living on bread and tea, saving their pennies for the day when they might purchase passage for the rest of the family.

And what a day it had been when Malka had arrived with their daughter Rivke and little Shmulka! The people from HIAS, the Hebrew Immigration Aid Society, had fluttered about them, forcing cakes on them; a band of musicians (Irishers, yet!) in fire department uniforms had played for them; a tall *goy*, a bald-headed man with a white beard, had made a speech to them in English. A young American Jew from HIAS had told them that the bald man was a minister, a Methodist, and he was welcoming the Jewish immigrants because they would all find jobs quickly and none of them would go to jail. Reb Yankele clucked in amazement at the memory. Such a country! The *goyishe* minister made speeches to welcome Jews; in Bessarabia a Jew might furnish a meal for the *goy's* pigs.

He glanced admiringly at his son. The boy's nose was red and runny under the whip of March's wind, but there was no fear in his dark eyes. The child had a large round head and a firm body. Secretly, the tailor was proud of his son's strength and agility, even though those were traits better suited for a gentile. A good Jew was concerned only with the mind and the spirit. These endured; flesh decayed.

The *kheydr* consisted of a draughty room in an ancient brownstone building adjacent to the synagogue. They trudged up scuffed stairs, the boy all but tripping on the new prayer shawl wrapped around his shoulders, thence through stained corridors redolent of cheap cooking and urine. The *melamed's* wife was a notoriously poor housekeeper. Of the neighborhood families, theirs was the poorest and most miserable. It was one of those curious paradoxes of the Jewish mind that the teaching of religion to children was deemed despicable and worthy only of paltry reward. To sell for cash your meager store of the law was considered contemptible. "One does not make an ax of the Torah," the elders would intone.

The *melamed's* name was Reb Kalman; his screeching voice could be heard echoing through opened rear windows, alleys, and side streets, during his classroom sessions. As the tailor and his son entered the opened door of the house of learning they found the teacher in typical tableau. His right hand gripped a screaming fat boy by the scruff of the neck. The left hand and its wicked birches flailed against the child's bare legs with a whistling noise.

"*Goy!* Pig! Horse!" Reb Kalman shrieked. "You should herd sheep! Your father will beat you worse yet, for reading so stupidly!"

The tailor cleared his throat. Twenty dark-eyed faces turned toward the newcomers, inspecting the initiate into their tortured fraternity. Arm poised in mid-air, Reb Kalman halted and managed a smile. Yellow teeth peeked between the pink foliage of his hungering face. He greeted the tailor cheerily.

"*Aleichem Sholem,*" Shmulka's father murmured apologetically. I have brought you my son as a student. He knows already how to follow the words in the book."

The *melamed* nodded approvingly. "A great rabbi, he'll become, I'm sure of it. I can see it in his face."

All that the teacher saw in the face, of course, was confusion and fear; but the prediction of great promise was expected of him. He led Shmulka Abelman to a front bench, a relic rubbed smooth by thousands of small behinds, and sat him down next to the weeping fat boy.

"I have brought some small cakes for the other scholars, Reb Kalman," the tailor muttered. "May I give them out to celebrate my son's entrance into your school?"

The *melamed* clucked in mock disapproval. "Such stupid boys, Reb Yankel, they don't deserve it, mispronouncing the easiest words in the *khumesh*. But to celebrate, all right!"

There were a few discreet yips of joy, and the tailor made the rounds of the class, doling out hard pellets of dough, soaked in honey. Then, leaving the near-empty bag and its remaining crumbs of pastry with his son, he admonished him, "Be a good boy and learn your lesson, Shmulka."

"Yes, papa." Then, glancing covertly at the looming figure of the teacher, he asked faintly. "He won't hit me?"

"Only if you're bad, Shmulka." He did not kiss him—such feminine displays were not for the iron precincts of the *kheydr*—and left. Plodding back to Ludlow Street, his heart was grateful and joyous: to have such a smart son, small as he was! How could he fail to be a great scholar?

Inside the schoolroom, the new boy sat in mute terror, struggling to follow the repetition of the Hebrew alphabet. On the east wall of the classroom sat the older boys, those who already knew the *aleph-bes*, the Hebrew alphabet, and had advanced to elementary readings. Shmulka sat with the smallest and most ignorant of the students: a shivering clutch of infants snatched too soon from their toys, and delivered to the *melamed's* merciless arm. The new boy pressed his primer against his chest. His skullcap—two sizes too big—fell over one eye, and he squeezed himself, for sanctuary and warmth, between two of his wretched confederates.

He could not escape the lookout's eye of Reb Kalman. In leaping strides, the teacher loomed over him. The tyrant smiled, a cracked grin obscured by the beard.

"So, Shmulka Abelman? Already in school ten minutes and you don't know what the book is for? Tell me, what is the book for?"

"T-t-to read," stammered the boy.

"So why are you clutching it like a farmer holds a whiskey bottle? Why shouldn't it be opened to the page?"

The older students across the room laughed politely at Reb Kalman's wit—he expected it of them—and in the wake of their laughter, the birches whistled across the new student's folded arms.

"The book! Open the pages, pig!" he shrieked.

Shmulka wailed unashamedly: the pain in his arms was unlike anything he had ever felt. Gasping, wiping tears from his eyes, he opened the primer and sought to catch up with the other students. But the pittance of instruction his father had given him was buried beneath Reb Kalman's disorganized assault. It seemed that everyone was reading something else at the same time. Rarely did the teacher pause to listen to a single student recite. Somehow his ear had managed to sift through a little of what each child was reading, and make mental note of the student's ability. The morning dragged on endlessly for Shmulka. Shivering at first, he now sweated uncomfortably in the crowded, unventilated room. His tiny stomach demanded attention; no less urgent was his bladder.

He had recited the *aleph-bes* perhaps fifty times (or so it seemed) and his head began to nod. The hum of voices grew dimmer, punctuated by the occasional whistle of Reb Kalman's birches and the injured yelp of some luckless boy. At length, he dozed, only to be awakened by a hand gripping his shirt collar and pulling him from the bench. Rubbing his eyes, he looked up at his tormenter.

"Sleeping in class, Abelman? One day in school and already taking naps, eh? From this kind of behavior your father expects a great scholar?"

"I didn't mean it," the boy whispered. "Don't hit me again." He backed a step away.

"An argument yet!" Reb Kalman smiled, nodding his head in simulated pleasure, to the delight of the boys. United in their hatred of the teacher, they were nevertheless amused by his novel techniques for torture. "You should be a lawyer not a rabbi! Now, lawyer, pull down the pants and turn around!"

Then, to Reb Kalman's horror, he heard the forbidden words— words which no boy had ever dared utter in his presence.

"I won't," said Shmulka. He backed away a few more steps.

The teacher's eyes widened in disbelief. The starveling chest puffed out with a sudden intake of soiled air; the left arm, holding aloft the birches, descended in vicious trajectory upon the defiant face.

It happened so suddenly that Reb Kalman, for a few confused seconds, was as dazed as if Elijah the prophet had walked into his classroom. The child, with uncanny agility, had ducked away from the weapon, recovered his balance, and, while the teacher's arm floundered against the floor boards, had seized the twigs from his hand and run off to a corner of the room.

"Now, Shmulka Ben Yankel, come to your teacher," he said soothingly. "I will have to punish you for what you did. Remember I am bigger and stronger than you."

But the boy stood his ground. Like a wingless prehistoric bird, red-ruffed and stilt-legged, the teacher stalked his prey, and again the unexpected happened. With magnificent co-ordination, the boy waited until the last minute—when the predatory claws were about to seize him—then feinted to the right and sped past the teacher's left, bowling over two of the smallest students and touching off a frantic chase around the benches.

"After him! Stop him! He is possessed by the *dybbuk!*" screamed Reb Kalman. But the tortured children of the *kheydr* had waited too long for rebellion; none volunteered. The accursed youngster could not be stopped. He leaped over low benches and scuttled underneath high ones; sped furiously down the main aisle, then braked his speed at the corners. Reb Kalman had now retrieved his birches, and with this added confidence, and the child's apparent exhaustion, he now put all his strength into one final onslaught. The boy was resting against the teacher's desk, his breath coming in agonized wheezes. He was clearly spent, incapable of further running. But as he saw Reb Kalman approaching him with the heavy tread of doom, he summoned up some last hidden source of strength.

"You won't hit me again," he cried. Simultaneously he hurled a prayer book from the teacher's desk at the oncoming knees, then turned swiftly and fled through the classroom door and down the steps. With Reb Kalman's unholy curses pursuing him, he ran all the way to his home, stumbling and sobbing.

The shame of Yankele and Malka Abelman coursed through the tenements of Ludlow Street: their son was, at worst, possessed of a *dybbuk,* daring to throw a holy book at the teacher. At the least, he was an incorrigible wretch who would grow up to be a *balegolah,* a wagon driver, or some other kind of common oaf.

Reb Yankele whipped his son soundly and never again spoke of the dreadful adventure of the *kheydr.* In a few months the boy would be old enough for the American school, where he would learn arithmetic and the new language and a lot of other barbarous things; all the beauty and dignity of the law would be denied him. Later he would enter him in the Talmud Torah, the school for routine Hebrew learning, as a part-time student. But little Shmulka would always have the mark against him: the boy who ran away from *kheydr*.

The tailor's life settled into the dull rhythms of poverty: the long hours in the shop, with Moishe working silently at his side; the younger children running into the wild, strange streets, speaking less Yiddish and more English every day; his wife, blessing the candles on Friday night; the single day of prayer at the synagogue and the resumption of labor on Sunday.

One night a week the tailor continued his attendance at the house of study, the room in the synagogue where ordinary Jews might come to read the law and discuss it with the rabbi and the other learned elders of the community. Since the shame of his son's first day at school, Reb Yankele had contented himself with sitting in a dark corner of the dingy room, burying his weary eyes in one of the holy books. No overt reference had even been made to his son's crime; but the nods and winks of the scholars were sufficient to inform him that his sorrows were known to them.

One night, into the gaslit room half filled with murmuring scholars loped the weedy figure of Reb Kalman the *melamed*. Normally he disdained the house of study; the law and the books had been unkind to him and when his teaching hours were ended he preferred not to immerse himself in their intricacies. Now, lurching through the room crammed with hard benches and worn tables, he spied the tailor. The remembrance of his humiliation burned anew and he clapped his hands to draw the attention of the part-time scholars.

"Reverend students," he intoned, "do you know the fable of the educated horse?"

"This is no time for riddles, Reb Kalman," a bearded elder reprimanded him kindly. "We are reading the *mishnah*."

"And I am being equally scholarly. I am about to relate a favorite story of the great rabbi of Lodz. All of you should listen. Especially any tailors among you."

Reb Yankele buried his gray face in his book and wrapped the prayer shawl snugly around his shoulders.

"In the village of Glebocka lived a farmer who owned a beautiful horse. Such a strong, handsome beast!" the teacher began. "It pulled the farmer's plow and hauled the wagon that took the farmer's family to market. It was the envy of the village."

The scholars listened attentively. For all you could say against Reb Kalman, he told a magnificent story.

"This simple peasant soon thought of his horse as a real person. He decorated the animal with bells and ribbons on the holy days. He spoke of it in terms of endearment. But this horse quite naturally remained a horse. To change all this the farmer decided he would teach this horse to talk. To *talk!*"

The tailor looked about him apprehensively, wondering if he could sneak out quietly. But with each sentence of his story, the teacher was advancing toward him.

"And so this poor fool of a farmer began to spend hours with his beloved horse. He spoke to him all day. At night he slept in the stall with him, whispering words in his ears. Words and more words! And, of course, the horse refused to speak. Soon the farmer was the butt of cruel jokes—neglecting his family, his plowing, just to make a horse talk. The elders said he had lost his mind. But he was determined. The horse would talk!

"Months later, when his children were going hungry and his fields were overgrown with weeds, the farmer had a dream. In this dream the horse appeared before him and told him: 'I will speak the day after the Sabbath.'"

There was an appreciative hum from the elders; clearly, Reb Kalman was leading up to an important point of law or custom. By now he was leaning over the tailor's desk, addressing himself to the shriveled little man.

"The farmer was overjoyed. He summoned his relatives, the villagers, the rabbi, all those who had made fun of him. And the day after the sabbath everyone assembled in the farmer's barnyard and the horse was led out. In terrified silence they listened. The farmer approached the cherished beast and commanded it thus, 'Beloved horse, speak!'

"With that the horse opened its great mouth and spoke. Do you know, reverend scholars, what it said? One little sentence. It said, '*Let me be a horse.*' And it never spoke again. You understand that, Reb Yankele the tailor, it said, '*Let me be a horse.*'"

There was a rising murmur of approbation from the readers. All of them knew of Reb Yankele's vain hope that his *prosteh* son would become a rabbi and how the child had disgraced him the very first day in *kheydr*. There was much smacking of gums and meaningful nodding. Reb Kalman folded his arms and leaned back, enjoying his triumph. The tailor glanced about him unhappily. Two of the elders were already interpreting the teacher's fable. He folded his prayer shawl neatly, gathered up his books, and shuffled out of the house of study.

In the morning, putting on his phylacteries and listening to his wife and daughter preparing breakfast in the cramped kitchen at the rear of the shop, he thought again about the teacher's story. It was true: he had been punished for his pride, for expecting too much from his son, just as the farmer had been put in his place for expecting a horse to talk.

Then, peering into the cramped and cluttered shop, he saw Shmulka sweeping bits of garments and thread from the warped floor, stacking the bolts of cloth, gathering up the tailor's instruments, and setting them neatly on the table. He worked swiftly and with remarkable strength; under the patched, graying winter undershirt he could see the boy's hard back, the muscular arms.

There was no disgrace in a man's becoming a good wagon driver or butcher, or tailor for that matter, Reb Yankele decided.

The rain had ceased and Dr. Abelman, after a few slams and curses, had succeeded in opening the other rear window. Through the copper screen, the rain-cooled night air rushed into the confined room bearing the scent of wet earth and soaked blossoms.

A black snout poked itself against the screen. In answer to the dog's whimperings, the doctor offered a gruff greeting. "Hello, you bum. Whoring around again, eh?"

The mongrel barked apologetically, and, in the reflected yellow light of the consultation room, Thrasher and Daw could see the saturated shape of the dog leaping against the screen.

"All right, you tramp. You stink, but I'll let you in." He gestured to his visitors to follow him. "We can have that ice-cream soda now."

They sat around the white enamel kitchen table; the dog curled beneath the sink and licked its underside. Thrasher found himself enjoying the physician's treat—an immense dollop of cherry-vanilla ice cream in a stein of root beer. Daw sipped ginger ale.

Thrasher sucked the syrupy liquid through a straw, wondering why he never drank ice-cream sodas any more. He was faintly annoyed with himself for all the scotch-and-waters he had never really wanted.

"You've given us some fascinating stuff, doctor," Thrasher said. "Of course we may use only a fraction of it, but it's important for us to get a total picture. You agree, Dec?"

Daw nodded sleepily. He was wondering if the old man had a secret bottle of booze somewhere. Normally, Daw would have asked quite bluntly for whiskey. But as brash as the young director was, he was growing increasingly aware of his alien nature in the physician's home. It was as if he were a Zulu suddenly thrust into an Eskimo igloo: centuries of divergent tradition stood between guests and host.

"It's funny my remembering all that about that louse Kalman," the doctor said. "Of course my father used to repeat the story to me, particularly after I was in medical school. I guess in his mind I still wasn't as well off as if I had become an old coot in a long beard."

"I think that teacher was unnecessarily cruel to your father," Thrasher said.

"Sure he was. But was he any different than a lot of wiseacres? He had to have the last word. I didn't like the idea of getting my ass whipped, so he had to humiliate my father!"

The doctor gathered up the empty glasses and brought them to the sink. As he ran the hot water over them, he peered over his shoulder at his sleepy guests.

"You know what he was? He was a crap artist."

"A what?" asked Daw.

"A crap artist. It's my own word. For anyone who craps people up. Oh, there's plenty of them today. Plenty. That's all that Kalman was, a crap artist. He'd clean up today if he could peddle those stories of his."

He was scrubbing the soda glasses vigorously when he half turned and spoke to Daw and Thrasher again. "Nothing personal there, you know. I'm not sure *what* you guys do for a living."

Thrasher and Daw exchanged glances, each wondering whether the reference to the *melamed* was intended as a comparison. Both decided against the possibility, and at Thrasher's signal they rose.

"We'll want to see you again soon, Dr. Abelman," the agency vice-president said. "Tomorrow night, if possible. We have a lot of work to do and we've just scratched the surface. Will tomorrow be all right?"

The doctor hesitated. "Well, tomorrow night is when I usually go out to Long Beach to see the wife. You can come along if you want. I leave about three or four, after the afternoon calls."

"Can I meet you there tomorrow night?"

"Sure, sure. It's no Ritz where the wife stays, but you'll get fed anyway. You can pump me some more and go home. I'm almost beginning to enjoy it. Kind of like analysis."

The nightbell suddenly rang. The doctor fell back as if stabbed, then ran for cover behind the refrigerator. Conspiratorily, he called out to his guests, "Hey, one of you guys answer the door! Tell them I'm not in! I've gone! My God—eleven o'clock at night and the bastards won't let you live!"

They looked at him helplessly, and Thrasher found himself asking, "But—but—if it's an emergency?"

"It's *always* an emergency! Go on, tell 'em I've gone!"

Obediently Thrasher went to the door. As he opened it, a Negro, his black skin dotted with glistening beadlets of rain, fell into his arms. Terrified, the agency man sought to escape, but the caller's bearish arms hugged him dearly. He was an immense man, wobbling slightly, his clothes torn and sweat-darkened.

"You de doctor? If you is, Ah owes you a gratitude."

"I—I—the doctor is not in," Thrasher lied.

"You de doctor. *Ah knows you is.* Ah owes you a gratitude cause you saved mah daughter's life. Dat Leueen Harrison. Ah done heard 'bout it from mah wife, dat bitch. But you okeh, doctor, so Ah come to pay you mah gratitude." He hugged Thrasher to his rain-soaked bosom. An aroma of cheap wine and vomit overwhelmed him. Thrasher tried to disengage himself from the loving embrace, but as they struggled, the colored man lurched forward and the two were propelled into the waiting room. Arms and legs entwined, they stepped off in a stately minuet, around and around the darkened anteroom, now dipping gracefully into one of the doctor's old leather chairs, now skirting the bookcase and the shaded double doors. With the Negro's soiled clothing and heavy body pressed against his own limbs, he smelled, along with winey effluvia, the rich aroma of an unwashed body. It was something like the odor of potatoes frying in cheap oil.

On their second waltz around the room (Mr. Harrison led, via the simple expedient of falling forward) Thrasher managed to unloose one arm, then another. Daintily he removed his partner's mahogany forearms from his waist and began retreating to the safety of the corridor.

"Yes, yes, thank you ever so much, ah—Mr. Harrison," said Thrasher. "Now it's getting on, it's rather late—"

The Negro stumbled toward him, and Thrasher ran into the hallway, moving a few paces toward the protective kitchen where the doctor was hiding. With the sodden pride of the drunk, the caller surveyed Thrasher mournfully.

"Ah, sheeet, man, Ah ain't gon' cut you up. Dat why you scared?"

Then, with wobbling dignity, he departed, muttering sadly as he opened the door, "Ah pays you a gratitude and you ain' man enough to shake mah hand. Ah comes fo' a little gratitude an' you chases me out. Sheeet."

Thrasher rested against the wall. He was nauseous. Behind him, he heard the doctor's heavy tread. The old man was chuckling.

"See what I mean, Mr. Thrasher? The bastards won't even let my friends live."

The agency man, at the moment, was too shaken to note that the doctor had called him a friend. Riding home later with Daw, he recalled the physician's words and was pleased by them.

IV

THE summer delighted and distressed Herman Quincy. It delighted him because the summer meant more freedom: freedom to roam the neighborhood, to spend long hours on the street corner, to rest leisurely in the cool confines of the billiard academy. It meant action and excitement and challenge. At the same time, Herman found the bright, hot mornings a source of annoyance. The August sun flooding into his bedroom awakened him too early. Under proper conditions, he could sleep till one or two in the afternoon—but summer found him rising before noon, sometimes as early as eleven. He was a creature of habit, and this dislocation of his routine was apt to set him on edge, to create an imbalance in his muscular tan body. Rising nude and coated with sweat in the oven of his room, he felt the lack of sleep, the prospect of two additional hours to kill on the street corner, the appalling prospect of loneliness. And there was that damned quick headache again: the pain lasting no more than two or three minutes, commencing as he rose, then slowly ebbing.

He saw only one solution. Sitting up in bed, he probed beneath the mattress for a small metal box which he had taped to a slat. He tore loose the tape, cupped the metal container in his hand, and then dumped the contents on the soiled sheet. First he picked up the severed head of a teaspoon and a small white capsule. Breaking the capsule, he emptied its white powder into the charred spoon, saying softly as he flicked out the last grains, "Good mornin', horse."

Rising awkwardly, he walked into his mother's kitchen. At the sink (it was clean except for a few dishes Herman had left when he retired at four in the morning) he permitted a few droplets of water to trickle into the spoon. Then, striking a kitchen match, he held it briefly under the spoon, watching, fascinated, as water and snowy powder amalgamated into a milky fluid. Cradling the spoon, so as not to lose a drop, he walked quickly back to the bed and picked up an eyedropper with which he sucked up the solution. Then, turning his left thigh outward to expose the soft interior flesh, he deftly jabbed the end of a hypodermic needle into the skin. Holding the needle firmly in his thigh with his left hand, he inserted the swollen eyedropper into the hypodermic's aperture and pressed the fluid into his body.

"Man, you a skin-poppin' fool," he said happily. He would be sustained and buoyant now for the remainder of the day; long before the tingling euphoria settled over him he would feel elated in anticipation of it. He did a little dance of joy, then dressed rapidly in pale-yellow pants which billowed around his knees and hugged his ankles. Over his lean chest he pulled a chartreuse polo shirt, allowing the long, slashed tails to hang languidly over his tight buttocks. From his dresser he took a pair of air-force style sunglasses and a brightly checked cap, virtually brimless. He was ready for another day.

His mother's apartment was on the top floor of a three-story stone tenement. It was a reasonably clean and well-kept building, but Herman detested it. He bounded down the creaking stairs, plunging joyously into the morning sunlight. A young white man in a blue sport shirt was resting against the wrought-iron railing, and Herman stopped abruptly at the head of the stone steps. His mode of life rendered him perpetually apprehensive and perceptive. He had known immediately that the young man was waiting to see him. And he was reasonably certain that he represented some kind of authority.

"Good morning," the young man said cheerfully. "Are you Herman Quincy?"

Herman paused briefly, then asked, in a soft, low voice, "Whaffo you wan' know?"

The young man smiled blandly. "I have a few questions to ask you. Maybe you can help me out." From the breast pocket of his sport shirt he took a rumpled pack of cigarettes, offering one to Herman. "Have a smoke?"

Herman grinned. Not merely his wide, full mouth with the sparkling teeth grinned, but all of his face—the large sepia eyes, the beautifully molded forehead, the luminous black fuzz on his pate.

"Why sho', man!" he said happily. "Why you didn' say you was a detach' worker? Man, I gets along fine with detach' workers. Does you know Ed Hoops—Joey Pennington? Dey all mah friends."

"I don't get you, Herman," the man said, holding a lit match as the boy leaned over and dragged deeply on the cigarette.

"A detach' worker—*detach*' worker, from deh Youth Board."

"Oh—a Youth Board worker! No, I'm not. What made you think I was?"

Herman exhaled magnificently, a thick spray of smoke through each wide nostril, and giggled. "Man, don't be a square. Dey ain' nobody goes around offerin' us free butts, he ain' a detach' worker. I swear, man, I git more free smokes from dat Youth Board! Dey mus' pay dose detach' workers in butts. When you extends me a sociable hand with a free smoke, what else is you tryin' to do but win me over?"

For a moment, the man in the blue shirt looked curiously at the grinning youth; he was no longer smiling when he spoke again.

"Herman, I'm a cop, if you must know. My name's Lou Kaplan, and I work out of the 77th. I'd like to talk to you a little."

The bubbling laughter vanished from Herman's face, but a flat, superior smile remained. He seated himself on the railing, lounging against the heated granite façade, where some small child had chalked: *THE MIGHTY BUGS: kings of the block.*

"Whaffo yo' wan' see me?"

"Well, I'm told you're kind of a leader among the neighborhood boys. We've been having a little trouble lately, and you might be able to help."

"Me? Sheeet. I ain't no leader."

"Herman, do you know somebody named Josh the Dill?"

"What kin' name is dat? Ah don't know no one dat name."

"Do you go to school, Herman?"

"Man, it's August. Ain' no school now. We on vacation."

The policeman flushed. Undismayed, he continued, "I mean when vacation's over."

Herman deftly flicked the glowing butt into the street. "Ah goes to Harvard. How come you ain' heard?"

Patrolman Kaplan controlled his temper. "That's a fine school, Herman. Do you know a girl named Leueen Harrison?"

"She a movie actress? Das all I 'ssociate wit' is actresses."

"No, Herman. She's sixteen and she was gang-raped by some boys."

"A *line-up!* Man, I don' mess wit dat stuff. Dat's fo' squares."

"Did you read about it in the paper, maybe? How they dumped the girl on a doctor's stoop?"

"Naah." Then, stretching his lithe arms, Herman rose from his perch on the railing and skipped gaily down the stairs.

"Hey, Lou," he said conspiratorially, leaning under the policeman's nose, "gimme another butt. I cain't answer yo' questions, but Ah sure can smoke dem free butts. Man you better den a detach' worker!"

The officer extended the package again, and as Herman lit up he spoke earnestly. "Herman, I want you to feel I'm your friend.

Sure, our skins are different colors—and I work for the law, and maybe you don't like the law. But that's no reason for our not working together. We should be good neighbors. I thought maybe I could interest you and your friends in a little sports. You play any baseball? We could get a neighborhood league up. I bet you can belt a baseball a mile."

But Herman was looking over his head, his eyes bright and disoriented, his small head wobbling faintly atop the pipestem neck. If he was hearing Patrolman Kaplan's speech, he was not reacting to it. In a desperate attempt at communication, the young cop seized Herman's thin wrist.

"Listen, Herman, I don't consider myself an ordinary cop. I'm a sociologist. I'm a member of a minority like yourself. I want to help you. I want to help create good conditions so you can be a credit to your race. I want *you* to help me. Sure, you're a minority, but what's the diff—"

Violently, Herman wrenched his arm away and bounded back a few graceful steps. He thrust his hands in the rear pockets of the yellow pants and, leaning far back, eyes half shut, jaw and lower lip protruding, the absurd cap yanked far down over his face, he spoke rapidly and with impatient annoyance.

"Ah, sheeet, man, you de same as de rest. Ah ain' no minority an' don' tell me dat. Ah'm deh majority, see? Ah in charge. Dat's sheeet about minor'ties. If Ah ain' de majority, how come all de cops and de detach' workers and de newspapers so concern' 'bout us? *We* important, *you* ain't."

Patrolman Kaplan moved forward a step. The sweat rolled in a warm curtain down his heavy face, into his eyes, and he saw the Negro youth dimly figured, as if he were looking at him underwater.

"Who are the Twentieth Century Gents, Herman?" he asked angrily.

"Nevah heard of dem!" Herman cried. Then as he skipped away he called over his shoulder, "Come roun' when you got more free smokes! An' make it *tea* nex' time!"

The daylight hours were but a period of delay before the excitement of the night. The afternoon wasted away; the monochrome telecast of the baseball game in George's billiard academy; the lazy clack of the balls; the endless aimless talk, salted with gutter filth; the speculation about women; the furtive search for alcohol and narcotics.

When night came, they gathered on the street corner, in front of

George's green-curtained window and the crumbling candy store where they could thumb through morning newspapers and magazines and learn that they were victims of social conditions; of slums; of poor parental supervision; of a faulty police force; of bad recreational facilities; of misunderstanding; of a lack of churches; of an industrialized society; of a lack of sympathetic treatment; of improper psychiatric care; of too much discipline; of not enough discipline.

All of the Twentieth Century Gents were not completely aware of this splendid situation; a situation which at once established their own innocence and the guilt of "society." It took a visionary like Josh the Dill, with rare powers of perception and analysis, to exploit this boon. He had, when only fifteen, made an impassioned speech before a notoriously tough judge in children's court.

"Whatchu expec' from us, jedge?" Josh the Dill (he was plain Herman Quincy in those youthful days) had asked after the jurist had denounced him for a brutal assault on a pretzel vendor.

"We too young fo' de army and we too old fo' de schoolyard. We runs a crap game and de cops takes a cut. We runs a sociable dance, an' de cops breaks us up. Mah ole lady go look for work. She do laundry for rich people. Deah ain' no one we can go to fo' hep; no one lissen. We human beens, jedge. We gotta right to live, have fun. We go to de recreation hall and deah ain' no one really hep us. We on our own. So we make our own club. Das all. Somebody give us a han', maybe we don' be so bad."

It was a speech destined for brief fame. Herman had appeared on two television programs (his back to the camera so that his standing as a juvenile delinquent might not be compromised), and the New York *Record* had run a three-piece serial on him, entitled: CASE HISTORY: *A Teen-age Gang Member Tells How It Happened.*

After this sudden notoriety, Herman Quincy had been watched rather closely by Youth Board members, the police, and the other dedicated social workers who covered Brownsville. But in two years' time Herman did little to indicate that this increased attention had noticeably affected his behavior. True, he had no police record, save for the incident of the pretzel vendor. But Herman Quincy had quit school after several run-ins with his teachers; he had never sought work; and he was distinguished mainly for lolling on street corners. Vaguely, the police—notably the diligent Kaplan —had heard of his association with a group called the Twentieth Century Gents.

In the hard light of the open candy-store window, his feet dancing

daintily on the heated pavement, Josh the Dill enacted his encounter
of the morning with Patrolman Kaplan. He was an expert at gutter
humor, and his mimicry of the officer's stupid sincerity was delightfully accurate.

"An' he say to me, Mistah Quincy, Ah wants to hep you. Ah you
fren'. Our skin diffren', but we both minor'ties!" Josh the Dill
giggled. "An'—an' Ah say to him, 'Sheeet, man, you a minor'ty but
Ah de major'ty!'"

His audience dissolved in wild laughter. One of them, a square,
black youth named Lee Roy, fell to the pavement. He folded two
massive ebony arms about his iron waist and pumped his stubby
legs.

"Oh, Josh, you de man! *Mistah* Quincy! Ah sure like to see dat
ole cop try stop us some night!" Lee Roy was ecstatic.

Josh the Dill placed a hand on one hip, and then, mincing by
effeminately, paused in front of another of his friends, a tall, broad-
shouldered boy whom they called Nobody Home, and spoke in an
approximate British accent.

"Ah beg yo' pardon, Mr. Nobody Home, but could you please
hand me dat piece? De one with the twenty-two-caliber bullets.
An' desist from stompin' dat boy, if you please? Ah a soshologist an'
Ah wishes to aid you!"

With a dancer's precision, Josh the Dill spun about rapidly, an
enraptured dervish. Then, jerking to a halt and springing upward
on his toes, he found himself facing a short gray-haired man in
a dark suit. The man was carrying a black leather satchel. Josh the
Dill pointed at the bag, and in mock horror jumped backward clapping a hand over his mouth.

"Man, what you sellin' in deah? Rubbers? Gimme a gross of dem
rubbers. Ah got a busy night!"

They laughed, Lee Roy rolling on his face and shaking his buttocks in helpless joy; Nobody Home giggling; a few others echoing
their leader's taunt.

"Yeah! Gimme a gross too!"

"Ticklers, man! French ticklers!"

The doctor breathed deeply, walking toward the candy store—
he was calling on the owner's consumptive daughter—and muttered, "You galoots should know better. A few kicks in the ass
wouldn't hurt."

Thus challenged, their laughter ended. They had been insulted:
their race, their religion, their honor, their good names, their
importance. In the half light they were suddenly menacing and

cruel. Dr. Abelman did not stay to see the deadly, flat looks directed at him, the humorless smiles, the indolent hatred.

"You know who dat is, Josh?" asked Lee Roy softly. "Dat's dat ole doctor."

"Yeah, Ah knows him," said Josh. "Man, you know how much dat doctor carry in dat fat wallet?"

"Yeah, he a crook hisself," said Lee Roy. "We do some good takin' him some night."

"He de one say he gonna get a baseball bat to us," Nobody Home recalled. He flexed a massive biceps. "I baseball bat him good. He got a big mouf'. Callin' us galoots. Ah sure like cut him up a little."

Josh the Dill was quietly thoughtful. "Ah knows him good, dat doctor. Mah ole lady go to him once. He a cheat."

Hatred intensified; some day they would avenge themselves on the doctor. Gloomy and grumbling they ambled in disorderly array down Rower Avenue, past the rows of dilapidated stores, the malodorous tenements, the garbage cans with their overflowing filth.

"How 'bout a little flashin'?" Nobody Home asked. Flashing was a relatively harmless pursuit: the smashing of electric-light bulbs. They were passing a city housing project under construction. More than half the windows had already been broken. A high wire fence surrounded the modern buildings.

"Know somethin' bout dem buildin's?" Josh the Dill asked. "Dey ain' nobody lives in de house get torn down gets to have an apartment in deah."

"Yeah, it's a damn racket."

"Dey sheet. Dey all sheet."

They gathered in a knot beneath a street light, looking over the wire fence at the red brick structures, solid and clean except for the jagged remnants of windows.

"Ah show dem," Josh the Dill said. "Dey don't mess wid the Twentieth Century Gents." He picked up a fragment of red brick, and, toeing an imaginary rubber, took a full, sweeping windup like a pitcher and threw the missile high and straight against the offending structure. The window shattered with a surprisingly faint tinkle.

A final loosened fragment of glass toppled, crashing on the stone steps far below. At the entrance to the project the door of a construction shack creaked open and the night watchman emerged cautiously. He was a bowed Sicilian, aged and crippled in his left leg, but possessed of the indestructible strength of the Italian laborer. He carried a pick handle, and he moved with the tread of a man who feared nothing.

"Who broke da window?" he asked thickly. "You break da window?"

They clustered together. Nobody Home, with one graceful swift gesture, scooped up a brick from the ground.

The old Sicilian did not halt. He limped toward them, the pick handle dragging at his side, making a shallow furrow in the sandy soil. "Beat it, you," he said softly. "I call cop, you don't beat it. I know who break da window."

"You a ole piece of sheeet," said Josh the Dill. "You a ole ginny sheeet."

"Yeah," Lee Roy joined in. "We ain' 'fraid you."

The night watchman spat fiercely at their feet; then with deceptive agility he raised the pick handle and, in an odd, unbalanced gait, ran toward Josh and Dill and swung the staff at the grinning brown head. Josh and Dill leaped backward, and the weapon grazed his shirt front. Nobody Home hurled the brick at the Sicilian's skull. It struck him above the bridge of the nose. Stunned, he halted as if a steel door had been lowered in front of him. He wavered briefly and then, the wasted leg crumbling as if it were a papier-mâché prop, he fell heavily to the ground. They were upon him in an instant, fists flailing at his old body. They struck him a hundred times: with fists, with bricks, with the pick handle. They laughed and cried and grunted, and when the leathery old form was pounded into a shapeless pile, they leaped away at Josh the Dill's signal and ran. At least a dozen people on the opposite side of the street had seen the incident; none pursued them, none called the police. They knew better.

Hearts pounding in their chest, they flew into a dimly lit tenement doorway. When their laughter had subsided, and they were breathing normally, Nobody Home had some second thoughts.

"How bad you think we beat up dat ole man?" the tall boy asked.

"Ah, he gon' be all right. He tough," said Lee Roy.

"Yeah. We fix dat ole doctor some night like dat."

Then they noticed that Josh the Dill was acting strangely. He had slowed down to an agitated walk the last few hundred feet of their wild sprint, and he had been gasping in great agonized heaves. Now, resting his head and back against the peeling wall of the hallway, they saw that his mouth was sucking air with abnormal speed. His right arm was twitching and shaking; now his face—

the right eye and right cheek—was jerking in a peculiar manner. The leader tried to talk, but no words came forth.

"Gaaah—gaaah—aaah—"

"What de matter, Josh, boy? You feel sick?" asked Lee Roy.

"Lie down, man, you got de shakes, bad. You need a cap, maybe? You wan' go find de handler and get a fix?"

But Josh the Dill did not hear them. A black, suffocating cloud was growing inside his head; a rush of pain assailed his skull, and he lurched forward from the wall. He moaned, and then slumped into the protective arms of Nobody Home, his head and right arm twitching violently.

"He done fainted," said Nobody Home. "He had a fit."

"Yeah, he sick," said Lee Roy. "He takin' too much horse."

"He gon' get cold turkey he keep dat up."

Nobody Home looked at them appealingly. "Sheeet, man, Ah ain' gone lug him 'round. Gimme some hep."

"Ah git a taxicab," said Lee Roy. "We take him home."

They carried the stuporous form of Herman Quincy to the curb and waved at a passing cab. The crazy jerking had now spread to his left leg. They rode, silently, to their leader's home, suffering with him. Finally, Lee Roy spoke.

"Watchu gon' tell Josh's ole lady?" he asked.

"I think of somethin'," Nobody Home said. "Das her worry see he get better. She take care of him."

The campus of Columbia University was one of Myron Malkin's few associations with a world he had never made, a kind of forged membership in an Ivy League that would have no part of him. Myron attended two classes (*Short Story Writing; Survey of the English Novel*) in the School of General Studies, under the GI Bill. His four hours per week of lectures permitted him the luxury of saying he was "a Columbia man"; it also gave him a place to bring dates. Admittedly, the gray flights of steps and dull red buildings of Morningside Heights were no match for Ithaca or Hanover, but it was all Myron could offer his young ladies, aside from the *mystique* of the fourth estate.

The role of impoverished intellectual, the hard young man pounding out perfect copy as the night editor's good right hand, was carefully nurtured by the doctor's nephew. In lieu of a ZBT pin, or a father who owned two Cadillacs, or an invitation to the Mask and Wig Show, Myron offered that most fraudulent of American stereotypes, the cynical newspaperman, complete with inside dope, baggy knees, and bourbon-on-the-rocks.

Unfortunately, his girl friends took him too literally. How could anyone as eccentric, as talented, as off-beat as Myron ever be viewed seriously? He was fascinating to talk to, but—

Hand in hand, of a summer's evening, Myron and his date, Sandra Dorgenicht, tiptoed up the steps of Low Memorial Library, past the matronly figure of Alma Mater. Myron informed Sandra that there was an owl hidden in the statue's bronze skirts: Sandra replied she knew about it, that she had once gone out with a TEP at Columbia College. The unintentional rebuff sunk Myron into momentary sullenness. It had been an uncomfortable evening, surrounded by Sandra's multitudinous aunts and uncles in the overdecorated eight-room apartment on East Eighty-eighth Street. They had quizzed him about Russia, Eisenhower, and the stock market—overweight men in suede shoes and shapely women in copper and blue permanents, and he had not let them down. Myron Malkin, the inside dopester, the young talker with his ear attuned to the events of the day, had given them the straight stuff. Yet his triumph, in front of Sandra's moderately admiring black eyes, had been a hollow one. In the long run, these successful shirt manufacturers and appliance distributors had the laugh on him.

And then Sandra with her snide remark about the owl and her TEP friend from Columbia College. He decided it was time to explode his bombshell.

They were seated on a curved stone bench near the Alumni House, and he tentatively snaked an arm around her white shoulders, covered only by a silken stole. Sandra wriggled slightly, undraped the arm, and smiled indulgently at him. She had a round pretty face, and an oversized red mouth; her body was full and a little shapeless in the hips but not without a certain enticing expansiveness.

"I got me a new job," he said casually.

"You're kidding. Why didn't you tell me?"

"With your family givin' me the old third-degree job, how could I?"

"Are you leaving the *Record?* Gosh, and you're doing so well there."

To Sandra, Myron was the assistant to the night city editor; to the *Record*, Myron was a copy boy, at twenty-five the oldest copy boy in the office. He was permitted, from time to time, to write filler or an occasional feature, this in keeping with *Record* policy of encouraging the lowest paid help to absorb the work of the higher echelons. The latter could then be fired more expeditiously.

"No, I'm keepin' my hand in at the shop," Myron said craftily. "This is a television deal. Strictly an outside operation."

Sandra sat back in surprised delight. "How wonderful! What is it, a free-lance deal?"

"Nah. More solid than that. A new program, kind of a telementary thing. I been hired as a consultant by the Whitechapel Agency for the series."

"How come?" she asked. Myron's success in talker society was almost too much to be borne; Sandra herself was looking for a job on a women's magazine.

"Oh, some wheel at Whitechapel read some of my stuff in the *Record* and got an idea for a new program. If it works out, I'll junk the old newspaper racket for keeps."

"You wouldn't, Myron. You like newspaper work too well."

"What's to like? Lousy hours, bad pay? Boy, what a myth. And the way everyone wants in. Like you. Your old man can buy and sell any newspaper guy in New York. I tell ya it's mythology. Pure and simple mythology. Meet the big people, by-lines, press card. What crap."

"What about the *New York Times*?"

"Some paper. Askin' Eisenhower to play nice. You know what newspaper work is? PTA meetings. Box scores. Social notes. A few paste-ups from *AP* and *UP* for national and foreign news. Ya could take ten high school kids, real smart ones, and teach 'em to put out any paper in the country in two weeks. It's all routine, mechanical."

"You sound frustrated. I know from the little work I did on the Cornell *Sun* that's not true at all. There's lots of room for imaginative writing and enterprise."

Myron struck a match and bent wearily over a cigarette, a Murrow in the making; his nose had the look of a melting taper.

A university policeman, with time clock and flashlight, lumbered by, studying them casually. Myron leaned back on the concrete bench and exhaled a rich cloud of smoke at the summer sky.

"Newpaper work. What a pile of manure," Myron muttered. "And every kid outa high school wants in. Let 'em push reefers."

"Tell me more about the TV program," Sandra said. "It sounds fabulous."

"Yeah. If it makes, I'm in. I can write my ticket with Whitechapel."

"What's the format? The subject matter?"

"Kind of an actuality based on a typical, ava-ridge American."

"Just *any* American?"

"Well, they picked my uncle for the first show," he said weakly. "You know, Uncle Doc, the guy I told you about."

"Oh. That's how you got the job as consultant."

"Like hell. This agency vice-president got the whole idea for the show on an article I did. He admitted it."

Sandra weighed the young man's improbable story. She had always regarded Myron as an engaging clown; now, there was a good chance he was developing into a worthwhile personality, someone almost as interesting as the off-Broadway director she had a date with the following night.

"Well, gee, that's wonderful, Myron. You're on your way."

"In more ways than one, doll."

He tried to get an inept hand on one inviolate breast, but she was fast and strong, and her father's only daughter. Her charms, like the fine bathroom fixtures Mr. Dorgenicht manufactured, could not be purchased in discount houses by bargain hunters like Myron.

"How 'bout a date next Saturday?" he asked hesitantly.

"I'd love to, Myron, but I'm going to Cornell for the weekend."

"Ya just graduated. Whatcha goin' back for?"

"I still have friends there."

"That guy in law school."

"Oh, not just him. A whole gang of kids."

Gloom oozed upward around Myron's slumping form like quicksand. He had a bloodhound's nose for success and failure, and now, after his brief and triumphal announcement, he was back in the bog. In the long run, Sandra and her family and her friends at Cornell had it, and he didn't. He thought of his Uncle Doc and the crumbling yellow brick house, the creaking Buick, the waiting room that was so rarely filled. Whatever it was that had defeated his uncle would not reach him. He would learn from Thrasher.

"C'mon," he said suddenly, bouncing from the hard bench. "I need a coupla quick bourbons. Let's go to the Wet End."

"The *what*?"

"The Wet End. I guess your friends in TEP and ZBT were too fancy for that kind of place. The West End Bar. Only I call it the Wet End."

She assembled her splendid virginal body and walked primly ahead of him, denying him even a moist palm.

The air-conditioning had broken down at Whitechapel during the night, and the ensuing discomfort lent a happy feeling of "roughing it" to the stratified office. There were jokes about the girls stripping down, speculation as to what kind of underwear old T.C. wore, rumors that Ben Loomer, a notorious tightwad, was opening a lemonade concession, and finally a pool, initiated in the art department, on what time the cooling system would resume operation.

Thrasher found the leveling banter tiresome, but he joined in with insincere vigor. He was unquestionably the most popular executive in the organization, and it was expected that he participate freely.

"Is it hot enough for you, Mr. Thrasher?" the receptionist asked.

"Is *what* hot enough, Porter?" The receptionist's first name was Porter; she was big-busted and deeply tanned and her triangular glasses had Scotch-plaid frames.

"Oh, you *know* what I mean. There's no air-conditioning today!"

Thrasher clutched at his throat. "Thank God! And I thought I had undulant fever!"

She giggled appreciatively, waving *Variety* at him as he went by and crying nasally, "You made *Variety*, have you seen?"

Louise had efficiently opened the windows in his office; she had located an immense floor fan, and it was whirring madly. She opened *Variety* to the Radio-TV section and was marking an item with red pencil.

"Gee, Louise, Porter Simpson pulled a funny one on me. She asked me if it was hot enough for me. Pretty good line, eh? How come you never say clever things like that?"

"She learns those clever things at Fire Island," Diane said. "All I can afford is Jones Beach. She'll probably get the new job in media because she says such snazzy things, and wears plaid glasses."

He peeled off his jacket and tie in one swift gesture; he rather enjoyed the heat for a change. It justified slovenliness and sweating, two conditions of life which the office generally frowned upon.

He sipped at his morning coffee, and read the *Variety* article which Louise had marked for his attention. The one-column headline read:

G & T Dumps Higgins;
Telementary Next?

Client and Agency unhappiness over low rating means an exit for the Brick Higgins Wednesday night opus. Last week's test run convinced Whitechapel biggies that the comic's half hour won't suit their purposes. Gatling & Theis, whose heavy coin is Whitechapel's biggest source of income, is said to have agreed to a brand-new telementary-type actuality program for the fall. While this kind of eggheadry is usually the network's bailiwick, Whitechapel executives feel their property is so hot they'll produce it themselves. According to Ben

Loomer, agency veep, the new format combines elements of *Person to Person, See It Now, This Is Your Life,* and *We the People.* Loomer and Tom Finucane, account exec for *G & T,* are riding herd on the project, tentatively titled *Americans, USA.* Woodrow Thrasher of the Agency is slated to write the new series, and Andrew Bain Lord is said to have the inside track for the emceeing job.

"It's very interesting, isn't it?" Louise asked. "You get equal billing with Lord—and he isn't even hired yet."

Thrasher patted his neck gently with his handkerchief. It served him right. He had been too damn secretive about everything, and he had underestimated, Loomer's jealousy. At least three dozen people, in and out of the agency, knew that Woody Thrasher had created *Americans, U.S.A.* and was producing it; to subvert history, to create a clear fiction which could readily be challenged was the rash move of an uneasy man. Thrasher was clipping the story from the page when Loomer walked in.

Loomer greeted him with a bland smile. "Hiya, Woody. How's the doctor's best friend?"

Thrasher tossed the *Variety* clipping onto his desk.

"This is a nice piece of publicity," Thrasher said evenly. "Must be a lot of trade interest in our project already."

Loomer winked. "Tom and I felt we had to give the project a little push. You know—working on such a tight schedule, and you running off to Brooklyn every day. Man, you're a bear for work. Can't do the whole thing yourself, Woody."

"Yes, I notice from your quotes that I'm not doing it all myself. It's a funny thing, Ben, I remember that first meeting we had after the Higgins fiasco, and I can't remember you suggesting—"

Loomer leaned forward. "That's not what the story says, Woody." Suddenly, in Ben's round, healthy face, he saw a quality of hardness that had eluded him heretofore.

"It says you and Tom are 'riding herd,' Ben. What's a herd-rider? You must be an executive herd-rider, at least. What does that make me?"

"Let's not be bitter, Woody," Loomer said. He was no longer smiling. "No one's trying to crab your act. But, frankly, neither old man Gatling nor T.C. like the way you're keeping them in the dark. Hiring Dexter Daw without telling anyone—a guy with his rotten reputation. Tom and I mean to keep an eye on the project. We have every right to. Dammit, Woody, I shouldn't have to explain all this."

The door opened and Finucane's flat Boston vowels assaulted them.

"I just spoke to Andy Lord, Ben," Finucane exploded.

Thrasher grimaced, ignoring Finucane and keeping his eyes fastened on Loomer. "What's this about Andrew Bain Lord working the show? How did all this happen?"

"Where you been, Woody? *G & T* has been sponsoring Andy Lord on radio for twelve years. Tom and I talked to them as soon as T.C. got the go-ahead, and, naturally, Lord's name came up. He's a natural for the job."

"Surprise, surprise," said Thrasher. "What if I don't want any talent on the show? What if I decide we'll go with real people for a change? What does that do to Andrew Bain Lord?"

"Oh, for Christ's sake, Woody," Finucane said wearily. "You're always so damned negative. We're only *talkin'* about Andy Lord. Maybe he won't emcee. Maybe he'll do commercials, maybe just intro the show."

"Maybe we won't do live commercials. Maybe just one filmed institutional. Maybe just a brief sponsor identification." Thrasher was looking desperately for some feint to set them off balance, something to regain his edge. There was no doubt they had gotten the collective ear of both T.C. and the client and had secured for themselves—even if it were purely a fictional designation— control of the program. But a well-publicized fiction, Thrasher understood grimly, was better than an obscured fact.

Loomer pursed his lips before answering. "I'm goin' to give it to you straight—"

"You and Sergeant Friday," Thrasher muttered.

"—and you know, Woody, Tom and I think damn highly of you."

"You bet we do!" Finucane clapped a fat arm around Thrasher's shoulders. "But you're a tough guy to reason with!"

Thrasher recoiled. Clearly, they were not prepared to edge him out entirely. They merely wanted to be included; sufficiently involved to claim credit for a success, yet sufficiently detached so that no onus would fall upon them in the event of a disaster.

"Let me say this," Loomer drawled. "You're the creative guy in this outfit. We know it. We want you to handle that end. But client relations—network contacts—and, well—over-all supervision has to be our responsiblity. Just as it is on *any* package this agency turns out. We're a team, Woody, not a bunch of grandstanders."

"Okay, Ben." Thrasher said quietly. "I'm a big boy."

"Something else bothers me," Loomer said, ignoring his proffered olive branch. "I think you're tackling too much. We're supposed to hit the air in ten days and you don't have a darn thing to show us in the way of a format, a script, not even a coherent idea."

"There's plenty of time," Thrasher said. "I work best under pressure."

"But you forget you're not the whole show. A lot of money and a lot of jobs are riding on this pilot program. If Gatling buys, we've got to be prepared to offer thirteen more solid shows."

"No problem," Thrasher said. "We have a hundred and sixty million shows."

"I have asked Ted Chilson to head up an advance unit for future shows. Ted will report to me. I'm authorizing a research staff for him. And after we cull out some fifty future subjects, I'm going to set up a rotational system for scripting. You'll get to do maybe one out of every four. Or, if you want, you can give up the writing altogether. Frankly, I'd be happier if you did. There's simply too much to do, and the only way we can succeed is if we leapfrog the work."

Thrasher studied the ruddy, round-faced man with frank admiration. He himself had never been good at that sort of thing; he was too prone to short cuts and labor-saving techniques.

"You're really organizing, aren't you, Ben?"

Loomer nodded slowly. "The only way to operate, Woody. I'd like you to sit in on an advance meeting ths afternoon. Ted wants to kick around some future show subjects."

"I can't," Thrasher said. "I have to visit the doctor again."

"Jesus Christ!" Finucane shouted. "You takn' the nine-day cure or somethin'?"

"Hold the meeting without me, Ben. You and Tom can block out the next show on the basis of Ted Chilson's research, I'm sure."

"I'd like you to be at the meeting," Loomer persisted. He had lost, for the moment, his Midwestern rhythms, and was speaking in pure New Yorkese. A dental "t" had crept into his carefully guarded speech patterns.

"What happened to your drawl, Ben?" Thrasher asked. "You'd better find it for that meeting this afternoon. No one'll recognize you with that Flatbush brogue. You can fill me in tomorrow on what happens."

Leaving, he punched Finucane playfully in his glutton's paunch. "Hot enough for you, Father Feeney?" he asked softly, and, ignoring their noncommital stares, he walked out.

For the time being all three of them realized it was a stand-off. They would need Thrasher to create and mold the new show; but he would need them simply because they were powerful and secure in a world which he had never fully joined. He would defy them and taunt them at the moment. But they would forget neither the defiance nor the taunts; and if somehow his value were to be diminished, they would be waiting for him. Apparently they knew something he didn't, something relevant to the client's attitude which they were shrewdly keeping from him.

Leaving Loomer's office, he saw old T.C., prim, cool, and maddeningly neat in a black suit and a stiff detachable collar, and he wondered if he might carry an appeal to him. But it was too early for this. T.C. Whitechapel liked to believe that everything hummed along smoothly and happily. His mind was like a peeled hard-boiled egg, smooth and slick and untroubled by dents or abrasions.

"Good morning, Woodrow," T.C. greeted him. There was not a sign of sweat on his soft pink face. Thrasher imagined he was desiccated inside—no liquids were left to seep through.

"Good morning, T.C. Is it true that some spy from BBD & O sabotaged the air-conditioning?"

The old man smiled feebly, and Thrasher wondered whether he understood the joke. "Is it hot enough for you, Woodrow?" he asked pleasantly.

"I should think so, sir. Two copywriters are prostrated from heat exhaustion, and a girl in media has gone stark raving mad. But if we can hold off Muhullah Khan another day the relief column from Lucknow, commanded by Victor McLaglen, should be able to save us."

It was the kind of nonsensical sally that was expected of him, but the old man just blinked his eyes a few times, turned abruptly, and walked into his office.

Dexter Daw joined Thrasher later in the morning, and they remained in conference through the day, Louise ordering lunch for them. He detested Daw, but he enjoyed the afternoon's work. They discussed placement of cameras; a basic routine; the emphasis that the half-hour program would take. The subject of Andrew Bain Lord came up, and Thrasher was pleased to learn that the director shared his unflattering view of Loomer's choice of talent.

"We will need a pro to cross the *t*'s and dot the *i*'s," Daw said. "But Andrew Bain Lord—he's goofed every television job he's had. He's great for that midmorning philosophy for housewives. But this deal needs somebody with a name. Stature. For example, Eisenhower. He'd be perfect."

Thrasher looked at Daw's inverted pear of a head with quiet admiration. He had a lot in common with the young director. Only someone with a genuine feel for the business, with a certain screwball daring, would dare to suggest that the President of the United

States introduce commercials for deodorants. But it was the kind of "big thinking" that enabled Dexter Daw to finance his extensive lunch program.

"Eisenhower," said Thrasher reflectively. He sipped his iced tea, and glanced sideways at Daw. "Yes, he'd be great, Dec."

"Or someone like Oppenheimer, if he hadn't goofed. Someone completely unexpected to introduce our typical worthwhile American every week. Not a performer, but someone with a name, a meaning to the public. A Helen Hayes, or a John Gunther. Maybe Roy Campanella."

Leaning forward to catch the fan's warm breeze, Thrasher found himself grinning. "Dec, it's just occurred to me that we're playing the great TV game 'Who Can We Get?' But has anyone ever played it on such a cosmic level? You've covered politics, science, the arts, sports, and you've even got the Commie issue. You're liable to convince me you're serious, and I'll replace you with Gadge Kazan. Hey—he's another name that always comes up in 'Who Can We Get?'

"And who needs the doctor anyway? We get Steve Allen to play the part!" Thrasher finished.

Daw drained his container of tea, making a sucking sound as the straw drew up the dregs. "You know, you're not a bad asshole for an agency fink, Thrasher. Do you ever talk like that at board meetings?"

"Too much, Dec, too much. You read *Variety?*"

"I saw it."

"I've got a couple of herd-riders over me."

"Is a herd-rider higher or lower than a project officer? We got project officers at our shop."

"Dexter, you and I should start a crusading newspaper in a small town in Vermont. Let's chuck the whole business, like in those novels where the highly paid whore goes off to be an honest *Life Magazine* reporter."

Daw was cracking ice cubes with his rodent's teeth. "I'd hate it. I love this disgusting business we're in. How else could I eat and drink so good? And have to do so little?"

From outside, Louise buzzed him and he picked up his outside line. It was his wife, sounding fresh, cheerful, and alert; a negation of the sour game he and Daw had been playing, and affirmation that they lived in a good, productive world.

"Can you make the early train, Woody?" Ann asked. "It must be unbearable in town."

"I can't, sweetie. I have to go to Long Beach tonight."

"*Long Beach!* What ever for?"

"Dr. Abelman goes out there every Thursday night."

"Oh, rats. Junior won't know his daddy pretty soon. Can't you come home after you're through with him? Where is Long Beach anyway?"

"South Shore. It'll be much easier for me to stay in New York. That's the trouble with this city. It's as far from one suburb to another as it is from New York to Boston."

"Okay," she said resignedly. "I'll spend the evening assembling the new redwood set. The braces for the legs still don't fit, but I'll saw them down to size."

"Why don't they fit? We've exchanged them three times already. We paid cash money for the table. Why shouldn't the braces be properly made? Isn't anybody responsible for a goof like that?"

"It's a six-foot table, dear, and all they had left were braces for a seven-foot table. Remember, it was a sale."

They both paused briefly; the minor domestic crisis had provided them with a subject for mutual concern. Now they had nothing left to talk about.

"Woody," she said querulously, "you're sure you're not in the poker game again?"

"Poker? Hell no. Baby, I'm working hard at this project. I've got a deadline and an internal problem right here to worry about. Whatever gave you that idea?"

"Nothing, Woods, nothing. I'm sorry. Have a happy trip to Long Beach."

"Have a good evening with the redwood table, dear."

Daw had flattened out the straws from his iced tea container and was snapping them together. "The suspicious wife, hey, Thrasher? Why don't you be like me? Don't try to cover up. Tell her everything. Clinical details. I drove my wife nuts with it, and she leaves me alone now."

"Shut up for a minute, will you, Daw?" Thrasher said. "And stop snapping those goddam straws."

From the outer office they heard the hysterical shrieking of several of the girls, the kind of abandoned noise which usually followed the announcement of an engagement or a pregnancy. Thrasher buzzed Louise.

"Now what is that all about?" For the moment, he felt like Dr. Abelman, cursing the galoots beneath his waiting room window.

"The air-conditioning just went on," she said.

"What's so hysterical about that?"

"Lucille LoPresti won the pool. She had three-thirty, and it's three-twenty-eight. You almost won, you had three-twenty."

"Second best, eh? Loomer must have a drag with building maintenance. They won't even let me win an office pool."

Even as he spoke, he realized that his words were born less from his role of office cynic than from a genuine fear of Loomer. The big man with the false drawl was not quite as dependable or friendly as he had thought. It was strange, he thought, how everything starts unraveling at once. He didn't like the tone of his wife's voice; he had no clear idea where his wild venture into programming was taking him; and the crisis in the agency was more serious than he had imagined. He looked at Daw, at twenty-seven, a drifter on the fringe of the industry—a professional lunch-eater and meeting-goer. Thrasher was pressing forty; he could not afford to be a middle-aged Dexter Daw.

He took a rattling Long Island Railroad train to Long Beach, then a taxicab to the address the doctor had given him. It was just turning dark as he walked up the brick path to the small boarding-house where Mrs. Abelman was spending the summer. The house was a malformed stucco and timber relic of the twenties. A large family of wealthy junk dealers had built it, a mass of small rooms and oversized baths.

A Negro handyman was wrestling the day's garbage to the curb. Under the awning over the open porch, a convocation of white-haired ladies sat nodding and chatting in muted voices. Thrasher asked a fragile woman with the pointed face of an aged vaudevillian where he could find Dr. Abelman. She smiled coyly and told him the doctor was inside watching television. He walked through a creaking screen door into a small dining room which led to a glassed-in porch. A handful of elderly people, the doctor among them, and some drowsy children were gathered about a television set. Spying his visitor, the doctor rose, gesturing to a short, gray woman sitting next to him.

"Hello, Mr. Thrasher. You're right on time," the doctor said. It was the kind of place where the most minute departure from routine was marked with extensive ceremony. No one was watching the screen; all eyes had turned to Thrasher. A few white heads were peeking through the screen door to study the caller.

"It's hot as hell here," Dr. Abelman said. "How about a walk on the boardwalk?"

"Oh, don't let me take you from the show you were watching."

"I've seen enough. All I really like is the commercial."

Thrasher looked puzzled. "You're joking."

"I mean it. The one where the fellow goes into the tobacco store and buys the pack of tobacco. He pays the clerk the money and walks out. Just the way you or I would do it."

"I never thought of it that way," said Thrasher, making a mental note that the doctor's estimate of commercials might make a useful gambit at a future meeting.

"This is my wife, Mr. Thrasher," the doctor said, smiling. "Sarah, this is the young man who wants me to be Boris Thomashefsky."

"I'm delighted to meet you, Mrs. Abelman."

A stout, gray-haired woman, with prim, bland features, she returned the greeting, smiling through rimless glasses, and immediately asking, with deep concern, whether he had eaten.

"I ate in New York before leaving, thank you," Thrasher said. "I hope I'm not interfering with your evening. I could see—"

"Interfering?" the doctor asked. "Who ever does anything here? C'mon, the boardwalk is nice at night."

The doctor's wife cautioned him against tripping on the darkened steps (he guided her gently by the arm), wondered whether he needed a sweater, and began to fret over Thrasher's train schedule.

"Where do you live, Mr. Thrasher?"

"Stamford, Connecticut."

"Oh, my goodness! So far to travel! How in the world will you get home tonight?"

He assured her he would manage. She was, he could see, a gentle and submissive person, one who went through life worrying about trivia and constantly cautioning those she liked to be alert against minor catastrophes. Trains would be missed, unbrellas forgotten, doors left unlocked, milk bills unpaid, friends offended, unless she were on guard to remind her family about these small impending disasters. If, while urging a beloved grandchild to finish his oatmeal, a bomb were to fall on her house, she would rise, unshaken, from the rubble and remind him that oatmeal was full of vitamins.

It was warm and misty on the boardwalk. They sat on a green bench beneath a lamppost, watching the ocean's rhythmic assault against the darkened beach. Stout elderly couples drifted by in postprandial smugness; glowing cigar tips illumined the foggy night; teen-age boys on rented bicycles sprinted amidst the stately walkers with the pointless defiance of youth.

"Dr. Abelman was telling me about the program, Mr. Thrasher, and I'm quite thrilled," the doctor's wife said. She spoke in a low voice, with no trace of accent. "And I want you to know *he's* delighted also, even though he probably is telling you that it's a bother."

"I'm sure we'll have a great show," Thrasher said.

"And it was very kind of you to give my nephew a job, too. Myron is a very talented boy. He just needs a break, the poor kid. He writes very well."

"I'm sure he does," Thrasher said, recalling with faint revulsion his promise to the ugly young man whose soupy prose had first brought him to the doctor's home.

Thrasher took out his notebook and pen, and the doctor almost on cue, asked him where he wanted his story to begin.

"I'd suggest, Dr. Abelman, you get into the early influences in your life that brought you to a career in medicine."

The doctor rose, resting against the boardwalk railing, and facing the agency man. "What do you think, Sarah? Should I leave out all about how we were kids on the Lower East Side?"

"It was pretty routine," she said. "Dr. Abelman's family was very, very poor. My own folks were a little better off. My father had a wholesale grocery business." She sounded quite proud.

"He was something of a windbag, too."

It was a little game they had, Thrasher realized. They had made the same jokes for many, many years, and if malice had ever been part of them, it had been worn away long ago by constant repetition.

"I ran errands for my old man for years," the doctor said. "His specialty was waiters' jackets. I used to do his delivery work. You ever try to lug a stack of boxes filled with alpaca jackets on and off a trolley car? I got to know every kosher waiter in New York, and what a bunch of tight bastards *they* were. The only ones meaner were the trolley car conductors. But what should I expect from an Irishman?"

He smiled, shaking his large head in amused reminiscence. "I kicked one conductor so hard in the shins one day I almost broke my foot. He tickled my father's chin whiskers. What right did he have to do that to an old Jew who wasn't bothering him?"

"Oh, Sam," she said wearily. "He tells it a million times, and I'm sick of hearing about it. He was always like that, Mr. Thrasher. Everybody's problem was his. His whole family were nothing but weaklings—the kind of people who give in to everything. So Sam had to defend them. If he wasn't fighting his brothers' battles, he was defending his parents. Once somebody called his brother Moishe a dirty name at the shirt factory where he worked. Don't you think my husband, who was fourteen then, had to go down and pick a fight for that big ox of a brother who wouldn't raise his hands to help himself?"

The doctor grinned. "Boy, did those Italians give me my lumps!"

A Brueghel panorama depicting the squalid jungle of New York's Lower East Side at the turn of the century began forming in Thrasher's mind. In a series of detailed vignettes, he saw the small, muscular form of the young Sam Abelman taking on his enemies— a streetcar conducter here, a policeman there.

"That's one of the reasons I became a gym teacher," said the doctor. "I liked the idea of being strong. Everywhere I looked people were shoving us around. Not just Jews, mind you, but anyone who wouldn't stick up for himself. If you were a greenhorn, you got shoved."

"A gym teacher?" Thrasher asked.

"Oh, didn't the doctor tell you?" Mrs. Abelman asked. "He usually makes everyone feel his muscles as soon as he meets them."

As if to amend for this oversight, the doctor rolled up his shirt sleeve, and shoved a mammoth, undulating biceps in Thrasher's face. "Feel that, young fellah. I can still handle myself."

Thrasher, with slight repugnance, touched the lumpy white flesh. It was like a granite slab; hard, unyielding, and as wide as Thrasher's thigh.

"That didn't come from reading poetry," the doctor said proudly, "although, as a matter of fact, we did a lot of that also, when we were kids."

"You're in excellent condition, doctor," Thrasher said admiringly.

"That's what Hector O'Bannion liked about me," the doctor said. His intonation indicated that he not only expected Thrasher to know who Hector O'Bannion was, but to be thoroughly awed by the doctor's association with him.

Mrs. Abelman, perceiving the visitor's blank expression, intervened.

"Hector O'Bannion was one of Sam's heroes when he was a young man. He was a physical culture nut."

"Says you," the doctor interrupted curtly. "He was a damn fine man, and he ran a damn fine school. He wasn't ashamed to be eccentric."

"He was *still* a physical culture nut," Mrs. Abelman said insistently. "If you want to talk about someone, why don't you talk about Mr. Comerford? He was a *much* better influence on you."

On the oak paneling behind Mr. Comerford's desk were mounted the memorabilia of what had clearly been the great experience of his life. There was a framed, fading picture of General Thomas F. Meagher, commanding officer of the Irish Brigade, in tailored battle coat, the silver stars thickly embroidered on black shoulder knots. He wore a sprig of evergreen in his broad-brimmed hat. There was a picture of three rumpled privates of the Union Army, thin young men of the 88th New York, resting, with the false arrogance of enlisted men, on their rifles. The center soldier, lounging a bit less flamboyantly than the others, and trying to look grim behind a fledgling mustache, was Mr. Comerford himself, then Private William Comerford, Company B, 88th New York. There was also a map of Fredericksburg, showing the deadly stone wall from behind which Confederate sharpshooters massacred the attackers. Beneath the map, mounted on cotton batting, was the misshapen lead bullet with which a Rebel infantryman had struck Private Comerford in the right knee, removing him from combat forever at bloody Fredericksburg. He was among the lucky: of fourteen hundred members of the Irish Brigade whom bumbling Ambrose Burnside had sent against the Confederate lines, only two hundred and fifty survived.

Every morning, Mondays through Saturdays, Sammy Abelman opened the street-level door of Comerford & Sons, Twine and Paper Bags, and, in the center of the office, he would pause briefly at his employer's battle shrine. There was a quiet awareness of the past in Mr. Comerford's display that intrigued him. On winter mornings, the sleighs tinkling by on snow-covered lower Broadway, he would warm his hands at the fire, listening to the kindling crack and spit, and imagining himself a part of Mr. Comerford's valiant company. He was somewhat jealous of Mr. Comerford: nobody in his family could summon up such a past—meaningful, romantic, a segment of history, even though it symbolized a great defeat. What would his father have to show? An old scissors and a needle?

He never was able to muse very long. After starting the fire, his next job was to sweep and dust. He could expect Hanratty, the bookkeeper, any minute, and Hanratty could always be counted on to make some nasty remark. He was a small, cranky man with an oversized head, a common type of Irishman in the commercial world, but one rarely celebrated in the mythology of jolly policemen, inspired revolutionaries, and Celtic athletes. He had cultivated a series of expressions and gestures which he assumed to be symbols of authority: narrowed eyes, outthrust jaws, thumbs hooked in vestpockets. No one, least of all Sammy Abelman, feared Hanratty, but it was much less trouble to pretend that the self-portrait was genuinely frightening.

He never said good morning. His greeting was usually a brief critique of Sammy's chores: "Ain't much of a fire!" "You dusted my desk yet?" "Where'd you put them new invoices?"

The proprietor of Comerford & Sons would greet his two office employees with the same words he had used for more than thirty years, words, he claimed, he had heard General Meagher cry to his raw troops just before the Second Wave marched to death and mutilation across the plain of Fredericksburg.

"Well, boys, are we ready for them?" Mr. Comerford would ask.

"Good morning, sir," Sammy would say, barely looking up from his own midget desk.

"Ready as ever, sir!" Hanratty would chirp brightly.

Mr. Comerford was in his middle sixties, yet aside from a small paunch, neatly molded beneath a black vest, his body was as lean and limber as it had been in his infantry days. The sparse mustache had flowered into a thick gray mat, liberally stained with tobacco.

Established behind his great mahogany desk, Mr. Comerford would sip a mug of Irish tea which Sammy had brewed for him on the glowing stove lid and would listen to Hanratty's recital of woe. The bookkeeper was a born apostle of doom, and, although Mr. Comerford chose to close eyes and ears to the storm warnings, there was a good deal of truth in Hanratty's dreary reports.

"Sir, if we don't move fast, we'll lose that whole Altschuler order," the bookkeeper would say.

"Now what makes you say that, Andrew?" Comerford would ask, in faintly shocked surprise. "Mr. Altschuler and I are very old friends."

"Friends or no," Hanratty would whine, "them smart salesmen from Acme have been chippin' away at our order every month. Why do you think Altschuler cut down on our number twelve Manila to ten gross, when we used to send them fifty?"

"I'm sure I don't know, Andrew. Perhaps they are using less of it."

"Aw please, Mr. Comerford. Altschuler just opened two new stores. That's a hot item. They're buyin' Acme's is all."

Mr. Comerford spun about slowly in his great chair. It was all getting much too difficult for him. He had built the concern himself, starting with a door-to-door business, carrying his sample twines and bags in a huge carpetbag. He had done quite well, sent two sons to law school, and lived to see them turn down the business for the more colorful pursuit of politics. Now he was watching the slow nibbling away of his customers by younger, more aggressive men. Over the years, his contacts had been established on two bases: personal friendship and a good product. He was discovering now that these were not enough.

"Now, Andrew, listen to me," he would say to Hanratty, as the latter's gnomish face twisted itself into sorrowful disagreement, "what in the world difference does it make if I run down personally to see Mr. Altschuler and take him to lunch? He knows me. He knows my merchandise. Why in the world must I go through the rigmarole of convincing him all over again?"

Beneath the Civil War display at the rear of his desk, Mr. Comerford kept a small bookcase, crammed not with business catalogues and ledgers but with a library of select works from which he could read during the slack late afternoon hours, much to Hanratty's disgust. There was a Riverside edition of Thoreau, a similar set of Emerson, and the works of Whitman, Poe, and Hawthorne. In addition there were scattered volumes, faded and stained, of Plato, Homer, Virgil, and a ragged, crumbling set of Shakespeare.

Sammy would bring his lunch from home and while Mr. Comerford would leave the office for a bowl of soup and a glass of beer at the nearby businessman's restaurant, he and Hanratty would brew fresh tea in the dented copper kettle and munch giant sandwiches at their respective desks. The bookkeeper would read his newspaper, studying the financial pages with great avidity; the young stenographer would borrow one of Mr. Comerford's books and struggle through a few pages, in between bites of a farmer-cheese-and-tomato sandwich.

"Whatcher readin' that stuff for?" Hanratty would ask. His eyes vanished, his pointed chin jutted forward belligerently. He had no particular contempt for the young man, it was merely Hanratty's attitude toward anything that intruded on his notions of what people should be and what they should do. A caricature of an office Irishman himself, he resented departures from the norm in anyone else.

"Trying to improve my mind," Sammy answered. He had a mouthful of farmer cheese and trying to eat, defend himself against Hanratty's thrusts, and absorb *Walden* was exceedingly difficult.

"Aaah," the bookkeeper sneered. "Whatcha wanna be? A cawledge professor? A poet?"

"I certainly don't want to be a secretary all my life. Or a bookkeeper."

Fresh kid. I bet you read that stuff because old Comerford reads it. I bet he don't even understand it. What do you wanna be like him for? He's on the way out, and he don't even know it. You read his kind of books, you'll end up like him."

"What's wrong with Mr. Comerford?"

Hanratty smiled, a cracked humorless grimace. "He's a sucker. He doesn't know he's outdated. Can't run a business like he does, depending on people he *thinks* are his friends. You gotta spread the word today, you gotta talk to customers, make 'em feel important. Like Acme does. Like Loewenstein does. *Oi vay,* dot Lowenshteen he gats costumers!"

Sammy closed his book slowly. "What was that last crack supposed to be? A dirty dig at me?"

"What crack?" the bookkeeper asked.

"You know. That business with the accent. I didn't like it."

"Don't be so sensitive, Abelman. Who's insultin' you? I meant it for Lowenstein. Everyone in the business knows he's a hustler, that he undercuts the price."

"Like hell you did. That accent was for my benefit."

Hanratty turned away. He didn't appreciate the way that young kike looked you over; his eyes were too dark, and he didn't have that softness, that apologetic look that most of them had. At a quick glance, with those dark eyes, and the black shock of hair, the sharp, hooked nose, he could pass for an Indian as much as a Jew.

In the afternoon, Mr. Comerford would dictate to Sammy, sign letters, check the sales and the incoming payments, and tour the small shipping and receiving office on the second floor. On this daily trip, Sammy would accompany him, clipboard at his side, taking notes and feeling a cut above the Irish and German workmen. He liked the pungent, fresh smell of the new balls of twine, the efficiency with which the workmen packed and banded the crates, the sense that Mr. Comerford, whom he admired and respected, had been responsible for creating all of it.

One afternoon in March—it was one of those freakish days when the temperature and the atmosphere belong to winter, yet some unseen, unfelt warmth creeps through to deny the cold—Mr. Comerford did not return from lunch. Hanratty winked knowingly. "You'll find out, Abelman. Your hero. All I can say is he's been pretty good this year. Used to do it every other week."

It turned dark on lower Broadway. Gaslight glowed in the waterfront mist and cabs clattered uptown, taking the wealthy merchants home to their brownstones in Harlem and along Riverside Drive. The last workman checked out, looking curiously at Sammy as he sat patiently at his desk, waiting for his employer. One of the packers whispered something to another and then spoke to the stenographer.

"Why doncha beat it, kid? The old man went on the town again. He won't be back."

Sammy looked at him innocently. "What do you mean?"

"He's drinkin' up the profits."

They slammed the street door and vanished. Sammy looked at the wall clock. He would miss his evening classes at Normal College if he delayed any longer.

Then he saw Mr. Comerford on the street. He was not wearing his topcoat; his derby was cocked crazily to one side of his head, and he was smiling stupidly through his gold-rimmed spectacles. Leaning against the glass window, he was peeking through the gilt script which read *Comerford & Sons* and rapping sharply to attract Sammy's attention.

He ran to the street, catching Mr. Comerford in his arms as the twine merchant wheeled unsteadily from the window.

"Yea, I have cavorted with Bacchus in Elysian Fields," Mr. Comerford said softly. A sour odor assailed Sammy's face, and he turned his head, still supporting his floundering employer. He wrestled him gently to the curb and a waiting hack.

"Unpleas—unpleas—unpleasant odor, Sammy? You shouldn't mind the odor of 'nebriation, m'boy. Oh. Forgot you are a Hebrew. Hebrews cannot abide alcohol. 'M I right? Curious people, you Hebrews."

"Sure, sure, you are, Mr. Comerford." Sammy shoved him through the opened door of the hansom. Seated, Mr. Comerford lurched forward, as violently as if some giant hand had slammed his back. His long arms dangled between his knees; the brown bowler toppled to the cab's floor.

Sammy stood on the sidewalk, hesitant, embarrassed. "You think I better ride home with you, Mr. Comerford?"

"Come aboard, Sammy! Always room for another rifleman in the old New York 88th!"

The driver winked at Sammy and jerked a thumb toward the cab interior as if to say, *You'd better go along, I don't want the responsibility.* He climbed in, gave the hackie the address of Mr. Comerford's brownstone on West 121st Street, and the horse clattered off.

As abruptly as he had collapsed, Mr. Comerford suddenly jerked upward again, resting his head against the black leather seat cushion.

"Curious people, the Hebrews." He belched comfortably.

"You said that already, Mr. Comerford."

"Did I? Getting old. Repeat myself."

The air was warm and moist; everything was bathed in a soft mist; fuzzy yellow halos encircled the gaslights. The first hurdy-gurdy of the season was singing its ratchety serenade on the street corner.

"Lovely city," Mr. Comerford mumbled. "Delightful city."

"It's all right," Sammy said.

"Why'd you come here then? Who sent for you?" Then, sensing some offense to his stenographer (through drunken eyes he could still see the youth's solemn face), he added, "Now, don't m'sunderstand me. I came here too nobody sent for me. Billygoat Irish, used to call us. Me. William Francis Comerford, billygoat Irish."

"Who called you that?"

"Old Americans. Know-nothing hoodlums. But bother me? Never! We showed them! Up the Irish Brigade and General Meagher! Showed 'em at Fredricksburg!"

"No one should insult anyone else because of their religion or nationality," Sammy said seriously.

"Right! Don' let 'em, Sammy! Curious, you Hebrews. Thought I'd never like you. But y'all right. You take some good advice, Sammy?"

"Yes, sir."

"Important thing," Mr. Comerford said, speaking slowly and with excessively careful enunciation, "is to have identity of your own. Very important in this country. Identity. Be *somebody*. That's why it was so important for me to be in Irish Brigade. We had identity. Accepted. You must do the same, Sammy. Don't join army, 'f course. Hebrews don't make good soldiers. But use your brains. Study. Learn. Advance. Have identity. You understand?"

"I think I do, Mr. Comerford. I'm going to night school now, making up credits—"

"Not 'nough. Set high goal. Law? Medicine? Teaching? But have identity. Be a whole person. Don't lead life of quiet desperation. Don't get lost in swarm."

He suddenly spun about, shoving his face into Sammy's trying, as much as his condition would allow, to look fierce and commanding—the young Willie Comerford, who charged the stone wall at Fredericksburg.

"'M not sure you're absorbing all this, Sammy. You Hebrews have strange turn of mind. Quite possible you're misinterp—misin—misinterpretin' every word I say. You doin' that?"

"No, Mr. Comerford, I understand you."

"Don't think you do." He leaned forward, slapping his hand against Sammy's knee to underscore his lesson. "When I say identity, I don't mean get lost in the crowd. I mean—be your own self. Be strong, don't let anyone call you billygoat Irish."

He belched as he realized the inanity of his admonition, and, with his mouth still opened wide, gulped air and resumed. "Thas' ridiculous. Couldn't call *you* billygoat Irish, but call you worse names. Ignore 'em. Get own identity. Fight back."

"I can take care of myself," Sammy said.

" 'M sure you can. But don't want to see you grow up forced into mold, restricted, stifled. Need all freedom you can get, Sammy."

Like an oversized, ungainly child, Mr. Comerford was now resting his aching head in Sam Abelman's lap. The pleasant clip-clop of the horses' hoofs, the rhythmic creaking of the axle, was putting him to sleep.

"For want of a man, there are so many men," Mr. Comerford whispered before plunging into a deep, drugged torpor. "Curious people, you Hebrews."

March merged gently into a hopeful April, April into an indolent May. Sammy Abelman was nineteen and restless. On Saturday nights (he went to night school Mondays through Fridays) he sat on the stoop of their sagging, stained tenement in Brownsville and talked with his friend, Sol Pomerantz. From where they sat, they could see green fields and the clustered treetops of Traficanti's farm. Like hundreds of other East Siders, the Abelmans and Pomerantzes had moved to Brownsville—*Brunsveel*—in search of lower rents, a slightly better standard of living, and the sight of grass. Six years after the turn of the century, much of Brownsville still looked out on wide, flat plains, choked with angry weeds and stunted trees. On the flat, sandy land where an honest-to-goodness Farmer Brown had once raised goats and geese, a new slum was burgeoning. Builders were buying up acreage as fast as they could raise the cash. Each day a new excavation would start. Swarms of gnarled Neapolitans and Calabrians, knights of the pick and shovel, brightened the neighborhood with their staccato chatter.

Sol was a small, wiry youth. An immense shock of luxurious chestnut hair, dipping in graceful waves over his intense face, gave him the look of a distrustful, irate bird. His pipestem limbs and narrow body, however, were like high-tension steel. If Sam Abelman's family had been poor, Sol Pomerantz's were impoverished, and, thus nurtured on insufficient foods, the fibers of his body had curiously formed themselves into stringy, elastic muscles. There had been nothing left over for fat or flesh. Sol also was a reader. He haunted the public libraries and attended lectures. Once he had shaken hands with Edwin Markham, and twice he had listened, enraptured, as Eugene V. Debs spoke out against the crimes of capitalism.

"This new book by Jack London," he was telling Sam. "It's the best he's done yet." He held it up proudly, showing his friend the title: *The Sea Wolf*.

"I liked *The Call of the Wild*," Sammy said. "But it takes me months to finish a novel. I'm not a speedy reader like you, Solly. If I ever get the time, I'll catch up with you."

"Reading is part of growing up," Sol commented solemnly. "It's especially important for us. To acquaint ourselves with a new environment, to be a part of it. That's why Jack London is so great; he's got the feel of the whole country in his prose."

Sam saw his father approaching. Another Sabbath had ended, and he was returning from the synogogue with a few cronies. Halfway to the house, they paused. From the stylized gestures and intonations, the youths could see that the oldsters were engaged in one of their interminable Talmudic arguments. Thumbs and fingers dipped and rose, voices became agitated, a bearded participant ruffled his whiskers to underscore a telling point.

"See what I mean?" Sol asked impatiently. "We've got to escape from that kind of thing. It's holding us back."

Silent, Sam thought about the way his relationships with his family had unraveled in the last decade. He loved his parents; yet they were becoming more alien to him than the *goyim* with whom he worked. His father, more stooped, more mute with each dragging year, lived for the tailoring shop on Ludlow Street, the crowded flat in Brownsville, the synagogue. The old man (he was in his fifties, yet he was undeniably old) had never in his life taken a vacation, read a book, expressed an opinion. And his mother had aged with him. The hope that the new country would rejuvenate them had been a delusion; the habits, the pressures, the miseries of the old world were too deeply entrenched in blood and bone. The poison of decay had been injected into them in the Czar's ghetto. If anything, the shattering, convulsive change of America had accelerated the degenerative process. They ate better, slept better, had more money and greater freedom; but they aged faster and died earlier. Their meek submission was mirrored in the children—all but Samuel. Moishe, a silent, shy young man, had learned almost no English. Daily he went to his sewing machine in the shirt factory, daily he returned. The girl, Rivke, fragile and

querulous, had married a broad-backed plumber, a gross Gali-
cian with boorish manners. The youngest son, Aaron, now fourteen,
showed some promise, Sam thought. He got excellent marks in school,
his English was good, and he had a feverish curiosity that pleased
the older brother. But he was a sickly child—Dr. Lemkau had told
them that his heart was weak, that they should not expect him to
lead a normal, active life. To Sam's mother, he was the eternal,
pampered baby: *mein kind.*

"It's hard for the old generation," Sam said. "You can't change
a whole way of life overnight, Solly. You should be more tolerant—
a hot Socialist like you."

"Socialists aren't tolerant! We're world changers, Sammy. I have
half a mind to organize a Yom Kippur banquet!"

"What the devil is that?"

"Back a few years ago," Pomerantz explained, "the young radicals
on the Lower East Side got fed up with all this religious junk. So
on Yom Kippur, instead of fasting and hanging around the synagogue all day, they'd rent a hall and have a huge banquet. They'd
eat pork, mix the milk and the meat, and get drunk as *goyim.* Just
to show the old fogies that they were outdated. They'd advertise
the feast for weeks in advance, sell tickets, and buy whiskey with
the proceeds."

"That's going too far," Sam said, scowling. "How come they
stopped doing it finally? I bet they turned everyone against them
with that kind of crazy affair."

"Oh, I don't know. I guess they proved their point."

"People still go to *shul.* They still fast on Yom Kippur."

"You don't. I don't. How many of our friends do?"

"We're the younger generation, Solly. We're in a new environment, adopting new ideas."

"So!" cried Pomerantz, holding his hands out to prove he had won
his point, "you agree with me!"

"I don't really. I have nothing against anyone who wants to stick
with the old ways. That's their privilege. Just like its mine to break
away. Furthermore, even though I don't go to *shul* any more, I'm
still aware of my identity as a Jew. I don't go screaming it to everyone, but I don't reject it. You don't go bragging about your arms
or legs, but you don't deny they exist either."

Sol leaped up the stoop, sitting beside him. He whipped from
under his arm a folded copy of the New York *Evening World,* and
opened it to a column facing the editorial page.

"Okay, Mr. Identity," Pomerantz said, "let's see if you have any
bright ideas today. Ever read John Sylvanus' column?"

"I glance at it sometimes."

John Sylvanus was the pseudonym for a journalist-nature lover who conducted a daily column in the *World*. He reported on larks and lizards, wild mustard, and Norway maples with splendid impartiality. No field mouse, no Mourning Cloak butterfly escaped his watchful eye. In addition, John Sylvanus' column served as free advertising space for innumerable hiking clubs, *vereins*, naturalists' societies, and assorted groupings of outdoor folk. It was particularly popular with young immigrants, who availed themselves of John Sylvanus' generosity to organize social clubs.

"Let's start our own club," Sol said earnestly. "We'll put in a free advertisement, asking young people with literary and outdoor interests to meet us at Jackson's Lot a week from tomorrow."

He jumped from the sagging gray stoop, slapping his hand against the folded newspaper. "I'm writing in to the paper today! And I'm signing both our names to it. We'll call the first meeting for next Sunday, right?"

"Go ahead, if it will keep you happy," Sam said.

"See you Sunday, Sammy! And bring lunch!" He bounded away joyfully.

From the narrow tenement door, Sam's mother emerged. She was shepherding Aaron, her youngest son. He was carrying a paper bag filled with leftovers under one arm, and a chipped tureen of soup under the other. The food was being dispatched to her daughter Rivke—a gesture dictated as much by charity as by the mother's need for binding her vanishing family together. She spoke in Yiddish to Sam.

"Sam, help Aaron carry this to Rivke's. It's a long way and it's getting dark."

"Ah, mama, it's two blocks. What is he, a baby?"

He looked at Aaron's translucent white face, the bluish lips, the black hair growing stringly at the ears and nape of the neck. He regretted his words, and he understood they stemmed from his own sorrow at Aaron's weakness.

"Who needs you?" Aaron said quickly. He had bright, quick eyes: there was no sickness in them.

"I'll show you who!" He jumped from the stoop, and squaring off, boxer-fashion, started to flick short left jabs—each missing by a fraction—in the direction of his brother's nose. It was a game they played constantly. Aaron giggled, bobbing his head to avoid the blows that would never land. Sam took the bundle of food and they walked off. He glanced over his shoulder at his mother. Her face was a fretwork of age and toil; hair, features, and clothes were a smudge of dull gray. He winced inwardly, thinking of the pathetic frailty of his people. They gave in, they surrendered without a fight, they grew old quickly. Maybe Solly was right: you had to learn, to adapt, to expand.

It was a classic May morning, the air clear and thin, a faint breeze ruffling the luxurious weeds surrounding Jackson's Lot. Sol Pomerantz' notice in John Sylvanus' column had called the meeting for ten in the morning, but, at half-past eleven, the two organizers were the only applicants present. They sat on a huge boulder, the site Sol had designated as a gathering point, and waited. They were dressed for the outdoor adventure in old neckband shirts without collars, old trousers, and tennis shoes. Each had brought his lunch in a shoebox: hard-boiled eggs, fragrant onion rolls layered with sweet butter, tomatoes from Traficanti's farm, thick slices of honeycake, and a quart bottle of milk.

Disconsolate, they waited on the sun-warmed rock, watching a lazy game of tennis doubles. A noon, they began to eat their lunches, an act both sensed signified the failure of their project. The last hard-boiled egg had been ingested, the last drop drained from the milk bottles. The sun was at its height, and they sweated freely on the hot rock.

Sam stood on the boulder, shading his eyes. "Let's give it five more minutes, Sol. Then we'll take our own hike. You can tell me all about Jack London—for the tenth time." At that moment he spied a party of seven or eight young people walking toward them, from the direction of the trolley line. They wore light, informal clothes, and each carried a paper bag or box.

"Hey, Solly, cheer up! Business!" He leaped from the boulder, and the two organizers went out to meet the arrivals.

"Good morning, I'm sure," said Sol. "Are you folks by any chance the ones who read the notice in John Sylvanus' column?"

There were eight of them: four youths and four girls. Like Sol and Sam, the boys wore collarless shirts, the dark trousers of ancient suits, and tennis shoes. The girls were dressed in white shirtwaists and tight, dark skirts; their thick halos of hair were gathered at the neck in bright ribbons. A tall youth, blond hair neatly parted in the middle and combed in delicate twin scallops, shook hands limply with Sol and Sam. He appeared to be the group leader.

"Delighted to meet you. I'm Louis Kosloff." He took from his breast pocket a pair of pince-nez, and in a gesture intended to impress the strangers fixed them on his nose with a professorial tweak. "We're all members of a club of our own in Williamsburg," Kosloff continued, "and we thought it might be valuable to meet another group with similar interests. Are there just two of you?" His tone indicated disappointment.

"Yes," Pomerantz said, "just Sam Abelman and myself. We thought we'd gather together a nice congenial group."

"Just two of you," Kosloff repeated unhappily. "Hardly worth our trip. We took the wrong trolley, too. That's why we're so late."

There was an uncomfortable pause. Clearly the Williamsburg contingent was distressed by the thin ranks of the Brownsville chapter. One boy kicked a stone, two of the girls stared at Sam and began to giggle. He flushed in embarrassment.

One of the girls stepped forward. "Well, really, Louis," she said softly, "it doesn't matter. I'm sure these gentlemen had the best of motives. What's the difference if there are only two. I'll bet they can take us on a lovely walk. Rome was not built in a day, Louis."

She was slim, yet gently rounded, Sam noticed uncomfortably. Her waist was pinched the tightest of all the girls, and her skin was white and smooth. Her voice had a cultured and delicate lilt— clearly a girl who read a lot and worked hard at improving herself.

"I'm Sarah Malkin," she said, "and these are the other members of the Cloverleafs—Anna Levinsky, Hilda Myerson, and Eva Cohen. Let's see, you know Louis, so why don't you other boys introduce yourselves?"

The Williamsburg contingent shook hands vigorously. Only the blond, bespectacled leader remained faintly aloof. But Sarah's diplomacy had saved the day. Soon they were joking and exchanging biographical data. Sol suggested they walk along King's Highway, a dirt footpath winding through wide pastures and scattered farms. Sam found himself walking with Sarah Malkin, but it was soon evident that he would have to share her with Kosloff. The lanky young man made it clear that no Brownsville upstart could monopolize his girl.

They strolled at a leisurely pace. Wagons creaked by them, moving slothfully in the spring warmth; butterflies skipped and danced in the high grass.

"What do you do for a living, Abelman?" Kosloff asked sharply.

"I'm a stenographer for a downtown firm," he said hesitantly. "But I'm studying at Normal College nights."

"For what?" Kosloff asked.

"I'm not sure," he said. "Medicine, maybe. Or teaching."

"Louis goes to CCNY," Sarah said. "He's studying to be an English teacher."

Kosloff favored Sam with an indulgent smile. "How do you manage to absorb anything at night school? Don't you sometimes think it's just wasted time and motion?"

"Maybe," said Sam. "I can't afford day college."

"It seems to me," Sarah said, "that you get out of education what you put into it. Day or night, it doesn't really matter."

"Tell me, Abelman," Kosloff said, "what made you and this other chap—what's his name—organize this group?"

"It was Sol's idea," Sam said. He hated having to defend the project. He had entered into it unwillingly, and now he had to take on the big brain. Sol, on the other hand, was having an animated argument about Debs' role in the Pullman strike with one of the new boys.

"Well, which of you is the literary expert?" Kosloff persisted.

"Sol reads a lot," Sam said.

"Yes, I'll bet he does. *Old King Brady* and *The Yaller Kid*."

Sam stopped walking, and Sarah and Kosloff, noticing that he was lagging, halted and turned. "Look, Professor Kosloff," Sam said acidly, "you can beat it right now if you don't like this arrangement. We can't help it if we were the only ones in the club, and we can't help it if you were too dumb to take the right trolley. We can't help it either if you don't like to walk. If you get tired let me know, and I'll carry you."

Kosloff looked down his nose through the fragile pince-nez; he had the appearance of an offended greyhound. "Don't get so uppity, Abelman," he said. "I didn't know male stenographers were so tough."

Sam advanced a step. Then, realizing that it would have been neither mannerly nor purposeful to pursue the argument, he halted. "Aah, to heck with it," he said, and turned his back.

Sarah was at his side in an instant. "Now, really, Samuel," she said, "you're both being childish." She was a born mediator; moderation, discretion, and calm deliberation were her watchwords. "Louis is really not a bad fellow. He's very artistic and high-strung. He writes poetry, and I'm sure he'll read to us when we stop for lunch."

They found a raised plateau beneath a grove of lindens, pin oaks, and poplars. They mingled Emerson and Whittier with hard-boiled eggs and seeded rolls; Poe and Longfellow spiced the farmer-cheese sandwiches and the buttered slabs of pumpernickel. Sam and Sol, victims of their own impatience, willingly accepted donations from the Williamsburg visitors.

"I think it's time for Louis to recite," said Hilda Meyerson. She was a dumpy little redhead, and her dark eyes rolled about too frequently for Sam's comfort.

"Don't encourage him, he will," one of the Williamsburg boys said.

"What'll it be, Louis, 'The Face on the Barroom Floor'?" another asked.

Sam was feeling better about things. Louis, in spite of his CCNY education, his pince-nez, and his poetry, was not immune to gibes; maybe even Sarah was aware of his vulnerability.

Kosloff, supine on the thick grass, raised himself to a sitting position, clasping soft hands about his knees. With evident disdain, he put aside his book of poems, underscoring the fact that he would recite from memory. When he spoke his voice had a deep luster; he would make a superb English teacher.

" 'The Raven,' " he began, "by Edgar Allen Poe."

Sol Pomerantz glowered from beneath his shock of dark hair. He preferred meatier stuff—something that sang of revolution and man's highest hopes. He made a point to memorize some Markham for their next meeting.

" 'Once upon a midnight dreary, while I pondered weak and weary . . .' "

Sarah was listening raptly, her small round chin resting on her clasped hands. Leaning over to whisper in her ear—the group was determinedly silent while Kosloff intoned his offering—Sam murmured, "I wish he'd quit his Raven."

She looked up at him sharply with a fierce "Shh!" But she was smiling appreciatively at his appalling pun. He felt that his jest had been as well, if not better, received than the poet laureate's recital.

It was evening when he brought Sarah home. Kosloff, her escort at the start of the long Sunday, had grown exhausted on the return hike.

The Ralph Avenue trolley took them to Williamsburg, an older, more crowded Jewish settlement. He made no effort to hold hands with Sarah. Instead they talked, about their families, their ambitions, their interests. Sarah's parents were Litvaks, from Vilna;

Jews with a modern, progressive outlook. Her father had a small jobbing business, distributing tea and coffee to Brooklyn grocery stores. She worked as a secretary for the MacReady Elevator Company on Vesey Street; she was seventeen and liked to read.

They walked slowly to the yellow brick tenement where she lived, anxious to prolong the evening, aware that the prying eyes of parents and neighbors would hasten his departure.

"I enjoyed this day very much," Sam said haltingly. "You are a very interesting person to talk to."

"You are too, Sam," she said. "You have a fine sense of humor."

"Will you come to the club's next hike?" he asked. "Say, I'll bet if we start early we can go to the Palisades or something like that."

"Oh, I'm sure I will. I think the Cloverleafs had a wonderful time. We might get some more members if you place the notice again."

He looked intently at her. "I don't care if we stay just as we are. I don't need any more members."

Her father was waiting on the stoop. He was a tall, portly man, his beard clipped short, neatly squared and combed like a Russian grand duke's. He wore a black silk vest and a high square skullcap. Seated on a wire-backed chair, his hands resting on a silver-headed ebony cane, he was clearly the neighborhood elder, a man not to be crossed or snubbed.

Sarah spoke to her father in Yiddish. She addressed him with evident respect. He was a *sheyneh yid*, Sam was sure, a man who held an honored seat on the Eastern Wall of the temple.

"Father, this is my new friend, Samuel Abelman."

The ebony cane tapped authoritatively on the stone stoop. "Abelman? I don't know any Abelmans." His basso profundo indicated that this circumstance reduced the youth to a convenient nonentity. He lifted horn-rimmed spectacles and squinted through the street lamp's half light at the black-haired young man.

"You're a Litvak?"

"No, sir, my parents came from Bessarabia. Near Kishinev."

Malkin the elder flipped the eyeglasses back in position. "Hoooy! A Rumanian!"

If he had referred to his daughter's new acquaintance as a Cossack, he could not have sounded more annihilating. His rudeness embarrassed Sarah and she blushed. But neither the patriarch's unprovoked insult nor the fact that he was without carfare and faced an hour's walk to Brownsville troubled young Sammy Abelman. He would see Sarah next Sunday and for many Sundays to come. Love, nurtured by Whitman, Lanier, and Longfellow, would bloom amidst the tenements.

Through the oppressive summer, the walking-and-literary club continued its excursions into the green pastures of the city and the prose and poetry of America. Sammy remained in the employ of Mr. Comerford, but there were portents of doom in the stifling office of the twine merchant. Increasingly, Hanratty would report on lost accounts, dissatisfied customers, dwindling sales. And more and more, Mr. Comerford seemed not to hear the bookkeeper. Unquestionably, he was looking pale and spent during the breathless August days.

The Saturday before Labor Day, Mr. Comerford did not appear at the office until early afternoon. He arrived, or rather was helped to his desk by his eldest son, a meaty man with thick brown burnsides and the coarse friendliness of a Tammany sachem. Mr. Comerford's creamy linen suit was disheveled. His eyes were dim and teary behind the gold-rimmed glasses and he exuded a corrupt alcoholic odor, as if the liquor within him was vaporizing through his limbs.

"Now, Billy," Mr. Comerford told his son, "don't you lecture your daddy. I am in complete command of my faculties. Am I right, Sammy? Sammy understands me."

The stenographer walked to his employer's desk, pushing the green eyeshade back on his forehead. "Can I help you, Mr. Comerford? Would you like something?"

"He's all right, Sammy," Billy said. He sat down wearily at the side of his father's scarred desk. "B'Jesus, you'd think he'd have a new desk around here. Who'd place an order in a slum like this? Sammy, don't you or Hanratty ever air this joint out?"

"It's all the ventilation we can get here, Mr. Comerford. All the doors and windows are open."

Young Comerford loosened his stiff collar and removed his checked jacket. It had light-gray velvet lapels; a pink carnation bloomed in one eyelet. "Ah, it's no matter any longer." He turned to Hanratty. "Michael, fetch me the books for the last quarter. Sammy, call in the boys from the stock room and the shipping department. Everybody."

The elder Comerford had appeared to be dozing. Now he jerked himself upright in the ancient swivel chair. "I shall handle this affair, Billy," he said stiffly. "I am equal to the occasion."

"Go ahead, Sammy," Billy said sharply. "Call them in."

They gathered in a respectful semicircle around the old man's desk. Mr. Comerford had slumped back in his chair in a semi-stupor. Billy sat on the edge of the desk and gazed reflectively through the dust-stained window onto lower Broadway.

"What I have to say is not very pleasant, so I'll be brief," Billy began. "As you know, Mr. Comerford's business has not been doing too well. Competition is getting tougher, costs are up. A lot of our line, quite frankly, is outdated. There are other problems, but why should I bother going into them?"

Mr. Comerford raised his hand as if to interrupt his son. Then he lowered it and moaned.

"Last Tuesday, my brother and I went over the company books and decided that Mr. Comerford could no longer stay in business. We have filed a petition for bankruptcy, and, as of next week, the assets of Comerford and Sons are being taken over by the Commercial Bank. I'm sorry you are all to lose your jobs, but we've no choice. The banks are closed through Monday, so why don't you all come in Wednesday and Hanratty will have your last pay envelopes."

No one spoke. One of the stock-room boys, a bloated Irishman who supported a wife, a mother, and six children, crossed himself and muttered, "Holy Mary, Mother of God."

Sammy said nothing. He knew it was not his place to speak. There was some uncertain shuffling of feet. Hanratty cleared his throat and took a step forward. "May I say for the boys, Mr. Comerford, we're sorry as can be this happened." The shriveled little bookkeeper was sniffling, Sammy noticed. He felt a sudden rush of pity for Hanratty—the man wasn't all meanness. He was genuinely fond of old Comerford.

The twine merchant smiled. "Why, Michael, that's a very nice sentiment."

"Okay," Billy said. "You might as well clean up and take off the rest of the day. I hope you all get work real quick."

"Just a minute, Billy," Mr. Comerford said. "Grant me at least a soldier's farewell to his troops."

The workmen, at the door of the stock room, halted. Sammy and Hanratty drew closer to the desk.

"Failure is not a pleasant circumstance," Mr. Comerford began.

"Oh, for Christ's sake, papa—"

"That's all right, Billy. I am clear of mind and firm of purpose. But if I have failed, I should like to think it is not because of some defect of character, but rather through a minor weakness . . . one which will not, I trust, bring on the contempt of my fellow men. Let us call it inflexibility. The practices of trade have changed since my boyhood. Instead of learning them, I read Thoreau. When a man falls out of step with the multitude, he has no right to feel neglected. He falls out of his own volition. He cannot blame his fellow men or what they have made of society. So I leave my business, and you, my associates, with no feeling of persecution. Each of us must cherish some small illusion when fortune turns against him. Mine is that I have been honest."

"Ah, papa, that's enough," Billy interrupted. "I'll take you home."

He ignored his son. "The best that can be said of illusions is that sometimes they transcend their fictitious nature and cross the line into reality. I trust my illusions are of that quality."

He rose from the desk, turning theatrically to the Civil War memorabilia on the mahogany wall. "A case in point on man's illusions," Mr. Comerford said huskily. "General Meagher, the proud commander of the Irish Brigade. For years after I fought under him, I believed implicitly in his heroism. Could any man have better looked and lived the part of a hero? And yet, years later, I read accounts of Fredericksburg where it was proven that General Meagher had left the field of battle early under the pretext of having been wounded. He was never wounded. He had never been under heavy fire. Yet the image of my hero persisted. I preferred to remember my commander as he looks on that old picture, not as some historian has portrayed him."

He stumbled, and for an instant it appeared he would collapse. Billy and Hanratty helped him to the door. They stood in the blinding summer sunlight waiting for a hack. Sammy, stunned by the events of the afternoon, walked out and joined them.

"Sammy, I shall be happy to give you the highest reference," Mr. Comerford said. "I suspect you will not long be a simple stenographer. You have ambition, strength, and a clear mind."

Sammy hesitated before speaking. His request, one which he had harbored for several months, seemed much too piddling in the wake of Mr. Comerford's disaster.

"Mr. Comerford," he said, "I'm very sorry about what happened. If you want me to work next week, to help clean up—"

"That's all right, Sammy," Billy said. "The bank is sending their own people over. Hanratty'll stay on a few days."

A hack drew up, and the door swung open. "Mr. Comerford," Sammy continued, "do you remember I told you about a kind of literary group of young people? You know, how my friends and myself go for walks and discuss famous writers?"

"Oh, for Christ's sweet sake," Billy said. "Let's get going."

"Well, I was wondering, Mr. Comerford, if you'd join us tomorrow and lecture to us on Thoreau. We have had some very interesting discussions. Mr. Madison from the Henry Street Settlement spoke on Whitman last week. And the assistant principal of Boys'

High talked to us about Emerson. It was my turn to get a guest speaker and I thought maybe—"

"Sammy, Mr. Comerford is tired and isn't feelin' well," Billy said sharply. "He's in no mood to be takin' nature hikes and lecturing."

Mr. Comerford shook himself loose from his son's arm.

"Quite the contrary, Sammy. Your invitation makes me feel brighter already. I shall be honored to speak to your young friends."

His step seemed springier, his eyes sharper as he climbed into the cab.

"Can you meet us at South Ferry at ten in the morning, Mr. Comerford?" Sammy called, as the horse trotted off. "We're going to Staten Island!"

"With my lunch under my arm!" the twine merchant called back.

Overlooking Great Kills Harbor, the literary club lolled on a tree-shaded plain. Sam and Sarah Malkin rested against a gnarled Norway maple; in semisolitary grandeur Louis Kosloff composed couplets. He had taken to wearing a flowing black silk tie; a black ribbon dangled from his pince-nez.

Coatless, Mr. Comerford sat on a folding camp chair (Sammy had rented it for the occasion and carried it himself) and opened his edition of *Miscellanies*.

"People equate Thoreau with *Walden*," Mr. Comerford began, "but since I am sure that this learned assemblage has already mastered the philosophy of that well-known work, I shall choose a different text for my sermon."

Eva Cohen and Hilda Meyerson giggled, and Sarah looked at them reproachfully. They were both exceedingly pretty girls, and Sarah suspected they had joined the group only to augment their friendships with young men. Mr. Comerford knotted a red silk handkerchief around his neck and resumed.

"I shall read first from *Life Without Principle*. When I have concluded my reading you may ask questions of me."

He read haltingly, as if somewhat confused by his role as teacher to these alien children, but they listened with profound gravity. Any scrap of learning was treasured. The lore of the new country had replaced the Torah.

" 'The ways by which you may get money almost without exception lead downward,' " Mr. Comerford began. " 'To have done anything by which you earned money merely is to have been truly idle or worse. If the laborer gets no more than the wages which his employer pays him, he is cheated, he cheats himself. If you would get money as a writer or lecturer, you must be popular, which is to go down perpendicularly. Those services which the community will most readily pay for, it is most disagreeable to render. You are paid for being something less than a man. The State does not commonly reward a genius any more wisely. Even the poet laureate would rather not have to celebrate the accidents of royalty. He must be bribed with a pipe of wine; and perhaps another poet is called away from his muse to gauge that very pipe. As for my own business, even that kind of surveying which I would do with most satisfaction my employers do not want.'"

Mr. Comerford paused and took a deep breath. "Now, before I resume, would anyone like to comment?"

"It seems to me," Louis Kosloff said, "that he is far too pessimistic. When he says that the ways of earning money all lead downward, he isn't setting much hope for us. I mean, young people like ourselves who wish to get ahead."

The twine merchant closed the book gently, using his thumb as a marker, and nodded slowly.

"In a sense, he was a pessimist," Mr. Comerford said, "but, like Dr. Johnson, he was, in his way, a pessimist with an enormous zest for living."

He hadn't really answered Kosloff's question, and Sam, sensing that his guest lecturer had been evasive, jumped in.

"Louis, when you read Thoreau you realize he always said things in the extreme to make people pay attention. When he says the ways of making money lead down, he wants you to sit up and listen, just as you did. Then he goes on and says, okay, earn a living, but do something fruitful, rewarding. Don't just work for the sake of money. Is that right, Mr. Comerford?"

He reopened the book. "You must have been reading this essay, Sammy. It's the very next part. Thoreau writes, '. . . it would be economy for a town to pay its laborers so well that they would not feel they were working for low ends, as for a livelihood merely, but for scientific or even moral ends. Do not hire a man who does your work for money, but him who does it for love of it.'"

Mr. Comerford tilted a glass jug to his lips and sipped tepid water. "And as you read him and learn to appreciate him, pray that some of his hard sense touches you. I have found Thoreau a comfort and a guide for many, many years."

"Isn't there a lot of the escapist in him?" Sol Pomerantz asked.

"I mean, the world, Mr. Comerford, is beset with terrible injustices and problems. Aren't we duty-bound to rise up against them, instead of looking for muskrats and loons?"

"Escapist? My boy, Thoreau went to jail for what he believed in. He stood up and was counted when the slavery issue came to a head." Mr. Comerford looked slyly at Pomerantz, shrewdly gauging the young man's turn of mind. "He was a revolutionary, yes, but his own particular kind of rebel. He would join no causes and follow no banners. But he preached a radical doctrine, you may be sure. When he said simplify, he was striking at the roots of our society. Imagine! Tons of paper work, memoranda, newspapers, aimless possessions, and useless social functions, swept away, if all of us were to follow his advice!"

Sam watched the old man as his voice trailed off. He was thinking of the bookshelf behind the mahogany desk; the long sad afternoons in the office on lower Broadway, the faded pictures of Fredericksburg, and General Meagher, who had never really been a hero.

"And may I impart one cautionary word," Mr. Comerford said, as if roused from a reverie. "Take your Thoreau in small doses. Do not try to swallow him whole. If you permit your entire life to be guided by his precepts, you will fall out of step, perhaps forever. A man may be out of step with his fellow men, Thoreau said, because he is listening to a different drummer. But the trouble today is that this different drummer may cause you to fall so far behind the line of march you will never catch up. So use your Thoreau sparingly. Listen to the different drummer now and then, but do not fall out of the parade altogether."

They were silent. Not all of them understood the old man's lecture fully, but they knew he had imparted to them something of himself.

Below them, in Raritan Bay, a steamboat whistle broke the summer quiet. A stir of wind fluttered the leaves of the sentinel lindens and poplars; it was turning cool in the natural classroom where the ghetto children listened to the veteran of Fredericksburg. Few moments of triumph would come to William Comerford in his remaining years on earth; but in his brief role as teacher to the young aliens he understood that something had been illuminated for them that summer afternoon on Staten Island.

With the collapse of Mr. Comerford's business and his enforced retirement, Sam was unemployed. Unable to find a satisfactory job, he compromised by helping his father in the tailoring shop on Ludlow Street. The new line of waiters' jackets was being turned out, and Sam did triple duty as delivery boy, order-taker, and assistant fitter. His father did not work Saturdays and Sam took advantage of the day off to meet Sarah. They would rendezvous in Prospect Park, and the conversation, as it invariably did, turned to Sam's future.

"It's that darn night school," he complained. "I can't seem to catch up. There's no time for me to study. Oh, the junk like English composition and history are easy enough. But the sciences! I'm way behind in chemistry!"

She slipped an arm through his. Such demonstrations of affection were forbidden at the meetings of the literary group. But alone, far from the jealous eyes of Louis Kosloff, who still envisioned himself as a contestant for Sarah's soft hand, they indulged their love.

"Well, I think you should make your mind up. You ought to take a full year off from work. Borrow the money for school and get all the credits you need for medical college."

"So who pays for medical school? It's four years, and the tuition with books and everything is more than two hundred dollars a year."

They rested on a concrete bench. It was early morning, and the park was virtually empty. A policeman ambled by slowly, eying them with bland contempt. Several well-dressed small boys with the inbred blond faces of Brooklyn's old founding families—proud Presbyterians who would soon be engulfed by the waves of immigrants—ran by. A sweltering German governess followed them.

"Sam, what in the world is that?" Sarah asked.

He looked first at the small boys who had run by, then realized she was pointing toward a sunken grassy plain, where a group of young men appeared to be walking on their hands.

Sam shrugged. "Search me. It's five fellows walking on their hands. I guess that's their privilege, since we live in a democracy. It's their America too."

"Oh, let's see why they're doing it!" she cried.

They walked down the slope toward the hand-walkers. The gymnasts wore identical uniforms: soiled white tennis shoes, white duck trousers, and white athletic shirts with red piping around the throat. One of them, still ambulant on palms, came to a stop and then did an artful flip, landing on his feet. On the front of the shirt (it had several small holes in it) Sam noticed the red letters "CC."

"What does the CC stand for?" Sam asked. "Cubic centimeters?"

The young man folded a pair of arms the color and consistency of oak beams across an abnormally developed chest and eyed the visitor coldly. He was a man in his late thirties, with the look of a tethered falcon about him. A thatch of red hair fell on either side of his bony head. Thick tufts of the same red growth overhung his fierce eyes and grew in a great irregular patch over his upper lip. But for all his feral appearance, his voice was high-pitched and almost apologetic.

"Now that wasn't very nice," he said. "You know very well that isn't the case and you said it to be funny. Probably to impress the lady."

"I didn't mean any harm," Sam said. "Just a little joke."

"It is not my idea of fun to make jokes about educational institutions," the red-thatched man said prissily.

"Well, I'm sorry. I didn't know you were having a study period here. I just mean to be sociable." He gestured to Sarah and they turned to leave.

"Just a minute, young fellow," the redheaded acrobat said, his voice getting higher and squeakier. "Where did you get those deltoids? For that matter your pronators and supinators aren't bad either."

"My who?" Sam asked. Smiling, he shook a finger at the chief hand-walker. "There are ladies present and you're getting very personal."

The muscular man leaped to Sam's side, and with iron fingers began probing his biceps and shoulders, like a woman examining a chicken. "You are in rather good shape, my boy. Have you read my book on muscle vibration?"

"I—ah—I don't think I have," said Sam. "What's your name? Maybe I've seen it in the library."

He stepped back and bowed stiffly, an Italian fencing master about to don his mask. "Hector O'Bannion, president and dean of Chelsea College of Physical Education. These gentlemen developing muscle vibrations are my senior class."

"Just four of them?" Sarah asked incredulously.

"I accept only those students who can live up to the rigors of my curriculum. Besides a thorough education in the well-being of the body, we teach the arts, the sciences, and the social graces." He fixed Sam with a predator's eye.

"What about yourself? In need of education? Anxious to further yourself? The New York City Board of Education has cited me twice for the excellence of my gymnasium teachers. If you can pass the entrance examination, you can get a teacher's certificate in two years."

Sam and Sarah exchanged puzzled glances.

"But—but—I was thinking of medicine as a career," Sam said "I don't particularly want to teach."

"Medicine!" O'Bannion cried. "Pill purveyors! Charlatans! My boy, seek health in the temple of your body. I can see you are endowed with strength and wisdom. Come to Chelsea College and make a career for yourself. Learn a philosophy of life with us!"

Sam shook his head. "It doesn't matter, Mr. O'Bannion. I can't afford the tuition anyway, and if I could, I wouldn't spend it to become a teacher. But I sure admired the way you jumped around and walked on your hands."

O'Bannion's steel trap of a hand reached out again and clutched Sam's wrist. "Less hastily, young man," he said. "What can you do for a living, right at this moment?"

"I'm a pretty good stenographer," Sam said.

"Splendid!" cried O'Bannion, "you may work your way through Chelsea as my own personal secretary!"

"But I—"

"You will report for classes Monday at nine in the morning. We can work out a method of having you sit in on classes and handle my correspondence at the same time!"

The four other young men, all wearing the same ragged shirts with the crimson "CC's" on the front, were upright now and were smiling at Sam and Sarah. He noticed they were a pleasantly conglomerate group: one had the square, blond look of a Scandinavian, another the pugnacious friendliness of an Irishman; the other two were nondescript, but were evidently not Jewish.

"Gosh, Mr. O'Bannion," Sam said, looking for help to Sarah, "I can't make any promises. I haven't even taken your entrance examination. How do you know I can qualify?"

"Indian hand wrestle?" O'Bannion asked abruptly. He staked out his right foot alongside Sam's and extended his open right hand toward the unwilling adversary.

"Okay," said Sam absent-mindedly. They grasped hands and began to bend their strength against each other. O'Bannion was incredibly strong; Sam could feel the power coursing from his massive shoulders and chest into the oak plank of an arm and the iron fingers. Yet for the first few moments, neither budged an inch. O'Bannion's face turned a flaming red, his orange mustache bristled and rose from his upper lip. He had not bargained for so much resistance from the young man with the admirable deltoids. But if O'Bannion was surprised, Sam was confounded. He had never met his equal at Indian hand wrestle, but pitted against

O'Bannion he felt he could no more move the gymnast than he could budge the Brooklyn Bridge. The veins swelled in his forehead, sweat poured from his head and collected in a pool at the juncture of his collarbones. They made brief, hesitant jerks, grunting with the effort, and still neither gave way.

Suddenly, with deft deceitfulness, O'Bannion relaxed his grip and yanked his arm backward. The unexpected termination of resistance caused Sam to lurch forward clumsily, and as he did O'Bannion tightened his grip again, and with one magnificent, sweeping thrust of his right arm jerked the opponent from his feet and hurled him rump first, onto the grass. Sam shook his head and smiled. He was a little annoyed that O'Bannion had tricked him. Rising, he heard Sarah's disapproving *tsk-tsks* as she dusted the grass and dirt from his trousers.

"My boy," said O'Bannion solemnly, "you have just passed your entrance examination. I shall look for you on Monday."

The semester at Chelsea College was not scheduled to start until late in September. But Hector O'Bannion, president and dean, was so enamored with the notion of having his own secretary that he hired Sammy immediately, paying him four dollars a week. When the school term started, the gymnasium teacher did not discontinue the stipend; he understood the poverty of his new student and the sacrifice he was making. Sam had raised the matter with him, offering to work without pay under the terms of their original agreement, but O'Bannion would not hear of it. The new student realized that the four dollars he received every Friday could have been put to excellent use by the president-dean to pay heat and lighting bills, to purchase textbooks, to keep the converted stable where the college was located from falling into complete disrepair.

Sam had inveigled Sol Pomerantz to enroll at the College of Physical Education with him, and the young revolutionary joined him each morning for the long trolley ride across the bridge and to West Twenty-fifth Street where O'Bannion ran his haphazard school.

And yet it was not quite as ridiculous as it seemed at first blush. The ancient stable, with its sloping floors and drafty corridors, was kept immaculately clean. On the ground floor, taking advantage of the high ceiling, was the gym itself: a jungle of rings, bars, horses, and ropes. O'Bannion himself taught all the athletic courses. He was an avid student of the Swedish school of gymnastics, and Sam and Sol were soon executing giant swings and the other stylized maneuvers. O'Bannion also taught calisthenics, playground games, folk dancing, and the standard sports—basketball, handball, volleyball.

There was only one other instructor besides O'Bannion. He was an aged Westphalian named Herr Gochanauer who imparted chemistry, physics, and biology through rattling false teeth and a tobacco-stained white beard. His combined classroom-laboratory, held together with electrician's tape and assorted nuts and bolts (Sam was always being called upon to perform maintenance chores), smelled of his cheap cigars, a circumstance which distressed O'Bannion. The president-dean advocated Spartan living: he eschewed tobacco, alcohol, coffee, tea, and meat. Vegetarian and abstainer, O'Bannion sought, with limited success, to instill in his pupils his own dietary rules. To entice them into the healthful pastures of vegetarianism, he served inexpensive lunches for the student body. A buffet of carrots, lettuce, and pulverized whole wheat was always available at noontime. Pitchers of fresh milk and bowls of fresh fruit were also provided, and, for the impoverished students, the nominal charge of ten cents for as much food as they could absorb was a distinct boon.

Sam, transferring his credits from his night classes at Normal College, remained at Chelsea for the full two-year course. He courted Sarah, helped his father in the tailoring shop, and he dreamed of respectability and a place in the community. But even with his new certificate stating he was a qualified teacher of physical education, and an appointment as a summertime playground instructor, he was not certain of his goal. Hector O'Bannion's diatribes against medicine had not really swayed him from his original hope of becoming a doctor. Rather it was the thought of four more years of schooling, the part-time jobs he would need, the endless studying that had caused him to surrender his hopes for a medical career. He was thinking now of another year of college, a baccalaureate degree, and certification as a full-time teacher in the city school system.

In June of 1908, Sam Abelman and Sol Pomerantz, the two newest members of the city's playground staff, rode the trolley to a public school in Red Hook, a neighborhood where the traditions of hoodlumism were deeply rooted. The mores of Red Hook demanded flouting of the law, and the weaker the symbol of authority, the more openly it could be defied and tormented. The two new instructors were aware of Red Hook's notoriety. But Hector O'Bannion's assurances that a strong right arm could handle any playground rebellion buoyed them as they rode out.

When they arrived, the playground was empty. The concrete pavement cooked beneath the summer sun. Little bubbles of tar erupted between the sidewalk cracks, and the morning sky glinted on spiked cast-iron fencing. The two instructors toured their steaming empire, eager to impart their knowledge of physical education, of sports and good sportsmanship to the children of Red Hook. The challenge was hurled at them from the filthy red brick tenements, from the squalid streets, from the sodden drunks sleeping in doorways. Completing their brief survey, they were met at the gate by a deceptively fat young man with a pink bald head. Slung over his shoulder was a lumpish olive-drab bag, which gave him the look of a beardless Santa Claus.

"You Abelman and Pomerantz?" he asked.

"That's us," Sam said. "Ready for our induction."

"I'm Charlie McDevitt, district supervisor for playgrounds. This is your gear. Basketballs, volleyballs, handballs, Indian clubs. You're personally responsible for the equipment. If it's lost or stolen, it's deducted from your salaries."

Sam scratched his head. "Are these kids in the habit of stealing?"

McDevitt dumped the bag at Sam's feet. "These kids will steal anything. Don't turn your backs for too long, or you'll be catching rocks."

Sol squinted under the great shock of chestnut hair. "How do you keep from turning your back in an open playground?"

The district supervisor smiled, showing a row of magnificent alabaster teeth. He seemed delighted by the distress of his new subordinates. "You can't really, Solly. Use your fists when you have to, and keep moving. Lock the joint up at five o'clock. Don't take any wooden nickels."

He walked off whistling. Through the opened gates a trickle of children started to drift in. Sam and Sol greeted them cheerfully, trying to overcome the sullen glances. The youngsters had the peaked, dirty look of the slum.

At ten o'clock there were enough children present for the organization of games. Sol took a younger group and started a game of club-snatch. When they tired of this, an underleg basketball relay was begun; soon a volleyball game was under way. A half-dozen little girls in pigtails were jumping rope.

At the rear of the playground, parallel to the high iron fence, was a basketball court, the cracked concrete hot as an oven. Sam took a party of five boys to the court. They ranged in age from twelve to fifteen. After some preliminary shooting and dribbling, they started a three-man game: Sam and the two youngest boys against the other three. The burning sky was merciless, but they played with the defiant vigor of sidewalk athletes.

Sam played well; Hector O'Bannion had neglected nothing in his ramshackle college. *Dribble, pass, shoot, weave in and weave out; cut for the basket, lay it up, throw it back.* They repeated the intricate rhythms of the game for almost an hour, losing track of the score, abandoning themselves—instructor and boys—to the pure delight of using their bodies. So absorbed were they in the game that Sam failed to notice his audience. A cluster of older boys had collected outside the iron fence, watching the game with bland, insolent faces. Pausing for a brief rest, Sam noticed them, remembered McDevitt's warning, and decided to try the friendly approach.

"You fellows like to join the game?" he asked pleasantly.

One lean youth cocked a pimpled face at the instructor and grinned. "Not with you, Rosenberg."

"My name isn't Rosenberg," Sam said. "It's Sam Abelman. And I think you're a punk. You have five men. Come in and play a little game if you're such a hot shot."

"Go back to Russia, Rosenberg," the youth shouted.

"Yeah, Russia, that's where ya come from," another called.

Sam clenched his fist a few times. He would have liked to wade into them, fists swinging. Already he could see his basketball players eying him curiously. They were of the gutter also; their rules dictated that a taunt had to be answered. But he would try to ride it out without a fight; once he antagonized them they would be his enemies throughout the summer. It would be a black mark against him in the school system—unable to maintain discipline his very first day out.

"Beat it, you bums," he said. "You want to play basketball, you're welcome. If you're going to stand there making faces, who needs you?"

He turned to the game again, distressed by the faint disdain on the faces of his own kids. When he dribbled through the entire opposition and curled in a beautiful one-handed shot, they failed to show any enthusiasm.

Again the taunt was hurled. "Oh, Rosenberg!" The lean boy, now puffing a cigar butt, had started it; the others took it up. "Oh, Rosenberg! Oh, Rosenberg!"

"Rosenberg! You're a *sheeny!*"

He had to move. Tossing the basketball to one of his team-mates, he sprinted for the gate, rounding the corner in full career. As he did, he saw what their strategy was. Two of the boys were helping a third over the high fence. The intruder leaped to the court below, knocked the boy holding the basketball to the ground, then seized it and hurled it over the high fence. *McDevitt's warning!* It had been a plot to steal the ball! Yet what was he supposed to do? Spend the afternoon letting them insult him? He was in a straightaway now, running as fast as he could. The hoodlums were running also. Pomerantz who had witnessed the theft, joined the chase.

The skinny youth carried the trophy under his arm, and fortunately for Sam he was the poorest runner. After half a block he was panting fiercely and loping with an ungainly stride. Wobbling, he turned into a cobblestoned alley, the playground teacher a few steps behind him. Separated from his own companions, he was helpless. Sam bounded into the alley. It was a dead end; he saw his tormenter backed against a sagging board fence, the basketball clutched under his arm.

"Ya sheeny bastard, don't touch me. My old man'll kill ya," he wheezed. "My brother'll mobilize ya."

Sam walked toward him purposefully. "You're a lousy, yellow punk, you're yellow, yellow, yellow, you cheap bastard. And furthermore, you're a galoot. Give me that ball."

The youth began to cry.

"Give me the ball. Throw it to me and say you're sorry."

"Ya sheeny—beat it!" he sobbed.

"I'll break your arm off," Sam said. He spit professionally on both hands and took a step forward. "I want an apology too."

The ball bounced toward him and he scooped it under one arm.

"Now I'm going to use one arm to kick the crap out of you," Sam said.

"I'm sorry, I'm sorry!" he screamed.

"You're sorry you called me Rosenberg. My name is Sam Abelman, right?"

"Yeah, you're not Rosenberg. You're Sam Abelman. Lemme out! Don't hit me!"

Sam turned his back. "I wouldn't dirty my hands on you, you punk." Then, looking over his shoulder, he said, "Bring your buddies to the playground when you learn how to act like men. But stay away if you want to be a bunch of galoots."

Turning the corner out of the alley, he heard a window slam open above him. Instinctively, he ducked as a flower pot sailed by his head and shattered into a thousand shards on the cobblestones. He ran back to the playground, meeting Pomerantz on the way.

"What did you do to him, Sam?"

"Nothing. Just made him apologize. Why should I belt him? Maybe they'll come and be good boys now."

Sol shook his head. "It's terrible what bad social conditions can do to young people. You think they'll give us any more trouble?"

"If they do, we'll give it back to them." He began dribbling with the ball; he had a vested interest in it—if it were to be stolen, he recalled McDevitt saying, it would come out of his own salary.

For several weeks there were no disturbances at the playground, and Sam and Sol decided they had won the battle for control of their little domain. Each day brought more children to the concrete square; each day the young teachers taught new games to new groups. They taught them songs and folk dances, gave instruction in boxing and wrestling on a tattered stained mat which McDevitt brought over one day, and got to know the neighborhood families. There were no return visits from the "galoots."

On the weekend of July Fourth, Sam and Sol, with McDevitt's help, organized a basketball game between a local athletic club and the instructors. They would charge admission, five cents per person, and use the proceeds to buy new equipment.

The neighborhood team, composed of young men who worked on the nearby docks and a local brewery, made up in brawn and height what they lacked in skill. The instructors' team, composed of Sam, Sol, McDevitt, and two of McDevitt's classmates from City College, were superior in technique and finesse. It promised to be an exciting contest, and the playground, outfitted with a bank of wooden stands, was rapidly filling with people in early afternoon. Outside the gate, at a folding table, Sol sold hand-lettered tickets to the crowd, dropping the nickels into a small canvas bag. Gate-crashers were common at playground games, McDevitt had explained, and he advised Sam to tour the crowd after the tickets were sold and collect the stubs as an extra safeguard.

The neighborhood people had gotten to know and like the young instructor. Over their beers, they told each other, "That little Jew-boy is strong as a dray-horse—you wouldn't believe a sheeny could have such muscles!" They said it not disrespectfully, but in sincere wonder. Now, circulating among the audience—women in merciless skirts and constricting blouses, and men sweating in Sunday collars and striped silk shirts, he joked with them, genially refusing to book their bets. The local club was a sentimental favorite, even though the instructors, now warming up with professional grace, appeared to be a more skilled group.

Sam had reached the end of the rickety grandstand, and had found not a single gate-crasher. The pack of soggy tickets in his fist made him feel good. He and Sol were proving themselves the best men under McDevitt's command. They had maintained discipline, stimulated local interest, gone far beyond what was expected of a summertime playground instructor. Approaching a short, squarely built young man lounging against the edge of the seats, Sam suddenly felt a premonition of trouble. He had become acutely sensitive to the attitudes of what he called "the professional galoot," and now he saw some of the symptoms in the short young man.

"May I have your ticket?" he asked politely.

"I got none." Sam looked at the arrogant face. The bridge of the nose had been broken and flattened, and there were scars across the broad cheeks.

"Well, I'll have to ask you to leave," Sam said.

"I don't wanna leave. I wanna see the game."

"Why don't you buy a ticket? It's only five cents. Here, I'll show you where." He stepped forward, grasping the young man firmly under the elbow. "Right out in front."

He pulled away savagely. "Keep ya sheeny fingers off me, Rosenberg."

Sam stuffed the tickets into a pocket. "Where did you learn that Rosenberg stuff?"

"*From us, Rosenberg!*" He looked through the fence, seeing for the first time the same gang that had tormented him the first day he had been at the playground. The lean youth who had tried to steal the basketball was there, and there were at least seven others with him, all cursing and shouting.

"Oh, Rosenberg!" they chanted in unison, the skinny youth leading them like a choirmaster.

"Try to throw him out, Rosenberg!"

"Yeah, Rosenberg, he's my brother!" the pimply one called. "Try to make him apologize, Rosenberg!"

A circle of people had run from the grandstand and had gathered around Sam and the gate-crasher. McDevitt, sensing a disturbance, left the basketball court and ran over.

"What's up, Sam?" the supervisor asked.

"It's okay, Charlie, let me handle this," Sam said. He walked again toward the stocky young man, who was now standing feet apart and braced, his thumbs hooked in his high side pockets. His square head was thrust slightly forward.

"Why do you have to be a galoot?" Sam asked. "Is there a rule written somewhere that says you must behave like a hoodlum?" He indicated the holiday audience in the stands, the circle of spectators waiting for inevitable bloodshed (and sensing that in some secret way they were pleased to see him in trouble), and continued, "Look at all these nice people. Why do you want to ruin their fun?"

"I ain't gonna ruin anyone but you," the young man said. Then he added—a bit tentatively it seemed, "Sheeny Rosenberg."

Sam moved forward and reached for the young man's forearms. He hoped to subdue him quickly without any fighting and escort him from the playground; there was no point in provoking a riot. The tormenter, all slum muscle and grace, recoiled; Sam had barely touched him. The playground instructor saw the white arms and dirtied fists spring into position; a second later it was as if someone had exploded an electric-light bulb in his face. He was stumbling backward on his heel, feeling a thousand needles stinging his offended chin. Numbness radiated through his teeth and cheeks, and a little bath of salty blood was forming inside his lower lip. He had not fallen, however, and as his head cleared he saw the gate-crasher bouncing professionally, fists in the classic boxer's pose, the abysmal face aglow with hoodlum joy. Irrelevantly he thought: Why do they smile so much? Who said they could be so happy about it?

The crowd had shrieked when the first blow was struck. Outside the fence, the boxer's supporters were urging him on.

"Mobilize him, Paddy!"

"Kill the sheeny bastard! Cut his eye out!"

Sam put his hands up. He was a poor fist fighter, strong enough but neither graceful nor well trained. The truth of it was he didn't like to hit people; during Hector O'Bannion's boxing lessons, he had been a reluctant pupil.

Paddy hit him a second time with a professional left jab—straight, fast, and with the fist grinding painfully into his right eye. The right cross struck him below the breastbone, and he grunted. Crouching low now, he was amazed to discover how quickly his eye was closing. Dimly he heard McDevitt shouting to him, asking him if he wanted help; Pomerantz was standing at the edge of the crowd, pale and helpless.

He buried his head inside hunched shoulders, and charged forward. The rush unbalanced the boxer slightly, but even falling away he struck Sam with the quick left hand. Again he tried to cross his right, but the instructor blocked it with an iron right forearm. It was purely a defensive move; but the boxer's fist had hit against something harder and tougher than it had encountered in any gymnasium or ring. The pain made him flex and unflex his left fingers sympathetically, and the gesture was not lost on Sam.

More confident, Sam tried the rush again, head down, fists and arms working like pistons in front of his face and body. He had the satisfaction of feeling his right land flush on the pugilist's chest; but in that instant the authoritative left jab found his teeth again, the right cracked against his cheek and made a noise like two wooden slats being slapped together. He shook his head and a spray of blood issued from his mouth. Already his new white gym shirt was speckled with red dots.

"Knock him down, Paddy!" he heard them shouting.

"Go 'head, Paddy, that sheeny's yellow!"

"Knock him on his ass! Go on, Rosenberg, fight back!"

Then, curiously, the boxer betrayed a gutter hesitancy. He glanced querulously over his shoulder, as if asking: How long must I keep socking him, if he won't go down?

The instructor was charging him again, head down, fists working. This time Paddy stepped neatly aside, and smashed a swift left hook beneath the pumping forearms. It caught Sam below the Adam's apple, made him cough, gasp, and stagger. Tottering, he felt a second blow (it must have been a right hand thrown from behind the boxer's ear) catch him on the back of the neck. He was on his knees, watching the drip-drip-drip of blood from his ripped mouth onto the pavement, hearing McDevitt asking him plaintively:

"For Christ's sake, Abelman, enough is enough. This guy is a pro, Paddy Lynch. He fights at the Velodrome. Let me call a cop."

Then he heard Pomerantz, his voice straining for confidence.

"Sam, call it off. So he beat you, so what? The punk threw a rabbit punch. That's illegal."

Still shaking his head, blinking, hearing the rabble's happily horrified murmur, he knew he could not quit while he could still stand and raise his fists. There was always someone out to beat you, to make you eat dirt: the teacher back in *kheyder* on the East Side, the streetcar conductors who insulted his father, the sharpers who had put Mr. Comerford out of business. You had to fight them, and on their terms. He was on his feet again. His head ached in a hundred places, and he saw only through his left eye. But his limbs, his body, the gymnast's huge muscles and tough bones were intact.

"Is a rabbit punch really illegal, McDevitt?" he asked, trying to sound genuinely curious.

McDevitt grasped his upper arms. "Sure it is, Abelman, you know that. Come on, we'll call it quits. Fight's over."

He shoved the supervisor away. "I just wanted an official opinion, because I'm going to be illegal also."

The crowd screamed, and the hoodlums danced and chanted as the instructor and the pugilist squared off again. The boxer bounced on sneakered feet; there was not a mark on him, not a cut, not a bruise. Yet he did not seem completely happy with his assignment. The rudimentary brain told him he might have to throw punches at this muscular Jew all day.

Paddy danced around him tantalizingly. His left fist, the knuckles now reddened and tender from having battered the hard face and body so many times, struck a half-dozen times. He varied them with the whipping right, pushing it against the iron chest and feeling it bounce away when it struck the Jew-boy's shoulders and forearms. He must have hit him fifteen successive times, but there had been no retreat. Instead the crazy instructor was closing in, burying his bloodied head on the boxer's lean chest, forcing him to move backward.

"Ya crazy sheeny," the boxer gasped. "D' I hafta killya?"

"No," he heard the instructor grunt, "I'm gonna murder you. I made my mind up."

For an instant, striking Sam again with the right hand and hearing the painful grunt, he believed it: *he would fight this Jew bastard all day and then he, Paddy Lynch, the best prelim boy in Red Hook, would be stretched out.* He believed it even more a second later. As they struggled apart, disengaging arms and heads, the boxer dropped his left arm in one exhausted lapse. In the unguarded interval, Sam, with no professional grace and in the poorest of style, had clouted him on the ear with his right fist. He had brought his thick arm around in a great sweeping arc, gathering momentum, and by the time the square fist landed with a dull *clack* on the boxer's skull, it carried enough force to bend him sideways. Paddy's aggrieved ear turned a deep crimson, a pained flush that spread across the contorted face. Sam saw his advantage. He accepted a somewhat discouraged flick of the left hand, and again, as they parted, swung the right hand. It landed high on Paddy's temple. This time the boxer swayed and looked at him dreamily, unbelieving. The fine blue eyes were crossed, and the jaw drooped. Sam charged, head down, feeling the mild prick of Paddy's fist on his forearms as they tried to stop him; the boxer collapsed like a rotting timber. He was sitting on his haunches, less stunned than humiliated, now turning slowly toward his horrified supporters outside the fence. Sam wiped a scarlet streak from his mouth across his arm. With excessive deliberation, he knelt, placing a knee in the small of Paddy's back and nailing him to the blazing cement. He grasped the boxer's floundering left arm and yanked it sharply backward and upward, stopping only when he heard Paddy's desperate wail.

"Now what's my name?" he asked.

"Rosenberg, ya bastard."

"No, it's not. I'll pronounce it for you. Samuel Abelman. Can you say that?"

A remnant of gutter bravado forced him to resist. "Nah, ya name is Rosenberg."

Sam looked through the fence. The galoots were studying him with grave, subdued hatred. "You tell him what my name is, you punks, or I'll break his arm. You dare me?" He yanked the arm viciously (it was an old trick of Hector O'Bannion's) and the boxer screamed.

"Ya sheeny bastard," the boxer's brother shouted. "We'll mobilize ya!"

This time he pulled the arm and twisted the wrist simultaneously. The violence of the gesture caused blood to spurt from his own mouth. It fell in a little line of red polka dots on Paddy's white shirt.

"Let him go," he heard the thin youth saying. "Ya name is Samuel Abelman."

"Swell," said Sam, "you're a real smart feller. Now, *you*, what's my name?"

"Samuel Abelman," the boxer gasped. "Now lemme up." He was whining.

Sam leaped back. Paddy rose painfully, first on elbows and knees, then on one knee and then upright. He was holding the left side of his head, the tenderized temple and cheek where the two blows had landed. Outside the fence he joined his friends, and the stream of obscenity assailed Sam again. But the cursing was less hearty. There were a few halfhearted "Rosenbergs" and a tin can was hurled.

McDevitt and Pomerantz were studying his smeared, swollen face with polite horror.

"You didn't have to go through that," McDevitt said. "I could have got him to lay off. They're my kind, you know. That Lynch. I saw him knock out a middleweight last year. Why did you have to push it?" He was wiping Sam's face off with a towel.

Sam smiled, feeling each ache and cut on his battered face intensify. "Why not? Who said he could sneak in? How about the basketball game now?"

The visiting team—they were neighborhood people and they had mixed feelings about the fight—were eying him with curious respect.

The captain, a Celtic ogre with a shock of orange hair and freckles the size of nickels, walked up and grasped his hand.

"Abelman, you're a battler. We'll be honored to be your opponents."

The others were nodding their heads. Pomerantz tossed the basketball to him and they were warming up under the basket, listening to McDevitt's gymnasium chatter. The crowd had really not cheered his victory, indeed he had felt a faint hostility when the tide of battle changed. But he never could have backed down. The world was full of galoots laying in wait to make it rough for you. Sometimes you hit back, and sometimes you won. The trouble with winning, he told himself, was that you realized how loathsome your adversaries were. He took Sol's pass, cut under the basket, and banked the ball off the cast-iron fretwork of the backboard, lingering long enough to see it bounce through the hoop.

A not unpleasant mist drifted in from the ocean. The night odors of seaweed and moribund shellfish surrounded them. The doctor and his wife were holding hands, an attitude which seemed to Thrasher more habitual than amatory, a closeness born of years of living together. The affection was unspoken, unevident. He sat with arms crossed on the cold railing, listening to the muted thunder of the waves, studying the doctor's large, creased face under the lamplight.

"I suppose I'm the world's greatest authority on galoots," Dr. Abelman said. "All my life I've been running into them. Even today there's something about galoots. They smell me out like I'm a natural enemy. Dog and cat."

"You don't help any yourself," she said petulantly. "You go looking for a lot of fights yourself. Or at least you used to, when you were younger."

"I guess I hate galoots because they get away with so much. I can always remember them, standing on street corners, never working, talking loud, living big. I think they enjoy life a lot more than I do. What worries them? Do they stay awake nights over a leukemia case? Do they worry about taxes or about losing patients? You think they're really happy, Mr. Thrasher?"

"I'm afraid my knowledge of galoots isn't as extensive as yours, doctor."

"I don't mean just the street-corner galoots," the doctor said thoughtfully. "They got them everywhere. There's all kinds of galoots."

Thrasher laughed. "You mean a kind of spiritual galoot?"

The doctor clapped his hands together. "Very good description! The world is full of those bastards. Just look at my next-door neighbors, the Baumgarts."

Mrs. Abelman stood up heavily. In the misty yellow light she looked older and more misshapen. She was long past the ministrations, the magic of the Sunday magazine girdle ads. She looked her age, no more or less, and Thrasher was suddenly disturbed. Where were all the old people who *looked* like old people? You never really saw any old people in his business; if you did they were so artfully preserved, molded, cosmeticized, and appareled that they gave the illusion of youth. He could not recall one of his associates bringing a fat, aged, wrinkled, or poorly dressed mother or father into the office and saying, "These are my parents." Where were they all hiding? Was everyone slim and young and fashionably dressed?

"Sam, don't start on the Baumgarts. You'll ruin what's left of my vacation," she said. "I think we'd better get back, Mr. Thrasher. It's getting late and you won't have any sleep at all."

She was worrying about someone else's impending minor disaster again, and Thrasher found it tended to worry him also. Descending the wooden ramp, she twice cautioned them against falling (it was not at all steep) and she scolded the doctor for not having worn a warmer jacket. At street level she complained that the lights were insufficient and, spying two teen-age youths returning from a night dip, wondered aloud how they avoided pneumonia.

"You were saying about galoots, doctor," Thrasher said, "that you can find them anywhere. How would you define one?"

The doctor halted as they stepped off a curb, in deference to his wife's warning to be careful, the drivers never looked where they were going.

"A galoot is a guy who thinks the world owes him a living," the doctor said. "And if he doesn't have it handed to him on a silver platter, he goes after it at someone else's expense."

It was an admirable definition, Thrasher felt: it included all galoots, everywhere.

At the boardinghouse, the doctor volunteered to drive Thrasher to the station. The Buick coughed and protested and lurched off. With what seemed to Thrasher excessive casualness he turned to his wife and announced:

"Well, *ketzeleh*, we're through with galoots. We're getting out."

"I've been hearing that for years," she said. "You know we decided against it a long time ago."

"Oh no. *You* decided against it. You were against the X-ray and the EKG and the basal metabolism, too. Just like you're against a new house. But this time, *I* made the decision. We're buying a new house."

"Now, Sam! Did you buy that house without telling me?" From her tone it was clear she *knew* he had not, nor would he ever without her permission.

"Dannenfelser is giving me a break on that beauty on Republic Street. He knocked his down payment down two thousand bucks. I told him to hold it. I'm buying it. You can't stop me."

She settled back peevishly. "You'll stop your*self* when you think it over. At your age. You're almost seventy. What are you doing with a new mortgage, new obligations, a new neighborhood? What are you, some kid who can tackle all these things?"

They were silent a few moments. Thrasher was deeply embarrassed. She spoke after a while, sounding wan and unhappy.

"Don't you dare buy that house, Sam. You'll clean out your savings and you'll be saddled with a terrible responsibility. And with our luck you'll get a lemon. How do you know it's worth over twenty thousand dollars?"

"Skip it, skip it," he said. "We're boring Mr. Thrasher."

The Buick rattled up to the Long Beach station, shivering as a dreadnought-sized Cadillac convertible, a chartreuse ark conveying two stout men in yachting caps and eight-inch cigars, brushed by and cut them off.

"Louse!" the doctor snarled. "Galoots can drive Cadillacs, too!"

Thrasher wrestled with the broken door handle. The doctor had to lean over the seat and pound it with the right fist that had downed Paddy Lynch. It swayed from the car body.

"You'd do better buying a new car than wasting your money on a house," Mrs. Abelman said.

Thrasher leaned through the window. "Many thanks for your help, doctor. Can I see you this weekend?"

"Yeah, sure. I guess so," the doctor said. He seemed preoccupied, inattentive. Clearly, the argument over the new house had unsettled him. Thrasher felt an urgent need to leave him in a more cheerful frame of mind.

"I thoroughly enjoyed your stories about Mr. Comerford and Hector O'Bannion and Pomerantz. By the way, what ever happened to Pomerantz?"

The doctor blinked behind his thick lenses. "Solly? He had that corner drugstore for years. The *tunkeles* held him up four times.

The fourth time he got disgusted and tried to throw them out. He died in St. Mary's Hospital with three bullets in his chest."

"I'm sorry to hear about it."

The doctor sighed, crossing his thick forearms on the wheel.

"Yeah, they're all gone." He shook his head mechanically. "I don't know what it is. There was a kind of gentleness in people then, something I miss more and more every year of my life. Mr. Comerford, what a gent! Are there any more like him around? Or Hector O'Bannion?"

"Whatever happened to O'Bannion? He was quite a guy!" Thrasher was trying to be, as his associates would say, upbeat.

"He lost Chelsea College. The bank got it. He went broke and died young. Lots of people thought he was a charlatan, and maybe he was in a little way. But he never hurt anyone, and he gave so many free scholarships to his school he never made a nickel. Lots of people were peddling physical culture then, stuff they stole from O'Bannion—including some doctors. But *he* never got a red cent out of it."

The train had arrived. The seashore crowd surged toward the gate: a bloated blonde in red knickers pushing an overfed dark boy; a herd of bony teen-agers, raucous and contemptuous; two swart Sicilians, garlanded with black curls and sideburns, shepherding a pair of bosomy young girls in peasant blouses.

"Everyone pushes and shoves," the doctor said sadly, "everybody is pushing somebody or something. Where's the gentleness? Nobody does anything for its own sake any more. That was the trouble with Comerford and O'Bannion, both of them. They couldn't get anywhere with what they liked to do. Comerford read his books when he should have been taking ads, and O'Bannion gave free tuition instead of rounding up students. They were gentle, that was their trouble."

Thrasher shook hands with the doctor. "I'd like to convince you that the world as it is today isn't so bad after all, doctor. Maybe we can argue it next time. There's plenty of kindness around, if you look for it."

The doctor shrugged. "Ah, I've been talking too much. I'm not as unhappy as I sound."

"Gloomy Gus, that's you," Mrs. Abelman said. "You talked so much you'll get a sore throat. Mr. Thrasher, you'll miss your train if you don't hurry."

She had pointed out two more impending catastrophes; her evening was a success.

V

The bulk of the doctor's office work was crammed together on weekends. Sometimes the waiting room would be filled from mid-morning through late afternoon and Jannine would have to set up bridge chairs to accommodate the overflow. If the weather was pleasant, several patients would adorn the doctor's front stoop, taking advantage of the sunlight filtering through the bright foliage of the Lombardy poplar.

He loved the ritual of the office: opening the double doors to the examining room, inviting the next patient in; the case histories, the preliminary interrogation, the probings. With old hands, he liked to discuss family matters, business affairs; they knew he expected it and they told him everything. With new patients, he delighted in learning the new facts, even though, more often than not, they were a dreary repetition of a hundred similar cases.

It had been a tiring day. A GI series on the Traficanti boy had kept him in and out of the darkroom most of the morning. He didn't like the irregularity of the duodenal shadow; it would gnaw at him all through the day. That was the trouble with medicine—nothing was ever isolated. Every case, every patient was a part of you all the time. Angelo Traficanti's duodenum would occupy him continually, infringing on his concern over Mrs. Abarbanel's arthritis, Shirley Feinman's fainting spells, Mr. McMorris' coronary, and Ed Dineen's gall bladder. All of them would force themselves like driven nails into his consciousness, until his mind was a swarm of problems, self-generating and self-propagating, feeding on each other and on him and shutting out his personal worries. He did not think about the new house very much on weekends.

At five in the afternoon there were still several people in the waiting room, sitting quietly in the dull heat, all of them flecked with the irregular spangles of the tree-patterned sunlight.

He had just given Rabbi Piltz his monthly check-up, and the snuffish odor of the old man lingered in the examining room. The patriarch departed, waving his authoritative cane and mumbling his incomprehensible blessing. Standing between the partly opened doors, the doctor chuckled, addressing the three people in the hot anteroom.

"Well, we're all in good luck today. The rabbi blessed us." He

151

did not notice that two of the people were Negroes, nor did it bother him. In the filth and noise of the savage street he saw an enemy in each dark face; in the office they became real people, identifiable, capable of salvation, worthy of a little dignity.

A stout Negro woman, draped in the outlandish dark clothes which denoted Deep South churchgoing and an eschewal of vulgarity, rose hesitantly. Gently, she guided a thin, café-au-lait youth toward the door. He moved lightly, head down, his manner one of contemptuous indifference. At the door, the third patient, a short fat man in a soiled white shirt leaped from his seat. Boldly, he thrust himself between the doctor and the Negroes, crying coarsely:

"It's my next!"

"It's your next?" the doctor asked pleasantly. "You mean it's your *neck*, and it could use a bath. These people were first."

The fat man looked from the doctor to the Negroes. He said nothing, but the curled upper lip and the eyes transmitted the message: *They are black and I am white and therefore it doesn't matter if they were here first.*

"So you don't take me foist?" he asked.

"If you were first, I'd take you first," the doctor said. "You know —the last shall be first. Ever read the Bible, Ballenberg?"

That was the trouble with most of the doctor's little *ripostes*: they pointed morals and they were much too far above the heads of his audience. Ballenberg ignored him.

"You'll take dem foist?" he persisted.

"Of course," said the doctor. With a deft shove he moved the fat man aside and, opening the doors wider, ushered in the Negro woman and the boy.

"You shouldn't touch me like that!" Ballenberg said. "I'll fix you, Abelman! I'll go by Baumgart! He wouldn't take a *schwartzer* foist! To your own people you do this, *hah?*"

He turned, irate and indignant, slum honor sullied by the doctor's insistence on fair play. The Negro woman looked distraught. "Ah'm sorry, doctor," she said in a barely audible voice. "Maybe you shudda seen him first. You gon' lose a patient."

"Who needs him. Who needs his kind?" And he knew, of course, that he needed all of them, the galoots, the boors, the villains. Yet somehow Dr. Baumgart never seemed to have these troubles with patients; you never heard him arguing with them, moralizing, ordering them out of his office. And how that young guy knew how to collect the big fees! They paid through the nose for his X-ray work, they called him in on consultations, and he sucked them dry.

The shades were partly drawn in the consultation room—a

mingled essence of summer flowers drifted into the dim room. Through the cracks between shade and window, slivers of late afternoon sun intruded, falling across the comforting face of Harlow Brooks. He sat the youth to one side of the great desk and the woman perched unhappily at the tip of the deformed Morris chair.

"I think I know you," the doctor said. He squinted over his glasses at the woman. "Are you related to the Jeffersons on Patchen Avenue?"

"No, suh," she answered faintly.

"Well, I'm sure I know *you*," the doctor said, looking at the boy. The youth silently lowered his head, an exquisite knob, molded and shaped like a bronze museum piece. The black burrs on top were an afterthought, a Greenwich village touch on an authentic Ashanti wood carving.

"Ah don' know you," the boy muttered.

"Well, it's a funny thing, I don't remember you in this office before, or seeing you as a patient, but I could swear I've met you."

The youth jerked his head, the kind of movement a dog makes when being annoyed by flies. "You don' know me. Don' nobody know me," he said flatly. Then, inexplicably, he looked up quickly and, with an impertinent grin, said, "Ah deh man of mystery."

The doctor settled back in the swivel chair, crossing his stubby legs. He enjoyed the challenge of the perverse patient, and the youth's mocking tone had not been wasted on him.

"That's very nice. We should get along fine, because, you see, I'm very good at solving mysteries. If you're a mystery, I'll find it out, young fellah. I'm a kind of detective. But you wouldn't know anything about detectives or cops, would you?"

The boy started to rise, the stringy body uncoiling like a snake. "Ah don' wan' stay here. He talk too much," he told his mother. "You make me come here. Ain' nothin' wrong with me."

She raised her voice and leaned forward, speaking in the hard voice of the deaconess, the church pillar. "You sit down dere, Herman, and be polite to deh doctor. You a sick boy."

The doctor turned to his desk, yanked out a fresh file card, and dipped the non-fillable pen in the clotted inkwell.

"You can stay or get the hell out, young man," he said sharply. "Excusing your presence, lady, I don't need him."

"He gon' stay," she said. It seemed to settle the issue for the time being.

The doctor began his interrogation, writing swiftly and illegibly, salting his notes with the shorthand symbols he still remembered from his days as a male stenographer for Mr. Comerford and Hector

O'Bannion. He learned quickly that the boy's name was Herman Quincy, age seventeen, that he neither attended school nor worked. He lived with his mother (father deceased) in a fourth-story walkup. He had no past history of serious disease, and from the doctor's cursory study of him appeared to be in good health, if somewhat sullen and ill-mannered.

"So what's bothering him?" the doctor asked Mrs. Quincy.

She shifted her dark bulk, layered with ungainly petticoats and skirts. "He havin' fits," she said.

"Ah, hell, Ah ain' had nothing but a little faintin'," Herman said, turning his head away again.

The doctor leaned forward. "What kind of fits?" he asked.

"Jes' fits is all," she said uncomfortably. "He done had three already. He had one las' week runnin' 'round with his no-good friends. An' he had two more at home. Ah' seen deh last one."

"Have you been to any other doctor?"

"No, suh. He don't like no doctors."

"Has anyone ever mentioned the word epilepsy to you? To you, Herman?"

They both shook their heads, uncomprehending.

"What was this fit, as you call it, like? Did you pass out right away, Herman? Do you remember anything?"

"Ah don' remember nothin'. Ah ain' sick."

"This last fit, the one you saw, Mrs. Quincy, what happened?"

"It skeer me awful, doctor. He come home late at night an' I hear him moanin' and thrashin'. He layin' on deh bed an' his fingers an arm, dey jerkin' and twitchin'—"

"Left or right arm?"

"Ah don' recall."

"Well, was it both arms and sets of fingers, or one?"

She ruminated, recalling the tan body writhing on the rumpled bedsheets under the glaring bulb. "Ah ain' sure, doctor, but Ah thinks at first only one arm and deh fingers, and den deh haid and one leg, and den deh whole body, twitchin' and jumpin'."

"What do you remember, Herman?"

"Nothin'. Ah fainted das all."

Dr. Abelman scowled. "You may be pretty sick, young man. You should realize I'm trying to help you."

"Ah don' need no help."

"What else, Mrs. Quincy? How long did this seizure last?"

"Ah ain' sure, seem lak a whole hour, but could'n' been more den five, ten minutes."

"What happened then?"

"He pass out cold a few minutes," she said. "He right, he fainted, but dat come *after* deh fit. Den he wake up and he say his right arm weak, he cain't move it. How long dat last, Herman?"

"Couple minutes. My arm fall asleep das all."

The doctor looked owlishly at him through thick glasses. His eyebrows bristled over the top rims authoritatively, demanding co-operation.

"How is that right arm now, Herman? Think it's strong enough to hand wrestle me on the desk?"

"Dat arm feel fine. Ah cud pitch a double-header." He was looking up, smiling easily, without the contempt he had evinced earlier.

"Okay big shot, put the arm down here and see who goes down first."

He moved aside his blood pressure apparatus and daybook, grasping the thin brown fist. Their elbows rested on the glass top. Herman looked apprehensively at the huge biceps under the short-sleeved shirt and widened his eyes a fraction.

"You pretty strong for a ole man," he said.

"Strong enough to knock some sense into you," the doctor said. "Ready?"

Herman nodded. They clamped hands, and, after a second of resistance, the doctor slammed the tan arm to the desk top.

"How does it feel now, Herman?"

"Feel funny. Mebbe a little weak." He was examining his right wrist and forearm curiously, wondering how he, Josh the Dill, could be afflicted with any kind of weakness.

The doctor invited him into the examining room, asking Mrs. Quincy to remain behind. You did better with them when you had them alone. Relatives got in the way, particularly when there was palpable hostility between family members. Herman stripped down to his shorts in the interior room. The doctor took his height, his weight, his blood pressure; listened routinely to his chest and heart and found nothing out of the ordinary. He seemed a perfectly healthy child of the gutter: limbs, heart, and lungs defiantly strong. Like so many of his companions, the absence of vitamins, pediatricians, and wheat germ had not affected Herman Quincy's physical well-being.

The doctor was examining his ears, nose, and throat, probing with spatula, the patient seated on a converted piano stool below him, when he noticed the pinpricks in the soft flesh of the tan thigh.

"And what are those, mosquito bites?" he asked grimly.

The boy stiffened again, the hostility returning. "Das my business."

"How much do you take?"

"What Ah can git."

"Can you do without it? Or are you hooked for good?"

He lowered the sculptured head, turning away from the doctor's outraged face, a face which said: *No goddam patient of mine has the right to be addicted.*

"Ah take it or leave it. Ah too smart to be hooked."

"You taking it now?"

"Ain't had it fo' a few days."

The doctor wondered idly if the strange convulsions, the loss of consciousness, the weakness in the right arm could be the result of narcotic addiction—or perhaps abstinence from it. He would have to consult the texts; crazy things happened to addicts, one-in-a-thousand symptoms which had to be taken into account before you even leaned toward other diagnoses. He'd have to probe the boy's medical history. They must have taken him to a clinic of some kind at some time, somewhere there was a medical record available. You couldn't leave anything to guesswork; you researched it as deeply as you could.

He flicked off the overhead chandelier and lit his ophthalmoscope. Preceded by the yellow cone of light, he walked toward Herman again.

"Herman, you get headaches, don't you?"

"How you know?"

"I just guessed. What kind of headaches? Morning, when you wake up?"

He was bending over him now, peering through the instrument into the luminous eyeball.

"Yeh. Dey come an' go quick in deh morning. Jes' a few minutes, das all."

"Every morning?"

"Three out of fo' mebbe. Sometime dey come quick when I go to deh bathroom, or bend over fast."

The doctor squinted into the eyeball, trying to focus his own tired eye on the optic disc. On the side of the disc nearest the nose, there was a faint blurring of the edge, and the entire disc itself appeared to be somewhat swollen—papilledema, the books called it. And papilledema could mean several things: hypertension, kidney disease, something worse. . . .

That was the challenge of the profession: the more you knew, the more possibilities you opened up. He was starting with papilledema, a swelling or choking of the optic disc; a slight engorgement of the veins, the blurring and dim streaking that might conceivably have been the start of a hemorrhage. Where would it lead him?

Turning on the overhead light again, he sat Herman on the creaking examining table. He had worn out a dozen leather examining pads on its smooth hard surface: the bright green plastic affair resting there now was his daughter's gift. It didn't ring true next to the smoky wooden sides and legs.

"Just lay still, Herman, completely relaxed."

"Ah relax real good. Man, Ah'm loose."

"Loose as a goose, is that what you fellows say?" He chattered on aimlessly, keeping the patient comfortable and at ease, seeking to avoid the slightest tensing or resistance to his probing fingers. The doctor began with Herman's face, poking at the forehead, the delicate musculature of the eyelids, the muscles around the thick African lips, light pink inside the darker red. He found nothing suspect. Gripping the right arm at the elbow, he tried rotating it, seeking some rigidity, some resistance to the passive motion. There wasn't any—the arm moved freely. The hands and fingers offered no stiffness either, nor did the left arm. Next he tested the extensors of the knees and the plantar flexors of the feet; there was neither resistance nor an exaggeration of the normal reflexes. The whole picture of the limbs was negative. Or had he missed something? Again, the worm of doubt gnawed at him. You could miss the slightest hint, the faintest suggestion of a symptom and go completely wrong the rest of the way. To assure himself he repeated all the tests, flexing and probing the bronze face and limbs again.

"Stand up, Herman," he said. "Now go to the end of the room by the door and walk toward me at your normal pace, no faster or slower."

The boy rolled off the table lightly, stood at the locked double doors, his figure sharp as a paper cutout against the bottle-green shades.

"Walk toward me, son," the doctor said.

Herman walked. The doctor looked intently at his arms and legs, studying particularly the right-hand members, seeking some variance from the normal gait, some faint betrayal of what he suspected. The boy moved as lithely and easily as an oiled machine. There was even a faint swagger to his narrow hips and small athletic buttocks. Did he imagine that the right arm was swinging differently? Was the right knee the slightest bit stiffer than the left?

"Now walk away from me, a little slower," he said.

Herman spun about and proceeded again, toward the shaded doors. The doctor took off his glasses and studied the right arm and right leg once more. It was his imagination: you sometimes started to see signs because you wanted them to be there, to tie together the loose ends of a diagnosis. He told himself that the boy's right knee was indeed stiff, that the right arm was not swinging normally. But comparing them again to their opposite members he decided the difference existed in his mind, in his eagerness to confirm his suspicions.

Herman, his tour of the office completed, stood in front of the physician gazing down at him with bored, detached eyes. The doctor leaned back in the swivel chair and pushed his eyeglasses back on to his forehead.

"Herman, I want you to repeat a sentence after me. You listening?"

"Sho."

"Fine. Say this: *Around the rugged rock the ragged rascal ran.*"

"Whuh?"

"Say it just the way I did. Go ahead."

"Ah don' recolleck it. Whuffo yo' wan' me say dat?" He was as suspicious as an alley cat.

"I want to get you a job as President of the United States, Herman, and you have to speak very nicely in that job. Now you understand? Come on, repeat it: *Around the rugged rock the ragged rascal ran.*"

Herman Quincy did not smile at the old man's joke at his expense; but, reluctantly, he repeated the strange sentence, slurring words and syllables together with deliberate contempt.

"Roun' de ruggah rock de raggah rascahran."

"Wise guy, hey, Herman?" the doctor said. Again he was in furious debate with himself: did the tongue-twister come out any more blurred or indistinct than Herman's normally slothful speech? Was there a hint that the faculty of speech had been impaired? He pointed to Herman's clothes.

"Okay, Herman, you've been very co-operative. Get dressed."

Throughout the examination Mrs. Quincy had remained seated precariously on the edge of the Morris chair in the consultation room. She looked as if she were about to topple over: the flopping black hat on the graying steel-wool hair added to the illusion of unbalance.

"Well, Mrs. Quincy," Dr. Abelman began, "there's something wrong with Herman, but I'm not sure what it is. I need your help and his. I want you to keep a record of his headaches and his fits."

She looked at him blankly, uncomprehending.

"Look. Get a piece of paper with lines and write down whenever Herman gets a convulsion. Here, I'll give you some."

He fumbled in the lower desk drawer, in a pile of old rolled-up

EKGS, electric bill stubs, and irregular stack of prescriptions, envelopes, and stationary, and found a ruled pad that Myron had brought from the newspaper office.

"Now listen to me, and you too, Herman. I want you to write down on this paper every time you get a headache. The date, and how long it lasted. Also if you became nauseated and had to throw up. I also want a record of the next fit you have. How long it lasted, exactly what happened. You, Mrs. Quincy, you watch him closely and tell your neighbors, if they're around, to watch him too. Now this is very important: call me when he has the next fit. I don't care how late it is, call me. If I'm in Long Beach, I can't come back, because it would be over by then. But if I'm in my office, or if I can be reached nearby, I want to see the next one—"

"Dey ain' gon' be no next one. Ah'm okay."

"Like hell you are. You're sick. I don't know how sick, but I'm going to find out."

He advised them that a series of X-rays would be needed. He himself would do the routine work in his office; if more specialized pictures were needed (and already he suspected they would be), he would take them to a specialist. She protested—they were very poor, wouldn't the clinic be better?

"No. If you're my patients you have to trust me. Don't worry about the cost. I'll see that you can afford it. What do you think, I'm a professor and charge Park Avenue prices?"

He took two dollars from her for the office visit. The two dollars already represented an hour's hard work and hard thinking; stuffing the rumpled bills in his trouser pocket, he knew the sixty minutes would generate an evening's worry, a few afternoons in the medical library, any number of phone conversations with the doctors he trusted.

The waiting room was vacant. He bid them goodbye and, motivated by a curiosity he could not explain, peered from the screened window as they descended the stoop. On the street, the youth pulled a ridiculous checked cap over his eyes and skipped lightly away from his unwieldy mother. The doctor watched him prance away down the cluttered, steaming street, thinking: *The little bastard, the little son-of-a-bitch.* It didn't have to be the same one, the one who rang his bell and called him names. They all looked alike in the dark. Besides, that cop, Kaplan, had told him his name was something else, Jess, or Joss, or something like that. He couldn't keep unimportant information in his mind any longer; there were too many symptoms and lab tests and techniques and diagnoses and prognoses and therapies to remember. Who could remember the name of a *tunkele* galoot? And suppose it was? Should he run him in—call the cops? To hell with all of them, he thought. Let the cops find him.

He plodded through the liquiform heat of the office into the back-yard. Under the cherry tree, Diane licking at his hands, he rested on the rotting slatted bench and reviewed the symptoms: three peculiar convulsions, apparently affecting the right side (if the colored woman's description could be believed), a history of brief headaches in the morning; a possible swelling of the optic disk (or something akin to that), and *maybe* an abnormal gait on the right side of the body. All he could be really sure of was the convulsion and the headache and he hadn't witnessed them. And there was the narcotic usage to be taken into account. Could headache and convulsions be associated with a bad reaction to heroin—or whatever it was that young punk was shooting into his system?

He rose from the sagging seat and walked with short, stiff steps into his cornfield. A breeze fluttered the tassels and he inhaled deeply. He did not cultivate his corn through any *mystique*; he did it to be witness to the process of germination and growth, to participate in the battle against worms and smut, to fertilize the tired earth, to cull the stones, to water the roots, and to pick the fat ears. He liked eating them, too. Like Thoreau, he only wanted the earth to say corn instead of weeds. Half aloud, he said, "Why do the bastards bother me? Why do they come to me all the time?" The pointless protest answered itself. Office hours were ended, but he would be a long time worrying about Herman Quincy's seizures. He allowed himself just a few more minutes in the cornfield, picking two ripe ears for his dinner as he left. There had been an article on intracranial tumors in an AMA *Journal* a few months back. Recalling it, he was impelled to read it at once.

Thrasher reached his home after one in the morning. The combined trip on not one but two commuter lines, from Long Beach to Pennsylvania Station, then from Grand Central to the shores of Connecticut, left him exhausted. The sight of his bedroom window alight, beckoning to him in the country night as he approached his house in a speeding cab (they always made more noise than necessary at night, he was convinced), started the ebb of fatigue from his body. It delighted him so much, it did not occur to him that his wife was still awake.

She was sitting up in bed, her long rectangle of a face with its flawless planes looking distressingly attractive.

"What's the big deal, O'Neill?" he asked. "Something hot on the late, late show?"

They kissed and he ran his hands over her teen-ager's limbs, strong and fuzzed with gold. "Seriously, Ann, baby, since when are you an insomniac? We're not the sleeping pill kind of young moderns. We sleep good because we're creative, remember?"

"Woody, you won't believe it," she said, half tearfully, "but it was that damn redwood table. I worked and slaved over it all afternoon. I said I'd be damned if I'd send it back to the Outdoor Livin' Shop and have them send me another set that I couldn't assemble."

"So? Sounds like you did the right thing."

"Oh, Christ, I worked all day on it! Look at my hands!" Her knuckles were raw and tender; as she turned her hands over he could see the painful white calluses on her palms. "I figured out that the braces had to be shortened—that they weren't a precise fit. So I sawed them down, bolted them in, and—"

"For goodness' sake, baby, what the hell is so disastrous about fixing a redwood table?"

She wailed, "I sawed them too short! The whole damn table shakes like lime jello! It's no good! And I'm no good!"

He put on his dacron shortie pajamas. "Baby, baby, what kind of carrying on is that? So we'll sue the Outdoor Livin' Shop. We'll get a refund." Solicitously, he wiped her eyes with a tissue.

"I don't know," she said, "it's just that I hate to be defeated by a real job, by having to do something myself, with my own damn hands. I want it to be perfect, to come out right. Why shouldn't I be able to assemble a redwood table?"

He plopped into his bed, turning off the lamp between them. She was using the inadequacy approach, he was sure, and he was aware that the guilt lay with him. Ann had deep suspicions (maybe she knew for a fact by now) that he was unfaithful on a fairly regular basis. The whole routine, he felt, was aimed at arousing his sympathy. But, on reflection, he altered his analysis. She had always been terribly concerned with her failures, no matter how small. After an enthusiastic start, she had given up golf because she couldn't improve her putting quickly enough. And the business about *doing* things—hell, Ann wasn't alone. All over Connecticut and Westchester there were wives making little things out of tile and clay, diddling around with ceramics, potsherds, leaf imprints, and filigree work. If not that, they joined organizations to lower, raise, or stabilize the voting age. The worst of it was he couldn't console her. He would have been even worse where the redwood table was concerned; he would either have left it to rot and warp unassembled in the garage, or would have paid his gardener five dollars to put it together, thereby negating the savings she had engineered by taking advantage of Outdoor Livin's end-of-season clearance. He would have lost either way without even a try.

"Well, nuts to the redwood table, Ann," he said comfortingly. "My good friend Dr. Abelman could have shown us how it worked. And if it didn't he would have spit in Outdoor Livin's flagstone eye."

"You sound like he has the answer to everything. Really, Woody, if I didn't know you better, I'd suspect you two of being *simpatico*."

"I could do worse." He slammed the pillow.

"Ben Loomer called twice tonight," she said. "He was trying like mad to locate you. He seemed a little annoyed you didn't leave word where you could be reached."

He jerked up in bed, betraying his concern. "What did Ben have to say?"

"He'd like you in an hour earlier tomorrow. You're all scheduled to meet Mr. Gatling for a progress report on *Americans, U.S.A.*"

Progress report: that was a good Ben Loomer phrase. He liked to deal in *progress reports, evaluations, tables of organizations*, and *co-ordinated plans of attack*. Normally a progress report was not too much to worry about; you went in armed with a few convincing catch phrases; you were terribly enthusiastic; you stressed the originality and attention-getting qualities of your program; and you assured everyone that it could *sell*. But why the meeting at Gatling's diggings? Normally the *G & T* people kept themselves far removed from the actual programming of their radio and television properties—the notable exception had been Brick Higgins, and Thrasher was convinced they had been burned badly in their insistence on using the fat slob. He was sure of two things: Finucane and Loomer had arranged the session, and if there *were* second thoughts on the part of the sponsor regarding *Americans, U.S.A.*, his own associates at Whitechapel had implanted them.

Getting to the office an hour earlier meant missing his usual express to Grand Central. He stood as far as 125th Street, and only got as far as the theater section of the *Times*. Not having read the book review left him with an incomplete feeling.

Loomer was all good cheer and straight talk. Finucane looked bloated and discolored; the alcoholic pouches under his eyes seemed to have a detachable, do-it-yourself quality. They sipped their morning coffee and Loomer explained, as considerately as possible, that Mr. Gatling wanted to know more about *Americans, U.S.A.* After all, it represented a big investment to them. Their radio, magazine, and newspaper campaigns were all set; they had some exciting new products they were introducing. Only their television showcase was lagging. Mr. Gatling wanted to know all about it, something about the first subject, the commercial pattern, the *sell*.

"I've asked Teddy Chilson to come along to this marshmallow roast," Loomer said casually. "The kid is going to function as assistant to the producer, Woody. That means he's your baby."

"I already got a baby," Thrasher protested.

Loomer and Finucane looked blankly at him. They probably knew by now—there were no secrets in their incestuous business— of his carryings-on with Alice Taggart. They were men of excessive morality, and while a little cheating was permissible, you didn't go around making public jokes about it. Thrasher waited for them to speak, and then, understanding their silent shock, he laughed.

"Oh—not that kind of baby! I meant I already hired an assistant to the producer. A kid named Myron Malkin. He's the doctor's nephew, a newspaperman on the *Record*. He can be very helpful on local color, anecdotes, etcetera."

Loomer turned a shade redder, a kind of patio terra-cotta.

"As executive producer, Woody, I think you would have consulted me."

"Who says you're executive producer?" Thrasher asked.

"There was a company memo put out on it late yesterday. If you hadn't run off to Far Rockaway—"

"Long Beach—"

"—for another of these crazy seances, you'd have known. Now it seems to me it's my prerogative to okay everyone assigned. If you insist on Dexter Daw, okay, I know he's talented. But this nephew character—"

Thrasher was a lot less stunned than he should have been. After the *Variety* article it was inevitable that Loomer and Finucane would follow up their attempt to grab the credit for the new program by creating jobs for themselves. They were playing the title game again. Everybody needed an identity, a label, just like a line of drug products. They tossed titles and positions around like an old vaudeville juggler manipulating oranges. Executive producer, producer, associate producer, assistant producer, assistant to the producer, supervisor, supervisor for the network, editor, director, associate director, manager, managing editor, project officer, coordinator, unit manager, business manager—there was no end to it. They dealt in symbols and slogans so much, Thrasher thought, that the designations lost their meaning after a while. Functions became blurred, indistinct, the higher you went. What did the executive

producer do that the producer didn't do? Where draw the line between a supervisor and an associate producer? He knew of one
program where the associate producer's job was to buy live chickens
every morning in the produce market. The comedian who starred
on the program gave six free chickens away to lucky housewives
every afternoon; the associate producer had to keep them fed,
watered, and caged, and clean up after them. Thrasher was envi-
ous of him: now *there* was an associate producer who knew *exactly*
what he was supposed to do and did it. No vagueness of job, no
overlapping with the executive producers and the supervisors.

"I'll make a deal with you, Ben," Thrasher said, "I won't raise
any fuss about Chilson, or about *you*, for that matter, if you'll let me
keep this Malkin kid. We can make both of them assistants to the
producer."

"If you insist, Woody. Hell, you know I'm a reasonable guy. And
I wish you'd stop feeling that I'm working against you. Tom and I
need you, boy. Right, Tommy?"

Finucane gargled, locating what remained of his voice. "You bet
your ass we do! We were tellin' Gatling only yesterday what a solid
citizen you are—how the whole thing was your idea—"

He stopped too quickly, and Loomer looked downward. Of course
they had been huddling with the client, and, of course, any misgivings the client had must have originated with them.

"Now that's funny," Thrasher said. "All through the Brick Higgins
fiasco, Gatling never once met with us. He'd send word through his
hunkers. Even the decision on Higgins came to us in a three-line
memo. Why is he suddenly taking such a personal interest?"

Loomer pulled his square body out from behind his desk. "Skip
it, Woody, you've made your mind up to be unreasonable. Let's go."

Ted Chilson was waiting for them outside the door. The lapels
of his blue cotton cord, almost invisible, were imperfectly ironed;
the roll of his Brooksweave shirt was properly unkempt, and his
dark-red foulard was knotted carelessly. Thrasher was annoyed with
himself for studying the young man so closely; annoyed even more
with the minute perfect symbols of his complete self-assurance, his
complete membership.

Lyman Gatling's office was enormous, severe, and functional
except for little illumined shrines which glowed from glassed-in
recesses in the battleship-gray wall. In each of the glass compartments, couchant on maroon velvet, was one of *G & T*'s numerous
products. A color engineer who commanded a five-figure consulta-

tion fee had been called in to select the proper interior lighting; the ruffles in the velvet beds had been molded by an interior decorator. In one shrine lay a blue-and-gold plastic Whiffo dispenser; in another the familiar rectangular box of Blanch; in another the stern, dark bottle of Vita-life.

"I hate the lousy things," Gatling told Thrasher when he noticed the agency man studying them. "Some pansy decorator sold Van Alst on them, and before I could say no they were having consultations."

He was a man in his sixties, everything about him stout, pendulous, and hairless. His round, bald head hung low over a flabby chest, and each feature of his white face drooped and sagged— the mournful blue eyes, the waxy nose with its tulip-bulb tip, the lower lip falling in a fat pink fold over the cushioned chin. Yet there was nothing flabby about Lyman Gatling's movements, his voice, or his mind. The firm had originally been founded by Parker Theis's parents. Gatling had started as an apprentice chemist under old man Theis, and when the latter had become a bedridden invalid, it soon became apparent that young Parker did not have his father's talents for manufacturing, marketing, and administration. Gatling had never consciously sought the high post he was eventually to get: it had come to him through natural evolution. He was competent and shrewd and possessed an unerring instinct for hiring capable people. Thrasher, looking at the great soft heap, an amorphous blob of white paraffin, wondered how many competitors had been deceived by Lyman Gatling's appearance. The agency man felt a secret little pleasure at meeting someone who, so ugly, misshapen, and asymmetrical, could rise so high and command such vast amounts of money and respect.

"Come to think of it," Gatling said, in his loud clear voice—he had spent many years making himself heard over the din of half a dozen steaming factories—"some of you birds had a hand in those things. Ain't that right, Van Alst?"

D. M. Van Alst, vice-president in charge of sales and advertising, seated at Gatling's right, nodded affirmatively. He had a gray crew cut and a face that succeeded in being roseate and bloodless at the same time. He held a gold automatic pencil in readiness over a memo pad.

Gatling looked indifferently at the four visitors, the alien salesmen, the dealers in words, whom he and his companions of the shop looked to for counsel. "I seem to recall there was a guy like one of you—some thin kid in a narrow suit. He kept talking about making my office a microcosm of the whole. I kept thinking he was saying *hole* and I told him I didn't particularly like our line of laxatives and didn't want their memory perpetuated in my office."

The little speech had unsettled all of them but Thrasher. He was smiling, feeling a growing affection for Lyman Gatling. What their previous encounter with the drug titan had been like, Thrasher could not guess; but it seemed a good bet he had saved a lot of himself for further meetings. He was that kind of a man, Thrasher knew: you were given only a little of him at a time. In reserve were great hoards of strength, wit, and intelligence.

"Mr. Gatling," Loomer began, bending forward and clasping his square hands into a huge red block, "when Tom and I spoke to you, we tried to give you a brief outline of our new show. Now, Woody Thrasher here is producing and writing the project and, frankly, he's been a sort of one-man task force to date. So we asked him up here to answer any questions you might have."

Gatling tugged at the pendulous lower lip until it seemed to drop below his chin. "Hell, I didn't send for him," Gatling said. "You birds came to me. I don't like being dragged into these artistic fights. I'm a chemist. I let Van Alst's bright boys in advertising worry about the programs, and I trust old Whitechapel because I know he's never gone out of his way to cheat anyone."

"Bu-bu-bu-but, Mr. Gatling, what the hell," Finucane spluttered, "you said yourself you wanted to know more about *Americans, U.S.A.* You said yourself right here, last time."

"Did I?"

"I might have misunderstood you, too," Loomer said.

"Oh, hell," the drugmaker said, wobbling the fleshy gourd of a head from side to side, "maybe I did want to know a little more. But one of you birds could have sent me a one-page memo. Would have been as good as a meeting."

It was magnificent, Thrasher thought. The old sloven had probably listened sympathetically to their recital of misgivings about the new TV property on which he was about to spend a million dollars. Gatling didn't know a good show from a bad show, but he could smell a conspiracy a factory block away. Gauging the true purpose of their original audience, he was playing it safe. They were all strangers to him, smart young men who talked well and used graduate school terminology. If the company were being stuck with a bad show (and after Parker Theis's insistence on Brick Higgins he was exceedingly wary of television), he would prefer to find out for himself—not have two birds in narrow suits tell him.

Loomer was smiling. "Fair enough, Mr. Gatling, let's call it a misunderstanding. Now suppose I let Woody take it from here. Go ahead, Woody, it's dealer's choice and you've got the deck."

"Suppose you tell me, Mr. Gatling," Thrasher began innocently. "What's *your* impression of the show?"

The drug manufacturer looked surprised. In his dealings with advertising men, public relations experts, publicists, and press agents, he was rarely asked anything. They usually were making presentations, throwing posters under his nose, reading from leather-bound folders.

"All I know is it's a half hour of expensive network time."

"You know more than that, Mr. Gatling," Thrasher said softly, pleased with the sinister-friendly note he managed to get into his voice.

Gatling spun about, showing a profile that was less a face than a series of pasty lumps. One sad eye stayed with Thrasher.

"What did you say your name was?" he asked.

"Woodrow Thrasher, and what's the difference? You no more care what my name is than you would if I were a hundredweight of potassium permanganate. You've seen plenty of smart kids like me, Mr. Gatling, and I'm sure you've looked at enough incoming shipments of potassium permanganate."

What might have been a smile sought unsuccessfully to invert the downward droop of the executive's lips. "I know what your buddies told me, and I got a report from Van Alst here. He read some of that stuff from that little grass-covered booklet with the faces on the cover."

"How much do you remember?"

"Something about real people doing real things. It sounded kind of dull, if you ask me. But hell, I'm a chemist. You birds are the experts. The way I get it, we stay with this one character—for a half hour and get his life story. You think this can sell Whiffo?"

"It depends on how it's done," Thrasher said quickly.

"And I assure you, Mr. Gatling, Whitechapel plans to do this right. That's why we're insisting on Andrew Bain Lord," Loomer said firmly.

"Always liked Andy Lord," Gatling said. "The wife and I wouldn't miss him. That man is a goddam genius, pure and simple."

Thrasher shivered at the thought of Andrew Bain Lord, the great Potemkin Village of American Journalism, a brainless wretch with a handsome hewn-rock face, a white crew cut, and the holy tones of a Baptist circuit rider. Every evening Lord assaulted the radio with what was advertised as a newscast, a bathetic conglomeration of neutral information, written by a ghost in a cozy conversational style, and delivered with the histrionic skill of a summer stock heavy. The bedrock ignorance of Andrew Bain Lord was common knowledge in the industry, so much so that his ghost writer, a stunted drunkard who had once edited the *Discoverist Review,* was an equally appreciated character in network circles. And yet a shrewd and capable man like Lyman Gatling could listen to Andrew Bain Lord's mellifluous nonsense and acclaim him a genius: it was the miracle of the word again.

"I'll take your word, gents, that this is a good idea," Gatling resumed, "and I'm sold on Andy Lord. His name alone should get people to look. But I'm concerned over the first show. I seem to remember, Loomer, you were the one who raised the doubts. Mind repeating them? You birds phrase stuff so much better than me."

He was doing all right, Thrasher thought. Getting Loomer to articulate his objections was his way of putting the problem back in their camp.

"All I said was that this doctor, this Abelman chap, whoever he is, may not be sufficiently—well, dramatic, or upbeat, for an opening show. I warned Mr. Gatling that there was a kind of depressing air about the neighborhood, about the doctor himself. We like to stress success, achievement. But I seemed to gather this doctor is just a kind of—well—stick-in-the-mud sort."

"That's because you don't know him," Thrasher said.

"If I don't—if none of us do—it's your fault. Keeping us all in the dark. Doing all the work yourself."

Loomer sounded petulant. Van Alst made a quick notation in his little book.

Thrasher shifted unhappily. "Okay, Ben. I'll give you daily reports if you want 'em." Then, brightly, he added, "Say, why don't you and Tom and Teddy—and even you, Mr. Gatling—come out to Brooklyn with me for my next session? It's only a short ride—"

Loomer was shaking his head and Thrasher congratulated himself. They wanted to be filled in, to get the reports, to be in the know: but the actual doing represented too much of a risk. You couldn't be blamed for anything if you were sufficiently ignorant.

"I think Ted should go along with you," Loomer said, "but Tom and I are too busy, and I'm sure Mr. Gatling can't be bothered."

Slumped deep in his seat, the drugmaker was studying them in mournful boredom. "Say, Thrasher," he said loudly, "what is there so special about this old pill-roller? I've known as many doctors as any man alive and, hell, they're the damndest bunch of stuffed shirts and woodenheads I've ever seen. What's this guy's name, Abelman?"

"Mr. Gatling," Thrasher said. "Dr. Abelman is a person leading a valuable, useful life. How many of us, particularly in our field, can say the same? Every act he does is worthwhile. And what makes it more amazing is that he's a man who's had innumerable setbacks and frustrations."

"Does that make him interesting to a big audience? The people who buy my drugs?"

"I suspect it will. We're subjected to drones, talkers, scroungers, and confidence men so much these days that a little fresh air might get people interested. A big industry like yours could do a lot worse than take the lead in improving the public taste and attitudes."

It was a wrong move, Thrasher knew, as soon as he saw the slumping figure struggle forward, the moist fat fingers fall to the green blotter.

"Back up a minute, Thrasher," he said, and he sounded like the old head of the refining department about to eat out a careless technician. "I didn't like that crack about drones and confidence men. Because if there are any drones in industry, it's you birds who have let 'em in. What do I have to apologize about? What does any American industrialist have to apologize for? Standard of living? The money we pay out? The way we support the government, the army, and everything else? You talk about useful and valuable lives—what's more useful than what we do, turning out good services for one hundred and sixty million people and doing it goddam well?"

"I didn't quite mean that—"

"Balls. Let me finish. You meant it, all you smart college boys in short-changed lapels and tight pants. You're always telling us what to do, what to say, who to be nice to. You know why? Because you got us scared. You like the color of our money, so you keep us scared stiff. I had some smart young son-of-a-bitch like you sign my name to an article for the *Saturday Evening Post* in support of GATT. I don't know what GATT is. I might have liked it if the kid bothered to tell me, but there it was "GATT Helps You" by Lyman Gatling. Is that supposed to make people love us? Like hell. They'll love us if we keep up the double time and triple time and make good products. And I don't like apologizing for what I do for a living."

He paused to gulp air into his soggy chest, and, surprisingly, it was Loomer who took up the challenge.

"I think I know what you're objecting to, Mr. Gatling," he said sincerely, "we at Whitechapel have never been too heavy on this so-called prestige approach. We don't do any public relations at all. Our feeling is that advertising is purely and simply an extension of a company's own sales program. We want to sell, not create any of these alleged favorable atmospheres."

Gatling seemed not to have heard him. "Drones and confidence men, eh, Thrasher?" he continued. "Where? Down in our lab? Our factories? Our shipping and receiving departments? It's you birds—you guys with the quick words and the presentations—who screw everything up. You keep telling us how rotten we are with all our money and how we have to make people think we're really nice. Well, I don't care if everybody thinks I'm a louse, just so long as they order Whiffo by the case and drink their Vita-life every morning."

"I don't see how you can separate the two," Thrasher ventured.

"Maybe you can't. And maybe all I'm objecting to is an attitude. Sure, we got our own salesmen, our own ad guys. We need 'em. We need 'em so badly we hire smart kids out of college as engineers at four thousand a year and if they're *real* smart they can make fifteen thousand as salesmen after a few years. The dopes remain engineers. But don't you or any of you other guys in tight pants drone-and-confidence me."

Loomer got up and took a little tour of the glowing velvet shrines, the artfully illumined crèches, dedicated to proper bowel movements, deodorizing, and polished white teeth. He was pounding one fist into another.

"I'm sorry this discussion has taken this turn, Mr. Gatling. Woody is one of these creative lads"—he laughed unconvincingly—"and he uses words he doesn't mean every so often. The only reason we came here was to get your reading on *Americans, U.S.A.* I hope you've been told enough."

The icy air-conditioner, humming faintly, did nothing for Mr. Gatling's dewlapped face—it exuded a hundred little streams of perspiration. He didn't mind the heat or the sweat. He could remember working in plants where it never went below one hundred, where the heat would soften windows and buckle cast-iron beams.

"That first show better be good. It better get people to look and it better sell Whiffo. Or screw Whitechapel." He might have been telling a wholesaler of oil of vitriol that his last shipment contained three broken carboys; one more like that and they'd lose the order.

"I'll take responsibility for that," Thrasher said quickly. Then, motivated by some wild need to change the direction of the discussion, to throw some new provocation at the drug manufacturer and his own colleagues, he added, "There's one thing you should know now about the costs for the first show, Mr. Gatling."

Loomer, Finucane, and Chilson were stunned. You didn't annoy the number one man of a giant company with details of a show budget. There were vice-presidents who worried about that. That's what Van Alst was on hand for.

"Part of the costs," Thrasher said firmly, "will be an eight-thousand-dollar fee for Dr. Abelman to help him buy a new house."

"What the hell does that have to do with me?" Gatling roared. "Am I running a charity? I know a little about what television talent costs, and for eight thousand bucks I don't want some broken-down sawbones."

"When did you decide on this, Woody?" Loomer asked. He was horrified.

"Yeah—I saw the budget that our unit manager drew up. There was no entry for a fee. Not on a public service show. It's—it's—like paying Bishop Sheen!" Finucane exploded.

"I just thought I'd let you all know at the start," Thrasher said innocently. "It's one of the conditions."

"Okay," Loomer said malevolently. "We can argue that later. Mr. Gatling, is there anything else you want to know?" Thrasher could see the boiling rage beneath Loomer's slow, calm voice. The pointless gambit about the eight thousand dollars had infuriated him, as only a slow-moving and logical man can be infuriated.

Gatling dismissed them without bothering to shake hands or thank them. He again mentioned Andrew Bain Lord as a *must* for the program. Proving he was not as ignorant or contemptuous of publicity as he had led them to believe, he advised Loomer to begin an intense campaign on the program. He cared less about the content of the show, it seemed, than the ways it could be promoted, tied in with the trade name, popularized in every corner drugstore in the country. Apparently his bitterness over drones and confidence men had in no wise affected his understanding of their value. As they departed, he was squinting at Van Alst's notes.

Returning to their office in a cab, the agency group was silent, Loomer nursing his private fury over Thrasher's behavior. If they were to lose the *G & T* account, he would be in very bad shape. A single poor show could be blamed on Thrasher and he could be sacrificed. But when a big account went—

Ted Chilson spoke first.

"Say, Woody, something that bothers me about that money to

help the doctor buy a house—" The china-blue eyes were utterly innocent: the president of student board asking the dean for a later curfew on prom night. No one looked at the young man, but, undismayed, he continued.

"If we pay the doctor, give him that money to get a new house, aren't we really negating the purpose of the show? I mean, his very integrity, as I get it, his complete honesty. Don't we destroy this whole atmosphere if we pay him? And especially so much money?"

"You're damn right we do," Loomer said darkly. "And I personally will make sure there's no such payment."

It was not until late that afternoon, meeting over iced tea with Dexter Daw and Alice Taggart, that it occurred to him that Ted Chilson's arguments against paying Dr. Abelman were identical with those he had voiced to Myron Malkin. There probably was a good deal of truth in them, too. If the story leaked to the trade that G & T, a drug firm, had paid a physician, it wouldn't look good for the donor or the receiver. But neither the unfavorable publicity nor the questionable morality of the transaction disturbed Thrasher. His mission now had assumed a double goal. He had to prove to his enemies (where had they all come from so quickly and where did they find their courage?) that *Americans, U.S.A.* would succeed simply because he was a better man than the lot of them. Beyond that, he wanted to be present on the bright morning when Samuel Abelman moved into the big house on Republic Street.

Dexter Daw had invited them to his home in Rockland County, and, wheeling his unwashed Dodge station wagon through Harlem toward the George Washington Bridge, Thrasher found nothing but displeasure in the project. His gloom, of course, had been born of the uncomfortable meeting with Lyman Gatling and Loomer's unconcealed rage that followed. The Saturday at home had done nothing to palliate his unhappiness. He had tried writing, drawing up an outline for the program, and had been distressed to find it was no easy task. The last dramatic scripts he had done were for a soap, on a free-lance basis, some seven years ago. The words did not come easily, they never seemed to say precisely what he envisioned so clearly in his mind. And the need to work in Andrew Bain Lord as narrator and guide impeded him simply because of his distaste for the commentator whom Gatling regarded as a genius. In the quiet basement study, cool and dark, Ann had beautifully accessorized his desk with the anal impedimenta of the writer— the beer mug of needle-sharp pencils, the neat stacks of onionskin and carbon, the scratch pads, erasers, calender, manila folders, and a mammoth ash tray. The very richness of his equipment embarrassed him; by early afternoon he had produced only a carpet of crumpled white sheets and a single page of notations. When his son pleaded that he accompany him to the Little League game, he agreed, even though baseball bored him. Woody Junior played right field, a position which Thrasher knew was the prize of the poorest regular. But at least he didn't sit on the bench, and while his team was badly beaten, young Woody caught a pop fly, walked twice, and scored a run. In a negative way, he had acquitted himself without being the goat. Thrasher found himself thankful that the kid had not committed some horrible, crucial error: he had sweated miserably through the seven interminable innings and was as happy as the winning pitcher when the last out was made.

Dressing for the evening, he had gotten into a pointless argument with Ann. She had accepted the invitation from Daw's wife, and Thrasher felt she might have fabricated an excuse.

"I see enough of Dexter Daw all week," he complained childishly, "and do you realize it's a two-hour drive from Stamford to Blauvelt or Grandview or whatever the name of that place is they live in?"

She only half heard him. She was pulling a new summer dress over her head, something severe and smart and bright green, with immense black circles. The sight of her headless form—only the lower part of the postage-stamp girdle, the lovely silken legs, and spiked emerald shoes were visible—aroused him. A spark of adolescent passion flickered, and while she struggled with the dress, he pinched her tanned thigh just above the stocking.

"That's the first cheerful thing you've done today," she said. Ann was always at her best before a party. The clean hard face, with minimal make-up, glowed; the close-cropped hair smelled of some honest perfume; her dress had an original, startling quality. A few harmless passes would be made at her, she would get reasonably drunk, and would get the best of at least one egghead in some kind of aesthetic argument.

"Isn't it disgusting the way a pair of detachable garters and high heels can change a man's outlook?" he said. He slipped to his knees, embracing her legs.

"Enough," she said, stroking his head. "Save it for later."

"I won't be fit for anything after that two-hour haul through the Eastern Seaboard. Why must Dexter Daw live in Rockland County?"

"Stop being negative," she said firmly, pulling away from him and straightening out her skirt. She began installing a series of immense Mexican bracelets on her lean brown arm. "And please do me a favor and forget all about *Americans, U.S.A.* and Ben Loomer and Dr. Abelman tonight. Get good and drunk. Get into an argument. But don't talk shop, please, Woody."

Crossing the George Washington Bridge, he found himself lecturing Ann on the folklore of suburbia. For some irrational reason, he was annoyed with Daw for choosing Rockland County, with its conscious rusticity and artiness, over conventional Westchester and upper-bracket Fairfield County. Moreover, he found himself sticking up manfully for Long Island. When he and Ann had first gone house hunting, having had their fill of drafty brownstones, he had seen any number of magnificent development-type split levels in Nassau County. They were huge, solidly built homes; room after room with immense closets, well-appointed bathrooms, dens, basements, and cavernous garages. For $22,500 he could have bought such a home—a model that could not have been duplicated in Connecticut or Westchester for $40,000. But Ann and his friends at the agency had dissuaded him. Nobody but stationery salesmen and dentists lived in Nassau, they warned him. There were copywriters earning half his salary who were *building* in Rye and Westport; on the vice-presidential level he had no right to get his money's worth on a mass-produced split-level. Often, Thrasher thought of the stocks he might have bought, the mutual fund he could have started with the cash he would have saved with the Long Island house. But it was out of the question. He wondered how all these small-town boys and girls, the seminarians of talker society, *knew* instinctively where to live. Did the Dexter Daws go to some clearinghouse where they were advised *not* to live on Long Island, *not* to live on the West Side, *not* to drive Dodges and Plymouths, but to acquire MG's or at least Hillmans? Who made the rules? He had seen youngsters fresh from Davenport, Iowa, or Billings, Montana, arrive in New York, and, with the innate motivation of army ants, make all the right moves. It was the native New Yorkers—the few he knew in the business—who violated the rules, who purchased development homes in Roslyn, drove large, utilitarian American cars, and bought their suits in Rogers Peet or Browning King.

With cruel delight, he retold an incident at the office last week when Dexter Daw—who made a point of introducing himself to any reasonably attractive woman—had begun a casual conversation with Lucille LoPresti, the assistant commercial co-ordinator. Lucille was a formidable Neapolitan beauty with aggressive breasts and a fine black mustache. She was loud, funny, and virginal, but Dexter Daw saw nothing to lose in some exploratory small talk. He had announced, with casual pride(after depicting himself as a key man at the network who might do things for her) that he lived in Rockland County.

"Whereabouts?" Lucille LoPresti asked.

"A charming little town called Piermont," Daw said airily. "It's really quite unspoiled. You know—none of this Madison Avenue pretense."

Lucille laughed a hearty Parkchester guffaw. "Piermont! Oh, dear, of all the places—Piermont!"

"What's so funny?" Daw had asked.

"Piermont," Lucille said flatly, "is where my father drinks beer with Vinnie Rotunda on Saturday nights!"

Daw had been properly crushed: the vision of Rockland County, the rustic, unaffected country place where artists and writers mingled in an atmosphere of honest stimulation, was annihilated. Instead, Lucille had put Piermont in proper perspective—a nest of cramped Italian homes and dreary saloons where Nick LoPresti and Vinnie Rotunda drank beer.

Daw's house was a mongrelized accumulation of dirty white revolutionary war walls, a feverish tile roof out of the twenties, and a yellow stucco wing, flaking and discolored. It squatted, surly and inhospitable, on an irregular mountainous plot, overgrown with crab grass and an ungroomed grape arbor. The guests seemed to have no center of gravity: the house had no true living room, and at least three crumbling patios. People drifted in the riverbank heat, from faded deck chair to peeling Adirondack bench, from the cluttered den where Daw purported to work, to the not-so-early American parlor, a patch of sloping boards built around a rock quarry fireplace.

"Not an appliance jobber in the lot," Thrasher muttered as they parked the station wagon on a precarious slant, an asphalt goat path, already jammed with MG's and other deformed foreign cars.

Most of the guests were from the outer fringes of talkerdom: a jolly couple who worked for the AP and came from Hastings, Nebraska; a junior copywriter at a major agency who had written an excellent first novel about life in his home town, Orono, Maine; an assistant professor of English at Columbia's School of General Studies, who told charming anecdotes about his "kinfolk" in Tulla-homa, Tennessee; and a middle-aged lady photographer who had lived on the same block with Freud.

Thrasher realized that Daw was paying him a sincere compliment by inviting him. These were creative people, *bright creative* people, as opposed to stodgy clods like himself (and Daw for that matter) who had sold out. Trudging up the impossible hill to Daw's checkered lawn, he resigned himself to getting drunk, aware that he would reap only a headache and a fit of yawning from Daw's cheap gin. They would run out of tonic and ice in a few hours, he was certain, and he would end up desperately sipping gin and lukewarm club soda.

He stopped short, halfway up the ascent, childishly terrified by the tableau on Daw's gingerbread porch. The youthful director, quite drunk and talkative, was sitting in between his wife and Alice Taggart, bobbing and weaving his fetal head like the moderator of a panel show warming up two recalcitrant guests. Daw's wife was a head taller than her husband. She was a perpetually morbid young woman, all bones and lank black hair, who had left Provo, Utah, for a modeling career. Of the trio, she alone seemed miserable; Alice seemed unusually gay. Thrasher felt a spreading numbness in his abdomen; there was no doubt Daw had invited her deliberately, another of his characteristic gestures. And there was no doubt that Alice looked marvelous—crisp and fresh in a pink button-down shirtwaist, the skirt billowing over crinoline. Enough of her thin legs was exposed so that any normal male would want to plunge both arms under the clouds of petticoats and explore the rest of her.

Daw staggered from the creaky porch hammock on which he was conducting his seminar and greeted the Thrashers effusively.

"Hi there, kids! Miz Thrasher, it's a pleasure . . . you coming all the way from Connecticut. We were taking bets old Woody couldn't bear to leave the flagstone patio district, but I see you convinced him the slumming would do his soul good."

Ann smiled pleasantly. "It wasn't a bad trip. And I've heard so much about Rockland County, I really was anxious to come. Your house is charming."

Mrs. Daw untangled a pair of stork's legs and stood up. "I'm Mary Jo Daw, Mrs. Th—"

"Ann. Hi."

"Hi."

"I'm Alice Taggart. Hi."

Thrasher shuddered faintly, noting at the same time that of the three nasally intoned "Hi's"—the official Eastern Seaboard greeting of the upper five percent income bracket—only Ann's had a true ring. They were all spurious, of course, but his wife *had* been in summer stock. She'd "Hi" them to death, those two yokels.

"Yep," Daw said, "li'l ole nymphomaniacal Alice. Alice works for the network and she's aiding and abetting ole Woodrow Wilson and young Dexter Daw on our doctor project."

"Oh—gee—it's a real *Americans, U.S.A.* party!" Ann said brightly. "What do you do, Alice?"

Daw ground a fragment of an ice cube in his teeth, and before. Alice could answer, he fairly shouted, "Know that old song, Ann— 'What she won't do her sister will'? Well, Alice here is the sister they wrote that about!"

Mary Jo Daw sank back, a collapsed contour chair, all aluminum tubing and saran webbing. Watching Alice's bony, self-controlled face, Thrasher had to hand it to her. Daw's disgusting rudeness had cut deep, yet she would not give him the satisfaction of a slap, or even a mild rejoinder. Instead, she turned to Ann and offered a harmless little lie.

"I'm delighted to meet you, Ann, really. Woody talks about you all the time."

They would be buddies to the end: soon Ann was sitting next to her in an unraveling wicker chair. She was asking Alice Taggart precisely what she did at the network, what an A.D.'s functions were, advising her how jealous she was of those lucky girls who had stuck to creative careers instead of vegetating as den mothers and PTA cake sale chairmen. Thrasher located the English professor and listened to a prepared text on the evils of television. He had hoped that the opening gambit would have varied, but the young man from Tullahoma was no different from the WQXR listeners he met at North Stamford parties.

"Television has great potential," the professor began, "but, really, when are you guys going to grow up?"

"You don't like it, turn it off," Thrasher said. "No one holds a gun to your head and makes you watch."

From there, Thrasher advanced his usual arguments: all the good stuff on television, the relative percentages of bad plays, bad books, and bad movies; the original writing and directing TV was creating; the possibilities of educational TV. Thrasher found these conversations like sports interviews or Greek tragedies—the laws were rigid, the sequence of dialogue predetermined. They always terminated in mutual agreement that television had a great future.

Returning to the front porch with a cracked tumbler of Macy's gin and soda, he paused, fascinated by the startling similarity of his wife and the girl he had been sleeping with.

Their blond, cropped heads were nodding at each other animatedly; two trim, sharply outlined faces, strong white teeth. Even the precise gestures of arms and hands were alike. He could hear his own name being kicked around, and he knew that there was a little too much enthusiasm in their voices, a little too much eagerness in their desire to be pals to hope that Ann hadn't gauged Alice Taggart's relationship with her husband properly.

He sat opposite them on a splintering porch rail, trying to be aloof and neutral. The gin, oddly enough, had calmed his nerves and he felt equal to the delicate balance.

"Topic of discussion number one," said Alice, laughing. "We're giving you the works, Woody."

"Alice seems to feel, dear, that this new job you've tackled is changing you. I told her I've noticed it too. It's like—well—as if you were a prize-winning playwright trying to outdo himself. It's not just that you're tense—"

"—we're past tense, we're living in bungalows now," he said lightly.

"That's from *Animal Crackers*," Alice cried. "And right after that they sing 'Abie the fishman.'"

She was the kind who went to Marx Brothers pictures at the Museum of Modern Art. As a kid back in Ontario, California, she never saw anything funny about Groucho. Today, she could recite whole scenes from *Coconuts*.

"Seriously," Ann persisted, "we both said how tense you've been lately, but we also feel—and tell me if I'm wrong, Alice—that you seem to be in a kind of, well, rebellion. You're negative. You don't like anyone or anything, really. And you don't get enthusiastic over things the way you used to."

Alice was nodding her head affirmatively. "You're like the fellows in those novels that are going to expose the advertising business. Nobody's any good but yourself after a while, and everything is rotten. He isn't really that way is he, Ann?"

"Hell no," said Ann. She was having her share of Dexter Daw's gin, ice or no ice, and the PTA in her was losing out. "Woody, I've heard you argue about all the good your business does—and I know you believe it. You know, about spreading goods and services, creating more jobs, and putting more money and products in circulation."

"And raising the standard of living," Alice said quickly.

"Girls, girls, for Christ's sake," Thrasher interrupted. "This sounds like Economics 1-2, Monday, Wednesday, and Friday at 9 A.M. three points, in the freshman curriculum at South Dakota State. Does anybody know any good dirty jokes for a change?"

"Oh, Hattie Loomer told me this one!" Ann said, with a faint hysterical start. It occurred to Thrasher she had been forcing herself into a state of strained gaiety with his mistress, and that the chance for a risqué story offered a handy release.

"This boss and his secretary—they were on the twentieth story of this building where his office was, and she said, 'I think I'm going to have a baby and I'm going to throw myself out the window.' So he patted her knee and said, 'That's a good girl.'"

"It's an old story, dear," Thrasher said. "I heard it about a movie producer and a starlet in an airplane."

"I'm terribly sorry," Alice said, "I'm not sure I get it."

Dexter Daw, a pitcher of water in his pink hand, fell into their circle. "She was knocked up, Alice, get it? And the boss knocked her up, so he was very happy she was going to commit suicide? Catch? You know girls get knocked up sometimes. You know the one about the pregnant lady and the lion cage?"

Their silence bleakly informed Dexter Daw that nobody appreciated his program notes. Ann suddenly found it mandatory to wash her hands; Thrasher discovered he hadn't touched all the bases in his dialogue with the English professor. Departing, he heard Daw mumbling to Alice, "It's cool in the root cellar, Taggart," he said huskily, "let's you 'n' me go looking for rutabagas."

The long ride home has scarcely begun when Thrasher heard his wife weeping. Her crying was not the kind he would have expected of her; it came in thin, almost inaudible squeaks, the tears trickling neatly down her flat cheeks in cadence with each high-pitched sniffle.

"How is she?" Ann asked. "Real good in bed?"

He sped desperately by the sordid New Jersey landscape of used-car lots and hot-dog stands. The gin was leaving a sour, raw feeling in the pit of his stomach. The first pinching pain of a headache was creeping up his right temple.

"If you insist, dear, she's not bad at all. Okay, you know. I slept with her. So did Dexter Daw and so did four or five other people. Shall I say I'm sorry? That won't help. Should I get on one knee and ask forgiveness? For Christ's sake, Ann, these things happen. There's more of this going on than *any* wife likes to admit."

"She looks like me," Ann said dully.

"She does, as a matter of fact," he said. "Enough to be a sister. I often wondered why she attracted me because of that. When a man cheats he usually looks for a different dish. Guys with washboard-thin wives usually go for the big, fat type. But me, I'm original."

"You're not making me feel any better," she wailed.

"Ah, come on, Ann, cut it out. You've suspected me a long time, and now you know. We don't suddenly drop dead, or get a divorce or get analyzed. It happened, it's over, we're still married."

"Was she the only one?"

"Yes, she was the only one." At this stage, he felt, a small lie would'nt be of any harm. And, actually, she was the only one as of *that moment*. Moreover, it had been a week since he had slept with Alice.

"And let me tell you a few things about marital infidelity," Thrasher said wearily. "It ain't nearly the fun you'd think it would be. It's all anticipation, daydreaming, desire at your desk in midafternoon. You're in, you're it, you're out."

"Maybe that's the way you feel about marriage too."

"No, there's never that much anticipation connected with marriage."

"Oh, this is the living end!" she cried, sufficently exasperated with him so that her tears ceased. "Is this a recent Thrasher platitude? Was this how you felt twelve years ago?"

"It's pretty recent. I've come to the conclusion everything we do is compromise. Marriage, particularly. There are no more big risks, big thrills, big loves, and big hates. Everything is sort of medium. And you shouldn't expect a marriage to be the be-all and end-all. If it's got flaws, so has everything else."

"Well, I hope ours isn't anything *but* flaws."

He was so incredibly exhausted that he had to keep shifting the position of his arms and hands on the wheel to prevent cramps from developing. The back of his neck and upper spine felt as if someone had worked over it with a hoe handle. He had enjoyed the thought of his wife's thin legs, the high green heels, the ridiculous elastic girdle. It had made the overland trek to the other side of the Hudson seem almost bearable because of the prize at evening's end. But he knew he'd never make it. It would be seconal and out for him.

"Woods, let's pull the big switch on suburbia tomorrow," she said eagerly, patting his knee. "We'll go to New York and drink double martinis at Camillo's and then take in a foreign movie. And maybe for old time's sake we'll drop in at Tim's for a nightcap with some of your friends."

"I'm sorry, honey, I have to go to Brooklyn again. Daw and I have some work to finish up with the doctor." By including Daw he had hoped to remove some of the burden of guilt for neglecting his family.

"I'm beginning to hate him. Your hero."

"Not quite, dear. My interest in Samuel Abelman is strictly business. I've committed myself to doing a successful show with him. If I flop, there's a good chance we'll be back in a brownstone walkup. For your peace of mind, I don't think I can lose everything.

I'm high enough up now so that the conspiracy will protect me."

"What conspiracy?"

"The one that says the high-up fellows have to be protected. If one flops, you find him another job. Makes it look bad for all the other high-up fellows. If you let enough of us prove publicly that we are fools and knaves, it's 'The Emperor's New Clothes' all over again."

"You don't act as though it's purely business." She sounded suspicious, keenly aware of some startling alteration in her husband—a change which this obscure, profane physician was working on him in some cabalistic fashion. "Why are you so set on buying him a house? Why is that so important to you?"

He slowed down briefly before approaching a hairpin curve, and then, recalling some advice from a friendly disc jockey who dabbled in sports cars, he accelerated on the turn itself, delighted to discover that the Dodge held the road nicely.

"Because the bastards won't let him live," he snapped "And they're starting on me now."

VI

HERMAN QUINCY had returned on Sunday for a series of head X-rays. He seemed less surly than on his previous visit, but whether it was through a realization of the seriousness of his illness and his need for the doctor, or simple street-corner indifference, the physician could not say. The doctor took four roentgenograms of the small bronze head—two lateral views, an antero-posterior and a postero-anterior. Turning and bending the boy's brown poll, studying the black indifferent eyes, the pneumatic lips, he wondered if this seventeen-year-old could really be so bad. It seemed impossible. *His* patients weren't galoots. Okay, the kid took dope, and he'd go to work on that as soon as he had figured out the current symptoms. Maybe he had dumped the girl on his doorstep and maybe not; maybe he and his chums had beaten up the old man in the park and the night watchman at the project. It wasn't his business to find out. Let the cops, that social worker Kaplan, worry about it.

Dismissing Herman and his mother with another warning to let him know the instant the boy showed symptoms of convulsions, he studied the moist plates on his illuminator. He knew what the neurologists said: standard roentgenograms rarely imparted information on intracranial tumors. But he had sometimes found that the tendency of specialists to minimize basic diagnostic methods was simply due to their unfamiliarity with them. They knew all about the fancy stuff, the ventriculograms and the pneumoencephalograms, but they ran like thieves when you showed them a simple plate and asked them to read it.

In late afternoon he was studying the pictures a second time. With him was another general practitioner, a doctor with whom he had graduated from Bellevue more than forty years ago, and whose office was located a few blocks away. He was a man a year or two younger than Dr. Abelman, with the ruddy glow of hypertension in his cheeks. The men were alike in many ways, yet the essential difference between the two might have divined from a study of the shirts they were wearing. Dr. Abelman's was a cheap blue sport shirt. The floppy, elongated collar had never been meant for union with a tie. Yet the doctor had, with casual contempt for high fashion, knotted a stained dark-brown four-in-hand around his

182

neck, and the ensuing disaster was evident in the ripples, folds, and asymmetry of collar, tie, and shirt front.

Max Vogel, M.D., on the other hand, cool and neat in the humid office, wore an imported Swiss voile job, the trim collar designed for tieless or dress wear. Its secret little slots held firm plastic stiffeners. A sky-blue tie of light silk was knotted artfully over the hidden button. Max Vogel could, after donning his navy silk mohair jacket, have walked into 21 and outbluffed the headwaiter.

"What do you see, Maxie?" Dr. Abelman asked. "You're a smart GP, let's see how much you know."

Vogel flipped a pair of gold-rimmed glasses onto his mushroom cap of a nose. He dressed like a dandy and drove a two-tone Mercury hard-top, but there was nothing of the fop in Max Vogel's attitudes or manner of speech. He spat his words out of the corner of a poolroom mouth—glib, articulate, self-assured.

"It looks to me like clap."

"Cut it out, Maxie," Dr. Abelman said. He chuckled, did a little dance step, and slapped his thigh. It was clear that in Dr. Abelman's eyes the world had never seen the equal of Max Vogel's wit. "Give me it straight, Maxie, what's he got?"

"Gimme some history. Who am I, Harlow Brooks?"

"Seventeen years old, Negro male. History of three convulsions, poorly described, maybe affecting the right side. Mother seems to recall fingers and hand started the seizure. Subject reports recent brief, morning headaches. No nausea. Papilledema, maybe."

Vogel squinted at a right lateral view. "You pessimistic bastard," he said, "I know what you're thinking already. How about weakness and paralysis in the limbs?"

"Not really. I hand wrestled the kid on the desk and he was as weak as a kitten in the right arm."

Max Vogel dabbed at his moist forehead with a spotless linen handkerchief. "What the hell is wrong with you, Sam? Are you still a goddam gymnasium teacher? No wonder you lose patients. If you ever got a coronary, you'd probably try running around the block a few times."

"I did it mostly to win the kid over."

"Will you do me a favor and stop winning patients over? You get personally involved with all these *shmucks*. Patients are slobs. You got to scare 'em, keep 'em scared, and bulldoze 'em. Don't make friends with a patient, ever. Don't even let him think you really care about him. Ah, you'll never learn, will you, Sammy?"

"What do you want me to do?" Dr. Abelman removed the lateral view from the illuminator and placed the frontal plate on it. The two of them peered at it, searching the deceptive shadows and lines for some clue. "He's a kid, seventeen."

"What did any boogie ever do for you?" Vogel sneered.

Dr. Abelman shrugged, defensively embarrassed. "Oh, I know, I complain about them a lot. But they got a right to live."

"Not by sucking my blood," Vogel said. "Better *yours*."

"What do you make of these shadows over here?"

He had placed the second lateral view on the illuminated box now, and they were both studying it intensely.

"It might be convolutional atrophy," Vogel said quickly.

"Yeh," Abelman said quietly, "digital impressions. It's supposed to be like sticking your fingers in clay. Have you ever seen any before?"

"A few. It's not necessarily typical. You get this when the intra-cranial tension has existed a fairly long time. Of course, this kid has a history of three convulsions and doesn't know how long he's been getting headaches."

Dr. Abelman stared at the plate as if he hoped that the toothy egg-shaped skull would come to life and supply him with the answers he needed. A single bead of sweat rolled down his strain-ing forehead, down the arched slope of his nose and dropped to the dark-brown tie. There did indeed seem to be an uneven absorp-tion of the inner table of the cranium; the absorbed areas ap-peared to be separated by faint ridges, little dark semicircles like the imprints of a child's fingers.

He was hoping that Max Vogel would make a quick, expert diagnosis, something in keeping with Max's own sure approach to the problems of life. But Dr. Vogel was too good a clinician to commit himself to a fast decision based solely on the deceptive shadows on the electric box. Dr. Abelman understood this, too. He rarely called in other doctors to aid him in reaching a judg-ment: but Max was somebody special. Max, for all his crudeness, his cake-eater clothes, and his wiseacre answers, was a superb medical man.

"I'll tell you a little secret about convolutional atrophy," Vogel said. "It doesn't mean a damn thing if there are no other manifesta-tions. I've seen it in normal children and adults also."

"You can't discount it, Maxie."

"No, but don't go basing a diagnosis on it. What else are you looking for, Sammy?"

Dr. Abelman squinted belligerently at the X-ray. "Calcification, only I don't see any." He placed the postero-anterior plate on the box.

"If you find any, write me a letter. I'll tell you something else, Sam. Calcification doesn't prove anything either. It happens in normal craniums where there's no trace of a neoplasm."

The host physician flicked off the illuminator and opened the office door. "Why is it, Maxie, that the professors always tell us to look for certain things, and when we find 'em, they warn us it's not necessarily the real thing?"

"That's why they're professors and we're *shnooks*."

Jannine loomed in the doorway. "Dem two men fum de television is here. Dey in deh yard wif deh rest."

"Oh, those two!" Dr. Abelman said. "Hey, Maxie, those two guys who are making a Boris Thomashefsky out of me are here. C'mon, you gotta meet them. You'll like them, two nice *goyim*. You, with the Broadway plays and the operas—you'll get along fine with them!"

He led his old classmate through the cool hallway, the narrow kitchen, into the bright heat of the backyard. Diane galumphed toward them, a slobbering mass of dirty hair and oversized paws. She tried to leap on to Vogel's knife-creased mohair trousers, and he sent her into confused retreat with a deft kick of his pointed black suede shoe. Under the natural awning of the cherry and magnolia trees, a hesitant little party had begun. The hosts were the doctor's daughter Eunice and her husband, and their seven-year-old daughter, Marsha. They sat on the doctor's odd assortment of old stools and frayed beach chairs, surrounding their two guests: Thrasher and Daw nailed to the ungentle slats of the half-buried bench. The little girl was passing around a tray of cream soda and a bowl of summer fruit.

"Well, I guess everyone knows everyone by now," Dr. Abelman said cheerfully. "Mr. Thrasher and your little friend—what's your name?—you've met my daughter Eunice Platt, and my son-in-law Harry Platt; and my little *ketzeleh* Marsha."

Thrasher and Daw nodded politely. "Oh, and let's not forget Maxie!" Ceremoniously, he guided his colleague to the bench, indicating that Max Vogel, M.D., held a special, revered place in his catalogue of associates. "Mr. Thrasher and Mr. Daw, you better be nice to this big clunk. If you're doing my life story, he's part of it."

Vogel shook hands firmly. His alert, quick eyes sized them up as aliens to Sam Abelman's world, but men with whom he, Max Vogel, would have no trouble communicating. They dealt in words, in guises, in moods—and Vogel had used these elements in his practice of medicine many years before either of them had dreamed of their careers as successful talkers.

"Whaddya wanna bother with this old *klutz* for?" he asked nastily. "Do a show about me! The biggest *goniff* in Brooklyn! Ask Sammy about me!"

The roguishness, Thrasher sensed, had a double edge. There was real affection in Vogel's manner; at the same time, he almost seemed convinced that he *was* a better subject for a wide publicity campaign, that Sam Abelman would never in a million years know how to turn the benefits of a TV program into cash. Vogel walked quickly to a sagging beach chair and sat down spryly. Watching him, Thrasher realized that something in his appearance didn't ring true. It dawned on him suddenly: Vogel was of moderate physique, almost lean, yet he had the movements, gestures, and speech pattern of a jolly fat man. The rolling gait, the red cheeks, the button nose, the falsely merry eyes, the glib manner of speaking: all these were the accessories of a Falstaff. He smiled at Vogel and said politely, "Dr. Vogel, I'll bet you once lost a lot of weight."

Vogel slapped his knee. "Another lousy internist, Sam! You're right. I took off fifty pounds three years ago. I had a coronary occlusion—a beaut. This old bum here pulled me through. I wouldn't let a specialist touch me, even though this guy almost killed me."

"*Hoo hah!*" Dr. Abelman crowded. "I put you on that diet, too, and almost killed you again! Boy, what a myocardial infarction!"

Thrasher could see the dovetailed precision of their relationship: Dr. Abelman, the worrier, the perpetually outraged, the tilter at windmills, and Max Vogel, the nose-thumber, the rogue, the irreverent opportunist who regarded patients as slobs.

"Ah, what do you know, you old *futz*," Vogel said. "You once treated a guy for yellow jaundice for a month before you found out he was a Chink."

The doctor's granddaughter, a pigtailed child, with sharp, precocious eyes, ran to Vogel, punching him playfully on the pleated pocket of his twelve-dollar shirt.

"Grampa is *not* old. You're old!"

"Marsha!" the doctor's daughter said sharply. "That's not nice. Tell Uncle Max you're sorry!"

"I'm not! He called my grampa old!"

"Eunice, you gotta stop cramming vitamins down this kid's yap," Vogel said. "They overfeed 'em today. If the body can't absorb all that stuff, it goes into the nervous system and look what happens."

The doctor's daughter and the son-in-law laughed, taking no offense. She was an attractive, mildly stout young woman, with the doctor's strong, dark features; her husband was a tall, quiet man, stoop-shouldered and long-armed. Both of them regarded Vogel with the same humorous affection as did Dr. Abelman; he supplied something missing in their orderly, moral lives.

"Marsha," Eunice Platt said, "tell Grampa what you're doing next week."

"I'm going back to school!" She ran to Dr. Abelman, squeezing between his knees.

"What do you like most about school, *ketzeleh?*" the old man asked.

She titled her nose up toward the thick green roof of the cherry tree. "Raymond DeVito is the worst boy in the class," she said proudly. "He never wears a white shirt and his sneakers have holes."

"Tsk-tsk," the doctor said sadly, "you shouldn't be so happy about it. Maybe his mommy and his poppy haven't enough money to buy a white shirt."

Thrasher felt a subtle justification for his choice of the doctor as a subject for *Americans, U.S.A.* How better gauge a man than from his sympathy for an unknown little Italian boy who had holes in his sneakers? He really didn't have to defend Raymond DeVito from his granddaughter's delighted denunciation.

Eunice rose from a deck chair. There was evidence of the doctor's own repair work in the patched seat. "Harry, we'd better get going. Marsha is getting overstimulated and she'll never sleep tonight."

Thrasher and Daw were on their feet, almost too quickly, as if they were more than willing to have the doctor's relatives depart. They had both been constructing their own private versions of Samuel Abelman and the intrusion of too much reality—particularly in the persons of these normal, middle-class people who were his family—was disconcerting them. Vogel was a different story: he was theatrical enough to mesh with their own world of make-believe.

The doctor shook hands warmly with his son-in-law.

"Take it easy on the nightwork, pop," he said, "and give our love to Mom. By now she's at least the mahjong champion of Long Beach."

"Night work doesn't bother me. To hell with 'em. I can take it or leave it."

"You'll get your coronary yet," Vogel said, and laughed loudly, as if he almost were anxious to see his dearest friend so afflicted.

Dr. Abelman kissed his daughter and his granddaughter, and the three of them, accompanied by Diane's frantic leaps and yelps, departed. Thrasher and Daw, coatless and perspiring, resumed their buttock-scarring perches on the slatted bench. The *wah-wah-wah* of a young Negro playing Tarzan in a giant poplar echoed through the yard. In the adjoining plot of ground, through the doctor's fading picket fence, the elder Baumgarts, two monoliths out of mankind's past, walked stolidly through their proud weeds. Four eyes peered from under venerable lids through the spaces in the fence; anyone in Abelman's yard was as much their adversary as the doctor himself. Arm in arm, they continued their stately promenade. Once, the white-thatched man stooped to pick up a loose branch sullying his otherwise pristine patch of useless growth.

"Don't throw it over, Baumgart!" Dr. Abelman cried. "We got witnesses!"

"Shud up you fresh mout'," the old man muttered.

"You sleep mit deh *schwartzer*," his loyal wife added. They marched, untroubled, through the wasteland.

"That young Baumgart sure inherited all the fine qualities of his parents," Vogel said. "I've seen him take patients from his own cousin. I gotta hand it to him."

"I don't," said Dr. Abelman. "What the hell is to admire in that?"

"It got him that mansion on Republic Street."

Dr. Abelman made a flat, disgusted gesture with his thick forearm. "What does it prove?"

Vogel jerked a thumb in the direction of his friend and spoke to Thrasher and Daw. "It's not that he's so honest, fellahs, he's just stupid. He makes friends out of patients, the worst thing you can do. Patients should be scared stiff of their doctor. I wear a white coat that buttons up to my neck and I hire an Irish nurse who wiggles her ass on schedule. I put red lights that don't mean anything on the diathermy, and I won't let a patient call me by my first name."

"And what did it get you?" Dr. Abelman broke in. "A coronary!"

"I think there's something to be said for both points of view," Thrasher said. "I'm no medical man, but I would think a doctor could be both a friend to his patients and at the same time command their respect."

"Impossible," said Vogel. "All patients stink."

Daw said nothing. Within his protuberant skull he was mulling over the admirable simile of the meaningless red light on the diathermy. His business was full of those blinking red lights.

Thrasher's pad came out of the folded cord jacket; his pen was poised. "Where would you like to start today, Dr. Abelman?" he asked.

The doctor stretched his short legs. "Might as well get into Bellevue. You're lucky Maxie is here because he went through the joint with me. Or better, I dragged him."

The thin-fat face laughed—more sincerely it seemed to Thrasher than he had before. "Oh baby, were we a couple poor slobs!"

"You were poorer than me, Maxie."

"Listen, my old man kicked me in the ass when I said I was going to medical college. He saw a great future for me cleaning fish in his store, the cheap bum."

"How about *your* father, Dr. Abelman?" Thrasher asked.

The doctor was staring mistily into his cornfield. It was a long way back to 1908 when he had entered Bellevue. He was thinking of what his father had said to him when he learned his son had been accepted by the medical college. The old man had told him that he wanted to add his share to Sam's expenses. Going to medical college during the day would mean that Sam's earning capacity would be cut down if not altogether eliminated. Now he would be able to teach gymnasium classes only during his summer vacation. These earnings along with his savings, and what he was borrowing from Malkin the elder, would just barely take care of tuition, books, and lab fees.

Reb Yankel the tailor presented his son with a new black suit, a fitting garment for a doctor-to-be, and informed him (to Sam's complete surprise) that he wanted to contribute fifty cents a day to his expenses. The old tailor had figured it out—twenty cents for carfare, a dime each way, and twenty cents for lunch. Recalling it, the doctor could almost feel his father's hesitant handclasp as he pressed the first half-dollar into his palm. He and his father almost never spoke any more: the son had entered the new environment wholeheartedly, and had shaken the old rules, the old man prayed every day and avoided gentiles.

"You remember the day I brought you lunch, Maxie, and we both had to walk home from Bellevue?" Dr. Abelman asked.

"We ate in the Physical Culture Restaurant on Second Avenue," Vogel chuckled. "For twenty cents, a bowl of black bean soup, enough to feed a roomful of internes, two slabs of whole-wheat bread, and a hunk of apple pie the size of an infected spleen. Oh, I forgot, a tumbler of milk! The best lunch I ever ate."

Dr. Abelman slapped his iron stomach, delighted by the reminiscence. "We didn't call you Crazy Maxie for nothing! When you had the dough you could eat *two* of those lunches!"

"Bellevue must have been a challenging and exciting place in those days," Thrasher said.

Dr. Abelman sighed. "I loved the lousy place."

> *Slonimsky is a bum,*
> *Slonimsky is a bum,*
> *He never sends no heat up,*
> *Slonimsky is a bum.*

Slonimsky was their landlord; the tune was "The Farmer in the Dell"; and Sam and Aaron Abelman, now sole residents of the dark, cheerless second bedroom of the railroad flat, would greet each chill winter's morning with the disrespectful serenade. Their bare feet curled from rugless floors. No hot water heater eased the frigid grip of Slonimsky's castle; they shrieked as they tossed the gelid tap water onto their faces. Sam, now twenty-three and in the middle of his third year of medical college, had a nine o'clock class to make each weekday. Aaron, the family baby, worked in a costume jewelry factory on Lafayette Street. He was nineteen—bright, intense, and so frail that Sam wondered how he got through a day's work. Yet, he had to admit, the kid had courage and he had brains. He was learning the business thoroughly. In a year or two he would go out on his own (if he lived that long).

Their breakfast was a seeded roll, thinly buttered, and a cup of tea. Through the peeling kitchen door, in the seven o'clock gloom, they could see their father saying his morning prayers, the tight thongs of the phylacteries bound about his head and right arm, a stern reminder of the old rules which his sons were so happily abandoning. Sam leafed through Cunningham's *Anatomy* while sipping the scalding tea. He had to squint at the minuscule type; they were not permitted to use the single kitchen bulb during the day. His parents shuffled in, bringing the sounds, the smell, the look of defeat with them. Sadly, Sam decided he was a mutant, a sport: where else did his strength and his ambition come from? Two and one half years of medical schooling had taught him the importance of family history. He had heard Harlow Brooks tell them again and again—study the family past, learn about the patient's antecedents. Yet how did you explain his own departure from these bowed and beaten people? The other children had followed the pattern—there was a damp sadness about them. Moishe, now living by himself in a hall bedroom, unraveling his life in a shirt factory; Rivke raising a family of small *galitizianers;* Aaron always a heartbeat away from the dark pit.

His father performed his morning ritual—pressing into Sam's outstretched palm two quarters, his daily allowance to help his son through the strange maze of the *goyishe* college.

"Thanks, papa," he said cheerfully. "You're a regular Rockefeller."

The old man nodded indifferently; he had no time for jokes. Sam knew the tailoring business was suffering. He could no longer work as fast as when he opened the shop on Ludlow Street; competition from the big manufacturing houses was taking customers away every day. More and more he would cart home work to be finished on the wheezing, earsplitting Singer in his bedroom.

It was January, the streets lumpy with filth-strewn snowbanks. Halfhearted attempts to burn garbage on the dirty white heapings had left blackened smudges, pockets of potato peelings, and eggshells, where stray dogs nosed about for breakfast. Aaron and his father took the electric trolley car over the Bridge to the Lower East Side. Sam had a fifteen-minute walk to the corner of Fulton Street and Saratoga Avenue, where he picked up the Brooklyn-Manhattan Elevated. The ghetto people were on their way to work —Brownsville *auslanders* making their sodden pilgrimages to the East Side, to lower Manhattan. The old-timers, the illiterates, the uneducated went to the garment lofts, the textile houses. The more ambitious younger folk, beneficiaries of the new land's liberal educational opportunities, worked in offices, in schools, in retail stores. Sam was among the lucky few who had insisted on something better. Watching his neighbors, wrapped in bulky dark coats, scurrying through the slushy underfooting to the elevated, he could not find time to feel superior. He had midyear examinations all that week—clinical medicine, special pathology, surgery, obstetrics, and therapeutics. They would come thick and fast, one delightful ordeal after another. He enjoyed the challenge; he knew he would do well. In two and one-half years of exhausting study he had never failed a course. He ranked in the upper third of his class, a quiet, studious young man, a year or so older than most of his fellows, a solemn commuter, in ill-fitting clothes, lugging the badge of the day student —the scarred, overstuffed brief case. He was reviewing in his mind the steps in a neurological examination—just the way Brooks had outlined them the week before—when he saw Dr. Lemkau standing beside his haughty air-cooled Franklin. Lemkau was the grand old gent of the Brownsville medical corps: a portly, goateed Senator of a man. He wore a swallowtailed coat and a floppy bow tie and looked down his nose at patients through a pair of octagonal specs on a black string. Sam saw him sniffing the cold morning air as if he owned it, flapping his long arms, then lifting his black calfskin satchel and climbing stiffly into the lofty perch of the Franklin. In a few years, Sam thought, he'd be competing with Lemkau for patients. He was not awed by the prospect. Indeed, he felt a little sorry for the old codger in his air-cooled buggy.

The elevated lurched and clattered off for the long jerking ride through Fulton Street, through downtown Brooklyn, the lair of the ward heeler and the ambulance chaser, and then across the great sweeping curve of the Brooklyn Bridge. Crushed in the narrow seat between a Calabrian laborer, whose rocky flanks all but bruised him, and an Old Testament prophet seeking new omens in the Social Democratic editorials of the *Vorwarts*, he remained isolated, eyes glued to his text. As he rode and read, he jotted shorthand notes on the back of an old envelope. He left his studies only long enough to change to the Third Avenue El at the Brooklyn Bridge station, resuming his reading now strap-hanging, cradling the book in his right arm, straddling the misshapen brief case, and protecting it from the milling feet around him.

His first lecture was in medicine at the Carnegie Laboratory on Twenty-sixth Street. He reached the austere red brick pile about five minutes before nine. Normally, he met Max Vogel outside the arabesqued door of the lab, but the fishmonger's son was nowhere in sight. Sam worried about him: Maxie was always just barely passing his courses. If he missed any of the concluding lectures he would be in hotter water than he imagined. And the lecturer that morning was the new dean himself—Egbert LeFevre, the one professor whose lectures were considered mandatory. Old Lemkau, himself a Bellevue man, had once advised him, "Cut classes, fail courses and be a bad boy, Sammy. But don't miss LeFevre."

He waited apprehensively for Maxie, pulling the peaked cap over his ears to close out the icy wind whipping across the street from the East River. At the curb a group of high-class Princeton and Yale boys in derby hats and fur-lined greatcoats, were baiting Otto, the *diener* in charge of the morgue. A fresh shipment of canvas-wrapped corpses from the City Hospital had arrived. The bleak, swaying wagon, driven by an Irishman with a pulverized scarlet face, had barely reached the front of the laboratory when the fun began.

"*Oi, oi,* fresh fish today!"

"Hey, Otto, your relatives!"

"Look—meat on the bones!" One of them had thrown aside part

of the stained canvas wrapper. A woman's arm dropped out, the mortised fingers scraping in the gutter snow.

Sam watched them with quiet revulsion. These were the class gentlemen: the kids who smoked Havana cigars and meerschaums. They had dates with girls from Rector's and the Hippodrome. They never seemed to study, yet they always seemed to scrape through. He didn't mind their carrying on. They left him alone and there were remarkably few unpleasant contacts between the gentlemen and the commuting Jewish boys with their crammed brief cases. But fooling around with the dead! Making jokes about those corpses! They had been real people once, people with hopes and desires and emotions. He shuddered. The stiffs never bothered him in the dissecting room, but, seeing the canvas bags stretched out on the cold pavement, now being picked up like so many sacks of cabbages by Otto's white-smocked attendants, he was drenched with vague misery.

Maxie was still not in sight. He greeted Karasik, the little refugee with the pince-nez and the black derby, who was his other close friend, and they walked into the drafty, semicircular lecture hall. LeFevre was not in sight, and, once in the classroom, the gentlemen resumed their gleeful play. They had seized the tan derby of one of their number; three others in sharp suits and silk waistcoats were tossing it around in a wild game of *salugi*. Suddenly a white-coated attendant entered, rapping for order with a yardstick. From a side door, Egbert LeFevre entered, his dignity and intelligence demanding immediate silence. LeFevre was in his early fifties. With the death of the legendary Edward G. Janeway that year, LeFevre had become dean. LeFevre's brown hair was parted neatly in the middle, falling in delicate semicircles over the high forehead; he had a full fleshy nose, a trim pointed beard, and a thick mustache. Hands gripping the lecturer's bar which separated the amphitheater from the professor's little empire of blackboards, slate-topped desk, and laboratory equipment, LeFevre surveyed the class. He endowed his third-year men with a professional intimacy they hardly deserved.

"Gentlemen," he began, "we will put your powers of observation to test this morning. Rather than wear you out with an academic lecture, we will attempt diagnoses with several subjects. Since most of you are now cramming your heads with words for your midyear examinations, I felt it would be politic to let you try your skill as true practitioners and offer you a bit of respite."

The voice was not in keeping with the frock-coated, bearded figure: it was high and nasal, and the last few rows of students were obliged to lean forward to catch the dean's words. LeFevre gestured to the *diener,* and the man standing at the sliding blackboard pulled back one wall-high panel to reveal a small anterior room. It was like the stage of a child's theater, black-curtained and bare, with a platform rising several feet above the classroom level. On three wooden chairs sat the subjects for diagnosis: an elderly man in a baggy workhouse suit; a bearded young Jew, sitting cross-legged, his distracted eyes roaming over the faces in front of him; and a girl in her teens, shivering in a black shawl.

"Now, gentlemen, take your time observing our subjects, make notes if you wish, and be prepared for questioning. Before we take up each patient, I shall offer you a little clinical history—but be assured it will be very little indeed," LeFevre intoned.

There was a clattering noise as the side door of the amphitheater was pushed open. The attendant rose crankily from his seat, *shushing* the late-comer. Sam cringed. It was Max Vogel, trying to sneak quietly up the side aisle, trying to hide his roseate face beneath a mangy fur cap.

"Late-comers will please remove their hats," LeFevre said gently. "Mr. Vogel, you are late for class, you're late for laboratory, you will be late for your first delivery, and you will be late on the Judgment Day."

Max maneuvered his ample rear end, straining within shiny blue serge, into the seat adacent to Sam's.

"Where the devil you been, Maxie?" Sam whispered.

Maxie's words, delivered from the side of his facile mouth (his eyes all this time fixed innocently on the lecturer), shocked Sam.

"I stayed in New York. You know that redheaded assistant in pathology? The one with the tits that dip into the test tubes when she bends over? I paid her a visit and slept late. *Oi vay!*"

Sam looked at him disapprovingly. How could Maxie get away with it? How did he find the nerve to live that way? He, Sam, had been engaged to Sarah Malkin for four years—ever since the formation of the walking and literary group. They were more than willing to forswear the intimate company of other young people. Sam had proposed at the first chance, advising Sarah he didn't want Louis Kosloff hanging around. She had accepted, and now they were both prepared to wait until he was practicing medicine. Thinking of Sarah, his attention drifted from the three wretches on the little stage.

"Vogel, what do you make of this case?"

Maxie stood up.

"I will inform you that the subect is a white male, aged fifty-five. A history of alcoholism, undernourishment, and irregular habits. He has worked in a nearby tool and die factory, performing arduous manual labor. Recent symptoms: loss of appetite, coughing spells, occasional bringing up of bloody phleghm on rising."

Max suggested consumption, the obvious answer. LeFevre questioned him unmercifully, pricking his confident response with several alternate possibilities, trapping the student with the latter's own glibness. It *was* a case of incipient consumption, LeFevre said, but he felt that Vogel had merely made a wild guess. It might have been any one of several ailments, and he wanted to stress the danger of snap decisions: better to be careful and thorough than to be too quick and sure of yourself.

They were discussing the little girl now, a cardiac case; blue-lipped and white-skinned, the transparent flesh like bleached bone. It was a congenital disorder, LeFevre said, and all that could be prescribed was rest, fresh air, and a good diet to build up her resistance. It did not seem like much in the way of therapy to Sam, and suddenly, with a sinking feeling of terror, he felt he was looking at his own wretched family. The ruined little consumptive could have been his father, the little girl with the leached-out, bloodless look of the congenital cardiac could have been Aaron. It distressed him that these people had to be paraded in front of the probing eyes of the students; what right had those clucks in the derbies and checked coats, puffing their twenty-cent cigars, to look them over like monkeys in a zoo?

LeFevre asked the young bearded Jew to stand up and speak to the class. He moved hesitantly to the railing, bowing his head as if flinching from a blow and running a soft white hand over hospital-cropped hair.

"Say something, speak," LeFevre said.

The young patient looked innocently at the dean. The gentleness in the professor's voice made him smile and he seemed happier about the ordeal. LeFevre gestured at his lips, moving his fingers outward to indicate speech. The visionary eyes opened wide with understanding.

"*Ich bin hungerich, Ich vill essen, Ich vill a schnappsel,*" the young man mumbled. "*Ich bin hungerich, Ich vill essen, Ich vill a schnappsel. Ich bin hungerich. . . .*"

His voice drifted away to a hoarse murmur; the imbecilic smile remained. LeFevre gave a brief history of the patient, and then elicited from the students an opinion of insanity; one suggested paresis; another, imbecility induced by an accident to the nervous system.

The patient, who had resumed his seat and was holding his head in his hands, was called to the railing again. "Insanity is well advanced in this subect," LeFevre said. "You will note when I ask him to speak, he will repeat the same meaningless gibberish that he uttered before. His entire range of speech, of articulation, possibly because of severe brain injury, is now restricted to these few words."

"You'll excuse me, sir, but I think what the subject is saying makes perfect sense," he said. There was an obscene hoot from the back of the lecture hall.

"What makes you say that, Abelman?" LeFevre asked, smiling. "When a patient who has shown all the symptoms of withdrawal, of inability to communicate, keeps repeating the same set of words, what are we to expect?"

"That's very true, sir, and I agree," Sam said. "I just want to point out that the words themselves aren't meaningless. All the man is saying is, 'I'm hungry, I want to eat, I want a little whiskey.' That's pretty good sense, to me. He's voicing sentiments which a lot of us feel from time to time."

"You make an interesting point, Abelman," LeFevre said. "I agree that my own—let us say—linguistic limitations prevented me from a complete and accurate reading of the syndrome. But, nonetheless, I think that, when taken in context with other symptoms, we cannot help but reach a verdict of insanity. However, there is a lesson in the point you make, Abelman. We must never take anything for granted. Had I been treating this poor soul, and had I failed to call in a person fluent in the language, I would have been guilty of an oversight. Thank you for calling our attention to this."

Sam sat down, flushed with the half victory. Vogel's elbow nudged his ribs. "Stop stickin' your two cents in, professor," he said bitterly. "He needed you like a hole in the head."

"Shut up and listen. You might learn something," Sam muttered.

The termination of the first hour's lecture was the signal for an outbreak of singing, whistling, and spitball warfare in the rear rows. A heated argument had broken out over the outcome of the last Yale-Princeton basketball game. Cigar smoke floated down to the lower rows. An Ivy League wit was doing a comical imitation of LeFevre, mimicking his nasal singsong, the precise phraseology.

Karasik, the voice of cultured Europe, shook his head sadly at Sam. "Such behavior," he said sadly. "No respect at all for the professor! Tell me, Abelman, why do they act like apes?"

Sam smiled indulgently. He liked Karasik, the solemn little Austrian with his polished manners, but he couldn't be bothered with philosophical discussions during midyear week. He had ten minutes between lectures, time enough to get his nose into the surgery textbook.

A spitball the size of a lemon whistled between them. Spinning by, it flicked the outer edge of Karasik's pince-nez and sent them flying into the back of the chair facing them. Karasik's Viennese poise was shattered, even though the spectacles were undamaged. He leaned over, a fat little foreigner, very conscious of how different he was from the vigorous Americans, and picked them up daintily, almost ashamed for having invited the humiliation. He was adjusting the pince-nez on his nose when Sam reached down and picked up the wad.

"I got a good mind to tell those lice off," he said to Max Vogel and to Karasik. "Are your specs okay, Franz?"

"Yes, yes, of course. Don't make any fuss over me."

"Sam, for Christ's sake, sit down," said Max contemptuously. "You're no lousy gym teacher any more. Siddown!"

But Sam was already pushing his way through the crowded rows of overloaded knees, heavy with overcoats, open textbooks, and brief cases, and was trudging up the steps to the rear seats. A basketball, fashioned of someone's cap stuffed with a muffler, was being tossed around. Sam vaulted an empty seat, and with the leap of a trained gymnast (Hector O'Bannion would have approved) intercepted the makeshift ball. A lean blond student with a gray derby, tilted over languid eyes, blew a cloud of cigar smoke his way.

"Don't tell me! It's the poor but honest Horatio Alger, Abelman the Great!"

"Ah, cut the crap," Sam said. "Which of you guys threw this?"

"What's it to you, Abelman?" another one of the rear-seaters asked. He had the prognathous face of a halfback.

"I just want to return it," Sam said. "I guess one of you lost it."

"Look, Sammy," the cigar smoker said. "What do you take everything so seriously for? Why get so excited over Karasik? The little professor doesn't care if we rag him. Why should you?"

"Did you throw it, Padgitt?"

"Sure I did. What are you so offended about?" He was genuinely anxious to appease his outraged classmate. To Padgitt, raised in an atmosphere of fraternity pranks, a spitball was part of the hazards of student life. Sam, a head shorter than the confessed thrower, walked up to him and with deliberate slowness stuffed the soggy paper ball into Padgitt's waistcoat.

"Well, all I wanted to do was return it," Sam said. He shoved Padgitt gently and then both were surprised to find themselves locked together, shoved unwillingly into each other's grasp by the halfback and two other members of the rear-seat clique. They struggled purposelessly, little Karasik running in a woman's mincing steps up to the scene to try to arbitrate. A surging crowd was gathering around the contestants as Hermann M. Biggs, professor of public health, entered the room. The austere beaked head with its curled black mustache looked in horror on the battle. His compelling voice, one that had once forced New York City's politicians to enact a venereal disease control program, dispersed the crowd in an instant.

"For a group about to enter its crucial midyear examinations," Biggs said, "such behavior is inadmissible. I find it hard to believe you must be treated like undergraduates. I will save what else I have to say for my office after five o'clock. All of you who participated in this exhibition will meet me there. Fitzpatrick here"—he indicated the little attendant at his side—"knows which of you were involved, so do not attempt to deceive me."

A cold gloom settled over Sam Abelman—of all things, to be trapped in a disciplinary mess! He slumped back in his seat, barely hearing Biggs start his lecture on the protection of child health. He jumped when Max grabbed him in the ribs.

"What the hell is the matter with you, Sam? Whose battles are you fighting?" he whispered. "So what if Karasik's cheaters got knocked off? What skin is that off your nose? And that argument with LeFevre! You think he liked it? Like hell he did. When he needs a Yiddish interpreter he'll hire his own!"

Sam said nothing. His despair was complete. Mox Vogel nudged him again. "And if you gotta stay after five to see Biggs, how am I gonna borrow your pathology notes without hanging around? Don't you ever think of me?"

They met in Biggs' office in the main building on First Avenue and Twenty-sixth Street. Padgitt came, and the halfback, and two other rear-seaters. Karasik had insisted to Sam that he come also. In his whining, apologetic Viennese accent he had advised Sam it was all his fault for looking so silly that any normal, healthy American would be perfectly justified in knocking his glasses off. He angered Sam thoroughly, hanging on his overcoat sleeve and trailing along, until they reached the entrance to the red brick building.

"Beat it, Franz," Sam said bitterly, "I didn't start the fight just to help you. I did it for my own reasons. Go home and study for the pathology exam."

"But really, Samuel, if you will only permit me to speak to Professor Biggs—"

"Vamoose!"

Biggs kept them waiting half an hour, all of them fidgeting, crossing and uncrossing their legs in the anteroom. Padgitt once offered him a cigarette; Sam refused but smiled and thanked him. It was dawning on all of them that the whole battle had been meaningless, unnecessary, and that essentially they were not bad fellows at all.

Hermann M. Biggs called them in finally. They stood in a sheepish semicircle around the vast desk, watching Biggs spin away from them in the leather swivel chair. The gesture seemed to imply his own weariness at having to treat with them like delinquent children; he was a man who dealt in campaigns to stamp out TB, diphtheria, syphilis. Teacher, clinician, administrator, he was probably the most brilliant member of the Bellevue faculty.

"Quite candidly, gentlemen," Biggs began wearily, "I don't know what to tell you. I have always felt that the practice of medicine, whether it involves the bandaging of a sprained ankle or the organization of a state-wide campaign for inoculations, demands a high seriousness; the kind of seriousness I like to see in our students. I know that the wild behavior in my class today can be attributed to the pressures and tensions of examinations. But that does not make it easier for me to see my students behaving like hoodlums when they should be applying themselves to learning all there is to learn in our complex profession."

They looked curiously at each other, wondering whether Biggs had finished his disciplinary lecture. Once having called them to his office, the great clinician had appeared too preoccupied to chastise them.

Biggs sighed. "Do any of you wish to offer any explanation for what happened? Do some of you feel unfairly treated?"

"Just horseplay, professor," Padgitt volunteered. He darted a quick glance at Sam; it had not been horseplay alone, it had started with the pointless baiting of Karasik, the *auslander*.

"That's all it was, sir," Sam said quickly. "We were playing basketball and a few of us lost our tempers."

Biggs spun away again. "High seriousness, gentlemen, high seriousness," he said. "Have your fun at times other than office hours." He dismissed them with a wave of his hand and as they trooped out, heads properly lowered, Sam heard Biggs calling his name. He halted at the door and turned.

"Abelman," Professor Biggs said, "what were *you* doing in that mess?" His tone was not unfriendly, and Sam sensed the vague compliment. "Me, sir?" he asked. "Oh, just a little fun. I guess we got carried away with ourselves." He wanted nothing of the Karasik matter discussed. It would be difficult—almost impossible—to explain what motives had impelled him to act as the Austrian's knight errant.

"You don't seem the type to me, Abelman," Biggs said. "Marks good, attendance excellent, and, if I may say so, an occasional streak of brilliance in diagnostic work."

He thanked Biggs and left, walking on a misty cloud all the way to the library where he spent an enchanted hour making last-minute notes, inscribing them carefully on a carbon and an extra sheet for Max Vogel who waited for him like a predatory bird outside the library.

"Where ya been so long?" Vogel asked peevishly. "I'm supposed to stay up all night for four pages of notes? And that handwriting!"

He had no harsh words for Max; he was lofted away by Biggs' brief praise. Jammed inside the rattling Third Avenue Elevated again, the textbook once more cradled in his arm, he only half knew what he was reading. The magic of learning, of maturing, was intoxicating him and the confrontation with Biggs was like an excessive inhalation of aromatic tobacco. After two and one-half years of medical college he had not lost his feeling of arrival, of initiation into some blessed fraternity. He loved the books, the heavy, finely printed texts, so loaded with information that they broke away from the dark-red bindings; the hours in the laboratory, squinting into microscopes, probing the luckless corpses; the sessions in the lecture hall where the great men of medicine came to share their knowledge. And what a group of men!

LeFevre, Biggs, Park, Wyckoff, and of course Harlow Brooks the assistant professor of clinical medicine, the friendly man with the Indian face to whom all students sooner or later brought their problems.

Transferring at Brooklyn Bridge to the Fulton Street El, swept along through slush and street dirt by the swarm of immigrants, Sam had a disturbing thought. It seemed to him he was almost *too* intoxicated with Bellevue, with the professors, the art of learning, to ever feel so strongly about anything in his future work. What if he did hang out a shingle in Brooklyn? Could anything ever approximate the pure sense of achievement he gained from a straight A in pathology under Wyckoff? Or a compliment from Harlow Brooks? Or even the little speech Hermann Biggs had made to him? Practice would mean Brownsville again, long, hard hours of work, in the mushrooming slum, a struggle for the first few years and maybe longer. Bellevue meant an association with the men who were revolutionizing the concepts of medicine in the United States.

It was after eight at night when he reached home. Dr. Lemkau's black Franklin was parked in front of the tenement. Innate pessimism propelled Sam up the stoop and the sloping stairs, through the odor of tired cooking and sodden garbage, into their apartment. He had a sense for disaster: Lemkau was seated at the kitchen table, scribbling on a prescription pad. The pince-nez were perched elegantly on the tip of his nose, jiggling in cadence with each jerk of the pen. Aaron, as pale as the faded white enamel of the kitchen sink, was standing at his side. His mother was hunched over in a kitchen chair, crying softly into a soiled handkerchief.

"It's Papa," Aaron said. "He collapsed at the place this afternoon and they wanted to call for an ambulance, but he wouldn't let them. He was afraid it would cost too much money. So the crazy nut had to come all the way home on the streetcar. How he walked from Ralph Avenue to here, I don't know."

Sam was horrified, his own guilt jabbing at him. Abelman the tailor had collapsed and refused to have an ambulance take him to his home because it would cost too much; and each day he gave his son fifty cents to see him through one more step toward being a doctor.

"What's wrong, Dr. Lemkau? Is it serious?" Sam asked.

His mother wailed, raising shriveled arms, the wrinkles on her face multiplying as she grimaced. Sam looked at her with annoyance and Aaron cautioned her to control herself. That was the trouble with old country Jews—they went around parading their sorrows publicly, breast beating, shrieking to heaven, convinced that every stroke of ill luck was directed against them personally by that stern and indifferent God who had been demanding excessive tribute from them for so long. Sam was glad to see Aaron was calm and self-controlled; he was thankful the boy had been around when his father came staggering home.

"It looks like a case of la grippe, nothing worse, I trust," Lemkau said. He had a rolling baritone voice, tinged with enough of a Russian accent to make him sound authoritative without being a greenhorn. "He was running a high temperature, one hundred and four, but, with aspirin and alcohol baths, it should come down overnight."

"How about his heart and lungs?" Sam asked quickly.

Lemkau's eyes appeared to smile indulgently, but he was not over-joyed with the medical student's query.

"You sound like LeFevre already, Sammy, asking questions like that," he said. "All right, professor. The heartbeat is normal, the pulse a little faint, but not enough to worry about, and the lungs don't seem congested. I wish he hadn't traveled all the way home like that. These cases where the patient refuses good advice—"

"Papa came home to save money," Aaron said bitterly. "These old-timers save a dollar and take their lives in their hands."

Lemkau stood up, handing the fly-tracked prescription to Sam, noting with distaste the way the young man scrutinized the specific, as if putting his approval on it.

"Sedative?" Sam asked.

"What did you expect, roast goose?" Lemkau asked loftily. "The aspirin every three hours, the sedative only when he wakes up, and an alcohol bath every three hours until the temperature goes down."

Aaron was helping him into his greatcoat, straightening the bear-skin collar. "I don't think it will be necessary to call me," the doctor said. "By morning he should be looking better. The fee is two dollars, please."

Other doctors charged a dollar for a house call, Sam knew, but Lemkau asked for two, and not only got it but was in the greatest demand. A vague feeling that the pince-nez, the fur collar, the swallowtail coat, and the rich baritone voice had as much to do with his popularity as his clinical knowledge fleeted through Sam's mind. He went to the bedroom, glancing at the shrunken figure of his father, breathing heavily beneath the drab blankets, and found two soiled bills in the thin wad of household money his mother kept in the dresser drawer. Lemkau tucked the money into a vest pocket, assured them that everything would turn out well, and left. His departure brought on another seizure of wails from Sam's mother, and both he and Aaron pleaded with her to be still.

"Ma, that hollering isn't going to help papa get better," Aaron said. "Go sleep in my bed. Sam and I will look after him tonight. Go on."

"*Oi gevald*, he'll die!" she shrieked. "He came home, sick like that!"

"Ah, ma, he'll be all right," Aaron said placatingly. He led her to the second bedroom, comforting her. He was her baby, Sam thought, sickly, spoiled, favored; yet he had a tough fiber inside him that made him more of a prop to his helpless parents than they were to him.

Sam was unpacking books on the kitchen table, brewing some

tea, and preparing himself for a night of study. Aaron returning from the bedroom, shoved him away from the gas stove. "Sit down and study, professor," the younger brother said solicitously. "I'll brew you up an Abelman special."

"Okay, Hackenschmidt," Sam said. "You're getting muscles like a wrestler, working at that shop. I think I'll get Hector O'Bannion to give you a scholarship if you keep it up."

"I should live on carrots and lettuce like you did? Nuts. I'll be eating steaks and blueberry pie in a few years."

It was past nine. He was two hours behind his normal study schedule, and he had to complete his review of a half year's work in pathology. What with tending to his father it would be a rugged night. But the challenge only made him more determined to absorb every shred of information he could, to conquer the endless words, sentences, paragraphs of complicated information, to prove to Biggs, to LeFevre, to Brooks, that he had the talent for the work. He bent to his books, again scribbling notations on scraps of paper: abbreviations, interspersed with neat, accurate drawings.

At midnight he heard his father stirring. It was time for the sedative, the aspirin, and the alcohol bath anyway. He tiptoed in, letting the dim kitchen light filter through. In the yellow gloom the tailor looked appalling weak and drained.

"Papa, you awake?" he asked.

"I'm not sleeping, so I'm awake." His voice was thick and frighteningly faint. "Shmul, it's my heart, my heart."

"It's not your heart, papa, you've got grippe—a bad cold." It was always the heart with the old people when they were ill. There must have been something in Mosaic Law or in some paragraph of the Torah that convinced all of them their heart was going when they took sick. He propped the old man up in bed, rolled up the soiled undershirt and repressed a rush of pity at the sight of the caved chest. Modesty forbade them looking at each other's bodies; he had forgotten how thin and weak his father was.

"Take it easy, papa, the great Professor Abelman is examining you." He proceeded with the stethoscope, using the worn instrument Sarah had bought for him in a Third Avenue pawnshop, looking for the clear sounds of health. Either Lemkau was inefficient, or the old man had developed new symptoms in the past three hours. There was, to Sam's ear, a distinct congestion in the right lung. He checked the chest again, convinced he was right. But Lemkau had assured him it was just la grippe; maybe he was imagining it. He sponged the shrunken limbs, feeling the temperature of the shriveled skin change as the cooling liquid was daubed on.

"Go back to sleep, papa," he said.

The old man's voice was so faint he wondered if he had heard him properly. "You'll have to stop going to school," he thought he heard him murmur, "it costs too much."

Sam left him, returning to his texts. This time he found it harder to concentrate; the tailor's mumbled admonition upset him. He knew what his father was thinking about—if he died or became incapable of working how would they get along? In addition to the fifty cents per diem Sam received, he also got his breakfast and evening meal, as well as his lodging and an occasional piece of wearing apparel. If the income from the tailoring shop ended, what would happen? He refused to think about it: the examination came first. At four, he stopped reading and, removing his shoes, tried to doze on the sagging, discolored living room sofa. He had been there no more than fifteen minutes when a rattling, rhythmic noise made him start. Softly, so as not to awaken his mother (all he needed was some more of her screaming), he roused Aaron. They tiptoed into the old man's sickroom. The tailor was sprawled, arms wide, in a stupor; the room smelled of tired sweat, as if he had carried the defeated steamy odors of the shop into his bed and saturated sheet and blanket with them. His mouth was wide apart and he was gulping and exhaling air in what appeared to be a supreme unconscious effort to pump life into his body.

"Oh, my God," Sam shuddered. "It's his death rattle. Papa's on the way out."

"He can't be," Aaron whispered. "Lemkau said—"

"Lemkau could be wrong. I swear I felt something in his chest. Aaron, you better run get him. Call from the candy store."

"Candy store? There's nothing open now."

"Then you'll have to walk over. I'll go if you don't feel strong enough."

"No, you stay. I'll go now."

It took an hour before Aaron returned with the irate physician. Victor Lemkau did not appreciate middle-of-the-night calls. Only the arrogant persistence of the younger brother had brought him out of bed, grumbling and cursing the profession. He had no sooner entered the apartment than, to Sam's great relief (and embarrassment), the old man's breathing improved. The rattling noise abated, and his heartbeat and pulse sounded almost normal.

"For this you woke me up?" Lemkau asked angrily. "For a slight change in breathing? Sammy, what kind of a diagnostician are you?"

"It sounded like a death rattle," Sam said. "Cheyne-Stokes breathing."

"But Cheyne-Stokes breathing doesn't necessarily mean death is imminent."

"I also listened to his chest," Sam said apologetically. "He seems to have developed something since you examined him."

"Well, an Osler already we have," Lemkau said. "What diagnosis, if you please?"

"Look, Dr. Lemkau, I'm not trying to be a weisenheimer. I know you know more than I do. I *said* he probably developed the symptom *after* you examined him. Could you please listen again?"

Lemkau walked to the bedside and re-examined the tailor's chest. He made a noncommittal gesture with his hands and pursed his lips.

"A little bit, a little bit," he said. "It's to be expected in these old garment workers. Nothing out of the ordinary. Call me in the morning if the temperature stays up."

The fee this time was three dollars, for a night call, and the dwindling roll of household money perturbed Sam momentarily. As Lemkau left he remembered his father's curious warning about his having to leave school. Fortunately, the clock prevented any brooding over it. It was six now—and, after a half hour's sleep, he would be on his way to Bellevue again for two examinations.

In the morning, he had three hours of special pathology; in the afternoon three hours of principles and practices of medicine. But for Sam Abelman, the allotted time did not seem nearly adequate to write down all he knew. He assaulted the written examinations as if they were his old enemies, the galoots, searching his well-arranged mind of every relevant fact, tying them together in clear and meaningful paragraphs.

At lunch with Max Vogel after the pathology examination, he gulped three scalding cups of black coffee, feeling the stimulant perk his brain, confident he could not be beaten. After all, he owed a good performance to Brooks and Biggs and LeFevre; a man couldn't let *them* down. He was unsympathetic with Max's whining complaints about the rigorous problems posed, the amount he had to write.

"A goddam good thing I had your notes," Vogel said. "I bet Winters had a hand in that one. All that crap about atrophied muscles! I'll atrophy him some day."

"Did you pass, Maxie?" Sam asked. He cradled the hot coffee mug.

"You bet your sweet ass I did," Maxie said slyly. He looked about him furtively, content that no one in the Physical Culture Restaurant was listening. "Get a load of these." He turned up the inner side of his belt, revealing two cards, filled with minute lettering, sewed to the raw leather.

"I stayed up most of last night getting this rig finished. The whole pathology *megillah* on two cards!"

"Are you out of your mind, Max? What if you get caught?"

Vogel seized Sam's unfinished bowl of bean soup and drained it greedily.

"They don't catch guys like me, Sammy. I was born to get away with things. Just like you were born to work for 'em." His round, red face looked about again for any listeners, and then he took from his coat pocket a second belt, similarly festooned on its inner surface.

"I got 'em for medicine, too," he said. "No one screws around with Maxie Vogel."

Sam needed no such mnemonic aid for the second examination. Twenty minutes before the examination period was over he handed in his paper, waved to the sweating Maxie and to little Karasik, and left for Brooklyn.

Fatigue began asserting itself on the elevated. When he debarked at Saratoga Avenue he thought he would be incapable of making the fifteen-minute walk to his home. A numbing weakness had seized his limbs, his iron chest. Enervation combined with a sudden sense of guilt. He had barely thought of his ailing father throughout the headlong rush of the day. His mind has been laden with the symptoms, syndromes, therapies, and diagnoses of abstract patients who existed only in heavy textbooks. His own father, feverish and wheezing, had never entered the ideal medical world of his examination booklets. He wondered again what could be the matter with the old man. Lemkau was probably right—it was la grippe, the usual winter infection so common in the slums. It would knock the old man out for a week or so, and then he'd be back in the place, bent over his machine, his stooped body obscured in the steamy clouds of the presser.

In the midwinter dusk he saw a small group of people gathered at the stoop of the house. He recognized two of his father's distant cousins, members of the same lodge, and then he saw Sol Pomerantz walking toward him.

"Sam, Sam, listen to me. Don't get hysterical and don't collapse," Sol began. His own eyes were red and swollen. "Your father died a few hours ago."

Sam stopped. The brief case fell from his grip and he put a hand to his forehead, as if someone had smashed a fist against his temple.

"Die?" he groaned, "Oh, God, Solly! How? What? Was Lemkau

here?" He could not weep; he had become a stranger to his father. In the old man's last hours he had served him more as a clinician than a son.

"Lemkau left a little while ago. He got here after your father died. He said it was his heart, it gave out suddenly. He said he might have lived if he hadn't taken that crazy trip back to Brooklyn and gone to a hospital when he collapsed yesterday."

"Oh, God," Sam repeated, "my mother—Aaron—what happens now?"

"Your mother is taking it pretty good," Sol said, "and Aaron— the kid is great." He missed completely Sam's implication: what worried him was their financial future, including his own. Tormented by his own selfishness in the face of his father's death, he could not help thinking of the year and one-half of schooling he had ahead of him.

In the apartment, candles flickered in the winter gloom. He heard the muddled chanting of mourners: some of his father's chums from the synagogue were there, standing around the coffin, mounted on trestles in the narrow living room. His father, an Orthodox Jew, would be spared evisceration and the other arts of the mortician. He wore a skullcap, a new white prayer shawl, and held a prayer book in his broken hands. Nodding and bobbing, the old words flowing from beard-muffled mouths, the elders interceded with God on behalf of Reb Yankele Abelman, the tailor from Brovo and part-time Talmudic scholar. Sam noticed the mirrors in the house had been covered—a custom brought over from the old country.

Aaron led him to the wooden box. In death, his father looked barely different than when he was alive.

"How did it happen, kiddo?" Sam asked.

"He started moaning about one o'clock. I just gave him a glass of tea with lemon. I stayed home from the place today, and he was sipping it, saying he felt pretty good. He started that heavy breathing again. I called Lemkau, but Papa was dead before he got here."

"How did you know?"

The mourners eyed them sorrowfully, the two apostate sons, shorn and English-speaking, discussing their father's last hours on earth in tearless voices, ignoring the holy chants.

"I held my shaving mirror up to his mouth and I saw he wasn't breathing. So I called Karnofsky the undertaker."

"Where's Mama?"

Aaron indicated their own bedroom. "She's in there with Moishe and Rivke. Hysterical! What can we expect? You should go in and comfort her."

Sam walked dutifully to the bedroom, to the conglomerate wails and shrieks. His mother was prostrate on his bed, sobbing in great, convulsive gasps. Rivke was crying in agitated sniffles. Moishe was Moishe—he crouched dumbly in the corner, muttering prayers and despairing commentaries. Sam knew he had to love them, to comfort them. But was he supposed to be the only one who was strong, who stood up under pressure? He sat down beside his mother, hugging the bony frame, feeling the coarse texture of the black shawl she always wore. He spoke in Yiddish, finding the words coming easily.

"Don't cry, mama, Papa was very sick. He never could have worked any more even if he had lived. He was a good, kind man and everyone will remember him that way. When you lead a good life, mama, a little bit of that life always remains in the world for people to think about and love. Mama, please stop crying! Don't cry!"

His speech, aimed at comforting them, only invoked new spasms of tears. His mother clutched at him, streaking his face with tears.

In the half light of the living room Aaron was sitting at the window, staring into the darkening slum street. A single ancient of the synagogue remained, an old world vestige, seated in respectful and self-sufficient silence. He was of a piece: skullcap, *tallis*, prayer book—all that he needed to sustain him in this world and the next and any other worlds he might be thrust into. Sam was almost a little jealous of him.

"Who's he?" he asked Aaron. His brother's invalid face was red-eyed and deeply enshadowed; yet the boy was as calm as a neurosurgeon.

"He's the one who stays up all night with the deceased and prays."

"Who appointed him?" Sam asked with some peevishness. "Do you want him hanging around all night?"

"Ah, come on, Sam. Papa would have wanted him. It's one of the old rules. He can't hurt anyone."

The patriarch turned a white-ruffed, cross-hatched face toward the brothers. He understood more English than they imagined.

"*Boychiklech*, you wouldn't pray with me?" he asked.

"I prayed already," Aaron said, not unkindly.

"And you, professor?" he asked Sam.

"*Zayde*, I am a scientist, a professor, as you said. We're a bunch of bad fellows, we don't pray very often."

The old man nodded disapprovingly, clacking false teeth.

"The Torah is a better teacher than the college, *boychick*."

Sam picked up his overcoat and cap. He felt he had done his duty—what more did they expect of him? They would demand that he sit *shiva*, stay in the house for one week for a period of mourning, acting as host to the scores of relatives and friends who would visit with gifts of fruit, candy, wine—sweets to sweeten the bitterness of death. He would refuse, of course, because of the examinations (he would have refused in any case), and there would be another shrieking scene.

"Where are you going, Sam?" Aaron asked.

"I'm going to see Sarah," he said hastily. "I'll be back in a few hours."

"Sam! You should be here! Mama needs you—and you have to study tonight! When will you sleep? When will you eat?"

"I'll manage." He was out the door already, leaving behind the dull hum of tragedy—the muted cries from the bedroom, the low rumble of the mourner at the coffin. Alone in the street, his tears were unloosed. He had been cold, indifferent in the face of his father's death, the detached medical man offering flat, comforting words and trying to keep his head. Sobbing now as he walked toward the trolley, he realized, with deep shame, that his behavior had stemmed from something more selfish, more personal, than the desire to soothe his family. His father's death had plunged him into crisis: at the back of his mind had been the appalling prospect that his education was at an end. They were almost penniless. Aaron would have to help support the old lady—and who could say how long Aaron would be able to work? There remained a year and a half of medical schooling to be paid for.

He burst into Sarah's kitchen as the Malkin family was having its evening meal. Malkin *père* had just finished his nightly upbraiding of Sarah's younger brother, Willie. Willie had opted against serving under his father's iron hand in the grocery jobbing business. Instead he had gone to work in a Pitkin Avenue clothing store, assuring unwilling customers that "it fits perfect." Between the tyrannical father and the rebellious son there was perpetual border warfare. They sniped from behind preconceived notions, set up small verbal ambushes, and peppered each other with interminable insults. Through it all, Sarah and her mother, a small woman of remarkable dignity who wore a wig on her shaven pate, would sit quietly and await the few peaceful moments when the warring parties would catch their breath.

"Pop, when are you gonna wise up?" Willie would ask, ladling chicken soup dotted with thick globules of fat into his mouth. "How long you think the big guys are gonna let you sell your tea and coffee a cent higher than them?"

"Look, it talks yet! Advice from a *prosteh yid*! From a salesman who sells suits they fall apart after you wear them once!" He looked up seeing Sam standing in the hallway. "Oh, *halloi*, Abelman! *Nu*, how is the professor?"

"I have some sad news," Sam said. "My father died today!"

"*Oi*, a shame," Malkin said. Mrs. Malkin and Willie made appropriate condolences. Sarah rose and came to Sam's side. Her father murmured a prayer and expressed his admiration for the departed tailor, who, though he worked with his hands, found time to study once a week. "Oh, Sam, I'm so sorry," Sarah said. "How did it happen? Was it sudden?"

"He came home sick from work yesterday. His heart gave out this afternoon. I was in school taking my tests when it happened." He discerned a cold look of disapprobation in Malkin's merciless eye.

"Mr. Malkin, I'd like to take Sarah for a walk. We won't be gone long."

"A walk? Your father's dead and you're walking with girls, yet? She's in the middle of dinner!"

Sarah rarely disobeyed the old man. But she understood Sam's urgent need. They hurried down the tenement stairs into the bleak January night. They walked—for hours it seemed—and Sam cried softly for a while.

"It's a terrible thing to say, kiddo," he told Sarah, "but now that Papa is dead I feel more sorry for the way he was *alive* than the fact that he's gone. What a waste his life was! Making other people's coats, pressing and repairing them for thirty-five years! What did he ever get out of anything? What kind of pleasures did he have?"

"Oh, it wasn't *that* bleak. He had his buddies at the *shul*, and his family."

"Some family. The sick and the tired. And me, the big boy who couldn't pay his way through medical school."

They locked arms and she squeezed his hand. "What are you going to do now, Sam?"

He stopped and withdrew his hand as she moved ahead a step.

"I'm going to quit, that's what has to happen! Now I know why I was so—so—indifferent when Solly told me Papa had died. I was feeling sorry for myself. He played a dirty trick on me, dying like that. He had no right to run out on me. Me, the only one in the family with any guts, with any ambition. What else did he have to live for except to help me?"

"Sam, bite your tongue!" She was genuinely angry. "You talk about courage! Think of what it took for your father and mother to leave Russia when they did, and how they did! How do you know what went on in his mind? He was more proud of you than anything. Don't you think that fifty cents a day and all the meals you never paid for was a strain for him?"

"He never told *me* that." He was rather enjoying the opportunity to feel sorry for himself.

"When did you ever talk to him? When did you try to know him?"

"Ah, what was to talk about? All he knew—his needles and the new Singer and the *shul* with the old guys with the spinach on their face."

"Sam, you sound awful. I'm a little ashamed of you."

"And I'm fed up with everything. Okay, no medical school. I can get back in the school system, get an appointment. I'll call McDevitt tomorrow."

She drew back a few paces. Under the street light he could see the blush of anger in her smooth cheeks, the anger in her eyes.

"You do that, Sam, and you can stop calling on me. You can forget about our engagement and everything else. You know what you said three years ago—you couldn't go on being a teacher, a *melamed,* instructing a bunch of wild kids in calisthenics. You wanted something better, something more useful to the world. Well, you get nothing for nothing, Sam. And if you won't work to become a doctor, you don't deserve it."

"You tell me how, " he whined. "I should work at night and weekends and never be able to study? What kind of job can I get?"

"That's your business. You don't seem to have thought much of your father, but at least he raised a family and gave you a start. Call your friends. What about Mr. Comerford?"

"I haven't seen him in years. He's bedridden anyway."

"Well, ask Hector O'Bannion. Ask somebody for work. Don't just lay around looking like a sick calf. And don't come calling on me until you know you're going to finish Bellevue."

She left him; the first time in their four years of friendship she had done so. It was easy enough for her to be so brave, he thought. She didn't know what it meant, trying to learn medicine and earn a living at the same time. And who would support his mother now? He might earn his subsistence, he might scratch together enough for tuition and books. But Slonimsky the landlord was not noted for charity.

Yet somehow he managed. They moved from Slonimsky's four-room apartment to a two-room basement flat, sharing a communal toilet with several other families. Sam made a deal with Aaron: the younger brother would manage the rent and the food for a year and a half, until Sam had graduated. They would keep a careful record of what Aaron spent, and as soon as Sam began practicing he would begin paying off his share of the maintenance money for that period., Meanwhile, he needed cash for tuition, books, and his daily expenses. It was a bad time to look for work—particularly part-time employment. He tried a few agencies, hating the hat-in-hand business of filling out endless forms and waiting behind the wooden railing where the smug agency people sat, calling names out like bailiffs summoning prisoners to the bar. With some uneasiness he turned to his old mentor, O'Bannion. The physical culturist had never forgiven his ex-pupil for forsaking the simple truths of raw carrots and handstands for the mumbo-jumbo of the "dispensers of false remedies."

"My boy," O'Bannion piped through his red mustache, "I act in your behalf against my better judgment. You showed great promise once—a man born to the crusade for good health through diet and muscle vibrations. Instead, you deserted me for the charlatans, the bone-breakers and flesh-cutters, the dolts who misrepresent nature and try to deform her, instead of co-operating with her in endowing suffering mankind with health. I would not exchange a plate of raw cabbage for all the aspirin in Bellevue."

But O'Bannion delivered a job. He had former students in every gymnasium in the city. There was a small athletic club in the financial district which was owned and operated by a Chelsea College graduate. Sam was hired as a semi-instructor and locker boy—mopping floors, supplying towels, assisting the masseur, leading the flabby businessmen in calisthenics or pounding a medicine ball into their mushy paunches.

He worked four nights, Monday through Thursday, earning a little extra in the way of tips by coming in Saturdays and Sundays to give special exercises to the club regulars. It paid enough to defray his daily expenses and left a little to store away for tuition. But he could tell in advance that he would need additional cash before the year ended. Charlie McDevitt had promised him a summer playground job again, and he hoped to make up the difference by returning to his beloved galoots. He prayed it would be for the last time—the problem of keeping up his studies with a night job and weekend work was already troubling him.

Toward the end of his third year, when the lengthening days

deceived him into thinking he could stay up longer, read more, absorb more, he began to notice that his strength was giving out. He felt he could barely make it through final examinations. Desperately he recalled the way he used to face up to an exam. He had been like a conditioned boxer, an athlete with inherent skills of strength and speed, looking upon each contest with calm confidence. He had enjoyed the tense challenge of the test: the sealed envelopes, the barbed queries, and he had plunged into his answers with a sense of wild joy. Now, he knew, examinations would be a struggle. He never began his studies before eleven o'clock at night, blinking into the unfriendly texts over his evening bowl of soup. Appreciation of what his beaten father had done for him dawned on him slowly; he would never be able to tell the tailor what his aid had meant. Guilt deepened, as he resumed each night his battle with the books. Concentration was harder; he had to read and reread, fight against dozing off.

In May, two weeks before examinations, Dr. Winter began his spring series of quizzes, aimed at reviewing the year's work. It was exactly the kind of hard refresher work Sam needed; but his mop-and-medicine-ball duties at the club made it impossible for him to attend. The sessions were of a practical nature, conducted in the Carnegie Laboratory. Sam, coattails flying, would leave the gym and reach the lab a few minutes after Winter's class adjourned. Usually he found one or two students who remained behind. If he was lucky enough, he borrowed their notes or pleaded with them to furnish him a quick verbal résumé of Winter's demonstration. The Thursday prior to examination week, a prematurely hot May night, he flew into the laboratory, his hopes shattering as he saw the empty room. Only Otto, the chief morgue attendant, was present, muttering his litany against students, professors, and corpses. The remains of an autopsied body, an immense Negro, gleaming blue-black under the ceiling lamp, lay on the dissecting table. Apparently the students had been performing an exploratory of the abdomen. The incision was still stretched open by clamps; Otto was in the process of dismantling the apparatus and stowing away his silent companion.

"Otto!" Sam called out. "Hold it! Give me a few minutes!"

The sour face, a roadmap of blue-red veins, looked at him contemptuously. "You again. Come on time, or to heck mit you. Dis vun to sleep has to go. Beat it!"

"Otto, please! Just this once! What was Winter discussing?"

"Who am I? Professor Biggs? Vat does it look like, a fractured leg?"

"Please, Otto, let me just look it over for an hour or so!"

"You crazy or somethin', Abelman? Vy you such a pest?"

"Look, Otto, I'll lock up for you. I'll clean up everything. And, I promise you, after exams I'll get you a bottle of schnapps."

Greed conquered churlishness. Otto gave him the keys and left him with the drained corpse. Sam tore off his jacket, rolled up his sleeves, and started to attempt a reconstruction of Winter's demonstration. There was a convulsion of some kind in the lower bowel that had been exposed for particular attention. He reached for scalpel and scissors and went to work.

He had no idea at what point he had fallen asleep, or how from a standing position over the dissecting table he had ended up flat on his back on the wooden floor, in the drugged stupor of total exhaustion. Just as it had been Otto, who had left him there the night before, so now it was the attendant, rousing him with a tirade of profane German. Sam raised himself on elbows, shaking his head. The stink of formaldehyde and the polite rotting of the corpse made him gag.

"Abelman, you liar!" Otto screamed "You gave me your void! You would close up for me und clean up!"

"I'm sorry, Otto," he muttered. "I guess I fell asleep. I'll clean up right now."

"Right now! Right now! Mit a class to begin in fifteen minutes! You see what I mean, Professor Brooks? Dese New York fellahs?"

Harlow Brooks was standing with the morgue attendant. The assistant professor of clinical medicine studied Sam quizzically behind rimless glasses. Sam scrambled to his feet. He had no time to be furious with Otto. He was brimming with shame.

"What happened, Abelman? Volunteering your brain and body for the future of medical research?"

"They won't get much out of my brain, Dr. Brooks," Sam said. "Can I resign now?"

"Any time you want." Brooks turned to leave, but a slight hesitancy in his walk, some faint beckoning prompted Sam to pursue him.

"Could I see you for a few minutes, Professor Brooks?"

"Of course, Abelman. But first give Otto a hand."

He grabbed mop and pail (he was an expert at it after his labors in the athletic club), sponged the table clean with disinfectant, helped the custodian return the remains of the corpse to the meat locker.

Brooks was waiting for him, his trim figure like the sachem of a tribe behind his desk. The walls were covered with Indian masks and artifacts. Sam stared at them curiously, forgetting his distress for the moment.

"Go on and ask it, Abelman, is it true that I'm part Indian?" He saw Sam's embarrassed smile and continued, "I'm not, if it sets your mind at ease. I guess it started because I was born in Mankato, Indian territory. It's a funny thing how fact fashions itself after fiction. People kept saying I was an Indian, although, I'm no more a redskin than you. Eventually I became interested in Indian life. Almost as if I were fulfilling what people expected of me."

Sam scratched at his unshaven face. He felt dirty and unkempt, unfit for the dignified precincts of Brooks's office with its library, its grotesque reminders of the nation's original inhabitants.

"What's eating you, Abelman?" Brooks asked. He sucked an unlit pipe.

"I'm no good," Sam blurted out. "I'll never make it. You know what happened to my marks."

"I've noticed. You turned in a pretty miserable paper to me last week."

Sam lowered his head as if ducking a punch.

"Can't take a little punishment, Abelman? Working nights will be the death of you, I guess. Seems a shame with a year to go."

"I have only so much strength," Sam said. "If I can't do well at something I won't do it at all. Look, Professor Brooks, when I studied shorthand I wanted to be the best shorthand stenographer in New York and I darn near was. I graduated at the top of my class in Chelsea College and I ran the best playground in New York City for two summers."

Brooks stoked the pipe, lit it, and puffed. "That's the trouble with perfectionists. One setback, one change of circumstance that forces a lowering of performance, and you fold up. Abelman, I don't go around preaching, even though people get the idea I'm some kind of an oracle and they keep trooping in here for advice. Heap big chief or something like that. But if there's anything a good doctor needs it's staying power. Sure, the fellow with the occasional stroke of brilliance is needed. But it's the day-in, day-out practitioner, the M. D. who isn't sure he knows all the answers, the one who knows he'll make mistakes now and then, who keeps the profession going."

"If you know how tired I was all the time. Work nights, study into the morning, no sleep."

"Stop whining. Either stick with it or I'll send you in to the dean now and you can resign. But after almost three years . . ."

He turned away for a moment, gazing at a magnificent Mandan

war mask mounted over the doorway. "Reminds me of some of my Park Avenue clientele," Brooks said, smiling. "Acute dyspepsia brought on by excessive indulgence in rich food. Let me tell you a little story, Abelman, before you go to see Dean LeFevre."

Sam, half rising, resumed his seat.

"Some years ago I had a seventy-year-old maiden lady as a patient. Since her sixteenth birthday she had suffered from paroxysmal tachycardia. Know what I'm talking about?"

Nodding, Sam replied, "Distressing heart spells, with rapid beating making it difficult to count pulse."

"I couldn't do a darn thing for her when she got these spells. But the old hen had invented her own therapy. She would lock her thumbs behind her head and bend to the floor several times. This crazy salaam, believe it or not, made her heart behave normally. I didn't believe her until I saw her perform for me when she suffered a spell. Last year, the lady had an attack of pneumonia, and while in the hospital she was seized by one of these characteristic paroxysms. I got an urgent call from the hospital in the middle of the night—seems the old bird was raising Cain and screaming for me. Well I got to the bedside, and there she was, standing in the middle of the floor going through her crazy calisthenics—thumbs behind neck, bending to the floor! The internes and nurses thought she was insane, of course, but in a few minutes she was all smiles, happy, content, free of her tachycardia, and back in bed, anxious to recover and be out and about again."

Sam was doubly puzzled—first as to the purpose of the story, and secondly as to the medical explanation of the patient's therapy.

"How did you explain it? Did you ever recommend it for other patients with a similar ailment?" Sam asked.

"I haven't the faintest idea what it did for her, Abelman, not the remotest. I thought about it a lot and then gave up." He set the pipe down in an ashtray—a Navaho bowl with geometric designs running around the base. "You look as if you're expecting a moral. Well, there isn't any. Just that there's so much beyond our understanding, so much that eludes us all the time and must continue to."

"Are you asking me to stay on, Professor Brooks?"

"I'm not asking you to do a darn thing, Abelman. You know your own mind. What were you going to do after graduation?"

"General practice."

Brooks nodded. "The best kind. We'll have specialists for the right and left toe if we keep on. Medicine isn't drugs and surgery and therapy. Medicine is people. We deal in people, each one different, valuable, worthy of some kind of special attention. That old lady with her calisthenics, for example. I can sometimes make a better diagnosis from a painting hanging on a man's bedroom wall than I can from the beat of his heart. After all, that painting is as much an expression of the individual as his heart."

Shamefaced, Sam stood up. He knew he could never quit. He might collapse from lack of sleep, his grades might plummet him into the bottom quartile of the class, he might be the biggest dunderhead in Bellevue's history, but he knew he could not give up.

"One more thing, Abelman. Every year I live it seems to me there are less and less useful things to do in the world. Everything seems to be getting pallid, conformed, stereotyped, people as alike each other as one epithelial cell to another. Medicine is one of the few places where nothing you do is ever a waste, a drain, a bore. You can stay in general practice in one small village all your life, Abelman, and each day will present a new prospect, new things to learn, new gifts to impart to people. It's the difference between being a spectator and a participant. If you want to be on the outside, looking through the window, go up to LeFevre and resign. But if you want to get your hands into the mess we're in, for better or worse, stay with us. I don't care if you end up with the worst set of grades in the Class of 1912. You'll learn more and do more in one year of general practice in Brooklyn than in five years of postgraduate work. That's the trouble with all you vagotonics—pessimism and perfection in equal doses. Too much vagus nerve."

They shook hands, student and teacher, and Sam left.

He was amazed how soundly he had slept next to the corpse in the dissecting room. A nine o'clock class in gynecology beckoned and he felt remarkably fit and strong. He'd even keep a carbon of his notes for Maxie—something he hadn't done in weeks.

The doctor was stooping low in the cornfield. The last ears of the season were ready for harvesting, and, on the completion of his reminiscences about Bellevue, he had retired to the tassel-topped enclosure, seeking out the remaining crops of his minuscule farm. Outside the makeshift gate, Diane leaped and pranced. She was never allowed in the sancrosanct farmland, yet she never tired of appealing for entree.

Under the trees, Thrasher and Daw talked excitedly about the role they would assign to Harlow Brooks in the television program. They knew, of course, Brooks had died many years before, but to Daw's way of thinking that made it even better.

"How about this," Daw was saying, "we have an overhead shot of the doctor at the desk, maybe with Lord sitting where the patient normally sits. Dimly, in the background, we see a glimpse of the Brooks photograph, enough to pique a viewer's imagination. As Lord asks Dr. Abelman who was the greatest influence in his life, he begins to talk about Brooks. Camera dollies in slowly, focusing on the Brooks photo, and then we roll some tape of Brooks—there may be a broadcast or a speech of his recorded somewhere. If not, we get a guy with a kindly doctor-type voice to read some of Brooks's ideas."

"I'm not sure I like the actor angle," Thrasher said, rising from the cruel slats. "And I doubt if there are any recordings of his voice." He called into the cornfield, "Dr. Abelman, when did Harlow Brooks die?"

"Bum! Got you!" Dr. Abelman looked up from his labors in the postage-stamp farm. "Not you, Mr. Thrasher. It was a lousy corn-borer. I hate the bastards. What did you ask me?"

"When did Harlow Brooks die?"

"Oh, around 1936. Very sad. He died of a liver abscess. It was caused by the Welch bacillus—the germ he investigated forty years earlier. They called him the 'beloved physician.' Usually when a doctor gets a handle like that you can bet he's a crap artist. But not Brooks. He was a real man."

"Even I liked him," Max Vogel ventured generously.

The doctor had an armload of corn. They looked thin and delicately green, smaller than the supermarket ears, but Dr. Abelman assured his guests they were sweet and juicy beyond a gourmet's dreams. He unloaded four or five ears on Daw and Thrasher, then, turning empty-handed to Max, tossed a small object at him.

"And that's for you Maxie!"

"Ah, you louse!" Vogel shrieked. He pawed frantically at the huge, malevolent insect on his starched shirt front, almost tumbling from the hazardous beach chair. "Some joke!"

"What's the matter, Maxie, afraid he'll make poo-poo on the twelve-dollar shirt?" It was not quite jealousy of Vogel's haberdashery that had prompted the move, Thrasher sensed; just a little resentment against his colleague's complete control over his patients, his life, his own person.

"Max, I want you to look at those head plates again." The doctor was moving toward the house.

"Dr. Abelman," Daw asked, "anything else about Bellevue we should know? Are any of those people you mentioned still around?"

"Anything else about Bellevue? Well, I graduated. That last year almost killed me, but I got out. Got married six months after graduation and bought a Dodge from Bishop, McCormick and Bishop."

"How about people like LeFevre, doctor?" Daw persisted.

"Sonny boy, they're all dead and gone. LeFevre died in 1914, what a loss! Biggs, Carlisle, Brooks, Park—all of them. Most of my classmates, like this clunk, are around. Karasik is a practicing neurologist and I send him work. Padgitt, the guy I had the fight with, he's a big gynecologist. He always liked sniffing around."

He was tiring of the interrogation, anxious to get back to his plates, to the urgent problem of Herman Quincy, his headaches and his mysterious convulsions. "What do you know about heroin addiction, Max? Can it cause headaches with any regularity?"

In the cool hallway of the house, the doctors left their visitors. No date was set for the next session, Thrasher hoping he could entice Dr. Abelman into meeting him in New York. He wanted to see the old man completely relaxed, at ease, in a different milieu for a change.

Leaving, they heard Vogel lecturing his friend—"Sam, for Chrissake, why don't you shine your shoes and get a haircut more often?" —and it occurred to Thrasher he had often wanted to ask Dr. Abelman the same thing. He had never seen Seymour Baumgart, M. D., but he knew that Baumgart's shoes were always bright with polish, his hair trimmed, his collar and tie firm and neat. It was so easy to do the little things properly, he thought. Why did Samuel Abelman insist on doing them all wrong? Even Harlow Brooks must have been well barbered and neatly shod.

At the vestibule door Myron greeted them. He was wearing what was evidently his lounging costume—the faded basketball trunks and the ragged T-shirt. A monstrous yawn distorted his face into a grotesque rubber mask, the kind favored by bank robbers.

"Hiya, men! How's the Madison Avenue task force?" Myron asked.

"Coming along nicely, Myron," Thrasher said. Daw looked bleak and uncomfortable.

"Hey, shorty," Myron said to Daw, "that your MG on the street? You better get out and rescue it from the boogies. They're having their annual barbecue and jitterbug contest in it."

Daw turned pale and left. He would have liked Thrasher to accompany him, but Myron had buttonholed the vice-president and was backing him into the waiting room.

"You're comin' along so good, ya got me to thank. Remember, I got Uncle Doc to go along. Which brings up two things. First, when do I go on salary? And, second, what about the dough—the eight thousand bucks for the house?"

"Don't rush the season, Myron. You'll never get anywhere in our field—and I take it that's what you want—by being in a hurry. Be slow, deliberate, take time to think, to talk, but never hurry. Buy a pipe and chew on it if you find you're talking too fast."

There were barbaric shrieks from the street; Thrasher was almost becoming accustomed to them, and he attached no importance to them.

"I'll ask ya again, Thrasher. When do I start work, and does Uncle Doc get the dough? He says he can get the job on Republic Street for twenty grand, but it has to be twelve thousand cash. Okay, he could take four grand out of savings and it wouldn't hurt him too much, not this late in the game. Eight thousand from you, and we're in."

Thrasher listened gravely to the mathematics. He was on Dr. Abelman's side, but he preferred not to have Myron know he was won over. And as yet he had not the remotest idea as to how the money could be raised, or accounted for.

"I'm working on the money, Myron, let's leave it at that. As for yourself, I plan a production meeting early next week and I'll want you to attend, to meet the gang."

"In the morning, hah?" Myron asked. "I gotta be at work by four in the afternoon."

"Production meetings are always in the morning, Myron. That leaves the rest of the day for lunch, drinking, and whoring. Aren't you going to love television?" Halfway through his assurance to Myron, he realized that he would be calling very few of the meetings from now on. He now had an executive producer, Ben Loomer, a specialist in meetings.

"I'll hear from ya then?" Myron pursued.

"My secretary will call. So long, Myron."

The late afternoon sun, after the shaded confines of the anteroom, blinded him for a moment. They had parked Daw's car a good distance down the block, near a public school. The street was lined with automobiles (Thrasher wondered how so many poor people were able to drive cars), but Daw's creamy white sports car, encircled by a curious crowd, was easily locatable. Thrasher walked quickly toward it, realizing at once that Daw was in trouble. The Twentieth Century Gents had taken over. Herman (Josh the Dill) Quincy sat at the wheel. Nobody Home was beside him, and Lee Roy was perched on the folded convertible top, the raven on the Pallid bust of Pallas. Several dozen Negro children, bare-chested and barefoot, eddied about the forlorn MG with the adhesiveness of sugar ants.

"They won't get out," Daw said to Thrasher plaintively. "I keep asking them and they won't."

"We comin' into deh home stretch at 'Napolis Speedway!" Herman Quincy roared. It was a rather accurate imitation of a sports announcer.

"Oh, man, we drivin' fools!" Lee Roy shouted.

"We doin' one hunnert fifty miles a hour, man!" Nobody Home cried.

"Why don't you be good fellows and let me in?" Daw asked. Thrasher felt sorry for him: a little blond man with a round shaven head and a cotton cord suit. Anyone could see *he* belonged in a sports car, not them.

"Man, you selfish!" Herman Quincy cried. "You got to share wid deh oh-pressed minor'ties!"

"Yeah! You selfish! Sheeeet!"

"Evabody invited on!"

The sugar ants swarmed over the functional chassis, on the hood, the folded canvas top, the fenders and bumpers.

"Oh my God, Woody," Daw muttered. "How can we get them off? Maybe the doctor can!"

"Make way for deh Twentieth Century Gents!" Lee Roy called. "We comin' down the stretch—we run you over and kill you daid, man!"

It seemed unfair to Thrasher to have to trek back to the doctor's office and ask him to rescue them. He didn't doubt that Dr. Abelman was equal to the situation. He knew them and he could handle them. But between them he and Daw earned over sixty thousand dollars a year. Somewhere in that sum of money, still a very large sum indeed to Woodrow Wilson Thrasher of New Arabia, South Dakota, there should have been an allocation for dealing with twelve Negroes on an MG convertible. Yet neither of them knew where to begin. Daw's sorrowful pleas had only inflamed them into greater bursts of joy. If they tried to force their way into the car, pulling the squatters off, they might suffer something more humiliating than insults. Thrasher imagined himself and Daw in bush jackets and pith helmets, Vickers automatics under sweating armpits in canvas shoulder holsters. The Mau Mau were on the warpath again and they were leading a punitive expedition into Kikuyu territory.

Salvation rolled by in low gear, a New York City Police Department Ford, Officers Moynihan and Kaplan in command. "Call them, Woody!" Daw cried. "For goodness sake, ask them to help!"

The Ford halted, but the dark usurpers did not budge. Lou

Kaplan jumped out of the driver's seat and approached the MG. To Thrasher and Daw's confusion, he smiled affably at the occupants, addressing himself to the young man at the wheel.

"It's my friend Herman Quincy," Patrolman Kaplan said softly. "How are you doing, Herman? Having fun?"

A gentle smile exposed Herman's teeth. Thrasher got a good look at the young Negro, impressed with his beautiful symmetry, the off-color tan, like some new decorator's creation—*mulatto brown, smoked beige, cream'n'sugar*—he envisioned the advertisement in a woman's magazine. The facing page would have an article called "*Get Out the Vote!*"

"We doin' jes' fine, Lou," Herman said easily. "We havin' a little harmless fun with these gemmun's racin' car."

"It's *not* a racing car," Daw protested, "it's a *sports* car. There's a world of difference."

"No sheeet?" Herman asked.

The sidewalk audience unloosed a chorus of *wah-wah-wahs*. Kaplan edged closer to the MG and gave Herman a strong push in the ribs. "Okay, Herman, the joke is over. Now you and your friends get out and let these men have their car back." Lee Roy, Nobody Home, and the small children bounced from the sagging car at the policeman's word, and the narrow, low vehicle seemed to spring back to its normal shape. But Herman had not moved. His long hands still gripped the wheel.

"No, Lou, don' you evah lay hand on *me*, no mo', see? Y'all wan' talk to me nice, talk, but don' lay no han' on me. I don' let no one touch dis boy. Dis boy private property like dis car."

Inside the hot Ford, Kaplan's partner grinned. He had chosen not to leave the automobile, knowing that all Kaplan would get would be abuse and back talk. It was just like that little sheeny, buddy-buddy with the boogies all the time and then getting insulted for it.

"Now, Herman, run along," Kaplan said firmly. "You and I are old friends, and we don't have to be nasty."

"Y'all jes' don' tech me, see?" The inviolate figure untracked itself from the cramped leather seat and hopped to the pavement.

"It's all yours, folks," Kaplan said politely to Thrasher and Daw. They climbed in, both looking straight ahead, trying to ignore the stares and profane comments of their audience.

"Scram, Herman, and take your friends with you," the officer said.

Herman rolled his eyes in mock terror and fell back into Nobody Home's arms. "Oh, pleeze, mistah cop, don' hurt me! Ah's sceered of you!"

The Twentieth Century Gents and their little friends roared:

Kaplan walked up to Herman and shoved him again, a little harder.

"Okay, Herman, wise up. I'm willing to meet you halfway, but I'll slap your teeth in if I have to. You're not such a big cheese."

"Y'all jes' don' tech me." He folded his arms, refusing to move back an inch.

Frank Moynihan called to the occupants of the car from his Ford, "Either of you guys wanna file a complaint?" He was grinning; the whole affair amused him.

"Well—well—aren't *you* going to do anything?" Daw stammered.

"What? Malicious mischief?" Moynihan asked. "We'd fill the poky by noon every day."

Thrasher, giddy, nudged Daw in the ribs. The director seemed stunned. "Doc, for God's sake, get moving," he said. The imported motor backfired with flatulent arrogance. Herman Quincy clapped his hands rhythmically. Patrolman Kaplan shook his head and walked toward the coughing MG.

"Are you the fellows who are working on the television program about Dr. Abelman?" Kaplan asked. "I read about it in the New York *Times*. It sounds like an interesting project. I once prepared a sociological survey on the effects of mass communications in a slum area when I was working for my Master's. Perhaps you might need—"

Another expert, Thrasher thought weakly. He was having his own troubles keeping his footing, yet everyone he met was convinced they could be helpful to him, especially the amateurs. Why didn't Myron stay on the New York *Record,* running copy and putting commas in the PTA story? Why didn't this idiot in the blue uniform remain in his prowl car? Even Max Vogel, M.D., had hinted he'd like to assist.

"Thank you very much, officer, but at the moment it's just in the blueprint stage. Perhaps later. Thank you."

"Dr. Abelman's social theories are kind of backward," Kaplan began. "I hope you won't—"

But Daw had finally engineered his escape. The cream-colored machine fled noisily. If its owners were too blind to understand that they did not belong on Haven Place, at least *it* knew where it wasn't welcome.

"Hey, Lou," Herman called from the admiring crowd, "y'all got any mo' free butts like las' time we talk? Wheah all dem free butts, man?"

VII

LOOMER was absent from the office on Monday. His secretary, apparently sworn to secrecy, would only say he was "on a special junket." Significantly, T. C. Whitechapel was not in evidence either, and Thrasher assumed they were off huddling somewhere on urgent matters—not necessarily *Americans, U.S.A.* and the troublesome *G &T* account. He took advantage of the lull—there was always a pleasant moratorium on meetings and executive lunches when Loomer was away—to do some organizing of his own. As producer and writer, he retained some prerogatives, and apparently Loomer was still willing to let him control the content of the show. He sent Alice Taggart to the Bellevue Library on First Avenue for some digging. Louise, a more capable researcher and a better writer than any of the higher-priced girls with Ivy League drawls, started assembling facts on general practitioners. Daw joined him shortly after ten; both the director and his MG were fully recovered from their encounter with the Twentieth Century Gents. They were rolling now, and it was a good, reassuring feeling. Daw had unearthed some excellent old footage of Castle Harbor and Jewish immigrants—it would play wonderfully in the brief sequence on the doctor's boyhood. A crew would be assigned to shoot footage in and around Bellevue—most of the old buildings where Dr. Abelman had attended class were not only standing but still in use.

They had worked for no more than half an hour when Louise buzzed him.

"Got your parachute, boss?" she asked. "You have a flying lunch date."

"What?"

"You and Tom Finucane have just been invited to lunch on Bugler's Island."

"Cut it out, Louise. Daw and I are busy. Order us some more coffee."

"I'm *not* joking. Ben Loomer called in from Bugler's Island just a few minutes ago. He's been in session with Mr. Gatling and Mr. Whitechapel at Mr. Gatling's home, and you and Tom are to meet them at the Bugler's Island Country Club at twelve-thirty for cocktails and lunch. Mr. Gatling's private seaplane is waiting at the Twenty-third Street dock. Mr. Loomer said please don't be late, it's important. You'll be flown home."

"How do we get to Twenty-third Street? Didn't Loomer arrange for Mr. Gatling's scooter to take us?"

"I didn't talk to him. He called Ted Chilson."

"Okay, Louise. If Chilson is calling him back, tell Loomer we're on our way. Where is Bugler's Island anyway?"

Daw was rolling his droopy eyes. He was palpably impressed with the invitation. "You've arrived, Woody, arrived," the director said, somewhat jealously. "Bugler's Island is it. They don't come any fancier. Southampton is Haven Place alongside Bugler's Island."

"Is that the place way off Orient Point? It never shows on the road maps—you know, a dotted arrow at the border and it says 'Bugler's Island twelve miles'?"

"That's it. Forty families and one country club. Reachable only by ferry, chartered plane, or private boat. I used to lay a dame who was married to a guy whose family had a summer home there. She divorced him because she thought the island was sinking into the sound. It had something to do with an immersion-womb complex. But Bugler's Island, whew!"

"You make it sound so nice," Thrasher said, "I may never come back. If I don't, Dexter, advise the police you suspect foul play. There's a good chance that if it's as isolated as you say, Loomer may try to bury me in Smuggler's Cove."

"Hell, you've *been* there!" Daw cried. "How'd you know about Smuggler's Cove?"

"Dexter, Dexter, there's *always* a Smuggler's Cove."

An hour later he and Finucane were aloft, flying noiselessly east over the gardenless garden apartments of Queens. Gatling's pilot had the leathery disdainful face of the aerial bum. He brooded sullenly at the controls, and Thrasher imagined he was recalling his days as a wingwalker at carnivals.

Finucane was unusually silent and sober. Thrasher had noticed the slow change in the effusive Irishman, and, as much as he thought he disliked Tom, he began to feel sorry for him. Looking at him now, the chunky face the color of a seed catalogue tomato, the fitted navy-blue suit wrinkling in the cramped seat, he wondered what was eating him. Finucane was a man of no talent. He had never in Thrasher's recollection made a single constructive suggestion, come up with a single original thought. He had risen through the sheer ebullience of his personality, selling himself as the brawling street-corner Mick, the kind of comical strong-arm man that every agency needs. Finucane alone could tell an anti-

Semitic story in front of one of their Jewish clients and get away with it. Even Jews liked—or pretended they liked—his crudeness.

"What's this big meeting about, Tommy?" Thrasher asked. "You've been pretty thick with Loomer. How does it look?"

Finucane looked at him blankly. "Should I know?"

"It's your account."

"What does that mean to Loomer?"

"Tell me this, Tom," Thrasher said earnestly, "you and I once were pretty good friends, so I feel I can ask you."

Finucane was looking at him like a sympathetic barfly.

"Tom, what soured Ben Loomer on me?"

Finucane looked out the window at the beige and green coastline of Long Island's North Shore. "Jesus, I can't say for sure, Woody. I think it was just the way you took over so completely at that meeting after Brick Higgins fell on his prat. You know Loomer is a funny guy. He's honest, and I suppose he's always given *me* a fair shake, but, Jesus, he's scared stiff of his job. I guess he figured you talked too good for his comfort, that your pitch was a little too brilliant. He knows his job is ten grand better than yours and he also knows old Whitechapel may want a board chairman under the new setup."

"You mean he made his mind up then, that far back, to start undercutting me?"

"I wouldn't call it that, Woody. He's an exec VP and he's got a right to supervise everything, to make changes, to, let's face it, take credit for your work!"

Finucane had phrased it very well. And his willingness to talk so freely assured Thrasher that Loomer was closing Tom out of the *G & T* operation. At least he had something left as producer and writer; Finucane, whose importance to the company was an abstract, an intangible, might wither away altogether if Loomer moved into his area of diplomacy.

"What about you, Tom?" Thrasher asked.

"What about me? I'll manage. Whitechapel knows I'm no slob, that I've kept Gatling happy for a long time. B'Jesus without me they would have yanked those regional spots years ago! I kept Parker Theis in World Series tickets and broads for longer than I like to remember. Oh, I'll be around."

They were the two kids who hadn't made Bones, who were left off the Dean's List, who didn't get the good jobs the college employment office had promised. There was something so desolate in Finucane's defense, his pride in having served as ticket speculator and panderer for the heir, that Thrasher wanted to pat his moist black curls. The man should have been standing by the River Liffey singing ballads to the sea gulls.

Now the plane was skimming over the sound, bumping along on the still waters, and coming to a jerking, bobbing halt. Gatling's timing was admirable: no sooner had the seaplane's propellers ceased whirring than a trim little launch was speeding toward them. Waiting for it, Thrasher could see a ferry slip, a drab gray pile of rocks and timbers. A few sun-scarred natives lounged about the forlorn dock. A macadam road wound away from the ferry slip, climbing through what appeared to be a deserted army post. There was a red and yellow sign, the colors of the old Coast Artillery, Thrasher recalled, and a series of vine-covered barracks and brick buildings which were once officers' quarters. An abandoned post theater, the shuttered box office standing dismally under a fading marquee, was visible; if they had been closer they could have seen what was playing when the station was shut down.

Ashore, the ugliness of the island appalled him. Finucane, aboard the plane, had confirmed Daw's awed estimate of Bugler's Island— one of the very last places where America's real wealth gathered in the summer months. Inaccessible, water-locked, its rocky terrain carpeted with stunted and malformed greenery, it seemed better suited to serve as a penal colony than a resort. The initial impression was confirmed when they transferred from the launch to an unwashed Plymouth station wagon with a cracked rear windshield. The scarred lettering on the door read *Bugler's Island Country Club,* but Thrasher felt that FRESH EGGS DAILY would have been more appropriate. Bouncing along the twisting roads, Thrasher was reminded of a landscape description he had read, in an old science fiction novel, something about "the bowels of the earth disengorging their foul and rank vegetation." Not a tree seemed over six feet tall. The undulating land—not hilly enough to be picturesque and not flat enough to provide a vista—was covered with low angry bushes and stout weeds. Occasionally, in the distance, they could see the eaves and dormers of one of the island's mansions.

The country club itself overlooked an inlet where an artificial beach had been deposited. The gray sand was strewn with seaweed and shells and looked bleakly inhospitable. A jetty separated the bathing area from a stretch of black rocks that formed a crescent in the shoreline, and Thrasher took this to be the inevitable Smuggler's Cove. As the mystery of Bugler's Island's supereminence in the hierarchy of vacation spots intensified, Thrasher blinked his eyes at the club itself. It was a misshapen pile of dull pink plaster, a Tudor hydrid of the twenties, the exterior beams, windows, and trim painted a gloomy green, the same doleful shade as the dirt-pocketed lawn surrounding it. A Filipino boy in a uniform designed, manufactured, and first worn in the Coolidge administration, eyed them unhappily when he noticed the absence of baggage.

"The power of the word," Thrasher said. "Make the myth big enough and everyone believes it."

"What's that, Woody?" Finucane asked.

"Nothing important, Tommy. Give me enough time and money and I could make acne popular. Why have a clean, clear skin when you can have it decorated with pimples and blackheads?"

Finucane mumbled something about "not before lunch," but it had been lost on him.

The spare, functional lobby contained a small registration desk, behind which were a gray-haired native lady, who looked like the village postmistress, and a glass-covered display case half filled with Hershey Bars, Oh Henrys, three brands of cigarettes, and a box of Roi-Tan cigars. Thrasher had been on several free junkets to Miami Beach, and it occurred to him that a fifth-rate hotel in that sunlit strip, one frequented by butcher boys, electrician's helpers, and shipping clerks, would have been infinitely more luxurious than this revered retreat. There was a twofold explanation, he felt. Bugler's Island represented the ultimate warped triumph of Thoreau, the dirtiest of dirty tricks on the Marxists. Partly it was the business of being "one of the boys," the chairman of the board calling the millwright by his first name, the full circle from Cadillac to Austin-Healey, back to Dodge station wagon. But the real beauty of Bugler's Island was that you didn't actually have to get your feet wet with the slobs. You could, if you were crazy, carry the simplification-and-modest-living theme to a very painful conclusion merely by vacationing in Coney Island or Miami Beach instead of Southampton. But then you ran the double risk of too-close association plus a baffling return to complexity and opulence. The fifty-dollar windows at the harness racing in Westbury, Thrasher knew, were invariably at the service of Italians in three-day beards, Negroes in upturned panama hats, and elderly fat ladies squinting at Jack Schultz's selections in *Newsday*. Anything the swells could do, they could do better. Thus at Bugler's Island you simultaneously simplified and closed the door. There were no colored men driving Oldsmobiles to remind you how disturbingly thin the line had become. When every bricklayer had his own three-way radio-television-phonograph and when every fireman's daughter took ballet lessons, what was there left to do but to run the other way?

Once you got it started, the *word* took over. The best families went to Bugler's Island, *ergo* it had to be the best place. Young men from Menominee, Michigan, and Pass Christian, Mississippi, all the eager hinterlanders dealing in the word in the New York talk factories, knew about Bugler's Island and hoped to be invited there. The few who made it, expecting a gilt and marble nirvana, were too stunned to be critical, to question the loftiness of the weed-choked rock. Returning to their converted brownstones and offices, they vigorously continued to perpetuate the myth. After all, they had come from towns where the victrolas were hand-cranked and broke down regularly, and where there was no one to *give* ballet lessons, let alone permit the daughters of the house to take them.

A series of dark corridors, each with a threadbare gray runner on the aged floor boards, led them to a dining room slightly less formal than a rear-echelon non-com's mess. Through glass doors they saw their host, Van Alst, Whitechapel, and Loomer seated on mail-order house furniture, hand-painted an emetic yellow. Gatling and Loomer greeted them cheerily, and Whitechapel, prim and precise in a black suit and starched detachable collar in defiance of the informality of the setting, shook hands with his boys. Van Alst only nodded. T.C.'s eyes had a special twinkle for occasions when he met with his people on a more or less social basis. At company picnics he was known to tell a risqué story to his top executives, and Lucille LoPresti once claimed that he had pinched her arm behind the grandstand during the softball game between the married and single men.

"I would have liked to have had Mr. Whitechapel and you birds out to my own place here," Gatling said, "but the old lady is up in Maine and I wouldn't trust that frog cook to make coffee. Besides, the chow's pretty good here."

Thrasher was relieved to see that T. C. Whitechapel was not included in Gatling's ornithological generalizations. The drugmaker may have come up from the Erlenmayer flasks, but he knew a high-class gent when he saw one. Just as he realized that Loomer, Finucane, and Thrasher were all "you birds," he understood that the agency chief was "Mr. Whitechapel."

"How 'bout some drinks?" Gatling asked. "They give you an honest count here!"

Whitechapel sipped sherry and Finucane took a double bourbon on the rocks; the rest of them settled for mammoth martinis. Thrasher was relieved to find there was no stinting on the drinks or the lunch. They were served a magnificent succession of summer dishes: fine seafood, perfectly mixed salads, and a plate of cold cuts that managed to transcend the usual synthetic display of cross-sections. The people who dreamed up Bugler's Island weren't carrying it so far as to grow and cook their own beans.

"If it's okay with you, Mr. Gatling," Loomer said, "we can get down to business with the coffee. I don't want to keep the fellows too long."

"Hell, they'll be home in a few minutes. My pilot's got nothing to do but sit on his can and wish for another war."

"As you know, Woody," Loomer began, "Mr. Gatling, and some of *us*, for that matter, have felt that *Americans, U.S.A* doesn't have enough zip. Thus far, you haven't given us a gimmick, a windup."

Thrasher pushed his chair out far enough to let him rest an ankle on the opposite knee. "Must everything have a gimmick, Ben, a windup?"

"In television, I'd say that most shows must!"

"I'm with you," Finucane said quickly.

Loomer continued. "Any dramatic play has a resolution, something is solved. A good comedy or variety show saves its best act for the end. Even your documentaries and discussion shows have some kind of bow on the package, some moral, some lesson. That's what *American's U.S.A.* is lacking. Or at least you haven't told any of us what it is. The way I get it, we merely do a chronological, on-location documentary on our subject, proving that he's been a good citizen, a worthwhile guy, doing an admirable day-in, day-out job."

"Where's the gimmick or the windup in *See It Now?*" Thrasher asked.

"The gimmick? It's those blinking monitors with the datelines, I always thought. You get the sense of *going* someplace, even though it's film rolling in a studio upstairs. The windup is the little summing-up Ed does at the end."

Thrasher nodded his head slowly.

"Ben has a point," Whitechapel said softly.

"You bet he has," Gatling said. The hardwood kitchen chair seemed to have pushed his droopy lower bulk upward, so that his chest and abdomen appeared endowed with several new lumps and flaps.

"What I'm saying, Woody, is, what are we really doing to get people to tune in?" Loomer drawled.

"A good show. A show with dramatic value, truth, and purpose."

"It's not enough," Loomer said. "You can write the world's greatest script, and I'm sure it will be adequate. This doctor may be colorful and exciting and everything else. Andy Lord will pull us *some* viewers. But Mr. Gatling feels, and I've felt for some time, that there's a missing part."

"How would you know, Ben?" Thrasher asked. "You haven't been in on any of our meetings. You haven't even met the doctor."

The round face went a shade darker, a progression on a hemoglobin chart. It was wrong to accuse a top man of lacking intimate contact with a project: he wasn't *supposed* to roll his sleeves up, and by challenging him to do so you were only further violating the rules.

"I don't care if it's your doctor, Woody, or any of the subjects Ted Chilson has selected for future shows. It's your format I'm dissatisfied with, not specific content."

Gatling selected a fat pale-green cigar from a box offered by the colored waitress. The Roi-Tans in the lobby were a nod in Thoreau's direction; if you knew where to ask, you could get the secret box of double claros.

"Well, with less than three weeks to go, what do you suggest?" Thrasher knew that something was going to be suggested and he felt obliged to give them their opening.

"Funny damn thing," Gatling said, carelessly blowing clouds of smoke in their faces, "but I've never messed with the TV end of the business. I'm a chemist, a manufacturer. But you birds—especially you, Brasher—got me all wound up. I went home to the missus and asked her what the hell was it so hard you guys did. Every one of you I've ever listened to, it seems to me you're peddling farts and belches over a counter, selling something that's got no shape, no color, just two cents' worth of air in a ten-cent bottle. Now frankly, gents—and Mr. Whitechapel knows this—I've got all I need and *G & T* isn't going to be in any trouble over one lousy show. We make good drugs. We got good salesmen. We pay high wages, and we were years ahead of Reuther with guaranteed annual employment. What I'm getting at is I decided to get into this television and see if an old quantitative analysis man can add something to the formula."

Thrasher leaned forward. "I'm sure we're delighted to hear your thoughts on *Americans, U.S.A.,* Mr. Gatling. It's been my experience that you practical men with industrial experience can often add something of real value."

"You bet I can," Gatling said. "I already told your bosses and they think it's great."

He was about to have it handed to him. Evidently Whitechapel and Loomer had already folded. His idea, his bold thinking, his hard work would all be forgotten by the time they were through with him. He could see the final move: they'd ring in William Faulkner to write it and his credit, if he were lucky, would be "Assistant Supervisor."

"You know I blew my stack at you, Brasher—"

"Thrasher."

"Yeah, and when I got home I realized you weren't a bad sort of bird. In fact you gave me the whole idea for the new slant we can give this show."

"I did?" They weren't merely going to hang him; they had let him tie the knot. Yet he couldn't believe that Gatling had anything personal against him. The saggy old chemist looked impartially upon all of them as "birds."

"I can remember getting you pretty mad with a crack about drones and confidence men, Mr. Gatling," Thrasher said calmly. "You wouldn't be thinking of a series on famous charlatans and deceivers?"

"Nah," Gatling burped. "It came to me after you started talking about the eight thousand bucks for this old sawbones. Remember that?" Behind the falling pouches, the eyes were slyly merry—a Falstaff of the acid baths.

"B'Jesus, I remember that!" Finucane said. "I thought Ben would flip his lid on the way home!"

"You see, Woody," Loomer said, slapping a huge square hand on Thrasher's knee, "how wrong I could be. You gave Mr. Gatling the idea, and I almost wanted to sock you when you brought it up!"

Was he yet to be saved? Did some idiotic train of thought that his request for money had touched off in Gatling's mind mean he was home-free? It couldn't be completely so—Loomer was too eager to be magnanimous.

"Look, Thrasher, let's say we do these programs about plain American slobs like this doctor, good, average people who buy G & T products, pay taxes, don't hurt anybody. Swell. We do it, like you fellows say, live, real honest-to-God stuff. But why leave the public with an empty feeling? Why not pay them off? I wouldn't make a laxative that just smelled, looked, and tasted nice. It would have to get you in the end—"

T. C. Whitechapel gagged slightly, but for several million dollars he was able to keep the lobster and shrimp salad down.

"I don't follow you, Mr. Gatling. What does the eight thousand dollars have to do with it?" Thrasher asked.

"I'll draw you a diagram. What do you want the dough for?"

"To help Dr. Abelman buy a new house. He surely deserves one."

"Great! Perfect!" He was elated. "That's the payoff! What does the old guy need to buy a house? You can't get a house for eight thousand?"

"No, but by selling his old one, and using some savings—"

"Details! eight thousand, ten thousand, the more the better!" He hoisted his drooping bags and pouches from the cruel chair and was on his feet, using the cigar as a schoolroom pointer.

"Wait till you hear the details," Loomer whispered. "It's the end."

"It's quite an idea, Woodrow," Whitechapel said, nodding his agreement.

"Get this, Thrasher. We tell the story of this poor guy. His life, his hard work, his value to the community, all that stuff. How he got where he is, why he's a poor slob instead of rich. And then—then—we have Andy Lord ask him his heart's desire! Get it, *heart's desire?*"

"See if I can guess, Mr. Gatling," Thrasher said. He had expected his tongue to freeze in his mouth, but the words came out, as if someone else had uttered them. "*G & T* gives it to him."

"A bright kid you got there, Whitechapel!" Gatling boomed. "Sure! It's the windup! Every man in the world has some single thing he wants above everything else. Why not use this as the key to the whole mess? After we tell the story—*heart's desire*. And we fill it. This Dr. Edelstein wants eight thousand bucks for a house, we hand it to him. Certified check, personally given by Andrew Bain Lord."

They permitted him a few moments of digestive silence. Both the rich cold dishes and Mr. Gatling's notions of programming needed considerable gastric action.

"I also suggested," Loomer broke in, "we might change the name of the program. Instead of *Americans, U.S.A.* we could call it *Heart's Desire.*"

"I like it," Gatling said. "I'm new in this racket but that has a nice sound—*Heart's Desire!*"

"I'll buy it," Finucane said quickly. "Of course it's a shame we've put out all that publicity on *Americans, U.S.A.* The network press department has daily releases going out. We were the lead story in *Variety* last week."

Loomer wrinkled his nose. "Doesn't really matter, Tom. A follow-up story on the new format will do us more good than harm. Look at what *Today* went through before it got on the air. Just getting the story in print creates interest."

Thrasher was desperately trying to drain what remained of his martini. They were giving him no time to think. The little fortress he had built for himself around the new show was crumbling. Any minute they'd bring up the battering ram and cave the door in. From Gatling's standpoint, it was a perfectly logical move. He was basically a good-hearted man, proud of his achievements, his company, his honest products, and his high wage scale. A man who had been ahead of the country on guaranteed annual employment would quite naturally think in terms of rewarding people like Dr. Abelman, the old librarian who couldn't make the trip to Stratford-on-Avon, the impoverished minister who wanted a new carillon. Thrasher had to admit: it had its value, it would draw an audience.

"I'd like time to think about it, if I may," Thrasher said. He turned on his appealing, younger-son manner. He hadn't had occasion to use it in years. "Mr. Whitechapel, in fairness to me, I think I should be allowed to sleep on this change a few days. After all, sir, you'll remember that *Americans, U.S.A.* was my baby. I invented it. I pushed it. I'm doing the bulk of the work now, under Ben's supervision, of course. I see a lot of virtue in Mr. Gatling's revision, but I see one big defect. Could we possibly postpone a decision until the end of the week?"

Whitechapel blinked his eyes a few times.

"Why wait?" Gatling shouted. "Your bosses went for it. Why must you guys always have to have meetings on top of meetings? You'd think your jobs were hard or something!"

He was surprised when Whitechapel interceded for him. "Mr. Gatling, I'm sure your suggestion will be the key to a successful show. By the same token, we owe Woodrow a few days to mull it over. I'm sure he will come around to our way of thinking."

"He better," Gatling growled.

"I'm convinced," Finucane said.

"I'll be damned if I am, Mr. Gatling. Want to hear why?" Thrasher unlimbered himself and leaned over the table. A breeze drifted up from Smuggler's Cove, from the gray beach devoid of bathers, and fluttered his batiste shirt away from his back in a white inflated arc.

"I don't have to. But go ahead."

"I'll tell you something, Mr. Gatling. People—especially the people I have in mind for my show, and especially Dr. Abelman— don't always like charity. They don't like being held up in front of forty million of their neighbors as failures, people who couldn't make the grade on their own, who need *your* money to get them their fondest wishes. You'd insult and humiliate Samuel Abelman beyond repair if you let it be known to the world that he couldn't afford a better house in a good neighborhood, that a drug company had to buy it for him."

"Balls. Every man's got a price."

"No, Mr. Gatling. Only bichloride of mercury and crystalline oxalic acid have prices. Do you know what Sam Abelman will do when Andrew Bain Lord hands him that certified check?"

"He'll stuff it into his wallet and buy that house, that's what!" Gatling's face was splotched with wrathful red circles.

"Oh, no he won't. First he'll belt Andrew Bain Lord right on his bobbed beak, and I hope he unbobs it for him. Then, in front of all those millions of people who buy *G & T* he'll tear your check into confetti and use some choice profanity. Besides, I know he'll refuse to go along with the deal as soon as he hears how we're going to take advantage of him. He may not belong to the Bugler's Island Country Club, but he grows his own corn. I ate a couple of ears yesterday and it's the best corn I've had this summer."

Gatling's bloated features reassembled themselves around the soaked cigar butt. Somewhere in the folds of his neck he gargled in search of his voice, and Ben Loomer had to rescue him.

"You're wrong, Woody," Loomer said slowly. "First of all, the way we've set it up with Mr. Gatling, the subject never knows what we're going to give him. We will research each subject so thoroughly that we'll *know* his or her heart's desire. But it will be kept completely secret. A real surprise on the air."

"Jesus," Finucane spluttered, "think of them great closeups! Tears 'n' all that stuff!"

"That's the idea," Gatling said breathlessly. "We keep it *secret*. Not even Andy Lord knows—just us. He opens a sealed envelope, reads a little story, and produces the *heart's desire*. That's the way it's got to be."

"How do you guarantee the person won't raise hell on the air?" Thrasher asked insistently. "I've just told you Mr. Gatling that Dr. Abelman will do just that."

Gatling pounded the table harder than he wanted to. Rubbing his reddening hand, he roared at Thrasher, "Why the hell are you always fighting me, Brasher? I told you he'll fall on his knees and kiss our asses when he sees that check! And if you're so damn sure he'll be offended, we'll lose him! There's millions of Americans willing to take my money and to use it for good purposes. Now if you want to drop him, fine with me!"

Whitechapel's firm little chin was trembling ever so faintly. "Woodrow," the old man said in a whisper, "I think you have no right to provoke Mr. Gatling. He is being very reasonable and generous—"

"You're damn right I'm generous! You think I don't know what charity is? There are Gatling scholarships in forty-three colleges and universities! There's a Gatling wing at the cardiac hospital in Des Moines! No one's ever turned down my money, and, let me tell you, Brasher, I *like* the idea of giving it to people who need it. I don't give it away because some kid in narrow lapels tells me it will make the public think I'm hot stuff and buy Whiffo! No sir, I *want* it put to good use!"

It was amazing, Thrasher thought, they really weren't very far apart at all—Gatling, Dr. Abelman, and himself. Yet there was almost no means of communication available to them.

"It's not the same, Mr. Gatling," Thrasher said desperately. "Everyone appreciates what you've done for charities. And I know your desire to help the people on *Americans, U.S.A.* is sincere. But you'll be doing more harm than good."

Whitechapel cleared his throat. It was a tiny, rattling noise, but everyone looked at him and waited for the cracked voice.

"I suggest, Woodrow, you are arguing to no purpose. Ben and myself are agreed that the heart's desire climax to your program is mandatory. I can make this no clearer. You must accede to our wishes. After all, Woodrow, we are in a majority. Do what you will for the first twenty minutes or so of the program, but conclude it with the presentation to your doctor."

"May I still have a few days to think about it?" Thrasher asked.

"You may. But we will not change our basic concept. A detail here and there, perhaps." Loomer was nodding mechanically, registering silent "yeses" to every word the old man squeezed out of his dried innards.

Thrasher stood up.

"Okay, Mr. Whitechapel. I've never let you down yet, in five years." Every now and then you had to do it that way. Surprisingly, it was not painful at all. "I'm young enough to take orders and I'm too old to start looking for work as good as this."

They shook hands all around. He and Tom were about to leave; Loomer and Whitechapel were staying over as the drugmaker's guests.

"One last thing, Brasher—"

"—Thrasher—"

"Yeah. Don't you dare go blabbing to this pill-roller about what we're going to give him as a surprise. If he finds out and starts acting up, we'll lose the both of you. I'm not really mad at you, kid, but I sure will be if you cross me."

Thrasher smiled. He had meant it to be his disarming, man-to-man smile, the one he used on board chairmen, but he found he was *really* smiling at the ugly, sagging, fat man.

"No hard feelings, Mr. Gatling. It's your privilege to pin my ears back." The manufacturer waved him away, thus minimizing their differences. Then he brightened. "Say, why don't you birds hang around? We can squeeze in nine holes of golf and still get you back early."

Finucane seemed delighted; Loomer and Whitechapel had no choice but to play. Thrasher had been a late-in-life golfer, learning it when he had to. He enjoyed the game and played fairly well. But he had to save something of his chosen role as the company rebel.

"Gee, I'm sorry, Mr. Gatling," he said, "but I don't play golf any more. Thanks very much, anyway."

Loomer was shaking his head in aggrieved disbelief as they departed. It was a poor trade—Thrasher had lost on a massive principle, and had won only the esoteric pleasure of having scoffed at a ritual.

VIII

Thrasher's next meeting with the doctor took him to the office of F. L. Karasik, M.D. The neurologist, Dr. Abelman's old classmate, lived in a three-story semidetached brownstone on a street of aging respectability in the Eastern Parkway section of Brooklyn. It appeared a focus of medical and dental offices. M.D. plates were in evidence on several parked cars, and the streets were noticeably free of children and baby carriages. The peaceful bordering rows of maples reminded Thrasher of how desperately the doctor wanted and needed a new home.

Dr. Abelman had asked him to meet him in Karasik's waiting room. He was bringing a patient to the neurologist, and they would have time to resume the interrogation as soon as the medical examination was concluded. Thrasher was met at the door by a uniformed nurse. He explained he was not a patient, that he merely wanted to meet Dr. Abelman there. Seated in the specialist's anteroom, he gathered that Dr. Karasik was quite successful. The furniture was modern and medium-expensive; all the chairs but one were filled. A middle-aged Negro woman, clad in old-fashioned heavy clothes, sat uneasily on the edge of a cane-back chair. The busy office, the respectable neighborhood, the well-appointed waiting room, and the starched nurse started Thrasher wondering. What did Karasik have, what did he do, that had eluded Sam Abelman—the tough young man who once had to fight his battles? Abelman had been able to protect the Viennese from the galoots almost half a century ago; it seemed almost mandatory that Karasik should have been able to assist his old champion in some way now that *he* was successfully adjusted to the world.

In a few minutes the office door opened and a young Negro walked out. Thrasher recognized him immediately. He was the serpentine young man, so beautifully tan and so malevolent, who had commandeered Dexter Daw's MG and had sassed the earnest young policeman on Haven Place. Shuffling in delicate little steps to a chair alongside the Negro woman (she was evidently his mother), he slumped deep on a flexible spine and lit a cigarette. Thrasher admired the theatrical manner in which he struck a kitchen match on a long nail, lit up, inhaled, blew out the flame, and then dropped it indifferently on Dr. Karasik's slate-gray carpet-

238

ing. The woman clucked disapprovingly and, retrieving the smoking match, dropped it in an ashtray.

Behind opaque cream-colored shantung curtains on the office door, Dr. Karasik studied the X-rays of Herman Quincy's troubled head. The neurologist was a trim miniature of a man, white hair and mustache immaculately barbered, his professional confidence sharply outlined in French-toed black shoes, a starched white knee-length coat, a loosely knotted maroon silk bow tie. Franz Karasik had long ago ceased apologizing to people. Each year of his life he had added a little more aggressiveness, a bit more certainty to his personality. As a result, at seventy, he appeared to Sam Abelman more youthful than when he was struggling through Bellevue as a target for spitballs.

"The syndrome is not complete, Sam," Karasik was saying. "You know, these suspected intracranial tumors. By the time we've got a definite diagnosis, something we're really sure of, the patient is often beyond saving."

"Those convulsions are what get me," Dr. Abelman said. "Idiopathic epilepsy, it could be. That's a handy name for whatever you professors don't understand."

"You can't eliminate it," Karasik said indulgently. He was accustomed to Sam's barbs, disappointed if he wasn't insulted a few times.

"We're old buddies, Franz. Make a guess. I won't snitch if you're wrong."

A *Mittel-europische* smile, part charm and part slyness, wrinkled the neurologist's mouth. "No sir. Not until after the electroencephalograms. Go ahead, diagnostician, you make it."

"Cerebral neoplasm, probably in the motor area. I think we'll have to try ventriculography in a couple of weeks."

"Why?"

"Just a GP's instincts, and don't tell me how dangerous those are."

Karasik nibbled at the temple piece of his gold-rimmed spectacles. "You're still the pessimist, hey, Sam? Did it ever occur to you that your own dismal view of everything colors your diagnoses?"

"Who's dismal? I'm happier than you are, you old louse."

"Slow down, Sam, slow down," Karasik said. "Two of us have given this boy the full tests, and what have we found? No genuine weakness or paralysis—"

"Right arm is weak."

"*Ach*, Sam, you with your muscles. You wrestled him like he was Hackenschmidt, you with your gymnasium mentality. Besides, was it real postconvulsive weakness or just the debilitation of a narcotic addict?"

"We aren't sure he's an addict. A user, yes."

"The gait seemed normal to me," Karasik continued. "And until we observe an actual convulsion and mark it for local diagnosis, until we can examine the patient *immediately* following the convulsion, we don't know where we are."

"All right, professor, how do you explain apparent papilledema and a history of morning headaches?"

Karasik squinted at his desk blotter. He knew that, like most of Sam Abelman's patients, the colored boy and his family would be able to pay only half of his normal fee. Yet he was obliged to give his old protector's patients every possible attention. The tortured hours in the Carnegie Laboratory had never been erased from his mind.

"Papilledema, possibly indicative of a lesion," Karasik said. "As for the headaches, he told you one story and told me another. Remember, Sam, we're dealing with a psychopathic personality here. This boy is a heroin user. Who knows what the drug has already done to his system? The headaches may be nothing but a manifestation of excessive use, or a reaction to involuntary abstention."

"I think he's getting 'em every morning, like he told me. My patients don't lie to me." The doctor peered over his horned-rimmed glasses, the dark eyes enshadowed and grave.

"Why shouldn't this little hoodlum lie to you or anyone else?"

"My GP instincts again."

"*Ach,* you annoy me, Sam. You and your reverse snobbery. Let's leave it at this. Tomorrow, he comes for electroencephalograms. Better make sure his mother brings him. He might try to diddle around with Miss Malloy, that little villain. After we read them, we wait a little while to see if any defects are evident in the motor area. If we get an unfavorable reading on the electroencephalogram, if we note additional motor defects in gait, muscle tone, strength, and if we can observe a convulsion, then we will know more."

"What about my X-rays?"

"Very lovely X-rays, Sam. But I would say negative. The digital impressions aren't pronounced enough. Absence of calcification. The brain keeps its secrets from general practitioners, Sam. It's open only for the professors to look in."

Dr. Abelman tugged at the ruffled collar of his lemon-yellow sport shirt. The knot of the dark-green tie had vanished beneath one flapping wing, and the tie itself dangled over the breast pocket.

"Stop crapping me up, Franz. I gave you my suspicion, give me yours."

"I have no medical instincts, Sam. I need more evidence. But if you press me, I'll give you two alternates. First, idiopathic epilepsy—"

"Idiopathic, my foot. It means you can't explain it."

Karasik ignored the rude interruption. "And second, depending on what we can observe in the next two weeks, possibility of a lesion of some kind in the brain. I won't be as specific as you."

Dr. Abelman looked grim; a sadness that seemed to weight his features pulled at his eyes, his mouth; the deep knifecuts at his nostrils lengthened. As the lower part of his face sank, the skin on the high, sweating forehead wrinkled upward quizzically. The spiked gray tendrils almost seemed to rise under the fluorescent glow of the chandelier.

"If it's epilepsy—" He shook his head. "I remember a neurology textbook's advice, how the patient should be encouraged to lead a regular life, associating with his usual playmates. He should finish school. No alcohol, narcotics, or irregular living. Some joke. How do you get that little rat out there to do that, hey, Franz?"

"It's not our problem, Sam. We didn't make him."

"And if it's a neoplasm in the brain—"

"Probably surgery," Karasik said. "But first we'll pump a little air into the ventricles and have a look around. All right, Sam. Do me a favor and don't worry. Why do you take it personally all the time?"

Dr. Abelman looked offended. "Who takes it personally? You think I'll stay awake nights over it?" The manner in which he asked the question told Karasik that his friend would not only suffer insomnia over Herman Quincy, but would live with the youth's ailment forever, for as long as whatever it was that was afflicting the Negro boy would let the patient survive.

Karasik deftly placed a cigarette in an ivory holder and inhaled deeply.

"So aside from business, Sammy, how have you been? How's Sarah, and your family?"

"Oh, everyone's fine, Franz. My little *ketzeleh,* she's going back to school, and Eunice and her husband are doing very nicely."

"But you, *you.* When are you getting out? Last time I saw you you were moving out the next week. That was two months ago."

Dr. Abelman removed his glasses and tucked them into the breast pocket of the malformed shirt. "Haven't you heard, Franz?"

He asked the question as if he expected the American Medical Association to have publicized the news in its last journal.

"Don't tell me, Sam—retiring?"

"Nah, what the hell would I do retired? Franz, I'm buying a house on Republic Street. Across the way from the Klopf Mansion. Maybe you know it—a brownstone job, three stories, semidetached, with garage in the back." He leaned over conspiratorially. "It's a steal. I murdered that real estate agent."

"Sam, I'm delighted." He was, too. "You know for so many years I wished you'd get out of that slum. You, the best diagnostician I ever knew. I mean it, Sam. And there are fellows who earn four times what you do who say so also. If you'd only stop loving and hating your patients and start treating them like customers."

He rang for the nurse and asked her to make an appointment for the Quincy boy for the following afternoon. Dr. Abelman rose, shaking hands warmly with his classmate. The trim little Viennese looked at him admiringly. "I hear they are doing some kind of television about you, Sam. That should be a good break. You tell me when it goes on. I must see how they handle my old guardian."

"Yeah, some kind of crap. My nephew Myron, the newspaperman, he got me into it."

Karasik rose. "It shouldn't hurt your practice any. People watch television and listen to what it tells them."

"Who needs them?" Dr. Abelman snapped with strange ferocity. "I still have a tremendous practice."

Through the opened office door, Karasik saw the massive colored lady and her lawless son. They were Sam Abelman's tremendous practice—the dregs and remains who somehow missed the clinics; some old friends who understood him; a sprinkling of neighbors who had overlooked his caustic tongue and his moralizing because they knew he charged less than the specialists.

Thrasher smiled and got up. He had hoped to meet Karasik, but the neurologist had returned to the cool interior office; the nurse was holding the door ajar. Dr. Abelman waved a greeting at the agency man and then spoke briefly to Herman and his mother. The colored boy listened sulkily, kicking with a tan suede shoe at the carpeting.

"You'll be all right, sonny boy," Dr. Abelman said. "Listen to your mother and to Dr. Karasik, and we'll fix you up."

"Ain' nuttin' wrong wit' me," he mumbled.

"Get in that office, or I'll knock your block off," the doctor barked. "You're a punk." Herman Quincy seemed stupefied, detached. He followed his mother back into the office.

A new Pontiac, the length of a submarine and painted mauve and royal purple, was parked bumper to bumper in back of the doctor. At the wheel of the wheezing Buick, he sweated and cursed trying to maneuver the reluctant car out of the trap.

"How about a louse like that?" he asked Thrasher. "What kind of consideration is that? Only a cake-eater who would drive a whore's houseboat like that would jam into a guy. And with the M.D. plates on, too. Some lice have no character at all. People like that should go to jail."

Thrasher had a sudden mental image of a jail jammed with cake-eating drivers of brightly colored Pontiacs; the doctor, in turnkey's olive drab, was laughing at them.

The doctor was sweating so violently from the exertion that Thrasher became concerned. The huge biceps were inflated with the effort, the sharply outlined veins on his temple swelled and reddened.

"Dr. Abelman, why don't you let me maneuver the car out?" he asked politely. "I'm used to this from parking in the city."

"Stop kidding me, son," the doctor said, as the car lurched out of the vise. "I can handle these whoremasters."

He made a right turn, and as they passed a corner candystore, a newspaper delivery truck sped by them with arrogant recklessness. A bundle of late afternoon editions went spinning over the Buick's hood and the doctor had to slam his brakes on to keep from running into the tailgate as it cut in front of him.

"Punks! Galoots!" the doctor called out. "All that speed for what? To deliver a pile of crap! Something you can start fires with! You should use all that energy for better things!"

A grimy delivery boy, hirsute and harelipped, spat over the tailgate.

"Blow it out of your ass, pop!" Two sidewalk loafers giggled.

"They all stink," the doctor grumbled, defeated for the time being. His warfare never ended, Thrasher saw. It was no use asking him not to knock himself out battling everyone who was rude, cruel, or fraudulent. Outrage seemed to sustain and invigorate him. Or did it really? He looked particularly haggard, the agency man had noticed, in Karasik's office. Perhaps it was the soggy August heat; perhaps it was the whole burdensome problem of the new house; worst of all, Thrasher's own inquisitions might have been wearing him down.

"Funny thing about the Negro lad," Thrasher said, "I could swear he was one of a gang who swarmed over Dexter Daw's car the other day when we were at Haven Place. I saw him give a policeman a very bad time."

"Nothing surprises me about that trash any more," Dr. Abelman said. "Why should they listen to a cop?"

"He seems to be listening to you."

"I don't care whether he does or he doesn't. I don't need him."

"I'd say he needs you. How sick is he?"

The doctor made a left turn onto a wide, tree-shaded avenue. "I'm no professor," the doctor said, "but I think he's in bad shape. You know what a glioma is?"

"It sounds like a malignancy of some kind."

"You're a smart boy. I think he's got one in the cerebral hemispheres. I had a case just like that about ten years ago. The symptoms played hide-and-seek for a couple of weeks, and then the thing grew like a weed."

"What hope is there for him?"

The doctor was wheeling the car slowly on the right-hand side of the street now, peering out first from one side of the car to the other. This had to be Republic Street: a series of solid dark homes, lawn-bordered and devoid of noise or children.

"There's all kinds of gliomas. Surgery is almost always indicated. After that, it depends on how far the brain has been damaged. You see, none of these things are ever encapsulated. So that means when you gouge 'em out, you have to take normal brain tissue with them. If it's a small tumor, a nodule, like an astrocytoma, you can make a complete removal and sometimes a permanent cure. But if it's the invasive type of glioma, what they call a glioblastoma multiforme, it's a lost cause. They usually affect both lobes of the brain. A hot-shot neurosurgeon can do a pretty good job of removing it, but there isn't much left in the way of a patient. They never last long. That lousy glioblastoma gets them very fast."

He seemed to regard the deadly neoplasm as a personal enemy; the affliction was an evil state of things, like a cheat or a galoot, and certain moral laws could be expected to work against it.

"I know that kid is just a little rat," the doctor said quietly. "But no one should have to die that way."

He had parked the car under a towering Norway maple, about a half-dozen houses from the corner. From where they were to the street's end, the solitary mansions had been replaced by a series of semidetached brownstones. They were now opposite the first such set of homes, a pair of monstrous Siamese twins, adorned with cornices, buttresses, and the ornate, ponderous masonry of the turn of the century. Yet it was not an entirely ugly house. For one thing, it might be expected to stand forever. No basement walls would crack, no beams would buckle, nothing would chip off the dark, solemn façade. He could picture the interior—narrow, high-ceilinged rooms, the walls thick with decades of painting.

"There she is, Mr. Thrasher. My beauty." The doctor pointed across Thrasher's chest to the left-hand half of the attached homes. A cement driveway ran to the rear, and he could see the corner of a detached garage peeking through the shade.

"It's a fine-looking house, doctor," Thrasher said. "Is there a backyard with it?"

The doctor shook his head. "Nah, just a little patch of grass. I could put in some dahlias, I suppose. But I can't have everything. I've been looking at houses for fifteen years now, and I know this is the one. It's a steal."

"It would be a shame to give up your cornfield and your trees— I don't think I've ever seen a magnolia like yours in the city."

"So I'll give 'em up. Getting out is what matters now."

Thrasher wanted to stick up for the cornfield, for the wonderfully helter-skelter backyard with the mammoth dahlias, the natural green arbor, the ancient slatted bench under the cool foliage.

"What are you going to do with three stories?" he asked.

"Listen, you're beginning to sound like my wife. Discouraging me all the time. So what if there's three stories? I figured it out already. I use downstairs for an office, next floor for living quarters, and upstairs we'll have a tenant. Perfect. Help me pay off the mortgage."

Thrasher winced. The notion of this irascible old man and his timorous wife, the one fuming with anger at the slightest provocation and the other seeing imagined holocausts on the hour and half hour, the notion of them ever putting up with the burdensome duties of landlords and listening to the eternal complaints of a tenant, upset him. Dr. Abelman could no more tolerate a tenant of the most compassionate variety than he could a plague of smut in his cornfield.

"You're convinced you can handle this thing from a financial standpoint?" Thrasher asked.

"Don't get personal," the doctor said, winking at him. He had no bitterness in his voice; it was merely the assurance of one man of the world to another that he would recoup his millions in a flier on the market. But Thrasher kept thinking of his first meeting with Myron—the arch references to the doctor's precipitous drop in income, the paucity of his savings, the added weight and responsibility that a new house, a new neighborhood would mean to him. Of course, Lyman Gatling would provide him with enough money to leave him reasonably secure even after buying the house. But what would that public donation do to the old man?

"I wish you a lot of luck with it, doctor. When are you closing?"

The doctor pushed the starter button and touched off a violent retching in the engine. "I'm really jumping the gun a little," he said. "I'm giving Danny, he's the agent, a down payment this week. First I got to get him to agree to a little deal, then I'm all set."

"Does Mrs. Abelman know?"

"And she's not going to. All I'll get from her is an argument."

Suddenly, he patted the nape of his neck, where the gray hair was growing in a slovenly unclipped fringe, inching over the lumpy collar.

"Oh, that reminds me—the haircut. The wife got home from Long Beach yesterday and if she sees me like this I'll catch hell."

Thrasher was completely on Mrs. Abelman's side. It seemed to him the doctor could have used a clipping when he first met him, more than a week ago. Now the untrimmed hair endowed him with the look of an intelligent vagrant. After driving less than a mile, he parked the car on Rower Avenue, the street running at right angles to Haven Place. A small, neat barbershop was jammed between a body-and-fender machine shop, spangled with grease and sun-heated hubcaps, and a billiard academy. The lettering on the barber's window read *A. Traficanti,* and Thrasher assumed that the proprietor was the neighbor from whom the doctor had bought tomatoes in the era of the walking club. In front of the billiard academy, three young Negroes played a slothful game of rummy on upturned Coke boxes. They slapped their cards down with minimal zest in the afternoon heat. Watching the doctor enter the barbershop, Nobody Home mumbled, "Dat's dat ole doctor."

"Yeah," added Lee Roy. "He takin' care Josh."

"He no good. He kill Josh 'fore he through. Josh ole lady nuts."

A rattling, whirring floor fan made conversation difficult in the shop of A. Traficanti. The proprietor, dozing in one of his two chairs, roused himself in irate delight on seeing the doctor.

"Hey, doc! Where you been? Why no come in? I bet your wife come home, hah?" He was an oversized gnome: a snow-white Umberto crew cut, more Madison Avenue than Thrasher's, crowned a wrinkled set of hyperactive features. The firm white teeth were clenched around the quarter-inch remains of a diNobili cigar. Gleefully, he guided the doctor to a chair, chuckling as he fastened the sheet around the reluctant client.

"I fool-a you today, hey, doc?" Traficanti asked. He addressed his next remarks to Thrasher and two other men who had drifted into the shop on seeing the doctor's car pull up.

"You know how he work, this doctor? I see him. He no fool me. He wait outside around corner, till all-a chairs fill up. Then he go home and tell missus—no gotta haircut, Traficanti chairs all fill! But today, no business, so he gotta no excuse!"

The visitors laughed at the story that they had heard many many times. Scowling, the doctor ignored them. "All right, cut the jokes, Angelo. Make it fast. I can't stand that damn tickling in my nose."

One of the men, a long-headed Irishman with a monochrome red face and curly gray hair, lounged in the adjacent chair. The other, a short blond man in greasy overalls, apparently the major-domo of the auto repair shop next door, seated himself on a rear window looking out into a grape arbor.

"Hey, doc, what's all this about the television they're doin' on you?" the Irishman asked.

"Ask him. He's doing it," the doctor said. He jerked a thumb toward Thrasher. "Mr. Thrasher is a television writer. This is Ed Dineen who lives on a fireman's pension that we pay, and over on the window is Louis Gruber, who louses up my car. And this bum torturing me is Mr. Traficanti."

They exchanged greetings, and Thrasher sensed that the barber-shop group was an insular little clique: a conspiratorial gang that gathered whenever the doctor could no longer contest his wife's demand that he get a haircut.

"You gonna get a new car outa it?" Gruber asked. "They can't show that old heap you got on the television."

"Car? You get paid *big* money for that television stuff. The wife's kid cousin," Dineen said in awe, "went on one of them quiz shows and walked off with a thousand bucks. And he never went beyond the fifth grade, the lug."

Traficanti waved the scissors in front of the doctor's nose. "You get haircut *here* for television! Me! I cut!"

He exhaled a noxious cloud of smoke from the black stub. The doctor coughed and waved the fumes away. "*Gevald,* blow that poison somewhere else!" he shouted. "You want to asphyxiate us?"

Thrasher edged over to the side of the chair where the doctor slumped, enduring the ordeal. "Doctor, why don't I catch you at your office in a few minutes? Your friends seem to—"

"Whose friends? These tramps? Because they're still my patients" —and his pride in them was unmistakable for not having deserted him—"who says they're friends?"

"Holy Mary, Mother of God! After what you did to my prostate!" Dineen intoned.

The mechanic winked at Dineen. "I got him to thank for my second kid. He saved him."

"Let's go, let's go. You want to hear about how it was when I started practicing, right? Well, Ed remembers some of it. Mr. Traficanti was here before I was."

"I be here long time after you go too," he said nastily.

"Why don't I tell you about the influenza epidemic? It started 1918, when I was in practice six years already. You guys remember it."

Dineen and Traficanti nodded solemnly. The barber stepped back and shook his scissors violently under the doctor's nose.

"I give you tree 1919, remember?"

"You sure did, Angelo." The doctor smiled.

"Damn good tree, hah? How many pounds this year?"

"Sixty or seventy. I got stewed cherries coming out of my ears because of that tree. Who asked you to plant it anyway?"

The barber relit the black stub, puffing out a new cloud of choking smoke. A troll's eye squinted at the doctor. "You no kid me, doctor. You love tree. I plant. You grow. Best tree on whole block."

Looking back, Dr. Abelman seemed to recall that Yolande Traficanti had been his first true case of "Spanish influenza," as they had called it during the first World War. Yolande, the only one of Angelo Traficanti's daughters whose name he could remember, had been stricken on a Saturday, September 21. A month later, when the pandemic was reaching its peak and the cemeteries were piling up corpses as rapidly as city officials were piling up excuses, it was decided that the "bacilli" causing the disease had been brought to New York aboard a Norwegian freighter which had docked on September 18. There had been known cases of "Spanish influenza" aboard, yet no quarantine had been invoked. The sick passengers were sent to the Norwegian Hospital and discharged; the other travelers had gone their way into the unsuspecting city.

As much as the doctor would have enjoyed blaming the careless authorities for failure to invoke quarantine for the brushfire spread of the disease, he had long suspected that the Norwegian ship theory was, as Max Vogel put it, so much *bushwah*. The ravages of influenza had been world-wide in 1918—not even the interior of Africa had been spared. Reports coming from remote settlements on the Congo River, from steppe villages in Asiatic Russia, from mining towns in the Bolivian Altiplano, told of deaths from the scourge. To blame a single Norwegian ship for an infection that had been world-wide and was to strike every major American city in time was the work of a crap artist, Dr. Abelman always felt, the snappy answer provided by some cake-eater in City Hall.

Twelve Traficantis—the barber and his wife, eight children, and Mrs. Traficanti's father, Mr. Speciale—had wedged themselves into the family Hupmobile for the trip to Holy Family. Yolande, in fluffy communion white, had been complaining of a headache all morning. But her parents, knowing her as a whining child, and anxious to have her undergo the sacred rites, had advised her the headache would vanish as soon as Father Bevilaqua pronounced his blessing. They assured Yolande that the ritual fasting was making her head hurt. When, after cranking up the overloaded automobile and bouncing off to Atlantic Avenue, she began to scream that her neck and her arms were hurting, they became apprehensive. Only one more symptom was needed to terminate the religious expedition, and Yolande supplied it two blocks from the church. She began to retch violently, her starved little stomach bringing up bile and mucus and staining the white organdy dress. After a violent Neapolitan scene in which Angelo Traficanti accused his wife of browbeating the girl and Vincent threatened to punch Dominic for taking up too much room, the party chugged back to the frame house on Calvert Street.

When Dr. Abelman arrived, the turmoil could not have been greater had Francesca, the oldest daughter, eloped with a Sicilian. Yolande had been put to bed. Efforts to stimulate her appetite first with warmed-over ravioli, then with bread and butter, and then with cornflakes had failed. The little communion girl, fasting since the night before, was unable to eat. She was running a fever, no question about it: her head ached, so did her eyes, her ears, the back of her neck, all her joints. Sam Abelman, reading the thermometer at one hundred and four, did not need that evidence to tell him she was sick. She *looked* sick. There was a dull redness about her eyes; the color of the skin was unhealthy; her motions were sluggish. He prescribed aspirin, alcohol baths, liquids, and light foods until the fever subsided.

"What she got, doc?" the barber asked.

"It's what we call la grippe, or influenza," the doctor said. He was sitting on the little girl's sickbed—one of three beds in the narrow room—sketching a rabbit for her on his prescription pad.

"This is for you, *ketzeleh*," Dr. Abelman said. "If you're a good girl and take your medicine and get better, I'll make a doggy for you next time." She watched him in fascination as the facile pen drew the outlines of a bunny. It was not so much the artistry that intrigued her, but the deft speed with which he sketched.

"Grip? Wassa grip, hah?" Traficanti insisted.

"She not very sick?" his wife asked. She was a muscular handsome woman, gold-fanged and hirsute. Her brothers were eminent men in the founding of the new plasterers' union, protean fellows who could wield a trowel or a guitar pick with equal facility.

"At the moment, she isn't," the doctor said, ripping the top sheet from his prescription pad and handing it to Yolande. "But she needs good care to prevent the disease from getting worse."

"I give best care!" Mrs. Traficanti exploded. "My Yolande my best daughter! Smart!"

"Well, let's see how smart *you* can be," Dr. Abelman said. "First, she needs a room of her own. Get the other kids out. I don't care where they sleep. She's going to cough and spit a lot. Let her do it in clean rags, then burn them. Keep a window open all the time in her room, but don't let her get a chill. Plenty of liquids, sponge bath, aspirin. If she starts to feel worse, or if the temperature goes up tonight, call me."

The barber assured him, over his wife's loud complaints, that she could not possibly give Yolande a room of her own, that they would observe all the rules. Pressing two half dollars into Dr. Abelman's hand, he walked to the door with him.

"Hey, doc, okay if I use-a cup?" he asked with some hesitation.

"Cupping?"

"Shue, cup, a match, you know. Bring up skin, bleed out bad blood."

"You do and I'll punch your nose," the doctor said angrily. "What the hell you think this is, the Middle Ages? Don't you bleed that kid with cups or anything else."

"No leech? Nice leech?"

"No leeches, goddammit! She may get very sick before we're through. Grip they get better from. But she might get pneumonia, meningitis, an inflamed ear. So be careful. Listen to me for a change. Would I tell you how to cut hair?"

"Shue, shue, doc. You boss. I call tonight." He lit up his precious deNobili, filling the dark hallway with thick clouds. The doctor used the smoke screen to make good his departure, running down the wooden steps, through the autumnal remains of Traficanti's grape arbor—all that was left of the original farm—and to his Dodge, surrounded by an admiring circle of Traficanti boys.

"Yolande very sick, doctor?" one of them asked. It was either

Mikey or Vincent, he wasn't sure. He knew Dominic—Dominic had a forceps mark on his temple; he had put it there himself in his first year of practice.

"She'll get better," he said, starting the crank, and waiting for the reassuring *puk-puk-puk.*

"You bet. Pop'll get out his ole cup and leeches—"

He climbed into the high seat, delighted by their waves and cheers as he pulled away from the curb. Cars were still a rarity; aside from the neighborhood doctors, one or two wealthy merchants, and the district leader, nobody drove automobiles in Brownsville.

The doctor refused to answer their taunt about the cupping. He knew that the barber would bleed his daughter anyway and, while it would do no earthly good, it could not harm the little girl. For six years he had been warning patients not to employ cupping—*bankas,* as his Jewish patients called it—knowing that they disobeyed his injunctions with impressive regularity.

Sarah was polishing his sign as he drove up. Haven Place looked clean and respectable in the prenoon September sun. It had been a warm fall. Leaves were just beginning to drop from the Lombardy poplar. An itinerant carousel, drawn by a sagging Percheron, piped a scratchy recording of "Hello, Hawaii." Down the street, a half-dozen little girls held hands and danced, singing a tune that brought back recollections of his playground days. Dismounting from the Dodge, he paused to hear their voices, in strident competition with the cranky merry-go-round.

> *Who wants to come to the sisters' praying?*
> *To the sisters' meeting,*
> *Who wants to come,*
> *Who wants to come,*
> *Who wants to come with me?*

Sarah gave the burnished brass plaque a final flick with her rag and turned to greet him.

"Another call," she said. "Ausnitsky on Herzl street. Mr. Ausnitsky has pains in his head and is running a fever."

"He can wait till after office hours," he said. "First we'll eat and then I have a few appointments." He pinched her backside. "If this keeps up you can have that Peruvian boom-boom coat or whatever it is they call it."

"Bolivian pompon, Sam, and we can afford it now."

"Okay, call up Meyer Malkin, your rich father, and let him buy it."

They used the rear chamber of the ground floor as their dining room—it was not until years later that the doctor converted it into a consultation room. He went first to the windowless middle room, where he examined, treated, and prescribed, and kept his equipment (two tables and a cabinet) and a desk. The soft black Homburg he hung on an oak clothes tree. Carefully he removed his suit coat, the black bow tie, the dapper Arrow collar—it was their newest model, a Marley 2¼—and washed his hands with alcohol. In the small mirror over the examining room sink he enjoyed a moment of Narcissism. His face was strong and hard, everything a young doctor's should be. The mustache he had begun in his second year of practice, aimed at convincing the skeptical neighbors of his maturity, was now firm and full and very black. A faint, incipient baldness at the temples added to the thoughtful, intense mien. He almost felt sorry for old Lemkau having to compete with a vigorous, determined comer like himself.

He heard his daughter calling him from the dining room. He stalked in, an Indian on the prowl. She was two and a half, dark-eyed and precocious, and this was their game. The doctor tiptoed around the circular oak dining room table (the set had been the wedding gift of Meyer Malkin) and halted in his tracks at the sound of the shrill infant's voice.

"I am de mack rider! *Bing*, I shoot you!"

"I'm shot!" he cried. He fell beneath the table, finding her crouched underneath the metal arms and gears used for expanding the table top. "But I caught *you*! I am the sheriff and I caught the masked rider!"

She dissolved in giggles; the joy was too great to be borne. He carried her out, the wiry arms and legs wriggling in gleeful rebellion.

"Were you good to Mommy today, Eunice?"

"Mommy's naughty. Is this a brand-new shirt?"

"Oh, yes. Everything is brand-new. This is my special shirt for playing masked rider with my *ketzeleh*."

Sarah brought in their lunch—onion rolls, snowy sour cream, moist, cold pot cheese, and smoked whitefish, resting beady-eyed on its bed of fresh lettuce. She shopped on the push carts and stalls on the adjoining block's open market place. If you got to know the owners and gained their confidence you could buy the finest foods in the city. The peddlers trudged to the wholesale markets every morning, selecting their own wares, pushing the four-wheeled carts all the way back to Brownsville where they enticed crafty housewives with characteristic cries, a penny off here and there, a bright display. As the doctor's wife, Sarah was entitled to special consideration. Moreover, she was polite and not given to haggling, and in return they saved their choicest vegetables, the best cuts of fish and meat for her shopping bag.

Sam looked through the window at his rear yard. Traficanti had helped him plant climbing vines along the rear fence: honeysuckle and rambling roses. Later he had put in lilacs, mock-orange, and Japanese snowballs. In a few years they'd be spreading their foliage throughout the narrow yard. He had begun a neat brick path, and would soon start growing his own vegetables. It would shape up nicely, he thought to himself. In fact, everything was shaping up pretty well.

It was six years since he had put up his shingle, since he had taken the Hippocratic oath and received his diploma from LeFevre, he and Karasik and Maxie Vogel and the rest of the class of 1912— although Maxie had not actually been present at the ceremonies at University Heights.

"I should spend a buck to rent that nightgown and the flat hat?" he had asked. And he had passed up the academic ritual, showing up instead outside the campus with a horse-drawn white wagon from which he sold hot dogs, peanuts, and pop to the sweltering thousands, including his classmates. He had taken a razzing for it, but he had also earned thirty-four dollars and sixty cents.

"What are you smiling about, Sam?" Sarah asked him. She played hide-and-seek with Eunice's locked lips, trying to wedge a spoonful of sour cream into them.

"I was thinking about Crazy Maxie selling hot dogs at our graduation," he said. "Boy, that Maxie!" Nothing Max Vogel ever did failed either to amuse or astound Sam Abelman.

"I sometimes wonder if he's a good influence on you. Why doesn't he get married and settle down?" she asked.

"Maxie? He's holding out for a millionaire's daughter! And he'll get it!"

She looked prim and disgusted, brushing a strand of hair back under the cleaning turban she had not had time to remove. "He's so smart he didn't get married—and what did it get him! Into uniform!"

Max was a lieutenant in the Army Medical Corps, but, as always he had found the angle. He was stationed at Fort Jay, and he spent a minimum amount of time there, continuing his private practice in violation of all army regulations, and doing quite well. Maxie knew how to turn the buck, no doubt about it, but he, Sam Abelman, wasn't doing badly either.

The first two years had been rough ones, true. He had earned less than fifteen hundred dollars those two years and had to borrow freely from old Malkin to keep going. The Williamsburg elder, he of the Edward VII beard and bearing, had paid for their wedding—a modest one, held in the Malkin apartment, and attended only by the immediate families. Sarah had come to him without dowry except for the dining room set. Theirs was a romance that had come to fruition with the aid of American poetry. To sully it with hard cash hardly seemed right. Besides, Meyer Malkin wasn't *that* happy about having a Rumanian in the family, even if he was a doctor.

From a modest beginning they were getting there. He had all the basic equipment he needed, he was gaining new patients every year. Obstetrics was proving particularly lucrative—he received nine dollars for each case, the fee including prenatal examination, delivery, one or two visits after the birth. One good OB a week really kept the household budget in good shape. In six or seven years they would be able to own the house on Haven Place outright. Not much money went into savings, what with the expense of a two-story house and a car—and the money he gave Aaron to help support his mother—but they were managing very well. People were getting to know Abelman the doctor. They were coming from East New York, Canarsie, and Flatbush to see him; he was on the staff at Beth Abraham, and active in the County Medical Society.

Before Sarah brought in their dessert, the phone rang. Sam leaped from the table—he always sat at the edge of his chair anticipating a call—and had the receiver off the hook.

"Mr. Traficanti? Yes? Yes? Oh—"

He looked grave, deeply concerned. Sarah wondered if other doctors reacted so personally to illness. Each new case Sam took on became part of him, for better or for worse, eating a little bit of him away, eroding his character and his strong body.

Hanging up, he walked to the examining room, washing his hands again, putting on the stiff Marley collar, the somber tie, the jacket, and the Homburg.

"What is it Sam? Is it the little girl again? Why did they call you so soon?"

"Little girl, hell! It's Dominic. He collapsed a few minutes ago—fever, aches, and pains, just like his sister."

"Have your dessert and your tea, first. You'll get indigestion."

He had grabbed the black calfskin bag and was out of the house already. Sarah would never get accustomed to it. She returned to Eunice, unco-operative as ever, for one more valiant effort with the sour cream.

Within ten days, Yolande and Dominic were joined by Mikey,

Vincent, and Francesca. Traficanti's sagging house resembled a pediatric ward. And as "Spanish influenza" spread—attacking the poor with special savagery—city officials advised everyone that there was really no danger at all. It was so simple to avoid infection! All you had to do was "sneeze, cough, or expectorate into your handkerchief." This would prevent the spread of the causative agent, and the disease (if it really *were* a disease) could not possibly reach epidemic proportions.

By October 5, the increase in cases was sufficent to permit the New York *Times* to run the influenza story on its front page (the Americans had broken the Kreimhilde line that morning, Haig was nearing Lille, and one hundred persons were feared dead in a munitions explosion in South Amboy). The day before, when twenty-six persons in Brooklyn had died of Spanish influenza, the city had reassured everyone that "there are no alarming symptoms about the spread of the disease in New York." A day later, a staggering of opening and closing hours for offices, stores, factories, and other places of business, was put into effect to alleviate subway crowding. Citizens were again ordered not to cough, sneeze, or spit. To show that they meant business, special sanitary police arraigned ten spitters in Yorkville court, where they were fined eight dollars each. Ten other miscreant expectorators were held in two-hundred-dollar bail in the Tombs to await trial in Special Sessions. Harlem courts fined twenty-two spitters and three others paid small fines on the West Side. No schools were closed, however; the Health Commissioner's Office advising everyone that "no epidemic is now in effect." (The previous day, there were reported 1,695 new influenza cases, and 188 new cases of pneumonia.) If everyone would stop spitting, it was felt, this figure could be brought down drastically.

" 'It has been the position of the Department of Health from the first,' " Sol Pomerantz read from his morning *Times*, " 'that no individual is in danger if he or she escapes the mouth or nasal secretion of some other person who has it.' " His irate bird's face peered at Drs. Abelman and Vogel over the counter groaning with patent medicines, razor blades, and baby products. "You need more proof of why we need socialized medicine, you guys?" the pharmacist asked. "Four hundred and twenty-one cases in Brooklyn alone—and they tell us we shouldn't spit!"

Sam pushed his Homburg back and scratched his forehead. "The way I feel today, I bet I looked at four hundred of them!"

"Stop bragging, ya draft-dodger," Max Vogel sneered. First Lieutenant Vogel overflowed his quasi-military uniform. Yet somehow he managed to remain dapper, poised, a man equally at home in his own office or in the Fort Jay dispensary. The overseas cap rested sideways on his round fat face, the Sam Browne belt created two bulging khaki spheres on his elastique blouse. There the martial note ended. He wore checked trousers, black pumps, and a swagger model London topcoat.

"One word out of you, Pershing," Sam said, "and I'll turn you in for practicing. How do you get away with it?"

"I should screw around at sick call when there's money in Brownsville? You know how many people we'll be seeing every day in a week or so? Come on, Sammy, smarten up! I'm gonna make a big enough pile out of this to furnish my office—everything new, the best!"

Sam shook his head and chuckled. Pomerantz made a sour face. But there was a good deal of cynical truth in what Max had said. The two of them—Vogel working only part of the time—had never been busier. Not only had "Spanish influenza" stricken the neighborhood with startling severity, but a whole host of related diseases were on the increase. Pneumonia, the sudden killer, appearing either on its own or as a complication of influenza, was much in evidence; cases of ear inflammation and meningitis were cropping up in the wake of the "grippe."

"I was lucky with the Traficantis," Sam said proudly. "Five cases in one house—and not a complication! Don't ask me how I did it!"

"Ain't you great," Vogel mocked. "Professor Abelman, a nifty guy with the aspirin bottle. You use any vaccine, Harlow Brooks?"

"Nobody uses it, Maxie," Sam said. "It only gives a few weeks' protection, if that. Dr. Parks said so himself. It isn't even recommended by a lot of the big shots."

"That shouldn't stop you, professor," Vogel said. "Any man who cured five ginzos in one house—"

In one swift move, Sam hooked his right arm under Vogel's garrison belt and lifted his classmate over his shoulder.

"Yiyi, ya bastard! Lemme down!" Max shrieked. "What if a patient saw me like this? Sam! Sam, ya louse, lemme down!"

"You see, Solly," Sam said to the druggist, "he's all wind inside. The fat slob talks a good fight, but there's no substance there. You know his type of doctor—every man gets a rectal, and every woman a rectal *and* a vaginal. And for this he gets an extra fifty cents!"

Max's face was the color of an uncooked smoked ham when Sam dumped him to the floor. "Goddam gym teacher," he puffed. "Can't take a little joke? Wait, wise guy, your patients will be dying like it was a pogrom here, and you'll get the migraine, not me. He cures five wops in one house and he thinks he's Biggs! What do you do for pneumonia, fellah, hah?"

"The same as you," Sam smiled. "Rest, fresh air, light diet, aspirin, baths. What else is there?"

A young man was standing in the doorway of the drugstore watching the professional men indulging in undergraduate horseplay. He was just nineteen, slight, fair. His sharp, small features were smiling indulgently. Much their junior, he still managed to attain a curious note of maturity, an awareness of his own superior qualities. He wore gold-rimmed spectacles and carried a stack of medical books under his arm.

"Can I join this consultation?" he asked politely. Concentrated effort had removed any hint of a Yiddish accent from his speech. Blond, neatly barbered, and dignified in a black suit, he might have been the son of an Episcopalian minister.

"Lemme outa here!" Vogel cried. "When Heshy Hemitz sticks his two cents in, I'm through. You got this whole, entire Spanish influenza figured out already, hah?"

"Dr. Vogel," the young man said easily, "please call me by my Christian name. It's Harry, Harry, H-A-R-R-Y. I don't know anyone named Heshy."

"I'll Christianize you, ya little *putz*," Vogel snarled. "What did ya learn in Bellevue today? How to treat clap?"

Harry Hemitz (he had been Heshy to the neighborhood before entering medical college) was the son of a widow who worked as the janitor of the tenement house on the corner of Haven Place and Rower Avenue. From the time Sam Abelman had opened his office, Harry had been shadowing him, pumping him for information, seeking advice on preparing for a medical career, baby-sitting for Eunice on the rare evenings when the doctor and his wife would go to a movie or visit friends. He was a peculiar young man: excessively formal in his manner, his ambition not evident in bursts of passion or rhetoric, but neatly packaged and secreted. His mother wrestled ashcans and wielded mops, seven days a week; they received their rent free in a two-room dungeon in the tenement basement; and yet Harry Hemitz was always trim and clean. Unlike Sam and Maxie, he was making his way through Bellevue without working. Somehow, somewhere, his mother—a silent, muscular woman who could crush a complaining tenant with one fierce eye— was finding the money to send her only child through medical college.

"Max, why are you always teasing me?" Harry Hemitz asked softly. "You afraid I'll take patients away in a few years?"

"Listen, kid," Max said, "by the time you're practicing, I'll have retired on my liberty bonds! Why aren't you up front dying for your country?"

"Medical students are exempt, haven't you heard?" he asked seriously.

"*You're* a medical student?" Vogel asked. "*Oi*, I thought you were a rubber salesman!"

"All right, Max, that's enough," Sam said firmly. "Leave the kid alone. How you doin', Harry? You knocking 'em dead on Twenty-sixth Street?"

Young Hemitz smiled again, a slight rearrangement of his neat face.

"We had an interesting seminar on influenza yesterday," Harry said. "Park spoke on the Pfeiffer bacillus. The lab is working over-time trying to get the vaccine out for family physicians."

"They recommend using it?" Sam asked.

Hemitz smiled again. "Yes and no. They're not sure how long it immunizes, or how high the percentage of immunization is. Really, it's still experimental."

"What else did they say?" Sam asked.

"Oh, that this is a different kind of influenza. You know it's not really Spanish, that's just a misnomer—"

"I'll give you a misnomer," Vogel snarled.

"Shut up," Sam said quickly. "Go on, Harry."

"Well, you know diseases can manifest themselves differently at different periods in history. This one is a particularly virulent variety. A lot of the professors felt the worst is yet to come in New York. It's only barely touched the city, and these things usually run a typical twin-peaked curve. We haven't even hit the first peak yet, according to the epidemiologists. They're talking about volunteer nurses and more hospital beds already."

Sam nodded thoughtfully. He admired the way Harry Hemitz, nineteen years old and in his second year of medical college, could reel off the information in that glib professorial way. He himself had never had the skill of articulation, the ability to talk so well. It was amazing—the kid being raised in a cellar by a lady janitor.

Behind the counter, Pomerantz made a wry face. "Someone oughta tell the Health Commissioner's Office and the rest of those people in City Hall. Don't you read the papers? There's nothing alarming at the moment, there isn't even an epidemic. Just everyone stop spitting."

Vogel rolled to the drugstore's open front door and hawked a wad of mucus into the gutter. "Look at that, Heshy! Howzat, Sammy? I just made forty more patients!"

Five days later, while the Americans mopped up in the Argonne, and Haig took Cambrai, Sam's first death attributable to Spanish influenza occurred. A young Polish laborer, all massive bones and muscular slabs, died suddenly. Sam had visited him the night before, prescribed the usual treatment, and had left him resting comfortably. At dawn, his widow, screaming and pressing the night-bell relentlessly, came to tell him that her husband had begun to breathe heavily and then had died without regaining consciousness. He had been sick less than five days. What distressed Sam was the absence of any symptoms hinting at complications—nothing in the chest to indicate pneumonia, no evidence of ear inflammation or meningitis. Spanish influenza, or whatever it was, was capable of doing its own slaughtering—it didn't need the more lethal diseases.

A day later Eunice came down with the typical symptoms—head-ache, fever, pains in the eyes, ears, and joints. She ran a spiked temperature, the chart showing precipitous peaks and valleys, and whatever time Sam had free from his multiplying outside calls he spent at the little girl's bedside.

"What else can you *do?*" Sarah pleaded. "What else can we give her?"

Sam sat wearily at his daugher's crib, listening to her faint moans. Medical knowledge and skills afforded him no special reassurances when members of his own family became ill; rather they intensified his own natural tendencies to worry. His mind would become restless, exploring endless possibilities, invariably turning to the most dismal prognoses.

"Nothing, Sarah, nothing beyond what we're doing. You think the professors know any more than we do? If it's just the grippe, we'll be okay. I just hope nothing else develops—"

He lost another influenza victim on October 17. This time it was pneumonia, the shadow, sneaking in after the grippe had weakened old Gruber, the gardener, filling his lungs with mucus and water and snuffing him out in the middle of the afternoon, the old Dutchman lying at his window, looking out on his backyard of fruit trees and landscape bushes, gasping his last breaths with a fragrance of autumn leaves and sheep's manure. He had done what he could for Gruber. Before he left, his efficient widow, tear-less, was burning sickroom rags and bedclothes. Everyone had suspected that Gruber, the old penny-pincher, had been secretly socking money away. The police and the family—even little Louis, the grandchild—spent a busy night searching his cluttered house and the pots and sacks in his yard. All they got for it, Sam was delighted to note, was a few handfuls of horse manure and some old peony bulbs.

He came home from Gruber's and collapsed at his office desk. He was too exhausted to eat. Sarah brought him tea and a buttered roll and he nibbled at it. It was rough on her also—her mother had had a mild siege of Spanish influenza, and her younger brother Willie was in the Argonne with the AEF. Luckily, Eunice was recovering (knock on wood); she was taking nourishment now and the color was back in her cheeks.

Sam reached into his pocket and took out a wad of crumpled bills and a fistful of coins. He would never learn to keep his money neatly folded in a wallet or with a clip. Payment of the fee always seemed to embarrass him. He wanted to stuff the money away, to hide it from view as quickly as possible.

"Well, *ketzeleh*, we're getting rich," he said wearily. "Soon we can buy the house."

She started to sort out the bills, smoothing them and stacking the coins neatly. "I wish you didn't have to work so hard for it, Sam. You're knocking yourself out."

"I wish people didn't have to be so miserable for us to make money," he said. "It's a crazy world. The only time we do well, the only time we can make plans—when people get terribly sick. They suffer, we benefit." He sipped at the hot tea, enjoying the sharp tang of the lemon, the soothing taste of the lump sugar.

"What do you expect, Sam? You didn't go into medicine expecting to be dealing with happy, healthy people, did you? Think of all the good you're doing. All the people you're helping."

"Yeh, yeh. Alcohol baths and lemonade."

"Now stop minimizing what you do. You wouldn't catch Max Vogel knocking his business." Throwing Max Vogel up to him was always a good gambit—Maxie had become a curious hero to him. He envied Maxie's audacity, his nerve, his defiance of the rules.

As tired as he was, the thought of Maxie made him laugh. "That Maxie!" Sam laughed. "He stole a thousand cc of experimental vaccine from the army, and he's giving shots for five dollars a throw! They were lined up outside his office!"

"Sixteen dollars and fifty cents," Sarah said. "That's one of your best days yet!" The money was entirely from house calls, the equivalent almost of *two* OB's. And collected in a single day's work, with a few evening calls likely!

She made the entry in her neat bookkeeper's hand in the accounts ledger they kept each day. There would be enough left at the end of October to buy another bond. Both of them had been touched by the full-page advertisement in the paper that evening about Private Treptow's pledge. He had been a battalion runner, killed by a German sniper. In his pocket they had found, in his own handwriting, his credo.

> *America Shall win the war.*
> *Therefore I will work*
> *I will save*
> *I will sacrifice*
> *I will endure*
> *I will fight cheerfully and do my utmost,*
> *As if the whole issue of the struggle depended on me alone.*

The charcoal drawing of Private Treptow's mangled body brought to mind Private Willie Malkin, 77th Division; Chief Petty Officer Hector O'Bannion; Lieutenant Charlie McDevitt; and Lieutenant Colonel Harlow Brooks, chief of medicine for the Second Army. Sam had not been called up. He was married, a father, in practice five years, past thirty. Occasionally, guilt assailed him, but Sarah assured him he was needed more in Brownsville. Who would have taken care of the influenza victims if every single doctor had volunteered?

He unloosened the stiff collar and rested his neck against the heavy leather of the swivel chair. "I feel like Hector O'Bannion just gave me a workout," he said. "I tell you, Sarah, it's a good thing I got the muscles I have. You know Lemkau put a limit on the number of calls he'll make?"

"Who can blame him? He's got all the money in Brownsville already."

She picked up a penny postcard, one of several on his desk. A form was printed on the message side. They had been distributed to all doctors the week before to enable the Health Department to keep track of influenza and pneumonia cases. Physicians were required to mail them in every twenty-four hours; they contained spaces for the number of new influenza and pneumonia patients visited, and for the number of deaths certified in each category.

"Don't forget, Sam. You didn't send your card in yesterday," she admonished him.

"Ah, some crap artist in City Hall is keeping his job with these," he grumbled. "Suppose the city gets the cards every day and keeps records? What will they do? Arrest two more guys who spit on the sidewalk? They'll fine a storekeeper for dry-sweeping? Who are they kidding?"

"Be safe, Sam, and send it in."

He made the entries: in the past two days he had seen six new influenza cases, and one suspected pneumonia case which he listed as pneumonia. He had certified one death from pneumonia (old man Gruber), and scratching in the figure with his desk pen he felt it was completely unfair to the gardener. The crabby old Dutchman had filled his yard with flowering shrubs and brilliant perennials for a few dollars; all he could do for him now was reduce him to a cipher—a single entry on a manila postcard.

October, brisk and red-brown, was in its third week, and the death toll hovered around eight hundred. Each day the city's physicians reported approximately five thousand new cases, and each day the authorities assured everyone that influenza was decreasing. *There is no cause for alarm; THIS IS NOT a true epidemic; obey simple rules of health and don't cough, sneeze, or spit.*

On October 20—a day on which 4,570 new cases were reported—Mayor Hylan put his finger on what was wrong with the handling of the epidemic. The doctors were at fault! Of course! They had to be! Reports kept trickling into City Hall about extortionate practices by doctors, druggists, and morticians, but mostly by doctors. Civic virtue was aroused; the city might not have had the sense to close schools (in keeping with the best medical advice) or quarantine the suspect Norwegian vessel (in keeping with standard health practices), but even a ward heeler knew a scapegoat when he saw one. The doctors, those extortionists!

"Maybe a law can be found," opined Mayor Hylan. "If not we will advertise them to the world and pin upon them a badge of shame that will last longer than their ill-gotten gains!"

A West Side practitioner asked the city administration to name the profiteers, reminding the officials that at the onset of the Spanish influenza pandemic, they were denying that there was any such thing. "To recognize a few cases as an epidemic would interfere with the progress of the war," one city father intoned. Besides, influenza wasn't causing the deaths, it was bronchopneumonia. How could anyone demand emergency measures, against influenza, when it was bronchopneumonia that was causing the occasional death?

It was the office of the health commissioner that discovered the true extent of the doctors' perfidy. Each day the commissioner would see no cause for alarm, assuring the public that the disease was on the wane. Yet the official figures indicated no such thing;

daily death tolls during the week of October 21 were running considerably higher than the previous week. And since the newspapers efficiently printed the totals each day, much in the manner of the standings in the baseball leagues, the numerical facts in agate type were continually at variance with the optimistic reports from the authorities.

The commissioner's office then put its collective finger on the source of guilt. Who else but the doctors could be guilty? If the commissioner said the disease was decreasing, it *had to be* decreasing. Obviously, the doctors were letting cases pile up, accumulating influenza victims by the score, by the hundreds, and not reporting them until they had a fat batch of cards. Thus cases which were a week or so old would be reported at a time when the number of diseased was *actually decreasing! They had to be* decreasing; the commissioner's office said so.

To fail to report influenza patients on a daily basis, the authorities warned sternly, "is a misdemeanor punishable by a fine of $250 or imprisonment for six months or both. Beginning tomorrow, we have asked the Police Department to have policemen from each precinct call on all the doctors having offices in that precinct to remind them that each day's new cases must be reported on that day and no other. We know that the number of new cases is decreasing rather than increasing. . . ."

To Sam Abelman, in drugged sleep at the wheel of his Dodge, the warning conveyed no terror. The finger of guilt pointed at him; he was among the busiest of Brooklyn's doctors, and among the most delinquent in reporting his cases. Time had become a blur, a cycle of ringing telephones, ascents of tenement steps, prescriptions, admonitions, advice, collections of one-dollar fees, and now, more and more frequently, certifications of death.

Twenty-four hours earlier, shortly after four in the morning, the phone and the nightbell called him simultaneously. At the door were two patients—the Shapover kid complaining his mother wasn't feeling good, and Ed Dineen saying his oldest son had caught it, Jesus God, and lookin' like death itself. The phone call was from the Leiberman family, his brother Aaron's inlaws. They suspected two cases. Before he had dressed, there was another call, in the same building where the Leibermans lived, and as he climbed into the Dodge with Dineen and Hymie Shapover, Sarah called from the window that Sol Pomerantz' cousin, on Saratoga Avenue, wanted him also.

He had never experienced anything like it. It was like the clinical descriptions of a malignancy—you excised it once, only to have it crop up in three other places, sudden, virulent, unpredictable. The early morning calls depressed him; the incidence of deaths was running higher this week, and maybe it was his imagination, and maybe it was based on accurate diagnoses, but it seemed to him the people were looking sicker, the bug was getting more vicious.

Back at Haven Place, after the dawn patrol, the phone interrupted his breakfast. It was going to be one of those days, one of the merry-go-rounds of general practice that neither LeFevre, nor Biggs, nor Brooks had warned him about. No, that wasn't quite accurate. Dousing his face with cold water, he recalled Harlow Brooks's advice about the "day-in, day-out practitioner," the doctor who lives for the routine, the house call, the office patient. The backbone of the profession, Brooks had called them. He may have been a backbone, Sam thought grimly, but his own could stand some propping. He had been averaging four hours' sleep per night for the past ten days, when the presumed "peak" was reached. It seemed more like a steady ascent now, even if the Health Commission *flatly denied* there was an increase in Spanish influenza.

He noticed that three new calls were on the same block, two of them in the same building. He suspected that the half-dozen wretched tenements on March Place had become a focus of infection. Crowding, poor ventilation, primitive sanitation all could speed the spread of the disease.

A twelve-year-old with matted blond hair and a steady drip of snot from his Slavic nose greeted him at the door.

"Doctor you? My papa Widzik. Family all sick. Papa, Mama, two sisters. You come-it with me now?"

"You bet, Polski," he said. "You can ride back with me like Pilsudski at the front." Widzik was a drunken house painter who had done some work for him when he had opened the office. He was an immense, lumpish man, given to executing dance steps on the sidewalk and crooning the folk songs of Lodz, whenever sufficiently sodden. But he was also violent and unpredictable; Sol Pomerantz had once told him to shut up and he all but tossed the bantam druggist through his front window.

As they parked in front of the tenement where Widzik lived, a knot of people gathered around the car. The spokesman was a flabby little man with a head of Brillo and the pallor of the garment loft.

"Dr. Abelman," he cried, "everyone's sick in there! The whole house. I swear, there's twenty cases in 1718 alone!"

He got out of the car and they surged about him with pleading, dumb faces. Selfishly, Sam imagined them as they would be when he asked for his fee: stupidity replaced by cupidity; their plea would become furtive whines.

"Doc, come by me first! My old lady is coughin' like a trained seal act!"

"Me next, doc, Apartment 4-H!"

"Stop by 5-B also. Sheregrodsky. You treated my uncle, Abe Blaufein."

He walked toward the stoop, fingers and hands clutching at his coattails, the frightened voices demanding his reassurances. A basin of sickroom slop sailed in a liquid arc from an upper-story window and he shouted angrily, "Slobs! Don't you do that again! I'll run you in if anyone else throws anything out of a window!"

He turned on them furiously. "Someone get a mop and some ammonia and clean up that mess!" he cried. They did not move. All that concerned them was their own little choked world, their own apartment with its sick and dying. Outside the door, blessed by mezuzah or crucifix, the world could go to hell.

"You!" Sam shouted. He grabbed the litle man with the Brillo hair. "You're in charge of the clean-up detail. You and three of these other big galoots, grab mops and pails and clean up the gutter, where all the crap is collecting." He pointed to the overloaded ashcans, crammed with bandages, gauze, sickroom offal. "And I want all the junk in those cans burned right now. Make a pile in the street and light it!"

"But, doctor," the spokesman pleaded. "My father! He's sick!"

"And he'll die, if you don't keep this place free from infection. Get the hell to work!"

Community effort was beyond their understanding; they lived their crabbed lives in little shells. But somehow they were shamed into action by his fierce Indian face, the authoritative mustache. An Italian lady, in eternal black mourning, appeared with a mop and a pail. Two small Yeshiva *bokhers*, earlocks and all, sullied their scholarly hands by rolling ashcans to the gutter. Mermelstein, the corner grocer, donated a bottle of ammonia.

Not all of them were won over. A toothless beshawled granny sneered at him in Yiddish, expecting that this *goyishe* young Jew with his short haircut and bow tie, would not understand her.

"*Ai*, better Lemkau should have come!" she murmured. "He is a gentleman, a *mensch*! He don't insult people!"

"So call Lemkau," Sam snapped. "You look like the kind who needs professors."

Brillo-head peered up from his sanitational duties. "We tried, doc. But he says he can only handle so much work. He won't recommend no young doctors."

He left the mopping, burning, and wailing, and, with the Widzik boy steering him, entered the house painter's apartment on the ground floor. He raced through the kitchen, steamy with cabbage smells, and into a bedroom. Two small girls, flat-faced blond children, lay on one bed; their wretched mother, a scarecrow at thirty, was stretched on the other bed. He took their temperatures, prescribed aspirin, sponged them all with alcohol, and was giving the boy the phone number of the visiting nurse service, when he recalled that the father was supposed to be sick also. He asked about the painter. The woman raised herself on one elbow. "He go crazy, doctor. Run from house, scream-it. All sick, he kill himself. He blame-it me for children be sick."

"Can you pay me for the visit?" Sam asked apologetically.

"No got-it money," she wailed. "Stashu take all money. Buy whiskey, I know it. Beat me up."

"To hell with him," Sam said. "Look, if the big galoot goes out and deserts you, let's at least use the other bedroom. Mrs. Widzik, we'll move you back in, and put the girls on separate beds. Sonny boy, you can sleep on the couch."

He resigned himself to not getting paid; but there was no point in not finishing the job. He picked up the frail woman, told the boy to take the sheets, and began carrying her into the other room. Halfway across the kitchen, the front door slammed open and the man of the house lurched in. Widzik may have been sick with influenza, but there was no doubt that he was very drunk. He had on his motley painter's overalls. In one hairy fist he wielded a ten-inch brush, dripping with thick scarlet paint.

"Gooddammit family, all sick-it," he crooned. "Paint-it up whole goddam house! Teach you lousy wife get-it sick!"

"Take it easy, Stash," Dr. Abelman said. "Put down that brush and get into bed. You're sick also. You'll drop dead if you keep acting like a horse's ass."

He carried the ailing woman into the room, hearing the painter's hoarse curses and moans. The galoot was chasing his son with the brush, swearing at him in Polish.

Returning to the kitchen, Sam was amazed at how much paint Widzik had been able to spread in a few seconds. The ceiling, the kitchen table, the dreary cabinets had all been liberally smeared with scarlet.

"You bum," Dr. Abelman said, "you should paint that well when you do my office over. You stink. You can't even hold a brush right."

The boy poked a head out from under the table. His silken hair was matted with scarlet ooze; pale-blue eyes peered from under a red mask. "Papa's paint-crazy again," the boy said, quite calmly. "Whenever he drinks too much, he goes paint-crazy. He paint-it whole milk wagon and horse yellow New Year's Day."

"Well, no drunken son-of-a-bitch is going to paint *me*," the doctor said. "Specially when he owes me a dollar and a half for three patients. Give me the brush, Stash!"

"You screw-it yourself, you doctor you. You lousy. You play wit' wife in bedroom. I see. You take money, no cure-it. You and lousy wife, make-it sick kids."

He was advancing, one lopsided step after another, brandishing the dripping brush in front of him. A little trail of scarlet dots followed him across the floor. The bloated, speckled face exhaled cheap whiskey. Sam set his feet wide apart, his hands held low, arms spread, like a wrestler. He had no doubt he could handle Widzik, drunk or sober. But the thought of all that thick scarlet slop smearing his new black serge disconcerted him. What did the textbooks on clinical medicine say about this *kind* of situation?

Widzik lunged, swinging the brush at him. He partially deflected the painter's wooden arm, but the worst had happened. A great sticky path had been smeared down his suit jacket, down the front of his trousers. Raging, he twisted Widzik's arm back and almost tore off the right hand at the wrist. The painter screamed and dropped the weapon.

Sam slapped him in the face, once, twice, a third time; not terribly hard, but with enough of a sting to assert his authority. The painter fell into a kitchen chair and wept.

"I sorry, goddammit doctor, I sorry sonofabitch. My lousy, lousy." He reached out for Sam, his two lumpish arms, reddened up to the elbows, pleading.

"Keep your hooks off me, you cheap bum," the doctor shouted. "Just give me a dollar and a half and get the hell to bed. You're no more sick than I am. But your kids are and your wife is. If you're any kind of a man and not just a drunken slob, you'll take care of them. This little boy has more sense than you."

Widzik bawled, softly, intensely. "No got-it money, doctor," he blubbered. "No got-it single penny."

"Spent it on cheap booze, hah, Stash?"

"Spend it all, pay later, I good for it. You know-it me, doctor. I love-it you. You good man. Treat me good like gentleman."

It was going to be a great morning at 1718 March Place, he could see. Done out of his first fee; his new suit ruined with red paint that would never come off, and for which he would never be reimbursed; and a wrestling match with a drunken Polack painter to perk him up.

He doused his face and hands with alcohol, removing most of the sticky mess. Leaving the Widziks for the Sherogrodskys, who lived down the hall, he found himself feeling sorry for the painter. He had had every right to turn the galoot in to the police. But what could you do with them? They tortured and badgered you (and ruined your new black suit) and then they looked at you like crippled dogs and licked your hand.

Sherogrodsky was an easy one—an old man in a skullcap, propped up in bed, spry and talkative. The family was Lemkau's and the patient was recovering. He gave him a routine examination, finding the heart and lungs normal, the temperature almost normal. They paid without a complaint—Lemkau's patients were conditioned to deliver the money without any arguments. The professor took no nonsense from them.

Up one flight, he called on a family named Oestreicher, strangers to him. They were a childless middle-aged couple, the woman a glandular case, freakishly obese, with a child's terrified eyes. He heard the coughing halfway down the hall and found her propped on pillows, alternating helpless gasps for breath with the coughing. She was quite sick; the fleshy face was dull with the look of grippe. Her husband trembled at the bedside while the great mound heaved, bringing up pink sputum into a soiled rag. After each spasm she fell back on the pillows, her lips pursed and petulant, in search of air.

Sam studied her closely. She must have weighed in excess of three hundred pounds; the flesh on her upper arms lay in little flaps and folds and the soft torso inflated the gray blanket.

"Does she always sleep lying down?" he asked the husband.

"Usual," he said.

"Did anyone ever tell you she might be more comfortable in a sitting position?"

He gestured indifferently and the woman hawked again. Hot tears trickled from the childish face as she fell back again, gasping.

"Well, we'll try an experiment," Sam said. "Sit her up in a chair near the window and let some air into this lousy place. I don't want her to lie down for anything. She can breathe easier and cough easier from a sitting position."

"I can't move her by myself, doc," he protested. "You sure it's the right thing?"

Sam tore off his paint-stained jacket, spitting on his hands. "Come on, muscles, get over there. You ready, lady? Wait till I put you on a diet, you'll be a regular Theda Bara."

She smiled coyly, hooking a hand around Sam's neck. Mr. Oestreicher, handling her port side, almost pitched to the floor as they raised the dead weight from the mattress. For a moment Sam thought he would have a compound fracture on his hands also; it seemed as if Oestreicher would buckle under his wife's heft and break one of his pipestem legs. But they made it, Sam carrying the payload, to an overstuffed armchair at the window, looking out on a vista of broken fences and weeds.

"Now keep her here," Sam said. "She should sleep here, take nourishment here, until she's stronger. She can't breathe flat on her back because of the weight pressing against her diaphragm."

They looked at him blankly. He dashed off a prescription, trying to ignore the husband's plaintive query. "A person is sick they should go to bed, no? I never heard a doctor made a sick person sit up."

"Well, you heard it now, sonny boy. And if you throw her back on her spine, you'll be calling Karnofsky, not me."

There was a coal stove, the pipe thrust out of a window, and a pile of egg-size coals in the corner of the kitchen. No effort had been made to keep the coal confined. It lay on the kitchen floor just as the man of the house had deposited it.

"What's that for?" Sam asked.

"To heat it up good," the husband said. "The landlord don't send up enough heat. He says he's a patriot. He's saving coal for the war."

Sam frowned. "Doesn't he know the city is ordering landlords to maintain heat during the epidemic? He can be fined if he doesn't get the heat up."

Oestreicher spread his hands helplessly. "It don't bother him."

"Well, it bothers me. I don't want that coal pile in the same house where there's a respiratory infection. Get it out. Keep it in the hallway and bring in just a little bit at a time. Besides, she isn't that cold. She's got plenty of insulation."

Stuffing the fee in his pocket, the scarlet coat over one arm, he left. His first thought was to get hold of the landlord and give him a little hell; but he never had the chance. They were clawing at his lapels, taking the satchel from his hand, guiding him first here, then there. In the next two hours he made six different stops, calling on every floor of 1718 March Place. The corridors echoed with hacking coughs, groans, and sighs, the whimpering of relatives. He chased visitors out of sickrooms, battled recalcitrant children who hid under the bed, put the match to infected rags, and threatened to punch an old witch, a sorceress of some kind, who refused to let him into Speciale's apartment. The old crone, waving some kind of dried weeds in his face and chattering away in a dialect out of the hills of Calabria, tried to keep him from the sickroom where Charlie Speciale was running 104.5 with a pulse so slow you could hardly clock it. She bit him once when he shoved her aside; a cuff in the neck pried the teeth loose and when he showed her his fist she slithered away.

He hurried back to the street. There were a few cases in the adjoining tenement, 1720, and he wanted to clean them up. There was an OB due in East Flatbush and he wanted to look at Eunice again; what with the disease intensifying, he couldn't be too solicitous of his own child's health. As he reached the sidewalk, he heard shrieking following him. It was Brillo-head, the pasty little man who had mopped up the street.

"Doctor, doctor! You missed us! Top floor—Feuerstein!"

The little man flew at him, pausing, even in his distraught condition, to mark the scarlet smears on the doctor's suit.

"My father, doctor! He's groaning, something terrible. How come you missed us?"

"How come?" he asked. "I made nine calls here. How can I keep track of everyone?"

He was being propelled up the five flights again, finding it tougher and tougher to make the ascent. Sam hurried through the kitchen to the rear bedroom; he heard the rattling breathing and understood he was too late. Brillo-head's father, a shriveled Orthodox Jew, was gasping his last. He heard the *râles*, felt for the fading pulse, and found almost nothing, and sat down at the bed. The old, stained mouth opened, emerging from the mass of white hair, and Sam imagined he heard a blurred, "*Shema Isroel. . . .*"

Women were weeping around the cluttered bed. Brillo-head was on his knees, sobbing huge convulsive gouts of tears into the old man's concave chest. Sam lowered the eyelids over the gummy orbs. He raised a bedsheet over the face, stuffing his stethoscope back in his pocket.

"You should have come sooner!" a woman screamed at him.

"I asked you, I asked you!" Brillo-head sobbed, looking up from the corpse. "Why didn't you come here first?"

Sam shook his head. "Listen, he was an old man and he was dying. I couldn't have done anything for him. I'm sorry I was late, but, believe me, he was going to die anyway."

"You're all the same, you doctors!" Brillo-head's wife shrieked. She was a lank sloven, a head taller than her husband. "You want the money, but you won't put yourself out! We won't pay you!"

Another woman seconded the move. "Not a cent! Papa died! The poor old man with no one to help him!"

Brillo-head and another member of the household were removing the body from the bed and placing it on the floor, in keeping with tradition. An old woman was draping sheets over the mirrors.

"When did he get sick?" Sam asked.

"When?" Brillo-head asked. "Two days ago, I guess. A cold, that was all. A little coughing and fever."

"Did you call a doctor?"

"No, of course not. Just a little cold—"

"Why, you fools," Dr. Abelman said. "The old man has been sick two days, and he dies of pneumonia and you blame me! What's the matter, too stingy to pay a buck for an examination? This man needed medical attention immediately! Not the day of his death!"

They looked at him with dull hatred. He was the most convenient object for their bitterness; not only had he been closest to the old man when he died, but in their primitive minds his tardiness certified his guilt. Sam would encounter it a thousand times; yet he never would be able to take it. It pained him that the blame-the-doctor attitude was most prevalent among his own people. A strangle hold on life, that was their trouble. Life owed them too much, including the one thing it could not possibly provide—a guarantee against death.

He made out the death certificate, getting the information on the late Avram Feuerstein, born in Galicia, from Brillo-head. The little garment worker sniffed tears, apologized for his rude behavior and that of his wife and sister, and paid him a dollar. Sam shook hands with him warmly; the little guy had volunteered to mop up the street, he wasn't a bad sort of *shnook* after all. Leaving, he heard the women screaming at the little man—the new scapegoat.

"You paid him, Hymie! You paid him his blood money? *Oi*, and he killed Papa!"

The shrieks unnerved him and he had to stop and remember what his next move was. The tenement next door, 1720, that was it. He still had a call from this morning hanging fire there, and it was now midafternoon. The encounter with Widzik had ruined his timetable as well as his suit; he smelled like the rear of a hardware store. Rather than make the climb down five flights and up five again, he climbed up the escape ladder and through the roof trap door. On top of 1718, he breathed deeply, resting for a minute. There was a four-foot jump across the alley between the houses and he vaulted it easily, landing on the tar surface of 1720. He had barely started toward the trap door when he heard a low growl. Alert as he was to the menace of dogs, he never anticipated the violent rush of black fur, the white teeth, the uncurled red gums. The mongrel, lurking behind the chimney, belonged to the janitor—a stern warning to neighborhood kids to stay away. He dodged the brute, swinging the satchel on the flat skull. The mongrel grunted, wheeled on wobbling legs, and came at him again. Sam ran to the roof door. There was no time to unlatch it before the black mutt was on him again. This time he used the calfskin bag as buckler and shield, shoving it into the snarling maw once, then slamming the heavy load of instruments at the stupid skull. He opened the trap door and descended. On the first landing he checked his bag. There was a row of teeth marks on it; inside, the glass on his sphygmomanometer had been shattered. He was sure that no course at Bellevue had covered what he had just been required to do.

It was early evening when he arrived back at Haven Place; office hours were already begun, and a few patients were waiting for him. He had eaten nothing since the morning, but his appetite was gone. Sarah insisted he at least have some tea and a sandwich. He obliged, visiting Eunice first for a bedside game of "masked rider."

He gave Sarah a wad of bills and a fistfull of coins—the day's work since four in the morning, more money than he normally earned in a week. It was impossible to tell how many people he had visited, and the day was not over yet. After office hours, he tried to fall asleep. But he had forgotten about the OB that was ready to pop—that cousin of Sol Pomerantz in East Flatbush. The urgent call from the father-to-be roused him from a black stupor shortly after ten o'clock, and he was off again in the rattling Dodge. The mother was narrow-waisted, a little pale thing with a contracted pelvis, and he earned his money squeezing the infant into the world on top of the kitchen table. The family forced a glass of sweet wine on him and it made him dizzy. Leaving, richer by nine dollars for his obstetrical work, he was stopped at the door by a short woman in the apron of the local candy-store owner.

"You're Dr. Abelman?" she asked him.

"Yes," he muttered. "Don't tell me—someone's got Spanish influenza, and it's on the fifth floor, and you didn't call the doctor yesterday because you were sure the patient only had a cold."

"Such a doctor! He makes jokes yet. Nobody's sick by me, thanks God, knock on wood."

"What do you want me for, then?" he asked. He could have slithered down the wall and fallen into a dead sleep at the head of the stairs.

"From your wife, a message. Three more calls you got, and she said it's better you should make them now than come home and go out again."

She pressed a slip of paper into his hand with the names and addresses of three new calls on it. He gave her a nickel for her services and walked slowly down the steps. He had changed his clothes on returning home, yet he still smelled from paint.

He was back at Haven Place after one in the morning, so enervated that he fell asleep at the wheel as soon as he had parked the car. Consciousness left him as abruptly as if he had been slugged by five Paddy Lynches. Two hours later, Sarah was shaking him. She was standing on the sidewalk in her flannel bathrobe, shining the flashlight in his face.

"Sam! Sam! What happened? You didn't get held up?"

"Whah—who? What am I doing here? What time is it?"

"It's after three in the morning! Are you all right?"

He felt as weak as if he were coming out of deep anesthesia. It took a few seconds for him to get his arms and legs in motion, and he struggled across the seat, lowering himself to the sidewalk. A chill autumn mist swirled about the deserted street and he saw Sarah only dimly. Toward Rower Avenue, he could see a smoky fire at the curb—somebody committing sickroom towels and gauze to the purifying flame. He wondered how much good these rituals did. A tinkling of wagon bells aroused him, and in the distance, moving slowly through the wet fog, he saw a horse drawing a creaky flat-bed.

"It's Karnofsky's assistant," Sarah explained. "He get so many calls now he keeps a wagon on the street twenty-four hours a day, picking up bodies wherever he can."

The makeshift hearse, four cheap pine coffins resting athwart the wooden boards, rolled by them. A Negro driver slapped the reins across the horse's butt and the bells tinkled wearily. Any minute Sam expected him to cry out, *Nice, fresh coffins, today!*

"Come in, Sam," Sarah said, taking him by the arm. "You're not to make a single call until noon. I want you to get some hot food and a night's sleep for a change. How can you keep it up? Let them call someone else."

He didn't hear her; he was watching the ghostly progress of Karnofsky's night prowler. A fat lot of good it would do the families, he thought sourly. Didn't they know the dead were piling up in the cemeteries? In Queens, the borough of the dead, there were already two thousand unburied stiffs! The city was asking for volunteer gravediggers, but there had been few applicants. Relatives were going out to Queens on the streetcar, armed with picks and shovels to intern their dead. It was particularly tough on the Orthodox Jews, whose law prescribed immediate burial. Karnofsky might be there waiting with his empty boxes, but the influenza victims would be forced into a lonely limbo somewhere on the flat plains of Queens County.

Sarah helped him undress upstairs. He was asleep as soon as he fell against the pillow. It seemed he had just closed his eyes when he saw her again, standing at his bedside, calling him softly. Sunlight was leaking through the drawn green shades; the clock on his dresser told him it was a little after nine in the morning. Dimly, he recalled having heard the phone ring a few times during the night, and Sarah politely making excuses.

"Sam, I hate to wake you," she said.

He sat up blinking, feeling uncomfortably unshaven and unwashed, fatigue clinging to him like a coating, something with mass, odor, a feel of its own. A faint pressure in his temples warned him that a migraine might be in progress; his throat was unnaturally parched, and rising from the bed he sensed a curious lightness.

"Sam, I wanted to let you sleep until noon," she said apologetically. "But there are a couple of people to see you, and they insisted they had to see you right away."

"Okay, okay, *ketzeleh*," he said reassuringly. "I'm fine, just a little weak in the knees. Who are they? Regulars? Or some of Lemkau's deserters?"

"They're not patients," she said timidly.

"Detail men?" he asked suspiciously. "Some guy with a new vaccine?"

"Oh, Sam, I warned you about sending those cards in to the commissioner! It's a policeman—a cop! And somebody who says he's the district health officer! They want to talk to you about not sending in the cards. Sam, why couldn't you have done something so simple?"

He grunted in disgust, walking to the bathroom. "Why didn't

you do it for me, wise guy?" He wanted someone to share a little of his guilt.

"Who can ever tell where you've been?" she complained. "You haven't made an entry in the daybook for three days! How do I know how many calls you've made—or how many deaths you've seen?"

"Ah phooey," he said.

"That's a very nice answer," she said, "very polite. For all I care, they can cart you off to jail."

He tried a scalding shower to unloosen the knots in his arms and back, shaved and threw some aspirins down his throat and drank two full tumblers of water. Superficially he felt a little better; but he couldn't set aside the uneasy feeling that something deeper than exhaustion was making him lightheaded.

They were waiting for him in the anteroom: Patrolman Pope of the 77th Precinct, and a small neat man in derby hat and chester-field.

"Dr. Abelman, the name is Saunders, G. M. Saunders, district health officer, working out of 590 Hopkinson Avenue. Nothing personal in this, I want you to know. Doing my job for the grand City of New York."

"Stop crapping me up, buddy," the doctor said. "You want to know why I haven't sent in my daily reports, is that right?"

"Now don't get huffy on me, doctor," the little man said. Gold teeth peeked through a cracked smile. Sam seemed to remember him at the polling place in the public school, handing out blotters just beyond the *No Electioneering* poster.

"You have been a prime offender in this matter," Saunders said. "As health officer, so appointed by the commissioner, I'm authorized to check on all delinquent doctors. It's you fellows who are ruining the city's fine record, not sending in your reports. Why, there's a fellah like you in Harlem who sent in an accumulation of six days' cases—two hundred and seventeen to be exact. Now how does that make the commissioner look?"

"No worse than not closing the schools," Dr. Abelman snapped. "Or quarantining a ship, or having enough nurses and enough hospital beds ready."

Saunders turned to the policeman. "Read the law to the doctor, officer."

Haltingly, Patrolman Pope read from a booklet.

" 'The penalty for neglecting to observe this provision of the sanitary code is fifty dollars for each offense. Furthermore, neglect of physician to carry out the provision of the sanitary code constitutes a misdemeanor which may be punished by one year in prison, five hundred dollars' fine or both.'"

Sarah had come in to the room. "Why, that's horrible!" she cried. "My husband has gotten three hours' sleep a night since this thing started—he's treated hundreds of people! If it weren't for people like him the city would be a graveyard. He admits he didn't fill out the cards. He was just too busy, too exhausted. We'll do it right now, won't we, Sam? Then, please, leave him alone!"

"Busy is right," Saunders said, showing gold fangs again. "You know what the mayor of our great city said about extortionate doctors getting rich—"

"Why, you cheap Tammany Hall bum! You goddam ward-heeling punk!" Dr. Abelman was advancing purposefully.

Saunders skipped gracefully behind the officer. "Don't try it, doctor," he said confidently. "You're in trouble enough as it is. Right, Pope?"

Pope said nothing. He had no kidney for the job, ever since the district leader had called him in the night before and given him the word. The city wasn't looking too good on this epidemic or pandemic or what the hell else you wanted to call it. And this was an election year, a big election. They had to get the city off the hook on Spanish influenza; and they already had the cue—lay it on a few doctors, make 'em sweat for it. Especially those guys not handing in their reports, making the daily statistics look so rotten, especially when everyone *knew* the disease was on its way out. The district leader had leveled a fat finger at Saunders, reminding him why he had gotten the job of health officer. There was a hint to Pope also that he could be helped if he played along.

"Lookin' through these records," the district leader told them, "I seen this guy Abelman, a young draft-dodgin' sawbones. He's been runnin' through whole buildings like Rochelle Salts. And he ain't handed in his cards for four days now. Let's start with him. Get him down to the district office to fill the cards out. We'll make an example of him, get his name in the papers, and let him go. I know these little Jew-boys with the mustaches. He'll see the blue uniform and he'll fold up. Just hold him long enough to get the information, then call the reporters at Brooklyn police headquarters. I took care of *them* already."

Recalling the briefing, Pope shivered a little.

"I'm sorry, doctor," the policeman said, "I got my orders. You're to accompany Mr. Saunders to the district health office and fill out the cards there."

"Why can't I do it right here?" Sam asked. "My wife and I—it will take us five minutes! Go, Sarah, get the book—I can remember most of them."

"Remember! You mean you got no records of your own?" Saunders asked. He was stationed a foot behind the sweating cop now, calling out his taunts.

"I said I could remember them," Sam said. "You think I'm a chump?"

Saunders shook his head and tugged at the cocky derby. "Not good enough. You will accompany us to my office, and we'll review everything you've done the past few days. We intend to make an example of a few of you fellows. Will you come along, doctor, or must Officer Pope assist you?"

"Oh, God!" Sarah cried. "You're arresting him!"

Eunice, in her mother's arms, started to laugh. "P'leeceman, p'leeceman! I am de mack rider! Bing, I shoot you!"

Pope smiled at them weakly. "It ain't the police station, lady, it's just the health office on Hopkinson Avenue. Doc, we'll make it as quick as possible, honest. We'll get you back in less than an hour, right, Mr. Saunders?"

"I am not promising anything," the health officer said. "I don't like the doctor's attitude one bit."

"Why don't you take a flying leap at a rolling doughnut?" the doctor asked. "Okay, I'll go. I'm too tired to argue any longer. *Ketzeleh*, I'll be back soon. If Sheregrodsky or Speciale get impatient, tell 'em I'm on my way."

Riding in the patrol car, he began to feel the dull ache in his temples again. Now his chest was hurting, and the back of his neck, too. His outrage, his fury with the crap artists, prevented him from worrying about his own symptoms. The nerve of the bastards! He's knocking himself out fighting drunken house painters, crazy relatives, old witches, and mad dogs—and they have to come arrest him like a thief, over a few lousy postcards. He'd complain to someone, the district leader maybe. That would show 'em—the district leader was a friend of Ed Dineen's. He'd take care of them.

The emergency health office had been set up in an empty store, the lower half of a peeling yellow frame building. As the police car approached, Sam could see a crowd of thirty or forty persons collected around the door. The office, which was supposed to supply home service and keep records on the progress of Spanish influenza, had only three nurses available. Two of them had been making calls since eight o'clock, when they came on duty. The third was trying with no success to keep order in the surging mob around the shabby store. She was quite obviously a volunteer—a pretty young *shicksa*, probably from one of the old Protestant families on the Heights, and her good intentions, her pleas for reasonableness, were lost on the aggrieved citizenry. All they knew was that the city was supposed to supply medical aid. Where was it?

"You run a pretty good office here," Sam said to Saunders. "You'll be cited for malpractice, you don't organize that place better."

Saunders glared at him as they started elbowing through the mob. Sam had brought his satchel with him, hopeful of resuming his calls as soon as the ordeal with bureaucracy had ended. Following Pope through the mob, he suddenly felt a hand gripping his suit collar.

"Hallo, you doctor!" It was Widzik, his speckled painter's cap towering over the crowd of stunted Jews and Italians. "You doctor, come-it my house, quick dammit! City no good, no got-it nurse! Tell us come here for nurse, no nurse!"

He heard a voice whine. "Dot's a doctor, yet?"

"He's a doctor! A doctor!"

"Doc, my old lady—570 Saratoga—Apartment 3!"

They were grabbing at his arms, his coat; someone snatched the bag from his hand. Widzik had him in a bear hug and was kissing him.

"Oh, you goddam gentleman, doctor! I love-it you! Come-it me first, I carry bag for you!" He located the satchel-snatcher, a fat little Greek, yanking the bag from his hands. "You give-it me doctor's bag! Everybody want-it Dr. Abelman, one goddam gentleman, I tell you, lousy people. You follow me, see my kids and old lady first, then take-it care all of you! Everybody!"

The mob, whom he would have occasion to detest, to fight, to moralize with, to preach to, and to curse for half a century, was rescuing him. Widzik was wrestling him to the curb, pushing him into the front seat of his paint wagon; the others were climbing onto the back, still shrieking at him, extracting promises that he would visit.

"It's me next, doc—Donoso—I'm a friend of Traficanti the barber!"

"Come by me, Dr. Abelman, I'm next door to Widzik, 1720, you were there yesterday!"

Saunders was screaming at Pope, "Stop him! Stop him, officer! Do your duty or you'll be reported! I'm warning you people—Dr. Abelman is guilty of not filing his reports! He has to answer to the great City of New York and our great Democratic party for this!"

Pope was looking the other way, grinning. He'd think of some excuse. What was he supposed to do? Keep the doctor from helping the sick? Saunders ran to the wagon, shaking a fist at Widzik.

"You're impeding justice, you! And you, doctor, you're an educated man, you should know better! I'll take care of *you!*"

"Ah, go fugg-it yourself, you piss, you," Widzik said. He slapped the reins and the horse trotted off, saving Sam Abelman from civic dishonor and plunging him into the diseased tenements for another day's work.

The work kept him from worrying about his own symptoms; if anything it was worse than the day before. In addition to the new calls, he felt impelled to drop by his old cases, charging them nothing for a quick visit. Mrs. Oestreicher, the three-hundred-pounder, was improving. So was Speciale and so were several others. But there had been another death in 1718, again from pneumonia.

Back home in late afternoon, he knew he had contracted influenza. It was inevitable, he felt, the way he had been exposed to it. He put himself to bed, trying to sleep off the awful pressing pains in his eyes, around his head, his ears. He vomited bile; he dozed in fits and starts; his temperature hit one hundred and five and then dropped precipitously when the aspirin took effect. Sarah called Max Vogel, and the quasi-military doctor came in that night from Fort Jay.

"You look like my Uncle Hymie after Yom Kippur," Vogel told him. "Whaddya trying to do, make all the money in Brownsville?"

"Why not?" Sam asked thickly. "Should I leave some for you?"

"Serves ya right. You'll be flat on your back for a month."

"Influenza runs a five- or six-day course, Maxie, read up about it."

"Not the kind you got, buddy. Why should I be nice to you? You're sick as hell, Sam. I'll tell you for your own good—I don't like your lungs or your color or anything." He turned to Sarah, pale and distressed. She didn't trust Max Vogel. She didn't like the way he always told Sam the worst—her worrisome husband believed implicitly everything the fat man said.

"Listen, Sarah, keep this guy on his back. He's damn sick. All he needs is to be getting out of bed too soon, with all the stuff he's been exposed to. You and the kid sleep downstairs."

Sam told him he was a rotten diagnostician, but Max Vogel was right. The bug turned his powerful muscles into mush. He wanted to leap from the bed, to resume his practice, but he couldn't find the strength to stagger to the toilet. It had been the long hours, the endless hikes up the tenement steps, the constant exposure, the irregular diet, and the more irregular sleeping, and finally the aggravation of the incident with the district health officer. Luckily, Saunders never bothered him again. Sarah personally brought the reports over, and another miscreant doctor was located.

What hurt as much as the illness—he skirted pneumonia, but the grippe itself was virulent enough to keep him bedded—was the loss of practice. He had no one to take his cases; it was dog-eat-dog in Brownsville, and he knew that much of the large practice he had built up, the good reputation he had earned during the pandemic would be dissipated by his prolonged absence from work. It was just his luck, he thought unhappily. Yet it wouldn't turn out too badly; he'd be up and around soon, with some new people to show for his hard work. With the cash he had taken in, he could get some new office equipment. The surgical supply house had a beauty of a sterilizer he had his eye on.

He lay in the double bed, looking out at his garden through the ending of the war in late October and the first week of November, listening to the sounds of the children playing in the yards.

> Nan-nan-nanny goat
> Sew sew sew,
> Sew my petticoat,
> No, no no!
> Sew my dress?
> Yes, yes, yes!

Little Harry Hemitz, the janitor's son, came to see him and asked, point-blank, if he could handle some of Sam's cases while he was ill.

"Are you nuts, Harry?" Sam asked. "You're a kid in second year medical college. You can go to jail for that!"

"Oh, not to charge money or anything," Harry said calmly. "Just for the experience. You know I treated a whole bunch of people in Mama's house. For nothing. I even tried out a little Park vaccine and kept records on it."

He took an ampule from his vest pocket and held it up to the light. "Pretty good stuff," Harry said. "I'll know after I match the results against my control group."

Sam looked at him in wonder. What nerve that kid had! Practicing medicine already, conducting his own experiments with vaccine—and still a punk in medical school.

"You're some guy," Sam said. "You'll be murdering me when you open your office."

"Oh, don't worry about that, doc," Harry said, unsmiling. His strong little hands were folded prissily in his lap. The butter-yellow hair had just been watered and neatly combed as if he were on his way to Sunday school. He was teacher's pet, but with a toughness that would brook no nonsense from the class bully.

"I'm going to specialize," young Hemitz said. "General practice is okay. But the real money, the real challenging work is a specialty. I've been talking to some of the men at Beth Abraham about surgery."

Sam laughed. "You're okay, kid. You sure have that old ambition. I guess you can handle almost anything."

Harry Hemitz nodded in complete agreement. "I know I can."

On Armistice Day, Sam was still convalescent, spending part of the day sitting at the window looking out on his backyard. He heard the band playing in the street, the cheering and shouts, the happy crying of the neighbors whose sons would soon be home. Sarah was overjoyed; her kid brother Willie, with a combat record, would be on his way in a few weeks. He heard someone calling his name and, looking below, he saw Traficanti standing on the brick path he had begun but never finished. The barber was holding an oversized twig in his hand. There was a clump of earth and a cluster of taproots at one end.

"Hey, doctor!" the barber cried to him. "I got tree for you!"

Sam waved at him. "That's a tree? It looks like a piece of kindling!"

"You joke, okay! But this very fine tree! Sour cherry—make wine, jam, pie. You see, taste very good!" He twisted the tip of an imaginary mustache and smacked his lips. *"Magnifico!"*

"Go ahead, Angelo, have your fun. Don't you know it's too late to plant trees? It's November already."

Traficanti spit into the dormant tulip beds. "Pah! You go by book! You once listen to Gruber, no-good gardener. I plant cherry tree now. Cherry tree grow, get big, healthy. You get better too. This good old country cure. Tree live, you live."

Sam gulped. "What if the tree dies, Angelo?"

"No die. I plant. By fence, there—tree never die!"

"Okay, Angelo, whatever you say. Did you bring a shovel?"

"I bring whole works."

And the barber went to work—neat and spotless in his white jacket, little clouds of acrid cigar smoke rising around his close-cropped Umberto haircut as he thrust the spade into the hard soil.

He was on his feet in December, weakened and more reserved, making his rounds again, limiting his night work until he felt stronger. A new year came and Willie Malkin came home from

France to open a dry-goods store. Hector O'Bannion returned from the Great Lakes Training Station to start another doomed college. He learned that Mr. Comerford had died quietly during the pandemic. One morning in spring, the strength back in his short body, his office agleam with new equipment, he walked through his yard and found Traficanti pruning the cherry tree. It had indeed taken, November or not, and the barber was proudly trimming its sad little garland of leaves.

"Take it easy," Sam said. "It hasn't got much to get clipped. You think it's one of your customers?"

Traficanti, disdainful, did not even look up, but continued his deft trimming. "You good doctor, doc," he said, "but no good gardener. You no think tree grow! I show you."

It was a pretty good life being a doctor, Sam thought.

The doctor had concluded his narrative while driving Thrasher to Eastern Parkway, where he could find a cab. Traficanti's tonsorial skill made him look eminently more respectable. But the barber's scissors had not removed the haggard look from the physician's face. Thrasher was surprised to hear him express concern over *his* appearance.

"You don't look too hot, Mr. Thrasher," he said. "You work too hard. I know the kind. You have an ulcer?"

"Not that I know of."

The doctor pursed his lips, ruminating. "You're a vagotonic, my boy, the same as me, only you show it differently. Anxiety, worry, compulsion. High intelligence, sensitivity. You get migraine?"

"No, but I'm willing to try it, if it will help your diagnosis," Thrasher said lightly.

"Stop kiddin' me, son." He double-parked near a hackstand. "Listen, I'm beginning to wonder about you. Do I really have to tell you all this stuff? Why are you so interested in me?"

Thrasher leaned through the window. "Any good reporter works that way, Dr. Abelman. You know the program is less than three weeks away. That's why I have to do such concentrated work."

"How do you know I'll be all right? I'm no actor—"

"You'll be fine, Dr. Abelman. Besides, Andrew Bain Lord is going to work with you. You know, sort of interview you, and guide you around."

The doctor smiled and nodded his head. "Hey, he's a very famous man! I listen to him all the time!"

"Why that's wonderful," Thrasher said. "You don't consider him a crap artist?"

"Oh, I suppose he is," the doctor said generously. "But he's a gentleman, an intellectual. It'll be a pleasure to talk to him."

Thrasher shook hands and hailed a cab. He had expected the doctor to bridle at the mention of Lord; he had almost been disappointed in his honest pleasure. Mulling it over, it wasn't too unnatural a reaction on the physician's part. Andrew Bain Lord's soothing optimism probably sounded wonderful after a day spent fighting for two-dollar fees.

IX

PORTER SIMPSON, the receptionist, had been promoted to commercial co-ordinator of the new Whitechapel package, and to mark her first meeting she wore a low-cut pink sweater. A few tired jokes were made about Porter's new look (Dexter Daw whispered to Thrasher that without the Exquisite Form "floating action" they came down to her navel), and the meeting got under way. It was the first big meeting on *Americans, U.S.A.*—Heart's Desire had apparently been abandoned—and Ben Loomer, while joining in congratulating the new commercial co-ordinator, didn't take too kindly to Porter's décolletage. It detracted from the business at hand, he felt, and he reminded himself to have a little chat with her later. Better than that, he'd ask Chilson to do it. The kid had a cold, competent way of telling the hired help off.

Loomer had begun by introducing everyone. There were four factions present. First there were the agency people, headed by Loomer, Finucane, Thrasher, and a half-dozen lesser employees including Chilson, Porter Simpson, Louise, and a man from research and development. From the network there was Daw, burping his way through a hangover, Alice Taggart, carrying an immense leather folder, through which she kept shuffling, and a technical director and his video man, the pair of them in dollar sport shirts and Robert Hall suits, discussing overtime and seniority. Andrew Bain Lord had his own little crew—his writer, Kevin McBee, and his agent, Terry Schwartz. And, finally, Gatling's chief of advertising was on hand, the silent Van Alst, jotting minuscule notes on a leather-bound memo pad with a gold automatic pencil.

It was to Loomer's credit, and Thrasher admired him for it, that he kept the disparate elements in a continual friendly ebb and flow. His honest face was in perpetual unspoken appeal for fair play, for sportsmanship, for teamwork, for everyone driving to a common goal.

Loomer had begun by introducing everyone. He then made a point of asking Thrasher where that special assistant of his was, what was his name Marlow, Mallet? Thrasher had to claim ignorance. He had told Myron about the meeting, but the doctor's nephew was not present. There was a small rebuke to Thrasher

284

in the query and he wished Loomer had not asked him in front of the whole gang. Next the executive vice-president summarized the program's aims and hopes quite expertly. Thrasher noted how frequently his own phrases were used—*stature in programming, improving tastes and attitudes, new concept in TV journalism, using the TV camera to mirror a slice of life.*

Loomer was now asking for questions, and Lord was in a behind-the-hand consultation with his writer and his agent. However, the commentator himself didn't ask the question. He limited himself to a thoughtful nodding as McBee, a hyperthyroid intellectual in shaggy tweed suit and dark-green woolen shirt, ran the errand.

"Andy's wondering, Ben, just how big is his role? Is he limited to a straight Q and A with the subject? Or does he narrate? Or what?" He spat the words out rapid-fire, tinging them with what he believed to be an educated Dublin brogue. Kevin McBee, a purveyor of inaccurate newscasts, fancied himself in the tradition of Joyce, Yeats, and Synge, although the closest he had gotten to the Republic of Ireland was Sag Harbor, New York.

"I think I'll let Woody handle that one," Loomer said. "The script is his baby, Kev."

Thrasher slumped deeper into his chair, catching Louise's disapproving frown. She was warning him regularly about overdoing his rebelliousness; it hadn't served him too well of late. Or maybe she was just sore at him for failing to get *her* the promotion to commercial co-ordinator. She was nine times as smart as that phony Porter Simpson with her big knockers. And with all she had done for him: protecting his exposed rear, filling him in on intrigue, doing all the hard research and digging. And he had never once gone to bat for her for the new opening. What good would it do to tell Louise that her brains and her competence were neutralized by her heavy legs and her Bronx speech patterns?

"It shapes up like this, Kev," Thrasher said amiably, "Andy is the key guy in many ways. Remember our subjects are plain people, not actors, unrehearsed, everyday Joes. Andy will need all his charm and intelligence to keep them topside. It's a rough go."

Lord nodded his magnificent head. He saved his words for airtime; a man who was paid four thousand dollars a week for talk didn't go around wasting the stuff. Thrasher wondered what went on inside that great square head with its white crew haircut. He was an elderly Clark Gable with overtones of a headmaster—the kind who was always ready to clasp two masculine hands around the trembling mitt of the new boy's mother.

"As a matter of fact, Kev," Thrasher continued, noting the dull silence from Lord's encampment, "I got part of the idea for *Americans, U.S.A.* from an old bit you used to write for Andy."

That was pure Thrasher: he had established before everyone that the show was *his* idea in spite of Loomer's big act; he had attempted to mollify Lord and his crowd; and at the same time he let them know he was wise to their act by stating publicly that McBee created everything that came out of Lord's facile mouth.

"Really, Woody?" It was delightful. Two men of letters kicking around old ideas—Dr. Sam Johnson and Bennet Langton recalling a witty epigram of Richard Savage.

"Sure. You used to write that little once-a-weeker for Andy when Amalgamated had him. It was called *People Are Good* or something like that."

McBee smiled crookedly, a conscious effort to look like Barry Fitzgerald. "*I Like People* it was called, Woody. I didn't think hardly a man alive remembered it, eh, Andy?"

Lord nodded, arching the tufted brows he used so effectively with his Sunday night television "sermonaire"; but the holy tones were not brought forth.

Loomer looked from Thrasher to Lord's group, imagining he had settled the issue. But Schwartz, the commentator's manager, was shifting in his seat as if a sand fly had sunk its stinger into his huge rear.

"That brings up something else, fellahs," Schwartz said hesitantly. "About the script, the writin'."

"What about it?" Thrasher asked.

"Well, nothing personal, Woody, but we figgered somebody with more stachoor maybe, you know, if Bill Saroyan was available, or Buddie Schulberg." Terry Schwartz was one of the white-on-white people. He had a white-on-white shirt *and* a white-on-white tie. Thrasher wondered if his drawers were similarly loomed.

He was delighted to see Loomer leap to his defense. It was part of a manager's job to question every move that would affect the client. And since Andy Lord rarely understood what he read so beautifully, Terry Schwartz had felt impelled to raise the question. Thrasher realized that his own recklessness in demanding the writing job made him open game—everyone knew he had never written anything of the importance of *Americans, U.S.A.* But Loomer, for his own reasons, was ready to back him.

"Let's understand one thing, Terry," Ben drawled with evident firmness. "Woody Thrasher is producing and writing this opus, under me and under Whitechapel control. No one is dictating to us on this baby. We feel that an agency has to be more than a clearinghouse. We want to create something valuable and free of pressures. As far as *Americans, U.S.A.* is concerned, neither myself, nor Woody, nor T. C. himself is going to permit a swaying of our intent. That goes for the network, the talent, the sponsor, everyone." He peered to the silent man from *G & T*, daintily jotting notes in his leather-jacketed pad. "And I know Mr. Van Alst, representing Lyman Gatling, is one hundred per cent in accord. Right, Van?"

The gray head gave a single nod and Loomer, waiting for a protest from Lord—he knew Dexter Daw, representing the network, would never say a word—winked at Thrasher, indicating their complete victory.

There was some more peripheral chatter. Porter Simpson, sticking her frontage out so far that it obscured his view of Alice Taggart's neater, yet more enticing charms, wanted to know about the commercials. Daw had some questions on behalf of the technical men. Chilson read a list of possibilities for the future. It was apparently decided that Teddy's old English Lit prof would be the next subject. Thrasher noticed that everything discussed could have been handled by the people involved without the need for an open forum. Yet to do this would destroy the vital seminar, the big meeting, the convocation of minds for the liquefying and mixing of everyone's brains in one giant electric blender.

There was a shuffling of feet as T. C. himself entered the conference room. He motioned them to remain seated and stood at Ben's side.

"You can see how much this new job for *G & T* means, Mr. Van Alst," Loomer said cheerfully. "The top man himself wants to give us the send-off. Morning, chief."

"Good morning, Benjamin. And Woodrow. And all of you fine friends," T. C. began. His eyes took them in in a vague sweep, surveying all of them in the mass, yet looking none in the eye singly. All of those bright young faces scared him a little.

"We are delighted with the challenge of this new project," Whitechapel said faintly. Thrasher could swear he heard Dexter Daw make a faint raspberry, but it might have been an upholstered chair squeaking. "We accept this challenge, because we believe our industry is not a static one, but a fluid one, a revolutionary one, if you will. And I hope a certain Senator won't get wind of that remark, eh, Benjamin?"

Loomer guffawed appropriately, and everyone else, on cue, laughed at the old man's little joke on himself. Imagine! T. C. Whitechapel being suspected of subversion!

"There is so much new and exciting in our world," Whitechapel continued, "so many people we must know better, so many things we can tell our audiences about. Worthwhile things. Good, educational things. Those of us blessed with the means to dispense information should be thus guided." He paused and gazed out the window at the midtown skyline, and they imagined he had finished his peroration. But he was merely stopping for breath.

"Now about these new things in the world. Take frozen milk. I am reliably told that frozen milk is just around the corner. When it comes, what will it mean? To the iceman? The milkman? The housewife? For that matter to the bottling industry and makers of paper containers. Frozen milk is only one of many new things we will have to face, things that we can explain and explore. I wish all of you the best of luck with your new project, and I look forward to a crackerjack of an opener. Benjamin, Woodrow, it is in your hands."

He turned away briskly, and left them.

"Thanks a lot, chief," Loomer called to him. "We won't let you down!"

There was a round of applause. Thrasher, sitting up straight and joining in, wondered how many in the room would dare to ask about the old man's reference to frozen milk. A few cynics, like Daw and Louise, would understand that the speech was the product of nothing but the old man's simple mind: he had read somewhere about frozen milk and it seemed a nice item to throw into a meeting.

Loomer was ending the session; a little chromium wagon from Schrafft's bearing hot coffee and sweet rolls had been pushed into the room. Ben was asking everyone to help themselves and get to know one another over morning coffee. He ran a superb meeting, Thrasher had to admit.

The usual chatter buzzed around him as he saw the conference room door burst open. Myron Malkin, an unnervingly discordant figure in the perfectly cast *Americans, U.S.A.* unit, was loping toward him. He wore a light tan suit of impossible checked rayon. The shoulders were padded so as to make him look deformed, the lapels were half a foot wide and dipped below his waist in a hideous curve. As usual, the makeshift spectacles kept sliding down his nose. The touch of his clammy hand made Thrasher recoil.

"I ova-slept, Thrasher," he said, with no hint of apology. "Hadda work late last night on the Queens bank job. We beat the pants off the opposition. I got the first exclusive with Falcone's wife."

Myron was talking rapidly and noisily—loud enough for all the others to hear, to understand *right off*, that he was that most admired of men, a working newspaperman, an honest toiler in the fourth estate, a man who without narrow lapels or a good school could hold his head up in any assembly of talkers. Porter Simpson was already looking him over, and Ted Chilson had edged near them, coffee cup and cheese bun in hand.

"Say, Teddy," Thrasher said, "you should meet Myron Malkin. You and Myron are the two assistants to the producer, namely me. Myron is Dr. Abelman's nephew and he can help us set up a lot of local stuff. You know, cops, characters, all the basics we'll need to make the first show hang together."

Chilson studied Myron coldly: the misshapen face, the badly fitting and worse-styled suit, the slouching, ill-at-ease figure. He shook hands limply.

"Where did you prep?" Chilson asked nasally.

For a moment Myron appeared hurt, a querulous dropping of his lower jaw betraying his own uncertainty in the immense office, surrounded by the successful talkers of the world he longed to join. And then, to Thrasher's joy, he smirked, a true gutter smirk from Haven Place, and answered.

"Yeshiva," Myron said. "I got my numerals for throwing the bagel."

Chilson managed a thin smile and invited him to a cup of coffee. For Thrasher, it was a good omen. Myron would be a very useful fellow to have around. He had met the enemy, and while they weren't quite his they weren't going to have him running out for cokes, either.

Ann had called in that she wanted to lunch with him, and he was delighted. She came to town about once a week, "to get the chlordane and peat moss out of my system," as she put it, lunched with some girls she had known back in her little-theater days, and then either shopped at Saks or went to a matinee.

She had left word for him to meet her at Bayard's, in the East Sixties, near First Avenue. The restaurant was housed on the ground floor of what had once been a bleak and rotting four-story tenement. Since the war, its resident Irish and Italians had been driven out of their warren by the decorators and realtors. A thick coat of washroom white now covered the building's tired bricks, and the ironwork and woodwork had been painted a funereal black. Like the subject of a gigantic hysterectomy, the decaying interior had been scooped out, replastered, rewired, resanded, repainted, and air-conditioned to make room for the young men and women from Maumee, Ohio, and Princeville, South Carolina, the bright creative people. One of the street-level windows, gold-curtained, bore the minute lettering *Bayard's*—a reluctant hint that food was served within.

Although the cuisine at Bayard's was advertised as French-Italian, the restaurant's name was by no means Gallic in origin. Rather, it was the family name of its sullen proprietor, a former public relations counsel named Okie Bayard, who, with the backing of a few old clients, had decided to open his own, as he put it, "booozery," instead of spending his earnings at the Pen and Pencil, Camillo's, or Danny's. He was an egg-bald man with a sodden purple face and a reputation for great warmth, generosity, and good humor. Yet when Thrasher had been introduced to him some months back, he had received only a distrustful eye and a symbolic handshake. Bayard had held his hand firmly enough, but the restaurateur's right forearm, stiff and forbidding, had kept him a good distance away as they mumbled their greetings. It was the instinctive gesture, Thrasher felt, of a man who despised people, who used the straight-arm as a warning not to get too close, unless he *wanted* you to.

Arriving a little after half-past noon, he peered over the crowd at Bayard's Lilliputian bar, looking for Ann. She was not in sight and he decided to wait at a table rather than loiter at the cramped bar. Okie Bayard, newly arisen, barbered, perfumed, and squared off in a black silk suit glanced at him malevolently and he smiled back, hopeful that the ungenial host remembered him.

"Hi, Okie," he said. "Got a quick table for two?"

Bayard fought back a belch. He was now able to purchase whiskey at a discount, a facet of the business that delighted him as much as the three-fifty he got for London Broil.

"Who you?" he asked Thrasher.

"Woody Thrasher, from Whitechapel, Okie. Jimmy Puttering introduced us a few months back. Ole Jimmy's doin' fine."

"Yeh? I doan remember you."

He was tempted to advise Okie Bayard to drown himself in his own jellied madrilene. Crawling before this sot was bad enough—but using Jimmy Puttering, a lecherous sports announcer who revolted him, as a reference was a debasement that appalled him. But he had agreed to meet Ann at Bayard's and there was no retreat.

"You got a reservation?" Bayard asked, turning away to wave at a blond woman who worked the panel show circuit.

"Ah, I'm afraid not. My secretary goofed."

"Well, you ain't got a reservation. Ah do the best Ah can. Dino, give him fourteen."

Dino, swart and silent, led him to a table the size of a scrabble board. It was wedged between the ladies' room and the kitchen. Processionals of women fumbling with their purses, and overloaded Latin waiters effectively screened Okie Bayard's solitary cell from the rest of the brave company. He curtly refused to order a drink, earning a Mediterranean sneer from Dino. His distress was complete when he saw Andrew Bain Lord, Kevin McBee, and Terry Schwartz walk in, to be greeted with warm embraces and honest laughter by Bayard. They were shown to a prized corner table, in full view of Bayard's clientele, yet sufficiently secluded so that they were, in effect, in their own private little dining room. Childish jealousy gnawed at him. Even the sight of Ann, cool and primly beautiful, failed to hearten him.

"Who do you know to rate the dunce's seat?" she asked, laughing.

"I got friends," he said archly. "I didn't make a reservation, and I guess good ole Okie Bayard didn't remember me."

"Oh, I don't really care, Woody. Just being in New York invigorates me and restoreth my soul. The master fuse blew again and we were without the electric for an hour this morning."

"Again? What kind of an electrician is that guy anyway? Wasn't he supposed to check all the wiring? It's the third time the master fuse has pooped out."

"He says it's just overloading. The wiring is all right."

"The house will burn down some night and he'll still insist the wiring is all right. Doesn't anyone *do* anything right anymore? The redwood table doesn't fit; the three-hundred-dollar coffee table had scratches on two legs; the last grease job on the station wagon, they forgot the transmission; the clown who put in the side steps for us had the wrong mixture and it cracked in a month. What happened to all the people who did things properly?"

She gestured helplessly. "They're probably in rebellion against the do-it-yourself racket, is all I can figure. The poor slobs like us who can't even hold a screwdriver have to suffer, too."

"You're the best-looking broad here, Annie," he said suddenly. "I'll bet that ridge-runner is sorry he sat me in the kitchen now that he's cased you."

She did look marvelous. Her face was tanned and there was a spray of darker brown freckles, generous, healthy splotches, across her nose and her lean cheeks. Her hair was short and neat, and the touch of purple lipstick was a magnificent startling effect in her natural, uncomplicated face. It made her equally at home in Bayard's or at the PTA meeting. She was that grand combination of aristocrat and democrat: the Old Westbury matron who worked as a receptionist in the community hospital, exuding politeness to the families of plasterers and milkmen two afternoons a week. The social graces came to her more naturally too—nobody in New Bern had played polo or ridden to hounds.

The waiter looked her over with furtive approval. Clearly, Thrasher's stock had risen. Ann wanted a vodka martini; he settled for tomato juice.

"Is this more of Dr. Abelman's common-sense advice?" she asked. "Abandonment of the ritual drink?"

"Not his advice, but a related phenomenon. This project isn't helping the old gut any."

Andy Lord waved at him, General MacArthur acknowledging the cheers of children shaking little American flags on the sidewalk. He found himself signaling back with more vigor than he intended, but Okie Bayard hadn't noticed.

"Who are you waving to?"

"Andy Lord. Another one of my burdens."

"Is this the day you feel sorry for yourself? I thought the project was coming along swimmingly."

"It is and it isn't. It's, you'll excuse it, like pissing into the wind. They've stripped me of the top job and left me on the firing line if it gets loused up. That isn't too bad. I've been used to that ever since I was rewriting cablese on the night desk. What hurts is the way they've goofed up the idea. You know—that cheap give-away business. That really galls me."

"Well, for goodness' sake, don't eat yourself up, Woods. You really haven't been looking too hot. 'Tain't worth it."

She was right. He had caught a glimpse of himself in Bayard's bar mirror, the kind of muted, bottle-framed setting that usually improved your looks. There were charcoal smudges under his eyes, and the tan he usually acquired at the beach or the club during the summer months was not deep enough to cover the pallor of worry. He had rather enjoyed a faintly harassed mien; it helped buoy his role of company aesthete. But you could carry these things too far.

"I haven't written a line yet," he said. "But it's all shaping up in my mind, thank goodness. I think a week's work at night in the office will be all I'll need. I can dictate a lot of it to Louise."

"How about Alice Taggart? Can she take dictation?"

He was hurt; she was all that was saving him from total oblivion in Bayard's and it was wrong of her to remind him of his caddishness. Moreover, as far as he was concerned, the Taggart episode was a dead issue. *Americans, U.S.A.* was draining every bit of energy from his limbs. There was no excess for fun and games.

"That was a low blow," he said, sipping at his tomato juice, and glaring at Bayard's nosy waiter, who had set the drinks down and had lingered at the scent of a good saloon fight.

"Tell Mr. Bayard this tomato juice is warm," he snapped.

"I take it back for you, sir," the waiter said quickly.

Thrasher glared at him. "No, I want to suffer. Go ask the chef what he recommends."

The waiter walked away, apparently subdued, and he felt a little proud of himself. He had always been very poor at this kind of thing.

"That little dialogue wasn't necessary," Ann said.

"Well, you got me all wound up with that Taggart crack. I wish you'd appreciate that I'm under terrific tension these days. You don't help any by making those smot-crecks, as Milt Gross used to say."

"I don't want to ruin your lunch, Woods, but that's exactly why I wanted to meet you today. I hardly ever see you at night any more, and when I do, you watch John Cameron Swayze, read the newspapers, and go to bed."

"I guess your opening line should be, 'Darling what are we going to do?'"

"I've thought of several. But can I ask you a question first?"

"Ask me anything, but don't think I'm feeling any better about this lousy trick."

She cocked her head and it made Bayard's tricky illumination dance in little winking lights on the stiff blond tufts.

"Why did you cheat?"

He was tempted to say "with whom" or "which time" or "under what circumstances," but he succeeded only in looking grave and pursing his lips. The truth was, he couldn't think of a fair answer; it was just something he had drifted into, not that he was any more lascivious than the next fellow, or disliked his wife, or was unhappy in his work. It had just happened; he had found it reasonably pleasurable and he had pursued it as other men breed beagles or grow dahlias.

"Tell you the truth, Annie, I think I did it because it gave me a kind of class, a sort of prestige."

"Oh, no! This is the living end! You mean people had to know about it?"

"No. Even if I were the only one who knew about it, it enhanced my stature. We're a pretty moral crowd, you know, all of us talkers, and if you can get away with a little diddling on the side, well, you become a sort of reckless, devil-may-care sort in your own eyes—"

"And the eyes of the women you diddle around with. How many were there?"

"Come on, Annie, that's enough. Let's just say I was conditioned to cheat, that's all. I am still very fond of you. I like our kid, even though he's only a right-fielder, and I think we're a nice little family. Okay?"

The waiter returned, stubbornly hovering at their elbows, until Thrasher placed the order. Ann wanted the cold shrimp and avocado salad and another vodka martini; he ordered London Broil.

"Well, I have some reservations about this whole deal," she said.

"Oh really?"

She took a deep breath. "Yes. I thought about it a lot, especially after that Saturday night at Dexter Daw's meeting your inamorata. I wondered about the different possibilities. First, I could just let you go on playing around and make believe nothing was happening. Maybe you'd stop and maybe you wouldn't, but in either case I'd keep my mouth shut. Then, I could get a divorce right away, and I think you might agree to it. In spite of your protestations about how much you like your family, I can't help but feel you're sick of all of us, including the redwood table. But there's a kind of compromise I've worked out, and that's what I'm coming to."

He fingered his hairline lightly. A delicate patina of sweat was forming there, and he felt his heart accelerating. Who would have supposed she'd have been so broken up over some simple cheating? Husbands, Thrasher had been told, did it every day. He was about to cite Kinsey, but she was delivering her windup.

"I'm going to get a job," she said. "I'm going to try to reassert my own personality, give myself an identity, expand my frontiers. Just vegetating in North Stanford at the age of thirty-six is for the birds."

"What can you do?" he gulped defensively. "You can't play ingenues any more. Not even at the Provincetown Playhouse."

"No, but I can type and I'm smart and well read. Do you remember that fellow Vickery we met at Daw's? The one who teaches at Columbia?"

"Sure. The little guy who kept asking me when was television going to grow up." He didn't know what was coming, but if he disliked James Brinton Vickery, Ph.D., on the basis of that one meeting, he was prepared to hate him thoroughly now.

"Well, Jim has just been appointed editor of the *Discoverist Review*, and he's looking for a Girl Friday. He mentioned it to me that night, and I didn't have the nerve to ask him then. In fact I wasn't really interested. But after that business with Alice Taggart and thinking it over, I called him yesterday, and the job is mine! It's only fifty dollars a week, but the hours are a snap, and it's real, creative work for a change."

She had so completely stunned him that he could only drain the warm tomato juice, look unhappily at his London Broil—they had honored him with one of those stringy end cuts—and wait for her to say something else. But she had evidently finished her emancipation proclamation and was now pecking hungrily at the gooey salad.

"So that's how you get back at me?" he asked. "By taking a job with a butcher-paper monthly that prints the lyrics to left-wing folk songs?" He started strumming an imaginary guitar, singing softly:

> *Oh, it ain't no bed of roses,*
> *To be sick with silicosis,*
> *In the mines,*
> *In the mines . . ."*

"Don't be boorish," she said, "people are watching you and you know how you hate that."

"And for fifty lousy bucks a week! We pay the mailroom boys more than that."

"You almost sound jealous, Woods. How'd you like to work for an outfit that didn't have to take orders from drug companies or carpet sweeper manufacturers? Where the stuff you write and print is all honest, uncensored, free of pressures?"

The London Broil refused to give way under Okie Bayard's dull knife. He gave it up, plunging his fork into a green salad inundated in liquefied blue cheese.

"You'll learn, cookie, you'll learn," he said. "There ain't none of us free of pressures. We're all victims of the word, slaves to talk. Everyone yapping at once and saying the same thing. Could you possibly read all the magazines, newspapers, books, and pamphlets made available to you? See all the television, the movies, plays? Listen to all the radios, loud-speakers, lectures? We're overwhelmed by words, drowned in talk. No time left to—to—to grow corn, or read Thoreau. We've upped the literacy rate and increased mass stupidity. Don't ask me how we've contrived to do it, but we have. And now, look at you. You could stay home and do useful things, like putting redwood tables together, or knitting Shaker sweaters, or even growing tomatoes, but instead you're joining us in the greatest gabfest of all time. More words, even though your circulation will be small, but more words nevertheless."

"That's a pretty anti-intellectual pitch for a fellow who fancies himself the company intellectual," she said, winking at him.

"I'm not being anti-intellectual," he said, almost pleading with her. "A lot of talk is good. Hell, I like a lot of the stuff on television and radio. I'm always the guy who defends television when our WQXR neighbors start insulting TV. I like the movies and I don't nearly read all the books I want to. It's the *mass* effect that troubles me: all of it going on full blast at once. And I'm not even getting into the *bad* stuff that we turn out, all the rotten words, and bum ideas, and cheap conformism. Forget about that. Just consider all the *good* material and you'll be stricken with terror."

"I'm sorry I brought all this on just by saying I'm going to work. I'm afraid to tell you anything else."

He hadn't even heard her. "Conformism! Thats' not too bad; nothing wrong with making people reasonably alike, so long as the model is a fairly good one. That's what keeps me in business, pays our rent and our food bill, and will send Woody Junior to Amherst. What kills me is that we no longer merely try to condition people to everything—condition their likes, their dislikes, their political views, their tastes. That's not inherently evil. But we've got everyone convinced that the only way they can act is through conditioning. People sit around waiting to be *told* what to do, how to act. They're unhappy if you don't tell 'em. They kick if there are no commercials—and thank God they do, for our sake. No one believes in choice any more, nobody wants to move; they're convinced someone will tell them sooner or later. That's the real crime. Heck, *someone* has to condition people. If we were on Yap Island, it would be the local medicine man; but the Yaps, if they want, can act without him, and they know it. We're reaching the point where *everyone* needs the medicine man for everything from buying a pack of cigarettes to going to church. Well, a few more harmless words won't hurt—especially if they're folk songs written on East Fourteenth Street. Welcome to the great gabfest."

She had polished off the avocado and shrimp salad while he had made his speech, and now she looked up at him brightly.

"All I can take is iced tea," she said.

He ordered two iced teas and swung around in his seat, hooking an arm over the back of the crimson leather chair.

"Well, no comment?" he asked.

"You're so full of contradictions that I don't know where to start. Let me ask you this, wise guy. If you're so darn critical of what you do, why don't you get out?"

"I'm conditioned, too. I've tried in my small way to preserve some element of choice in what I do. It's only a compromise, but I have to settle for it."

"Now you know how I feel going to work," she said triumphantly. "I made my choice. My conditioning told me to stay home and be a docile wife; but I chose to do otherwise."

The check came to twelve dollars. He left the waiter a ten and four singles and got up. "I can almost guess what else this great exercise in free will is going to lead to. Are you planning on climbing into bed with Professor Vickery?"

She got up and four or five male heads turned to admire her.

"Could be," she said. "At least I'll be circulating in the kind of company where that kind of thing is done naturally and with good grace."

He was furious; she was much too beautiful, too good, the mother of his son, his wife for twelve years, to be cozying around with a phony egghead like Jim Vickery. A horrifying mental image, chilling in its detailed clarity, made him trip—he was seeing Vickery and Ann together, his wife's delicious long legs, the high heels, and the sheer stockings—

She had walked ahead of him, stopping at Andrew Bain Lord's table to exchange pleasantries with the commentator and his friends. Lord had both massive hands clasped around her waist. McBee and Schwartz were rising, and in the dim foyer he thought he saw Okie Bayard eying her with lecherous favor. Thrasher joined her, and there was a loud, enthusiastic exchange of handshakes and locker-room camaraderie. Ann always mixed beautifully in these all-male sessions. Leaving, Lord called after him in his rich, firm voice something about "See you bright and early, Woody, boy!" Barflies and diners watched them in pure admiration.

At the door, Okie Bayard was standing in their way. He offered Thrasher his hand, and this time, there was no straight-arm.

"Hey, boy, how come y'all didn't tell me yew was a buddy of Andy Lord? Ah'm sorry 'bout that warm tomato juice. Y'all come back here real soon and Ah'll take good care of yew. And bring Miz Thrasher. Lady like that gives the joint a little class, 'sted of the newspaper bums Ah get."

There were no newspapermen in Bayard's, of course; none of them could afford it. The little deception, as much as the astounding change of attitude, filled Thrasher with a numbing disgust. He wanted to tell the saloonkeeper that his London Broil was inedible and that he would no more think of returning to his overpriced hash house than he would of buying him a drink at the cluttered bar. But Thrasher understood that he was totally conditioned; that his own powers of choice were more limited and confined than he had imagined. He found himself pumping Bayard's hand, smiling into the rotting face, assuring him he'd be back soon.

"I enjoyed that muchly," Ann said, when they were on the street. "He's an awfully charming guy."

"You won't get those kind of lunches down at the *Discoverist Review*," Thrasher said sulkily. "When do you start work?"

"I'm off to see Jim at Columbia right now. *Doctor* Vickery. Gee, I hadn't thought of that! We've both got our pet doctors now!"

She climbed into a cab, and the sight of her trim, co-ordinated figure, the simple-yet-luxurious orange sheath outlining her spare delectable hips and thighs, made him desperately angry with Columbia, literary magazines, and English professors.

Dr. Karasik squinted at the six wriggly tracings, first with his gold-rimmed spectacles on, then with the glasses removed. He gave the rolled paper to Dr. Abelman and sat back, humming to himself, something he had sung in Vienna as a young man, and placed a cigarette in the dandified holder.

"You don't smoke any more, Sam?" he asked.

"A cigar, now and then," Dr. Abelman said. "Sarah doesn't like me to stink up the house." There were six wavy lines, each one the recording of the electrical activity of a different area of Herman Quincy's cerebral cortex. Each jagged line, the penmanship exercise of a stupid child, was labeled with a set of initials: L. F. and R. F. for left frontal and right frontal; L. P. and R. P. for left parietal and right parietal; L. O. and R. O. for left occipital and right occipital.

"Sam, I will let you make the first speech," Karasik said softly.

For two hours that morning, Herman Quincy's head had been subjected to the pressure of Franz Karasik's searching electrodes, the electrical activity of the cerebral cortex registering on a revolving drum. With his agitated mother standing by in stricken silence—her son was in no pain, but the mystical gadgetry was sufficient to terrorize her—Herman had, with quiet patience, subjected himself to the diagnostic technique. The initial set of six tracings were now in Sam Abelman's hands.

"Well, this is what you guys call very slow," he said cautiously.

"And very abnormal. Maybe three waves per second, highly compatible with a convulsive state," Karasik added.

The little valleys and peaks hypnotized Dr. Abelman. He peered at them looking for some clue, some deviation in pattern.

"Okay, very slow waves, you say, abnormal at any age and suggestive of brain damage—"

"I didn't say that," Karasik said quickly. "I said very abnormal at any age. Look at them—slow, lazy impulses, like the brain doesn't know where it's going. But not necessarily brain damage."

"What is it then?"

"Let's be careful, Sammy. Let's say *suggestive* of epilepsy or a related disorder in our young friend out in the waiting room."

"You're a big help," Dr. Abelman said rudely. "We're back where we were. Maybe epilepsy. Maybe a lesion. Maybe brain damage."

Dr. Karasik took the tracings from his friend's hands and held them at an angle, that both of them might study the irregular lines.

"You see, Sam, while the tracings are almost—I say almost— abnormal for someone his age, there's no startling variation in any of them to suggest abnormality in any single area."

Dr. Abelman studied the electroencephalograms again and said nothing.

"What I hoped to find was a marked irregularity in one area, let's say right parietal, or left occipital," Karasik said. "That would be strongly suggestive of localized disease in that area, some kind of brain damage. I wouldn't be prepared to say what exactly the pathological process was, but I'd be fairly sure there was something nasty going on there. But while the over-all picture here is one of abnormality, there isn't anything to show us where the abnormality lies, or whether it's idiopathic—"

"Stop with the idiopathic, Franz," Dr. Abelman interrupted.

"What you're saying is the pictures tell us he's sick, but we don't know what it is. That I need like a yesterday day. I knew he was sick in the head when he walked into my office."

Karasik smiled, indulging him. "Are you sorry we went to this trouble, Sam?"

"No, no, of course not, Franz. You know me. I take everything personally. Listen, I know the limitations of this kind of stuff. Don't you think I know that the electroencephalogram is good only for lesions involving the cerebral cortex? Sure I do. I read the same books you do. This kid may have something deeply buried, working its way out. You'd never get a reading on it. Right, professor?"

"Yes, generally speaking. But a finding of generalized abnormality without a focus may still indicate a deep tumor. That is exactly why you *don't* get a focus of abnormal activity."

Dr. Abelman scratched the short, newly clipped hairs at the nape of his neck. "Suppose you had found a focus on this tracing, Franz?"

The neurologist pushed the gold-rimmed spectacles up on his forehead. "First, I would take four or five additional tracings. Under induced sleep and natural sleep, if possible. If I continued to get the abnormal, irregular waves, with little plateaus maybe, or deep valleys, from one area—I'd say surgery was indicated. In more than eighty-five per cent of these cases, Sammy, when the localization is consistent, you can go ahead and operate. Mind you, you won't be sure of what it is you're operating for, because many kinds of gross lesions cause the same kind of abnormal picture. But, in any case, the pumpkin has to be carved."

It was purely a hypothetical exercise. They were still uncertain, the neurologist more so than his colleague. Before Herman Quincy's skull could be opened, they would need more evidence.

"What's next, Franz?" Dr. Abelman asked.

"I need a few more of these." He indicated the paper sheet with its six wriggly lines. "Let him come tomorrow. I'll give him another neurological—motor function, reflexes, gait—you know, the same as you did."

"Don't trust the old man, eh, Franz?"

"Of course I don't. I know what a big dope you are, like all those GP's."

Dr. Abelman raised his eyebrows appreciatively. "The kid said he had headaches the last two mornings. No nausea, no fainting, or anything like that. I asked him to keep a record, but he didn't."

"He's such a liar. I wouldn't believe anything from his mouth," Karasik said distastefully. "What is very important, Sam, is that you should observe him in convulsion. It's several days now since he's had one, and if there's pathology upstairs, there should be seizures downstairs."

"All right. A few more electroencephalograms, observation of seizure and postconvulsive state and then?"

"If we're still in doubt, we pump a little air in. Ventriculography. I wouldn't mess with pneumoencephalography, if we suspect a tumor. It might kill him off quick. You increase intracranial tension and poof—out they go!"

"What's so much fun about ventriculography? Trephining the skull, puncturing lateral ventricles, replacing the fluid with air? They die from that, also, even before you can do the craniotomy."

"They do, Sam, they do. But what choice do we have if the boy gets worse and if we can't localize the neoplasm? It's all we have left."

In the confident office of Franz Karasik, air-conditioned and upholstered in rich, lifetime leather, the dark paneled walls and the mahogany-framed diplomas and citations bursting with professional competence and the assurance that all who entered there would be saved, Dr. Abelman felt weary and unfulfilled.

"*Ai*, Franz, we sure are a bunch of *shmegegies*. What we don't know!" It wasn't just Herman Quincy with his convulsions, it was the Goldman girl with the rash that wouldn't go away, Louie Gruber and his erratic vision and hearing, the whole damn Kooperman family, some malingerers and some honestly sick with whatever it was that made them skinny and neurotic. It was the entire sorry bunch, the thousands and thousands he had looked at in forty-three years, loving them and cursing them, and making each one of them, the best and the worst, part of him.

"Well, Sam, what keeps us going is our ignorance. It wouldn't be any fun if we knew it all. You know there are more than twenty-five different identifiable kinds of intracranial tumors; not to mention the crazy things that turn up and we mark unclassified."

The nurse brought Herman Quincy and his mother in, and the doctors, like two high-benched jurists, turned to look at them gravely.

"These little wavy lines you see, Herman," Karasik began, "show what's going on in your head. And it shows, Herman, that you are a sick boy and need medical care. Now I'll let Dr. Abelman tell you what you are supposed to do."

The family doctor folded his hands into an iron mesh on his paunch. "Now, Herman, you're going to get better," he began. A little lie never hurt; Brooks used to say that all doctors have to lie every now and then. And, of course, there was a chance Herman *would* get better.

"Ain' nothin' wrong wit' me now," the leader of the Twentieth Century Gents mumbled.

"Herman, would it be very hard for you to stop being a horse's ass?" Dr. Abelman asked, adding quickly, "You'll excuse the language, Mrs. Quincy, but that's the only way I can talk to your son. He is sick, there's something wrong with him. Now Dr. Karasik and myself are going to try to cure him, but he has to help."

Herman sighed. He was bored, aloof, weary of these two old squares, who kept asking him to move his arms and legs, poking at him like he was a chicken. Man, you'd think they was queer or something. That was it—he'd have Nobody Home and Lee Roy and the rest of the Gents on the floor with that one. A couple of queer old doctors!

"Now the first thing, Herman, Dr. Karasik will want you here again tomorrow to take some more of these pictures of the waves in your head," Dr. Abelman said. "But you must also start taking better care of yourself. You must eat regularly, sleep regularly, and no drinking or the other stuff. Absolutely none."

"What other stuff?" Herman was innocent. The small bronze head was cocked—a puppy trying to interpret its master's command.

"You know, wise guy," Dr. Abelman said. "Those marks on your thighs aren't mosquito bites."

"This is very, very important, my boy," Dr. Karasik said. "You simply cannot continue to take narcotics of any kind. You may have something very serious in your head, and that is the worst thing you can do. I will be as cruel as I can—if you keep injecting heroin into your system it may kill you."

Mrs. Quincy let out a controlled little shriek. "Oh, sweet Jesus, dear Gawd!"

Her distress was not shared by her son. Who did these old queers think they were fooling with? Some high school boy, some little punk? He was Josh the Dill, the head man of the Twentieth Century Gents. He broke windows and street lamps; he sassed cops; he robbed groceries, and shook down squares, and jackrolled drunks, and beat up anyone who crossed him and a lot of people who just happened to be in his way; he was Josh the Big Man, who had tricked Leueen Harrison into a line-up and dumped her on the doctor's doorstep; he was Josh who made the speech in front of the judge and got written up in all the newspapers. He wanted to tell all these things about himself to the two old dopes trying to scare him; but they wouldn't have appreciated it anyway, and what his ma didn't know wouldn't hurt her.

All he said was, "Ah ain' scared."

"That's fine, Herman," Dr. Abelman said. "It's good to have a confident attitude toward illness. You'll get better, I'm sure. But, meanwhile, either you take our advice and start living like a human being or you might as well forget everything. You can expect a lot more headaches, and a lot more fits, and worse than that."

"Ah see he be a good boy," Mrs. Quincy said firmly.

"And one other thing," Dr. Abelman said, pounding a fist into his palm. "I must, I absolutely must see Herman the instant he has another fit. I don't care where it is, or when, or what time of day, call me. Even if you think it's over call me. That's important to all of us, Mrs. Quincy."

"Ah calls you," she said. "You heah, boy? Ef you somewhere Ah cain' reach you, you have yo' no-'count friends call de doctor. You heah?"

Herman gazed about the room, the deep brown eyes longing for escape, ignoring the fancy framed pictures and the crammed bookcases. The street beckoned; Nobody Home was making fun of him because of the way his mother was leading him around to doctors. The Twentieth Century Gents needed him.

"Yeah, yeah. Les' go."

He sauntered out of the office, thumbs hooked in his belt, the cap pushed down over his eyes, the insolence not lost on the physicians.

"Ah try teach him good manners," Mrs. Quincy stammered apologetically. "But nothin' doan seem to take. His daddy leave me years 'go and me workin' all deh time . . ."

She shifted from one elephantine foot to another, the great black-draped bulk swaying with unease. Dr. Abelman sensed she wanted to say something additional. He almost knew what it was that was bothering her.

"Doct' Abelman," she said, "yo' frien' doin' lot of 'spensive work on mah boy, dese pictures an' 'zaminations an' all dat. You ain' tole me what Ah have to pay. Ah got some money save, not too much—"

"Don't worry about it," Dr. Abelman said quickly, "Dr. Karasik will present you with a fair bill. I'll guarantee you'll be able to pay it. Now just try to keep your son from taking dope, and remember to call me when he has a fit."

She thanked them and left, the characteristic odor of her Deep South hairdressing lingering in Karasik's office. The neurologist knew what would happen. He would keep the bill as low as possible. She'd complain to Sam and Sam would call him and plead on her behalf to have it further reduced. He would end up doing the work, the hours of concentration, for a fraction of his normal fee. Yet what else could you do with Sam Abelman and his patients? Most of them belonged in the city hospitals and clinics. It was Sam's tough luck that he had been left behind and had to scrape his clientele from the slums, from the few and far between who were too proud to go to the dispensaries. There were specialists he knew, "big men" with swarming belt-line offices, nurses for this and for that, who wouldn't take a case from Abelman. They knew that it would end up with an embarrassed plea from the old fellow to knock the bill down a few bucks more. He, Franz Karasik, got one hundred dollars for an hour's consultation, and he knew there had been weeks when Sam Abelman hadn't earned that much. Yet you could not hurt the man who had fought your trivial battles half a century ago.

Passing through Karasik's office, Dr. Abelman noticed the new sterilizer had been partially dismantled. A few spare parts lay on the floor, and a tangle of exposed wiring was visible.

"What's wrong with the sterilizer, Franz?" Dr. Abelman asked.

"Who knows? I'm no mechanic. Something with the resistors, the transistors, whatever they call them. Surgical supply is sending the fellow over. He was supposed to be here yesterday, but you know how they are. They take their sweet time."

It was a challenge that Sam Abelman could not let pass. He was outraged. Those bums, those frauds, not servicing their machines properly!

"Got a screwdriver?" he asked Karasik. "Who needs those crooks? He'll splice a wire and charge you forty dollars. I fixed my own three times already. C'mon, get me a screwdriver and a pliers. Take me a minute."

"Sam, please, it's not necessary—"

But the neurologist's protests were useless. You couldn't explain to Sam that doctors didn't get down on their hands and knees like mechanics and fiddle around wiring. He would never be a professor, not in a million years. Karasik's nurse, starched and superior, looked at the old coot curiously. In the sweaty blue sport shirt, the tie now stuffed into his pocket, jabbing the screwdriver into the helpless guts of her employer's expensive machine, he negated everything she had been taught a doctor should be.

"Ah, you louse, loosen up!" the doctor muttered at an unyielding bolt. "Come on, ya bastard, move!"

She shivered, convinced that the beautiful piece of office equipment would never work again. Karasik knew otherwise.

Thrasher was battling his own indifference to the project. Ever since Lyman Gatling had injected his concepts of programming into *Americans, U.S.A.*, he had felt the lassitude growing in him. He had always had trouble sustaining interest. He bored easily, of people, projects, places. Sedentary vacations made him ill and he deliberately kept his neighbors at a distance, fearful that they would bore him to death at close range. *Americans, U.S.A.* had delighted him at its onset because it had been all his—his conception, his raw lump of clay to mold, knead, model, and bake. Now that they were closing him out—and at the same time expecting him to carry the load—he found it harder and harder to be hyperthyroid about the job. The worst of it was, he couldn't goof off, couldn't shift the burden of responsibility on anyone else. To take on a writer now would be an admission that he wasn't good enough, and, worse, that he had bowed to the pressures of Andrew Bain Lord's managers. In the midst of everything, he might even lose his wife; at least he would know the dull anger of cuckoldry. It amazed him how much he thought about it, and how filled with photographic details his mind was on the bothersome subject.

He resolved to plunge himself wholeheartedly into the script. He would make it the best script, the greatest television documentary ever written, an award winner, the kind of tasteful, subdued, and sincere thing that even Gould and Crosby would applaud. And this meant he had to step up his interrogation of the doctor. The trips to Brownsville, which he had enjoyed so much, were now a drain on his energies, and his efforts to entice the old man to lunch in New York were fruitless. "Who me, sonny boy?" Dr. Abelman had asked. "Save your money. I hate to drive into the city and I never enjoy restaurants. Waiters are a bunch of bastards."

A call to the doctor's office to determine when he could next see him produced only a series of surly mumbles from Jannine, the mammoth maid. Wondering why after all these years the doctor did not employ a standard answering service, he took a cab out to the steamy slum again. The doctor was at the hospital, Jannine informed him, and she had no idea when he would be back. He was about to leave, when he saw Mrs. Abelman. Her placid face was peering at him over the banister of the second-story stairs.

"Oh, hello, Mr. Thrasher," she called down. "One of the doctor's patients is being operated on today at the hospital. I really don't know when he'll be home. It's a shame you made this big trip and then didn't find him in. You'll get overheated. Come up, but watch your step."

Listening to her precautionary warnings, it occurred to him that he wasn't being quite the thorough reporter he was imagining himself. By rights he should have been questioning a lot of people other than Dr. Abelman—his wife, his daughter, Vogel, Hemitz— all the others with whom he had spent his forty-three years in practice. It was an ideal opportunity to get some information from her.

As he climbed the steep stairs he thought of the doctor and his wife, plodding up and down, almost half a century of ascending and descending, to eat, to sleep, to leave the house on Haven Place, to return, to treat the thousands of patients who drifted through the quietly reassuring waiting room. It distressed him that the waiting room was so empty now, and he realized, with some discomfort, that he wanted to talk with Sarah Abelman to ascertain, for his own secret satisfaction, why the doctor was still piddling around in a slum. He resented Sam Abelman's driving a 1947 Buick and being unable to buy an impressive house in a respectable neighborhood. Had the profane old man with his outraged vision and his compulsion to fight galoots brought it on himself? Or had the world sized him up and decided he could never make it?

"Sit here, near the window, Mr. Thrasher," she said. "You might get a breath of fresh air. Let me get you something cold to drink."

He refused politely, but she was calling down the dumbwaiter shaft to Jannine to send something upstairs. The cowed shape of Diane ambled into the room, the splay-footed dog working hard at being unobstrusive, and failing. She plopped into a corner behind a couch, panting in moist rhythms.

"Now, Diane, that's naughty," Mrs. Abelman reprimanded. "You know you're not allowed upstairs."

Diane contracted into a furry ball. A rear leg wagged in conciliation.

"It's so terribly hot in the yard," she explained to Thrasher, "I really haven't the heart to order her out."

He noticed she had been eating grapes from a cut-glass bowl and reading a lending library book. He recognized the title as one of those invariably well-reviewed and unpurchased novels of English village life written by a former Commando officer now returned to his ancestral estate in Dipping Stenbury. He asked her about it, wondering how many placid afternoons she had spent reading novels and eating grapes.

"Oh, I'm immensely fond of the English," she said. "They have a calm approach to life that I admire very much. I've always been interested in literary things. I think Myron gets his literary talents from me, being my brother's son."

"Yes, he's a bright lad," Thrasher said. Jannine rolled into the narrow living room bearing a copper tray with two tall glasses of root beer.

"When my son-in-law, Mr. Platt, was in England during the war," she continued, "he became very friendly with a lovely family, well-to-do farm people, in the Midlands. I still correspond with them every two months. We exchange all sorts of interesting books and information. It almost makes up for my never having gone to England."

"Yes, it's a shame you never got to visit England. It's fascinating. They have a real sense of the past; they're proud of their literary traditions."

She drank delicately from the soft-drink tumbler and patted her forehead with a folded cleansing tissue.

"Well, I've never been one to eat my heart out over things I couldn't have, Mr. Thrasher," Mrs. Abelman said. "I have a knack for accepting whatever life gives me and making the best of it. I don't go around battling everybody and everything."

The reference to her husband was intentional, but he said nothing.

"You know, when we had our little literary club when we were young folks," she continued, "the head of our settlement house, Mr. Munro, a very kind gentleman, arranged for one of his wealthy friends to offer a four-year scholarship to Vassar to the girl who wrote the best essay. Everyone in the club knew I was the best writer and had real literary aspirations. But there was another girl in the club, and I certainly won't mention any names because she'd be known to you, who used to roll her eyes at Mr. Munro and was very beautiful and something of a sneak. Well, naturally *she* got the scholarship and went off to Vassar for four years, and married a magazine editor. She's a very big name in the magazine field today. I read her articles all the time, and I can't help feeling that I might have been writing them. Yet I've never really complained to anyone about that scholarship, and I wonder why I'm even bothering to tell you."

"Those things happen all the time," Thrasher said. "It's wonderful that you can be as philosophic and calm about it. Some of us would have taken it a lot harder."

"Oh, don't tell me, Mr. Thrasher, I live with it every day."

She must have listened to a thousand profane tirades by the doctor, a thousand denunciations of cheating patients, thieves like Baumgart who stole his old-timers, of the clinics who took the poor patients, and the "professors" who grabbed off the wealthy and the gullible, polemics against the drug companies, the supply houses, the auto manufacturers, the utility companies, and, of course, the galoots and the crap artists. He could see her unruffled bland face, the gray, waved hair, and the hexagonal rimless glasses, listening silently as he raged and cursed. Yet he could not avoid the uncomfortable feeling that some of the physician's fury might have stemmed from, or at least been intensified by, her very placidness, her willingness to accept the world and all its evils, to turn other cheeks and come up smiling. In the street, he heard the colored boys screaming and swearing in one of their interminable stickball games. The doctor would have been pacing to and from the window, sawing the air with angry gestures. But for all Mrs. Abelman seemed to care, they might have been sitting on the White House lawn.

She noticed his glance toward the windows.

"This was really a very nice neighborhood once," she said defensively, with a hint in her voice that she *still* considered it a fairly decent place to live. Thrasher gulped the cold, sweet pop and pulled the memo pad from his coat pocket.

"Do take your coat off, Mr. Thrasher, you look warm," she cautioned him.

He complied. "Now, Mrs. Abelman, I had hoped to spare you the kind of inquisition I've subjected the doctor to. But maybe you can give me a few different angles."

"I'd be very happy to." She smiled primly, more than ready and willing to participate in a creative project. Maybe she had failed to win the Vassar scholarship, but she had never lost the literary dream.

"Well—quite bluntly, Mrs. Abelman, and please be assured that anything you tell me that you don't want used will go no further than the two of us—why is Dr. Abelman still in Brownsville? I have the feeling he's a marvelous doctor. I've heard about his talent as a diagnostician from Drs. Vogel and Karasik. How do you feel about it? Don't you feel that there's an injustice somewhere?"

She pursed her lips. "Not really, Mr. Thrasher. My husband feels sorry for himself sometimes, but I think at his age he's more or less adjusted to his lot."

Thrasher shook his head. "Maybe that's because you're too close to him. I've only known him a week or so, Mrs. Abelman, and I'm inclined to disagree."

She offered him the bowl of white grapes, refusing to sit down until he had clipped a bunch for himself, and then returned to the armchair, slip-covered in a blurred pastoral.

"You're trying to say that my husband is a failure, aren't you?"

"I certainly am not, Mrs. Abelman, and please accept my apology if I gave you that impression. Failure is something relative, and it doesn't necessarily involve money or power, or anything like that." He phrased it so well that he wished he could believe it.

"Well, let's say that, for your own reasons, you're a little unhappy over the fact that he hasn't done better financially. Is that accurate?"

"I'd say so, yes. Forgetting about the television program, I have a strange—oh, not an obsession, but an interest—in the doctor, and I'm genuinely curious about him. Everything he's told me so far indicates that he was an ambitious young man, a fine doctor, a hard worker. Is that true?"

"Of course it's true."

"Well, I'm still puzzled then as to why he—my apologies again— didn't get further than he did."

She sighed, struggling with another stem of grapes. He noticed that her fingers were gnarled with the cruel signs of arthritis; she had difficulty tearing the stem off.

"Everybody will tell you something else," she said wearily. "If you talk to Max Vogel, he'll put some of the blame on me, and if you talk to Dr. Karasik he'll say it was because Sam didn't shine his shoes."

"What do you say?"

"Well, to begin with, I don't consider my husband a failure."

Thrasher smiled. "We're agreed on that, I'm sure."

"But if you ask me why he remained a GP all these years, working his head off for nickels and dimes, I'd have to put a good part of the blame, not all of it mind you, on Harry Hemitz. Oh, a lot of it is Sam's own fault, and I suppose some of it is mine. But Dr. Hemitz did *not* treat Sam very nicely at all."

"That was the young lad who lived across the street?"

"Yes. The janitor's son. When I think of the way Sam was good to him, and helped him out, and loved him like his own kid brother! Why, to this day you won't get Sam to say a bad word about Dr. Hemitz. He still thinks the world of him, praises him all the time."

"Did he become a surgeon? I seem to recall Dr. Abelman mentioning that."

"Harry Hemitz was one of the very *biggest* surgeons in New York, Mr. Thrasher." Then, noticing him unloosening his tie, the sweat dripping from his lean face, she was ready to fend off another minor disaster.

"You're perspiring terribly, Mr. Thrasher. Are you sure you don't want a salt tablet?"

Hilda Oestreicher's soft bulk lay supine on the operating table in the classic Trendelenburg position. The fleshy mass was at an angle of almost forty-five degrees from the floor. Her anesthetized baby's head was lowermost. The dimpled knees were highest. The legs, dwindling to absurd thin ankles and tiny feet, dangled over the table's edge. White drapes covered most of the doughy torso. The lower abdomen lay exposed, awaiting the first incision of Dr. Harry Hemitz' scalpel. The instrument cut at the pulpy skin, through the layers of fat. Hilda Oestreicher's blood oozed lazily through the cruel gash and Sam Abelman dabbed at it with the surgical sponge.

It was Harry Hemitz' first professional case, and the operating room at Beth Abraham had drawn an interested, if cynical audience. Pivarnik, the chief of surgery, had made a point of attending along with his retinue of worshipers. Young Hemitz had assisted him for over a year, and it was common gossip around Beth Abraham that Pivarnik would have been happier if the eager kid had sought his staff appointment elsewhere. But a few of the hospital regulars— Sam Abelman in the forefront—had insisted that Harry Hemitz get the next opening. Beth Abraham was growing rapidly, Brownsville was becoming more populous every day. Two general surgeons, even in a small private hospital, were certainly not too many. Besides, there was something about Harry Hemitz that demanded recognition. Maybe it was the deliberately casual way he tied knots with one dextrous hand. Or the speed with which he did the routine work, and the casual confidence with which he attacked the difficult. With never a change in his deadly monotone, with no dramatics and with a disdainful absence of emotion, the janitor's son dominated the operating room. Even when he was an assistant, Pivarnik had sensed it, resented it, yet was constrained to reward it.

Sam Abelman had undergone no such vacillation in his feeling about Harry. The young surgeon was his boy: the kid who had baby-sat with Eunice and answered the office phone. He had watched him mature at Bellevue, race impatiently through two years of interneship, and had made him promise that his first professional operative case would be one of Sam's patients. Now, under the glare of the overhead lamps, he was a little sorry that the bloated form of Hilda Oestreicher had been elected for Harry's debut. Those big fat ones, all soggy tissue and blood, were distressing to any surgeon, and while subtotal abdominal hysterectomy wasn't the hardest thing in the world to perform, there were all kinds of pitfalls involved. Injuries to the bladder and ureter were common; hemorrhage and shock could follow. And who could tell with certainty where the arteries were hidden under all that fat?

He saw Pivarnik exchange a solemn glance with him, and he knew the chief of surgery was granting grudging approval to Sam's protégé. The operative field had been exposed; already Harry had packed the intestines out of pelvis with moist gauze. Now the young surgeon was ligating and dividing the round ligaments; he worked so quickly that Sam felt like telling him to slow down. The severed end of each ligament was neatly knotted; they looked like the primordial heads of two bloodworms.

"Tenaculum," Hemitz said softly.

Forbes, the chief surgical nurse, slapped the hooked probe into his hand. She almost seemed to be smiling behind the mask. Pivarnik ran surgery like an army post; Harry's quiet authoritativeness apparently delighted her.

The surgeon slipped the tenaculum beneath the pinkish, diseased uterus, the barren pod which had borne Hilda Oestreicher no fruit save a benign tumorous growth of uncertain pathology.

Harry was dissecting the bladder peritoneum now, dividing the tough tissue at its reflection on the uterus and cutting downward below the level of the internal opening. The scalpel now changed direction, slicing the protective membrane laterally and exposing the uterine vessels.

"Hey, slow down," Sam muttered. "You trying to set a record for indoor hysterectomy?"

Harry looked curiously at Sam. "Who's hurrying? Do the routine stuff quick. If you know what you're looking for, why wait?"

Now the tubes and utero-ovarian ligaments lay naked before

the surgical scissors. Hemitz was snipping and tying again, letting Sam's strong hands dart in and out of the raw, red cavity with the sponge.

"You could just clamp 'em until you take the uterus out," Sam said. "Shouldn't you amputate first and get it over with?"

Harry made a minimizing gesture with his bloodied gloved hand.

"Do 'em while you got 'em, Sam," he said impatiently. "I want to get this one out of the anesthetic as soon as I can. She's got trouble enough breathing under the best of conditions."

"Guess you're right," Sam said apologetically. He glanced at Hilda Oestreicher's stupefied head. Five years ago he had pulled her through Spanish influenza, watching the obese body, so badly designed for resisting disease, fight off the bug, while stronger people died around her. She sent him a loaf of honey-cake, her own, every Passover, and had referred quite a few patients to him. Hilda Oestreicher, for all her absurd appearance and infantile brain, was surely worth saving. He was wrong to let his personal interest in her creep into the operating room.

The snipping and ligating were preliminary, yet in many ways were more demanding than the major step of the operative procedure, the amputation of the uterus. With the same quick, confident moves, Harry was now cutting a deep cone into the cervix, the base of the diseased organ. The blade dipped in and out of the pink-gray flesh, like the beak of a predatory bird tearing carrion. Maybe Max Vogel was right: it wasn't much different from cleaning fish once you learned where and how deep to cut. Yet there was a professional neatness and precision to Harry Hemitz' technique that transcended any crude comparison of Vogel's. Sam knew it and prune-faced Forbes knew it, and Pivarnik not only knew it, but feared it a little.

The blade flashed again under the antiseptic glare of the lamps. Sam looked at it transfixed, hearing Pivarnik murmur generously, "Neat, very neat"—and then he was wiping blood from his eyes. The tortured wound in Hilda Oestreicher's huge abdomen had come alive; a red fountain spurted from somewhere beneath the half-severed uterus. It was hard to believe there was so much energy and so much blood in the woman. Forbes gasped and looked to Harry for instructions.

"What the hell, Harry?" Sam muttered. Another spurt of warm blood pumped out of the gaping red hole in a rhythmic streak and sloshed against his nose.

"Ovarian artery," Harry said softly. "What in the world was it doing back there?" He sounded as if the misplaced vessel had deliberately concealed itself to thwart him.

"Tie it off, son," Pivarnik said. "It happens to the best of us."

He was probing for the damaged artery, not frantically, but with quick deliberation, peeling back the surrounding fatty tissue in an effort to track the violent bleeding to its source.

"Go get it, Heshy," Sam said out of the corner of his mouth.

He hadn't called him by his boyhood nickname in years. But watching him struggling to stanch the violent flow of Hilda Oestreicher's blood, seeing his proud exhibition verging on failure, he thought of him again as the skinny boy who had answered calls for him ten years ago.

"There it is," Harry said. He smiled, a flat humorless smile, at Sam, and proceeded to pass a ligature through the injured vessel. It was just a minute nick, a faint scratch caused by Harry's impatient scalpel, but it had been enough to soil their gowns and masks with bright-red splotches and to push Hilda Oestreicher a step closer to the grave. Clamps held back the furious pulsating bleeding as Harry manipulated the aneurysm needle and the suture. The bleeding ceased. There was a collective sigh of relief from the audience. Pivarnik murmured something about "good boy" and Harry Hemitz, an alien to both their distress and their praise, proceeded with the amputation. The rest was mechanical to him: anchoring the ligaments to the cervix, lateral sutures to cover the raw surfaces, and folding the protective flap of the bladder peritoneum over the bleeding stump.

It was an hour and three-quarters since Sam had stood by as Harry made the first abdominal incision. Now, the loose ends knotted, the truncated tips of the organs and vessels properly tied and protected, he worked a prim, symmetrical blanket stitch around the wound. He seemed fresher and more vigorous than when the operation had commenced. The fact that it was his first case, that he was on his own and no longer Pivarnik's shadow, had never entered his mind.

"Beautiful, Harry, beautiful," Sam said admiringly.

"My congratulations, too, Dr. Hemitz," Forbes added.

Pivarnik, tall and goateed, came to his side as Harry tied off the last stitch. "Very well done, son," he said. "Too bad about that nicked artery. But it happens. I must say you recovered admirably."

"Why even mention it?" Harry Hemitz asked. Pivarnik said nothing. A few weeks ago, Harry Hemitz was doing everything but polish his shoes, and probably would have done that, if Pivarnik had asked. Now, at twenty-six, in practice a few days, he was already filled with short answers. It was amazing what the first taste of blood did to them.

Scrubbing up afterwards in Beth Abraham's cramped dressing room, Sam bragged about his young friend.

"You should have seen him, Max," he said proudly. "This stuff comes up like a geyser—who would know the ovarian artery was buried there? I turned green around the gills. You know what can happen with a fat one like that Oestreicher dame, with the lousy circulation and the poor respiration. But Harry didn't bat an eye. Right, kid?"

Hemitz smiled uneasily. He didn't object to the older man's lavish praise. At the same time he was mildly uncomfortable under the curious eyes of his colleagues. Locker-room informality was not for him. A few of the doctors had heard about his rudeness to Pivarnik, and he sensed unspoken disapproval in their indifference. He even welcomed Max Vogel's rude outburst.

"He sounds like a friggin' genius," Vogel spat. "He's the kind of guy who'll confuse the lower sigmoid and rectum with a pecker some day and chop it off. Heshy, you don't even look like a surgeon. Grow a beard. Wear a plug hat. Take singing lessons. Don't you know surgery is more bull than poetry? Make 'em think you're somebody, Heshy."

"Please don't call me Heshy," Hemitz said primly. "And, as far as my professional skill is concerned, Max, I'll let my work speak for itself."

"Tell him, kid," Sam said happily. Then, as they departed, he turned to all of them. "We'll all be taking lessons from Harry, soon," Sam said. "He's got what it takes."

"And he's gonna take everything he can get his mitts on," Vogel shouted after them. "Watch out he don't lift your watch, Sammy!"

Later that day Sam took Harry to Williamsburg, Sarah's old neighborhood, to buy the young surgeon a tuxedo. Brooklyn's Broadway, permanently enshadowed by the elevated, was a center for clothing stores. Shirt-sleeved entrepreneurs, uniformed in black vests and skullcaps, stood on the curb and pulled customers in. Sam smiled as he observed the ritual entrapment of the unwary passers-by. He himself had done a short hitch as a "puller-in" in his youth. It had been one of his less rewarding jobs. The proprietor, a lodge brother of the elder Malkin, had hired him on a straight commission basis, and since Sam was a singularly poor salesman (he had no knack for tugging at coattails and gently guiding customers toward the door), he had soon quit.

As the doctors approached the establishment of *P & J Bleibtreu, Fancy Men's Coats and Suits,* the puller-in, a bearded gnome with thumbs hooked in vest pockets, glided toward them.

"Something nice in a topcoat, professors?" he asked. The hands had unhooked themselves and were at the ready, prepared to seize a jacket, an elbow, a hand.

"It's okay, *zayde,*" Sam laughed, "we're going to Bleibtreu's anyway."

The gnome winked at Sam and spoke in conspiratorial Yiddish. "Do me a favor, professor, walk away and let me catch you. Bleibtreu is watching."

Sam looked at Harry. "Come on, Harry, give *zayde* a break. He must be working on commission. He'll get an extra ten cents if he lands us on his own."

Hemitz frowned. "Isn't that kind of silly, Sam? We're coming here anyway."

The bearded troll's rheumy eyes pleaded with the older professor —the one in the derby and black suit, a nice Jewish fellah, a doctor, the son of a greenhorn like himself. The other one—that blond with the gold-rimmed glasses, he might even be a *shagitz,* for all he knew. No beggar's appeal would ever move that neat face.

"Oh, come on, Harry. Here, look up at the store and then follow me down the street. That must be Bleibtreu peeking in between the crack in the door. I hate him already."

Sam looked at Bleibtreu's window, peopled by a family of pink-laquered eunuchs. Then he pointed down the street and carried Harry off with him, noting the baleful eye in the doorway as they left. The puller-in took his cue with magnificent timing, permitting them to drift a few paces away. When they were nearing the adjacent clothing establishment (Morris Steingesser & Sons) the troll skipped nimbly to their rear and clamped a firm hand on the vent in Sam's jacket.

"Just a minute, professors!" he cried. "You'll make a mistake going by Steingesser! Inferior workmanship and old styles! Jacob Bleibtreu is having a special bargain week. Discounts for professional men!"

Sam roared. He pushed the derby over his eyes and staggered back, laughing wildly at the salesman's inspired oration. He punched Harry playfully in the back. "Oh mamma, did you ever hear such a line? How could we let him down after such a pitch?"

Hemitz scratched at his tight starched collar. "He isn't *that* funny, Sam. Are we going in or not?"

The puller-in rashly hooked an arm inside of that of the young blond man. Then, pushing the older professor by the seat and dragging the younger man by an arm, he delivered them to J. Bleibtreu, proprietor.

Half an hour later, a sidewalk photographer memorialized the occasion of Harry Hemitz' first tuxedo with a streaked brown print of the two doctors, arm in arm, the surgeon unsmiling, the GP, derby in hand, grinning. The tuxedo set Sam back twenty-four dollars, but it was worth every cent of it. He had helped launch Harry Hemitz on a career of surgery that would make academicians sit up and take notice. Looking at his protégé, trim in the narrow jacket, the satin lapels glistening under Bleibtreu's harsh light, he felt assured of their friendship.

Sam decided that a further celebration was necessary. They would call their wives, and have the girls meet them at Gage and Tollner's, Brooklyn's most expensive restaurant down on Fulton Street. Sarah protested. Gage and Tollner's charged too much, she had no sitter to look after Eunice, there was a call to the Tabbernoy family waiting, and she would have to dismiss Rabbi Piltz who had come for his weekly prostate massage.

"Tell the rabbi to let his wife work it over for him. It'll do them both good," Sam laughed. "Tabbernoy can wait. It's only the old lady, and she's a hypochondriac with a spastic colon."

"Why do you have to treat?" Sarah complained.

"Oh, Sarah, stop it, willya?" Sam protested. "Don't you know it's a celebration? Harry's first case! I sent it to him! If you saw what that kid did to fatty Oestreicher. Pivarnik's eyes popped out of his head. He'll make the old-timers look like butchers in a year!"

In his expansive moods, there was no stopping Sam. The wives met them at Gage and Tollner's before six o'clock. Sarah looked lovely in a new white linen shirtwaist and a tight maroon skirt; she wore her hair in a high pompadour. Harry Hemitz' wife was three year his senior, a bony woman with bad skin and drab brown hair. Her maiden name was Glaberson, and she was of the wealthy Glabersons, early Brownsville settlers who had accumulated fortunes in real estate and wholesale groceries. Her father owned a summer home on White Lake and once had his picture taken with the mayor on Rosh Hashonah. Myra had married the janitor's son upon his graduation from Bellevue, and while he was still an interne the overjoyed father-in-law had set the couple up in a roomy, three-story brick house on Montgomery Street. When Harry

was ready to practice, Menachin Mendel Glaberson had equipped
the office and installed, with a few sly pinches, a starched Norwegian
nurse who kept the surgeon's patients in perpetual terror.

At Gage and Tollner's they dined on shrimp cocktail and steak
and Sam toasted his young friend with sparkling burgundy. Sam,
goggle-eyed at the endless menu and the awesome wine list, had
to be rescued by Harry. It was not that Harry was any more con-
versant with the foods and wines; it was just that he took control
of the situation so thoroughly. When the headwaiter, an aged
Negro with the bearing of a colonel of marines, cautioned Sam on
using the wrong fork for the shrimp, Harry sent him off in confused
retreat with a demand for more cocktail sauce.

But, all told, it was an evening of triumph and promise. The four
young people would grow rich and famous together. Harry's scalpel
and Sam's diagnostic acumen would make them the finest medical
team in Brooklyn.

"To my pal, Harry Hemitz, M.D.!" Sam said, raising his glass of
wine. "A great guy to know and a great guy over the operating
table!"

"My handsome husband!" Myra Hemitz crooned.

Harry smiled in mild appreciation. He agreed with them completely.

In a few months, a dozen other GP's were following Sam Abelman's lead in directing surgical cases to Harry Hemitz. The new
office on Montgomery Street was invariably filled; his operating
schedule became increasingly crowded. At Beth Abraham, the
young surgeon's reputation soon threatened the dominant figure of
old Pivarnik. He charged less, he was quicker and defter, he had a
flair for showmanship and self-dramatization that attracted other
physicians and their patients as well. The populous Glaberson
family, influential and wide-ranging, spread the gospel about their
talented son-in-law. At the core of the growing legend of Harry
Hemitz stood Sam Abelman, praising him to patients and friends,
elaborating on his young friend's deeds until they assumed an air
of mystical invincibility. Dropping in at St. Mary's to visit a patient,
he would find a group of physicians and regale them with Harry's
latest marvel.

"So the kid opens her up," Sam would say, "and there's this
sarcoma—the size of a basketball. Everyone gasps a little when
they see the way it's anchored to the connective tissue. But not
Harry. The kid starts cutting and he shells it out as neat as scooping
ice cream out of a carton. Patient in her sixties too—but Harry did

it in twenty minutes, sewing her up and everything. He's submitting a report on it to the State Medical Journal."

One of the young doctors smiled. "You make Hemitz sound like he's a genius, Sam. Some people say he's closer to being a butcher."

Sam scowled. "That's jealous crap and you know it. The kid *is* a genius. Come watch him operate some day and you'll see why."

"Still tying knots one-handed?"

"You bet your sweet life," Sam said. "Better than most punks do with two."

The patients kept coming. They came for exploratories and for hysterectomies, for simple appendectomies (Hemitz had perfected a swift, neat procedure that left a minute horizontal scar), for operations on breasts, inner organs, reproductive organs, and limbs. He had the cold courage to try anything. If he lost an occasional patient, it was not for carelessness, or ignorance, or incompetence. The old-timers watched him with despair and admiration. Never had they seen anyone dominate a medical field so quickly and so completely.

Sarah did not wholeheartedly share her husband's adoration of the young surgeon. Driving home one Friday night after an evening at the RKO Albee (a movie and eight vaudeville acts), they argued about Sam's relationship with Harry. It started when Sarah accused Myra Hemitz of becoming, as she put it, "snooty." The Hemitzes had accompanied them to the theater and, later, to the Waffle Shoppe. The couples saw a good deal of each other socially, often in the company of other young Brooklyn physicians. Hemitz drew the line only at Max Vogel—he had had his fill of the fat man's insults.

"I didn't like the way Myra kept making cracks about the Broadway theater," Sarah said. "How she so much prefers a good play to a movie. You'd think that's all she did."

"Ah, Myra's all right," Sam said defensively. "You're too sensitive."

"I'm sensitive? I beg your pardon, Sam. You're the one who can't bear to hear anything critical about your darling Harry. Why, when Is Newman dared to suggest that Harry was too quick to operate on his brother for bleeding ulcers you almost punched Is in the nose—one of your best friends, too!"

"Is Newman is a dumb schoolteacher. Hey, I made a song! Is Newman a dumb schoolteacher? *Yes he Is!*"

"Stop being so smart and don't change the subject."

"Who's changing anything? I knew you were annoyed with Myra and maybe even with Harry."

"Well, I have a right to be. She didn't stop talking all night about her servants, and the summer home in White Lake, and the Broadway stage. Putting on the ritz like that when her dear husband is a janitor's son. A lady janitor, yet."

"More power to him, for going so far."

"With your help," she said quickly.

"Of course with my help, Sarah. How else does a young surgeon get started without help from other doctors who trust him?"

"Well, I'll tell you this, Sam, and I'm an excellent judge of character—"

"—I'm innocent, judge," he interrupted.

"—and I know people very well. You may trust Harry Hemitz and he may be the world's greatest surgeon. But *I* don't trust him and neither do a lot of people. He's all for Harry Hemitz, and to heck with the rest of the world. Goodness knows I don't care particularly for that homely wife of his, but the way he treats her! Acting like she isn't even there. And where would he be without the Glaberson money, and the house they bought for him, and the patients they drum up for him?"

"I'll tell you where, *ketzeleh*," Sam said firmly. Gently, he braked the Chandler as they approached a stoplight. The Brooklyn side streets were pleasantly deserted and calm. Bowers of maple leaves cast checkered shadows over the endless hood of the automobile.

"Harry Hemitz would be right where he is. He didn't need his inlaws' *gelt*, or me, or any of the other GP's who send him cases. All Harry needs are his hands and his brain and his eyes—"

"—and his gall—"

"Yes, Sarah, and his gall, or nerve, or courage or whatever you want to call it. Because Harry has got what it takes. I've seen surgeons in Bellevue, and at Jewish, and Mount Sinai, and they all act like a bunch of kids getting their first piece, if you'll excuse my rudeness. But Harry Hemitz doesn't crap around. He knows what he's doing every inch of the way. He's born to surgery. He'll make those big-shot *goyim* in the frock coats and the pince-nez crawl on their knees to watch him operate in a few years. So don't go saying Myra's money made him what he is. Sure, it helped, it helped him get up faster. But Harry would get to the top with or without her, or me, or anyone else."

She settled back in the seat, silent for a while. Rarely had she heard her husband wax so eloquent in anyone's behalf. It was almost as if Harry Hemitz had bewitched him and put the words in his mouth. They were driving now across the unmarked boundary between respectable, middle-class Crown Heights, into the tenements of Brownsville, their own territory, the crumbling neighborhood from which Harry Hemitz had so quickly escaped, and to which Sam Abelman appeared to be rooted.

"Oh, maybe you're right, Sam," she said wearily. "But I wish you wouldn't worship Harry the way you do—in public, so much."

"Who worships him? He's my best friend. I have a right to praise him."

She shook her head sadly. "It almost seems you do it at the expense of yourself."

"What was the meaning of that remark?"

"Just that you talk so much about Harry and how great he is, and everything he can do, that it kind of makes you a shadow. You should build yourself up more, you should talk about yourself. Or at least don't go telling the world what a genius this other doctor is. It makes you just a salesman or a publicity man for him."

"Ah, you've got it all wrong," he said. "You just don't understand us."

He parked the car at the curb in front of their home. The Chandler was the only car on the block, an object of awe and deep respect. Sam did a quick tour of the high automobile, checking for nicks, dents, and impending breakdowns, and joined Sarah on the stoop. He unlocked the street door, yawning prodigiously.

"I'll sleep good tonight," he said happily. "Between that lousy movie and the rubber waffle and your arguments, I'm really ready for a snooze."

But sleep eluded him. Long after Sarah began her gentle snoring, he lay awake, listening to the unrelated night noises of the city. The trolley clattered by; a neighbor's mongrel yapped in idiot rhythms; a weekend drunk across the street cried to a furious Sicilian wife to grant him entry, and she replied with a dousing of water.

He wondered about his relationship with Harry. Sarah's probing bothered him more than he would admit. Was he permitting himself to vanish in the surgeon's shadow? On the face of it, it was ridiculous. General practitioners and surgeons worked as a team. If he recommended more cases to Harry, and Harry operated in his competent manner, how could his own reputation help but be enhanced? They would grow wealthy and famous together: the one as Brooklyn's finest surgeon, the other as the wise diagnostician, the clinician whose shrewd groundwork would send the ill to Harry's healing knife.

Yet it was not that simple, nor had it really worked out that way in the year and one-half since Harry had performed the hysterectomy on Hilda Oestreicher. Sam was forced to admit that he had been standing still. His income had remained almost stable. He saw the usual quota of new faces in his office, yet seemed to lose the same amount to new men, to specialists, even to a fat chiropractor with oily hands who had opened a store-front office around the corner. The way his finances were working out, he had more than enough to cover expenses, to pay for a vacation for Sarah and Eunice, to employ a colored sleep-in maid. But a new home, for example, was out of the question. Already Brownsville was showing signs of decay. As Sol Pomerantz put it, "a lower element" was moving in. Overflowing bags of garbage now dotted the sidewalk with more frequency.

Moreover, Sam was beginning to feel the need for "going some-place." He had been in practice now for thirteen years, and while he still loved the work, the challenge, the mystery, the rude cama-raderie of the hospitals and the dressing room, he often wondered whether he was right in remaining in general practice. So many of the young punks were specializing: obstetrics, pediatrics, ear-nose-and-throat work, roentgenology. . . . It was no secret that the big money, the easy regular hours, the dignity of being a "professor" lay in the magic of specialization. X-ray work fascinated him, and he often thought about doing postgraduate work at Bellevue. It would be fun going back to the old red brick pile on First Avenue, rubbing elbows with Harlow Brooks and his other heroes. But it would be no easy chore. It would mean giving up several nights a week, and with new MD's popping up all over Brownsville, he'd be sure to lose patients. Besides, he was two years shy of forty, and he had a family to worry about, bills to pay. He would have to cram for boards, pass oral and written tests before getting a diplomate in radiology. When he mentioned the possibility of returning to school to Sarah, she registered strong disapproval.

"At *your* age, Sam?" she would ask, in her maddening, calm manner. "And what about your family? Not just Eunice and my-self—but your mother, and your sister, and the rest of them stand-ing around with their hands out! There's nothing wrong with general practice. You have a lot of fine patients. Why gamble on a new career this late? As for a new house, we'll have one some day. I'm perfectly happy here. This is the nicest block in Brownsville."

And so it would rest. The reference to his own relatives par-ticularly galled him because it was true. He was supporting his widowed mother, who now lived with Rivke. Moishe, gray and worn at fifty, drifted in and out of their house, silent and shy, filled with solemn wonder at his younger brother's wealth, fame, and knowl-edge. Only Aaron, sickly and fragile, was standing on his own feet. He dedicated himself to a growing costume jewelry business. Yet he too needed frequent medical attention—his attacks of tachycardia were becoming more numerous. They were all leaning on him, people who somehow were not in the mainstream of life. More and more, they turned to him for sustenance, even if it were in the form of a ten-minute visit for a cup of tea. Reflecting on his family only sharpened his sense of incompleteness, of yearning for something better and more fulfilling in his own life. He lay awake for hours, feeling the first twinges of migraine at his temples, knowing that morning would find him blinking at the aura and battling the vise of pain.

The dream of specializing lingered with him, but he rarely spoke about it to Sarah again. His practice was picking up, in spite of a growing tendency to lecture his patients. It alarmed Sarah to hear his voice rising, drifting upstairs through the office skylight and airshaft, advising some miserable couple that they were afraid to face life.

"Why the hell do you come to me with your *tsuris?*" she would hear him shouting. "There's not a goddam thing wrong with either of you medically! The X-rays were negative, the laboratory tests were negative. If I give you a diet, you won't follow it, and if I give you medicine, you'll call up after the first dose and complain you're still sick. What do you want from me? Go home and live like human beings, love each other, get interested in your kids, get a hobby. You're not sick!"

She wondered why he felt impelled to rail at them like a slightly demented preacher. Max Vogel would never lower himself in that manner; he greedily welcomed the malingerers, scared them into thinking they were terribly ill, and socked them with a fat bill, after subjecting them to half a dozen unneeded treatments.

One evening, in the midst of their weekly bridge game, Sarah heard the irate voices of an office argument, and she winced. The three other members of the foursome—her sister-in-law, Esther Malkin, and two old-maid sisters, Louise and Martha Kobernick —glanced at her in apprehension. Willie Malkin, lolling shoeless on the living room sofa, blew a smoke ring toward the ceiling and flicked a rich white cigar ash into the standing tray.

"Doc is off again," he said happily. "I sure like to hear him cuss out a patient. He's better than my old topkick in the 77th."

Military service in the AEF had been the zenith of Willie Malkin's young life. Nothing could ever surpass the romance of his khaki uniform; all events and persons had to be related to his glorious year under General Pershing.

"I don't think it's so funny," Sarah said evenly. "Two spades."

"He really does get wrought up," Esther simpered. She had a blond doll's face and a giggly manner that failed to mask her jealousy of her fortunate sister-in-law, married to a rich doctor. Her own husband, still in fearful combat with old Malkin, was now trying his hand at selling a new line of hairdressing to neighborhood barbershops and pharmacists. His only customers, Traficanti and Berkowitz, had come to him only through their friendship with Dr. Abelman—a circumstance that only served to heighten Esther's bitterness.

"Bid, Esther, bid," said Martha Kobernick.

"Two hearts." Esther's ear was cocked and alert for the increasing vigor and volume of the argument in the office. Two people—one a semi-hysterical woman—appeared to be screaming at the doctor. A door slammed, and they heard Sam Abelman's steady trudge as he ascended the hallway stairs.

"You can't bid two hearts after two spades, Esther," Martha chided. "If you'd stop listening to what's not your business, you'd play bridge better than you do."

"I'm sorry, I'm sorry," Esther said, with mock contriteness. "I pass."

Sam appeared in the doorway. He looked grim and overwrought; his thumbs were hooked in the lower pockets of his open vest.

"Well, I told *them* off, once and for all," he announced.

"Sam, please, can't you talk about it some other time?" Sarah pleaded. "What did you bid, Louise?"

"You sounded in great form, doc," Willie said. "Really gave 'em a chapter from the Torah, hah?"

Willie's goad made his lined face darken. He slammed a square fist into his palm with violent impact, and the bridge game, limping along politely in the face of the explosion, ground to a dead halt.

"Now, Sam, why don't you and Willie have a game of casino?" Sarah asked. "Go downstairs and have a salami sandwich and let us finish the rubber."

"Those lousy Tabbernoys!" Sam shouted. "They won't bother me any more! The whole damned lot of them! I told them off once and for all!"

Sarah shuddered. The Tabbernoy family had been among Sam's first patients. They were a well-to-do clan, people who had risen above the Brownsville level rapidly via a lucrative coal and ice business. Tabbernoy's trucks now serviced all of Brownsville, East New York, and the nearby areas of Flatbush. The aged parents, their four muscular sons and three fat daughters, had moved to Crown Heights some years back, but they still came to Sam Abelman.

They were loyal, albeit demanding and possessive, and Sarah knew that their financial contribution to her husband's income was considerable. What had motivated him to alienate them in one stupid, unreasoning argument?

"It was that bitch of an old-maid daughter!" Sam suddenly exploded. "That lousy schoolteacher with the flossy accent!"

Martha and Louise, both old maids and schoolteachers, looked stricken and helpless, and Sarah shuddered again.

"Who the hell is she to threaten Harry? To say we're incompetent? After all the care that old lady of hers is getting! And neither of us charging a nickel!"

"What's the story, doc?" Willie asked eagerly.

"Harry did a resection of the rectum on old lady Tabbernoy last week, and, let me tell you, it was a masterpiece. Not a single complication! He took that lousy tumor out like he was shelling a pea! I've seen resections, but this was the cleanest ever!"

"So what's the fight about?" Esther Malkin piped. "If Hemitz is so great, why should they complain?"

"Because they're rats!" Sam shouted. "Two days ago, the old lady had a lot of pain, and Harry was making his morning rounds. The old bitch wanted something to ease the pain, so Harry gave her a shot of morphine. Normally, the interne or the nurse does it, but it was my patient, and Harry always gives them special attention. So he talked to her a little and then jabbed her rear with a hypodermic, and that lousy, friggin', defective needle broke off! That's what they're so mad about!"

"But, Sam, that isn't so terrible," Sarah said quietly. "Can't they locate it and remove it?"

"I did already," he replied. The irrational fury left his voice for a moment, and he sounded puzzled and weary. "In all those goddam layers of fat you couldn't even see it on the X-ray. Let me tell you I really had to look. Then her behind developed a secondary infection, and the place where the needle entered is draining pus. Harry sees her every day, and I've been in and out of Beth Abraham —just for her—a dozen times since I extracted it. I'm not charging them a nickel for it. So tonight in walks the old man, that dumb Litvak, and that old-maid daughter, and she starts bawling me out, and insulting Harry and threatening to sue! We're negligent, we're cold-hearted, Pivarnik said her mother never needed surgery anyway, and the usual crap. Well, I took as much of it as I could, but when she said she was seeing a lawyer tomorrow, I really let her have it!"

"I heard you," Willie said proudly.

"Be quiet, Willie," Sarah said sharply. "Sam, can't we discuss this later?"

He ignored her. "I told her to take that goddam shyster of hers and they could both go to hell, with my compliments! As if that's all Harry and I have to worry about. We're doing our damnedest to get the fat old slob on her feet again, and she's going to sue."

"Why didn't you reason with her, Sam?" Sarah asked. "You could call Jerry or Harvey Tabbernoy. The boys have always trusted you, and you could have explained to them, at least to wait awhile if their mother wasn't in danger. Why did you have to fly off the handle?"

"Oh, so you're on their side?" he asked. "Always the *fekokteh* patients are right and I'm wrong, eh?"

"I didn't say that," Sarah protested.

"Well, I'll tell you something. I'll tell all of you something. I'm through with this lousy general practice. I'm going to specialize. I'm going to be a professor in a white coat, so I can look down my nose at patients and don't have to hold their dirty hands and love them, and then get blamed by them when any little thing goes wrong."

"Atta boy, doc!" Willie cheered.

He turned to leave, and Willie, shoving his stocking feet into untied shoes, rose to pursue him.

"We gonna have that casino game now, doc?" he called after his brother-in-law.

"Play solitaire, Willie," he said. "I'm going to see Harry."

A Japanese houseboy—the only one Sam had ever seen outside of a movie—answered the door. He was a recently acquired possession, hired by Myra Hemitz shortly after they had moved from Montgomery Street to the fourteen-room, three-story granite mansion on Republic Street a few weeks ago.

"Oh, harro, Dockah Aberman," he grinned. "Sorry, Dockah Hemit reave word not be disturbed tonight. Sorry prease."

He began to close the door, and Sam shoved it open violently.

"Stop crapping me up, sonny boy," he barked at the servant. "Where's Dr. Hemitz? I can see him any time, anywhere, understand?"

"He be very unhappy, dockah."

"Bull. Where is he? In the office?"

"He in prayroom downstairs."

Sam had been in the new home once before, and as he strode hurriedly through the ornate, mahogany-walled living room, toward the cellar stairs, he marveled at Myra's exquisite taste and Harry's fantastic income—there was a ceiling-high breakfront alone that must have cost three thousand simoleons!

The arena-size basement had been transformed into a paneled hobby room for the surgeon. The lighting was bright yet unobtrusive. There were three folded music stands in one corner; a violin case lay on a chair alongside them. At one end, Sam saw a laboratory table, complete with Bunsen burners, an array of flasks and tubes, and a series of cages containing live white mice. Nearer the stairs was a new padded gymnasium mat. A massive victrola gave forth a scratchy recording of Caruso singing a selection from *La Juive*. One entire wall was lined with books—not medical works, but an overwhelming library of the classics and contemporary works. At the end of the room, in the corner formed by the books and the music stands, Harry Hemitz stood in front of an easel, daubing oil paint from a splotched pallette onto a large canvas. He was painting an orange, a banana, and three apples, the models resting on a black velvet drape atop one of the musician's chairs.

"Hey!" Sam called out from the foot of the steps. "Get a load of Rembrandt! What's this all about, Harry?"

Hemitz squinted at him across the cluttered basement room, pushing the spectacles on to his forehead and leaving a bright green smudge on the bridge of his nose.

"Hello, Sam. How did you get past Hiro? He has instructions not to let anyone in on Wednesday nights."

"I threw him a fish and he went nuts," Sam said jovially. Depressed and outraged a moment ago, the very sight of Harry Hemitz restored his confidence, his buoyancy.

"Boy, what a layout, Harry! What's all this crap you've got down here? Violin—books—victrola—your own lab! What is this, Hemitz University for backward boys or something?"

Harry turned away and smeared a blob of emetic yellow oil paint onto the misshapen banana on his canvas. "It's my retreat, Sam. Myra finished fixing it up for me a week ago. I guess I never took you down here. Something to relax me, to help me get away from medicine whenever I feel the need."

"You mean all this stuff is for you?" Sam asked in wonderment. He was standing in back of the surgeon, grimacing at the clumsy representations of fruit.

"What the hell, Harry, what do you need it all for?"

"To prove I'm good at all these things, I guess. I just took up painting a half a year ago, and look at me now. I used to have a fellow from the Brooklyn Museum come over and give me lessons.

But, frankly, Sam, I paint better than he does now." He cocked his head at the half-finished canvas. "I like the way I've contrasted the yellow with the black drape. You notice, Sam? It isn't a true black—suggestions of purple and red."

Sam scratched his forehead. "You say you paint better than the guy who taught you?"

"Much better. He's a traditionalist."

"Well, I wouldn't want him to teach any kid of mine, if you're *better* than he is." He laughed happily and did a little jig. "Come on, Heshy, I know you better. Don't kid me with oil paints and violins!"

Hemitz smiled bloodlessly. "Sam, you'll never understand. If you didn't think the world began and ended with an Ace bandage and a bottle of Burow's solution, you'd be a finer doctor than you are."

Sam made a rude raspberry with his lips and strolled over to the laboratory table.

"You got mice already in this nice new house, Harry?" he asked innocently. "Myra can't call an exterminator? And white ones yet!"

"They're part of my experiments."

"What are you experimenting on, Harry? You're the fastest guy in the world with a scalpel, already. What do you need mice for?"

"I'm making a genetic study of the effects of anesthetics on different generations of rats. Tolerances for chloroform, and so forth. There's a kid from Long Island College comes in and does most of the work weekends. Fascinating stuff."

Dr. Abelman poked a finger through the wire cage at one of the albino rodents. "Kootchy-kootchy-koo!" he said.

"Please don't disturb them, Sam. We record their reactions every morning and any kind of unusual stimulus can affect the behavior charts."

Leaping back in mock terror, Sam cried out, "Oh! I beg your friggin' pardon! Will he accept my apology?"

Hemitz continued dabbing paint at the canvas. He was now investing his apple with dollops of visceral red paint. It resembled one of the savage growths he excised from people's abdomens more than a fruit. Sam sat down on one of the empty chairs alongside the folded music stands. He rapped with his iron knuckle on the violin case.

"And this? I suppose Paganini himself comes down and gives you lessons?"

"Not quite." Hemitz' voice betrayed a faint annoyance, yet Sam was totally oblivious. They were Harry and Sam—old Brownsville friends enjoying a good-natured ribbing. "But if you must know, I play with a little string quartet, a few fellows from the Brooklyn Academy who come down once a week."

Sam snapped open the hasps on the violin case.

"Some fiddle," Sam said. "You really any good, Harry? Or are you just doing all this to confuse the public?"

"You know, Sam, you can be pretty crude sometimes. It so happens that my hobbies are aimed only at improving myself. To prove to myself I'm capable and competent at anything I care to try. Or wouldn't you understand that?"

"Ah, cut it out, kid. No one loves you more than me, Heshy. Goddammit, you think I'm *really* needling you? Anything you do is okay with me, Harry, don't you know that?"

"Of course I do, Sam. I do wish you'd put that violin down. It cost me nine hundred and fifty dollars."

Quickly yet gently he laid the violin in its green velvet coffin. "Holy smoke! For a lousy fiddle?"

So captivated had he been by Harry Hemitz' playroom that he had almost forgotten the purpose of his hurried visit. In the silence that followed Hemitz' reprimand, broken only by the terrified squeaking of the mice, he remembered what had impelled him to come to the surgeon.

"Listen, Harry. Why I came here tonight. That lousy Tabbernoy family—they're threatening to sue us. You and me, because of the needle I took out."

Hemitz was not the slightest distraught. "Really? They'll lose an awful lot in lawyer's fees. I've kept the base of the hypo and the point, and I've gotten affidavits from the attending nurse and interne. I've had Myra's brother Al, the lawyer, call the manufacturers who make the needles. They've admitted they occasionally turn out a defective one. Absolutely no way of testing them beforehand that's foolproof. They're insured and so are we, so let them sue. They'll never collect."

"Jesus, Harry, you scare me, you're so thorough."

"That's part of surgery, Sam. Why stay awake nights worrying whether some idiot is going to pull you into court? We deal in variables, calculated risks. Things are bound to go wrong—but don't let the patient ever get the idea he's got anything on you. You're the master and he's the slave, Sam. If he says he'll sue, stare him down and show him out of the office. But don't lose your temper or raise your voice. Then make sure your lawyer has you covered." He turned from the easel and smiled at his older friend.

"I'll be you blew your top tonight at the Tabbernoys, didn't you, Sam?"

"I chased them the hell out and told them they were liars and cheats and that you were too good for them!"

Harry dipped a brush in the little cup of linseed oil, dabbed at a blob of black paint on the pallette, and applied a few strokes to the ebony background. He had failed to drain off the excess oil and it dribbled in dark rills down the lumpy fruit. The surgeon dabbed at the paint with a soiled rag.

"So you lost some of your best patients, is that right, Sam?"

"Who needs them?"

"You do. I do. We need them, Sam. It's a question of handling them. Why do you have to reform the world?"

"I don't want to reform any of these lice. What gave you that idea?"

Hemitz laid down his pallette, and removing his smeared blue smock, wiped his hands on a turpentine-soaked hand towel. He lifted the violin from its case and tentatively ran the bow across the strings a few times.

"Listen, Harry. I got an idea tonight, after that battle I had with the Tabbernoys and after listening to Sarah give me one of her talks again. I want to study surgery."

The constricted screeching of the nine-hundred-and-fifty-dollar violin echoed in the basement room; it seemed an accompaniment to the squeaks of the caged mice. Hemitz lowered the violin from his chin and laid it back in its case, tapping the taut bow thoughtfully on his knee.

"Just like that, Sam? A fight with a patient and you want to be a surgeon? You're thirty-eight, Sam."

"Thirty-seven, wise guy. Listen, you know I've wanted to specialize for a long time. I never had the guts to go through with it. But, after tonight, I decided I'm sick of holding hands with these slobs, comforting them, worrying for them, and then getting abused by them. Harry, why can't I be like you? Do your work and screw 'em. Keep 'em at arm's length. Make 'em respect you because you're so powerful they won't dare open their yaps about negligence or give you any back talk."

"All right. Suppose you study surgery. What makes you think you've got a talent for it?"

Sam stood up. He flexed his gymnast's biceps and practically shoved his fist in Harry's face. "What's this, a weakling's arm? I've got strength to spare, Harry. That's my trouble. All these muscles being used to tape ankles and deliver screaming brats. Why not put 'em to use properly? I've watched you so often, Harry, I swear I could operate tomorrow. And how about all the minor stuff I've done in my office? Listen, don't kid me. It's not as hard as you guys pretend. You're different, Harry—you're a genius—but the rest of 'em. Pivarnik and the Krampf brothers and all the others—I could do what they do."

Hemitz wandered along his library wall, lazily pulling books from the shelves, examining the tooled leather bindings with possessive gratification. In the soft light, he looked like a graduate student in philosophy wandering through the stacks.

"Surgery isn't all mechanical, Sam," Hemitz said softly. "A lot depends on your mental approach. Your attitude, your nerves, your state of mind. That's almost as important. No, it's more important than the sheer technical skills. Do you really think, Sam, you're equipped to stand over a half corpse, some nice young woman with three children, and look at the big red gouge in her abdomen, while her pulse drops and her breathing becomes erratic and you don't know whether you should continue snipping and cutting, or close her up?"

"Don't make it sound so terrible, Harry. You do it a few times every day and it doesn't bother you."

"That's me, Sam. How about Sam Abelman?"

"I'd get used to it. You got a set of Thoreau there?"

Hemitz stooped down and searched a lower shelf where his wife had installed sets of American classics.

"I don't see it. Hawthorne, Melville, Prescott, Longfellow—"

"I'll buy you a set. You won't read it, but it'll do you good just to have it around."

"Why should I read him? Thoreau hasn't done anything for your peace of mind. You're the only Thoreau student I know, Sam, and you're also one of the most excitable people I know."

"I'm not excitable. I just act that way."

Hemitz slammed a red leather volume of *Plutarch's Lives* shut and laughed lightly. "That's the *non-sequitur* of the week, Sam. No why don't you go home, call up the Tabbernoys, and tell them you want to reach an understanding with them—"

"Like hell I will."

"All right, be stubborn."

"Now, look, Harry, you owe me a few favors. I've never asked you for a thing, have I?"

"Of course not, Sam."

"Well, I want to study surgery under you. I know I'm eleven years older than you and you used to baby-sit for me. But I've made my mind up. There's room for another surgeon at Beth Abraham. I wouldn't even try to do the big stuff, the way you do. I'd settle for appendectomies to start with. I just have to get the hell away from all those sniveling bastards trying to eat my heart out."

"What about your practice?"

"I can still practice and work with you. I can even take some postgraduate work at Long Island or Bellevue at night. But I can't do it without your encouragement, kiddo."

Dr. Hemitz turned, hearing quick footsteps descending. A short, muscular man with a shaved head bounced into the basement room. He wore a white T-shirt, white duck pants, and gym sneakers, and carried two pairs of boxing gloves. His face was scarred and lumped, dulled with the impact of a thousand fists; yet it maintained a kind of comic poise.

"You ready for the lesson, doctor?" he asked Harry servilely.

"Why, yes, Vincent, just let me change into my sneakers and trunks."

The sight of the boxer evoked a dozen wonderful memories in Sam Abelman. He was back in Hector O'Bannion's gym, executing a perfect giant swing; he was organizing a basketball game in the Red Hook playground, oblivious to the catcalls of the galoots.

"For the luvva Mike, you taking boxing lessons?"

"Why not? Just a little conditioning now and then to get me in shape."

Vincent grinned irregularly. "He does very well, too. Got a great left jab."

The doctor approached the white-clad instructor warily. "You in pretty good shape, sonny?" he asked.

"Work out allatime. I have classes at the Crescent A. C. three times a week and a few private clients like Dr. Hemitz."

"Do any wrestling?"

"A little. Mostly I box, throw medicine balls, calisthenics. Why? You want a little instruction?"

"Hah! Tell him, Harry! Sonny, I was the best gym teacher ever graduated from Chelsea College! I've knocked more galoots on their asses than I care to think of."

Vincent nodded appreciatively. "You look in good shape. Want to put on the gloves?"

For a moment Sam hesitated. He moved forward to take the maroon leather balloons from the instructor's extended arms. The temptation was irresistible. Then he shook his head.

"Sorry, son, not for me. I'm pushing forty. But I wouldn't mind wrestling you. A little intercollegiate style. I think I could knock you flat on your can, if you'll excuse the expression."

The boxer shrugged, unoffended. Harry Hemitz, his spindly white legs issuing from flapping black cotton shorts, emerged from behind a screen. Vincent laced the gloves onto the surgeon's gifted hands. They squared off, and then Hemitz dropped his guard and turned to Sam.

"Sam. I'll let you have your way. You just proved to me maybe you're growing up. Five years ago you would have insisted on going a few rounds with Vincent—and getting your teeth knocked down your throat."

"Stop crapping me up, Harry." Dr. Abelman grinned happily. Harry would help him after all. He'd work with him, learn from him, and operate on his own. "When can I start?"

"Tomorrow morning. I've got a cecostomy at 8 A.M."

A whole new world was opening for Sam Abelman. At thirty-seven he would start all over. Being the second best surgeon in Brooklyn would suit him fine—no one could hope to outdo Harry Hemitz, his friend, his teacher, his former baby-sitter.

The surgeon and the boxer jabbed at each other tentatively; Sam was surprised at Harry's deftness, his quick, sure movements, the neat way he blocked and ducked punches.

"Not bad, Heshy," Sam said proudly. "But I still think I can knock both of you on your asses."

After six months he was ready to try his first case. Harry had kept his promise. Whenever possible, he had used Sam Abelman as his assistant; quite naturally on all the cases referred to him by Sam and a few other times when no assistant was designated by the recommending physician. He had stood at Harry's side, for years it seemed, watching the quick, graceful fingers, listening to his calm small talk, hearing the voice crack with authority in a crisis, absorbing a hundred little tricks along with the standard procedures. One night a week he attended a lecture course at Long Island. He was the oldest student in the class, and he found that his capacity for retaining book information had diminished markedly. Moreover, the lecturer told him nothing he did not already know from his thirteen years in practice. He found his mind tended to wander during the classroom sessions; when he concentrated on the professor's droning voice, he invariably found himself comparing the dry words to Harry Hemitz' dramatic, electric interpretation of the textbooks. *The sphincter muscles are gently dilated and the hemorrhoids are grasped with forceps.* Professor Willard

McCabe made it sound just like what it was: *piles*. Only a Harry Hemitz could make something beautiful out of a hemorrhoidectomy.

Sam's first chance at operating came via a call from Harry. It was a little before six in the morning, but the surgeon's voice was crisp and as clear as if he had been awake for hours.

"Look, Sam, I think we've got one for you. The resident in surgery just called me. They brought in a colored boy with a deep gastric wound. Knife fight. Bleeding seems to indicate a perforation of the wall. I think it's a nice one for you to start on. You can run over, scrub up, and start immediately. Okay?"

It had come so suddenly, so unexpectedly, that Sam had trouble finding his voice.

"Ah—you think so, Harry? I mean, doesn't this call for a complete exploratory of the abdomen?"

"I can't say without an examination. It might be a simple wound, or it might be something worse."

"Maybe I should assist you."

"Don't be silly, Sam. This is ideal. Some drunken nigger. If he goes out, who cares?"

"Well, Harry, what the hell. He's got a right to live."

"Of course, of course, Sam. Look, you'd better get moving. I told Forbes to meet you in surgery in forty-five minutes. She'll line up an assistant and an anesthetist."

"Will you be there, Harry?"

But Harry had hung up. He dressed hurriedly, hearing Eunice call after him as he left, "Daddy, will you buy me skates when you come back?" He stopped at her bed to assure her he would, waved goodbye to Sarah, and left, not wasting time for breakfast. The Chandler, strewn with catkins from the Lombardy poplar, awaited him in the fall dawn. Driving through the empty streets, he suddenly felt an urge to have Max Vogel with him, and he stopped at Max's long enough to waken the fat man and invite him to Beth Abraham.

"Screw you, Sammy," Vogel mumbled from his upstairs bedroom window.

"Come on, Maxie, look over my shoulder," he called. "I need someone to insult."

"Whaddya need me for? That little bastard Heshy will be there, won't he? Sooperman and you, what a team. The butcher and the gym teacher."

Sam laughed. "Just shut up and get dressed, Maxie."

He had almost no time to examine his patient. The resident filled him in quickly: Negro male, age twenty-five, brought to Beth

Abraham's emergency ward an hour ago suffering from a deep knife wound in the abdomen. They didn't even know his name. A cop had found him moaning in an alley off Watkins Street. He had refused to tell the police anything and shortly after arrival at the hospital had gone into shock. The bleeding, while not arterial, had been profuse; he had had one transfusion, and surgery was mandatory.

Events seemed to be jamming together, like a half-dozen automobiles in a highway pile-up. He had scrubbed up, conferred with Forbes and the anesthetist, greeted Max (exchanging a few routine insults), and was now at the table, looking down at the ugly crimson gash on the hard abdomen, the color of chocolate syrup. The room seemed almost deserted. The usual quota of internes and kibitzers was not in evidence. Sam held his hand out for the scalpel, felt Forbes's authoritative slap as she smacked it into the surgical rubber glove.

"Did Dr. Hemitz say he'd be here?" he found himself asking her.

"No he didn't, Dr. Abelman. He merely told me to prepare the room and wait for you."

"That's funny. I understood him to say he'd be here." He turned to the resident, a thin youth with bad skin. "Feibelman, could you call Dr. Hemitz please and ask him if he's on his way?"

They were all watching him curiously. Delaying the operation, scalpel in hand, with questions about Harry Hemitz seemed an odd way for a surgeon to begin.

"Make the lousy incision, Sam," he heard Max muttering. "You want I should make it for you?"

The resident departed, and Sam, sensing that there would be no Harry Hemitz to stand at his side while he probed the wound in his nameless patient's abdomen, bent to his work. He made the left transrectus incision, cutting firmly and deeply into the leathery brown flesh and the pink-gray muscle beneath.

"What's hard, Sammy?" Vogel asked. "Who needs Heshy?"

Sam smiled. "Yeah. But look at him bleed from that thing." The wound lay to the side of the incision, a six-inch gouge, still oozing rich blood through the sutures put in by the resident.

"Nothing like trying it out on the dog, hah, Sam?" Max whispered.

For the next half hour, he had only a marginal awareness of what he was doing, the instructions that came out of his mouth, the quick moves of his hands with the scalpel, scissors, or needle. Assuring himself that it would all end correctly, that he would do everything the way Harry would, he plodded on. Yet he could not overcome a vague feeling of disorientation. It was almost as if he were in an alcoholic or narcotic stupor—like one of those drunken newspapermen he had heard about who write flawless prose before collapsing.

He swabbed the ugly exudate around the damaged stomach, calling for a suction tube when the damned icky stuff kept oozing. It took a little clumsy probing, but he found two injured vessels, isolated them, and did a neat, if slow, job of ligating them. The wound in the gastric wall was deep and true: it lay perilously close to the liver, and he was delighted that the laceration had been confined to the stomach. He was about to begin suturing the tear when he felt Max nudge him rudely.

"Take a look again, Sammy," he whispered. "The goddam posterior wall is cut also. Whoever stuck that boogie stuck him good. You don't want to patch him up halfway. His relatives will sue."

Vogel was right: whatever blade had been thrust into the young man's hard abdomen had made it way through both anterior and posterior walls of the stomach. Sam took a minute to pause and study the pink, pulsating sac. He handed the needle to Forbes, avoiding her noncommital face, feeling the need to think for a moment. The heavy dullness in his head made it difficult for him to focus. For a fractional second his vision blurred and he felt a twinge at his temple—his old buddy, migraine, was coming along for the ride. He looked up—at no one in particular—and, clasping his bloodied rubber fingers together, asked, "Has anyone heard from Dr. Hemitz?"

Feibelman, the resident, answered in his East Side singsong. "The answering service said he left a few minutes ago, Dr. Abelman. He's supposed to be on his way."

"Stick your friggin' hands in and do it, Sam." It was Max again, this time whispering hoarsely and wickedly in his ear. "You wait for Heshy you'll have a dead boogie on the table. You know what to do, do it."

Vogel's rudeness penetrated the cloud of uncertainty. He had to expose the posterior wound. This normally meant opening the gastrohepatic omentum, the fold of the peritoneum connecting stomach and liver. But even as he studied the conformation of organs, he knew that his heavy, clumsy fist would never be able to manipulate sutures from that impossible angle. He hesitated, blinking behind misty glasses, and called for the scalpel. Deliberately, he began enlarging the *anterior* wound, added a few inches to the murderous slash inflicted by the assailant. He heard Vogel whistle appreciatively; when the expanded wound was large enough to pass his hand through, he did so, forcing an opening in the gastrohepatic omentum. He was home-free: with the rear wound exposed and accessible, he began suturing, stitching three rows approximating the serosal surfaces. He tried to work rapidly and with Harry's careless, offhand gestures, but he found that even the routine suturing was draining him. By the time he was working on the anterior wound (he had expanded it from three inches to a good five-inch gap) his arms were concrete slabs, his hands as lifeless and heavy as lead weights. By the time he was closing the brown skin with through-and-through mattress sutures, just as he had seen Harry do, he felt the full force of the migraine come crashing down on his skull. Someone had clamped the cruel vise on his head, sneaking it underneath the white surgeon's cap—the damned blinking aura was dancing around the operating table. In the midst of rising pain, he found an instant of humorous reprieve: a half-dozen yellow dots were bouncing on Forbes's virginal bosom.

He left an opening for drainage from the lesser peritoneal cavity and told Feibelman to continue gastric suction and decompression. Turning from the table, he pressed a palm to his forehead and shook his head. The gesture was meant only as a small protest against the headache, but the group around the table took it for a sign of resignation.

In the doctor's lounge, he gulped three aspirins and two glasses of water. He sat dully in one of the scarred chairs, half listening to the locker-room badinage, the early morning boasting and joshing in which he always was a leading participant.

"Lost your cherry today, hey, Sam?" he heard one of the young wise guys mutter. Max Vogel was arguing with Lemkau's older son about X-ray therapy; someone goosed Frank Karasik and his wild *whoooops* brought on a series of painful jokes about the neurologist's sensitive behind. It was lost on Sam: they were people he had never known.

"How did it go, Sam?" Herry Hemitz was sitting next to him, the small hard hand on his knee, the emotionless eyes studying him from behind gold-rimmed lenses.

"Oh! Jesus, I'm glad to see you, Harry!" He had been half asleep, nursing the dreadful ache in his head. "I got a bitch of a migraine, so I'm a little dopey."

"Feibelman says you did a swell job."

"Did he? I guess I did. I got a little confused on the posterior wound. But I widened the anterior cut and stuck my hand in. I suppose it came out all right."

"I'm sure it did, Sam."

Dr. Abelman closed his eyes tightly and ducked his head; sometimes the accursed thing was a physical presence and you had to dodge it.

"I wish you had been there, Harry," he said, opening his eyes. "You know—first time out. You could have made it easier for me."

"I really meant to, Sam," Dr. Hemitz said earnestly. "But I had this call at Cumberland, and then I got tied up with the chief of surgery—"

"Balls," Max Vogel interrupted. "You didn't want to come. You wanted Sam to look like a bum, right, Heshy?"

"Max, you're not only vulgar, you're a liar."

The fat man's face, each little feature cunning and alert, bloomed into a rich purple.

"Don't crap me, Heshy. I been wise to you since you used to get the other kids on the block to hustle old newspapers for you so you could sell them to Junkman John."

Plaintively, Sam tried to intervene. "Cut it out, Maxie," he pleaded. Ordinarily he would have threatened to knock Max's block off; but the pounding in his skull rendered him soft and weak. Vogel was on his feet, standing in front of them, the white-coated globe of his gut threatening them with its immovable bulk.

"Sam, you're a jerk. I'm your best friend and I'll tell you so. *You gotta stop worshiping this guy.* You gotta be yourself—Sam Abelman, a pretty good GP. You'll never be a surgeon in a million years, because you're all nerves. If a patient farts off-key you lay awake nights worrying, don't you? What the hell will you do opening people up, when they die of infection, hemorrhaging, adhesions? This little guy here, he don't care what happens to *anyone!* It's all part of his business. But you with your migraine, and your vagotonia, and that habit of kissing your patients' asses one minute and hating their guts the next—you'd last one week."

"Ah, shut up," Sam said resignedly.

"Sit back and enjoy your headache. You know something, Heshy? Sam did a *great* job in there. He doesn't know it, and he probably thinks you could do better. But that's because he thinks you're King of the Hill. Anyway, he didn't make one wrong move, and he stitched that boogie up so he'll be better in a week than he was before. He'll be able to stuff all the pork chops and collard greens he wants into that stomach. But Sam isn't *you*, Harry, so he *looked* lousy, he *acted* lousy, and Forbes and Feibelman and the rest will tell everyone that. Don't crap me up about surgery. You guys are mechanics with a dramatic school education. That's where Sam's no good. He can't *act* like a surgeon. He made one mistake, and you saw it on that dumb face. He got tired and he let everyone know. Worst of all, he wanted you there, and he acted like he couldn't button his fly without you around. That's exactly why you didn't show up. You knew Sam would look like a bum. Maybe he'd louse the whole thing up and the coon would die. What's the harm? A jigg nobody knows? Meanwhile, Sam proves he can't make it. He's no surgeon. He can't compete with you even if it's to do a small case now and then. Right?"

Sam was rising, feeling the peculiar dragging weight of the headache pulling his head down. "Lay off Harry, Max. You talk too much. I don't want to hear you insult him again. I'll tear your head off if you do." Vogel understood the dull menace in his voice. It was useless: Harry Hemitz could do no wrong.

"Don't bother with him, Sam," Hemitz said. He had moved not a muscle, betrayed not the faintest hint of anger, or fear, or embarrassment during the fat man's tirade.

Attaboy, Sam," Vogel snarled. "Keep coming back for more. It must feel good being screwed by a surgeon." He walked out angrily, a lurching white balloon of a man, trying to hide the welling of tears in his roseate face.

Sam tried his hand at surgery three more times. On each occasion he acquitted himself well, gaining new confidence with each case. But the work left him utterly enervated. All his energies—his physical strength and the powers of concentration he had developed in college—were greedily absorbed by the operation. He had no reserve left when the day ended. It became apparent to him after his last operation—a complicated resection of the large bowel, which involved three harrowing hours over the table—that he must abandon his brief career as a surgeon. He talked it over with Sarah at length, and she concurred. Sarah had never approved of the venture and she complained vociferously about the hours he had wasted, the neglect of his general practice, the toll it had taken on his health and his nerves. His work was bound to pick up, she told him: times were good and there was money in circulation, even in Brownsville. He agreed to forget about specializing for the time being. Secretly, he was glad to plunge back into the day-to-day routine of vaccinations, tenement calls, taped ankles, and the pleasant hum of a filled waiting room on weekends.

By 1927 Harry Hemitz was ready for a major move. He would build his own hospital, staff it with loyal friends, and break away from the conservative, restraining shackles of Beth Abraham. Just past thirty, the young surgeon had become a legend. In beauty parlors and at bridge games women talked about him endlessly.

"He invented his own way of taking out an appendix. Such small scars!"

"Three big doctors—the *biggest* in Brooklyn—said he couldn't operate. But Hemitz did, and, thanks God, my sister is still alive."

"Such a man! They say he made a hundred thousand dollars in the first six months of the year!"

"My own family doctor, I'm ashamed to go by his office after visiting Dr. Hemitz. Two nurses and two assistants! He don't even talk to you until the last minute!"

Aloof, unreachable, the little blond man in the gold-rimmed glasses was transformed from another successful young surgeon to a demigod of the operating room. They knew his impoverished background and they admired him the more for it. It was inevitable that the culture hero seek his own temple—in Hemitz' case, the New Hill Hospital for which his affluent inlaws were already raising money.

Sam had remained on excellent terms with the surgeon. True he and Sarah saw less of the Hemitzes socially, and Myra now greeted Sam with a brisk hello instead of the informal cheeriness of their early friendship. He was therefore surprised and delighted to get a warm hug and a delicate peck from his friend's homely wife one afternoon.

She asked him to join her for coffee in the living room—an acre of maroon carpeting and baroque lamps. The grasscloth walls were covered with paintings and etchings created by the surgeon himself. Winter sunlight filtered through red velvet drapes as they sipped coffee and Myra dropped her broad "a," reverting to the warm intonations of Brownsville. She started by asking solicitously after Sarah and Eunice, inquired about Sam's mother, and squeezed his hand as he recalled Harry's first case. They enjoyed a good laugh as he retold—for the thousandth time—the story of Bleibtreu's tuxedo. By the second cup of coffee, she got to the point: Harry was having trouble finding enough physicians to make up an adequate staff. As she put it, winking, the *alta cockers* at Beth Abraham were forming a conspiracy. They were jealous of her husband; Lemkau and his sons were doing everything in their power to keep the best men from leaving Beth Abraham. Apparently they had spread the word around at the last meeting of the County Medical Society. There had been terrible gossip about Harry splitting fees— a bald lie—and his ethics, particularly in regard to his readiness to operate, had been maligned. The old-time GP's, the fellows with the big practices, the busy offices, were not leaping at the chance to aid him in his new venture. More than enough money had been raised for the New Hill Hospital. But what good was a building without a staff?

"Those lice!" Sam shouted. "They'd better come with Harry!" He set his cup down so ferociously that coffee spilled on to the gleaming mahogany table top. A few drops fell to the carpet and he hastily bent to one knee, dabbing at it with his handkerchief.

Hemitz, standing in the arched doorway, wearing his artist's smock, winced. If you could only stop Sam Abelman from mopping floors and wanting to knock people on their behinds!

"Hello, Sam," he said casually. "Has Myra been giving you her song of woe about New Hill?"

"Why, those bastards!" Sam shouted. "Listen, Harry, who needs 'em? You and me—we can run the whole damn thing! They'll come on their knees! I'd like to belt old Lemkau one in the nose!"

Harry smiled. He sat primly on a Moroccan ottoman at the edge of the table, and, sipping delicately from a Rosenthal china cup, spoke of his plans for the hospital—the streamlined operating facilities, the high quality of the nurses he would employ, the new system for admitting and discharging patients, a whole new concept of hospital administration he was evolving.

"I'll need your help, Sam," he said finally. "Myra is exaggerating about the staff. But it is true I need more good men."

He went on to explain that he needed a few big names to round out the staff—Franz Karasik, for example, as chief of neurology. And a couple of good, steady GP's would help also. He knew Max Vogel didn't like him especially, but Max had a gigantic practice, and he felt they could forget their old feuds and get together. That's where Sam could be helpful. Doctors respected him. Surely Karasik and Vogel could be won over, and if Sam spread the word at the Medical Society meetings and at Beth Abraham, he might line up a few others.

"Why, just say the word, Harry! I'll start today!" Sam said. "I'll get you the best staff in the city! I'll get Max to join in no time flat!"

Dr. Hemitz opened the collar of the paint-daubed smock and stroked the lean muscles around his neck.

"It occurred to me, Sam, that you're the kind of fellow who would make a fine chief consultant. With your knack for diagnosis, and the way people trust you. I know you lose your temper easily, but with me around to restrain you a little—"

He barely heard the rest of what Harry Hemitz said. It was unbelievable: Samuel Abelman, chief consulting physician for New Hill! The conversation meandered through the autumn afternoon and he had trouble speaking coherently. He kept mumbling his gratitude, his appreciation, promising Harry he'd get him a staff, unwilling to grasp the total joy of the surgeon's promise all at once, harboring the delight for later hours when he would be by himself.

In the month that followed he more than fulfilled his part of the bargain. Harry Hemitz had not spelled out the agreement regarding a consultant's position in exchange for Karasik, Vogel, and whoever else Sam Abelman could bring to the new hospital, but the implication had been clear. He walked on air: Harry had asked him to tell no one about the impending appointment, but it was too rich an experience to hide. He told Sarah, he bragged to his relatives, he held court in Sol Pomerantz' drugstore, informing the doctors who drifted in and out that he was to be Harry Hemitz' right-hand man. And, worst of all, he dropped hints to everyone at Beth Abraham.

"Sam, it hasn't happened yet," Sarah cautioned him. "You'll notice Harry hasn't said a word to you in weeks about it."

"Ah, you're a sourpuss," he told her. He picked up Eunice, tossing her high and catching her again, a bundle of elbows, knees, and lank brown hair. "You, *ketzeleh*, you'll go to Vassar, like your mommy wanted to! We'll be out of Brownsville in a year!"

One gray morning in January—it was 1928, and he was quite busy thanks to a combined abundance of cash and colds—he stopped in at Pomerantz' for a dozen cigars and some razor blades. Sam found the druggist sorting his morning mail. The pinched face of the young radical had grown fleshy and calm behind the cluttered counter. Surrounded by sagging cartons of laxatives, headache powders, baby pants, and cough drops, Sol Pomerantz' sharp edge of rebellion had been softened into gray compliance. Karl Marx had come out a poor second pitted against the brightly packaged oils and pills of the capitalist industries which furnished the druggist's livelihood.

"Letters from H. M. Hemitz, M. D., no less," Pomerantz said. "What's he writing to me for? I can't do anything for him."

Sam made a raspberry. "You jealous, Solly? Why is everyone sore at Harry? Because he's got what it takes to get ahead? Look at me—I love him for it."

"Yeh, yeh, Sam. The great Hemitz can do no wrong."

He opened the letter from H. M. Hemitz, M. D., extracting a heavy vellum folder and ran his finger over the raised lettering, appraising its high quality. "Heshy's announcement of the hospital opening, Sam," Pomerantz said. "Didn't you get one?"

He hadn't opened his mail that morning. Most of it was circulars, bills, assorted junk. Sarah usually weeded it out for him and left the important items in a neat pile on his desk. Eagerly, he snatched the folder from the druggist's hand, reading the Old English lettering aloud.

" 'Dr. Harry Marshall Hemitz is pleased to announce the opening of the New Hill Hospital, St. Francis Place and Sullivan Avenue, February 15, 1928. H. Marshall Hemitz, director and chief of surgery.' "

He opened the folder, and, reading silently, felt a cold tremor germinate in his groin and spread through his limbs, with the persistence of a general anesthetic. He sensed a strange dimming of his eyes; not an onset of tears, but a mistiness born of confusion, frustration, and disbelief. It was like one of those dreaded moments when you told relatives the worst: *Mrs. Savitsky, your son has leukemia, but we'll do our best for him.*

He read it again.

HARRY MARSHALL HEMITZ, M.D., F.A.C.S.
Director and Chief of Surgery

✿   ✿   ✿   ✿   ✿

MORRIS MEYER APPELBAUM, M.D., F.A.C.P.
Chief Consultant

There were other names listed—men he knew well, and a few he barely knew. Karasik was on the list, as chief of neurology. On the rear page of the folder he found his own name included in an alphabetical listing of "staff physicians."

Pomerantz saw the grayness in his friend's face. At forty-two, Sam Abelman looked six years older—now in the wintry sunlight of the drugstore he seemed to be aging as he reread the little folder. The pharmacist came from around the counter and took it from the doctor's hand.

"Why, that bum," Pomerantz said softly. "That double-crosser. A punk like Morris Appelbaum with his fancy *yente* of a wife. He isn't half the man you are, Sam."

"It's a mistake," Sam said.

"Nah, it's no mistake. I heard about it from a couple of guys last week. You know, Sam, the guy who gets it is always the last to know. That'll teach you about Heshy Hemitz. Harry Marshall Hemitz! Where did he get that middle name?"

He put an arm around Sam's iron waist, feeling the hard muscular torso of the gym teacher recoil. "Forget it, Sammy, you're still the best man," the pharmacist said reassuringly.

An aged woman in ragged head-shawl and colorless overcoat, lugging a cloth shopping bag, had entered. Unloosing a flood of Yiddish, she waved a prescription under the druggist's nose. Outside, a snowball fight was in progress—they could hear the profane cries of the contestants.

"It's a mistake," Sam repeated. "I'll call Harry and have him change it. I know it's a mistake."

Protesting, Pomerantz found himself backed behind the counter by the old woman; he wanted to buoy his old friend, to comfort him, but he was helpless. Somehow Sam had always been that way. His misfortunes and his despair were peculiarly his own. No one could ease them.

He trudged back to the house on Haven Place, ignoring the wet snowball that skidded past his feet, the cheery greeting from Traficanti as he walked by the barbershop, unable even to summon up his normal quota of outrage at the garbage accumulating on the dirty snow. Outside the house he saw Eunice, heavily layered in warm clothing, on her way to school with two of her friends. She wore a wool-knit cap, a muffler, long stockings, a bulky plaid overcoat, and red mittens. She grasped his arm as he walked, unsmiling, through the gateway.

"Shirley Flaum said we're not moving to Crown Heights, daddy, and I said we were," she pleaded with him. "Didn't you tell Mommy we were the other day? Tell her so, daddy."

"Yeh, sure, *ketzeleh*, whatever you say is right. Shirley is talking through her hat."

He walked slowly up the stone steps, dotted with rock salt he had strewn earlier that morning, knowing that he would gain nothing by calling Harry Hemitz. There would be a terrible scene with Sarah, recriminations and accusations, and he would end up burying himself in the medical library for the rest of the day. The books didn't talk back and the printed page made no promises that had to be broken.

Thrasher twirled the little stem between his thumb and index finger. The radiating branches, each with a tiny shred of fruit, looked like something a surgeon would find in a diseased abdomen. Sarah Abelman had stopped talking and was nodding her head slightly. It was neither a negative nor a sleepy movement, but rather a kind of rhythmic reminder of her own quiet existence.

"And do you know something, Mr. Thrasher?" she asked, after a few silent moments. "My husband simply adored Dr. Hemitz the rest of his life."

"Even after he betrayed him?"

"I wouldn't call it a betrayal. Dr. Hemitz had his reasons. Morris Appelbaum was and still is a very fine physician. He was a tall, dignified man. He never cursed and he never lost his temper. A real gentleman. I'm sure I know what went on in Dr. Hemitz' mind. Imagine my husband having to be a diplomat! Wearing expensive suits and getting his hair cut every week!"

"That certainly doesn't make what Dr. Hemitz did to your husband any more acceptable," Thrasher protested. He heard a faint screech of brakes and a car door slamming beneath them; Dr. Abelman had apparently come home.

"No, it certainly doesn't. But it was partially my husband's fault for believing in him so implicitly. I guess he worshiped Harry simply because he was so completely in control of himself—and other people too. Harry always had a plan. He always thought ahead of everyone, and he never was in doubt about anything. There was a way Harry had of sitting back and looking at a patient with those pale eyes. Sam's patients always acted like Sam was their father. The kind of father you talk back to, and you love sometimes, and you hate other times."

"What happened to Harry Hemitz?"

"He was killed driving a speedboat, of all things. He had to prove that he could do anything. One summer he and Myra went up to Tupper Lake in the Adirondacks, and Harry had to have the fastest, biggest boat on the lake. Nobody really knows how it happened, but he smashed into a dock, and the boat went up in flames. It was a terrible shock to Sam. He never got over his feelings about Harry, even though he only saw him occasionally during his later years."

It was always that way with the Harry Hemitzes of the world, Thrasher thought. Their idolaters stood fast; long after a Harry Hemitz had forgotten fat Hilda Oestreicher and the spring afternoon on lower Broadway when he wore his first tuxedo, the Sam Abelmans would remember.

"I guess the doctor is back," she said. "I can tell the noise that old car makes a block away."

Diane had risen painfully and was standing at the window, shaggy forepaws on the sill, the absurd tail wagging lazily. Thrasher walked to the dog's side, looking through the leaf-shaded screen to the street below. The doctor was making his usual tour of the sagging automobile, kicking at the weary tires. On the sidewalk, he busied himself collecting an accumulation of tin cans and old news-papers (Thrasher suspected that old man Baumgart had left them there) and stuffed them into a burlap trash bag suspended from the cast-iron railing above the brick wall.

He was about to enter the house when a Negro youth, several shades blacker than Herman Quincy and much broader in the shoulders, ran up to the doctor and clutched his arm. Thrasher could not hear their conversation, but the boy appeared singularly agitated. The doctor was listening attentively.

"Someone's just grabbed your husband," Thrasher said. "Probably one of those emergency calls he hates so."

She reached for a fresh sprig of grapes. "Oh, he complains about them all the time," she said softly. "But, really, that's what general practice it. You'd think he'd be used to it by now."

Thrasher rose, somewhat annoyed by her lack of sympathy.

"I think I'd like to accompany the doctor. Do you think he'd object?"

"Not at all, Mr. Thrasher." She rose slowly, her shapeless form somehow compressed into the rude outlines of the overstuffed arm-chair. "The doctor is very fond of you."

He thanked her for her information, bade her goodbye, and ran down the stairs. The doctor and the Negro lad had just entered the car, and he called out to the old man to wait for him.

The overworked engine was coughing and gasping when Thrasher opened the rear door and sat on the edge of the faded seat. Dr. Abelman waved a greeting; the old car lurched off, narrowly, missing a stickball player.

"How long since your friend Herman had the fit?" the doctor asked the Negro boy.

"It jes' happen."

"This minute? You ran over from the market as soon as he fell down?"

"Yeah. Das right. He fow down, twitchin' and movin' his arms. I remembeh he say he call you ef he gits a fit. So Ah run over."

"You oughta get a medal. You're a smart fellah remembering me. I ever see you before? What's your name?"

"Lee Roy Bishop."

"You have an uncle William Bishop? He had cancer of the rectum two years ago and I took care of him?"

"Yeah. Das my fambly."

"A very nice fellow."

Thrasher leaned against the heat-sodden seat, marveling at the old man's double vision: he would shake his fist and curse eloquently at a dozen Lee Roy Bishops as they shrieked beneath his window—yet a single Lee Roy Bishop had to be invested with dignity and a sense of importance.

They had driven only two blocks when the doctor wheeled the Buick against the curb. Before them was a market block, a street of stores and street stalls, lined with double rows of cluttered pushcarts. It was something out of a different era, a vestige of New York City fifty years ago. Thrasher had passed by the market once before; this was his first close view of it, and it confounded him. For one thing, it was virtually impossible to get an automobile through the traffic lanes. Whatever area the pushcarts did not occupy was crammed with delivery trucks, piles of open crates, assorted garbage, and the overflow of shoppers and merchants. The ramshackle carts sold everything imaginable: plump fruits and lush vegetables, costume jewelry, corsets, eyeglasses, smoked fish, kerchiefs, and men's ties. The stores—most of them specializing in food—were in the ground floors of tenement buildings, and, while the proprietors appeared to be uniformly Jewish, the tenants of the upper stories were Negroes. They leaned from soiled sills and rusted fire escapes, gazing down on the milling swarm of buyers and sellers.

The doctor made his way through the throng with quick, nimble steps. He apparently was accustomed to threading a path through the market block; Thrasher had trouble following Lee Roy's muscular body as it trailed the old man. The late afternoon heat intensified a dozen strange odors, and soon Thrasher felt a little dizzy. A store labeled APPETIZING (Appetizing what? Appetizing who? Thrasher wondered) gave forth a miasma of garlic and fish; from the gutter arose the rich stench of garbage; all about them was the characteristic smell of unwashed Negro bodies.

The doctor made an abrupt left turn into what appeared to be an arcade of some kind. Over the entranceway was a sign in Yiddish and some crude drawings of chickens. Following Lee Roy into a dark, cool court, his nostrils twitched at two new odors. Thrasher was a country boy, and he knew chicken droppings and chicken blood when he smelled them. The arena was a slaughterhouse for fowl. To the rear he could see crates of chickens, piled ceiling-high. About them were lidless steel drums, and in several of these he could see the dripping carcasses of chickens enmeshed in wire frames to permit the blood to trickle downward. In one, the dying fowl was still screaming and thrashing as blood drained from its half-severed neck.

Dr. Abelman's short legs wheeled around a corner of the slaughterhouse. Lee Roy was running at his side, pointing to a cluster of people gathered about the supine form of Herman Quincy. The boy's lean body was splotched with blood, and for a moment Thrasher thought he was bleeding to death. Then he saw one of the steel drums overturned nearby, and he realized that the huge crimson stains were merely the drainage from a murdered bird. The left side of Herman's face—one sightless eye, lips, and jaw—was twitching irregularly. The long fingers of his left hand lay on the blood-smeared chest, and these too jerked with involuntary imprecision.

A bearded elder in sanguinary white apron and an undented black Homburg greeted Dr. Abelman and addressed him in guttural Yiddish. From the comments of the other observers, Thrasher gathered that Herman and Lee Roy had been making nuisances of themselves in the slaughterhouse, had been ordered to leave, and that in the ensuing argument a drum half filled with chicken blood had been upset. Herman had been struck by the drum and had pitched to the floor in convulsion.

"How long has he been twitching like this?" the doctor asked. He was on one knee at the boy's side, feeling the delicate wrist for the pulse, placing a burlap bag underneath the beautiful head.

"At least ten minutes, doc," a young man in a soiled undershirt volunteered. "He just pooped out in front of us. He's a pleptic, ain't he, doc?"

"Yeah, sure, professor. Is that your diagnosis?" The doctor set his spectacles on his nose, wiping the lenses on an atrocious orange and brown tie.

The bearded slaughterer, gesturing with his lethal knife, indicated he wanted the body removed, and Dr. Abelman protested vociferously. Without the remotest knowledge of the alien tongue, Thrasher understood that the doctor had reprimanded and silenced the chicken-killer in one rude sentence.

Suddenly Herman's twitching became more pronounced. The jerking of the left eyebrow and cheek quickened, until the entire left side of the face was shaking. The spastic movements of the fingers spread rapidly to include the entire hand, then the forearm, and then all of the left arm. Now the left foot was affected, the dandified tan suede shoe flopping about the bloodied cement floor and making the ridiculous tasseled laces fly up and down. From the foot, the agitation diffused to the left leg, and in a few seconds all of Herman Quincy's left side was a mass of clonic motion.

"He gon' die?" Lee Roy asked shrilly. "Man, Ah better git his ma. He look lak he gon' die."

"Not yet. Stay here and shut up."

"Do something for him already. We don't want he should drop dead here!" the young man in the undershirt pleaded. "Somebody dies in a kosher slaughterhouse, it's a whole *megillah* to get it kosher again!"

Dr. Abelman peered up from Herman's bouncing limbs. "How'd you like to take a flying leap at a rolling doughnut, buddy? Just hold your water. He'll pull out of this in a few minutes. Go cut up some chickens."

But Herman gave no sign of recovering. Indeed, the convulsive seizure was now affecting his entire body. Whereas a moment ago only his left side had been in motion, now his entire form was indulging in the crazed dance. The brilliant yellow slacks billowed and rippled as his lean legs kicked and jigged; the arms thrashed from side to side, and the hands grazed knuckles and fingers on the harsh floor.

"He's out cold," Thrasher heard the doctor mutter. "Perfect goddam syndrome."

Around the corner, the wild screeching of another stabbed bird riocheted off the unpainted walls; the crowd around the prostrate youth now numbered more than twenty. The normal quota of sidewalk practitioners were advising the doctor on therapy, and with every proffered bit of treatment, the doctor would respond with a tired snarl.

"If you'll all keep your traps shut," he muttered, looking up at them through misty lenses, "he'll snap out of it. The next wise guy who tells me to put ice on his neck, I'll turn him in for practicing without a license."

Gradually the convulsion diminished in intensity. The thrashing of arms and legs subsided, the jerking of fingers and face became less pronounced. Soon, the bloodstained form was still except for labored breathing. The doctor felt Herman's pulse again, nodded approvingly, then placed his stethoscope on the frail chest. One fearful eye opened and looked appealingly at the old man. Herman sighed deeply as the murky cloud of the convulsion lifted. Both eyes open and alert, he parted purple lips and sought his voice.

"Just lay here and take it easy, buddy," the doctor said. "Who told you to go running around a chicken market? You're studying to be a *shochet*, maybe?"

The bearded butcher did not think the doctor's joke was funny. *He* was a *shochet*, a ritual slaughterer, an honored professional man. To hint that a Negro, a *goy*, even in jest, could aspire for such a lofty vocation was disrespectful. Again, he admonished the doctor to remove his patient, and again the doctor answered him in one snappish phrase. The butcher raised his voice and the doctor raised his. It was an impasse.

Dr. Abelman propped Herman into a sitting position. He squeezed his left arm, raising it above the boy's head and watching it fall to his side like deadwood. He grasped the underside of the young man's knee, taking a handful of bright-yellow cloth in his massive fist, and jerked the leg into a jackknifed position. The leg fell back lifelessly.

"You feel anything in that leg, Herman?" he asked.

"Feel sleepy. Lak it asleep."

"How about your left arm. Try lifting it."

"Ah cain't. It asleep too."

"Try moving your right arm. Lift it up."

Herman did so. The right arm seemed normal. The doctor made him flex his right leg, and that member, too, betrayed no post-convulsive weakness.

"It's only temporary, Herman. It should go away in a few minutes."

"Yeh. Ah awright. Kin ah have a butt?"

"A what?"

"Cigret. Lee Roy, you got a butt?"

Lee Roy offered his friend a cigarette and struck a kitchen match on the slaughterhouse floor. Herman Quincy inhaled deeply, shutting his eyes and luxuriating in the redeeming smoke. Tobacco vapor spurted from his wide nostrils in thick twin streams.

"Okay, Herman, I'm going to stand you up now and let you walk. Try your left arm now. And jiggle your left foot around."

Hesitantly, the youth tried to raise his left arm, and this time he got it to the level of his neck. Likewise, his foot responded. The doctor placed one powerful arm around the narrow waist and lifted the boy to his feet. Herman swayed and ducked his head a few times and appeared ready to topple, but the doctor's arm sustained him. He gave the boy a slight push.

"Take a walk, buddy. Make believe you're chasing a couple of chippies."

There was a mild laugh from the audience; the butcher turned away disdainfully. It was bad enough having a *schwartzer* almost drop dead in your holy slaughterhouse—but to get a *meshugeneh* for a doctor, one who made dirty jokes, that was too much for one hot day. He clucked reproachfully and wandered off to dispatch a few more hens.

Herman was walking now, around the corner and toward the high sunlit doorway that led to the market street. The doctor was a few yards behind him, squinting at the youth's legs, grasping Thrasher's arm as they followed the wobbling figure.

"Boy, look at that," the doctor whispered. "Perfect. Perfect goddam gait. Was I right or wasn't I?"

"I don't follow you," Thrasher said.

"Yeah, but I follow him," the doctor whispered, grinning at what he took to be a magnificent display of wit under trying circumstances. "Look at that kid wobble like that. The *gait*, the *gait*. Just what you'd expect in a neoplasm of the cerebral hemispheres. I suspected it all the time."

Herman continued his painful excursion toward daylight. The doctor trailed him like a pointer on the track of a wounded bird. Now Thrasher noticed that the youth was walking in a peculiar fashion. The left knee and ankle were not flexing freely, and the entire leg appeared stiffly extended. Moreover, there was a tendency on Herman's part to circumduct the entire left limb; the outer anterior margin of his left shoe appeared to scrape the floor. When he reached the open doorway, Herman rested against the wall, shading his eyes from the burning sun.

"You feeling a little better?" the doctor asked.

"Some. Mah leg still sleepin' a little. Ah cain't feel it too good."

"You wait with your buddy. I'll bring the car over and take you home. I want Dr. Karasik to look at you tomorrow. You may have to go into the hospital today."

"Ah ain' goin' no hospital."

"We'll argue later. Go sit on that milk crate over there, in the shade. I'll be right back with the car."

The doctor patted Herman on the shoulder and resumed his hurried steps toward his parked car. Thrasher had trouble catching up with him. Once he almost tripped over a barrel of redolent pickles standing on the oven-hot pavement.

"What was that all about, doctor?" Thrasher asked breathlessly. "Have you made a diagnosis?"

"The same one I made a week ago. All that crap from Karasik about epilepsy. Idiopathic, my foot. That kid's got a tumor of the motor area of the right cerebral hemisphere. I was right all the time." He sounded fatigued and heavy with despair; his diagnostic triumph was affording him no pleasure.

"How can you tell?"

"That was a Hughlings Jackson convulsion. And a Jacksonian convulsion is typical of an intracranial tumor. Neoplasms in the motor area of the brain causing focal convulsions and generalized attacks. I saw one once before. This was the same thing all over. Followed by Todd's paralysis—weakness in the limbs. The whole damn picture was there, perfect, so perfect that even a crap-artist specialist could figure it out. Did you see him walk? Spastic hemiplegic gait! I'll bet you a plugged nickel if I examine him right now I'll get an exaggerated patellar reflex and the Babinski sign will be present. A lousy, stinking abnormal picture all the way around."

They were in the aged car now, the doctor honking furiously and cursing at assorted peddlers and truckmen in his way, the tires crunching on protesting vegetable crates. Thrasher felt that a blowout was imminent.

"What's next, Dr. Abelman? Surgery?"

He sighed, a long, weary *Hiiiiiii*. The gears jammed in neutral, and he wrestled them angrily for a second before answering.

"I guess so. Karasik will take some more encephalograms, and maybe we'll need ventriculography to localize the vicious son-of-bitching thing."

Thrasher wiped his forehead. "Well—I mean—does anyone live after these operations?"

"Yeah. You can keep some of them going a long time. But that poor little bastard! I think it's eating him up."

Double-parked at the entrance to the chicken market, they saw that the colored youths had vanished. The doctor leaped from the car, rushing inside the blood-smeared courtyard. But Herman Quincy had reverted to Josh the Dill; he and Lee Roy had vaporized.

"You made your mistake mentioning the hospital," Thrasher said solicitously. "He's probably scared stiff."

He cursed Herman, Lee Roy, the butcher, the neighborhood. Then, pounding his fist against the strident horn in an effort to dislodge a van unloading sides of beef, he included the driver in his litany.

"You'd think these lice would let somebody through. The bastards won't let you live."

X

STARING at the notes he had made on the ruled pad, Thrasher sensed the impossible, unbridgeable gap between Samuel Abelman's actual life and the fictionalized version that would emerge on the debut of *Americans, U.S.A.* He had written *Basic Elements* at the head of the page, and below it, neatly numbered, he had scrawled a series of names, places and incidents. The list read:

1. Lib. film? Immigrants.
2. Mobile unit—Bellevue
3. M. Vogel—live.
4. Traficanti family—use throughout.
5. Films—Lower East Side, Brownsville early days (?)
6. Dineen, Gruber, etc.
7. Still pix: Brooks, Biggs, LeFevre (influences)
8. Maybe have Lord rd Hippocratic oath?
9. Negro angle gud. Sympathetic. Mrs. Quincy.
10. Negro church across street? Possible service?
11. Old rabbi. Maybe expand to include local priest, minister.

He had made the notations upon returning to his office, taking time only to have Louise order him a sandwich and coffee. It was past six, and she had remained loyally at her post waiting for him, long after the other employees had run for their various trains, taxis, and subways. Now she was standing at his desk, her round face refreshed by a ten-minute paint job in the ladies' room. She looked weary and peevish. Losing out on the promotion had cut her deeply.

"Everything piled up today," she said. "Didn't you know that would happen when you tackled the writing yourself? It's so much easier producing—long lunches, all afternoon to dictate memos. Every time you run off to Brooklyn, six more problems pop up."

"Let's have a quick résumé before you go. Louise, doll, I trust you to make all the decisions in my absence."

She raised unplucked eyebrows in exasperation. "Well, you tell *me* how a ninety-dollar-a-week secretary goes about getting Dexter Daw reinstated at the network?"

"What's this about Daw?"

"You haven't heard. Your genius director goosed a vice-president's wife in the elevator this afternoon. She wasn't the gooseable type and she marched him right into a board meeting. He's been indefinitely suspended. The directors' guild is trying to get him a hearing."

Thrasher moaned.

"I asked Daw's boss, the fellow who co-ordinates staff directors, if we couldn't hire him outright for the series, but they won't even let him inside the building."

Thrasher ran his hand from the trimmed nape of his neck over the fuzz-covered crown of his skull, squinting and baring his teeth as if the gesture pained him.

"Let's call Hank Pulsifer at the network. He's high enough up to get Dexter back on the payroll. It wasn't Hank's wife he goosed, was it?"

"No. Some VP I'd never heard of."

Crises came in the strangest guises; anxiety had a thousand faces and costumes. By all the established rules of human behavior he had no right to be upset because a twenty-eight-year-old man, riding in a crowded elevator, had tweaked the buttocks of a strange woman. A morose guilt assailed him as he compared his own immediate worry with that of Dr. Abelman, whose delinquent patient, probably dying of brain tumor, had run away. In a way, his mode of life was more difficult than Sam Abelman's: while he and his associates walked a tightrope over the gorge of despair and failure, perpetually balancing and counterbalancing, the doctor had plunged into the canyon a long time ago and had, in his own way, adjusted to the cold and cruel realities. The illogic consoled him.

"What else?" he asked wearily.

"You ought to leaf through these reports. One from Ted Chilson on the next three shows—"

"Three?"

"Ben Loomer and Mr. Whitechapel are worried about all the time it's taking you to lock this one up. So they've asked Ted to draw up a future book. Kevin McBee is going to write the next show, and then maybe John O'Hara, and they're discussing Ben Hecht and James T. Farrell."

A week ago he would have been horrified. He had envisioned himself as the permanent historian of the program he had invented. But he realized that Louise's point about his neglect of his other duties was well taken. He would, of course, continue as producer of the series—assuming it succeeded—and it would be nice sitting around at idea sessions with a John O'Hara or a Ben Hecht.

354

"Chilson is hiring people," she said meaningfully. "Researchers, assistants—"

"Okay, Louise. I'll see that you get one of the jobs. You know it might not pay more than what you get for taking dictation for Uncle Woodrow."

"I don't care. I want to go to editorial meetings and be in on the two-hour lunches at Bayard's."

"I'll make you a deal. Stick with me through the first show. I need you very badly now, Louise. If the series catches, if old man Gatling buys the whole thing, I promise you a production assistant's slot with the unit. Okay?"

She half smiled. Louise Farber had been passed by so many times that she never believed promises and never could summon up excessive enthusiasm. She wished him well in his night's work and left for an evening of bickering with her impatient Bronx parents. What kind of job was that for a nice Jewish girl—with all those drunken *goyim*? No wonder she couldn't find a husband! Nice Jewish boys became dentists or opened stores or started successful businesses.

Thrasher leafed through the stack of accumulated papers she had left for him.

A massive publicity campaign was under way. In addition to the usual trade stories in *Variety, Billboard,* and *Radio-TV Daily,* most of which were concerned with the amounts of money involved, and contained arch references to *G & T's* rumored unhappiness with the agency, there was a surprising amount of material aimed at the general press. Andrew Bain Lord was to be interviewed by Bob Considine; *Life Magazine* had been contacted on doing a picture story at the rehearsal; Ben Loomer was writing a guest column for John Crosby entitled *Madison Avenue Looks to Its Responsibilities.* The "press kit" prepared by the promotion department had only one reference to him: a simple listing of his name with the credits. An explanatory paragraph noted that the writing chores would be rotated among three or four of "America's best-known literary figures."

He drained the rest of his lukewarm coffee, distressed by its brackishness, moved the electric typewriter into position, and decided to start at the top of the show and see where his ideas led him. A thousand troublesome details needled him. Could the doctor take instructions well enough to sustain the mood of the program for thirty minutes? Was Lord the right choice—would his pompous air negate the whole concept of the show? How about the neighbors —the people he was counting on—the Traficantis, Max Vogel, Mrs. Abelman—would they fall apart on the air? Could they possibly absorb enough of what you wanted them to do without appearing as inarticulate dolts? He kept coming back to Lord as the key: his poise, his skill with words, would have to carry the show. He shuddered. At best, they would get two or two and one-half days of rehearsal. He had a chilling mental image of the whole program collapsing in missed cues, paralyzed amateurs, wrong moves, technical failures. In a way he was glad to be assailed so thoroughly with doubts and fears: it kept him from worrying about the most dread potentiality of all—the doctor's reaction to Mr. Gatling's public generosity.

He began pecking at the handsome machine, using the double-index finger method he had perfected on the overnight trick at the press association years ago. It was pleasantly still in the office. The lamps dimmed, the summer evening calm settling over the plaza outside his window, the winking of lights in the functional gray skyscrapers around him, were soothing. It was good to be a boy from South Dakota, a graduate of New Arabia High School, not yet forty, working for thirty-five thousand dollars a year in Rockefeller Plaza.

He wrote steadily, for more than two hours, pecking methodically at the machine, letting ideas tumble onto the white sheets. It was almost nine when he paused to read over his output. He had written in twin columns, in the approved script fashion, the left-hand side of the page labeled *Video* and indicating the picture on the television screen, the right hand side *Audio,* denoting the accompanying text and the speaker.

Video	*Audio*
FILM: Montage of Typical American Faces: farmers, workers, teachers, children, etc.	MUSIC: INSPIRATIONAL, America-on-the-March theme.
SUPER OVER FILM: AMERICANS, U.S.A.	ANNCR: Americans, U.S.A.! The story of your neighbors, your friends, the story of *You.*
SUPER OVER FILM: Presented as a Service of *G & T* DRUGS.	Presented as a service of *G & T* drugs, providing the American Home with products of lasting merit for three generations.
DISSOLVE FROM FILM TO MOBILE UNIT.	
LONG SHOT: Haven Place (Boost Lighting).	LORD: (OFF CAMERA): Good evening. I'm Andrew Bain Lord, and I'm delighted to be invited into your homes once again.

Video	Audio
MCU: LORD STANDING IN FRONT OF DOCTOR'S HOUSE.	Tonight I'm happy to join the *G & T* folks in presenting a brand-new series of programs. We call this program *Americans, U.S.A.* and its purpose is as simple—well, as simple as the facts of everyday life in this vast and many-sided country of ours. We want all of you to get to know your fellow Americans a little better. We want the lumberjack in Oregon to know the tugboat captain in Baltimore. The oil-field rigger in Texas should be able to shake hands with the millwright in Lynn, Massachusetts. A professor of history and a wheat farmer in Nebraska; all of us have a common bond. And it is our hope to choose a particular kind of American—to tell you about his life, his work, the people he associates with. Yes, and his hopes and dreams. We are going to find the unsung heroes of our age—the quiet, workaday people who get no medals or honors, whose financial rewards may be small, but whose strength sustains and gives meaning to an entire community. I'm sure you have known such Americans in your own home town. We want you to meet one such man tonight.
CAMERA DOES SLOW PAN TO DOCTOR'S SIGN. LORD POINTS TO IT.	Samuel Abelman, M.D. That's our man. You see that sign? It's a little weather-beaten, and Dr. Abelman has been meaning to paint it for some months. Since 1912—a long forty-three years ago—that sign has meant compassion, help, sympathy to the people of this neighborhood.
CAMERA LOOKS DOWN STREET. CUE IN TYPICAL RESIDENTS: NEGRO CHILDREN, TRAFICANTIS, RABBI, ETC.	We are in Brooklyn, a borough of the city of New York. This section is called Brownsville, a poor community, settled mostly by immigrants, minority groups. You're looking at some of Dr. Abelman's people. There are Negroes — Italians— Greeks— Irish— Poles—

Video	*Audio*
	Jews. Many people from many lands, each with different backgrounds, different problems. Yet somehow Samuel Abelman, M.D., has found the key to helping all of them. Let's go inside and visit the doctor.
CAMERA FOLLOWS LORD UPSTAIRS AND INTO HOUSE. PICK HIM UP IN WAITING ROOM.	I'm standing in Dr. Abelman's waiting room now.
GENERAL SHOT WAITING ROOM, FOLLOW WITH SLOW PAN AROUND, ENDING AT MAGAZINE TABLE.	Forty-three years. The first time I came to this quiet little room I thought of the thousands and thousands of people—mothers-to-be, the aged, frightened kids, and troubled grownups—who have come here for medical help and departed with perhaps a little more than a prescription. A half century of eased sorrows, of lifted burdens in these old chairs.
CAMERA STOPS AT LARGE UPHOLSTERED LEATHER CHAIR.	(LORD CHUCKLE) That overstuffed fellow there. Dr. Abelman did the re-upholstering himself. He says that kind of work relaxes him.
ZOOM IN TABLE, LORD PICKS UP CALLING CARD. CU: CALLING CARD.	There's the story on one small card. Office hours, 1-2 and 6-8, Sunday by appointment. Now let's see where Dr. Abelman is.
CAMERA LOOKS THROUGH OPENED WAITING ROOM DOOR, THROUGH DARKENED OFFICE, TO WELL-LIT REAR ROOM. FIRST SHOT OF DOCTOR: NARROW SQUARE OF LIGHT IN DARKENED FRAME. HE IS AT DESK, FEET UP, READING THOREAU. BACK TO CAMERA. IN VEST, SHIRT SLEEVES.	Dr. Abelman is taking it easy tonight. There haven't been too many patients this evening, and he's reading. Probably a medical book.
CAMERA FOLLOWS LORD THROUGH OFFICE. (DRAMATIC EFFECT AS DOCTOR IN LIT REAR ROOM BECOMES MORE CLEAR AND VISIBLE.) AS LORD APPROACHES DOCTOR TURNS AROUND, LOWERS FEET FROM DESK.	LORD: Good evening, Dr. Abelman.

Video	*Audio*
	ABELMAN:
	Hello there, Mr. Lord. Have a seat.
LORD SITS AT SIDE OF DESK, WHERE PATIENTS DO, FOR CONSULTATION.	LORD:
	What have you been reading? Something from the medical library?
	ABELMAN:
	Nope. This is *Walden.* I read a little of Thoreau every night. Keeps my head above water. He reminds me that life is best when you keep it simple; that nature comforts; and that you can pile up a lot of money and still be miserable.
	LORD:
	These are morals that all of us can find valuable these days. What part were you reading?
DOCTOR REPLACES GLASSES ON NOSE, READS. CU DOCTOR, CU OF TEXT, OVER DOCTOR'S SHOULDER.	ABELMAN:
	Right here . . . Page 153, where he says (READS) ". . . Let us spend one day as deliberately as Nature, and not be thrown off the track by every nutshell and mosquito's wing that falls on the rails. Let us rise early and fast, or break fast, gently and without perturbation; let company come and let company go, let the bells ring and the children cry,—determined to make a day of it. Why should we knock under and go with the stream?" (PAUSES)
	LORD:
	And have you tried to follow Thoreau's teachings?
	ABELMAN:
	Not too well, Mr. Lord. I lead a pretty hectic life. Let's say that just reading a little Thoreau does me good, even if I can't pattern my life on his ideas.

Video	Audio
CU: LORD.	**LORD:**
	Doctor, my purpose in dropping in this evening is to learn a little about you—to tell your American neighbors something about your life, your work, your beliefs. Where would you like to start?
CU: DOCTOR REMOVES GLASSES. SCRATCHES HEAD.	
	ABELMAN:
	I'm a pretty old bird, you know. You think you want to go into ancient history?
	LORD:
	The past is always with us, Dr. Abelman. Our yesterdays are very much part of our todays. Why don't you tell us a little about your boyhood?
	ABELMAN:
	All right. My family lived in a ghetto in a little town called Brovo in Bessarabia. It was Russia then, Rumania later. My father left first, when I was four years old, and went to work as a tailor in New York City. Two years later my mother brought me over with the rest of the kids.
ROLL FILM: LIBRARY FOOTAGE, IMMIGRANT SHIP AND ARRIVAL.	
	It was no picnic, I can tell you. That boat—I was just five, but I remember the way we were crowded into the steerage. My parents had a lot of courage. All those old country people— Italians, Jews, Poles—it took a lot of spunk to pick up their lives and make the move.
	LORD:
	(OVER FILM ROLLING)
	Yes, that was a dramatic chapter in the history of our nation—the mass migrations of the late nineteenth century. All these oppressed people streaming in to freedom, a new life.
DISSOLVE FROM IMMIGRANT FILM TO FILM: LOWER EAST SIDE SCENES.	**LORD:**
	And you spent several years on the East Side, didn't you, doctor?

Thrasher stopped reading. He liked the sound of what he had created. It was a little corny, true, but Andy Lord was a cornball character, and besides he was shooting for a mass audience. Culture was all right at three o'clock on Sunday afternoon. They were in a prime time slot—nine at night—and they would be competing with obese comics and murder mysteries. Briefly he thought of the rest of the script. There would be the mobile unit outside Bellevue (he wanted to check Daw on some dramatic special effects he had in mind: supering photographs of Brooks, Biggs, and the other Bellevue greats over the live shots of the medical college); there would be the real people—Vogel, the Traficantis, Mrs. Abelman—and there would be an actual examination and diagnosis in the office, as dramatic and poignant as he could make it.

A luxurious feeling of fatigue born of fruitful mental labor settled over him; the thrill was almost sensual. There was no greater pleasure in the world than writing, he felt. Some day he would live in an old clapboard house by the sea and write novels.

It was half-past nine and he had been on the move since eight that morning. He felt the need for the restful assurance of his home, his family, his bed. Dialing his number, he found himself —for the first time in months, it seemed—looking forward to his wife's voice with boyish eagerness, a kind of teen-age expectancy.

" 'Lo." It was the curt offhand greeting of his son.

"Hello, Woods," Thrasher said. "What are you up to this fine evening?"

"Watchin' the Giants."

"Brooklyn's clinched the pennant already, buddy. Haven't you heard?"

"Yeah. Mays can still win the home-run crown."

He winced at the sports page jargon; the kids sounded more and more like Dan Daniel every day. He'd call a halt if Woody Junior ever dared use the verb "veheme."

"Is Mother there, Woods?"

"Nope."

"Where is she, over at the Willises'? Shopping?"

"Nope. She's workin'. At the magazine in New York."

He paused. Butcher-paper jobs like the *Discoverist Review* required slightly less work than an undergraduaate literary monthly.

"Oh. She's at the office now?"

"I guess so. That creep Mr. Vickery spent the afternoon here. He and Mom were reading stuff. Typewriting and all that. Then they went out to dinner and Mom said they had more work to do in New York."

"Well, what the hell. Who fed you? Are you alone?"

"Mrs. Willis came over and cooked dinner. I'm okay. Johnny Scarpinato is with me."

"Okay, son. I'm catching the nine-forty-eight. See you."

"Okay, pop."

He replaced the phone. His life was like a house filled with disorderly small children; no sooner did he straighten out one room than another would be wrecked. All the pleasure he derived from the good start he imagined he had made with the script was suddenly nullified. He had opened the bedroom door and found his shirts and socks strewn on the floor.

Sig Dannenfelser had never graduated from the twenties. His life had come to an admirable halt in 1929, and, while his face and his body had aged in the intervening years, he had preserved what he could of that glowing era. He wore double-breasted gray vests; his shiny blue serge trousers flared lavishly at the cuff. The gray fedora, now arest the ancient clothes tree, had the dashing contour of the hats seen in photographs of prohibition gangsters.

Looking through the reversed gold lettering of the realty office window (DANNENFELSER & TROY, FINE HOMES, ROOMS, STORES. *Notary Public*), he could see Dr. Abelman's Buick pull up to the curb, and the doctor and his dopey nephew climb out and walk toward his open door. Sig Dannenfelser lit a fresh White Owl and extended a welcoming hand to the visitors. For anyone else he would have put on his natty blue serge jacket, but he had known Sam Abelman for over thirty years, and moreover the sale was all but complete.

"Hi, docky!" the realtor cried. "What can I do you for?" He winked archly. Sig Dannenfelser worked hard at cultivating an air of brazen shrewdness; it helped him forget his own incompetence.

"Hello, Danny," the doctor said. "You know Myron? My nephew?"

"Sure. Willie Malkin's kid, right?"

"I ain't Jack the Ripper," Myron muttered.

"Hah! A sensayuma, like his old man!" Dannenfelser cried. Seated at the side of the cluttered desk, Dr. Abelman reflected a moment on how alike his late brother-in-law and the real estate man were. They were of the world of small, fast-talking, slangy little men in straw hats, whose lives ended in 1929. They were full of bad jokes, dyspepsia, and uncertainty.

Thumbs hooked in yellow galluses, Dannenfelser leaned back in his swivel chair. "So ya making the big plunge, hey, doc?" he asked. "Well, I gotta hand it to ya. Anyone's a good doctor like you shoulda been on Republic Street *years* ago."

The doctor smiled. "If guys like you didn't go running off to professors, I might have been able to." He said it without malice; he was merely putting it on the record.

Dannenfelser shrugged. "Listen, doc, it was my missus, you know that. You had her coming along fine with the treatments. It was the old lady's idea to go running off to Mount Sinai."

"Yeah, and she never came running back," the doctor added bitterly.

"Come on, Uncle Doc," Myron whined, "we ain't here to discuss lost patients."

Dr. Abelman ignored him. "I guess I wasn't fancy enough, Danny. Considering your wife took all her relatives and the kids to professors also."

"Ah, cut it out, doc. Don't I still come to ya?"

The doctor's fingers drummed rhythmically on the desk top. "Sure, Danny, you're a pretty good guy for a real estate *goniff*. I have no complaints about you." He said it with sufficient emphasis to indicate that he was not ready to forgive the rest of his family.

"Well! That's settled!" Dannenfelser said happily. "Some guy, your uncle, always ready to knock somebody's block off!"

Dr. Abelman wiggled his eyebrows appreciatively, and, reaching inside the breast pocket of his pale-green sport shirt, took out an envelope and gave it to the realtor. Danny opened it and regarded the contents solemnly—a certified check for a thousand dollars made out to Dannenfelser & Troy.

"That should do it. A thousand bucks now, the balance when we sell your own house. I figure eight thousand on the joint if we're lucky, another seven thousand cash from you, and a six-thousand-dollar mortgage. That shouldn't be too bad for you to manage, right?"

The fast arithmetic eluded the doctor. He had gone over the financing scheme with Dannenfelser a dozen times and each time it became fuzzier and more meaningless to him. All that mattered was the respectable, dark-brown house on Republic Street. How he got there, the money he needed, the means of raising it, had become unimportant. He knew, for example, that Sarah would raise a hundred arguments against the move when she found out. Even Myron was sitting there now looking droopy and worried, his mind acrawl with dread prospects. But as far as Dr. Abelman was concerned, they could all kiss his foot. For once, he would do something *big*, something he really wanted to do more than anything in the world. Neither his wife's damned caution, nor his nephew's doubts, nor his own waning confidence would deter him.

"Yeah, yeah, whatever you say, Danny. When do you figure I can move?"

Dannenfelser shrugged. "As soon as we sell the old place." He indicated a strikingly handsome Negro seated at the rear of the office, at a blond mahogany desk.

"Mr. Troy will handle the sale for me. He'll be over tomorrow to case the joint. We'll have to put a FOR SALE sign up in the window and make it a regular listing."

Mr. Troy said nothing, nodding and smiling frigidly at the doctor. He had golden skin and a fine black mustache. From an exaggerated tab collar, a black knit tie, no wider than a half inch, descended to a contracted waist.

"You're gonna make a rooming house out of it, aincha?" Myron asked. "Ain't that the usual procedure?"

Dannenfelser's face brimmed with offense. "What makes you say that?"

"Come on, Dannenfelser, I'm a newspaperman. I know the racket. You'll sell it to an operator or run it yourself. Chop it up into five compartments, stick an extra john and a kitchenette upstairs, and suck rent outa the joint from five families. Pretty good deal. Right, Mr. Troy?"

The handsome Negro ignored Myron. Dannenfelser relit his White Owl. "So what? You're getting class. You're moving out. Why should it bother you? It don't bother Doc, does it?"

"Nah. Do what the hell you want." The doctor had barely been aware of the casual argument.

"It doesn't mean nothin' to me. Except you'll make up that eight thousand bucks in no time and have a source of income as long as you want. Not bad." Myron winked at Mr. Troy, but Dannenfelser's partner was looking out the window.

"You're so smart, kiddo, you should go into the business," Dannenfelser said sharply. "You tryin' to louse up a sale for me or something?"

"Hey, Myron, how about piping down?" Dr. Abelman said suddenly.

"Atta boy, doc," Dannenfelser added. "These wise kids today—"

"Butt out," Myron snarled. "You all set, Uncle Doc? Let's go."

Dr. Abelman rose. "So we're agreed, hey, Danny? She's mine, right?"

"Right with Eversharp," Dannenfelser chirped happily. "Of course, it might be a month or so before we can unload the old place, but it'll happen sooner or later. The party at the Republic Street location will wait."

Mr. Troy nodded at them as they departed. Dignified indifference had proven an incalculable asset to him.

Sig Dannenfelser walked to the unwashed window with its half-dozen black lunchroom boards advertising his prize real estate parcels. Chewing thoughtfully on the cigar, he battled successfully against a mild wave of guilt. He would, of course, buy the old house on Haven Place himself; not under his name and not for eight thousand, but for six thousand dollars. He consoled himself with the assurance that the Republic Street job was an excellent buy for the doctor. Naturally, the plumbing and the heating needed an overhaul and the electrical system would have to be yanked out by the roots. What could it come to? Another two or three thousand? Maybe four? Then there would be closing fees, legal fees, taxes. What the hell, the Doc hadn't asked about any of that extra stuff, so who was he to tell him?

The doctor and his nephew were silent as they rode back to Brownsville. The old man had stopped at an exclusive grocery and fruiterer, a hangover from the Bedford section's vanished days of elegance, and bought some fat Belgian grapes, each as big as a plum, and a casaba melon for Sarah. He would need some kind of tribute once she learned that he had put down a binder on the new home.

Myron was going to suggest a celebration of some kind, but that was the trouble with Uncle Doc. You couldn't get him to celebrate because all the normal manifestations of celebrations—drunkenness, parties, the theater—were lost on him. The nearest he ever came to a wild time was sitting on Max Vogel's back porch and eating salami and imported cheese. As for himself, he found no elation now that the doctor was on the verge of reaching what apparently was the only goal remaining in his cramped life. Myron had wanted him to have the new house almost as desperately as the doctor himself had coveted it, yet now the whole enterprise had a barren air about it. He attributed it to the mental image of his uncle's beloved back-yard swarming with barefoot colored children, stripping the bark from the magnolia, desecrating the wild cherry tree, trampling the rosebushes into the dusty earth. He took a marginal amount of consolation in Thrasher's promise. Eight thousand dollars would make the whole business easier to take. He refused to subject himself to the dread alternative. If no money were forthcoming from the agency man and his client, Myron understood grimly, the purchase of the new house and its concomitant responsibilities might easily destroy his uncle.

"I think I'll take a run past Dean Street. That little rat Herman might be whoring around. Boy, wait till I get my mitts on him." The doctor let go of the wheel for a second to spit on the palms of his hands. "He doesn't know it, but I'm escorting him personally to New Hill, if I have to break his arm."

Delighted with the fluid manner in which he had begun the script, Thrasher decided to conclude his research as rapidly as possible. His meeting with Mrs. Abelman, while a little unsettling, had shed a good deal of light on the old man. Seeing him through the eyes of others gave him a different vantage point, a view that could not help but improve his own understanding of the first protagonist of *Americans, U.S.A.* Or so he told himself.

The notion that he was pursuing the physician's past, not so much for the perfection of a television script, but rather because of some obsessive urge, popped into his mind every now and then. Ann had virtually accused him of an abnormal compulsion where the GP was concerned. She had come home at two in the morning from her mysterious nighttime editorial work with James Brinton Vickery, Ph.D., and they had had one of those low-keyed venomous bedroom arguments, neither of them permitting themselves the luxury of pure hatred. He had contented himself with acerb remarks about literary people, evoking a dignified "go to hell" when he started to hum:

> Oh my grand-pappy died for the minimum wage
> But I won't be doin' the same, the same
> But I won't be doin' the same. . . .

The tortured atmosphere denied him sleep, and, rising at five in the morning to keep a fishing appointment with Max Vogel, M.D., he had the lightheaded, strained feeling that came to him during his navy career after a tour as deck officer. Crossing the Whitestone Bridge in the dawn hours, listening to the pleasant, private hum of the car radio, the intimate conversation of the disk jockey, he felt kindlier toward the raffish physician. When he had called Vogel, requesting a few hours of his time, Dr. Abelman's friend had advised him that he had been going fishing on Sundays for the past thirty years, come obstetrics or piles, and if he wanted to bend his ear, he could come along. Vogel assured him he had enough tackle for a guest, so all he had to do was bring himself.

Thrasher had expected a private boat, a neat forty-foot job like those run by his wealthier associates. He was distressed to find Dr. Vogel grinning at him from the crowded deck of an open fishing boat tethered to the Freeport public dock. It was the kind of re-scraped and repainted vessel, circled by a cold cast-iron rail, that invariably was involved in a major disaster on the July Fourth weekend: *The toll of one hundred and thirty-five dead for the metro-politan area includes the forty-seven people drowned in the tragic explosion aboard the open fishing boat Ocean Beauty III.*

Ocean Beauty III (where were I and II and what had they looked like?) had roughly thirty people aboard. There were colored ladies in natty straw hats; several small boys with their proud daddies; and several lithe young Neapolitans, sharpies in sideburns and mus-taches, accompanied by pulpy blond inamoratas. A cantankerous old German held out a calloused palm and demanded five dollars from Thrasher as soon as he stepped from the splintery dock onto the wet deck.

"Pay up, buddy," Max Vogel advised. "Admiral Doenitz here gets you out in the rip, hits you over the head with a knockwurst, and feeds you to the crabs. How the hell are you?"

Thrasher dutifully gave the cranky Teuton a five-dollar bill.

"You vant to be in pool, mister? Vun dollar more."

He looked in bewilderment at Dr. Vogel.

"The pool, the pool," Max explained. "Everyone puts up a buck and whoever catches the biggest fish gets it all. I won it four times already this year. Go ahead."

He surrendered another dollar, then, as the German grumbled something about the doctor's cheapskate friends, found a niche at the bow of the creaking boat, a three-foot space of iron railing that Dr. Vogel had thoughtfully reserved for him. The physician had tied two burlap bags to the rail. A fiberglass rod with an inexpensive reel rested alongside Thrasher's apportioned area.

"Is it always this crowded?" he asked apprehensively.

"This is nothin'," Vogel laughed. "You should see it when the fluke are biting."

"I mean—isn't there anywhere to sit down?" The redolent odor of rotting fish and of giant clams—the latter hacked into bait-size chunks and doled out to the passengers in little blue basins—was making him giddy. With no sleep and just a cup of coffee for break-fast, he wondered how he would possibly last the day.

"The only place to sit here is on your ass," Vogel confided. "You'll get used to it. When she starts rocking a little out in the rip, you won't even notice. Think a shot would fix you up?"

He took a quart bottle of I. W. Harper, 100 proof, out of a huge canvas satchel at his feet and offered it to the agency man. The sight of the fiery liquid make him queasy.

"I—I don't think so, Dr. Vogel. I didn't bring anything to eat. Can you buy anything on board?" Thrasher asked.

"Yeah, old fishhooks and warm beer. Never mind, I always take a whole salami, some blue cheese, and a pumpernickel. Like red onions? Cherry peppers? I got a bagful."

Smiling weakly, Thrasher grasped the rail firmly. "Not at the moment, doctor. Later, perhaps."

The doctor made a have-it-your-own-way gesture, then proceeded to rig and bait his own pole and that of his guest. He was apparently the best known of *Ocean Beauty III's* regular guests and everyone joked with him. The colored ladies roared when he called them "girls," the young Italians were convulsed when he accused them of being "mountain ginnies," the small boys were fascinated when he showed them how to operate their reels.

The wobbly boat was now churning through the inlet (everyone had to take time out to gawk at Guy Lombardo's house), and Thrasher found it not unpleasant now that a slight breeze slapped against them and the sun made a welcome appearance.

"You really enjoy yourself out here, don't you, doctor?" Thrasher asked. Sam Abelman's best friend was carving himself an inch-thick slice of kosher salami. Garlic fumes enveloped Thrasher, but this time he found the odor almost stimulating.

"Why shouldn't I?" Max Vogel asked. He spat the words out of the side of his mouth. "Know what I am? I'm a cardiac. I got a bum heart. It almost killed me thirteen years ago and it could kill me any minute. I walk up a flight of stairs, I strain at the toilet, I tear off a piece—I could go out *like that*! So why not enjoy myself? What else is there?"

"It's too bad you couldn't teach Dr. Abelman a little of your philosophy. I often feel he'd be so much better off if he could relax completely the way you do."

Vogel bit a huge crescent out of the salami slice. Chewing reflectively, he waited a few seconds before responding.

"Ah, that old *futz*. He's got his dahlias and his corn."

Thrasher looked out, over the bow. They were in a broad channel now, approaching a concrete bridge. Dozens of vessels, private and public, ranging from simple rowboats with outboard motors to forty-foot cruisers with hot and cold running water within, were in motion around them. He thought of the hundreds of people out for the day, wasting pleasant hours on the water, and he felt pained that all this was denied his friend Samuel Abelman.

"Don't kid yourself about Sammy," Vogel said. "Sure, he bitches and curses and gets mad at everybody. But he enjoys himself. He gets a kid off a sickbed, he lances a boil, he lowers a fever, hell, he prescribes kaopectate and stops a guy from crapping his brains out—he enjoys all that. More than I do, I can tell you."

"I never thought of it that way. He always seems so bitter, so angry at the world. Was he ever any different?"

Vogel leaned against the soiled white bulkhead of the cabin. Above them, they could see the crabbed face of the skipper as he piloted the overcrowded boat toward the bridge.

"Different? You mean any happier? I guess so, when we were kids. But that's so long ago I don't even remember. Sure, Sam was different."

Thrasher took the rod the doctor had prepared for him from its resting place against the rail and gripped the circular wooden handle. It had a nice, solid feel in his hands.

"How about the last twenty years or so? Since the depression, and the war and all that? I was talking to Mrs. Abelman yesterday and she told me about his relations with Dr. Hemitz, the big blow he suffered when he didn't get the job as consultant at New Hill Hospital. What was he like after that?"

"When ya mention Heshy Hemitz, spit, please," Vogel said. He hawked an oyster into the channel waters and pounded the butt end of his own rod on the deck.

"Between that bastard Heshy, and his wife telling him to stick in the mud, and his lousy patients, no wonder Sam wanted to knock it off."

"Knock it off?"

"She didn't tell you?" Vogel asked warily.

He was not looking directly at Thrasher now. His eyes were off on the mist-laden horizon, out beyond the surging waves of the rip, where the ocean tides crashed against the bay currents.

"Sam tried to kill himself once."

"Really? What brought it on?"

Vogel threw his hands up. "Who the hell knows? Nothing special. Just general disgust with himself, with everything. You know these bastards can get at your heart till you figure it ain't worth going on. If you're like Sammy and worry about all of them, you might as well be dead."

"I'd like to hear about it."

On the opposite side of the bow (the engine had been turned off and they were drifting now), one of the young Italians was reeling in a bouncing silvery fish; a row of spines arched on its scaly back.

"A porgy!" Vogel cried joyfully. "Broke your virginity!"

The young men roared and the girls simpered.

"Hey, *walyo!*" the doctor called to them, "porgies are good for stuffin'!"

"No kiddin,' doc? How do ya stuff 'em?"

"*Stuff 'em up your ass!*" Vogel called through cupped hands.

They howled at his gutter wit, and the young Italian, honored by the professional man's insult, bought the doctor a can of beer. Vogel, beer can in hand, threw his line over the side and advised his guest to do the same.

"You could stick a piece of flannel on your dick and throw it over and a porgy would snap at it," he advised Thrasher. "So you should catch a whole bagful. You still want to hear about Sam?"

"Very much so."

"Okay. You look half sick already, so I'll make you a little sicker."

The radio newscaster read crisply:

. . . Nazi Germany has informed the League of Nations that the problem of German Jews is none of the world body's business. Commenting on Ambassador MacDonald's report on the refugee question to the League, the semiofficial newspaper Volkische Beobachter *said today that the recently enacted Nuremberg Laws are Germany's concern alone, and that the League has no jurisdiction in the matter. The newspaper, which reflects the views of Herr Hitler's regime, added: "After three years' acquaintance with the emigrés from Germany, it has become clear to many people outside Germany for what human garbage they have entered the lists, partially as a result of ignorance. . . ."*

Hitler didn't surprise Sam Abelman at all. Everybody was wringing their hands now that the little bastard was proving he wasn't fooling, that he really meant to kill every Jew in the world. Where were all of them when the lights went out? What was so hard to predict? Kicking Jews in the ass was a fine old European custom. Dimly, he seemed to recall something about pigs eating Jews in the streets of a Russian village. Here was the final equation, truer and more inevitable than anything Einstein could formulate: *A pig may eat a Jew, but a Jew may not eat a pig*. Well, they'd be stuffing them into gas chambers and furnaces now and everyone would act horrified, "ashamed for the whole human race." And plenty of them would be a little happy secretly, delighted with those cultured, well-organized Germans for doing what *they* had only been able to dream about.

The doctor slumped deeper in the green leather desk chair, propping his feet on the outpulled double bottom drawer of his desk. *Concord and Merrimack Rivers* lay folded on his lap. Thoreau was not much comfort: you couldn't calm a man's mind with acorns and loons when evil was winning the battle for the world. Harlow Brooks looked down at him from the mottled wall above his cluttered desk; he hadn't seen him in fifteen years, at an alumni dinner that Sarah had insisted he attend. Since that time he had lost contact with Brooks, Bellevue, and all but a handful of his classmates. It was his own fault: he never seemed to get around to doing the things he wanted to do. For years he had wanted to visit Walden Pond; but somehow he and Sarah always ended up in the same boardinghouse in Long Beach, an incestuous crumbling mansion, tenanted by slangy Riverside Drive German Jews who spoke harsh New Yorkese and wore cake-eater clothes. Sarah liked it there; there was a regular bridge game, so they kept returning and Walden waited.

Outside, a hesitant snowfall swirled about the dead cornstalks and barren branches of his yard. It was the first week of the New Year. The morning *Times,* opened to the radio page, informed him that at eight that evening Dr. Walter B. Pitkin would lecture on "How to Make the Most of 1936." Also featured on the program were Block and Sully, Eugene List, and Rudy Vallee. He flicked the newspaper pages idly. The book reviewed that day was called *The Coming American Fascism,* and the author was described as "an intelligent and honest man." Ethiopia was protesting the bombing of a Swedish Red Cross unit by the Italians, and in Germany thousands of Christian servant girls were destitute and homeless because the Nuremberg Laws had forced them to leave Jewish households. The bastards had really taken over; they were running the whole show. He tossed the *Times* aside; the limits of human bastardry were appalling—people *liked* a Hitler, *wanted* a Mussolini, were willing to believe that the fellow who advocated Fascism in America was intelligent and honest. Why didn't someone punch Hitler in the nose? Knock his block off? He'd like to get that little louse in the playground, just for a few hours! He was no different than those galoots he used to contend with. That was it! Hitler was a galoot, a galoot come to power. Only he had been smart enough to organize all the other galoots, then form an alliance with the crap artists, the slick liars like Goebbels with his newspapers and radio and magazines. His analysis of Fascism delighted him for the moment: a mass organization of galoots, led by a supreme galoot and directed by crap artists. People laughed at him when he carried on about the galoot population of the world; well, they had their proof now. Galoots lurked everywhere, not just in front of the corner poolroom. It took a cynical louse like a Hitler to get them all lined up and organized. Galoots had to be punched in the gut and kicked in the ass regularly. If you didn't, they would overwhelm you.

It was two-thirty. Office hours had ended thirty minutes ago and not a single patient had called. He opened the dog-eared daybook: his gross income for the week was less than twenty-five dollars. The week was half over, and he'd be lucky if he earned seventy bucks. The sight of his own scrawls, the brief notations about each visit— *Mrs. Sol Fleischacker, bld prs, prscrbe pills, sdation. Chck in one mnth. $1.50.*—saddened him momentarily. They gave form and substance to his gnawing worries. Where were all of them going? The answer was multiform: to the clinics, the professors, the young punks with their fast talk and easy cures. Times were supposed to be getting better—tomatoes are cheaper, potatoes are cheaper—but he hadn't noticed it yet.

In the kitchen, he reheated the percolator and sat at the Lilliputian table, munching a slab of rye bread, alternately daubing it with butter and dunking it in hot coffee. He had one call to make that afternoon, to his sister Rivke. One of her kids was sick; it would be a charity call. His relatives wandered in and out of his life whenever illness or despair overwhelmed them; there were no joyous family celebrations around a festive table for the Abelmans. They seemed to live on the edge of disaster, in a barren land where the need to survive eliminated nonessentials. Only his younger brother Aaron had had the spark of life. Aaron had married, fathered a son and a prospering jewelry business, and had died of a heart attack before he was thirty. Sam had taken care of him to the end, the last gasping hours in the oxygen tent, hastily rigged in the summer bungalow at Far Rockaway. The miracle was that he had lived as long as he did. The old irony made him shake his head: Aaron with his knack for living, for adusting, for creating, had not reached thirty, while old Moishe, stumbling from one garment district job to another, would live forever, content with his Yiddish newspaper and glass of tea.

Someone was pounding at the rear storm door. He turned and, seeing the top of a wool-knit cap, bouncing in cadence with the knocking, knew that it was Myron. He unlatched the door, finding him standing on the threshold. The boy was not crying, but his expression betrayed fear. A ribbon of mucus adorned his upper lip. The bulky leather jacket was smeared with mud and the brown "Tim" cap was sitting sideways above his pinched face. One earflap dangled over a moist eye.

"What's the matter, Myron?" Dr. Abelman asked. "Can't you play for even two minutes by yourself in the yard without bothering me?"

He was seven years old. Three years earlier Willie Malkin and his wife Esther had died in a four-car pile-up on the Sunrise Highway. Sarah had debated for a long time whether to adopt her brother's child. Only after Sam had assured her he had no objections had they taken Myron from the Brooklyn Hebrew Orphan Asylum into their own house, to raise as another child. Eunice was in high school at the time, and they knew they would never have another child of their own.

"Murray Kantrowitz and Sheldon Kaplow were playing *salugi* with my hat." He blurted the words out bravely. In ignoble defeat he could salvage only the dim honor of refusing to cry.

"Sock them in the nose," the doctor said. "Don't let anyone push you around!" What was wrong with the world? Did everyone have to pick on somebody to be happy? Were the galoots setting *all* the patterns of behavior?

"They played *salugi*," Myron continued, "and then they chose up sides for two-hand touch and didn't pick me."

"I'll buy you your own football. To hell with them."

Myron pushed the "Tim" cap around so that it sat properly on his narrow, blond poll. He tugged at ane of the earflaps pensively.

"You bought me a baseball and it made it worse," he said truthfully. "The tough kids wouldn't let me play with it. They called me a sissy."

Tears were imminent. A few houses removed (the fences were down and the Haven Place kids enjoyed considerable freedom of movement) they could hear the wild shouts of the touch football game.

> *Sig-a-nals—eighteen—twenty-one—hike!*
> *Trow it, trow it, Murray!*
> *Waddya handin' me a touchdown? I haddim! I haddim!*

The doctor patted Myron's cheek. "Come in out of the snow, Myron." he said. He dusted snowflakes from the child's hunched shoulders, yanked the cap off with friendly roughness, and pulled one protruding ear.

"Listen, Myron," the doctor said firmly. "Fight back, even if you get your nose broken. When I was your age, I was turned loose on the East Side and I couldn't talk a word of English. They called me a greenhorn. There was always some lousy Mick or Dutchman waiting to knock my block off. But I'd never let them. I took my bloody noses and my black eyes but I fought back. You have to do the same. The next time those brats grab your hat for *salugi,* pick up a stick and give it to them in the shins. Make 'em afraid of you! Okay?"

Myron kicked at the scuffed linoleum adjacent to the door saddle. "I think I'll go upstairs and read my book," he said dully. He was unconvinced, unwilling to test his uncle's theories in the jungle of the backyard. Murray Kantrowitz had already give him three bloody noses that year—two without provocation and one when he had argued with him about the Pittsburgh Pirates' infield. The boy shuffled through the kitchen, leaving a wet trail of melting snow. Dr. Abelman heard his rubbered feet trudging up the stairs, seeking security and reassurance in his library books.

The phone rang. It was the relief office, asking him to make a call. He hated relief work. Each call required endless paper work. The city acted as if they didn't believe a word you said, and the payments were as much as a half year delayed in reaching you. At least six times his records had been sent back to him because of some minor clerical error; failure to note a patient's age, misspellings, faulty arithmetic. The call was to a family in Canarsie, the name strange to him. He jotted it down dutifully. Some day's work! A charity visit to his sister and a relief call which meant an hour's secretarial work and a half year of waiting for two dollars.

The empty afternoons depressed him. Sarah was at one of her bridge games, Eunice had a late lab at Brooklyn College, Jannine was off. Only Myron, huddled behind the safety of his books, was at home. Outside, the January snowfall was intensifying. Thick clouds of white powder softened the drab gray-brown of the yard and muffled the cries of the football players. He'd make his calls, spend a few hours in the dark calm of the medical library, and pick Sarah up at the Newmans'.

The upright Buick skidded away from the curb. The snow was wet and sticky, and the darkening sky promised a prolonged spell of nasty weather. He was annoyed with himself for not having put the chains on the tires, the thought of an accident bothering him less than his own laziness. It wasn't like him to neglect a simple duty, yet in the last few months he had been shying away from the chores he once liked so well—painting a chair, rewiring an old lamp, fixing the drip in the basement faucet.

Rivke lived in a sagging tenement a few blocks from Haven Place. His mother stayed with her, and he received the usual moist and proud welcome from the withered little woman. He was her successful son—*the doctor*.

He spent less than fifteen minutes with his sister. Her youngest daughter was ill, a solemn little girl who smiled reluctantly when he sketched a rabbit on his prescription pad. She had the fevered eyes and dull look of grippe, and as he prescribed for her on another blank, he mused about the changing nature of the disease. Back in '19 the kid would have had run the risk of dying. Today, influenza, or grippe, or whatever the professors wanted to call it, was minor stuff. If he were one of the smart young crap artists now in practice, he'd write a paper on it for the *County Medical Journal. Observations on the Changing Nature of Spanish Influenza.* Resisting his mother's frantic attempts to force a glass of tea on him, and brushing aside his sister's offer to pay, he made his retreat from the crowded apartment, through the flaking corridors heavy with cooking odors and the aroma of cats' urine.

The snowfall had become heavier. It was still melting as it struck the pavement, but the chill in the air told him that driving would be treacherous in an hour or so. Riding out of Brownsville, toward the unpeopled wastes of Canarsie, the Buick skidded a few times, once carrying him in an uncontrollable semicircle as he rounded a corner. In the dumps and reclaimed swamps of the ragged edge of Brooklyn, with nothing to break the wind's force, the snow was settling thickly. The windshield wiper piled up little hillocks of slush on the hood. Through the cleared arc on the glass he squinted at the desolate countryside—the edge of the world. Peering at the camouflaged cross-streets, in search of the relief patient's home, he suddenly recalled a Jack London novel he had read years ago. What was it? *People of the Abyss? The Abysmal Brute?* The landscape, cold and snow-blurred and barren, reminded him of the final chapter in the London book: the last subhuman survivors on earth, drifting through a misty bog, digging for shellfish in the frozen mud. You could ride fifteen minutes out of the heart of Brooklyn and find the same desolation.

The patient's house—a crumbling cottage at the edge of one of the bay inlets—lay at the foot of a sloping catwalk. He had to take each step with extreme care. The fierce wind, whipping across the flat bottomland, seemed eager to hurl him into the frigid marsh below. Apparently the house was a bait station. A fading hand-lettered sign read:

KILLIES
SPEARING
SKIMMERS
SQUID
COLD SODA

A dog's muted snarl warned him to wait before entering, and through the partly opened door he heard cuffs and kicks and the animal's whine. Inside, a brood of dirty children raced furiously about a coal stove; the dog had been tied to a table leg. The woman of the house was sick, the usual winter symptoms of grippe, and he prescribed the same treatment he had just given his niece. The husband—their name was Tellefsen, or Tollefsen—grunted at him as he left, restraining the slavering dog.

The car refused to start and he began to sweat a little. There probably wasn't a phone available for miles and the garages were few and far between in Canarsie. The desperate wheeze of the starter finally found a response in the engine, and he drove off, feeling the tires swerve on the slick roadway.

He had driven a little over a mile, on a narrow road winding through catkins and reeds, bordering a brackish half-frozen creek. The driving snow now all but obscured vision on either side, but he knew he was traveling in the right direction and that eventually he should strike Flatbush Avenue. When, perhaps five minutes later, he detected the dread wobble of a flat tire in his rear right wheel, he sensed he was lost. Cutting speed, but afraid to use his unreliable brakes on the snowy asphalt, he pulled the Buick to roadside. The wild, wet gust smacking his face made him pull back inside the car momentarily. He turned his overcoat collar up and, spitting on his hands, climbed out of the car. The tire was indeed flat, the hard rim sitting on a loose fold like a flap of gray flesh. Changing a tire was child's play to him. How many had he changed? Fifty? A hundred? Yet a slow, dull rebellion was germinating in his mind. Each blast of the wind, each bucketful of wet snow hurled in his eyes and nose, weakened his inbred sense of duty. All his life he had responded to calls—not just the urgent pleas of patients, but the nagging requests of family, the gnawing demands of being a householder, a taxpayer, a father, and husband.

Defying the needle of defeat, he started unloosening the bolt that held the spare in place on the fender. The snow and cold had frozen it fast. As fiercely as he twisted it, feeling the pigskin fingers of his glove rip, it held dumbly to the bracket. Under the front seat he found a small wrench and applied it to the bolt. It was useless. It could not be budged. He looked at his square, hard hands and wondered what was happening to him. Helpless, he blinked at the snowfall, looking from the unyielding bolt to the dead tire. It was idiotic: you didn't let a flat tire defeat you. He would walk to the nearest house, call a garage and wait for them. Or maybe he'd find a couple of strong young kids to change the tire. Thus solving his dilemma, he refused to act. Instead he returned to the car, resting his hands on the wheel and feeling the sweat collect beneath his arms, in the hollow of his neck. He was trembling slightly now, and his old friend the migraine headache was pecking at his temple. The calfskin satchel sat alongside him on the front seat. Thrusting his hand into its cluttered interior and fumbling for what he was not quite certain, the bleak elements of the day assaulted his memory in relentless succession: Myron sniffling in the kitchen, a victim of the local galoots, his helpless sister and her sad children, the unremunerative afternoon in his office, the daybook with its paucity of entries, the dull lone-liness waiting for the patients who never came. And now this small disaster on the edge of the world, in the primordial marshland, amid the savage reeds, whitened by the murky snowfall. He looked at the small pillbox he held between his gloved thumb and index finger.

Sarah was playing bridge at the Newmans'. At five-thirty she became uneasy. Sam was always right on the dot of five-fifteen to take her home—come rain, snow, or hurricane. When he failed to arrive, she phoned Eunice, but her daughter could tell her nothing. Myron recalled the doctor leaving about three o'clock with his bag. Beyond that they could establish nothing regarding his whereabouts.

"You'd better start supper, Eunice," Sarah advised. "Use the left-over meatloaf and the beans and make a nice salad. And please be careful with the oven. Make sure it's lit."

She took a taxi back to Haven Place, warning the hackie at every corner to be careful and drive slowly. Home after a shattering ride through Crown Heights, she immediately cautioned Eunice about using too much vinegar on the salad, took Myron to task for wearing his rubbers in the house, and made a mental note to have her husband buy some rock salt—the front steps would be frozen with a thick glaze in a few hours.

"For goodness' sake, mama," Eunice pleaded. "Is that all you can think about with Papa not home? How do you know something didn't happen to him?"

"Your father is perfectly all right," she said. "He probably got into one of those long-winded talks with some patient. I think he was going to his mother's anyway. He likes to sit around and gab there and complain about me. He'll be home any minute."

A half hour later she was less sure of herself. She called her inlaws, waiting anxiously as the candy-store owner located a small boy to run the errand and summon Rivke to the booth telephone—the plumber's wife was still unable to afford a phone. The tearful tremor in her sister-in-law's voice distressed her more than her own doubts. They were people sensitive to tragedy; despair was their normal state, and the faintest hint of bad luck set them off. No, Rivke had no idea where Sam had gone after he had left her. Sarah tried the New Hill Hospital, the medical library, the surgical supply house—he had not been at any of his haunts.

Masking her apprehension with a warning to Eunice to turn the fire down under the soup, she tried Max Vogel, waiting for the service operator to summon him from his bachelor's dinner.

"Max, have you seen Sam this afternoon?" she asked calmly.

"Whaddee do? Run away with a chorus girl?"

"He was supposed to pick me up at five-fifteen. I came home from my game, and it's after seven already. I have no idea where he is."

"He'll be home when he gets hungry," Vogel muttered thickly, as if munching a mouthful.

"Max, I'm worried. Sam has been acting very peculiarly lately. You know—depressed, not talking to me, mumbling about how terrible the practice of medicine is."

"He got *stuck* somewhere! It's snowin' outside, Sarah, what's so unusual?"

"That's not like Sam. He always calls when he's delayed."

Max Vogel held the receiver away from his ear. In her maddeningly calm way, Sarah Abelman's soft voice could be as grating as a fishwife's. He knew she was telling the truth: Sam had not been himself lately. The violent rages, the bitter curses were too frequent; the savage, mocking humor that had tempered them in the past had been absent.

"What do you want I should do, Sarah? Call the cops?"

"I'd rather you wouldn't, Max. Could you check around?"

"With who? Where? How the hell do I know who his patients are? Which one he went to see?"

"I just don't know, Max. Maybe he discussed some cases with you lately—"

"Awright, awright." He was getting worried himself. Sarah Abelman always had that effect on him. She had a way of removing certainty and action from a man's life and substituting a kind of mincing, apologetic caution.

Vogel, after hanging up, paused for a moment to analyze the problem. He had the shrewd, fast mind of a claims adjuster, and, recalling that perhaps half of Sam's outside work were relief calls, he phoned the local office. After the usual amount of red-tapery, one of the girls informed him that Dr. Abelman had been given a call to one Tollef Tollefsen in Canarsie that afternoon. Calling Sarah back, he told her of his discovery and advised her he would set out for Canarsie immediately in search of his friend.

"Please dress warmly, Max," she said, "and drive slowly. It's *so* slippery outside."

Christ on horseback! Her husband could be lying dead in an accident, or mugged and rolled, and all she could worry about was whether he dressed warmly! He couldn't resist baiting her.

"Hey, Sarah, while your hubby's away, no fooling around with the detail men!" he snapped.

"You're *awful*. I don't know how Sam stands you."

He rolled into his LaSalle, an endless black hearse with a sixteen-cylinder engine and an iron body. Once, when the LaSalle was new, he had rammed the Bergen Street trolley. The automobile was unharmed in the collision; the streetcar had sustained a dent the size of a beer keg.

Vogel knew the Canarsie roads. He was an old fisherman and he had fished from dozens of small boats anchored in the little inlets. He knew where the boat yards were located; the bait and ice depots; the marine railways; the crumbling little stores where you could buy hooks and sinkers, cheap cigars and linen caps. Tooling the immense car through the flatlands, he wondered about his friend Sam, finding it hard to believe that he could meet with violent misfortune in the desolate marshes, or cause himself harm through intent or ignorance. Sam was down in the dumps, sure, but he still could handle himself *anywhere*.

The snow had abated. He found the Tollefsen shack more by instinct than anything else. Vaguely he recalled stopping there some years ago to fill a Killie trap. The old Swede, holding back the snarling dog (Max had his bag in readiness to let the mutt have it in the snoot), told him the doctor had been there a few hours ago; he had no idea where he went. He asked for the prescription the doctor had left and they showed him two: one with the physician's scrawl for medication, and another with a hastily sketched rabbit. That was Sam Abelman: he would be ready to knock himself off, maybe, and he'd still find time to draw a rabbit on the pad. Vogel left, negotiating his great round body down the creaking boards of the walk. He paused before entering his car, looking at the bleak bogs around him. A great place to go looking for someone! The old East New York gangs used to dump stiffs out in the swamps. He remembered that only a few months back a Sicilian traitor had been burned alive by some of his countrymen, not far from where he was parked.

He decided to cruise through the winding roads, in the vague hope that his friend might have wrecked his car on the slippery asphalt. Inwardly he was beginning to worry about Sam. In a few minutes his headlights, the long beam projecting far ahead of the elongated hood, picked out the rear of an aged Buick. There was no mistaking it—it was Sam's car. Vogel parked behind it. The rear windshield was thickly coated with snow and he could not tell whether Sam was inside or not.

With amazing agility, he ran across the icy roadway and pulled the Buick's door open. Sam's arms were crossed over the wheel; his head rested on his left forearm, his face turned away.

"Sam! Sam, ya bastard! You all right? What the hell is this? Halloween? You're playin' jokes?"

He heard his friend mumble some obscene rebuff and he felt better.

In Dr. Abelman's right hand he saw an opened cardboard pillbox. Grabbing it from his fingers, he read the name of a common barbiturate—the kind that required a doctor's prescription, and which were the constant subject of physicians' warnings "not to use in excess of stipulated dosage."

"Hah! Wise guy!" Vogel shrieked. "How many and how long ago, Sam? How come you're awake, ya bastard?"

Sam turned his face toward Vogel. The hollows beneath his reddened eyes were smudged with soot, the creases alongside his lips were too deep, and the flesh hung loosely around his neck. Vogel's fat hand grasped Sam's lapels.

"Come on! Tell me!" he screamed. "How many? When? Why the hell aren't you out? Dead?"

"I—I threw 'em all up," he gasped. "Never took a sleeping pill in my life before. No goddam tolerance for the bastards. Irritated stomach wall and all the sonsabitches came up. Gastric irritation. See?"

He indicated a puddle of bile and mucus on the flooring of the Buick. Vogel sniffed the sour odor of vomit, and, freezing as he was, unnerved a moment ago by the possibility that his closest friend had killed himself, he burst into ribald laughter.

"*Oi*, Sam, such a killer! What a screw-up! Couldn't take a lousy dose of barbiturate without puking his guts! What kinda jerk are you, Sammy—can't even swallow a pill?"

"Shut up, Max."

"Come on," Vogel roared. "Get your hat and I'll take you home. Unless you wanna drive."

"I can't. I got a flat. I couldn't get the spare loose—"

"—so you decided to commit suicide. That's very logical. Anyone could understand that."

He helped his friend from the Buick. In the snapping waterfront air, Sam revived. The faint drugging vanished and his head cleared. The simple act of regurgitation made him feel better. Max Vogel's presence brought him back to the world of ampules and stethoscopes, of GI series and pilonidal cysts.

Driving back, Sam cautioned Vogel grimly, "Not one word of this to Sarah or *anyone*, Max. Promise me that or I'll kill *you*. I'll break your fat head."

Vogel found his hands were shaking. He had reacted to the emergency properly, roused Sam from his black despair, and now the deadly truth of the terrible last few hours his friend had lived through was becoming apparent to him. A patina of tears clouded his eyes; he felt Sam's powerful hand squeezing his knee, underscoring his demand for secrecy. He was assuring himself that he needed Max desperately and was limitlessly indebted to him.

"Get your clappy hands off me," Vogel snarled. "You and your old lady. I think I'll tell her you were in a whore house."

From the corner of his eye he saw Sam smiling in appreciation; the crisis was over.

They concocted a story about Sam getting a terrible migraine headache after the flat, and falling asleep inside the car. Sarah had her doubts, but she made a rule never to pursue misgivings. It was more to the point to worry about a current problem. An unbuttoned sweater in the here and now was her meat; the possibility that her husband was verging on breakdown she banished from her mind. Yet seeing him brood and grow silent after the strange episode in the Canarsie flats, she wondered. Business was poor yet somehow they got along; all their needs were taken care of, and if Sam didn't become a professor, or even a wealthy GP, what of it? She couldn't teach him *not* to insult patients, to stop lecturing them, to stop taking them into his confidence so that they lost all respect for him.

One evening, another of his violent rages (they were becoming more frequent) brought her hurrying down from the upper story, her lending library book, and her bowl of fruit. Eunice had been doing her homework from Brooklyn College and Myron was listening to Eddie Cantor when they heard the shouted arguments, the slammed street door, and then a strange, crashing sound. Eunice turned white. She was growing increasingly sensitive about her father, ashamed to bring boy friends home because of his bleak, unwelcoming manner. Myron buried his skinny head in the Zenith as his aunt rose quietly and left the room.

She found Sam looking at his bloodied right fist. He had smashed the glass top of his desk with it. A shattered nucleus at one end sent jagged radii across the once pristine surface. A few small pieces of glass clung to his bleeding palm, and he studied them with hot, intolerant eyes, furious with himself.

"Why is the practice of medicine the worst sonofabitching thing in the world?" he asked.

"What now?" she asked. "Who did you tell to go to hell now?"

"None of your goddam business!" he roared. "They all stink!"

"Look. Your hand is bleeding. Sam, what's the matter with you? Why must you carry on like this over every little thing?"

"The bastards won't let you live! That's the whole thing. They've made their mind up. They won't let you live." He was picking bits of glass from his clenched fist, inspecting the bloody scratches with curious detachment. It might have been the injured hand of a patient.

"Those lice, the Ravitches. That's the end of them. I'm through with the whole lousy crew." He spoke to the room in general, to the bookcase, the Morris chair, his desk, his wife, and the faded picture of Harlow Brooks on the wall.

Sarah sighed. "Oh, Sam, and they were some of your best patients. Why did you have to fight with them? You sit around and brood when you don't have enough work and then when a patient comes in you antagonize him. Why, Sam? Why must you do this?"

"Who antagonized who? You're on their side! You always are. Those punks! It was that rotten daughter-in-law, that skinny little schoolteacher bitch with the fawncy ideas." He minced around the desk in little high-heeled steps, in excellent mimicry of the lady in question. Sarah wondered how he managed to inject these wild flashes of slapstick humor into his most frantic tirades.

"That little frump! She comes in here with the old man, the old *kocker* who almost died of bleeding ulcers two years ago, and the only reason he's alive is because I diagnosed him and nursed him and held his hand and because Harry Hemitz did what nobody else could do on his duodenum! And he sits there with his stupid wife, and the big klutz of a son, while that little bitchy blonde tells me she doesn't like the way he's looking and her brother is a specialist, a *professor* yet, a big shot with an office on Eastern Parkway and she wants the records to take to him. So I ask her, what specifically is wrong? He doesn't eat well? He has any pain? No. Nothing. The old guy—and when I think of the way I held his lousy hand through the case—sits there and doesn't say a word. This blond bitch has them all scared, with her fawncy little behind and the earrings, so she keeps talking, and before you know it they all agree they want the records. You'd think that louse of a son, I delivered him and got him through scarlet fever and diptheria, would open his yap. But no! That blondie with her skinny voice—"

He commenced to imitate her walk again, lifting his trouser legs above his hairy calves and tiptoeing around the consultation room, his lips pursed and his large, graying head cocked daintily.

"Sam, stop! You look ridiculous."

"Well, I told her off! All of them! I threw the goddam records at them and told them to all kindly go to hell with my compliments! I never want to see the bastards again!"

He was in the office now, washing his bleeding hand, pouring freely from the alcohol bottle. Sarah shuddered. The Ravitches had been Sam's patients since his first year in practice, and now they were gone, gone irretrievably. She knew that the loss of the family was not really his fault. Yet somehow she felt he might have salvaged something; the arts of diplomacy, of soft talk, of negotiation always eluded him. He could have reached some modus vivendi with them. Other GP's managed to keep patients in spite of the growing encroachments of the specialists. Why couldn't her husband do the same? Why did every challenge result in one of his violent rages and the inevitable amputation of relations?

His hand bandaged, he collapsed in the Morris chair and covered his eyes. "Ah, to hell with all of them. The practice of medicine stinks. What the hell am I doing in it?"

She sat in his swivel chair and spun around to face him, appalled by the grayness of his face, the deep, cutting lines around his mouth. He was only fifty years old.

"Sam, I am terribly worried about you. You should talk to someone who can help you."

"I don't need any help. I'm fine. I don't need any professor telling me what's wrong with me."

"I'm going to take you to see Dr. Brooks. He'll talk sense to you. I know he can help you.

"Who needs him?"

"You do. I'm going to call his office tomorrow."

Sarah prevailed, and they went to visit Harlow Brooks. They waited, flanked by ladies in mink and workmen in ten-dollar suits, looking at the Indian masks and clubs on the walls of the physician's anteroom. Sam had not seen his former teacher in years. When the nurse showed him in, he was surprised to find Brooks totally gray, bespectacled, and a little heavier. They shook hands briskly, and Sam, in the uncomfortable role of patient, sat at the edge of the wide desk, in a black leather chair.

"You were the fellow I found asleep on the floor of the Carnegie Lab, isn't that right? How've you been these years?"

Sam settled back. "Oh, can't complain. General practice in Brooklyn. The usual dollars and cents stuff. I never specialized, but I guess I prefer what I'm doing. I have a tremendous practice."

"Good. GP's are still my favorite doctors." Brooks studied the furrowed face, the great caverns beneath Dr. Abelman's eyes; they didn't mesh with the jovial, confident manner.

"How can I help you, doctor? Your wife didn't indicate what the trouble was."

Sam gestured at Sarah. "Ask her. It was her big idea."

Brooks laughed lightly. "How about it, Mrs. Abelman?"

"I think my husband is bordering on a breakdown, doctor. He's depressed, moody. He gets terrible migraine—"

"—had 'em for years," Sam interrupted.

"He looks awful," Sarah went on, "he doesn't sleep well, he's irritable, and not a day goes by when he doesn't scrap with somebody—patients, myself, anyone. He's not himself, Dr. Brooks, and he won't admit it."

"You exaggerate," Sam said brusquely. "I'm not nearly that bad, Dr. Brooks. Look, I can smile! She makes it sound like I'm an ogre of some kind. Sure, I have my worries and my problems, but nothing like the way she described it. You know these women. They haven't got enough to keep 'em busy with bridge games and movies, so they invent things."

Brooks got up slowly. "Well, I'm a clinician not a psychiatrist, so I'll start with a simple medical check-up. I don't know if I can help you if you insist there's nothing wrong."

"Doctor, you're one of the few people in the world my husband respects. That's why we came here," Sarah said earnestly.

"That's very kind of you, but I still won't promise miracles. Dr. Abelman, go inside and strip down. And, Mrs. Abelman, would you wait outside, please?"

Brooks took him through a routine check. The clinician commented on his former student's magnificent physique; at fifty Abelman's musculature was like that of a man in his twenties. The powerful body didn't match the guant and weary face, so ill-colored and so cruelly lined. The heart was as firm and as regular as a youngster's; Brooks jokingly told him he'd trade hearts with him willingly. Lungs, blood pressure, pulse all betrayed no abnormality.

"I'm not even going to bother with X-rays or any lab work," Brooks told him as Sam dressed. "What's bothering you is in your head, it's not organic. Let's sit and talk about it a little."

Brooks waited for his patient to speak, studying the consternation in the man's face. When the strong went to pot, it was always that much worse; the weaklings never showed it so badly.

"Ah, I guess I'm just fed up, doctor."

"With what? Yourself? Medicine? Your family?"

"Everything, I guess. I do all right financially. I make a living. But what's it all about? I stay in one place. Still in Brownsville, losing patients to the professors, if you'll excuse the expression. They run off to the kids, the easy talkers. Once I wanted to be a surgeon, and I flopped at that. It took too much out of me. Harry Hemitz, he was a dear friend of mine. You know him?"

"By reputation." Brooks left the implications hanging—that the reputation wasn't necessarily a good one.

"Well, Harry tried to teach me surgery. I learned, don't get me wrong. I could operate with the best of them. I did some pretty neat stuff. But I couldn't sleep, I couldn't eat, I kept thinking about the case all the time. If I didn't worry about the sutures, I'd worry about the anesthetist. So I gave it up. That was twelve years ago. I stayed in general practice, and what have I got? An attached house in Brownsville and a lot of aggravation from a bunch of lice who don't appreciate anything I do for them."

His voice had risen to a vaguely hysterical climax, and Brooks, adjusting his glasses on his nose, glanced at him sideways through the temple.

"What patients do, Dr. Abelman? You think mine spend their spare time writing love letters? What makes you think you're an exception?"

"Well, you're a little different, Dr. Brooks. You have a reputation. You have everyone's respect. I have to fight for every fee I get."

"You still have a knack for feeling sorry for yourself, don't you, doctor? I seem to recall you were ready to quit medical college once."

"Who's feeling sorry for myself? I'm as tough as I ever was! I can handle anything! Listen, I've been climbing tenements and ringing doorbells in dark alleys for almost twenty-five years and nobody's ever scared me yet. You know the epidemic of '18? I used to start at the roof and work my way down and make a call in every single flat—at fifty cents a call, and I was damn glad to get it!"

"Why don't you settle for that?"

"For what, for fifty cents a call?"

"No of course not. For the pleasures you get out of simply being a good doctor. I'll bet you loved the hard work you did in 1918. Why can't you make your work the most important thing in your life?"

"It is, it is. It's not the work that gets me. I love it. It's—it's the *bastards*. The haggling, and the ingrates, and the cheats, and the inlaws who are always ready to steal the patient for their brother, the doctor. They eat me up, they won't give me a chance to enjoy my work."

Brooks leaned back in his chair. "Abelman, I won't prescribe a thing for you. You have to learn to make your own adjustments. You're a typical migraineur—bothered by details, worrisome, demanding perfection in yourself, which is understandable, and in others, which is very dangerous. All I can tell you—rather ask you— is to get away from your work for a while. Go somewhere, rest, get in the sun. Then go back to your practice and meet it halfway. Don't make a million demands of it, and don't feel let down when the arts of medicine and the people who come to you aren't perfect."

"I should take a vacation? Who ever heard of a vacation in January?"

"Go to Florida. It won't cost as much as you imagine. Swim, sit in the sun, fish—"

"I get seasick."

"Stop looking for a way out. I'm asking you to make a complete new start. You'll be surprised how it will help. Do you think you're alone in feeling weary, worn-out, disgusted with everything? Once a year I take off to the woods and hunt, get to know a few Indians, cook my own meals. It helps."

Dr. Abelman turned away, and, seeing his large head in profile, the aquiline nose and the sharp-cleft chin, the crown of gray-black hair, rising from the high forehead, Brooks saw him again as the tough young medical student at Bellevue.

"I'll tell you one of your troubles, Abelman. You're like a caged eagle. You'd like to soar, fly, raise a little hell. But you're in a cage— an office in Brooklyn with office hours one to two and six to eight. Well, it's too late to be free. Too late for all of us who have given ourselves over to the stethoscope and the bottle of Dobell's solution; but at least we can temporarily liberate ourselves every now and then."

"Caged eagle, hey? That's pretty good, Dr. Brooks. Should I be flattered?"

"No. Just try and remember that the cage isn't too bad a place. Canaries like it, and a smart eagle makes the best of it. Now I want you to assure me you'll take a month away from your work. Forget about it completely. Then try a new start. If you're still in trouble, call me."

Sarah returned from the anteroom. Brooks told her his advice, and they shook hands again. He escorted them to the door.

"Please don't call me again," Brooks said cheerfully. "Doctors are the worst patients in the world. Frankly, I can't stand them."

Sam clasped his hand firmly. "Listen, doctor," he said, "you have no right not to accept a fee. It's wrong. I want to pay you. Why should you work for nothing?"

Brooks turned to Sarah. "Take him out of here. He's breaking my heart." He winked at both of them and returned to his crowded office.

They left for Miami in a week, taking Myron with them, and leaving Eunice at home to wrestle with her mid-term exams at Brooklyn College. A creaking coastal steamer of the Clyde-Mallory Line took them to Florida. In years to come Myron was always able to remember the steward with the English accent who solicitously brought them tea and chicken sandwiches in their cabin during an agonizing night of rough weather. He was a wizened little man, bravely fighting his own nausea as he ministered to the stricken passengers.

The beach was still fairly primitive. The collapse of real estate values had left vast barren stretches of sand; half-finished hotels loomed in the tropic night. They stayed at a small hotel on lower Collins Avenue, dutifully went to the beach every day and to the movies on nights when Sarah did not have a bridge game. Myron was able to recall the small, stuccoed building in minute detail. There was a stone piazza to the rear, and he could still see his uncle arguing loudly with two broad-shouldered builders, white-haired and bronze-faced men, who advised him they had come to America only to make money. Dr. Abelman lectured to them on the glories of liberty for an entire month; he waved Thoreau under their illiterate eyes, stressed moral values, and took his rebuffs good-naturedly. One of the old goats (he was close to eighty but not above pinching the Irish waitress's soft flank) would fix the doctor with vigorous eyes and bleat:

"I came here to make money, und I made my money, und dot's all."

A month passed swiftly, and they returned to Brooklyn by train, happily surrendering Clyde-Mallory's attractive round-trip deduction. Arriving in New York, Sarah sensed Sam's old moodiness returning. He settled back in the cab, gazing dully at the dark February sky, heavy with mist and soot. Crossing the Williamsburg Bridge, he began to talk about the problems of resuming practice, the cases he had left hanging, the unpaid bills, the ugliness of the neighborhood. Sarah asked him to go easy, to be patient.

"Sam, you're just coming back from vacation! You're not even in your office yet and you're griping as if you never went away. Dr. Brooks sent you to Florida to relax your mind, to give you a fresh start."

"Who's complaining! I feel fine. Me and Myron, we're a couple of hot shots, right, Myron?" He pinched his nephew's frail arm, well padded with suit jacket, sweater, and overcoat.

"I learned how to swim," Myron said.

"You sure did, Myron," the doctor said. "Are you going to take any crap from the galoots now?"

"I'll knock them out, *pow!*" Myron said loudly.

The cab pulled up to Haven Place, and Sam, after wrestling the suitcases onto the sidewalk, stopped to survey the street. After the clean air and clean sun of Florida, the dirt and cold dismayed him, more than it ever had before. The ragged stores across the street proudly displayed their banners:

NRA   WE DO OUR PART

Jannine was opening the door for them, and Eunice was hugging and kissing them as they entered. Myron was informing them he had learned to swim and that he had shaken hands with a "Seni-mole" Indian. The doctor left the valises on the threshold and walked quickly into his waiting room. It was almost as if he hoped to find it filled with patients, that the simple act of taking Brook's advice and going off to Florida for a month would bring his practice back.

The green-shaded doors to the office opened, and Max Vogel, in shirt sleeves and rubber apron, thrust his paunch toward Sam.

"Who sent for you?" the fat man snarled. "Go back to Miami and chase a few blondes."

"Maxie! Maxie, I love you!" Sam hugged him and dug a fist into the rubber-sheathed gut.

"Cut it out, Sam. Take off your hat and coat and siddown. I got a surprise for you and you might faint. Sarah!"

She came in, greeting Max warmly enough, but sensing something not quite to her liking. His presence alone upset her, and seeing him in rubber apron, his round, rufous face flowing with more than its usual cupidity, put her on guard. Husband and wife sat down dutifully. Vogel, standing to one side, one chubby hand on the doorknob, like an Elizabethan master of the revels revealing a new *divertissment* for his lord, pulled the door open. Sam gasped and started to rise.

"What the hell is this, Maxie? Your idea of a joke? Who ordered all this? Who paid for it?"

"You're payin' for it. Through the nose, wise guy. Me and Eunice worked it out."

Sam walked slowly into his office. The huge chandelier splashed its yellow light on a shining new X-ray unit, a chrome and black beauty, complete with a control panel, a set of tracks, a Bucky diaphragm, and an attachment for fluoroscopy. But the X-ray was not all. Along the opposite wall was a new electrocardiograph unit, high on a maple cabinet. At its side was a basal metabolism machine. Its table secreted a neat little oxygen tank between its legs.

"Stop crapping me up, Max. This is a joke."

"You bet. The joke's on you. Wait till you see the darkroom in the back. That's what I got the apron on for. I was getting the solution ready, when you hadda walk in. I figured I'd take a plate of your stupid skull to see if I could find out what Brooks couldn't."

Entranced, Sam wandered about the room, touching the glistening new machines, the medical equipment he had so long debated buying, the basic units that would enable him to expand his practice, and be more than just a giver of hypos and aspirins.

"I don't like this," Sarah said suddenly. "I don't like this at all. What's the catch, Max?"

They were all gathered in the middle of the office, the three of them standing on the faded oriental rug. Myron and Eunice were peeking through the parted doors.

"What's the matter, Sarah? You want this guy to really go nuts? He puked up the pills last time, but maybe he'll make it stick next time. What do you think he was doing out in Canarsie? Digging clams? He's got to work his ass off, get patients, *charge 'em for everything!* That's all that'll save him. Brooks! Sure, you can be a philosopher if you got Brook's practice and you can go to Florida if you're rich. This is what Sam needs. Work! Ideas! He's the best diagnostician in the city, and for Chrissake's he deserves more patients! So I got him these to keep him outa trouble."

"Take it easy, Max," Sam said. "The kids will hear you."

"It'll do them good!"

"I still don't get it," Sam said. "This rig must have cost over two thousand bucks. Who paid for it? Who's going to pay?"

"You!" Vogel roared. "I laid out the dough, but you'll pay me back. At four per cent, too. I ain't lettin' you get a goddam thing for nothing. You'll send me a payment every month, and it'll be your ass if you're late."

"So that's it," Sarah said. "A trick to put more money in your pocket. You're very shrewd, aren't you, Max? Foxy Grampa."

Max turned to Sam. "I give up. How about it? Should I call surgical supply and have it all taken out? Or are you going to be a man and start practicing medicine and charging patients like they like to be charged?"

"I—I don't know," Sam stammered. "It's a big layout of dough. Sarah, don't you think maybe it's a good idea?"

"I've given you *my* opinion," she said tartly. "Eunice, help me unpack."

Sam gestured helplessly. "She's against it. It'll cost me a lot of dough. I'll be paying you back for years, with interest. Who knows whether I'll really get more patients? Or make more money."

"Screw you," Vogel spat. He headed for the phone. "I'm calling Savitsky and he'll come haul this away. I'll pay the installation and hauling charges. To hell with you."

Sam heard Vogel dialing. His eyes wandered around the office as he debated Max's proposal; the fat man had hoped to present him with an accomplished fact. But Sarah's opposition and his own doubts had spoiled everything. His eye settled on the trim little set of tracks that had been installed at the rear of the X-ray table, for the purpose of moving the tube. It was really something the way they worked these things out. He walked around the shiny black table and, studying the tracks, called to Vogel:

"Hey, Max! These tracks aren't set straight. I could do a better job with a screwdriver! Tell Savitsky I said so!"

"What do you care?" Vogel called back. "You ain't keeping it."

"We—ell, I don't know. Tell him to send his serviceman over. We'll see if we can get 'em straight."

Inside the consultation room he could hear Vogel convey the request to the surgical supply proprietor. Max was standing now in the doorway smiling at him.

"Taking the big plunge, hey, Sammy?" he asked. "What makes you think you're an internist?"

"Let's find out, Maxie. C'mon, I'll take your picture!" He started wrestling the fat man toward the cold table top.

Ocean Beauty III threaded its way through the channels on its return trip to the Freeport dock. It had been a good day. The porgies and the sea bass had been biting, and Thrasher, much to his own distress, had a burlap bagful of fish. Dr. Vogel had spent the afternoon baiting the agency man's line and pulling the fish from the hooks for him. There was something primitive and horrible about the damn things, Thrasher couldn't help feeling, bleeding from the gills and pushing out their red cloacas. Who would ever eat a fish after catching them?

They rested against the bulkhead, letting the late afternoon sun warm them, watching the assorted pleasure boats chugging back to their docks. One of the young Italians had won the pool with an immense sea bass (Vogel assured him it would be tough and stringy and fit only for a ginny), and they were now purchasing the last of the captain's warm beer. Beyond a small queasiness stemming from the foul-smelling bag at his feet, which Vogel insisted he take to his wife (he could see Ann yanking at the bloody guts and scraping the metallic scales), Thrasher felt upset. Vogel's story of the old man's attempt at suicide had unnerved him. He found himself asking Vogel over and over again whether the doctor ever relapsed into the depressed state that had moved him to attempt his life.

"Nah," Vogel said. "I fixed him up. Sure, he never became a millionaire, but that X-ray kept him going. He never learned to charge for his work, but at least it gave him more work to do. Sam likes all that stuff I got him. He paid me off in a couple of years, and pretty soon even Sarah stopped crabbing."

"Why doesn't he charge more?" Thrasher asked.

"Don't ask me. He always sells himself cheap. Scared stiff some lousy patient will get offended. Here, have an onion."

He handed Thrasher a peeled red onion, and the agency man bit into the crunchy, fiery vegetable, wincing at its sharpness. He had been eating continually, sampling Max Vogel's hard salami, cherry peppers, and sharp cheese. Surprisingly, it had kept his stomach calm and had supported Vogel's counsel to "keep eating, keep stuffing it down."

Ocean Beauty III bumped gently into the dock; her old boards were almost apologetic. The fisherman were debarking, waving their goodbyes to the sullen old Dutchman. Vogel collected his various burlap bags, satchels, poles, and reels and climbed out with Thrasher, accompanying the younger man to his parked car.

"I think I'll run out and visit Dr. Abelman," Thrasher said. "Is it far from here?"

"About an hour," Vogel said. "Take the Belt Parkway. Get off at Pennsylvania Avenue, then ask somebody. Don't forget your fish. It was a pleasure."

"Thanks, doctor, I enjoyed it immensely." Vogel tossed the burlap sack, heavy with porgies and bass, into the rear of Thrasher's station wagon. They exchanged goodbyes and Thrasher drove off.

He was on the parkway soon, weaving his way impatiently in and out of lanes, feeling an urgent need to reach the old man and tell him—what? The image of the doctor slumped over the wheel of his car, waiting to die in the snowy marshland, had remained with him since Vogel had told the story earlier in the day. He could see it in startling detail: the empty pillbox in his hand, the steam-covered windows, the wind whipping the flakes outside the warm interior where the physician had elected to end his life. Suddenly, Thrasher was thinking of his father, the thin, hunched science teacher at New Arabia High School, the quiet, harassed academician who never earned enough and tried to augment his salary with astronomy lectures in the summer months. Thrasher could remember traveling with his father through a hundred dusty prairie towns, in the creaking model-A Ford. His father had ripped out the rear seats and rigged up a narrow bed, where they could sleep. There was enough room left to store the charts and the globe he used in his lectures on the solar system. They would arrive in a town, tack up a few hand-lettered posters, and then set up a small folding table in the square, and wait for an audience to assemble. Sometimes no more than two or three people wanted to learn about the planets. His father charged no admission and would simply pass the hat at the end of the talk. After a few years, he gave up the summer lecture business—it had never really been a success and the small returns barely covered the expenses for gasoline and maintenance of the Ford. Thrasher could still smell the bitter dust of the little towns, could see the reddened, lean faces of the farmers who would come to hear his father, in his high schoolroom voice, discourse on the Milky Way.

It was almost seven by the time he had entangled himself from the parkways, cruised aimlessly through most of Brownsville, and located Haven Place. The usual stickball game was in progress and he parked in back of the doctor's car. A new Pontiac was parked ahead of the old man's Buick, and he recognized it as that of the son-in-law.

Jannine welcomed him with her usual malign sneer.

"Dey Jes' started dinner, but ef'n it's impo'tant, g'wan up."

Thrasher had brought the burlap sack of fish with him to present to the doctor. Lugging it with him, he sprinted up the stairs, made the hairpin turn into the living room, and found himself facing a family dinner. In addition to the doctor and his wife, Eunice, her husband, and their daughter were seated at the table, together with Myron and a pretty young girl, dark-haired and white-skinned. It was apparently a feast of some magnitude: an immense roast turkey rested before the doctor and he was sharpening a carving knife on a stone as Thrasher entered.

"Oh. Oh, I beg your pardon," Thrasher said. "I—I certainly don't want to intrude. I should have called—"

"Just in time to join us!" the doctor called jovially. "Eunice, get Mr. Thrasher a seat. There's plenty for all!"

"No, really, I can't—"

They were all greeting him effusively. Myron was proudly introducing him to the young lady (her name was Shirley or Sandra or something like that), and Mrs. Abelman was heaping his plate with cranberry sauce and some kind of dumplings.

"What's in that bag there?" Myron asked him. "Ya been sellin' potatoes or somethin'?" He grinned crookedly—a witty aide-de-camp who was permitted the luxury of small jokes at his boss's expense.

"I was fishing with your friend, Dr. Vogel. I was going to give you the fish."

"With Maxie?" Dr. Abelman's voice brightened and he laughed at the thought of his rascally friend. "Boy, that Maxie, he's tried to get me out with him a million times. I tried it once and quit. That *goniff*!"

And, expertly carving the bird, he launched into a comical monologue about a fishing adventure with Max. He acted it out with gestures and grimaces, his muscular body gyrating and bouncing with theatrical skill. They all listened attentively, laughing at his exaggerated moves, and Thrasher found himself laughing too. The doctor was a superb raconteur, and it was apparent he had told the story many times. This time it was largely for the benefit of Myron's date—the white-armed girl from East Eighty-eight Street whose junket to the bad smells of Brownsville could be redeemed only by her host's performance. She laughed, too, clapping a chubby hand over a red mouth. The doctor was describing how Max Vogel squeezed a salami under his nose to rouse him, how he had pushed Max so hard they both fell overboard, and how a Coast Guard picket boat fished them out.

"He exaggerates terribly, Sandra, dear," Mrs. Abelman said.

Sandra dabbed at her eyes. "Oh goodness, I can't remember when I've had such a laugh. Myron, you didn't tell me your uncle had such a *wonderful* sense of humor!"

Eunice looked at her father admiringly. "We've heard Pop's stories a hundred times, but they always give us a chuckle."

"How about the fellow who went paint-crazy, Pop?" the son-in-law asked.

"*That* comes after the dessert," the doctor said. "I have to get warmed up for that one." He held a glass of red wine high and offered a toast. "Well, here's to it, folks. To your program, Mr. Thrasher, even if I'm not Boris Thomashefsky."

They all raised glasses, the little granddaughter joining with a tumbler of ginger ale.

"Doctor, I really can't stay, and I would like to talk to you for a minute before I go. I promise I won't keep you from your dinner for more than five minutes."

"Can't you tell me here?"

"I'd prefer to talk to you alone. Downstairs, if possible."

"Oh, go ahead, Sam," Mrs. Abelman said. "You're always running away from the table for some patient, so you can certainly give Mr. Thrasher a few minutes. Considering all he's doing for you."

"Here, *ketzeleh,* for you." He deftly placed the turkey's oyster on his granddaughter's plate and rose.

Walking downstairs, the agency man found it hard to match the cheerful, cluttered atmosphere of the dining room with Max Vogel's portrait of the doctor nineteen years ago, sitting in the disabled Buick and waiting to die. He had seen the old man truculent, bitter, irate, had turned and examined him endlessly so that these grim facets had come to light. What joy there was in the physician (and he had underestimated that from the start) had eluded him. He remembered him as he had first seen him: in the tattered work clothes, spreading horse manure among his dahlias. Maybe he should have left him there and pursued Ted Chilson's professor. They sat in the consultation room, the light from the doctor's desk filtering into the adjoining office, where Max Vogel's equipment cast misshapen shadows on the rough walls.

"I have to tell you one important thing about our program this Sunday night, doctor," Thrasher began.

"What could be so important? That fellah Lord isn't coming on maybe? I told all my friends already. I really would like to meet him."

"No, doctor. Andrew Lord is all set. And most anxious to meet you, too."

"Okay, shoot. I want to get back to dinner."

Thrasher leaned forward. "Doctor, do you know what a giveaway program is?"

"Yeah. Like those quiz shows. The sixty-four-dollar question and that kind of stuff."

"That's the idea. Doctor, what I've failed to tell you is that the program on which you're going to appear is a *kind* of giveaway. Nothing has changed from what I've told you before. Of course we'll tell your life story and talk to the people who have known you. But at the end of the show, the *G & T* Company is going to give you enough money to buy the new house you want so much . . . whatever it is . . . eight thousand, ten thousand dollars."

The doctor looked baffled. He squinted at Thrasher earnestly. "The jokes on them, hah hah," he said. "Who needs them? I already bought the house!"

Thrasher was startled. "You bought it? Already?"

"Well, just about. I paid the down payment. I'm signing papers in a few days. Tell them to keep their money."

"That won't stop them. They'll give it to you somehow. They'll make it a gift to buy up the mortgage or something like that. Don't you understand? The whole idea is to make a big charitable presentation to you publicly. Mr. Gatling wants to show his appreciation."

The doctor's bafflement was disappearing. He rubbed a hand across his forehead. "Wait a minute. Now I catch on. They're playing me for a chump. That's it. In front of everyone, the whole world, in front of Sok Paulyak, they're going to tell them I can't afford my new house and they have to buy it for me, right?"

"Well, not really—"

"Like fun. You know what the score is, Thrasher, but you were too nice to tell me. Why didn't you tell me about this two weeks ago?"

"I was sworn to secrecy. I may lose my job for telling you now, but I felt in fairness to you you should know."

The doctor got up and paced the room. "So that's the whole idea. I'm a poor slob, like those cripples, those cancer patients, they get on the television in the morning to answer questions about the presidents. A charity case. A wheel-chair case, I became. Give a look everybody at this gray-haired old fart, he can't even buy his own home, so we'll buy it for him. Well, I fooled the hell out of *them!* I bought my house already!"

"I tell you, Dr. Abelman, that doesn't matter. They'll make the gift to you publicly anyway."

"That's what you think, sonny!" he cried. "I just quit! Get another sucker! You think I'm going to let those Baumgarts next door think I'm a charity case? I need benefits yet? I'm through with the whole deal! Tell your Mr. G & T *that!* Get someone else, a nice old lady on crutches maybe, with advanced carcinoma of the lower bowel. Now I want to finish my dinner."

"Is that final, doctor?" Thrasher asked. "Eight thousand dollars is a lot of money. Can you recall how hard you worked for that much?"

"You bet I can. But I didn't stand in front of the world and cry for it. Sorry, sonny boy."

He was leaving the room, heading down the corridor toward the stairs, Thrasher following him, feeling oddly relieved and unshaken. He would pay the penalty in the morning; for the time being he could enjoy his brief false reverie.

He shook the doctor's hand at the base of the stairs. "Well, I may not see you again, Dr. Abelman. I've enjoyed our little chats, and I hope I haven't been too much of a pest."

"You're a good kid, Woody. But you know how it is. I can't go accepting money in public like that. What would the AMA say?"

Thrasher blinked. Only Dr. Abelman could have injected so blithely an irrelevancy like the American Medical Association. He had done so without missing a beat, as if the censure of his professional peers had been in the back of his mind all along.

Myron was peeking over the banister. Thrasher didn't want to be around when the dread bulletin would strike the young newspaperman.

"Ya forgot your fish, Woody, boy," he called, tossing the heavy sack down the stairs. It landed with a dull *klumpp*, and Thrasher dutifully picked it up, averting his head from the fierce odor.

"If I had time, I'd clean those for you," the doctor said. "It isn't too hard. Buy one of these fifteen-cent scalers in a hardware store. Scale 'em first, then cut the guts out."

"Thank you, doctor, I will."

In the street he hesitated for a minute, wondering whether he could safely leave the burdensome bag in a trash barrel. The faint chance that Max Vogel might see it there, and be offended, deterred him. Driving back to Connecticut he wondered why. In all likelihood he had made his last trip to Brownsville, to the yellow brick house on Haven Place and Drs. Vogel and Abelman.

The doctor waited until the dessert was served to announce his decision. As he uttered the fatal words, Myron gagged on a mouthful of vanilla ice cream and chocolate sauce. There were a few seconds of pained silence, and finally Mrs. Abelman spoke.

"Now you didn't really, Sam, did you?" she asked softly. 'You told Mr. Thrasher you wouldn't go through with the program?"

"Sure I did. He was going to make a fool out of me."

"What are you talking about, pop?" Eunice asked, almost tearfully. "You always say how much you like Mr. Thrasher—he's such a gentleman, not like your patients. What was he going to do that was so terrible?"

"He's a crap artist like the rest of them."

"Sam!" Sarah said sharply. "That language is all right in front of the family, but we have a guest here. Please."

The guest in question, Sandra Dorgenicht, was looking stricken. She had made the long subway ride to Brooklyn unwillingly; her dates normally drove new Buicks and lived in Manhattan. All that had saved the evening was the thrill of being party to an adventure in the magic world of television journalism, as Myron had termed it. The skinny young swain with the long nose, the drooping spectacles, and the studied cynicism had sold her on the evening on that basis. "My Uncle Doc, whatta character—he's gonna kill 'em on that show. An' I'll prolly get a permanent job with this Whitechapel outfit, no more lousy newspaper work." Now it was all vaporizing: all that was left was the melting dessert, the confused looks of the family, the most panting of the ragged dog at the doctor's elbow.

"Ya kiddin' me, Uncle Doc," Myron said. "Ya had one of ya fights and ya told Thrasher off. Let's call him in an hour and tell him ya reconsidered. Okay?"

"I'll have some more ice cream, Sarah," the doctor said.

"Pop!" Eunice called. "Stop being so stubborn. What went on with you and Mr. Thrasher downstairs?"

"He tried to crap me up, so I told him I wasn't interested. They were going to make me a present of eight thousand bucks on the program. In front of the whole world, so the Baumgarts and everyone else could see I couldn't afford to buy my own house. That was the whole darn shooting match from the start. To make a chump out of me."

"And you turned down the dough?" It was Harry Platt, the quiet son-in-law, who asked the question. Harry built houses and knew the value of cash; he also had an inkling of the doctor's amateurish realty dealings.

"Sure I did. Who needs them to buy me a house? I bought my own."

"What did you do?" Sarah asked. "You what?"

"Oh, Jesus," Myron moaned. "Now she knows."

Sandra looked at the family in growing terror. The whole affair was deteriorating into a squalid, dreadful quarrel, the kind her parents used to have when she was a little girl and her father was staying away from home three and four nights a week.

"So you bought a house, did you?" Sarah asked. "Which one, the seventeen-room mansion on Crown Street that needed four thousand dollars' worth of repair? Or the one on Union Street where the roof leaked? What lemon did Dannenfelser unload on you, realty expert?"

"Okay, so you know!" the doctor shouted. "To hell with it! I wanted a new home in a respectable neighborhood and I got it. It's the semidetached three-story brownstone on Republic Street, and I got it for a steal! I'm not backing out and I'm not taking a red cent from anyone to help me get it! Not a word out of you, Sarah! You've stopped me too long from doing the things I want—"

"At your age," she said primly, "doing maintenance on a house that size. With a tenant yet!"

"Pop, pop, it's not for you," Harry Platt pleaded. "I've looked it over and I know."

"At least go on the television show and take Mr. Thrasher's money," Eunice implored him. "Then it won't be so bad."

"What do you know?" the doctor cried. "What do all of you know? I'm doing it my way this time. I've lived too long to worry about it, and I don't have too long to go. I want to die in a house that looks like a doctor's house, not in a goddam slum surrounded by the scum of the earth, who are my darling patients, if you please."

"You are calling Dannenfelser tomorrow," Sarah said, "and you will get back from him whatever money you put down."

He leaped to his feet. "Like hell I am! You can kiss my foot! You can all kiss my foot! You won't call Danny and nobody's going to call Thrasher and tell him I've reconsidered. That's final!"

He maneuvered his way around the crowded table, past Myron, now pale and shaken, past the girl with the white, fat face and the wet lips, Diane trailing him through the living room and down the stairs.

"He'll change his mind tomorrow," Eunice said hopefully. "Isn't that just like Pop? He finally has a chance to get his house, to have enough money for it, and he turns it down. Why must he do everything the hard way?"

"Grampa was very mad," Marsha said.

"Everyone eat their ice cream, please," Sarah said. "It's melting. Eunice, dear, call down to Jannine for some fresh coffee."

Mr. Whitechapel had done virtually no talking. He had posed the problem to Lyman Gatling, and now it was evident to Loomer, Finucane, and Thrasher that the drug manufacturer was engaging their chief in a long and violent response. T.C. held the receiver daintily by its base, nestling it against his translucent pink ear, nodding his perfect little head, blinking an eye and pursing his lips as the harangue intensified. At length he spoke.

"So be it, Mr. Gatling. Goodbye, sir. Goodbye. My very best wishes to Mrs. Gatling and to Everett."

"How bad is it, chief?" Loomer drawled.

"As bad as it can be, Ben," the old man whispered. "Mr. Gatling feels he has been betrayed, that we went back on our word. He will not change the format of *Americans, U.S.A.* and he will not hear of a new program. He feels we have let him down twice now. As for continuing as our client, I am afraid that only a miracle can save the account."

"W-w-well, w-w-what did he say?" Finucane stammered. A crimson dye was spreading upward from his tight collar; the thick black curls seemed more unruly than usual. If *G&T* pulled out, poor Tom Finucane, teeth, smile, curls, and Scollay Square accent, would be without a job—and through no fault of his own.

"He said he is revising his entire estimate of his firm's radio and television requirements and he seems to feel a new approach is in order," Whitechapel said.

Thrasher tried to hide himself in his chair. It meant, of course, that Lyman Gatling was through with them and that there would be bleak days ahead for Whitechapel. They were a small firm, a modest firm, and *G & T* was a mainstay. When one of the big houses lost an account like that, they could look to a reservoir of other business. But at Whitechapel it would mean a major disaster. It was curious how they kept ignoring him. He alone was the architect of their tragedy; yet after T. C. had called him in, none of them had greeted him or exchanged a word with him. Their conversations glided around him, their glances just missed him, their movements in the room always managed to exclude him. What he had done was so monstrously evil, so beyond normal criticism or rebuke, that they had simply shut him out of their lives.

"Chief, do you think it would help if I got out our survey on what we did for $G \& T$ with the vertical saturation plan last year, and maybe suggest a renewal of it?" Loomer asked.

Whitechapel shook his head. "In Mr. Gatling's present frame of mind, Ben, we would be prudent not to seek him out at all."

"I could get to Parker Theis," Finucane said quietly, "I always rated pretty high with the kid."

"No, Thomas," T. C. cautioned. "We have been guilty of a lapse of honor. Whitechapel's strong point has always been our honor, our honesty. If we keep pursuing Mr. Gatling or Mr. Theis we only compound our error. We must bravely and freely admit our guilt. Perhaps a year from now . . ."

His voice wandered off into a soft, phlegmy gurgle.

"I'll call the network and cancel all the arrangements," Loomer said. "I sure hate having to pay them all that dough, and not a darn thing to show for it."

Whitechapel sighed. "Ben and Tom, you may leave. The trade press will be calling and I think we must tell them the truth. Ben, will you handle that please?"

They left, still avoiding Thrasher, walking circumspectly around his isolated chair, as if he were a diseased animal.

"Why, Woodrow? Why?" Whitechapel asked him. "What impelled you to this rash, pointless deed?"

Thrasher ran a thumb and forefinger along his nose; he half closed his eyes. That was the hell of it: he liked old Whitechapel and he liked his job and now he had hurt the old man and destroyed his own livelihood. And the reasons still eluded him.

"I don't know, sir."

"You don't know, Woodrow? A milllion-dollar account is gone, your own job is gone—I have no choice, you understand—and you don't know?"

"Call it a protest, chief, and let it go at that. Not much of a reason, but the best I can offer on the morning after."

"What are you protesting against?" the old man asked. "Your salary? Your home? The security and good friends you have found with us? I recall once, Woodrow, you confessed to me that one of our major press associations paid you sixty dollars a week for writing their entire night news report, and that you would be ever grateful to our company for rescuing you from this durance vile."

"I am grateful, sir. My actions had nothing to do with T. C. Whitechapel, or yourself. I know how much I am in your debt." Thrasher meant it, but it sounded sticky and insincere as it came out.

"You have explained nothing to me. I will be sorry to see you leave us."

Thrasher felt the need to leave the old man with something more substantial than a vague reference to an unspecified protest on his part. He uncrossed his legs and leaned forward.

"You ask me what I'm protesting against, T. C., and maybe I can explain it this way. I'm fed up with talk. With bad talk. With people saying it over and over and over, the same damn words, the same dull ideas. It's making me sick to my stomach."

Whitechapel's hooded eyes narrowed; he was not nearly so stupid as everyone liked to think, and Thrasher could see now that he was aroused.

"And what has that to do with the betrayal of a trust?" he asked. "You broke your word by telling the physician we would pay for his house. How in the world does this relate to this—this sensitivity —you seem to have developed for, as you put it, talk?"

"I'm not sure I know. Maybe it's because he never was any good at it."

"I gather the contrary from your script and your conversations about him. He seems a most colorful man, capable of expressing himself rather well, if somewhat quaintly."

"No, that's not the point, T. C. It's the things that talk, words, can do that have eluded him. We're experts in this talk business and we put words to work. We create symbols, illusions, states of mind; above all, we substitute fiction for reality. The doctor has never been able to do this. He doesn't even know enough to dress like a doctor."

"And you admired him for this?"

"How could I help but admire him? And I feel sorry for him, even though I'll guarantee you he doesn't want or need my pity. The trick today is to live an illusion, create an atmosphere, go along with our little playlets and soap operas. He couldn't do it when he was five years old and refused to let his teacher wallop him with the birches, and he can't do it today when he's almost seventy."

"Ah! So you reward this fine man, Woodrow, by stealing from him the chance to make his life happier—to have his new home!"

"I admit it. I refused to let him be eaten up by the talker world. Maybe he would have accepted Mr. Gatling's generosity in good grace, in front of millions of people. But I'd be darned if I'd let him have the opportunity."

"Woodrow, Woodrow. You are like those anthropologists who refuse to let the sanitary engineers clean up the Amazon villages. It's fine for the Indians to live in filth, just so long as the old ways are preserved. In the long run, Woodrow, the engineers have their way."

"Maybe you're right," Thrasher said wearily, "maybe Dr. Abelman deserved a better deal from me. From all of us. And maybe it's simply my own rebellion against words that made me do what I did. I look at a newsstand and I get dizzy. We're drowning in bad talk, T. C. Not just us in advertising—but the whole gang of us. The most overwhelming fact of the twentieth century is the assault on the public ear and eye, the incessant, relentless avalanche of useless information. Take the news business, journalism, an area of talker society which most of us regard as useful, informative, dedicated to making our citizens better informed, all the usual good things we think we're doing for society—"

Whitechapel poured himself a quarter glass of water from a carafe and sipped it slowly.

"Let's take a for instance, T. C. Let's say a bus falls off a bridge in Ayacucho, Peru, and twenty-three people are killed. The story is transmitted to New York via cable; sent out on the wire services via leased wire; printed in afternoon newspapers; rewritten for the morning newspapers; read on radio newscasts; repeated on television newscasts; films are shown two days later on the TV shows; stills appear in the dailies; a two-page layout in *Life*; not to mention theater newsreels, weekend reviews on TV, and maybe even a Sunday supplement eyewitnesser written from the standpoint of each passenger's rendezvous with destiny. And when we're all done, who the hell cares? What have we done to make better people out of our eager listeners, viewers, and readers? Not a bloody thing. And, believe me, T. C., that's what almost all of contemporary journalism is. Buses falling off bridges in Ayacucho, Peru. Twenty-three Quechua Indians die, and three thousand members of our glorious profession, including five Pulitzer Prize winners and twenty-four members of the Overseas Press Club, go into action. More words! More talk! And I reiterate—this is news game, T. C., good old valuable, informative news game, as opposed to show biz, huckstering, or the other areas of talker society, the ones which aren't necessarily supposed to be uplift movements."

The old man rose from his high-backed chair and walked to the window. It offered a splendid view of the busy, sunny plaza. He motioned to Thrasher to join him.

"What you say of journalism may or may not be true, Woodrow," Whitechapel began. "I suspect you exaggerate and load the dice against our friends in the Associated Press Building across the street. But I cannot speak for them. I do intend to speak for my own profession."

He pointed one desiccated finger toward the sunlit throng below.

"Who clothed all those pretty girls and handsome men, Woodrow? Who built this great complex of buildings, stores, offices, restaurants? Made all those gleaming new automobiles? We did, Woodrow. The talkers you despise so heartily, or think you despise. We are the greatest force in the history of the earth for the redistribution of wealth. Compared to us the New Deal was a crackpot's program, run by incompetents. And the Marxists! What a dirty trick we have played on them! With all their boasts about leveling society, equal shares for all. How could they ever distribute wealth the way we have? Have you seen the parking lots outside our steel mills? Did you know that coal miners' daughters take singing lessons? A policeman's daughter in the Bronx can wear a twelve-dollar dress which, save to the eye of a couturier, is a duplicate of a Paris model costing three hundred dollars!

"And who has made this possible? Who has caused our great wealth to be shared? So readily available to all? We have, Woodrow. Not the Lyman Gatlings with their crucibles and retorts and narrow vision. But *us*. The power of the word! I know what you are thinking. That there are among us liars and cheats. But these scoundrels are less than one per cent of our ranks. Sooner or later they are exposed and driven out.

"Rather, Woodrow, think of the cars in use, the homes sold, the vast quantities of food purchased, through our stimulative efforts, our great crusade to make the full and rich life easy to attain."

Thrasher was silent. How could he disagree with old Whitechapel? There was a logic to everything he said.

"One other thing you should keep in mind, if you are again to seek employment in our field. Think simply of the jobs we create. Think, Woodrow, of the secretaries, writers, office help, editors, salesmen, the thousands and thousands who find respectable, decent employment. Is that something for me to be ashamed of? Must I write a letter of apology to some left-wing critic or some tainted novelist because we create jobs for good people? I would guess that there are as many people employed in our field and its allied arts as there are in the manufacture of steel. And I, for one, am proud to have helped create these jobs, to enable my fellow citizens to find work."

Whitechapel turned from the window. He held a tiny index finger up and waggled it at Thrasher. It looked like some kind of pink grub.

"Remember one final thing, my boy," the old man said slowly. "Remember what the book says. *In the beginning was the word.*"

There was the ultimate equation: it was the point all of them got around to sooner or later, from the little shrines in Gatling's office, to the quiz contestant making the sign of the cross before he tried for the million-dollar question; the magazine biography of the big wheel containing the line: *he is a religious man.* He was glad they were ending on an ecclesiastical note. The bland idiocy of the old man's thesis—that the Holy Book itself condoned and fathered talker society—seemed not at all illogical to him. As he reflected on it, turning from the window, he saw in the baptismal atmosphere a faint opening, a slim edge of light.

"Chief, may I ask a final favor of you?"

"Anything within reason, Woodrow."

"I want a final chance to win Lyman Gatling over. I want to go over to his office right now. I have nothing to lose."

"Ah, but Woodrow, *we* do. You will not succeed, I can assure you. And you may well prejudice our future relationships with *G & T*."

"On my word, sir, that won't happen."

"Your word?"

Thrasher wet his lips quickly. "I know you have no right to trust me. But I ask this as a final favor. I think I owe it to my wife and my son and my mortgage. If Gatling won't let me in, I'll empty my desk and leave. But I have a hunch I can get the account back."

Whitechapel inserted himself creakily in his mahogany chair.

"Go ahead, Woodrow. You have my good wishes. But make clear to Mr. Gatling that you come as a free agent and *not* representing me."

"I will, sir. Thank you. I'll call if it's good news."

Loomer and Chilson were standing outside the office as he came out. For a moment he thought Ben was going to punch him; the bald, ruddy man took a purposeful step toward him and he saw the huge right fist clench.

"I got a good mind to belt you one," Loomer drawled. "You were my friend. Some friend."

"Worst, sleaziest kind of thing I've ever seen, Thrasher," Chilson said. He indicated a thick sheaf of manila folders in his hand. "Look at that! A month's work for nothing! We've had researchers and writers blocking out the next thirteen shows and now it all has to be junked. All out-of-pocket costs, too. You have any idea what it's cost us?"

"Ah, to hell with him," Loomer said thickly. "He isn't worth it."

"Don't either of you make any bets against me," Thrasher said. "I still have my two weeks' notice and I'm not through with Gatling. If I were you, Ben, I'd wait till tomorrow before calling the network to cancel everything. And you, Teddy, hang on to those scripts. *Americans, U.S.A.* has a very good chance of making the electric television this Sunday night."

He walked briskly past them to his office. The word had already reached Louise and she was misty-eyed, dabbing at her nose with a paper tissue. A chastised Dexter Daw was sitting behind his desk, feet propped on the trash basket.

"Is it true, Woody?" Daw asked. "Everything canceled?"

"As of the moment, Dec. Louise, will you please stop blubbering? If it's my last act here, I'll get you your promotion. Dexter will get you a job at the network. You can drive a Hillman and wear ballet slippers."

"Hah!" Daw coughed. "I'm on the list. Say, I never did thank you for getting me reinstated. That took real doing, boy. Damn shame we lost the show."

"What are you going to do?" Louise said shakily. "I mean, where will you get a job? Does your wife know?"

"Louise, doll, we're always protected on my level. I'll land somewhere."

Even as he said it, he wondered whether he would. His "betrayal," as Whitechapel had put it, might even keep him out of a public relations spot—the kind of jobs that were reserved for high-level agency and network people when the iron ball hit them.

"Woody Thrasher rides again," he said. "Now the two of you listen to me. Dexter, go over to the network and make believe the show is still on. Your bosses will tell you otherwise, but just say it's touch-and-go, and that *G & T* is reconsidering. Louise, give me fifteen minutes to get over to Mr. Gatling's office—don't make an appointment for me—and then call Mr. Loomer. Tell him Mr. Gatling *called me over*, and that I suggested nothing be released to the press. I may have a bulletin before lunchtime."

Daw's embryonic head wobbled on its thin white neck. "What are you up to now, mastermind? A little blackmail? From what I hear Gatling is ready to dunk you in one of his lye vats."

Thrasher paused dramatically at the door. "I am a king talker, a manipulator of the word. If I cannot win this toothpaste baron over with words, I should turn in my Diner's Club card. I plan to run a strange banner up on Mr. Gatling's flagpole; maybe he'll stand up and salute."

Ten minutes later he had bluffed his way past a receptionist and a private secretary and was in Lyman Gatling's office. The drug king growled at him and buzzed for Van Alst. When the advertising manager arrived, leather book and gilt pencil in hand, Gatling advised Thrasher he had five minutes to say what he had to say.

"Make it swift, wiseguy," the drugmaker said. "You double-crossed me and I ain't forgetting it. Nothing you say rates around here. Right, Van Alst?"

The gray-haired man nodded icily. Thrasher crossed his legs and clasped his hands confidently on his belt buckle. He was absolutely calm and self-assured. All the pressure was off him— he was the eighth man in the batting order on a cellar team.

"Mr. Gatling, what do you know about the Traycon Watch Company?" he began casually.

Gatling shot a confused look at Van Alst. "Mean anything special to you, Van? All I know is that they make watches. Never owned one."

The sales manager shook his head. Gatling scratched his bald crown, and Thrasher, seeing him for the moment confused, the pouchy face puzzled by the strange opening move, suddenly felt sorry for him. Their world was ruled by handsome men and pretty women, slim, symmetrical, and co-ordinated. Lyman Gatling, homely and clumsy, was worthy of his admiration and respect, not the trap he was setting for him.

"Traycon used to be a pretty big name in watches," Thrasher went on. "The firm is located in southern Illinois and it was built from the ground up by a little man with an accent named Solomon Byk. Mr. Byk had an excellent reputation as a businessman, a watchmaker, a gent. He put Traycon stock on the Exchange and about eight years ago he was set up as Chairman of the Board. Traycon was really on its way. I won't go into the financial involvements that followed the stock issue. You're familiar with what can happen when a bunch of smart operators start moving in. In this case it was particularly bad for little Mr. Byk because the operators were the Chicago law firm that represented him. The head of the firm—you'd know his name probably, so I won't mention it—decided that Mr. Byk was old-fashioned, conservative. Besides, he was becoming something of a public figure, appearing at brotherhood dinners and getting written up in business magazines. So the Chicago operators went to work and, before you knew it, they had him outvoted on the board, controlled most of the stock, and told him to resign. Mr. Byk resigned; he was well into his seventies anyway and wanted to take it easy. The Chicago gang took over with a big expansion program—a big advertising budget, a new luxury line, a new two-for-one split. They waited for the orders to come in, for sales to go up, for the stock to rise. But a funny thing happened. People stopped buying Traycon watches. The stock fell to an all-time low of eleven cents. The firm went bankrupt and they had to put in an urgent call for Solomon Byk, accent and all, to come back and straighten things out. Luckily, he agreed and Traycon is in good shape today. You can buy a share for nine dollars and it's considered a fairly good investment."

He stopped, to see if any impression had been made on the lumpy, puffing man, hunched over his desk. Gatling's flabby chest, bursting a white shirt, rested on the gleaming desk top like a fat woman's frontage.

"What the hell are you driving at, Brasher?" he said slowly. "Get to the goddam point."

"I will in a minute, sir. Maybe Mr. Van Alst knows what I'm talking about."

A slow negative nod and a tightening of bloodless lips was all that he could elicit from Gatling's aide. He had hoped they would discover the moral themselves and spare him the need to spell it out.

"Mr. Gatling," Thrasher continued," do you know what percentage of retail jewelers in this country are Jews?"

Gatling's hulking torso made a faint convulsive jerk in the restraining chair. "You son-of-a-bitch," he growled.

"About sixty per cent, Mr. Gatling. That's an awful lot of retail watches. And do you know what they did when Solomon Byk was kicked out of Traycon by the smart money boys? They just stopped ordering Traycon watches. No one told them to. It wasn't organized. It didn't happen all at once. But, little by little, the Traycon salesmen were told to go chase themselves. There wasn't even any attempt made to determine whether Byk had really been canned because of his religion or his accent or his brotherhood speeches. They just stopped buying. Just before Mr. Byk was invited back in to reorganize the firm, Traycon's sales had fallen fifty per cent."

He paused to let the story have its effect.

"Now what the hell does that have to do with me?" Gatling asked.

"I'll be delighted to tell you, Mr. Gatling. Samuel Abelman is a Jew. You have just cancelled a program in which he was the star. There have been columns of advance publicity on him, on your show. Your drugs are identified with him. Now you've given him the business. Got any idea how many Jewish druggists there are in this city alone? I can't remember ever seeing any other kind."

"You little bastard," Gatling whispered, "you dirty, sneaking little narrow-pants bastard with your goddam narrow brim and narrow shoes and narrow lapels. You lousy little word peddler, selling your farts and belches across a counter. You know goddam well my decision to cancel had absolutely nothing to do with this pill-roller's religion. I never mentioned it once. I never objected to it once. You're trying to scare me so I'll put the show back on the way you want it, without the money at the end. I won't scare."

"How big a drop in sales can you stand, Mr. Gatling?"

"I won't lose a single sale over this. Not a cake of soap or a tube of shaving cream. I'll tell the truth. We dumped the show because you spilled the beans to this doctor, and besides we never had any faith in it. Who's to say no?"

"Truth is old stuff, Mr. Gatling. It's illusion that's important. When the New York *Record* and the professional bleeding hearts get to work on you, the societies to protect minorities and to make us love each other, you'll be tagged as a bigot. That's all your friends the druggists will need. *G & T* salesmen will be as welcome as the hoodlums in front of the plate-glass window."

"Get out," Gatling said. "Get out of my sight."

"Chasing me out of your office isn't going to keep you from being blackballed in every drugstore in New York City, and a good many of them in the hinterlands. There's nothing like an offended minority, Mr. Gatling." Thrasher got up; his legs should have been trembling but they weren't.

"You narrow-pants bastard, get out."

"I'm on my way, sir. As of this moment no one outside of our organization knows that *Americans, U.S.A.* has been canceled. Even in our shop it's not official. No word has been given to the network or the newspapers. You're still in the clear. All you have to do is let me put the show on the way I want to do it, the way it was meant to be done, a simple story about a decent man. Forget the cash prizes. You can buy Dr. Abelman some sheep's manure for his dahlias."

Gatling's secretary was holding the door open for him.

"You've got until noon, Mr. Gatling. You can call me direct, but it might be a nicer gesture if you called Mr. Whitechapel. I can't tell you how upset he is over this turn of events. Goodbye. Goodbye, Mr. Van Alst."

The last thing he noticed as he made his way past the little illuminated shrines was Van Alst making notations in his little book.

He returned in glory: Van Alst had gotten on the phone to Whitechapel ten minutes after he left, and the agency was given a free hand. Loomer looked at him in disbelief and young Chilson pumped his hand. Finucane had left a quart of John Begg on his desk. He had done the impossible. None of them wanted to know how it happened, what magic he had wrought. He could see the glowing adulation in Porter Simpson's eyes, and exchanging it for a long look at her unbelievable bosom, he felt a sudden urge to try her, a kind of sexual dessert to the feast of success he had just enjoyed. Rejecting the pleasurable notion as fast as he had entertained it, he realized that he had had his share of duplicity for the day, probably for the week. What he had done to poor Lyman Gatling was way in excess of the normal calorie count for deception.

"You're a genius," Louise said. "How did you do it?"

"What a guy to have in a fellah's corner," Daw muttered. "Gets me off the hook and gets the account back in two days. Woody, I love you."

Thrasher tore off his coat, yanked open his collar, and was at his desk in a single motion. He had used cruel means to reach his end; he would be obliged to see to it now that the end was worth it all. *Americans, U.S.A.* would have to be more than just a television program; it would have to make better people out of its viewers, open their hearts and their minds.

"Let's move, gang," he said. "Dec, you and Alice should run out to Haven Place today and start setting shots. Got your technical director?"

"The best."

"See if Andy Lord can go along. We'll pay him an extra hundred bucks if he spends the day with you. It always helps when the talent sees the layout in advance, especially on these remote jobs. Louise, get me Dr. Abelman, so I can tell him it's on again. Then call his daughter for me. Her name is Mrs. Harry Platt and she lives somewhere in Queens. I have to talk to her today. I also want to be checked out on commercials, openings, and closings. Have Porter Simpson draw up a film routine. We're rolling, kids! Just four days to go. Are we all with it?"

Ted Chilson was standing in the doorway. He waved the folders at Thrasher. "Care to look the advance shows over, Woody?" he intoned.

"Only if we can work it in at a business lunch. How's 21 sound?"

He was back in the swing again; the long lunch meeting, the fast talk, the brash assurance that everything in the world turned out for the best after all. Old Whitechapel was right: they were engaged in a mighty redistribution of America's wealth and had every right to feel proud of their work.

"Okay if I invite Ben and Tom?" Chilson asked happily.

"Sure. Bring the whole team. We all love each other again."

They were the last of his dahlias and the doctor was treating them with special solicitousness. He preferred not to cut them. Rather, he let them wither on the tall stalks, watching them turn brown and fall, to enrich the tired earth of his garden for another spring. He trimmed and snipped, fastened a sagging stem here and softened the black earth there. It was late afternoon of the dying summer's day, and he was thinking, for no particular reason, of Mr. Comerford, sitting on the folding chair which Sammy Abelman had carried out to Staten Island, and lecturing the young people on Thoreau. The work in the garden was like a mild sedative for him. The fading sun warmed his pate; the earth felt rich and soggy beneath his work shoes. Distantly, a dog raised a rhythmic protest and Diane went speeding down the unfinished brick pathway, slamming on her mushy brakes at the cornfield gate and leaping upward for the thousandth time, knowing she could never clear the chicken-wire barrier.

"Bums outside!" the doctor called.

His words, softly spoken, were enough to bring the mongrel flying back to the dahlia beds, waiting on haunches outside the forbidden area, the dustmop tail kicking up little clouds of dirt.

Jannine, accompanied by another colored lady, appeared on the porch, and Diane, running frantically for the wooden steps as she heard the screen door creak open, did a complete turn and scrambled back to the doctor. She and Jannine observed an armed truce.

"Dis lady say she got to see you."

He didn't look up. "Tell her to wait where she's supposed to, in the waiting room. You know I don't let patients back here."

"She say it's amergency."

"Iz me, doctor. Miz Quincy."

He shaded his eyes, resting the trowel on the short picket fence. "Oh, hello there, Mrs. Quincy. Has your boy turned up?"

"Yeah. Das what I wan' see yo' 'bout. He come home yestiddy an' have another fit. I ast him how come he doan let you treat him. He say yo' goan cut him open an' he doan wan' no hospital. I beg him come wid me heah, but he run off agin'. He run off wid dem no-good frien's, dat Bishop boy and sech, an' I 'spect he goin' fo' some of dat stuff he stick in his laig."

It was always the *other* boys who were bad; Herman was innocent, of course, the dirty little rat. He climbed over the fence slowly, feeling the arthritic twinge in his spine as he negotiated the short pickets. Hector O'Bannion would laugh at him, suffering from arthritis after all the exercises he had taught him.

"Where do you think he is now?" the doctor asked.

"In deh poolroom, I 'spec. I wish yo' all come wid me and fin' him," she pleaded. "He need you but he won' admit he need you. Ef'n you say he's got to go to deh hospital, Ah see dat he goes."

The doctor wiped his hands on an old towel and returned it to a nail at the edge of the porch.

"All right. Let's go. Let me call Dr. Karasik first and tell him to get a bed ready at New Hill."

She sat stiffly at the edge of the seat as they cruised the streets looking for Herman. They passed his usual haunts—the schoolyard, the candy stores, the motion-picture theater, before they approached the billiard academy.

The doctor saw a lean figure dart from a card game around an upended orange crate. A glimpse of baggy yellow pants and a checked cap told him it was Herman. He parked the car quickly, and, leaving the motor running, jumped out and walked into the dark confines of the pool parlor. A few Negroes were engaged in lassitudinous games around the green tables; they glided in slow-motion lethargy, aiming their cue sticks, chalking, moving the markers overhead. A television set brought in the hazy outlines of the last inning of a baseball game. Behind a fly-specked cigar and cigarette counter, the proprietor, an asthmatic Greek, whom the doctor knew slightly, looked at him with goiterous eyes.

"What can I do for you, doc?" he asked. "Lookin' for someone?"

"Yeh. That fellah who just ran in. Herman Quincy." He shaded his eyes and peered into the enshadowed rear of the wide, deep room, silent now except for the solid clack of the balls.

"Well, there you are, Herman," the doctor said. "All crouched down near the soft-drink machine like you don't want to see me. Be a nice little boy and come out."

"G'wan lemme loan," he heard Herman mutter.

"You're a sick boy, Herman. You had another fit. Your mommy is out in the car. Come along nicely, and I'll see you're taken good care of."

Three young Negroes, members of the card game, had gathered on the steps. The doctor, seeing them out of the corner of his eye, and recognizing one as the Bishop boy, wondered if he might appeal to them to assist him. Then he rejected the idea; Herman was his charge, his responsibility. He walked in quick, jerky steps toward the soft-drink dispenser. Against the bright red enamel surface, Herman, all bright yellow and light tan, looked like a circus poster.

"Come on, sonny, I'll take you by the hand."

In the dimness, he barely saw the glint of the switch-blade, although he clearly heard the *snap!* as the cutting edge sprang from its handle.

"Well, aren't you brave!" the doctor said. "Still a horse's ass, hey, Herman?"

"Hey, Josh!" he heard one of the boys call. "Put dat ole knife away! Why yo doan lissen to dat doctor?"

The doctor stepped forward. "Put that knife away, you lousy galoot!" the doctor shouted. He moved swiftly for Herman's right wrist, and before the youth could strike he had bent his hand backward. The knife clattered to the floor and Herman flopped at the end of the doctor's huge fist like a hooked porgy. Kicking the knife away, the doctor twisted Herman's arm behind his back, so that the boy's hand lay between his shoulder blades.

"You lemme be, damn you!" Herman gasped.

It was amazing how weak he was, the doctor thought. Paresis was evident in his limbs; not quite paralysis, but well on the way. He was like a man made of brown salt-water taffy; you could pull and knead him and his body would assume new shapes.

"Lemme go. You done shamed me in front of mah friens! Lemme go!" Herman was wheezing the words through thick, liverish lips; his soft eyes rolled about without focus, avoiding the horrified stares of his gang. Forever and ever, he had lost status with the Twentieth Century Gents—disarmed, shamed, marched off by a sixty-eight-year-old man who refused to be bluffed.

In the bright sunlight, he prodded Herman into the rear seat of the Buick. It was like throwing a giant doll in. The boy had the feel of one of his granddaughter's oversized teddy bears.

"Mrs. Quincy, go sit in the back with your son. If he tries to run away, belt him in the kisser."

She complied, taking his slack arm firmly in one hand, patting his lovely tan forehead with another.

"You goan be awright, son," she said. "Dr. Abeman heah, he goan fix you up. Das right, ain' it, doctor?"

Dr. Abelman squinted at the perfect head. Herman's eyes were open, yet unseeing, his jaw hung loosely and there was a faint twitching about his mouth.

"Semistupor already," the doctor said. "Faster than I thought. We'll take him off to New Hill right away. Dr. Karasik will look him over as soon as we get there."

All the way to the hospital the boy moaned, sometimes a whimpering little cry, sometimes a long, low sound.

"Tell him to shut his yap, willya please?" he asked the tearful mother, addressing her by way of the rear-view mirror. "Have a little consideration for *my* nerves."

Karasik took an electroencephalogram immediately upon Herman's admission. It showed nothing beyond the generalized pattern of abnormality that the previous tracings had indicated. After Dr. Abelman described in detail the observed convulsion, typifying it as "a perfect lousy Hughlings Jackson if ever I saw one," Karasik suggested at least one more day to make tracings, in the hope that the brain damage might be localized.

"You won't find a damn thing, Franz," Dr. Abelman said, then added, "Wow, I'm tired. Chasing that little rat into a poolroom, and then having to knock a knife out of his mitt. Imagine that little punk, trying to stick me!"

"Sam, you should turn him over to the cops and be done with him."

"Well, you know how it is. My patient, and all that. His old lady is a decent person. When do you start with the drilling?"

Karasik shrugged. "We give one more day for observation, keeping him under heavy sedation. Then on Thursday maybe we'll try some ventriculography."

"I'll be here for it," Dr. Abelman said. "You want me to assist?"

"No, no need to. There's a resident here, a smart young kid who wants to be a neurologist."

"Sure, sure, Franz. You won't hurt my feelings."

The neurologist accompanied Sam to the hospital door.

"And how is the great television show coming? I thought I heard something about your backing out?"

"Oh, just a little argument. Yeh, I'm going through with it, mostly for Sarah and the kids."

Karasik smiled. "I'm very proud of you, Sam. To think, my friend chosen for a big TV program just like that. I'll be watching you."

"What is it?" Sam asked. "Just some more crap by a bunch of crap artists. Call me tomorrow on the new pictures, Franz."

The doctor's daughter lived in a surprisingly large and luxurious red brick home in Forest Hills. Evidently the builder Harry Platt was a good provider. There was a Plymouth station wagon parked in the two-car garage, and Thrasher assumed that Platt drove the Pontiac to work. It pleased him that Eunice had married a success-ful man; the years of bitterness in the old attached home on Haven Place, the house to which she was ashamed to bring her boy friends, and in which she had listened to so many rages and curses, were all behind her.

They sat on a screened-in rear porch, shaded by a bank of lovely tall poplars. In a bright flower bed bordering the trees he could see the doctor's hand in a row of immense, startling dahlias.

"Pop comes around and works on them every chance he gets," she said. "Show him a few spaces of earth and he's at it with a trowel and his beloved manure."

Thrasher told her the story of his first meeting with her father, of finding him shovel in hand in the minuscule cornfield, and they both laughed. He hoped to get some family material from her, some in-formation about the doctor's home life, his relationships with her, her mother, Myron, some odds and ends that had eluded him in his interrogations. But there was very little she could add. They had been a happy family in spite of the old man's insistence on going through life in a state of fulminating outrage. She seemed most anxious to praise her father's medical skills; her dark eyes glowed with missionary fervor when she described a half-dozen cases in which he had proven the professors wrong, in which he had made the right diagnosis from the start, in which he had bested suspicious relatives and nosy neighbors.

"Pop always underestimated himself," she said, passing a bowl of fruit to Thrasher. He took a handful of cherries.

"When I was eighteen I came back from camp; I was working as a swimming counselor that summer in the Adirondacks, and I de-veloped a high fever, a cockeyed blood count, and a lot of other bad symptoms. I was in bed for six weeks. At the very start—the first day I took sick—I heard Pop mumble something about acute infectious mononucleosis. I became sicker and sicker, with a spiked temperature, sore throat, and what not and Pop got more and more concerned. By actual count, I know, because I kept track of them, he brought in *fifteen* different specialists to look at me. There were consultations, and special lab work, and professors, and goodness knows what else. Pop personally dragged in the chief of medicine at Bellevue, an old man with a bad heart who complained about climbing the stairs. And when it was all over do you know what all the professors decided? You guessed it, Mr. Thrasher. I had acute infectious mononucleosis. *His* diagnosis on the first day I took sick! Yet he couldn't believe his own judgment—he had to call in half the physicians in New York to discuss my case. And the way he carries on about specialists! But that's Pop."

Thrasher laughed. She had told the story with much charm and vivacity; he could see the crowds of doctors in the little rear bedroom, Sam Abelman moving them about like an anxious shepherd.

"I hoped to get some assurance from you," Thrasher said, "that your father wasn't quite as gloomy and unhappy as I imagined him to be. He does enjoy himself most of the time, doesn't he?"

"I'm sure he does. He just doesn't show it very well. He likes his garden, his corn, Thoreau, his family. And, really, he does love his work. He wouldn't have it any other way."

"I guess Dr. Vogel helped a lot. The X-ray and so forth."

"Oh yes, Max did Pop a wonderful favor with that. It changed his whole outlook. I really think that if it weren't for the Baumgarts, Pop could have been *really* happy these last fifteen years."

"The Baumgarts? The neighbors?"

She made a wry face. "They've done everything in their power to torment Pop. From the day their darling son entered medical college, and it appeared Pop wouldn't move, they made it miserable for him. It's funny. They were our neighbors for thirty years, and they never once invited us in, or vice versa. I used to hear Bing Crosby sing 'Love Thy Neighbor' and wonder if he knew the Baumgarts."

"They can't be that awful."

She looked at him gravely. "But they are, Mr. Thrasher. I lived next to them a long time. When I was younger I often got to thinking of Job, and how God put him to the test by visiting afflictions on him. I would see Pop as a modern Job, and the Baumgarts as a visitation from God to test Pop out, to see if they could break him."

Thrasher smiled. "I suggest your father didn't quite have Job's patience."

At night through the attached walls of the two old brick houses, Eunice, lying awake in bed, could hear the Baumgarts. They were a large and cohesive family and they seemed to hold frequent meetings in the rear room. Apparently their home was differently laid out than Dr. Abelman's—the large rear chamber adjoining

Eunice's bedroom was their living room, the site of their noisy, cabalistic gatherings, secret conclaves that ran far into the night.

Eunice would envision them squatting around the floor in a tight circle, like Australian aborigines holding a corroboree. There would be the old lady, the black hair drawn back in a bun; the father, lean and straight, his flat blue eyes betraying neither love nor hate, but a shrewd acceptance of the world; there were three sons, all with the father's neat, hard features; one was a dentist, a beanpole of a man with a long bald head; another a wealthy baker, short and fat, but with the same firm, unyielding face; and there was Seymour, the youngest, the darling, sleekly dark and compact. There were also two old-maid daughters, a bookkeeper and a beautician, bloodless, thin girls with tight mouths and narrow hips; and there were always visiting cousins, aunts, uncles, and inlaws to augment the family ranks.

To Eunice, hearing their blurred voices trickling through the walls in the winter night, they seemed strangely insular and united. She could rarely hear what they were talking about. There was an occasional woman's shriek at a joke, sometimes a long, low discourse by one of the men. They seemed to her completely allied, presenting one confident face to the world, afraid of no one, unassailed by doubts and fears. Hearing her own father rage and yell at patients, bemoan his fate, curse the galoots on the sidewalk, she wondered how they had so beautifully gained control of their environment. She was, admittedly, a little jealous of them.

Her first clear recollection of the Baumgarts was perhaps the grimmest. In a way, it had colored everything she knew and felt about them in the years that followed. She was seven years old when it happened, old enough to know that there was right and wrong in the world, lies and truth, but too young to have witnessed the carnage and pain resulting from the essential clash of the two.

It was a late spring day of startling clarity. Seated at her bedroom window, reading a public library book, Eunice could look out on her father's yard, now in luxuriant bloom. It was office hours and she could hear him below, his voice filtering upward. It made her happy to think of her father curing and helping people. She was happy also with the flowering trees and shrubs of the yard which her father and old man Gruber had planted. Towering above the roses and lilacs and Traficanti's stubby cherry tree was the magnolia, now in full bloom, heavy with giant pink-white blossoms. Once the girls in her class had derided her when she told them she had a magnolia tree; they assured her these grew only in the South. She had taken them into the garden, and one of them, Lila Shapiro, who always was so smart, still denied it. Her father had called Lila a *Galiti-zianer,* someone who always knows better; Eunice wasn't quite sure what he meant, but he always was right about people, so she accepted his explanation.

A door slammed below and she could see some people on the Baumgarts' porch next door. There was the father, in his buttoned vest, and one of the older sons, and a couple of girls. One of the girls was Mildred, the oldest daughter, and the other was probably a cousin of some kind—there were always cousins and uncles and aunts at the Baumgarts'. She couldn't quite hear what they were saying, but the son was pointing to the magnolia tree. A second later the two girls ran down the porch stairs and skipped nimbly over the fallen midsection of the picket fence. They were in her yard. The girls looked about quickly—from her window Eunice could see the oldest daughter clearly, her eyeglasses picking up glints of sunlight, her brown hair braided around her skinny head. And then, to Eunice's horror, the two trespassers began tearing branches from the magnolia tree. She could hear the ripping noise as they yanked the flower-laden twigs from the trunk. They worked swiftly, and when each had an armload of branches they fairly flew over the ruined fence and ran into their house. Eunice heard the door slam again. She got up from her seat, terror-stricken and numb.

Downstairs, she rapped gently on the office door. The doctor, in shirt sleeves, a spatula in one hand and a wad of cotton in the other, peered through the door.

"What is it, sweetheart?" he asked.

"I—I just saw them. They stole branches from the magnolia."

"Who? What are you talking about?" He set the spatula and the cotton down on his desk.

"Mildred Baumgart and some other girl. They came out in the yard and they ran into ours and took a whole lot of branches right off the tree. Then they ran back into their house and shut the door."

"You sure, baby?"

"I saw them! I saw them!" she cried. "The whole thing, from my window!"

"Lice," the doctor said. "Come on, we'll see about it."

She followed him into the yard and they inspected the magnolia. The scars left by the raiders made him wince. There were great naked strips on the trunk of the handsome tree, and twisted, agonized stumps where the branches had been snapped off.

"Why those bastards. Those four-flushers."

He looked toward the closed screen door on the Baumgarts'

porch. There was no sign of anyone in the kitchen, not a soul stirring in or about the house.

"You stay here, *ketzeleh*," he said. "I'm going to ask them about it."

"Should I call a policeman, daddy?"

"Nah, I can handle those punks. You stay right here. Don't come with me."

He strode purposefully over the fence, into the wild weeds of the Baumgarts' yard. There was a cemented area surrounding the wooden porch and he stopped just at the edge of it, calling into the house.

"Hey, Baumgart! I want to talk to you!"

There was no answer, and he shouted again.

"Hey! Who tore the branches off my magnolia?"

Mr. Baumgart's spare face appeared at the screen door. "Vat you vant, Abelman? Vat you hollering like a crazy man?"

"I'll crazy man you, you punk! Did your kid come in my yard and strip branches off the magnolia?"

"You crazy," Baumgart said flatly. "Nobody came in your yard. You dreamed it." There was a flurry of laughter from behind the screen door.

"Come out here like a man and say that, you louse!" Dr. Abelman called. "What way is that for a neighbor to behave? Trees are property, trees have life! You don't tear them apart and destroy them. Why the hell didn't you ask me for some flowers? I'd be glad to give them to you!"

"Who needs your flowers? Dey stink up deh neighborhood."

There was a burst of laughter again; the cackle of teen-age girls and the deeper laughter of men.

"Why, I got a mind to beat your face in!" Dr. Abelman's own face was scarlet.

The screen door suddenly swung open, as if violently pushed by a strong hand, and a bulky man rolled onto the porch. He had the hard, small features of the Baumgarts, nose, eyes and mouth crammed together in the middle of a large doughy mass. He was one of the eternal relatives, a cousin, an uncle, or an inlaw.

"Say that again, you son-of-a-bitch!" he called to the doctor. "I'll kill ya, I swear I'll mobilize ya!"

The doctor surveyed him carefully. He was in his early twenties, with the look of a kosher butcher or a moving man about him. The doctor flexed a biceps and turned it sideways so that the young man could see it.

"Come on, galoot, I'm waiting," he said. "Come down here and get it."

"I'll kill 'im!" the young man screamed. "Uncle Sol, lemme get 'im!"

He made a somewhat tentative start down the stairs, and as he reached the bottom step a half-dozen people spewed out of the open screen door and descended on him, dragging him bodily back up the steps. They were there in full force—the father, the squat mother, the sons, the daughters, and a crowd of adults, some strange, some known to the doctor, all hauling the young champion back to the porch, and turning to confront the doctor with defiant, guiltless faces.

"Let him down here!" the doctor said. "I'll make him eat a little dirt. Come on, fatty!"

The young man struggled and tugged, his pulpy bulk writhing helplessly in the network of restraining arms.

"He ain't worth it, Irv," one of the boys said.

"Yeah, some doctor! A doctor should live on Haven Place!" It was the mother who offered this.

"You're a liar, Abelman! You couldn't prove we took anything!"

"You couldn't prove nothing!"

"You're a lousy doctor! You stink! Your patients drop dead!"

Now they were in full cry; all of them standing behind the safety of the porch railing, shrieking abuse at his head, like citizens of some medieval town emptying buckets of slop on a condemned criminal on his way to the gallows. The doctor remained motionless; he faced them unafraid, waiting for the fat young man to be released. But the family held him in effective check. They cursed the doctor and insulted his ancestors, interlarding their cries with continuing denials, absolute denials, unequivocal denials that anything had been pilfered from his garden. Who would steal anything from such an ugly tree?

Eunice, watching her father facing them, alone, his arms folded on his chest, the spring breeze fluttering his black forelock, would never forget him thus. She was crying, the tears flowing freely onto her white middy blouse, and she was trembling, fearful that fat Irving would be freed to beat up her father. Or maybe all of them would suddenly fly screaming down the porch steps and trample him into the ground. All her life she would think of her father thus. He would deliver her child, see her through a dozen illnesses, advise her, comfort her, help her. But nothing would ever thrill her or arouse her love for him as the image of his lonely stand against the people on the porch.

"Who needs your lousy trees?" one of the daughters screeched.

"Who needs you?" one of the sons cried.

"Yeah, who needs you? You're a lousy doctor!"

The fat youth still struggled, but with less vigor. They were turning from him, satisfied that they had bested him, that the challenge he had hurled against their little crime was successfully buried under their avalanche of denial.

In a loud, clear voice, the doctor called at their vanishing numbers:

"You are a gang of scoundrels! You are not fit for human society! Scum of the earth!"

A final convulsive lurch by the fat young man was stifled by the other members of the clan. Dr. Abelman turned his back on them, recrossing the fence and joining his sobbing daughter.

"What's the matter, *ketzeleh*?" he asked. "Afraid of those slobs? I'd lay that young punk out on the ground. Look at Daddy's muscles!"

He made his biceps wiggle and jump, but she could not be diverted. They walked back to the house, father and daughter, and she managed to control her tears.

"They were going to hurt you, daddy. That man wanted to hit you!"

"He's a galoot. No galoot ever got the best of me."

"Why did they say they didn't steal the branches? They did. They did. I saw them, right from my window up there!"

The doctor hugged her. "Who knows, sweeties? Some people tell the truth and some lie. Some people like to lie. The more you show them the truth, the more they deny it."

"Why?" she pleaded. "Why should they? Why didn't they say they stole the flowers? Why didn't they ask beforehand, like you said, and you would have given them some?"

What could he tell her? "Who knows, sweetheart?" he said, pausing at his office door. He dug in his pocket. "Here, go around the corner to Rubin's and buy an ice-cream cone, with chocolate sprinkles, the way you like it. And no more crying, okay?"

After the incident of the magnolia tree, the two families settled down to a state of border tension. The incidents were uniformly provoked by the Baumgarts; the bigger battalions were on their side. They learned to operate furtively, careful that there would be no recurrences of the unfortunate raid which the little girl had witnessed. The elder Baumgart was particularly expert at hit-and-run tactics. He specialized in tossing garbage and debris into the doctor's yard. So softly did he work that Dr. Abelman rarely caught him at it. A rusted stove lid, a bag of potato peelings, the limb of a dead tree would suddenly materialize in the doctor's flower beds. Later, he would recall old Baumgart strolling through his yard, gazing about, stiff and proud in his black vest and white shirt. Snow removal was another of Baumgart's specialties. He would wait until Dr. Abelman had shoveled the snow from his sidewalk. Then, silent, and swift, he would emerge with his own snow shovel, glance about warily and work on his own pavement, depositing immense chunks of snow and ice on the doctor's newly cleaned frontage. It was virtually impossible to catch him at it. Once Eunice hid behind the blinds, hoping to see him in the actual commission of the crime, but some warlock's intuition told him he was being observed. Only after she gave up the spying game did he pursue his passion, working with amazing speed and even more surprising strength.

There was yet another facet of the Baumgarts' existence that intrigued her. They seemed to have an infinite capacity for avoiding the normal run of aggravation in a slum area. For example, a gang of hoodlums might slash tires, but the Baumgarts' Nash would remain untouched. On Halloween, their door alone would be unchalked, their gate alone unharmed. When dogs bayed at night and drunken husbands assaulted screaming wives, the Baumgart windows were never hurled open in protest: it was as if the night noises never reached their ears. Eunice could not explain it.

So barren were the relationships between the families that it was not until Seymour Baumgart, the youngest son, was in his second year in medical college that the Abelmans knew that he was preparing for a career as a doctor. Learning of this development, Eunice realized at once that his entrance into medical school had coincided with a stepped-up war of nerves. There had been the incident of the plumb line, when, after twenty years of living alongside one another, Mrs. Baumgart decided that Dr. Abelman's fence was encroaching on their yard. A plumb line was lowered from the roof by her spouse, and after lengthy debate they conceded sullenly that they were in error. But the argument, the dropping of the line, the recriminations, absorbed most of Dr. Abelman's afternoon and gave him a migraine.

One day in the spring of 1940, while shopping on the market block, Sarah was amazed to see one of the multifarious Baumgart cousins standing on the corner and distributing yellow handbills to the passing crowd. Diligently, he stuffed them into shopping bags, forced them on peddlers, showered them on storekeepers, tucked them into pockets and aprons. Sarah hesitantly accepted one—he did not recognize her, or if he did he chose to ignore her—and she read it hurriedly as she proceeded toward the first pushcart. Its message startled her.

ANNOUNCEMENT

GRAND OPENING: JUNE 5

OFFICE OF DR. SEYMOUR BAUMGART, M.D.

❅ ❅ ❅ ❅ ❅

ALL THE LATEST EQUIPMENT AT YOUR SERVICE!

❅ ❅ ❅ ❅ ❅

❅   X-RAY   ❅   BASAL METABOLISM   ❅   ELECTROCARDIOGRAPH   ❅

❅ ❅ ❅ ❅ ❅

Why Go to the Old Fashioned Doctors? The Young
Men Are Best!

SEYMOUR BAUMGART, M.D.
1555 *Haven Place*

Sarah blinked her eyes. Hastily, she purchased her eighteen oranges and dozen grapefruits and hurried home to show it to her husband. Sam studied the garish yellow flier with rising anger.

"Isn't this terrible, Sam!" Sarah said. "You should report them to the County Medical Association!"

"Ah, the hell with him. He doesn't bother me. It doesn't mean a thing."

"But he's sending these out to your patients."

"If some of my patients go to him, they'll deserve a guy like Baumgart."

She made an exasperated face. "What kind of logic is that? Must your patients all be paragons of morality? You can't bear to treat anyone unless they conform to your standards?"

"He won't get anywhere."

They were totally unequipped to cope with this new menace to their little world, with its limited security, its reasonably steady income from Sam's calls, the new business from the X-ray and the EKG. All dreams of glory and specialization had vanished from Sam's mind when Harry Hemitz, his idol, had been killed in a speedboat accident the previous summer. If Harry, so inviolate and so manifestly successful, could die suddenly, what was the sense in killing yourself for the extra buck, the extra hundred, the extra thousand? Harry Hemitz was getting a thousand dollars a throw for some of his cases, and was turning them away. Yet when his inboard cruiser smashed into the dock at Tupper Lake, Hemitz the great surgeon might as well have been an orderly in New Hill emptying bedpans.

Yet Harry's memory could not be put to rest. Sam talked about him incessantly, recalling his greatest cases, his omniscience, his perfection, his skill, and his colossal nerve.

"Harry showed 'em," he'd tell Sarah's weekly bridge companions. "He had all the answers. He was too smart for all of 'em."

For all of Harry's perfidy, he remained Sam's happiest recollection of the past. His old friends and associates were vanishing: each week he scanned the obituaries and read about someone he knew. A half-dozen of his Bellevue professors had passed on; his mother had died of a massive carcinoma a year ago; Sol Pomerantz had bled to death from an unknown gunman's bullets.

If Sam's past was being populated by the dead, his present was being dominated by Seymour Baumgart, M.D. Soon the shingle was up in front of the house next door, or, more properly, a glittering array of signs and advisory emblems. Seymour Baumgart had an immense gold and black sign bolted to the front gate; there was a huge illuminated box in one window, a smaller electric sign in the adjacent window, and a bronze plaque on the front door. The young physician's car bore innumerable badges and insignia, official and unofficial. There was a caduceus on the rear license plate, several stickers on the windshield, a large metal tag reading "M.D." on the front bumper. On the day on which Seymour Baumgart opened his office, his mother appeared in starched white uniform, nurse's cap, white shoes and stockings, to welcome the first patients. Catching a glimpse of her resolute figure, Sarah could only blink. Why in the world had that never occurred to them? Why hadn't she ever dressed as a nurse to aid Sam in the office? The question answered itself: *she was not a nurse.* This consideration had not deterred the Baumgarts, and for a moment Sarah felt a twinge of guilt for not having had the acumen to abet her husband as Seymour Baumgart's mother was now assisting him.

The network of relatives, the clannish, wide-ranging people who attended the nocturnal cabals next to Eunice's bedroom, now went to work. The dentist son, with an office in distant Jamaica, began to send patients to his young brother; the baker, located in Williamsburg, also delivered; all the other cousins and uncles and aunts joined in. Automobiles with license plates from virtually every section of New York City began parking in front of the new office. Sam Abelman observed them, tried to ignore the fantastic success of his new colleague, and muttered, "To hell with the *shtunk*. He won't get any of my old-timers."

He was wrong. The elder Baumgarts themselves undertook the task of appropriating Sam Abelman's patients. They were quite blunt about it. They simply stopped them on the street and warned them that Dr. Abelman would kill them sooner or later. The old woman specialized in grabbing unsuspecting passers-by by their coattails; the old man would hook an iron hand on the arm of some person he knew only slightly.

"Come by my boy, mister. He is a great doctor."

"What's the matter you went by Abelman?"

"He sleeps with the *schwartzer*."

"Abelman is an *anti-Semit*. He never goes by *schul*."

"You didn't know? Abelman killed Mr. Feigenlaub. He gave him the wrong medicine."

"The young doctors got all the new machines."

"My son the doctor was the smartest boy in college. How could Abelman know so much?"

So it went; two devoted old people working in precise shifts, sometimes on street corners, sometimes in front of Dr. Abelman's front gate, sometimes outside the neighborhood drugstores, where they knew patients would come after a visit to the doctor. And they reaped a rich harvest of the gullible, the frightened, the ignorant, ready to believe the worst about the stiff, moralizing old man who had thrown so many frauds out of his office, had delivered so many lost lectures, had told so many of them to kindly go to hell. They came to Seymour Baumgart and found him neat, cool, and aloof in a white coat, a model of professional competence who charged them twice as much, made no effort to become friends with them, and looked over their heads when he spoke. They appreciated his loftiness.

In a few years, Seymour married a tall woman who was rumored to have brought twenty-five thousand dollars into the kitty. The office was redone, his Ford was replaced by a Chrysler, a new flood of handbills appeared advertising new equipment, and the overflow from his waiting room spilled out on to his front stoop.

Inside 1553 Haven Place, Sam Abelman treated his "old-timers" and read Thoreau; he would admit to no one that Seymour Baumgart had stunned him, rendered him numb and devoid of his usual vocal outrage.

As it became apparent that they had won the victory they had sought for young Seymour, there was no relaxing of the Baumgarts' warfare against the Abelmans. A broken chair would appear in the cornfield; Diane would run yelping from some unseen missile; a rusted shovel head would appear under Dr. Abelman's car. In the street they still did not exchange greetings with the Abelmans, in the medical library and the hospitals, Seymour Baumgart, M.D., always managed to look the other way when Sam Abelman walked by.

Eunice could remember the final crushing blow: the news that Seymour had purchased the fabled mansion on Republic Street, a house of luxury beyond belief. It towered four stories, rooms set upon rooms, marbled floors and hand-worked mahogany balustrades. It had once belonged to a notorious abortionist, a slightly insane man who practiced his bloody trade with the aid of a loyal wife, a blond daughter of a clam-digger. The loving couple had gone to jail for their sins and the house had been up for sale for more than five years.

"That's some story," Sarah said bitterly. "In practice less than fifteen years and he's buying that place."

"Is that a dirty dig?" Sam asked. "Is that intended for me?"

"Not at all. Why are you so sensitive? You always think I'm referring to you when I mention him."

"That little punk. Charges one hundred dollars for a consultation! That's what he charged old lady Koff—you know—the ones on Saratoga Avenue. I used to treat them years ago until the daughter got fawncy ideas. How does he get away with it?"

"He just charges and gets it. He scares them, I guess."

"What good will it do him?"

Sarah shook her head. "Why knock it, Sam? He got the house. He's got the practice."

"Good riddance. I'll be glad when the *shtunk* moves."

And he wandered off to change into his overalls; Angelo Traficanti was coming over to help him dig up the dahlia tubers and store them for the winter.

"The awful thing," Eunice Platt said to Thrasher, "was that the Baumgarts had their whole campaign figured out from the start."

"How do you mean?" he asked.

"Well, if what they did to Pop had just been the result of plain rottenness, that they were just mean people, I might be able to excuse it. You know—it was in the genes, or they weren't loved when they were little. But it was all a concerted, planned campaign. They knew for many years their son was going to be a physician, and they decided from the day they moved next door to us that they would wear Pop down. Every time the old man—and I can see those flat, nasty eyes right now—pitched an old pot over the fence, he was scoring a point for his son."

Thrasher shook his head. "I find that hard to believe. That people would work so hard at it—"

"All I know is they never waged any warfare with their neighbors on the *other* side. They weren't exactly friendly with them; they didn't have any close friends. But there was never the business of the snow removal, or the plumb line, or the magnolia branches."

She pointed to a small magnolia bush at the rear of her garden. "You see that? That's a cutting from Pop's tree. I'm sometimes a little sorry I took it. Every time I look at it I remember that awful afternoon—those people denying the truth, denying the evidence, calling *us* liars. You'll think I'm being a silly PTA member, but that whole incident scarred my psyche, as they say."

Thrasher looked solemn. "I don't think so, Mrs. Platt. I think that in a way your father and yourself were lucky to have been exposed to it. So few of us ever have the issues drawn for us in total clarity. A man might live a lifetime and be unable to establish value judgments or the difference between right and wrong. You and your father saw the whole thing that afternoon."

She laughed lightly. "For me, maybe. Pop never needed any lessons in wrong and right."

In the driveway, they heard the Pontiac pulling in and coming to a stop, the elated squeals of the little girl as she ran to her father.

"I have to prepare dinner now, Mr. Thrasher. Will you join us?"

"No thank you. I have a lot of work between now and Sunday."

She escorted him to the front of the rambling, tree-shaded house, shaking her head at a final recollection of the story she had related to the agency man.

"All that rottenness, all that torture of my father," she said in a low, grim voice. "For what? Just so another man could succeed."

Thrasher was silent. All he could offer was a television program, but maybe it would be the best revenge of all—someone had to prove to the Baumgarts of the world that the Sam Abelmans were also rewarded.

XI

AGAIN, they stood around an illuminating box, this time at New Hill Hospital, studying a new set of X-rays of Herman Quincy's skull. Franz Karasik and Sam Abelman looked again at the shadows and lights that were supposed to tell them what process was at work in the boy's brain. Three floors above them, in a charity ward bed, Herman Quincy slept in drugged bliss. His shaved head was bound with thick white bandages. Two burr holes, each the size of a quarter, had been drilled in the parietal area of the cranium: two buttons of bone had been removed to permit the injection of air into the ventricles of the brain. Cerebrospinal fluid had spurted out as soon as the needle had been introduced, an indication that the pressure inside the brain was above normal. Immediately after there had been a second bad omen—the air had failed to bubble through to the opposite ventricle. Something was interfering with the circulation between the cavities within the skull.

While Herman still lay on the operating table, they had looked at the still-moist plates and Karasik had decided against immediate surgery. Now, studying the pictures for a second time, he wondered whether a craniotomy would have been in order. Some younger man, he was sure, would have proceeded to remove a flap of bone and attempt subtemporal decompression. It would be purely palliative, of course. But what else was left besides palliative measures? That old pessimist Sam, he had been right from the start: a massive invasive tumor of the cerebral hemispheres.

"Look at it. Look at it," Sam said. "What a monster." He almost seemed to be taking it as a personal affront.

"It's remarkable," Karasik said softly. "The entire ventricular system shoved to the opposite side. Can you imagine the size of that thing?"

"Tell me if I'm right. I read the professor's books also. All the dark stuff is where the air went in, right? And this crazy light patch here—that's our baby, whatever it is."

"It seems to me," Karasik added solemnly, "that the temporal horn has been pushed down. You know, Sam, it normally lies inferior to and lateral to the ventricle. But here—my God—that thing in there has shoved it away. Look at the body of the ventricle, all pushed up and over."

426

Sam Abelman scratched his head. He was all but proven correct in his grim diagnosis, but the victory gave him scant pleasure.

"You still think it best not to have operated?" he asked the neurologist.

"I could have, I could have. Maybe I'm getting old and cautious. You know, Sam, every now and then I wonder if I'm developing a kind of what's-the-use attitude. After I looked at the first set of films, I was tempted to. But when I got an idea of the size of it . . ."

"Yeah, yeah, I know, Franz." Dr. Abelman collapsed into one of New Hill's unkind oak chairs. "This place has gone to hell since Harry got killed," he said with angry irrelevance. "You'd think they'd get some chairs that didn't deform a man's can for life."

Karasik inserted a cigarette in his onyx holder. He puffed a fine white cloud toward the grinning negative on the electric box. Herman Quincy's skull, with its deadly shadows and patches of light, smiled at him through the lazy smoke.

"It's really amazing," he said, "how he has managed to keep going so long. Even the convulsions you described, the limited loss of motor function, the occasional stupor. He should be much further gone with what he's got."

"That little rat," Dr. Abelman said. "He chases chippies and takes narcotics, that's what keeps him going. If he were a student, or an intellectual, he'd be dead already."

"Oh, Sam, don't be ridiculous. You with your crazy moralizing."

Dr. Abelman folded his hard, square hands on the comfortable rise of his paunch. A couple of loud young residents breezed through the gray-walled room; they were discussing some new wonder drug, something that cured everything from schizophrenia to gout. His eyes following their lean figures as they strode by him, Dr. Abelman made a loud raspberry with his lips.

"So what do wo do for my patient, Franz?" he asked, almost plaintively.

Karasik spread his hands out. "Palliatives, palliatives. Let's try a little radiation, maybe a simple subtemporal decompression. You know what I mean, when I tell you I sometimes feel what's-the-use?"

Dr. Abelman nodded his agreement.

In T-shirt and shorts, Thrasher sat at his desk in the paneled den of his home, completing his script. He had left the office early, eager to finish the work. Only three days remained and he and Dexter Daw would have to start "blocking shots" for the program tomorrow.

He looked at the stack of onion skin he had accumulated, the pages scarred with corrections, rows of *x's*, penned and penciled additions and deletions. He prided himself on his neat, almost anal, editing. It had been his peculiar skill when he had ridden the night desk at the press association years back. He could redo a complicated, slovenly paragraph with new clauses, reworked punctuation, lengthy excisions, and make it completely readable. The teletype operators, that clannish and knowing breed of men in green eyeshades, used to call any piece of well-hacked yet legible copy a "Thrasher masterpiece."

Studying the irregular pile of papers—he had just placed a final sheet on the Colonial coffee table, complete with hand-hewn wormholes—he experienced a splendid sense of total achievement. The creative process, after all, was all that mattered. Whether you grew dahlias, or wrote copy for an ad to sell laxatives, or pounded out a half-hour television script, the trick was to engulf yourself in the creation of whatever your task was; to insist with yourself that it be as close to perfection as possible.

Outside, his son was playing catch with Johnny Scarpinato. Thrasher was tempted to join them. He was basking in a mist of euphoria; everything was turning out well; his show would be a resounding success; he had won all the preliminary skirmishes, and the last engagement would prove to be ridiculously easy. He was like the contestant on a quiz program who correctly answers all the buildup questions, each one a little harder than its predecessor, and now faces the ultimate query with utter confidence—he knows, from previous shows, that it is always a snap.

A snap. That's what *Americans, U.S.A.* would be. It could not miss. There were a few bugs to be ironed out, some of the details were a little unclear, but Daw and Andy Lord and the network's competent technical people would have plenty of time to resolve that. He got up from his desk and stretched out on the daybed, annoyed for the moment by the rough nubby fabric. He would ask Ann to change it. There were a lot of loose ends about the house he wanted to work on. With the first installment of *Americans, U.S.A.* out of the way, he would start giving them his attention. The patio wanted repaving; the tilework in the basement bathroom was cracking; the front lawn needed top dressing and reseeding. He resolved to do the work himself, knowing that his usual lassitude and revulsion for manual labor would defeat him. But at least he'd prepare a list and see to it that Ann hired people to do the work.

A taxicab stopped at the front of the house. He heard the door open and Ann calling a greeting to Woody Junior. Apparently she had returned early from her job at the literary magazine.

"You goofing off also?" she asked brightly.

She looked enchanting: all creamy tan and glowing blond in a white sheath, some kind of hard-finish material with a faint sheen. She wore the massive, blocky jewelry that looked so good on her firm arms and straight neck.

"Look." He pointed at the stack of typewritten sheets. "Finished, *Finito*. All done. Wrote the last deathless line five minutes ago." She sat down alongside him and the feel of her firm thigh under the stiff white fabric pleased him.

"How goes it with you and Dr. Vickery in the world of sustaining literature?"

She wrinkled her nose. "Pretty dull, if you must know. There are only four of us in the office, and the other three are usually discussing folk art."

He shook his head. "Poor Annie. You're too small town and too literal to fit in with that bunch. Folk art was never meant for folk. Why don't you quit?"

"Mind reader! I may stick it out for another week. Till we get the book out."

"The *book*! That's real publishing talk!" He stroked her leg. "Where you been all these weeks? Where have I been? Did you ever make that rash move with the good doctor?"

She puffed out her lips and looked at him slightly cross-eyed; she was just a little embarrassed, and it always helped her to play it for laughs.

"I chickened out, Woods. Kept thinking of those skinny hairy legs of his and that little pot under the tweed pants. You were right, husband dear, just like you usually are. What did you tell me? It was all anticipation, all the advance thinking about it. Half the time I guess people don't get the courage up—I was going to say screw up their courage—and when they do, it's a letdown."

"Thrasher's Law," he said solemnly, holding up a pedantic index finger. "The pleasure derived from an adulterous sex experience is in inverse ratio the amount of anticipatory excitement. Or something."

"How 'bout you? Won much at poker?"

He sat up quickly and hugged her. "You won't believe it, but I've given up all of that. New man. Reformed character. Blame it on Sam Abelman, or maybe the fact that I've been battling to survive."

She pointed to the manuscript. "I'd say you've survived and

prospered. Whitechapel must think you're number one boy after the way you got Gatling back into line."

"Yeah. Me and him are big dubs."

Thrasher shut his eyes. He thought of the agonizing tightrope he had walked in the past few weeks, amazed that he had come out so well. The crisis had been thrust upon him willy-nilly. After the Brick Higgins debacle, the collective accusative finger had been pointed at him. No one had planned it that way, neither Whitechapel nor Loomer nor anyone else. He was the croppy boy, the Inca's virgin of the sun, who had to be sacrificed. Miraculously he had talked his way out of it with *Americans, U.S.A.* At the time he had been half convinced that it was a good idea, a sound and valid principle. Now, he told himself, he believed it. There were Dr. Abelmans all over the country whose story had to be told, if only to balance the scale against the Baumgarts and the Hemitzes, the galoots and crap artists. There was a new surge abroad in what the doctorate boys called mass communications. A lot of jokes were made about upgrading people. But what really was so funny? Who was to say that the talkers did not have it in their power to improve human behavior?

"I never really did get the complete story on Gatling's switcheroo, dear," Ann said. "How'd you get Old Lumpy to change?"

He covered his eyes. "Let's say I ain't proud of what I did. I did it and that's that. He didn't deserve it, but my goal was a noble one. Ends and means and all that."

"You bet it was. I like this house and this income bracket and this husband."

"Thank you, doll. But I didn't mean it that way. Sure, I had to survive. But I also owed something to Samuel Abelman."

"What did you do that was so terrible?"

"I used the magic power of the word, the word manipulated and distorted to get that poor old chemist to give in. I told him every Jewish druggist in the nation would boycott him if he dumped my doctor. A lie, of course. And a terrible thing to accuse old Gatling of. I found out later the head of research at *G & T* is named Weinberger. Gatling had his own FEPC long before New York State thought of it."

She looked grave. "He'll be grateful to you some day," she said.

"Maybe. But the hell of it was, here I was using words, talk, fiction to put the screws to this pretty decent guy who knows his way around a retort. I shouldn't have such power. Suppose I was a real louse?"

"You couldn't be one, baby. And stop being so damn introspective. Have a great show. That's all that matters."

Thrasher sat up. He pulled his wife's head on to his lap and kissed her, a long and thoughtful kiss. Her strong arms locked around his neck, and they enjoyed each other's feel and smell—he redolent of male sweat and tobacco and she of some arch, lingering perfume.

"Woody, you smell," she whispered in his ear.

"Nay, madam. You smell. I stink. Samuel Johnson."

"Cut it out. *Stop.* Junior will be in here any minute and wonder if we're his parents. Hey, let go."

"You're great. The greatest. I like you. Stop working and be my wife. I'm through playing poker."

She broke away from him and moved to the foot of the daybed. "What's all this about?"

"Man regaining composure, confidence. I tell you, Ann, there's nothing like the creative process to make a man appreciate the simple, regular rhythms of life. Family, home, children, meals. You look much too good to be ignored. I won't apologize for having been a heel. Since I'm now a creative artist, you have to make allowances for that."

"Can I keep my job until we get the book out?" she asked.

"Sure. The book is very important. Then come home and be my mommy again."

He reached for her eagerly again, anxious to unruffle the hard white sheath of her dress, to jangle the immense jewelry, but she darted away, rising and leaving him with the promise of love and companionship and everything that was bright and fresh when they were first wed. He watched her departing figure, the straight back and the pleasurable roundness of hips, buttocks, and thighs and felt as if he were ogling a strange woman on Fifth Avenue.

"What a doll!" he called after her. "Don't I know you from somewhere?"

The window fan hummed much too noisily, Sarah thought. Sam had insisted on installing it himself, rather than let an electrician do it, and she was convinced he had hooked it up incorrectly. Tossing about, she heard him padding barefoot, in his pajamas, toward the bed and she mumbled her complaint.

"That fan is awful, Sam. Please turn it off."

"It's hot as hell. Let it go a while and cool us off." He sat down heavily, settling back on the mattress with a sigh and then a little grunt as the prone position touched off the arthritic snap in his spine.

"When we get into the new house, we'll get an air-conditioner," he said flatly. "Maybe I'll air-condition the office also."

"I don't want to hear a word about the house. It upsets me, and you know you're *not* really going through with it."

"Ah, be quiet. What do you know?"

She shifted about in the bed, fussing with the hairnet which she had placed over her new permanent. It was the evening before the television program. In the living room and below them in office, waiting room, and consultation room, coils of cables, lamps, tripods, and assorted heavy gear had been left that afternoon by the advance guard of network technicians.

"Did you look over that script Mr. Thrasher sent you?"

"Oh, I read it. He says I don't have to memorize all those lines. Mr. Lord asks questions and I answer them, and sometimes I can read the stuff off some kind of lantern with big letters on it. He showed it to me this morning."

"Sam, are you nervous?"

"Me? Nah. An actor, yet. Boris Thomashefsky. My *melamed* should see me now. Hey, I forgot to tell Rabbi Piltz. We could put him on the television and call it 'What's My Beard?' "

She sighed. "What a crazy world. You work and slave almost fifty years and no one knows you're alive. Then a strange man comes along and you'll be famous tomorrow. Maybe twenty million people will see you."

The fan clattered away; it seemed to grow louder as the night matured. Even the barking of the backyard dogs seemed deadened by its relentless *whirrrr*.

"I hope you do all right, Sam. Maybe when you changed your mind and didn't want to do it, it was because you really didn't want to do it all along. Are you sorry you changed your mind again?"

He turned his back to her and gathered the sheet up to his neck.

"No, of course not. I like this *shagitz* Thrasher, A very high-class young man. Why should I let him down? And Myron. He'll get a big job out of this, if he learns to keep his trap shut."

"He'll never learn it from you." She yawned prodigiously, and they murmured their good nights, only to hear the phone shatter the night stillness with its insistent scream.

"Ah, poop," the doctor said. He sat up slowly, grunting again, picked up the phone, switching on a bed lamp.

"Hello. Dr. Abelman speaking. Oh, hello, Franz."

Sarah looked at his hunched shoulders, the large, strong head with the gray hairs now rising in disarray from the scalp, the half light of the lamp smearing his face with harsh shadows and coarse lines. The frown she knew so well, the unhappy downturning of the lips that she had seen so many times was now apparent, and she knew that Karasik was conveying bad news. She could only guess, and her guess was that the colored boy had died or was dying. Sam would get no sleep if that were the case. He took death as a personal insult. In almost half a century of healing he had never gotten used to the idea of people dying.

"Yeh, Franz. Yeh. I see," he was saying. "Okay, let's see what happens. Right. Call me at once. Nah, don't be silly. I wasn't asleep. The house is filled with a lot of television crap. Who can sleep?"

He replaced the receiver, but kept the light on, remaining seated on the edge of the bed, shaking his head in disbelief.

"Is it the Quincy boy?" she asked. "Is he on his way out?"

"His way *out?*" Sam asked. "Yeah, *all* the way out! The little rat ran away from the hospital tonight!"

"But my God—as sick as he is!"

"A couple of his *tunkele* friends came to visit, and they sneaked him right the hell out, down the back stairs and through the service entrance. Whoever thought he had that much strength left? And with two holes in his skull the size of quarters! His whole damn head in bandages!"

"All right, all right, Sam, don't get so overwrought. Try to sleep. You have a very busy day ahead. Please, Sam."

He flicked off the light, and, falling back to the mattress, conscious now of the annoying rattle of the fan, he muttered his threnody.

"The bastards won't let you live."

Myron sat with Sandra Dorgenicht in the rearmost booth of a dark and dirty saloon on Third Avenue which had a minor reputation as "a newspaperman's hangout." The bar was inhabited by elderly Irishwomen in sneakers and baggy cloth coats, ambitious copy boys, and those curious residents of New York's East Fifties, eternally young middle-aged men whose lined, tanned faces never quite matched their cashmere sweaters, dirty white shoes, and oxford-gray flannel pants. Myron suspected they were interior decorators.

The doctor's nephew had a copy of Thrasher's mimeographed script in front of him, and was checking it against a list of the people he was responsible for. Thrasher had assigned him the job of keeping the dramatis personae in readiness for their entrances and exits. It was no mean job. There were eleven Traficantis alone, including two infants; Ed Dineen, Louis Gruber, Max Vogel, and all of the doctor's family. Myron had to figure out areas where they could be kept standing by, out of camera range. Sandra, seated beside him, and nursing a watered scotch-on-the-rocks, watched him work with new respect.

"What's so hard about the whole thing?" he asked. "I got it figured out. When this is over, I hit up Thrasher for a job. He'll deliver."

"You're very optimistic," she said. "You need training for advertising, Myron. This fellow I know at Cornell—he's been taking courses for *years.*"

Myron pushed the glasses back up the bridge of his nose.

"He's nuts, whoever he is. This whole racket is a game. I'm learnin' the rules."

"You'd better get a new pair of eyeglasses first."

He squeezed her hand, lowering it to her lap and sneaking a tweak of her thigh—edge of girdle, garter, and flesh—delighted that she did not recoil or reprimand him.

"I got that figured also. New eyeglasses, real thick black rims; crew haircut; nose bob; new dark suits. The works. I might even take diction lessons. *Hah!*"

"You're a nut, Myron."

"I used to be. Lookin' for a career as a big newspaperman. Cover Civic Association meetings and water supply hearings the rest of my life. Nah. If ya got brains ya get out. Like this guy Thrasher. What is he? A rube from South Dakota who wore the right clothes and met the right people."

"He seemed very charming. I liked his looks. Kind of a Gregory Peck. You know, boyish and serious."

"He's a phony," Myron said, with dripping contempt. "I can handle phonies. He'll get me a job."

Myron turned the pages in the thick script, making authoritative notations with a red pencil as he went along. He was very much aware of Sandra's admiring glances as he marked up the neat, double-spaced mimeographed sentences.

"Is Mr. Thrasher going to help your uncle buy the house?"

Earlier, Myron had bragged that, even without the giveaway ending to the program, his uncle would benefit financially from the television show—he, Myron, would see to it. Now, recalling his proposition some weeks ago to Thrasher—*get my uncle his house, and I'll deliver him*—he wondered whether he could swing it. Thrasher had no reason that he knew of to aid the old man now. Moreover, where would the money come from? Flushed with new

435

success, with the anticipation of Sandra's moist mouth and round breasts, he felt a stab of guilt. Everybody was getting what they wanted except Uncle Doc. He'd get his house on Republic Street, of course, but without outside help it might break him.

"I'll take care of Thrasher tomorrow," he said grimly.

The great silver and blue truck was parked alongside the doctor's house. It had arrived before eight in the morning and Haven Place had been all but deserted. Now, at a little after ten, an expanding mob was forming around its edges. Inside its aluminum hull the technicians started its massive electronic heart beating, tested its mechanical pulse, breathed life into its metallic lungs. From beneath the immense steel chassis, a series of black veins and arteries, of varying width and character, spread out toward the doctor's yellow brick house, snaked their way through the front gate, thence into the basement windows and cellar door, and from there radiated out to the various power boxes, cameras, earphones, and lights that were needed to perform the communications miracle. Atop the great truck's roof stood the dish, the receptacle which transmitted the micro-wave impulse to a tower erected on the Williamsburg Bank Building, some ten miles distant. From there the impulse was relayed to the Empire State Building, and then to the network itself, to be sent out across the length and breadth of the nation.

Around the electronic miracle of the age stood the products of the age, the people of Brownsville, mouths agape, eyes wide with contemptuous curiosity. They gathered with the same skeptical interest they had displayed the night Leueen Harrison, ravished and drubbed, had been deposited on the doctor's doorstep.

Four or five small Negro boys had already climbed on top of the truck. The crew chief, Ritola, a rarity among television people in that he was past fifty, had already discovered that friendly jokes, appeals, or the threat of force did not move Dr. Abelman's young friends.

Despairing, he called inside the control room to Dexter Daw.

"Hey, Dec, what do I do with them? They won't vamoose. I never seen kids like this before."

The director, earphones on head, eyes fixed on the four bright television screens on the panel, and the green oscillographs below them, had already heard the *pat-a-pat* of small feet over his head. He had met Dr. Abelman's dark neighbors before and he knew that moral suasion would not move them. The awful humiliation of the day they had commandeered his MG was fresh in his mind. He poked his fetal head from the truck door and handed Ritola a wad of bills.

"Here's two hundred, Rit," Daw whispered, "find some cops and get 'em lined up for all-day protection." Dexter had worked dozens of mobile units. He always carried a healthy advance from the network's liberal cashier to ease emergencies such as the present one. Ritola looked at the thick stack of legal tender.

"I could buy a whole precinct with this," he said admiringly.

Above them the little sneakered feet of the children beat a happy rhythm on the aluminum roof. Their loud, clear voices made it difficult for Daw to relay his instructions to the crew.

"We on deh telewision!"

"Yeah, man, Ah'm Superman! Look out foh Superman!"

"You ain' no superman—you sheeet!"

"Lady wid a baby! Comin' troo!"

Daw rested his protuberant forehead on the palm of his hand. "Good Christ," he murmured, "what a hole! Whatever made Thrasher go through with this?"

"Chin up, Dexter!" Thrasher called from the bottom step of the truck doorway. "I heard you, and I must say that isn't the old fighting Dexter Daw I know and love. Not the old gooser of vice-presidents' wives!"

Daw turned around sheepishly to find Thrasher laughing at him. The engineers, a breed apart from both the director and the agency executive, snickered appreciatively at the sally. They were the untouchable, unreachable knights of overtime and turn-around penalties and they delighted in the bandied insults of their superiors. This Thrasher, this agency fink, he didn't seem a bad Joe: wearing a faded plaid shirt and old navy chinos.

"Woodrow Wilson Thrasher, boy executive!" Daw called. "What's new, father? Are we with it?"

"Come out of the black hole and find out. What in God's name are you guys doing in there, growing mushrooms?" Thrasher understood that a limited amount of leveling with the technicians was mandatory; not enough to render them quite equals, but sufficient to establish his own earthy origins.

"Hey, Mr. Thrasher! You the boss here?" A rufous troglodyte at one of the sets of knobs was addressing him rudely.

"You mean who died and left me boss?"

They guffawed; the redhead grinned. "Yeah, that's the general idea. No kiddin', Mr. Thrasher, where do we eat here? I ain't seen a good restaurant for blocks. The contract says we gotta—"

"Steady, men," Thrasher said innocently. "I realize this isn't Paris, fellahs, but I promise you all a steak dinner on me tonight, after we wrap up. You name it—Pen and Pencil, Press Box."

"No kiddin', Mr. Thrasher?"

"On my honor as an agency fink."

They roared at his self-deprecating comment, and as he and Daw departed, they became involved in a heated discussion of seniority, back-up pay, turn-around, overtime, and the next contract negotiations which were not due until the following April.

Thrasher and his director pushed their way through the adhesive crowd, hopeful that police protection was on its way. They would surely need wooden barriers well before nine when the program was scheduled to go on. There was a determined stickiness in the air, a gummy heat that left a faint mist over everything and caused Thrasher to blink. Already his light cotton shirt was soaked through; under the merciless lights inside Dr. Abelman's narrow house the afternoon rehearsal would be unbearable.

Walking up the stoop of 1553 Haven Place, Thrasher saw two sets of eyes squinting at him from behind an opened slat in a venetian blind in the adjoining house. The Baumgarts were observing everything with baleful eye and he was happy to be their adversary, resolute in his desire to do his best for their ancient enemy, Sam Abelman. Across the street a Hillman convertible stopped at the curb; a Thunderbird and a jeep station wagon soon joined it.

"Here comes the rest of our gang," Daw said. "On the button."

"Five minutes late," Thrasher corrected him. "I called the meeting for eleven and by God that's when we meet." He winked at Daw, as if to say, *I can be tough when I want to.* Leadership was his again.

They gathered in the doctor's waiting room, where a dozen rented folding chairs had been set up. Ben Loomer, in flawless white linen suit, sat next to Thrasher; behind them Finucane and Chilson took discreetly subordinate posts. Alice Taggart was there, looking surprisingly fresh on four hours' sleep; Porter Simpson, the new commercial co-ordinator, who had brought the fiery red Thunderbird to the slum street, exhibited her rare frontage in a trim polkadot shirt. Both girls had stuck pencils behind their ears and had their shorthand books at the ready in their laps. Ritola wandered in, looking old and out of place. The noisy blast of a Jaguar announced the coming of Andrew Bain Lord. The great commentator pushed his way through the crowd, lifting his nose from the odors of heated garbage and dog turds. Kevin McBee, the gnomish ghost writer, followed a pace behind.

"We all set?" Thrasher asked when Lord was seated.

"Where's the doctor?" Loomer whispered. He had become remarkably subdued since Thrasher's victory over Lyman Gatling.

"I gave him the morning off to make calls, go to the medical library, do whatever he wants to do until we're ready for final rehearsal," Thrasher explained. "I just want to work with our own gang for the moment. The amateurs need special handling."

Myron ambled into the overcrowded room. He had a thick folder under his arm and he sported a pair of new black-rimmed glasses.

"What about the people, Woody?" the nephew called noisily.

"The people, yes," Thrasher said. "Carl Sandburg said that, Myron. We won't need them until two o'clock, for final run-through. Keep 'em out of our hair while Dec is blocking shots and finalizing the lash-up."

"Check." Myron was right in step.

"Now, to sum up quickly," Thrasher said. It was stifling in the room, even with both windows wide open and the front door held ajar by an antediluvian umbrella stand.

"Yesterday, Dec, Andy, and myself got a magnificent head start. We did two dry runs out here with Dr. Abelman. So, essentially, he knows the routine. Of course, a lot will depend on Andy and the floor managers to keep it moving. We've kept the routine simple and logical, so I don't look for any big goofs. Andy, there *will* be autocue on two cameras, but I'd prefer your using it only in a pinch. Don't expect the doctor to use it or any of the participants, for that matter. It's strictly a backstop for you."

Thrasher was standing now, warming to his subject. He was glib, confident, and supremely optimistic, just as he had been that morning at the office when he had dreamed up *Americans, U.S.A.* in a magnificent burst of enthusiasm extempore.

"Between now and twelve-thirty, let's wind up all engineering problems. We break for lunch then for one hour. Everyone back at one-thirty and we start full rehearsals at two. Break for dinner at six, preview the remote at Bellevue and all film at seven, go to test pattern at eight, final briefing at eight-thirty, and the show hits the road at nine pip emma. Everyone with me?"

They all nodded. Daw mumbled something about "no time for indoor sports," but nobody laughed. The heat and the pressure were mounting; Alice and Porter were looking messy and distraught already.

"Okay," Thrasher continued, "there are a few loose ends. Porter, will you please double-check the commercial films? I don't trust those seedy network editors. They may have slipped in some old stag reels by mistake. Dec, you or Alice make sure the PL to the Bellevue remote is working. On the montage of old newspaper headlines about the flu epidemic—you got 'em, Myron?—make sure they're not thrown too quickly. I want people to be able to read them. Floor managers, for goodness sake stay out of each other's way and work strictly with Andy. Don't give signals to our participants, especially Dr. Abelman. He's liable to start cussing you out."

He gazed about the room, realizing now how fully all of them were dependent on his leadership. They were about to undertake a shaky and uncertain venture; no one but Thrasher had faith inviolate in the program. True, they were all professionals, people wise in the techniques of the business. But the strangeness of the setting, the wild mob around the truck, the oppressive heat, the problem of dealing with nervous amateurs, disturbed the calmest of their number. Thrasher knew this, and he had to tread a fine line to buoy their spirits.

"One question," Loomer asked slowly. "Woody, how do you plan to—"

Thrasher spun about quickly. "Let me talk to you privately, Ben," he stage-whispered. "I think I know what's bothering you. Okay, gang, disband and go to work!"

He herded Loomer into the office, backing the executive vice-president against the X-ray. Finucane, dreadfully hung-over, and Ted Chilson, fresh and scrubbed, joined them.

"Look, Ben, I know you have some misgivings, but not in front of the kids. We're working with unknown quantities here, and I want to keep everyone at ease," Thrasher pleaded.

"Just what I wanted to bring up," Loomer said. "These darn people—not so much the doctor, but that Italian family, the Irish fellow, the others. How do you know they'll be able to become actors in a few hours?"

"Not actors, Ben. Real people. I want them to be just what they are."

"L-l-liable to be pretty d-d-damn dull!" Finucane exploded. "B'Jesus I wouldn't want to see my old man and old lady on the TV!"

Thrasher patted his forehead with a soaked handkerchief.

"Look, both of you. You've got to stick with me. I'm the only wheel in town. If they stutter or stammer or don't get their lines right, that's fine. They're *real people*."

Loomer chewed a huge knuckle. He was thinking about the impending reorganization of Whitechapel and the new board chairmanship. It was really unfair, Thrasher suddenly realized, to have his career at the mercy of eleven people named Traficanti.

"I don't know, Woody, I just don't know," he said grimly.

"I'm with Woody on that angle of naturalness," Ted Chilson chimed in. The pale-blue eyes were fixed on Thrasher; he had chosen what he assumed would be the winning team. "If television is to go anywhere, it's in that direction."

"Why didn't we do it with actors?" Loomer insisted. He sounded genuinely worried; the small-town drawl had been abandoned.

"Come on, Ben," Thrasher said peremptorily, "cut the disaster act. You're my boss on this deal, but if you start having the GI's in public, it'll infect the whole gang. Dexter Daw isn't noted for calm nerves, and I don't like the looks of that technical crew. We can blow the whole thing by acting like we're scared."

"J-J-Jesus, yes!" Finucane exploded. "And in this friggin' sweat-box!"

"All right," Loomer said softly. "But if this thing floppolas you're all going down with me."

In the store-front church directly across the street, the Wholy United Army of God had begun their service; the wild voices of the congregation, led by the powerful lungs of Mrs. Quincy, rose in morning worship.

> Go tell it on deh mountain
> Go tell it on deh mountain. . . .

"Do we have to put up with that too?" Loomer asked.

Thrasher turned away from him, throwing open the office door. If he stayed around Loomer any longer the runs would hit him also. He had to keep busy every minute to sustain his belief in the program.

Ted Chilson had been put in charge of food. A little before noon a caterer's truck showed up with white cake boxes filled with sandwiches, cake, and fruit; a coffee urn was set up alongside the mobile unit. There was a picnicky, roughing-it atmosphere about the whole operation that pleased Thrasher. By now a detachment of police, taken care of via Dexter Daw's largesse, had set up barriers around the great truck, and the network and agency people were enjoying a reasonable amount of privacy. Loomer's mounting nervousness had not been contagious. Daw and his engineers, Lord and his writer and the various assistants, all seemed in a holiday mood. Thrasher wanted to keep it that way.

Dr. Abelman, returning from a morning at New Hill and the medical library, insisted that Andrew Bain Lord be his guest at luncheon. Around a table laden with chicken salad, a half-dozen varieties of cheese, corn from the doctor's field, and a pitcher of iced tea, the doctor and his wife played host to the commentator, McBee, Thrasher, Loomer, and Finucane. The latter had started things off with resolute dullness by telling a long-winded and pointless story about a quaint little Jewish tailor he had known in Dorchester. It was meant, of course, as a friendly offering, but it only left the doctor with a puzzled look on his face.

"What a life, a tailor," the doctor said. "My father was one, and was he miserable. The world is full of lousy jobs. You fellahs—you television people, you're damned lucky."

Lord arched his magnificent tufted brows. "May I say, doctor, we don't realize how lucky we are."

The doctor looked at his idol with undiluted admiration. "I think *you* do, Mr. Lord. I like the way you admit it when you make a mistake on the air. Takes a big man to do that."

Kevin McBee, sweatless in flannel shirt and tweed jacket, sucked on his unlit pipe. Andrew Bain Lord's apologies, just like his mistakes, were carefully scripted, placed on a machine which magnified them out of camera range, and read aloud.

"Doctor," Lord said earnestly, "we are no different from you—or your neighbors—those people gawking at us in the street. We are frail, human, perhaps a little luckier in that we can *communicate*."

There was a single ear of the doctor's corn remaining; he offered it to Lord.

"Go ahead, Mr. Lord, you'll be doing all the work. I want you to have it. Better than any of the junk they sell in the supermarkets."

"You're very kind," Lord said. "But really—"

"Go on! Go on! I insist!"

Perspiration trickled freely down Lord's tanned cheeks, but he took the ear, buttered and salted it, and bit in. Opposite him, on the grasscloth wall, was an appalling rural landscape, an original by some unheralded realist who liked his yellows blinding and his greens feverish. Lord had an incipient ulcer, psychosomatic, his internist assured him, and the heat, the garish painting, and the superheated ear of corn were rendering him queasy.

"You feel relaxed, doctor?" Thrasher asked.

"Great. I can handle you young punks. I'm still in good shape."

"He was awake all night," Mrs. Abelman said primly. "Tossing and turning until I thought I'd go out of my mind."

"Ah, phooey," the doctor said. He speared a slice of tomato and popped it into his mouth. "Good tomatoes. From Traficanti."

"I'm sorry we ruined your sleep," Loomer said helpfully. He seemed distracted throughout the meal, his gaze and his mind wandering, reviewing all the sinister possibilities that could ruin the program.

"I'm fine!" Dr. Abelman shouted. "Pay no attention to her!"

Sarah leaned forward, speaking to Thrasher, who symbolized to her all the rich and powerful people at her table who had come to pay homage to her angry, frustrated husband.

"They simply won't let Sam alone. Not for a minute."

"The penalty that all physicians pay," Lord intoned.

"And that's God's truth," McBee added. "Hasn't changed since frontier days."

"But why Sam?" she pleaded. "At his age. . . ."

"Age! What's age got to do with it?" Dr. Abelman cried. "These galoots, these punks out there! What do they mean to me?"

"Says you," she persisted. "You're always reforming them. Why did you have to get so involved with that Quincy family? Why didn't you just turn him over to the clinic?"

"Because, goddammit, he's my patient!"

Thrasher had to halt the burgeoning argument. The doctor could not go into rehearsal upset, and his wife had no right to be baiting him just before they went before the cameras. He decided not to abandon the topic but to divert its direction.

"Is that the colored lad I met in Dr. Karasik's office?" he asked.

"Yeah. My buddy."

"What's new with him? Any hope you can save him?"

The doctor drained an entire glass of iced tea, reached in for the squeezed half of a lemon, and sucked at it, shaking his head in sour delight.

"The little rat ran away from the hospital yesterday. With two big holes in his skull where they performed a ventriculography. I don't give a damn what happens to him now. I'm through trying to help the ungrateful bastard."

Myron, accompanied by Max Vogel, rounded the corner and walked up to the table. Vogel placed a quart bottle of bourbon on the table, shook hands all around, and demanded his script.

"I can't memorize the formula for Epsom salts," he snarled, "so make it easy for me. Go ahead, have a drink."

Finucane eyed the amber liquid longingly and Loomer pronounced it off limits.

"Not right now, doctor," Loomer said slowly. "At nine-thirty, when we are celebrating our successful show, fine. But we're working people."

"I thought that's all you guys did, drink and screw. Oops . . . excuse me, Sarah!"

"Everybody's waitin' and ready," Myron said crisply. "I got eleven participating Traficantis and twenny who ain't in the script ready downstairs. It looks like the feast of San Gennaro on Mulberry Street. Whaddya say, Woody?"

Thrasher dabbed at his lips and got up. "Shall we do it, gents?"

"Doctor?" Lord asked warmly. "Will you come along with me?"

Thrasher had never been a fan of Andrew Bain Lord's but at that moment in their acquaintanceship he was prepared to offer him his heart, his wife, his money—anything that the commentator desired. They trooped out of the narrow living-dining room, stepping around thick cables, banks of lights, a camera.

"You did a job on Hitler once," Dr. Abelman was saying to Lord, "and boy, did you let that louse have it! I wanted to punch that galoot in the nose, but you really did a job on him! That rat!"

"You are very generous," Lord said modestly.

In the control room, two hours later, stationed behind Dexter Daw, Thrasher began to tremble. It had been a shambles, a disaster from start to finish, a disoriented and unraveling operation. Like a drunk falling downstairs, the rehearsal had always been headed in one direction, but had bumped and bruised itself, and scared numberless onlookers in its journey. Nothing had gone right. Lord, sweating furiously, had trouble reading the autocue, and as a result he kept asking the doctor wrong questions, or questions out of sequence. The narration of film—there were two filmed inserts, one on Ellis Island and one on the flu epidemic—had been worse than amateurish.

The lighting left much to be desired, and the cluttered narrow rooms of the old house restricted the mobility of the five interior cameras. But all these were minor considerations which could be corrected before airtime. The overwhelming defect of the program was the inability of the people, notably the doctor, to fall into the rhythms of the script. Thrasher had written suggested lines for them, in the hope that they would paraphrase the idea in their own language. He did not want them memorizing his script or reading it from the "idiot sheet"; nor did he want them to come before the cameras inarticulate and tongue-tied. He had hoped for a happy medium, something that could be achieved by talking it out with them. He had spent all of the previous day with Andrew Bain Lord and Dr. Abelman, discussing the manner in which the doctor was to answer questions, tell anecdotes, introduce the other people. Now, in rehearsal before the cameras, it sounded stilted, and what was worse, dull. All of the doctor's naturalness, his enthusiasms, his wild, colorful speech, his gestures, seemed to be missing. In the introduction to the Bellevue sequence, for example, he suddenly appeared indifferent. Yesterday, talking it over with Lord, he had made a wonderful little speech.

"Bellevue? That was a long time ago for me, Mr. Lord. I was a kid and I loved it. What men! What names! Real giants of medicine, LeFevre, Biggs, Brooks. I guess it was the most exciting thing that ever happened to me. Those old red brick buildings . . ."

From that, they were to cut to an actual live shot of the Carnegie Laboratories, its façade illuminated by a battery of floodlights. But the listless manner in which the doctor had spoken his prelude to the Bellevue sequence in the rehearsal set Thrasher to wondering whether the segment would have any life at all. It was a tour de force—a gimmick—that depended solely on the dramatic impact of the doctor's words, an old man recalling a happy time in his youth.

If the doctor's performance had been lackadaisical and halting, it glittered by comparison with that of the other participants. The various Traficantis, led by the gnomish barber (diNobili cigar clamped between aged lips), stammered and choked up when Andrew Lord spoke to them; Ed Dineen, the retired fireman, forgot the anecdote he was supposed to tell; Max Vogel's glib gutter speech, when cleaned up and edited, emerged singularly colorless. Of all the members of the cast, only Sarah, calm and clear of purpose, fulfilled the role Thrasher had envisioned for her.

Standing behind Daw, Loomer at his back, they perspired through two hours of missed cues and slovenly dialogue. Daw would call instructions to Lord and his floor managers, his thin voice growing hoarser and more frantic as the inept rehearsal stumbled along. At least a half-dozen times, he would leap from his hard swivel chair, run from the truck into the house, and try to assist the faltering actors. It was after five when he made the last of his flying junkets, and this time Thrasher and Loomer followed him. In the bit of business that had just finished, Dr. Abelman had forgotten the point of the sequence. He was supposed to take Lord to the wooden rear porch, and while the exterior camera, aided by two scoops, limned the garden, passing from dahlias to trees and shrubs to cornfield, he was supposed to philosophize about the beauties of nature, the solace that his patch of greenery afforded him. Lord had kept drawing him out, but the doctor would respond only with a curt "Yeah, I like it here," or "Gardening keeps me out of trouble."

The agency people and the director gathered around Lord and the doctor on the creaking porch, and Thrasher tried to explain his desires to the doctor. He was beginning to feel the tremor of fear in his gut, and he was amazed how calm he managed to seem in front of Loomer.

"I'd like you to talk a little more, doctor," Thrasher said easily. "Point out to the cornfield if you will. Describe the tassels, how relaxed you feel when you stand in it, like you did for me that day."

The doctor looked confused. He was sweating heavily and his face betrayed exhaustion. Even as he pleaded with him, Thrasher felt a stab of guilt.

"Woody, there's no monitor back here," Daw whined. "I'd rather the doctor took a cue from the floor manager—"

"To hell with the floor manager!" Thrasher snapped. "Listen to me!"

His womanish outburst brought looks of distress to Loomer, Daw, and Lord.

"Well, for Christ's sake," Daw said. "I don't have to—"

"Hold it, hold it," Loomer said shakily. "It's hot and it's late and we have real problems. Now the two of you cut it out."

"Yeah," the doctor said apologetically. "I'm sorry I'm not Boris Thomashefsky. Tell me what you want and I'll try to do it."

Thrasher dabbed at his forehead. "Fine, fine, doctor. Let's go into the garden sequence again. Don't try to remember everything, just be relaxed and natural. Dec, why don't we skip this bit for the time being? You can get a better idea of your shots when it's darker."

They trooped back through the house, and Thrasher noticed the doctor took the opportunity to sit down wearily in one of the kitchen chairs. Jannine poured him a tumbler of iced tea and he gulped it down. The consultation room and the office swarmed with Traficantis; the old barber called to Thrasher, and two of the sons (Joey? Dominic? Vinnie?) wanted to know when they'd be finished; one of the infants began to cry. They had been standing around since two o'clock, listening dumbly as instructions were hurled at them, responding haltingly as they were herded about like goats. Thrasher marveled at their patience and good humor. One of the older women, a Brownsville Circe in square black draperies, had commandeered a corner of the office and set up a buffet of peppers and olives, loaves of bread and plates of various barbarous sliced pressed meats.

Outside the truck he apologized to Daw. "Look, Dec. I think the heat is getting all of us. I think the best thing we can do is take a break. Then you and myself, let's take the people aside and talk it out with them. I'll work with the doctor. We can do more just discussing it with them than subjecting them to any more lights and cameras and signals. Okay?"

"You name it," Daw said happily. He was full of dexedrine, Thrasher knew. He had seen him popping orange pills into his mouth at noon.

"It's awful rough," Loomer said. "Those people need a lot of work. Why the hell did you depend on them so much, Woody? Why didn't you come out here two days earlier?"

Ignoring him, Thrasher followed Daw into the truck, taking his post behind him again, facing the bank of monitors.

"Let's try the last bit, Dec," Thrasher said. "Cue Andy Lord to start on the bottom of page fifty-six and clear the office."

The cameras transmitted legs, arms, and torsos of people scurrying out of range, clearing the lines of vision for the electronic eyes. A floor manager, a blond youth in an imported Italian Riviera striped shirt, was pushing a group of giggling Brooklyn Neapolitans in Gimbels' finery toward the office. In a minute or so Lord was in place, and Daw, relaying his orders via the youth in the striped shirt, called out, "Cue Lord."

The commentator was on the front stoop now, seated against the yellow brick façade, beneath the doctor's shingle.

"Thus, Samuel Abelman, M.D.," Lord said slowly. "And as office hours end this warm evening at 1553 Haven Place, we would like to peek again into that small room where so much misery has been eased, so many burdens lifted—the office of the general practitioner."

At that instant, Daw called for an interior camera. "Dissolve to two!" he snapped.

The image of Lord melted away, and on the screen came a picture of the interior of Dr. Abelman's office. He was bending over the examining table, listening with stethoscope to the heartbeat of a squealing baby. On the opposite side of the table, looking on intently, were Yolande Speciale, old man Traficanti's favorite daughter, and the barber himself.

"The third generation is now coming to 1553 Haven Place," Lord's voice continued. The baby's cries were brought in underneath the commentator's narration, a plaintive obbligato.

Slowly, the camera limning the group in the office began to draw back toward the opened double doors.

"Jesus, what a shot," Daw said breathlessly.

"Like a Dutch master," Loomer added.

"Quiet!" Thrasher cried. "Listen to Andy. . . ."

"Yes, forty-three years in one house, on one street, listening to the troubles of thousands of people—the poor, the humble, the ordinary people of this weary world of ours, people with hearts and heads and problems. A general practitioner must be more than physician.

He is counselor, priest, friend, lecturer, companion. All these roles Samuel Abelman has filled. And three generations of Traficantis, along with scores of others, will vouch for him."

The camera was now outside the office and the picture within the room was framed in a black border formed by the partially spread doors. There was no mistaking it; they had something. There was a perfection of composition, an honesty and warmth to the little group, that left the sophisticated and hardened people in the silver truck awed. The doctor was holding the infant up now; his creased face wrinkled with laughter as he spoke to the giggling child; the mother, dark and graceful, was tucking a diaper back into the rubber pants; the old barber was chattering away, unheard, and pinching the infant's fat thighs approvingly.

". . . Sam Abelman, M.D., Bellevue, 1912, one of our one hundred and sixty million *Americans, U.S.A.*"

Lord's voice reached a sonorous, uplifted climax. As he began his last sentence, Daw cued in a record, a few inspirational bars of instrumental music.

"And fade 'er out. Go to black," Daw said.

The screen darkened, obliterating the figures of the doctor and the Traficantis. They all remained silent for a few seconds. One of the knob-turners destroyed the mood.

"We knockin' it off now, Daw?"

"Okay, Woody?" Daw asked.

"Yes, yes. Let's break. You decide when you want the film previewed. Very good, Dec."

The engineers, freed from the control panel, began a four-way debate on overtime. The video man's arithmetic differed from that of the lighting engineer. They would be able to spend their dinner hour checking their sums.

Daw spun around to face his producer and his executive producer. "How'd it look?" the director asked hesitantly.

"That last bit," Thrasher said. "The greatest. The end. God, if we can only sustain that mood, that soft, sincere atmosphere, throughout."

"I have to admit it," Loomer drawled. "It got me. A helluva picture. And Lord gave it everything. Gave me the shivers—that kid crying, the old Italian gent and the mother. Like a darn painting in a museum or something." He was drawling again.

"That lighting man is a friggin' genius," Daw said. He announced it loudly enough so that the engineers, assembled outside the truck, could hear him. They had been growing mutinous in the last half hour.

Thrasher took Daw's arm. "Listen to me. You, too, Ben," he said intensely. "We've got a winner. I know it. That ending. It'll hit everyone who sees it the same way it affected us. Now, Dec, let's get going. I'm taking the doctor in the yard for a seance. Just the two of us. You grab a script and get hold of Myron, who knows these people, and work on them. *Work on them, dammit!*"

"Anything I can do to help?" Loomer asked. He sounded happier about the project. Somewhere in the magic picture they had just seen on the monitor, he saw a chairmanship of the board.

"You can, Ben," Thrasher said. "Get hold of the press outside. There's a skinny broad from *Life,* and reporters from the metropolitan dailies."

"I'll handle them," Ben said happily.

They left the truck again, shock troops deploying for the final assault, all of them buoyed by the striking climax to the program that had turned out so well in rehearsal.

Under the cherry tree, Thrasher, script in hand, sat on the wicked slatted bench, talking to the doctor. The old man appeared relaxed in one of his jerry-built, home-repaired chairs. Diane licked his hand and chased fireflies with idiotic abandon in the fading summer light.

"We can just take it easy now," the agency man said. "I really think we've covered enough ground." He had been reviewing the program, scene by scene, asking the doctor, over and over again, to rephrase his comments, his responses to Lord's queries. Away from the curious cameras, the blinding lights, and the hand signals of the young men wearing earphones, he fared much better. Thrasher had the feeling, too, that there was a little ham in the old man. He was underplaying his role in rehearsal, saving his best manner, his choicest anecdotes for the show itself. The busy chatter of the technicians drifted out to them.

"Get that flood moved over, Sal."

"We need another ten feet of cable. Check Ritola."

"Hey, Morris! Where does Daw want autocue?"

The doctor pushed Diane away. "What a mess!" he said. "All that fuss! For what? To sell soap? So people can know who I am? I looked at the inside of that truck before—those knobs and wires and switches. It almost gave me a migraine. What a complicated world! What would Thoreau say? You know his idea. Simplify, simplify."

Thrasher smiled, made a notation on his script, and looked up.

"I've just gotten a wonderful idea, doctor! Have you ever been to Walden Pond?"

"Nah. Every time I decide to make the trip, something comes up. Sarah hates the mountains and doesn't like to ride in the car for any distance. We always end up in Long Beach."

"I want to go to Walden with you. I tell you what. Let me get through the next show, and then the weekend after we'll drive up to Concord together. It's lovely there this time of year. We'll walk around the pond, and visit the historical society, and you can see Thoreau's old bed and chair and the pencils he made—"

The doctor leaped from the chair, almost upsetting it. Diane took it as a signal for play and draped two huge paws on his midriff.

"It's a deal! Let's go! Just the two of us! No women! Sarah wouldn't like it anyway. Your wife won't mind?"

"No, of course not. We'll take my car. I know the way."

"That's the best offer I've had in years. Thoreau had the right idea. Everything else is crap. Say, have you been there?"

Thrasher told him he had. He did not tell him that a public beach, complete with lockers, refreshment stand, diving boards, and loud teen-agers, existed at one end of Walden Pond. There was no marker, no plaque, not even a wooden sign to tell the literary tourist where the cabin had been situated. He seemed to recall something about a campaign to raise funds for a bronze tablet.

"We'll take a nice leisurely trip," Thrasher said.

"Boy, you've made me feel great. I'll give you a performance like Thomashefsky, all right." He walked up and down the path, slapping his thigh in delight. Turning around swiftly, he saw old man Baumgart squinting at him through the fence.

"Dat truck has got to move," Baumgart muttered. "It's blocking the front of my house."

"Ah, go chase yourself," the doctor said.

"Vot's deh metter you became a big television actor, Abelman?"

Abelman turned around. "It kills the old louse that I'm going to be on a television program. For thirty-five years he's been tormenting me. He can't even let me alone now."

Baumgart moved toward him. "I told you, Abelman. You, you television fellah. Dot truck should be moved. It's illegal."

Thrasher got up wearily. "Mr. Baumgart, it's perfectly legal. We have police permission to park there. I'm sorry if we're inconveniencing you."

"What the hell does *he* know about Thoreau?" Dr. Abelman asked Thrasher.

Daw, Alice Taggart, and Myron joined them under the cherry tree.

"Lord and McBee just gave me hell," Daw whispered. He had been getting hoarser and hoarser as the long, humid afternoon dragged along, and now he was reduced to a painful croak.

"What are they mad about?" Thrasher asked. Thus far Andrew Bain Lord had been a model of co-operation. His performance had been admirable, his handling of the doctor magnificent. Thrasher was feeling a new respect for the commentator; the man he had once called the Potemkin Village of American Journalism was, after all, a professional, a performer, a man you could depend on. He was a little annoyed with himself for having spoken so disparagingly of Lord a few weeks back.

"He says he can't read autocue," Daw croaked.

Autocue was the magnified script—"the idiot sheet"—which rolled beneath the camera and enabled Lord to read his lines.

"Oh no," Thrasher moaned. "And it cost us an extra five hundred bucks to lug that gear out here. Isn't he familiar enough with it so he can just glance at it now and then?"

"Nope. He feels he isn't getting enough attention from the brass."

A wave of exhaustion inundated Thrasher. The momentary relaxation of tension with the doctor—the happy agreement on the pilgrimage to Walden—was gone.

"I have a suggestion," Alice Taggart said. She looked surprisingly neat and fresh, although she had been in the control room as long as any of them. There was a healthy Westhampton Beach tan on her face and arms, and she had just redone her nicely angled face.

"Not that, Alice," Daw said. "Not with Andy Lord."

"Be quiet, Dec," Thrasher said. "What is it, dear?"

"Well, I can letter very well. If I could get some large white cardboard, maybe three by four feet, I could letter most of Andy's cues, and any stuff he was unsure of. I couldn't do his whole script, but at least he'd have some kind of backstop."

Thrasher looked at his watch. "It's six-thirty. You have two hours to dig that stuff up and get it lettered. What do you think, Dec?"

"Worth a try. Where do you find an art supply store open on a Sunday?"

Myron poked his antelope's nose into their agitated midst. "You might find one of them stationery and art stores, kind of, open on Pitkin Avenue. A lot of 'em stay open Sundays. But you better hurry."

"Myron, why don't you go with Alice? You and she should be very happy together," Thrasher appealed to his assistant.

"I'm in the middle of Traficantis," Myron whined. "I got 'em goin' good, Woody, and, Jeez, I'd hate to dump 'em now. Look, Alice, it's easy to find. I'll show you how to get there. C'mon."

They left for the house. It was cooling off slightly and with the easing of the heat, an excited confidence was growing in the television party. Thrasher sensed it in the way they had overcome the crisis of Lord's autocue, in Myron's progress with the Traficantis, in his own success in relaxing the doctor.

Dr. Abelman was wandering through the cornfield. "Last of the season," he muttered. Then, to Diane's slavering leaps against the wire fence, he added, "Bums outside."

Alice Taggart lowered the top of the Hillman convertible, and inched the small auto through the mob. There must have been a thousand people outside the wooden barriers. A dozen patrolmen, beneficiaries of Dexter Daw's expense account, struggled manfully to control them. Alice was a small-town girl; her conception of New York was the East Fifties and Westhampton Beach—protected little apartments in tall buildings guarded by uniformed doormen, and pine-paneled cottages with Thunderbirds in the driveway. The savage, surging mass of people—at least half of them black —filled her with a fleeting terror. The worst of it was they didn't come to gawk as fans, like the people at movie openings. Rather they seemed possessed of a skeptical hatred for the giant truck and the people who controlled it. From inside the Wholy United Army of God she heard the hymn singers and took heart: Alice came from a hardshell Baptist family, and the reminder of her devout parents in Ontario, California, heartened her.

With its canvas top down, the British automobile had the look of a rich child's toy, misplaced in the littered slum. As Alice motored through the streets, she became uncomfortably aware of the leers and whistles of street-corner loafers. She ignored them haughtily, trying to remember Myron's instructions. The neighborhood appeared to grow shabbier and shabbier and now she was on a block of peeling frame houses. The residents were uniformly black; little children raced madly about parked Oldsmobiles and Buicks and adults assessed her with hostile eyes.

She was driving on a street that appeared to have been destroyed by saturation bombing; the leveled-off rubble was the start of a public housing project. On the opposite side were a few closed stores, an auto repair shop, also locked, and a high, weather-darkened plank fence enclosing a junkyard. Where the sidewalk had been chipped away, the junkyard doors were partially ajar. She wondered why the establishment was open on a Sunday.

A young Negro, excessively muscular and quite black, was lounging against one opened gate of the yard. He wore a pink T-shirt and an absurd red cap. Alice, looking for someone to instruct her to Pitkin Avenue, braked the Hillman. As she did, he stared at her languidly and then tilted a pint bottle of red wine to his lips and drank deeply. Beyond him, she could see the rusted remains of dozens of automobiles, piles of ancient furniture, skeletal mattresses and bedsprings, and a family of abandoned iceboxes. Amid the ruins was a shack constructed of rusted corrugated sheets and packing cases.

"Which way is Pitkin Avenue?" she asked, smiling.

"Whuh?"

He walked toward her slowly, draining the bottle and then hurling it viciously against the old board fence. It shattered noisily and he grinned. Taggart had a sudden urge to drive off, to continue her search without benefit of his dark knowledge. Then she realized how ridiculous were her fears. It was as yet daylight; she was in the middle of a populated and policed city; all she had to do was scream.

"I'm looking for Pitkin Avenue. Am I going the right way?"

She had kept the car in gear, clutch and brake pressed to the floorboard, and now, as he walked toward her exuding a fruity, corrupted odor, she nervously lifted one slippered foot from the clutch. The convertible jerked forward, spluttered, and stalled.

"Oh, dear," Alice said. She slammed the shift into neutral and started the engine again.

"Wheah you wan' go?" he asked. He was leaning quite close to her and she could see his eyes were misty. Somewhere she had read something about a drink called "Sneaky Pete"—cheap wine and gin.

"Pitkin Avenue. Am I headed the right way?"

"Yo' way off. Ah jes' move heah. But mah fren's knows. Hey, Josh! Lee Roy! Come on heah! Dis lady wan' some hep!"

The door of the packing-crate shack swung open. Two other youths emerged. One was squat, blockish, the color of coal; the other was thin and beige-hued. He carried a half-full quart of red wine in one arm, and walked in a curious, wobbling gate. A thick swath of white bandages peeked from beneath a ridiculous checked cap; it wound over his ears and circled back of his skull. Evidently, he had recently been invalided, a circumstance he tried to negate with an arrogant, self-assured air that was not lost on Taggart.

The three of them ringed her now; winey vapors smothered her and she could see that all of them were faintly stuporous.

"Dis lady wan' go Pitkin Avenue."

"Ah neveh heerd of it," the squat black boy muttered.

The youth with the bandaged skull said nothing. His luminous eyes, half closed, studied her dully from beneath the tiny brim of the cap.

"Well, really, thank you very much," Alice said. "I'll ask some-one else. Thank you for trying to help me."

The tall youth placed two immense ebony hands on the door. "Whuffo yo' runnin' away? We ain' gon' do you no harm!"

Nobody Home was intrigued by her looks, her smell, the funny little automobile with its red leather seats.

"Look at dis chick!" Nobody Home cried.

"Please get off the car," Alice said. "I must go." She put the Hillman into first and as she came up on the clutch, the Negro boy yanked the door open. She ought to have screamed, she realized, but it all seemed so improbable. It was broad daylight! There were people in the block just beyond her, and in the street ahead, she could see a stickball game in progress. You could not be kid-naped and raped at six-thirty in the evening of a summer's day. A massive hand was clamped around her mouth. Someone else had grabbed her ankles and she was being carried, like a sack of cabbages, through the junkyard doors toward the shack. She saw the pale-tan boy, the one they called Josh, jump into her car and pull it to the curb; the offense against her beloved automobile angered her as much as the terrifying prospect of sexual assault. She managed to bite the pink palm around her mouth and unloose one loud, reverberating scream before they dragged her inside the corrugated rusting walls.

Louis Kaplan was an expert in short cuts. He knew every vacant lot in Brownsville and East New York, and he prided himself on being able to travel, on foot, from the precinct house to his home in just five minutes more than it took to drive the distance in his Ford. His tour had ended at four, but he was a remarkably con-scientious young man. He had stayed on at the station house an extra few hours to prepare a special report on his folk-dancing group. The reports would go to the lieutenant who would read them aloud to the other cops when Kaplan was not around and everyone would have a good laugh.

In civilian clothes now—knitted gray sport shirt and cheap navy slacks, he managed to look even less like a cop than when he was in uniform. Blue-bearded, round-faced, a bald spot the size of a silver dollar nestling amid his black curling hair, he looked more like a shipping clerk as he hurried across the weed-choked lots. He carried his police .38 wrapped in a brown paper bag. In the summer, he always carried his gun in this manner. It embarrassed him to have it bulging out of a hip pocket.

He was about thirty feet from Friedman's junkyard when he heard the scream. Wild yells and shrieks were of course part of the daily routine in this ragged edge of the neighborhood. A good many cops would have ignored it and hurried on; but there was in Patrolman Kaplan the dull determination of the graduate student. The scream, evidently a woman's, had come from inside the six-foot fence surrounding Friedman's cluttered acre. There was no entrance at the rear of the yard, and to run around the block to the front might involve a disastrous delay. Kaplan removed the revolver from its paper bag, jamming the gun into a rear pants pocket. Then, with the speed and sureness of a schoolyard athlete, he took a running start for the fence, anchored his hands on its rough top, and lifted himself over, landing with a noisy crash on the remains of a Singer sewing machine.

Through the partly opened doors of the yard he could see a small foreign car parked at the curb. It was a disturbingly incongruous note, and as he walked toward it he heard sounds of scuffling, and the thick whispers of conspiracy. They emanated from the sloping shack where Junkie Friedman kept a cot and some of his more prized items of merchandise. Kaplan took the gun from his pants pocket and cocked it. He walked to the shack, stepping gingerly over an old radiator, a cracked toilet bowl, a rusted kerosene stove. Stealthily, he leaned against the shack door. Now, unmistakenly, he heard voices.

"Come on, come on, man. Git it off."

"Git her haid down! Damn it, doan let her holler 'gain!"

"Y'all go first. Ah hold her."

"Man, you sure you ain' takin' a chance? De law doan 'low dis."

"Ah, sheeet."

Perhaps Kaplan imagined it, but he also seemed to hear a kind of muffled gasping. Gun drawn, he pulled at the latch and the ancient patched door, creaking on rusty hinges, flew open.

"What's going on here?" he asked. "Who've you got in here?"

He needed no response to tell him. The postures and attitudes of the residents of Friendman's shack were sufficient. A white girl, struggling and writhing, was being held down by two youths; a third was standing over her. There were two empty wine bottles on the floor. He knew them at once as his old friends, the Twentieth Century Gents, and he knew Herman Quincy by the white bandages coiled about his head. Kaplan kicked the door back so that it was fully open.

"Get out here!" he said. "Get against the fence and face it. Go on!"

Herman Quincy looked at the patrolman with stuporous, contemptuous eyes. "She ast for it. She stop us on deh street and ast for it."

"Yeah. We ain' done nothin'," Lee Roy added.

"Move!" Kaplan said. "Lean against the fence, with your backs to me!"

They trooped by him sullenly. Who was he to intrude on the mighty deeds of the Twentieth Century Gents? He kept the revolver pointed at the three backs, and peered inside the shack. A young woman was sitting up on the cot, a very high-class young woman, he could see. She had her hair cut short the way the girls in the ads in the Sunday *Times* magazine wore their hair, and she was tanned. She was rearranging her skirt and sobbing softly, little gasping noises that made her thin shoulders and small breasts start and jerk.

"Are you all right, miss?" he asked. "Did they—"

"No. They were just about to. They tried. You—" She began to tremble and covered her face.

"Miss, you got to help me. I need someone to call the station house for the wagon. I'm an off-duty New York City patrolman, miss, and there's nobody with me. Can you make a phone call for me?"

"She a liar!" Herman Quincy called over his shoulder. "She ast us! You know dem fancy white gals! Dey wants it! She stop dat ole car and ask Nobody Home to hep her out. Din' she, man?"

"Sho she do," Nobody Home protested. "Ain't you Officer Kaplan? You mah fren', man! You Herman's buddy! We ain' done nothin' bad!"

Lee Roy joined in. "We play baseball, gotta team our own. Man, we jes' kids!"

"Ah, shut up," Lou Kaplan said. "I'm going to take you all in."

Alice had stopped crying. Aside from a little rough handling, she had not been harmed and now she came to the policeman's side, patting her eyes with a handkerchief.

"My God! It was a nightmare. To think that these things can still happen. In daylight, right in the middle of New York!"

"You're going to have to file a complaint, lady. This is a felony," Kaplan said solemnly. "Can you remember this? Haddingway, that's HA, 3, 0, 7, 8, 9. That's the station house. Ask for Sergeant Felice and tell them what happened. My name is Patrolman Kaplan and we're at Friedman's junkyard. They'll come right down for us. Okay? Can you do it?"

She said she would be able to. Kaplan watched her climb into the little automobile. A very high-class young lady in every way. What was she doing in the middle of Brownsville?

"All right now. Who wants to tell me exactly what happened?" Kaplan called.

"She done ast—" Lee Roy began.

"Shet up," Herman interrupted. "Dey gon' ast you plenty inside deh station house. He ain' got no right ast us questions now. He jes' makin' deh arrest."

"You couldn't stay out of trouble could you, Herman?" the policeman asked. "It wasn't bad enough running away from the hospital with your head all bandaged like that, and you being sick. But you had to get into this trouble now. How much Sneaky Pete did you drink? Boy, Dr. Abelman was right about you all the time."

"Man," Herman asked, "yo' got a butt? Ah recalls you deh best man fo' free butts next t'deh detach' worker."

The other two youths giggled.

"You'll find out how funny it is," Kaplan said ruefully. For the moment they seemed to be in command; giggling and mocking him, forcing him into defensive statements. They were still leaning against the fence, heads resting on crossed forearms, their legs several feet back from the wall. Sneaking a glance over his shoulder, Herman Quincy caught a glimpse of the sweating face of his captor. There was nothing really menacing in Lou Kaplan's attitude or his voice. The gun in his right hand could have been a toy. He had made a fool of this square cop before and he was prepared to do it again. Herman straightened up and stretched his skinny arms.

"Oh, man, dis fo' deh birds!" He turned around to face the officer.

"Herman, get against the wall." Kaplan sounded more unhappy than angry.

"Nah, man, das uncomfortable. I ah invalid. Yo' all gotta treat me gentle."

"You didn't treat that girl very gently," Kaplan said.

"Ah, sheeet, she ast fo' it."

"Turn around and face the wall, Herman."

"Nah."

"Go ahead, Herman, I'm not kidding. I was once your friend and all that, but you're a criminal now as far as I am concerned and you have to obey me."

Herman shook his head in disbelief. In a million years that square would never pull the trigger on him. He was Josh the Dill, who laughed at cops, especially this bald man with the nervous wet face.

"Man you know whut Ah'm gon' do?" Herman asked. "Ah gon' walk right out dis place and yo' ain' gon' do nothin'. Das 'cause you chicken."

He turned toward the gate, and with his odd, wobbling shuffle began walking toward the street. His sharp tan shoes scuffed at the impacted dirt of the yard; the bandaged head bobbed slightly with each step.

"Hey, man, come on back!" Lee Roy called. The pleasant alcoholic dream was evaporating. Lee Roy was feeling sick and a little frightened.

"Josh, dat ole cop gon' get mad!" Nobody Home cried.

Herman stopped briefly and addressed all of them. "Ah, sheeet, he jes' talk a lot. Him an' his minor'ties. He ain' gon' shoot me. He love me, das what."

"Come back here, Herman," Lou Kaplan shouted. "I don't want to hurt you. You're sick and it would be wrong for me to harm you."

He thought of running for Herman and knocking him down. It was evident that the boy had only limited powers of locomotion and that he was terribly weakened. But Kaplan was fearful that if he did so, the other two, healthy young animals, even half drunk, would vault the fence and escape him. He cried out once more.

"Herman! I'm not kidding! Get back here!"

The wobbling figure did not even turn around.

Lou Kaplan felt the sweat trickling rapidly down his armpits, his neck, his temples. He had never used his gun on anyone. Blinking, wiping his sweat-flooded eyes, he raised the .38 and pointed it at Herman's shuffling figure. He squeezed off the shot, as he had been taught at the academy, knowing that the noise would frighten him and that the force of the bullet would surely slam the sick, frail youth into the junkyard dirt.

Max Vogel's quart of bourbon had found its way to Angelo
Traficanti, and the physician, delighted in finding a drinking partner
in the midst of the businesslike sobriety of the television people,
had encouraged the barber. The two of them, rosy with alcohol,
joined Thrasher, Daw, and the technicians in the garden.

"Look at all these high-priced guys!" Vogel snapped. "Hey,
Angelo, how'd you like a job in television?"

"Shue. What I do?"

"Just learn to talk nice. Talk fast. Get ideas. Like Mr. Thrasher
over there. Ask him what he does." Vogel's face was the color of
uncooked roast beef. Liquor made him loquacious and bellicose.

"Hokay. Whadda you do, mister? Hah?"

Thrasher laughed and Daw smiled. Pleased by the friendly reception, the little barber pursued the rest of them. He punctuated
each challenge with puffs of malodorous smoke from his black
cigar.

"Whadda you do, hah? You fellah, whadda you do? How you
make a living, hah? I cut hair. He doctor. How you earn a-groceries
an' a-rent, hah? Whatsa big secret?"

"They feed the public crap," Max Vogel belched. He leaned
against the magnolia tree and loosened his collar. Thrasher was
glad that his role was only a small one in the program, a little
contribution worked into the influenza epidemic sequence.

Dr. Abelman, bearing a pitcher of iced tea, came down the
brick path. "Hey, Maxie, stop bothering the people," he said
severely. "Who told you to start drinking?"

"Ah, go stick your head in the hypo. Ambulant proctology, that's
your life story." There was a surprising lack of humor in his tone.
"Big television star. Can't even buy a house. You going to move
to Republic Street and be fancy, hey, Sammy? And go broke your
first year!"

Dr. Abelman gave the tray to the audio man and shook an ad-
monitory finger at Vogel. "I can still knock you on your fat ass,
Max! So please stop acting like a *nudnik*. You, too, Angelo."

"Shue, shue. We just make-a joke. No hard feel."

Thrasher got the attention of the crew again and they continued
their final rundown. Now that the hour was approaching, all of
them—from Loomer, the executive producer, who was entertaining
the girl from *Life*, to the lowliest of the grips—sensed a pleasurable
excitement, a confidence growing out of their special skills and
the feeling, as Thrasher had put it in the truck, that they had "a
winner."

Dr. Abelman was peering curiously over Daw's shoulder, study-

ing the director's notations, thinking of his own vanished expert-
ness as a note-taker, when he heard his wife calling him. Sarah
was standing on the porch.

"Sam, telephone."

"Tell 'em I'll call back. To hell with 'em."

"You'd better come to the phone, Sam. It's the police. They found
Herman Quincy. They also want to talk to someone from the program. Maybe you'd better come, Mr. Thrasher."

The agency man and the doctor exchanged puzzled glances. In
the consultation room, the doctor took the phone from his wife and
heard Lou Kaplan's voice.

"The louse," Thrasher heard him say, "the little rat. Yeh. Yeh.
I'll be over. Well, he needs medical treatment anyway. You'll
have to get him back to New Hill. Okay. All right. This is Mr.
Thrasher. The little girl worked for him."

Thrasher took the telephone. Under the harsh office light, he
turned a sickly white as the events of the previous half hour were
related to him by the young cop. It all had an air of complete
fiction, he thought, a half-hour television drama. His people had
no right to be involved with these shameful, atrocious incidents.
He nodded, told the policeman he would come to the station house
immediately, and hung up.

"Isn't that awful?" he asked the doctor. "What are these people
anyway? Isn't anyone safe?"

"What do you think I've been living with all these years? Now
you know why I have to get out. Just have to get out, that's all."
He pointed an accusing finger at his wife. "I hope you heard it,
too. Now you won't scream so much about the new house. Come
on, Woody, let's go."

Thrasher looked at his watch. There were less than two hours to
airtime. They would have to wind up their business at the station
house quickly. Moreover, the disaster that had befallen Alice Taggart would have to be kept from panicking the crew. And there
was the immediate problem of filling her job.

The doctor picked up his black calfskin bag, and with urgent,
jerky steps walked through the equipment-cluttered office, through
the waiting room, and out to his car. Thrasher, on his heels, paused
in the waiting room to take Loomer aside. The executive was holding court with the lady from *Life* and four other reporters.

"Ben, can I see you a minute?" Thrasher asked.

Loomer excused himself and they found a corner of the room
where they could huddle.

"Now stay calm when I tell you this and don't act like the world is coming to an end," Thrasher began. "Alice Taggart was the victim of an attempted rape a little while ago. Some hoodlums grabbed her out of the car and roughed her up, but luckily they didn't do any damage. An off-duty cop broke it up and herded all of them in. She's at the local station house now, shaken up but okay. The damndest thing—one of the young punks was a patient of Dr. Abelman's, a kid undergoing treatment for a brain tumor. He escaped from a hospital bed two days ago. So both of us have to get down to the station right away. I'll see it that we're back on time. Get with Dec and have him promote one of the floor managers to A.D. Ted Chilson can take the floor manager's job. I have to beat it."

"God, what a blow," Loomer said. "We're jinxed. What the hell did you ever bring us all into this mess for anyway?"

"Too late now, Ben. Think of what's riding with us. White-chapel, G & T's millions, your promotion, my promotion. Come on, be a big boy and organize the joint."

One of the reporters stopped him as he headed for the door, pointing to the doctor, who was now standing in front of the house, waiting for Thrasher and trading friendly insults with the engineers.

"What's up, Thrasher?" he asked rudely. "Anything that'll keep this new concept in television journalism from getting off the ground?"

He smiled politely. "No, of course not. The doctor just had a last-minute emergency call. He told me he'd feel better if he got it out of the way before the program."

"Why you goin' along?" asked another reporter. He was a short man with thick-lensed spectacles which reduced his eyes to two sets of blurred, concentric circles.

"Just to keep him company," Thrasher said innocently.

Through the opened waiting room window, he could see the doctor waiting for him. With characteristic changeability, he now appeared to be in splendid humor despite the grim advices from the police. Apparently one of the technicians had kidded him, and he was flexing an enormous biceps under the grinning knob-turner's nose; the other knob-turners were laughing. About them the thickening mob ebbed and flowed, the clotted bodies moving lethargically in late summer, late afternoon heat. Above the doctor soared his magnificent poplar (NO PARKING: DOCTOR'S HOUSE), and seeing him thus framed in his truest milieu, surrounded by his beloved galoots and his dear lousy patients, Thrasher suddenly had the sensation that the old man was utterly indestructible, inviolate, undefeated. The disappointments had been many, the moments of triumph too few, and his sixty-eight years had been, to a great extent, a succession of losing battles. Yet he was not a man to pity, or to shed tears over, or to offer charity. Far from having been beaten, he was ascendant: as Herman Quincy's gray champion, he was still in the race, conceding nothing, compromising nothing, challenging everything. He would always be around, Thrasher assured himself, succumbing to his boiling temper, employing his outrage as a moral censor against all the cruelty and cant in the world, drawing rabbits on prescription pads, and cursing the crap artists who knew the arts of control.

Now Thrasher knew what had impelled him to pursue the doubtful goal of the program. *Americans, U.S.A.* had been born accidentally, a talker's gambit to save his neck. He could have abandoned it somewhere along the way, backed out gracefully, surrendered for the time being to Loomer and his other adversaries. But he had refused to do so. *Americans, U.S.A.* would have to succeed, if only to show the old healer to the world that had snubbed him, to repudiate the Baumgarts and the others who had tormented and deceived him.

Dr. Abelman was waving to him now. There were great dark stains under the arms of his appalling sea-green sport shirt; a breeze ruffled the wispy hairs on his crown. And the agency man understood in that moment of recognition that he loved the old man as dearly and as passionately as he had ever loved anyone.

"Come on, sonny boy!" the doctor called to him. "We got work to do!"

He was delighted to find him in such a cheerful frame of mind; hurrying down the stone steps, a few of the engineers called to him. As he and the doctor climbed into the Buick the photographers took their picture. Thrasher could see the caption in *Life*: *Emergency call pulled doctor away from rehearsal less than two hours before airtime.*

En route to the station house, the doctor railed against Herman, cursed Herman's teachers, his friends, his neighbors. When he had finished his tirade he suddenly conceded deep concern for Mrs. Quincy; he reminded himself sadly that she had been worshiping in the store church across the street and he could have brought her along.

"I can't think of everything any more," he said. "What the hell do they want from me? Do I have to worry about each and every one of them?"

They walked up the steps of the precinct house, into the dark lobby and then into the reception room. Lou Kaplan, still in civilian clothes, called to them from the top of a narrow stairway.

"Dr. Abelman! He's up here!"

The doctor started toward the steps, then, his attention diverted, he walked toward the desk sergeant. A small wooden plaque on the high desk read SERGEANT FELICE, and it struck a responsive chord with Dr. Abelman. The sergeant, a low-browed man of middle age with a head of inky Brillo, was on the phone as the doctor approached. Setting the receiver down, he stared insolently at the visitor carrying the black satchel.

"Yeh?" he asked.

"Are you Sergeant Felice?"

"That's what it says."

"You're a very smart fellow. That's why I want to tell you a few things. I'm Dr. Abelman, Dr. Samuel Abelman, 1553 Haven Place. You know me?"

"I heard a you." There was something so dogged and insistent in the physician's manner that, even behind his protective bench and his neatly lettered name plate, Sergeant Felice was uneasy.

"About a few weeks ago, sergeant, I called you about my tires getting slashed. Some galoots went crazy on my block and destroyed my sign. You remember that?"

"So what? I get lotsa calls like that. Yeh, yeh, I remember."

"When I made that call, sergeant, you called me 'Petey.' You used it in a disrespectful manner, to try to lower me to your level, sergeant. I'm glad to meet you to tell you to your face that you acted like a galoot. You know why? Because I'm a physician. A physician is entitled to some respect. I worked hard to become a doctor. I didn't get it by graft or by influence or by knowing somebody. I worked my ass off to get M.D. after my name and I'm proud of it. I don't care if you wear a uniform and represent the city of New York. You are a galoot if you don't know enough to address a physician with a little respect."

His homily concluded, he turned away, not waiting for a response, not seeing Sergeant Felice make a halfhearted gesture of *cuckoo*, a circular motion of his finger alongside his ear. Why? Thrasher asked himself. Why was the speech necessary? Herman Quincy lay dying upstairs, Alice Taggart had almost been raped, a million-dollar program hung in the balance, and all that had concerned Sam Abelman had been to put a fresh cop in his place.

At the head of the stairs Kaplan shook their hands and took them into a small room off the corridor. It smelled of alcohol and urine. The walls were a stained smoky brown; plaster peeled in great chunks from the ceiling. On a folding cot, covered with a faded army blanket, lay Herman Quincy.

"Mr. Thrasher," Kaplan said, "the young lady is downstairs with a policewoman. She's not hurt, just a little upset. We gave her a little sedative. I'll take you to see her in a minute."

Herman's eyes were half shut, his breathing labored. The bandage around his head, now soiled and unraveling, gave him the look of a Hindu ascetic, a starveling fakir, stretched on a bed of hot coals. Kaplan pulled back the blanket. One of the yellow trouser legs had been cut off to reveal Herman's thigh, wrapped in a bloodstained bandage.

"He tried to run away. Or I should say, walk away," Kaplan explained. "I had to shoot him in the thigh." He sounded sorry about the whole thing.

"It serves the little rat right," Dr. Abelman said. "Well, Herman, you had to know it all. You had to run out of the hospital and get in with those *fekokteh* friends of yours. Don't you know you're very sick? Don't you know I'm trying to cure you? Haven't you enough to worry about without going out and attacking people in broad daylight?"

"Go 'way," Herman muttered. "Evah since Ah seen you Ah been in trouble."

"Oh sure," the doctor said, matter-of-factly. "I've been very mean to you." Suddenly his calm manner changed and he was raging and screaming at the ruined boy. "What the hell is the matter with you?" the doctor yelled. "What the hell is eating you that you have to be a louse, a rat? Who ever did anything to you? Why must you be a dirty little punk instead of a human being? Don't you love anyone? Don't you ever want to do something for somebody? Who said the world owes you anything? Listen to me, Herman! It doesn't owe *anybody* anything! Who ever did anything for me for nothing?"

Herman moaned and covered his eyes. "Ah, sheeet. Stop yellin' at me. Who evah hep me? Dey all agains' me."

"Oh, is that so?" shouted the doctor. "Am I against you? Is Mr. Thrasher here against you? Is this policeman here against you?"

Herman turned his head away. "Ah ain' gon' lissen to you."

"Yeah, you bet. Well, I used to feel sorry for you, but I wonder why I did."

Thrasher fought nausea; he rested his head against the dirty wall and immersed himself in guilt. He could not possibly explain it to Dr. Abelman, or the boy, or to Louis Kaplan, but the guilt seemed to him so obvious that he was almost annoyed with them for not pointing the finger at him and driving him from the room. He was the custodian of the word; and the word determined what people thought and did; and when they turned out like Josh the Dill and the Twentieth Century Gents, where else could guilt lie?

Dr. Abelman appeared to be raising his right arm, almost as if he wanted to smash the tan, contemptuous face beneath him; but it was a gesture of despair, not anger, and Thrasher felt bound to alleviate his torment.

"It's really not all his fault," the agency man said hoarsely. "You know—what he reads and sees and is told—all of us—I'm sure the policeman understands—all of us have some responsibility—"

"You keep out of it!" the doctor said quickly. "What the hell are you talking about? This punk doesn't need your excuses. He likes what he is."

Kaplan shook his head sorrowfully. "Mr. Thrasher's on my side. We're all responsible to some extent."

"Sure! Sure we are!" the physician cried in agreement. "But so is he! That's all I'm saying." Then, wearily, he raised his arms and let them flop to his sides. "What did you call me here for anyway, Kaplan? Can't you see he hates my guts? He hates me even more for trying to help him."

"He asked for you."

The doctor scratched his head. "He sure doesn't act that way. Come on outside. I want to talk to you."

The three men walked into the dark hallway, out of earshot. They could hear the Negro boy's heavy breathing, a rhythmic, moribund noise.

"He has to go right back to New Hill for radiation, maybe surgery. He's sick as hell. Who can say how long he'll live? How he kept going with those two holes in his skull, I don't know," the doctor said.

"He's under arrest, doctor," the policeman said. "He can only go to a city hospital, to the prison ward. It'll have to be Kings County."

"Okay, Kings County. Karasik is on the staff there. See that he gets there right away. I suppose you'll see to it that your slug is taken out of his leg. He's got enough *tsuris*."

"Sure, doctor. It was nice of you to come. He's very ungrateful, I must say."

"You think he's any worse than the rest of my lousy patients?"

They walked back to the little room. "Herman, you're going to another hospital in a little while. Dr. Karasik and I will come to see you later tonight. Now try to be a good boy for a change. I'll call your mother and tell her. Shall I tell her you asked about her?"

"Go 'way," Herman muttered.

"You're a punk, Herman," the doctor said contemptuously.

They started down the stairs again, Kaplan remaining on the upper story, and promising to notify Dr. Karasik as soon as the patient-prisoner was removed to Kings County. He told Thrasher where he could find Miss Taggart, thanked both men again, and returned to the inner room.

At the bottom of the staircase, the doctor shot a parting glance at Sergeant Felice, but that worthy was not eager for a new exchange. He buried his two-inch brow in the blotter.

"Let's get out of here," the doctor said.

They had taken a step or two when they heard Kaplan's voice calling to them from the stairs.

"Oh, Dr. Abelman! Herman would like to talk to you for a minute."

The doctor turned around. "What does that punk want?"

Kaplan smiled weakly. "He says he wants to apologize to you. He's sorry for what he did."

"Oh, he's sorry, is he? That's just dandy. He shoots up a few people, slashes tires, beats up an old man and rapes a little girl and tries the same on Mr. Thrasher's assistant and then he's sorry. Not to mention getting fresh with me. I'm very glad he's sorry."

"I think he really means it," Kaplan pleaded. "As soon as you left he began to cry. He wants you."

"Tell him to go to hell!" the physician shouted. "I've had enough of his crap! And that goes for all of them!"

Thrasher thought he was going to faint. He battled an attack of vertigo, and, steadying himself, grabbed the doctor's arm.

"Time is running out, doctor," the agency man said. "I do think we should get back for a last-minute check. Remember, we've got a program to do yet. I don't want you to get upset. That boy seems to have unnerved you. Really, he isn't worth it."

"I wish you'd come up, doctor, only for a minute, it might help Herman if you did." The young policeman would not be denied.

"All right, all right. Didn't I tell you something once, Woody? The bastards won't let you live. You go see your little girl and I'll accept His Royal Highness's apology, the louse."

He began trudging up the stairway, his muscular, bent figure growing dimmer in the crepuscular light of the station house.

Thrasher watched him, walking a little stiffly from the arthritis, and then turned, looking for the room where Alice Taggart was being comforted by the policewoman.

The noise that made the executive spin about, a kind of grunt or cough, the noise that a man would make when punched unexpectedly in the groin, had come from the head of the stairs.

At the top step, the doctor was doubled up, leaning against the banister. Kaplan was standing over him solicitously and again Thrasher heard the peculiar grunt. He raced toward the stairs, flying up the steps, putting his hand on the doctor's back, on the sweat-soaked green shirt.

"What's the matter, doctor?" he cried. "What's wrong?"

"I don't know what's happened," Kaplan said breathlessly. "He was walking up toward me, and when he got to the top, right here, he made that funny noise and bent over, with his hands on his chest."

"Ah. Ah. Ah, you son-of-a-bitch," the doctor groaned. "Oh, you louse. You dirty rat. I'm all right. Not a word to Mrs. Abelman, either of you punks. Oh, you bastard."

He straightened up and they were horrified by his face. It was gray and moist; the creases and wrinkles appeared to have been dug deeper and the dark hollows beneath his eyes seemed to have widened and grown blacker.

"Oh. Ah. Like a lousy vise, closing right in," the doctor said. "Let me lean on you a minute, Woody. I'm fine. I'm all right."

The pain had struck him suddenly—a giant vise squeezing his breastbone. No sooner had it commenced compressing his chest than he felt it radiate to his jaw, his neck, his shoulders, his left arm, right down to the wrist. Resting against Thrasher for a moment, he began to massage his chest, rubbing his right palm and fingers against the offended sternum, cursing and grunting alternatively.

"Ah. Bastard. What a louse. Won't get the best of me. I'm too tough for any lousy coronary."

Thrasher's legs trembled; they were dissolving and for a minute he feared he would tumble down the narrow stair well. What amazed him was that the doctor could diagnose his case so quickly and still appear unperturbed. The occasional grunt, accompanied by a hunching of his shoulders and a painful grimace, seemed to be involuntary: gestures that only intractable pain could wring from the stubborn old man.

"Little morphine be very good now. That crazy Maxie, will he have the laugh on me."

It seemed the ultimate in irrelevant nonsense that at this critical point in his life he could be distressed about Max Vogel having the laugh on him. He was still rubbing his chest, trying to ease the relentless pressure, grunting and grimacing every few seconds.

"Can I help?" Kaplan asked. "Would you like to lie down and rest? We have a bed. . . ."

"The officer is right," Thrasher added. "You do look a little pale. A rest might help you catch your breath."

"Rest? Don't kid me, sonny. I got a coronary. Nice thing about being a doctor. Don't you know I'm a helluva diagnostician? I figured it out right away—ah—ah—ah, you bastard."

The policeman and the agency man exchanged terrified glances; at the base of the stairs a group of uniformed cops and detectives had gathered.

"What do you want us to do, doctor?" Kaplan asked. "Shall I call an ambulance?"

"Nah. To hell with them. It would just scare Sarah and Eunice. Help me to the car. Woody, you can drive. Now, damn it, when we get home, not a word to Sarah or Eunice. I got indigestion. I ate too much. Don't worry them or I'll knock your block off."

They paused momentarily. From the room where Herman Quincy lay dying they heard the boy's voice drift toward them.

"Whuh happen out deah? Deh doctoh okay? Ah wan' 'pologize. Ah' ain' mad at you, Doct' Abelman. You done try hep me. Y'all gon' see my ma? Y'all tell her Ah ain' mad at you . . ."

Dr. Abelman squinted at Kaplan.

"What the hell do you know. He's a human being after all."

"I don't think you ever doubted it, doctor," Thrasher volunteered.

"Ah——ah——bastard," he grunted. Then, raising his head, he looked toward Herman's room. "I guess I should talk to the little rat. C'mon, Woody, give me a hand."

"I think not," the agency man said quickly. "I think we'd better get you home."

"Yes, I agree," Kaplan added. "I'll convey any message you wish to Herman. I'm sure glad he said those few words."

They each took one of the old man's arms, Thrasher finding it hard to believe that the enormous iron biceps could ever be destroyed, and began the slow descent.

"That little louse Herman," he muttered. "Apologies from him yet. Well, he's not my worry any more. I did what I could."

Step by step, they aided him down the stairs, watching him wince every few seconds, watching the color drain from his face, amazed by the vigor with which he kept massaging his chest. They guided him through the cluster of law officers, down the stone steps and and into the ancient Buick. Thrasher climbed behind the wheel and Kaplan sat in the rear.

"I forgot my bag," the doctor complained.

"I'll come back for it," Kaplan assured him. "I think we better get you home in a hurry."

A sooty dusk descended on Brownsville, a warm mist that seemed to soften the tired buildings, the trash-filled streets. Thrasher had found nothing but ugliness in the squalid tenements and cramped stores, yet now they seemed to radiate a warmth and a repose that had eluded him. He glanced at the physician's hunched-over, pained figure and he knew that it was only the shattering possibility that it might be the old man's last view of his ministry that had softened his own sentiments about the ragged slum.

"Ah. Ah. Not too bad now. Recovery statistics are remarkably high for this kind of thing," he said confidently. "Oh, that's better. Lousy pressure on the chest is letting up. I'll be fine."

"I'm sure you will," Thrasher said. "It may not even be what you suspect."

"Sure," Kaplan volunteered. "It could be you ate too much, that's all. Same thing happened to my brother-in-law, Saul Plotkin. You treated him, doctor, remember?"

The old man said nothing for a few blocks. They passed a boarded-up motion-picture theater and it moved him to a tirade.

"That stinking movie house. That used to be Jackson's Lot, and Solly and I used to play tennis there years ago. Nothing but farms. So they built a theater to show rotten movies and debauch people and then it closed down. Served the bums right."

"You must be feeling better to get annoyed like that," Thrasher said. He sped through a red light and headed for the house.

"A little morphine will fix me up," the doctor said, lowering his head. "Sixth of a grain intravenously."

Thrasher brought the Buick to a slow, soft halt and ran out to aid the doctor. He and Kaplan helped him from the car. At first he refused their arms, but as he took his first step on the pavement, he winced and accepted the assistance of the younger men.

A patrolman called to Kaplan, "What's up, Lou? What you doin' here?"

"Dr. Abelman isn't feeling well. I thought I'd come back with him to see if I could help."

The mob eddied about them and the police shoved them back. With surprising speed, the doctor walked up his front stoop, leaning now on Thrasher. Already the slum dweller's instinct for disaster was at work. The word of doom spread from the front ranks of children to the oldsters on the periphery.

"Deh doctoh sick. He sick."

"Yeah, Ah seen him. He look bad."

"You head whut dat cop say? Dey gon' call off deh show."

By the time it reached the toothless patriarchs and earth mothers at the fringe, the doctor had been shot, stabbed, poisoned; was drunk again; had been carried in dead.

In the lobby they paused for a moment as the reporters, a beat behind the mob in nosing tragedy, gathered at the base of the stairs. Thrasher refused to tell them anything, advising them that he would be downstairs in a minute, and asking the little man with thick glasses to find Dr. Vogel immediately. A flash bulb went off and Thrasher cursed: the camera had taken a picture of Dr. Abelman resting on Lou Kaplan's arm.

They made the laborious ascent and escorted Dr. Abelman into his bedroom. Sarah and Eunice, cleaning off the dining room table, saw the three men pass silently to the rear of the house. They hurried into the room—wife, daughter, and son-in-law—to find him already seated on the edge of the bed, removing his shoes and socks.

"These shoes stink. They hurt my feet."

"What's wrong, Sam?" Sarah asked. If she was frightened, if she had the faintest suspicion of doom, she masked it miraculously. Thrasher wondered if she were really concealing terror, or whether her view of life as a series of small problems prevented her from comprehending the gravest tragedy of all.

"I got a little indigestion," Dr. Abelman said lightly. "I started feeling faint in the police station so I came home."

"It's nothing serious, is it, pop?" his daughter asked. She could not conceal her concern; there was more of her father's volatile nature in her.

"Of course not!" He was actually smiling now, even though his face remained the color of damp putty. Thrasher found it inconceivable that he could be happy.

"What about the program?" Eunice asked.

Thrasher gasped for air. "I—I'm afraid Dr. Abelman isn't up to it, Mrs. Platt, although I won't make up his mind for him. You decide, doctor." If the old man was playing a game, pretending that he was perfectly healthy except for a little gastritis, he would go along with him.

"Woody, I hate to disappoint you, but I think it's off. Maybe we can do it tomorrow." He lay back, sighing gently and resting his head on the pillow. "Ai—ai—that's a pleasure."

Mother and daughter were looking at each other, watching the beginnings of terror grow in each other's eyes; the one camouflaging it behind rimless glasses, the other having evident difficulty keeping it from convulsing her.

"What the hell is this?" Max Vogel, loud and brash, shoved his way past them and stood over the bed, looking blankly at his friend. "What's the matter, Shmul? All right, everyone, beat it. I'll take care of him. Eunice, send Myron up here. Everyone else get out. Hey, Sam, how about some handball?"

"Let's go," Dr. Abelman said, winking. "Three games out of five."

"What's wrong with him, Max?" Eunice pleaded. Her voice was a fraction removed from tears.

"How the hell do I know? He probably got the bends. *Beat it!*"

Thrasher left them. Downstairs, in the waiting room, he hurriedly called everyone together, after first meeting with Loomer. There were at least thirty of them huddled in the small room.

"I have some bad news for all of us," Thrasher began. "Dr. Abelman collapsed a few minutes ago while making a call to a patient. We don't know what is wrong with him. It might be indigestion, or a chest disorder or plain nervous exhaustion. In any case, he is under a doctor's care and the program cannot possibly go on. I would like you, Dec, and you, Ritola to strike the unit and all the gear immediately. Please be very quiet because we don't know how sick Dr. Abelman really is—"

Loomer broke in. "It seems a shame, Woody, after all this work, all these people. Could we possibly do the show without him? I mean, tell the story of his life through the people who knew him?"

Thrasher blinked. "No, Andy, I'm afraid we're licked for the time being. It simply won't work. There's no need to panic. Ben, I would appreciate it if you'd call Mr. Whitechapel and Mr. Gatling and talk to the press. Dexter, if you will get your boss at network, I'll talk to him. They'll probably have to run a standby film."

Daw moaned. "Oh, God—on class A time."

"All right, Dec, that's not necessary. We know this means a big loss to the network and to Whitechapel, too, for that matter. All I can say to all of you is that I'm terribly sorry things turned out as they did. I think we had a great show, a winner. That we suffered a bad break shouldn't keep us from looking ahead to the next installment of *Americans, U.S.A.* I, for one, intend to keep fighting to get it on the air. Thank you all."

For several seconds, none of them moved. The exhausting day, so rich in promise, had come to a barren end. The engineers shuffled off to undo their endless cables, unplug their various scoops and deuces, break down the intricate electronic tools.

Angelo Traficanti grabbed Thrasher's arm and his clan gathered around the agency man.

"Whatsamatter with Doc hey? He sick?"

"I don't know how sick he is, Mr. Traficanti. Dr. Vogel is with him now."

"We stay. We help."

"No, I think it would be better if you left. Dr. Abelman will need a lot of rest and quiet. But thank you for your offer."

He had suddenly become a member of the household, making decisions, giving advice, looking after the patient's welfare. The Traficantis trooped out in a sad, interminable file, and the sight of Yolande, so dark and pretty, holding her fat child, reminded him of the superb picture he had seen on the monitor a few hours ago, and the hopes he had pinned on the dramatic impact of that striking scene.

Andy Lord and Kevin McBee, stunned by the unwelcome encounter with reality, were departing. Gradually, the rooms were being denuded of people, cameras, props. He could hear Loomer in the consultation room making embarrassed explanations to Lyman Gatling and he felt momentarily guilty for not having spoken to the sponsor himself. The little reporter with blurred eyeglasses materialized under his chin.

"Mind if we hang around for a while?"

"I suppose I can't chase you. What's the big idea—a death watch or something?" Thrasher was so exhausted that his words came out spaced too far apart; his voice was unusually thin.

"No, no. Just a great yooman interest story here."

The girl from *Life* and her photographer were also seeing it through; so were a half-dozen other newspapermen and photographers. They took up positions in the emptying waiting room; in an hour or so most of them would be on overtime.

Myron came galumphing down the stairs, arms flapping as he raced for the front door.

"Myron!" Thrasher called. "What did Dr. Vogel tell you?"

"I can't talk ta ya now. I gotta get to the drugstore."

"Didn't he say *anything?*" Under the harsh light of the vestibule, where the two men now stood, the open door revealing the busy engineers, the dimmed truck, and the eager crowd, Myron appeared terrified.

"Uncle Doc is sick as hell. Very sick."

"His heart?"

"Vogel says he thinks so. Says he can't be sure. But he's just tryin' to ease the shock. See this prescription?"

Thrasher read the doctor's scrawl, deciphering the words *heparin* and *dilaudid*.

"I ain't been raised in a doctor's office for nothin'. Heparin's an anticoagulant and delaudid is a kind of morphine. Ya give 'em both in coronaries. That's what Uncle Doc got."

The last words came out as a wrenched cry, the sounds twisted and blurred by Myron's tears. The nephew raced down the stairs to the Buick, shoving aside two elderly women who clutched at him for information.

Loomer and Finucane sat down with Thrasher in the waiting room; Chilson stood somberly in the corner.

"B'Jesus, what a jolt," Finucane said. He had been at Vogel's bourbon and he was breathless and damp. "Poor guy. What is it?"

"Coronary thrombosis, in all likelihood," Thrasher said professionally.

"We're jinxed," Loomer said. "This whole project was jinxed from the start. What impelled you to get us into this, Woody? What? And why did we all go for it like such idiots? First, almost losing the whole *G & T* account. Now this. I'll bet we would have flopped even if we had gotten on the air. I still say Brick Higgins could have made it with a new format."

He could not be wroth with Loomer; actually, it was unfair of Sam Abelman to take sick in the middle of their project, their illusory world of formats, of concepts, of progress reports, of stewardships, of ratings and sponsor identification. All his life Sam Abelman had dealt in the dull realities of the world: in birth, life, death, pain, anxiety, hatred, and love. He had been a congenital enemy of symbols and illusions, of the mythology and fairy tales of the new talkers; even in death he was going to make it tough for the people whose coin they were. Poor Ben Loomer had more of a case against the old man than he imagined.

"I still stand by *Americans, U.S.A.*, Ben." Thrasher was arguing as a matter of form. He really cared very little whether the program went on the air, whether *G & T* pulled out, whether Loomer made his chairmanship, and he in turn got Loomer's job.

"It *would* be a shame to lose it after all the work we've put into it. We're all set for next Sunday, Ben," Chilson said. He rubbed his golden crew cut. "God, what luck. What awful, awful luck."

"How's Alice?" Loomer asked dazedly. He was like a man in the middle of an earthquake, so utterly stunned by bricks and plaster dropping about his head that he can only be mildly curious about a high wind that blew out his front window two days ago.

"Just a little shaken. Ben, I wish you or somebody would pick her up at the station house on your way back to town," Thrasher said.

"Will do. More complications. That little incident will require a report in triplicate to the whole bloody network." Loomer got up. "Well, we might as well shove. Gents?"

Thrasher accompanied them to the door. They had to stand aside while a cursing grip ported out two scoop lights.

"What did old Gatling say?" Thrasher asked.

"What could he say?" Loomer asked. "He couldn't get mad. He stuttered a little and said something about us being unreliable and failing to deliver. I think he saved his choicest comments for the chief."

"And what did T. C. say?"

"The chief? Not much."

"I mean—I guess I'm fired—or something about how mad Gatling will be with me?"

"Nope," Loomer said. "T. C. took it gracefully. All he said was he was very sorry the doctor was sick and asked if he could help. He really meant it too. Wanted to know if he could get some specialist down here tonight. Some big heart man who treated his wife."

"I'll be damned," Thrasher said.

An olive-green truck was double-parking next to the mobile unit. Two men in gray work clothes jumped out, yanked open the rear doors, and unloaded an oxygen tank and the gear for an oxygen tent. The incident touched off another tremor in the crowd.

"Give a look—oxygen dey're bringing."

"Dat mean he *real* sick, man."

"Yeh, dey *damn* sick when dey give 'em dat ole ox-gin."

The agency people stood aside as the delivery men wrestled the tank and the tent through the vestibule and up the stairs.

"That's usually for bad cases, isn't it?" Chilson asked.

"Not necessarily," Loomer said. "Most doctors order it immediately as a precautionary move. I read up on this stuff when Eisenhower had his."

Thrasher watched the delivery men vanish at the head of the stairs.

"So long, Ben. I'm sorry it all turned out so terribly. For all of us. Maybe Gatling won't . . ."

"Okay, okay, forget it, Woody. I guess you've got other worries. You really went for that old guy, didn't you?"

"I'm quite fond of him."

He waved his goodbyes to Finucane and Chilson. No sooner had they pulled out in Loomer's car than a taxicab drew up in the space it had occupied. A woman in a nurse's uniform, carrying a square wooden case by a leather strap, got out and worked her way through the mob.

Thrasher held the door open for her.

"I suppose Dr. Vogel is upstairs," she said. She had a competent, hard look about her. Her hair was tinted a bright blue and her figure might have been that of a woman twenty years younger.

"I'm Miss Banahan, the doctor's nurse," she said. "He asked me to bring the portable EKG. How is Dr. Abelman?"

"I really don't know," Thrasher said. "He seemed in quite a bit of pain. He's upstairs in bed now."

He offered to carry the wooden case for her, but she had hurried up the slanting stairs and he could hear Vogel greeting her obscenely and then the unmistakable sound of a hand slapping a starched buttocks. Dexter Daw, a sheaf of scripts under his arm, wandered into the waiting room. They looked at each other helplessly.

"Network is rolling an old film of the Philharmonic," Daw said.

Max Vogel could read the tracings of the EKG as they were made; his shrewd diagnostician's eye told him all he needed to know before the inky trail was completed. His friend had suffered a massive coronary occlusion. There was clear evidence of severe posterior wall infarction and auricular fibrillation: Sam Abelman had half a heart left. It was miraculous, on the face of it, that he was still breathing, talking, thinking, and insulting people.

"You take a lousy EKG," he said thickly to Vogel.

"Why don't you please shut up?" Vogel asked patiently. "Do I try to tell you how to spread manure on your dahlias?"

"There is a lady present." Dr. Abelman winked archly at the nurse.

Banahan smiled. "Thanks, doctor. It's a pleasure to hear a polite word after hanging around Dr. Vogel all day."

"Hang around this, willya, Banahan?" Vogel sneered.

Dr. Abelman, in faded pajamas, his head on a raised pillow, peered at the oxygen tank in the corner of the room.

"What's all that crap for?" he asked. His voice was faint.

"I got some welding to do," Vogel snapped. "I'm gonna weld

your behind to a dahlia tuber and see if it will grow up your rectum. Will you please shut up?"

Vogel was in shirt sleeves. The hypertension that had all but killed him thirteen years ago was now painting his deflated cheeks a fiery red. His quick expert movements (he was removing the jelly-smeared electrodes from Dr. Abelman's chest) were those of a young interne, not a cardiac case almost seventy years of age. Deftly, he peeled the EKG tracing from the revolving drum and dropped it in his pocket. Dr. Abelman held his hand out.

"Let's see it, Maxie."

"*Gotzongoole.*"

"Come on, Max. Do I have to get out of bed and grab it from you?"

"Grab something else."

Dr. Abelman made an effort at rising; he winced, clapped his right hand against his chest, and fell back. Infuriated, Vogel screamed at him.

"You goddam idiot! You stupid son-of-a-bitch! Lay back there and rest! I'm in charge here! I'm taking care of you! Banahan, if he tries any of that again, you got my permission to hit him with a bedpan."

Dr. Abelman had smiled slightly through the tirade. Now he winked at the raging, ruddy man. "Who you kidding, Maxie? What are you going to tell me? A little tachycardia maybe? You going to try to crap me up?"

"You talk too much. I think I'll fill you full of delaudid, that'll shut you up for certain. One-sixth of a grain of morphine and you feel like you can lick the world. What a hero. Now for Christ's sake, be still. *Don't move and don't talk!*"

He took Banahan outside, and in the corridor talked to her in conspiratorial whispers.

"He had a big one. Keep the old louse quiet. I'll call Brooklyn registry for a night nurse, so you hang around till she shows up. If you hear a change in his breathing, or if he seems to have a sudden attack of pain, holler for me. I want to talk to the family. A big friggin' help *they'll* be."

He waddled into the living room, in his spurious fat man's gait (in times of stress it was more pronounced) and, fingering the EKG in his pocket, eased himself into an armchair. They were a physician's family: they knew illness and the onset of death. The smells, tastes, and atmospheres of the sickroom were not foreign to them. Vogel knew he could not deceive them.

"Sam had a coronary," he said calmly. "A beaut. A real beaut."
Eunice began to cry; her husband put his arm around her.

"I suspected it," Sarah said flatly. "They way he looked when he
came in. I assume you're doing everything you can, Max?"

"Nah. I'm gonna let him fight it out himself. What the hell is
wrong with you, Sarah? Thirteen years ago I got mine and Sam
got me on my feet. The least I can do is prove I'm as good a
GP as that old *futz* is."

"Will he get better, Max?" The tremor had intruded on Mrs.
Abelman's calm voice; she removed her spectacles and blinked a
few times.

"Who knows? I think he will. If he gets by the first forty-eight
hours, he's over one hump. Then the next two weeks—if he gets by
them he's as good as recovered. But you can't tell with coronaries,
Sarah, you know that. He could turn around in the bed and it would
be over."

Eunice was sobbing softly, and Harry Platt was pleading with
her to be quiet. "Look, honey, that's the last thing Pop would want
you to do. He'd probably get sore if he knew Max told us as much
as he has. Right, Max?"

"Yeah. The last thing he did before I walked out was cuss me out."

There was no point in telling them all the truth. The message of
the EKG might destroy their last hopes, and Vogel owed them at
least a thread of optimism. How could he tell them that the old man
had no right, no right in the world, to be alive with the fraction of
muscle he had left for a heart?

Sarah shifted slightly in her armchair and folded her hands. "I
would like Dr. Applebaum to look at Sam."

"Applebaum? That phony? Sam would throw him out."

"That isn't so, Max. Sam has always thought very highly of
Dr. Applebaum. He respects his judgment in heart cases."

Vogel reached for his bourbon bottle, poured himself half a
tumbler, and drank it as quickly as if it were spring water. "What
about *my* judgment? I'm not good enough for Sam, hah? You got to
run to specialists also? Especially the guy who ruined Sam's career
and got his job."

"That is not so," she said.

"Balls. Call him yourself." He reached for the bourbon again.

Banahan was summoning him, and he rolled to the little hallway
where she stood, hidden from both patient and family.

"His breathing is becoming labored," she said. "He *acts* as if he's
feeling better—he won't stop talking. But he's sighing more now."

"Let's stick him in the tent."

They returned to the bedroom. The nurse, in deference to her employer's own scarred heart, rolled the oxygen tank across the floor and did the heavy work.

"You think I'm pretty sick, don't you?" Dr. Abelman asked.

"I always use oxygen in cases of chronic bedwetting," Vogel said. "That answer your question?"

Dr. Abelman smiled and Vogel found it incredible that Sam could carry out his deceit so thoroughly. He tried to recall his own coronary, and he seemed to remember crying a good deal; the notion of dying never left his mind for a moment. Asleep or awake, he had pondered the awful possibility of having to leave everything he loved and enjoyed. Maybe Sam Abelman's inability to savor the pleasures of life made it easier for him to confront oblivion.

"What'd you tell Sarah and Eunice?"

"Acute indigestion. Now will you please clam up?"

"What were you arguing about in there?"

In extreme exasperation, Vogel smacked a hand to his forehead. "Did I ever have a jerk of a patient like this one, Banahan? I can't keep him quiet. When Myron gets here I'm giving you more morphine, and if that doesn't keep you quiet I give up." Then, almost as an afterthought, he asked softly, "How's the pain, Sam?"

Sam winked at him. "Still there, Maxie. Dull sort of pressure now. None of that tightening I had before."

"See, you're better already."

"Yeh, yeh, I'm doing fine." He turned his head toward the window. The sky was darkening over the leafy tops of his cherry tree and the giant magnolia. The bed lamp enshadowed half his face, and on the other half Max Vogel saw the ashen moist pallor, the drawn and anxious lines that the old man was camouflaging with his crude banter.

"Hey, Max, shake hands with me."

"Why? Who the hell are you to me?"

"I want to show you how good I feel. You think I'm weak. Come on." He had lifted the edge of the transparent tent and was extending his right hand. It betrayed none of the ravages of the face; rather it was still strong and confident.

"You're screwy," Vogel said. He shook his friend's hand and cried out. "Sam! Leggo! What kind of joke is that?"

Dr. Abelman smiled at him and released Vogel's injured hand. "Now tell me who's sick, Maxie."

Vogel rubbed his fingers: it was a miracle if one of them hadn't been fractured. The strength in Sam Abelman's right hand was not merely undiminished; indeed it appeared to have intensified, reasserting itself in defiance of the disaster in the coronary artery. To the end, Max knew, he would do things the hard way. Death was a galoot; not a crap artist, to be sure, but a lousy galoot sitting on the edge of his bed and getting fresh and you had to treat him like a galoot.

Where the mobile television truck had stood there now lay an empty stretch of gutter, flanked by two mounds of coffee containers, empty lunchboxes, newspapers, discarded scripts and routine sheets, the detritus of an encampment of talkers. It was as if a raiding party from a rival network, savages in charcoal-gray suits and black knitted ties, had descended upon them, forcing them to fold their tents and flee in the night.

It was just ten. Already the period allotted to *Americans, U.S.A.* had vanished. Instead of Woodrow Thrasher's bold new concept in television journalism, the network had dusted off a half hour of music, a wobbly film replete with artistic close-ups of violinists' hands and French horns. The people of the word had vanished, all save four reporters and a photographer from the *News.* They had begun a halfhearted poker game in the waiting room, dime and a quarter.

Thrasher sat on the front stoop, smoking, watching an interminable noisy game that some Negro children were playing with a tin can. The can had to be kicked from one side of the street, across the littered gutter, to the opposite sidewalk. The contest was accompanied by wild screams and curses, and the agency man wondered if any of the bedlam was filtering through to the rear of the house and the doctor. They had been at the game for over an hour, it seemed, and their energy was undiminished. He imagined that far into the warm night, while people tried to sleep, they would be kicking the clattering tin can across the street and shrieking. (Except the Baumgarts: somehow the dreadful noises would never reach their ears. They would sleep deeply and healthfully, and rise prepared to torment the doctor again if he were alive.)

Myron sat down alongside Thrasher.

"What did Dr. Applebaum say?" Thrasher asked.

Morris Meyer Applebaum, chief consultant at New Heights, had arrived a half hour ago. Dignified in white mustache and black silk suit, he had examined his old colleague, read the second EKG tracing that Max Vogel had taken, and had conferred first with the attending GP and then with the family.

"He says Uncle Doc is gonna get better." Myron sounded unconvinced.

"You believe him?"

The nephew shrugged. "I dunno. He said Uncle Doc looked remarkably good for having sustained so much heart damage. He said he was resting comfortably and that his mental attitude was very important."

"What did Dr. Vogel say?"

"Well, I didn't hear what they talked about, but after Applebaum left Vogel told me Applebaum always says that. He ain't changed that speech in forty years."

"It is remarkable the way your uncle keeps talking and joking. Doesn't Dr. Vogel think that's a good sign?"

Myron pushed the crosspiece of his new spectacles back up his nose. It annoyed Thrasher: the glasses were brand-new and still they didn't fit.

"Well, you know Max. Took me aside and said it looks very bad. He said the only reason Uncle Doc is bein' so cheerful is he don't want to worry anyone. He says he diagnosed his own case the minute it happened. Uncle Doc knows just how serious it is and just what's gonna happen to him. His mind is clear as a bell, Max says. He shook hands with him before and almost tore off Max's fingers."

"What do *you* think, Myron?"

Myron looked over his glasses at the agency man. "I think Uncle Doc is on his way out. It hasta be. He gotta go this way, the hard way. Who told him to make that call to that friggin' boogie anyway?" The nephew lowered his voice as he pronounced the last few words, as if fearful that the can-kickers in the street might hear him and accept the challenge; Myron had been drubbed by Negroes too often in his boyhood.

"Ah, what a rotten way to go out," Myron sighed.

Thrasher inhaled, then let out a cloud of thick smoke. Through the opened vestibule door he could hear the poker players: *once for laughs, hit me light, all pink.* The game of kick-the-can continued; a group of older girls was cheering the players now. Thrasher had never heard such a din in his life.

"Boy, there's an easy way to live and a tough way," Myron whined. "I learned my lesson from Uncle Doc. I'm not gonna have to live his way."

"What are you going to do about it?"

"Plenny. I'm gonna get inta your racket. I got it figured out. First, I'm buyin' the right clothes. Then a little plastic surgery to shorten my smeller. Maybe a plane job on my skin to knock off the acne scars. Crew haircut, speech lessons, a coupla more courses at Columbia. I'm smarter than mosta you guys. I can write I'm young. I got ideas. What's to stop me?"

"You'll never make it, Myron. You'll miss by miles."

"Says who?"

"Says me and I'm an authority. You'll be tabbed as an intruder as soon as you poke that bobbed nose past the receptionist's desk."

"You're an intruder too. Ya never went to Yale. You're from some dinky town. Jalopy, Nebraska. *You* made the grade."

"South Dakota and you miss the point, Myron. This business isn't run by the Ivy League, by inherited wealth, or the high-type people of the Eastern Seaboard. Far from it. There are a few Yales and Princetons among us. But essentially we're a small-town business. New York's talker society, Myron, is controlled by people from Great Bend, Kansas, and Camden, South Carolina. The sooner you learn that the better off you'll be. The worst thing you can be is a native New Yorker. This is a captive city, Myron. Walk through the East Fifties at dusk and hear the rich rolling r's of the California valleys, the slurred vowels of the Tidewater, the sharp nasal twang of southern Illinois. Maybe it's as it should be. The bigdomes over at the *Discoverist Review* claim that jazz is our only native art form, but as usual they're wrong. It's talk. Mass talk. The word in its many shapes and forms. It's appropriate, I guess, that New York's talk factories be ruled by us, the sons and daughters of small-town America. You wouldn't last for one meeting, Myron, in your too-narrow lapels and the shirt collar that didn't bloop properly. Your cordovans would be the wrong shade and you'd be a giveaway every time you opened your mouth. You'd be labeled New York, the worst sin of all."

Myron, unembarrassed, smiled at Thrasher and pushed the drooping spectacles back. "You're a pretty smart guy, Thrasher," he said with grudging admiration. " A lot smarter than I ever cased you for."

"Let me expand a little, Myron. When I came to New York after the war I decided I had to be very Ivy to succeed. It killed me to be from New Arabia, South Dakota, because I hadn't realized what a marvelous edge that gave me. So I went to one of those men's clothing stores—you know, second story on East Forty-eighth Street, with a single gray jacket in the window, the kind with branches in New Haven and Cambridge. I bought a suit and a sports coat and I imagined I was all set. A few months later I had the suit hanging in my office, and the kid I shared the room with, a genuine Yalie, and a very decent sort, noticed the inside label.

He began to laugh, and when I asked him what was so funny, he told me I was a 'wide-stitch phony.'"

"Whaddee mean by that?"

"It seems that at this fine old establishment they distinguished among patrons by means of the stitching on the label. If the stitching was small and tight, it meant you were one of the elect, a genuine Ivy. But if they tabbed you as an *auslander*—and don't ask me how they could tell—they sewed the label with wide straight stitches. That damn suit set me back one hundred and ten bucks, too."

"Ah, phooey. How many guys go around lookin' at label stitches?"

"You're hopeless. All that was necessary was for *me* to know. If the lad in my office hadn't discovered it, someone else would have. In any case, I knew. I understood my failure."

Myron made a sour face. "What's all that got to do with me?"

Their meandering conversation was like the talk Thrasher used to hear in the landing barges during his naval career. Reflective, analytic, detailed, it covered everything but the imminent prospect of death. Above them, in the transparent tent, the old man gasped and joked, refusing to submit to the galoot camped on the edge of the bed, insulting his attending physician and still finding the strength to curse and scoff and scowl at the world of crap artists.

Across the street the *Wholy United Army of God* filled the night air with a wild, melodic chant, something out of the Gold Coast by way of a Georgia swamp. It was a rather pleasant sound.

"They really go at that beautifully," Thrasher said. Some day a man with a tape recorder would come to the store church and put out an album entitled *Dark Voices: Spirituals of the Slum.*

"Good thing Uncle Doc can't hear them," said Myron. "At least it's nice 'n' quiet back there in his room."

They rested against the yellow brick façade, listening to the street noises: the can-kickers, the singing from the church, the yelps of assorted dogs, the clattering of the Rower Avenue trolley. The crowd had vanished, evidently satisfied that the evening's entertainments were over.

Eunice's voice, distorted with fear, summoned them.

"Myron! Come up!"

The nephew unlimbered arms and legs and darted through the opened doors and up the stairs. Thrasher was a step behind him. The reporters had stopped their card game; a photographer was yanking a plate from his case and was moving toward the steps.

"Stay the hell down here," Thrasher said.

"Who you?"

"Just stay here till you're sent for. You'll get your overtime."

They burst into the bedroom. Mrs. Abelman, her daughter, and her son-in-law were gathered at the side of the bed. Harry Platt had his arms around them. Myron, disdaining their useless alliance against the inevitable calamity, braced himself at the foot of the rumpled bed, hands anchored to the mattress, his eyes goggling at the ultimate struggle.

Dr. Abelman lay with his head thrust back. The great cage of his skull stretched the fibrous neck and his eyes bugged from their sockets. Pulsating, his mouth tried vainly to suck air into his choking lungs. The dark, undefeated eyes and the gasping mouth seemed all that were left of his face: cheeks, nose, neck, and forehead were all of the same gray, tallowy vagueness. Each succeeding gasp was louder and more agonized than its predecessor, and with each the popping eyes protruded further from the cavernous sockets. It was, Thrasher imagined, no more horrible or racking than any death from coronary occlusion and its complications. What rendered the physician's last moments so unbelievable was the presence astride his trunk of Max Vogel. The attending doctor had straddled his friend's thick torso, and, with slow, forceful motions of his hands, was trying to pump air back into Dr. Abelman's flooded lungs. He squatted on his high perch, an unhealthily ruddy man of seventy, cardiac and alcoholic, angrily trying to squeeze a final drop of life into the patient's moribund chest. As he labored, he talked to him.

"Sam! Sam, you son-of-a-bitch! Listen to me! Stay with me, Sam!"

No tears, no panic intruded in Max Vogel's sermon. He was quite simply angry, furious with the unseen agents, the defects of physiology that were destroying his classmate. Against Sarah's soft crying and Eunice's hysterics, his voice, loud and rich with slum defiance, refused to concede anything. Who would lend Max Vogel the anatomy notes if Sam Abelman died?

"Sam! Breathe! Breathe, you old louse!"

"Please, Max," Eunice bawled. "Please stop! He's dead."

"The hell he is! Come on, Sam, once more for Max! Don't be a *futz*! You're fine! You'll play handball tomorrow!"

Dr. Abelman's eyes were sightless; he heard nothing. His mouth reached for a final swallow of precious air, failed, and he lay silent. Vogel remained astride him. His hands were still pushing at the sides of the patient's iron chest, trying to infuse life into a corpse. Abruptly, he withdrew his hands and climbed off the bed to face the mourners.

"He's shot an embolism. That always gets 'em when they're that old. I could have told that jerk Applebaum with his good news."

He spoke matter-of-factly, as if he were discussing a case he had worked on many, many years ago, an obscure patient whose fate had concerned him no more than that of a pet cat or dog.

Harry Platt herded his wife and his mother-in-law back to the living room. Myron lingered, staring in disbelief at the remains of his uncle. Dutifully, Miss Banahan pulled the bedsheet over the tortured head. Thrasher grasped Vogel's arm as the doctor, picking up his satchel, started to leave the bedroom.

"Could anything have been done, Dr. Vogel? anything at all? Was there any chance for him?"

"A chance? He had no goddam right to live as long as he did. Banahan, call surgical supply and tell them to remove all that junk. You better hang around and give the family a hand. I never saw such a helpless bunch."

Appalled by his callousness, his refusal to show emotion, Thrasher followed him downstairs. The reporters clustered around him. Yes, the doctor was dead. He had shot an embolism, Dr. Vogel said. They could talk to him for the details.

Vogel brushed by them, turned the corner, and headed for the consultation room. A flash bulb popped as he walked by. The little man with thick glasses asked for the exact time of death.

"I'll see you guys in a minute. I got some calls to make and a certificate to fill out."

Vogel slammed the door of the consultation room, and Thrasher sent the reporters back to the waiting room. Lingering in the darkened corridor, resting against the walls, lumpish with fifty years of repainting, he heard Jannine sniffling quietly in the saffron kitchen. Then he heard a louder crying, an abandoned, hopeless wailing, the kind of noise he imagined was made by parents of children killed in bombing raids. It seemed impossible that a man would make sounds like that. Yet there was no mistaking Max Vogel's voice in its private agony.

A clattering of clumsy feet brought Myron down the stairs. He wheeled around the bottom step like a Mack Sennett policeman changing direction. Sighting the agency man in the dim hall, he ran to him and pinned him against the wall with cold, sweating hands.

"Okay, that's it. The whole thing together. The bastards won't be botherin' Uncle Doc any more. No more doorbells ringin'. No more night calls. No more walkin' up four flights. Know what Max told me? Uncle Doc was carryin' nitroglycerine around in his pockets for six months. That's for angina, pain around the heart. Did he tell us? Nope. He didn't even tell Max. Just carryin' pills around and poppin 'em in his mouth when he couldn't stand the pain. And in between still fightin' for his lousy two-dollar fees. Who helped him? Me? You? Max? Those bastards in the street eatin' him up? He didn't want any help. From nobody. You couldn't even buy him a house and you couldn't keep him alive."

Thrasher pulled himself rudely from Myron's moist hands.

"He was going to Walden with me," he said defensively. "We had it all worked out. Just the two of us."

"Hah!" Myron laughed. "Ya can go by yourself now!"

He fluttered away from Thrasher, a wingless bird, and pounded on the locked door of the rear room. A light went on inside and Max Vogel opened the door. He appeared dry-eyed and preoccupied; he had a fountain pen in one hand and the certificate of death in the other. Myron did not pause in his wobbly flight. He hurled open the drawers of the doctor's desk and kicked open the mahogany closet beneath the electrocardiograph. Then, like a housewife gathering up prized pieces of bargain merchandise, he began collecting old EKG rolls, stuffing them in his pockets, into the wastebasket, into a paper sack he found on the darkroom floor. When he had accumulated as many of the tight little rolls as he could carry— hundreds of signatures of hundreds of hearts—he sprinted madly for the front door. Thrasher raced after him.

On the lamplit pavement, Myron emptied the contents of the basket and the bag. The rolls scattered about the sidewalk and the gutter. Then, emptying his pockets under the poplar tree, he flew back wheezing into the house, emerging a few minutes later bearing a load of old X-rays. These, too, he hurled into the street. As Thrasher observed the idiotic performance, Myron made four more trips into the house, each time bringing forth more EKG's more X-rays—GI series, chest plates, skulls, pictures of broken limbs—and finally the contents of the doctor's slovenly files, the cards, papers, notebooks, letters he had accumulated until they bulged the cabinets and spilled into the recesses of his desk and examining table.

His work done, Myron stood shivering and hoarse in the midst of the assorted papers. Under the half light of the street lamp he appeared singularly triumphant.

"Howdya like that, hey, Thrasher the nephew called joyfully. "Just let one of them bastards come around now and ask for his records. Just let 'em come. I wanna be here to tell 'em we threw 'em all out. They can't touch Uncle Doc. They can't annoy him. They can't even get their mitts on the X-rays or the EKG's. Let the bastards run to the professors now. Let those old bitches sit around the beauty parlor and say what a lousy doctor he is. An' the school-teachers and those Baumgarts. They can't hurt Uncle Doc. The garbage truck'll take all this away tomorrow and that's the end!"

"Come in the house, Myron," Thrasher said indulgently. "You're carrying on like a damn fool."

"Oh, let 'em come, just let 'em come," Myron crooned. "I wanna answer the door. I wanna be the first to tell 'em. *You can't have a goddam thing.* Dr. Abelman's dead and I, me, Myron, I threw all the records out!"

His aunt leaned from an upstairs window.

"Now, Myron, you come in this minute," Sarah Abelman said firmly. "You will wake up the entire neighborhood with your stupid yelling. People are trying to sleep."

She was there at the last with her cautionary advices. It was essential that the neighbors not be disturbed.

Myron kicked at a stack of file cards and they scattered in front of the Buick. He shuffled through the mounds of old films, cards, papers, now deflated and despondent, and walked into the house. No sooner had he vanished than the children playing kick-the-can ended their game to plunge into the new treasure. Thrasher, resting his agonized body against the yellow brick, watched them wallow in the mysterious leavings, tossing the rolls of cardiograms against each other, tearing the half century of medical records into confetti, and holding the X-rays up to the lamp light in sly hope of discovering some sexual secret on the shadowy images. Like the Twentieth Century Gents, Thrasher felt, they were his children, and their behavior was of deep concern to him.

"Man, look at dat!"

"Whuchoo lookin' at, man?"

"Das a lady's c—t!"

"Aw sheet, dat ain't no c—t!"

"Yeah dat is. Ast Henry. Ain't it, Henry?"

"Naw, das a man's somethin', das what."

"Dey say dat ole doctoh dead."

"Ah, he jes' ole sheet. He talk too much."

"He ain' gone talk no moh. Look at dis, man!"

They began an impromptu little war, hurling the cylindrical EKG's at each other with amazing strength and speed, bouncing them off black polls and glistening arms. Thrasher walked down the steps and called to them as sternly as he could.

"Hey, you kids! Don't you know somebody died in this house? There are people mourning upstairs. Go on! Play somewhere else!"

A boy no more than twelve, a future member of the Twentieth Century Gents, studied Thrasher with placid contempt, and then, accurately, swiftly, hurled one of the rolled films at him. The agency man ducked, raising an arm, and caught the missile on his wrist. He fled down the steps after them but they were gone, vaporizing into the slum night, leaving only a trail of mocking *wah-wah-wahs!*

XII

HE CALLED Louise just before ten in the morning, having been awake since five despite a sleeping pill and a double scotch at the hotel bar. She extended condolences; inevitably they all would act as if the doctor's death was his personal tragedy.

There was an edge of excitement in her voice as she asked, "Have you seen the morning papers?"

"No, dear. I've been imprisoned here in the St. Francis Hotel in the heart of downtown Brooklyn. Are we murdered?"

"You kidding? We're page one in the *News, Mirror,* and *Tribune* and page thirty-eight in the *Times.* Want to hear the *News* story?"

"Go ahead."

"On page one it says *Doctor's Death Halts TV Show* and the subhead *Dies Aiding Wounded Thug.* Then, on page three, with photos, the story goes like this: *The premiere of a coast-to-coast television program was abruptly canceled last night when the Brooklyn doctor upon whose life the show was based was stricken with a fatal heart attack after treating a teen-age thug for wounds received from police during an attempted rape. In a grim coincidence, the woman involved in the alleged assault by three Negro hoodlums, Alice Taggart, 26, was the assistant director of the video program. The physician, who died shortly after ten o'clock last night after suffering a coronary thrombosis, was Dr. Samuel Abelman, 68 . . .*"

"Enough," he interrupted.

"There are pictures of you with Dr. Abelman. Also Herman Quincy in jail, and Mrs. Abelman crying."

Thrasher moaned.

"And you're quoted as saying that the progrom will go on, that in spite of your sorrow over Dr. Abelman's death the show is by no means canceled."

He cleared his throat. "Is that what my colleagues are saying?"

"I only know what I read in the papers. Mr. Gatling is quoted as saying he's going to start a medical school scolarship in Samuel Abelman's name. Oh—and the *Mirror* is going to run his life story in four parts. They got hold of a bunch of photos of him as a student and a young doctor."

Already he knew he was saved. Talker society worked in curious ways its wonders to perform; the tightrope he had been balanced on since Brick Higgins' collapse was as stout as a cement sidewalk.

"Okay, Louise, get me Ben Loomer."

"Woody—"

"Yes, precious, if the show continues, I'll get you slotted with the new research unit. I promise."

How could he be angry with Louise Farber for being concerned about her promotion? People died all the time; an awareness of death did not call for avoidence of life. It worked the other way. The only way you could cheat the terror was to immerse yourself in trivia. Sarah Abelman, worried that Myron would awaken the neighborhood, had the right approach.

Loomer was cautiously cordial. After condolences, he broached the subject of the morning newspapers and the impact of the doctor's death.

"I take it from what you say, Ben," Thrasher ventured, "we came up smelling like a rose."

"Makes a guy feel a little guilty. You know, the old fellow dead . . ."

"Well, Ben, we can't change it. A million dollars' worth of free publicity . . . Sam Abelman wouldn't have begrudged it to us. I didn't kill him. You didn't. Goodness knows, Lyman Gatling didn't. I'm still sorry they never met. By the way, has he given his verdict?"

"T.C. spent the night with him. We're still his boys. Seems he read the stories and cried his eyes out. He said if we could find decent, honest people like Dr. Abelman for our programs, we would have the greatest shows in the history of television."

Thrasher leaned back on the rumpled pillow, resting the receiver against his ear. "Where am I?" he asked.

"Same deal, Woody. Of course, Gatling isn't exactly in love with you, but I figure I can keep you busy enough in production so the two of you don't tangle again. I'll do the diplomatic work. Fair enough?"

"I'll buy it."

"Look, Woods, Chilson and I are running out to Princeton today to meet Professor Van Tebbel. Can you join us? Kev McBee's script is almost set."

"I can't, Ben. The funeral, you know. I'll be in bright and early tomorrow. We can't let McBee sneak any Lordisms past us. I got the blue pencil sharpened."

"Good boy, Woody. Why not check me out tonight about nine or so?"

"I will, Ben. Thanks for everything. I mean it."

How good it was to be back in their malleable, rhythmic world of symbols, fictions, little one-act plays extempore! He and Loomer were so good together: the big, bluff, honest man and the nervous artist.

He showered, got a shave and a trim at the hotel barbershop, reading the newspaper accounts as he sat in the chair. Herman (Josh the Dill) Quincy had been hospitalized again and was to undergo brain surgery; the other gang members were being held for attempted rape, assault, and various other felonies. Alice Taggart, evidently unharmed for her sojourn in Friedman's junkyard, had been sent home in care of a matron. He wondered if the male animal would ever look the same to her, and he felt a deep pity for her.

Back in the room he called his wife at the *Discoverist Review*.

"That poor old doctor," Ann said. "For once he was going to get some recognition, and to die just before it could happen."

Thrasher sighed. "I still can't believe it. We were going to Walden Pond together."

"You really liked him, didn't you, Woody?"

"I loved him." He laughed, thinking for no good reason about the doctor's sly waiting game with Traficanti—when the chairs filled up, he went home without his haircut. "All of him—those rages and screwy notions about people, and being so completely out of step he was left behind. Yet it's a damn strange thing. I never knew anyone who had a keener idea of what it was all about."

"What what was about? Medicine?"

"No. The whole thing. Living, dying, working, loving, hating. He knew that none of them are easy. He didn't go to the bargain counters. You couldn't convince him otherwise."

"How're his family?"

"No better or worse than you'd expect. I have a feeling they feel the way I do right now—that some organic part of me has been wrenched loose, amputated."

"Poor Woody."

"There aren't enough people left who get mad, plain mad. Not mad for a cause or a purpose, but just generally mad at all the bitchery and fraud. We take fraud for granted. We accept it. We like it. We want to be had. That's where he was different. He knew he was being cheated and he didn't like it one tiny bit, whether it was some old biddy doing him out of his two dollars or a corporation telling him they made better cathartics. He was the last angry man."

"But, honey, we all can't be like that. Didn't he carry it too far?"

"He had to. He was the only one left."

"Only one of what?"

"The doers. The pure doers."

"Woody, pu-leeze. You sound like an editorial in the *Discoverist Review*."

"Fine magazine. When do you quit, baby?"

"End of this week."

They paused, waiting for each other to affirm that their breach had been healed. He stammered a concession first.

"Listen, darling, I am very fond of you. I'm not Woodrow Thrasher, reborn and redeemed through the dying god. I can't go off to Vermont and start a crusading daily newspaper. But I think we can settle for some minimal gains. There's nothing wrong with either of us, really. Will you be waiting for me behind the picket fence, newly baked pie in hand?"

"I promise."

"I love you."

"I love you, too. Goodbye, Woods. I must read page proofs."

The simple fact of the doctor's death could not possibly make their union a thoroughly happy one, and he knew it. Life never followed such a neat cause-and-effect. But he had to believe that somehow through his association with the angry old man, he had absorbed some of his archaic, uncompromising morality; the morality that had forced Sam Abelman to pursue an ungrateful hoodlum, the least of men, through summer heat in city slums, vainly hopeful to the last that he might be saved.

It had rained, lightly but steadily, at the grave, and now in the sanctuary of the limousine, Thrasher removed the plastic raincoat he had purchased in the hotel drugstore, folded it over the jackknifed jump seat, and stretched his legs forward, resting his aching feet. The uniformed driver had been told by Myron to deliver the passenger to Connecticut via the Belt Parkway and Whitestone Bridge, and although the cemetery was but a few blocks distant from the four-lane highway, his chauffeur had difficulty locating an entrance.

"All the goddam houses look alike," he confided to Thrasher. "I could swear this is where we hit it, but it's a dead end."

He was quite accurate. The houses did look alike; thousands and thousands of houses filled with people who lived by the word, who took their daily infusions of talk from Woodrow Wilson Thrasher and the others who told them what to believe, say, like, dislike, eat, drink, think, accept, and reject. He felt no guilt because of his power; indeed he never had. Old Whitechapel, of all people, had articulated what he had secretly believed for a long time: *they were engaged in the most impressive plan to redistribute wealth that the world had ever seen.* Whitechapel's corollary was equally reassuring: *they created jobs.* He could argue with neither. Moreover, you couldn't turn back the word; you couldn't make illiterates of people, you couldn't deprive them of sight, sound, perception, understanding. All you could do—and it was admittedly a modest goal—was to improve the quality of talk, restrict the bad words, and sneak up on them with more good ones. So Thrasher told himself as the rain-splotched limousine found the parkway and sped him toward his home.

Earlier that afternoon he had arrived at the funeral parlor. It was teeming when he got there, some ten minutes ahead of time, and already the dim anteroom and chapel were crowded. As the time for the service neared, it became apparent that there would not be enough seats. The funeral director and his sons began setting up camp chairs, but even with the emergency seating arrangement many of the mourners would have to stand. He had drifted in and out of the room where the doctor's body lay, thankful for Mrs. Abelman's decision to bury her husband quickly. The mortician's art had neatly camouflaged the agony on the physician's face. He reposed, serene and cosmeticized, in skullcap and white prayer shawl. There was a Bible in his hands, and a stethoscope in his pocket. The Viking's funeral, he imagined, had been Myron's idea.

The people who had been part of the previous night's festivities in praise of the doctor now came to mourn him. There were all the Traficantis, in various stages of tears, together with collateral Speciales, DeBonos, Coluccis, and Calabreses; there was the Gruber family, descendants of the old gardener, all of them a little stained with mechanic's grease; there was Ed Dineen and his crippled wife; there was a collection of towheaded Poles whom Thrasher imagined were the Widziks of epidemic fame; and there was a large delegation from the Wholy United Army of God, led by Mrs. Quincy, bulking large in shapeless black layers and dropping her unabashed "sweet Jesuses" to the horror of the funeral director.

Standing alongside the widow for a few moments (she was remarkably calm and had gone out of her way to tell Thrasher how much the doctor had liked him), the agency man eavesdropped as mourners paid their condolences. Louis Kosloff was there, the gangly aesthete who had once contested Sam for Sarah's hand; Myra Hemitz, in mink stole and an imported black gown; Patrolman Kaplan and his wife; Curtis Harrison, the father of the wronged girl whose misadventure had first brought doctor and agency man together; and a trim little man in a black Chesterfield with an unlikely skullcap perched on his utterly Irish head. "Do you remember me, Mrs. Abelman?" he had asked. She lifted her glasses, peered at him a moment, and answered unhesitatingly, "Why of course. You're Mr. McDevitt." It was: the playground supervisor for whom Sam Abelman had worked a half-century ago.

Thrasher wanted to grasp his pink hand and reminisce with him about the day Sam Abelman fought the middleweight, but he thought better of it. He had been an intruder all along, and there was no point in pursuing his nosy probing any further.

Waiting for the service, he joined Myron outside for a cigarette. The nephew appeared to have recovered from his wild outburst of the previous night. Like most bench-warmers, Thrasher realized, Myron was able to withstand the shock of tragedy better than people who succeeded in getting what they wanted. His normal pessimism, his knack for expecting the worst buoyed him. All would be worked out in time: the old house would be sold (by Dannenfelser, of course, who now owed them one thousand smackeroos), Aunt Sarah would live with Eunice, and he would get his own apartment, sharing it with a fellow on the night side who was looking for his own place. What of Sandra Dorgenicht of the red lips? Myron shrugged. She would have to wait until he made his move into television or advertising or some other exciting business. For the time being, he realized, he could not compete with the weekends at Cornell. Thrasher owed him something: he could not honestly offer him a job at Whitechapel, but he promised to ask around and see if a bright creative kid was needed somewhere.

The service was about to begin. They found seats on the jam-packed benches, the room redolent of rubbers, galoshes, and damp clothing, and listened as a young rabbi, a moon-faced boy with beautiful diction who had never known Samuel Abelman, delivered the eulogy. It surprised Thrasher that it was all in English save for a few ritual pronouncements in Hebrew. It surprised him even more when the rabbi held aloft the doctor's copy of *Walden*, reading from it a passage about a man who lived in a hollow tree. It had to do with a visit to a king, who offered a delicacy-laden table, but whose manners were rude and whose conversation pointless; by comparison the impoverished man in the hollow tree had "manners truly regal."

The reading was a peculiarly apt one, and as he mused about the rabbi's good instincts, he received a nudge from Myron and a *sotto voce* advisory that it had been his, Myron's, selecton. There was a good deal of sobbing and sniffling by now, and the service was over; the coffin was being borne to the hearse; and in the corner of the room Thrasher could see Max Vogel, partially supported by his nurse, surveying the surging mass of weepers. Vogel himself was dry-eyed, and it seemed to Thrasher a little disgusted. He appeared ready to snarl some obscenity at the wailing mob, some nasty reminder of their unfailing talent to torment his friend while he lived. Max had done his crying privately the night before; he would not adulterate his feelings by blending his tears with those of the mob. Thrasher wanted to take him aside and tell him how much he had admired his doomed efforts to save the doctor. But Vogel and his nurse were departing, and he knew that no matter what he told the cynical old GP would be reduced to an unwelcome invasion of privacy.

One incident occurred at the cemetery that was to remain fixed in Thrasher's consciousness for many years to come. They had assembled on the soaked funerary earth, several dozen people in raincoats with umbrellas, drained of emotion and sorrow, anxious that the final ritual be concluded. The rabbi had begun the Hebrew prayer for the dead, and the mourners responded, most of them haltingly and ineptly. Myron read phonetically from a leaflet; some of the people present said nothing at all. Suddenly, from the assembly of mourners, two relics of a vanished age stepped forward, and, standing beside the coffin, led the praying in loud, affirmative voices. One of them Thrasher recognized. In undented black Homburg and black caftan, it was Rabbi Piltz, the fierce bearded prophet whom Thrasher had met on the first day he had made the pilgrimage to the office on Haven Place. Alongside him was a shorter, more ragged man. His gray beard was untrimmed, his hat was a sweat-stained felt lump, and his black overcoat was held together by a single forlorn button. Thrasher studied the ravaged face, a mask of persecution, now mouthing with proud emphasis ancient Biblical words. It could only have been the doctor's older brother Moishe. His face had the same conformation as the doctor's except that where Sam Abelman's features had been sharp and firm, Moishe's were soft and blurred, worn away by the attrition of cramped sweatshops and jeering gentiles. He remembered Myron telling him at the funeral parlor that they were fearful of informing Moishe that his brother was dead, that the shock might kill the old garment worker. Yet here at graveside was the denial of their fears. With each purposeful nod of his ruined head, the doctor's brother uttered another syllable of the venerable prayer. He did not cry; he was not afraid; he had accepted the physician's death and was now bolstering himself with the words of antiquity. There was almost,

Thrasher felt, a little defiance, a little mockery in his recital, a lesson for the unbelievers and modernists at the grave who did not know the words and who could not properly pay final tribute to the dead healer.

That was it: the words, the sacred words. Thrasher thought about it as he traveled the rain-swept parkway. He was proud of old Moishe. In his prideful declamation, he had reminded Thrasher that the word need not be destructive, or fraudulent or malign. The usages of the word were multiform, and if the word could be used to debauch and deceive, it could also be used to create and to uplift. He comforted himself with this assurance, thankful that the incessant rainfall blotted out the endless rows of look-alike homes, with their look-alike fences and gardens and look-alike automobiles parked in look-alike driveways.